Barton in a Jam!

Barton spoke to the Demu on the screen: "Now I want information. Lots of it. How much fuel time do I have in this kite? And look, don't anybody try to crap me about anything. Because, anybody gets tricky, nobody can stop me from using this bucket to kill myself. They know damn well I've been trying to do that for a long time. And the Director's child will go right down the spout along with me. You got that straight?"

The Demu nodded, scuttled back to exchange shrill communications with the Director.

You may be the King of the Demu, thought Barton, *but to me you're just one damned big overgrown crawdad!*

THE DEMU
TRILOGY

BY
F.M. BUSBY

A TIMESCAPE BOOK
PUBLISHED BY POCKET BOOKS NEW YORK

A Timescape Book published by
POCKET BOOKS, a Simon & Schuster division of
GULF & WESTERN CORPORATION
1230 Avenue of the Americas, New York, N.Y. 10020

CONTENTS

Cage a Man

FOR ELINOR

I.

A Cage There Was

The ceiling above him was low and gray; Barton's first thought was, What am I doing in the drunk tank? On second thought it didn't stink like a drunk tank, and Barton was far enough awake to know that he was not hung over. So he sat up and looked around. The first thing he noticed was that he was naked, along with everybody else. If this were a drunk tank, it had to be the first coeducational nude drunk tank in his limited experience.

He could make no guess as to where he was, or why. Presumably there was some other place he'd rather be, somewhere he belonged—but when he tried to think of one he drew a blank. Briefly, he wondered why the lack didn't bother him.

He seemed to be the only person awake; at least no one else was sitting up. Looking, Barton estimated about fifty persons sprawled in the room, neither crowded nor widely separated in a space about twenty-five feet square. He stood, and found the ceiling claustrophobically low: not much over six feet, clearing his head by a few inches but heavy-heavy-hanging over it. He didn't like that.

Floor and walls were gray, as well as the ceiling. Solidly. There were no openings that he could see, anywhere. There was light, a little yellowish, but no visible sources; the light was simply there. The gray surfaces were not luminous and the air did not glow. Barton skipped that; it wasn't important. What was important was that he had to take a leak.

No place. He stepped gingerly over and around the sleeping bodies, noting little about them except that they breathed. When he accidentally touched one, it was warm. The floor was at body temperature also, with a slight degree of "give." After exploring the room thoroughly, Barton was faced with the fact that it was not only solid but seamless. Yet the air (warm, like the floor) was fresh and clean. It seemed to move against him gently from all directions, though he could detect no gross air currents.

He still had to pee. Going to one corner of the room, he considerately rolled the nearest occupant out of splashing range and faced the corner. At first he couldn't do it; all the times he'd stood in line (at theaters during intermission, at overcrowded facilities in tourist haunts), with impatient others waiting behind him, came up to clamp the sphincter tight. Waiting, he finally relaxed and the flow came. The interesting thing was that at the floor it simply disappeared: no splash or gurgle. The floor might as well not have been there. It looked dry, felt dry (Barton felt it) and had no telltale smell at all (Barton smelled it).

He had a sudden wild thought that perhaps the whole room was an illusion, and gathered a few bruises trying to launch himself through the floor, a wall, and even the ceiling, before he decided that in this case liquids had certain advantages over solids. His guess might be wrong, he knew, but that didn't mean it was stupid.

Other people were beginning to wake, sit up and even move around. Barton realized that he hadn't paid enough attention to the resident population, of which he was perhaps 2 percent. So he stood quietly in his corner and looked.

The people ranged from ordinary to exotic, in Barton's view. Some were as usual as anyone can be among some fifty naked persons in a sealed room. Others were notable for such things as highly stylized patterns of tattooing, possible cosmetic surgery, and selective depilation. Still others, Barton thought, must have come out of a freak show. Some of them he found hard to believe, but there they were. The frightening thing, though, was that these people were beginning to speak among themselves, and while Barton spoke French and a little German, and could recognize several other languages, he heard not one familiar word from anyone near him. Well, yes—there was one over there!

"Anybody here speak ENGLISH?" he bawled out suddenly. From the far side of the room came a "YES." Accented, but unmistakable. Barton began shouldering his way toward the sound, shouting "ENGLISH" now and then as a navigational aid.

"English" turned out to be a Doktor Siewen, a tall wiry man with a great bushy shock of white hair, and some alarming ideas. He and Barton traded names and shook hands, the ritual prelude to any constructive activity between strangers.

"I know considerable languages, Barton," said Siewen, "and some of them I hear in this place, but not many. Also I hear people talking in languages I didn't think exist."

"I thought I knew a lot of ethnic types, myself, but some of these people don't look like anything I've ever seen, even in pictures."

"There is also that," Doktor Siewen began, but just then he and Barton were knocked apart. A woman pushed between them; two men were chasing her. There were strangenesses about all three. One man caught her; the two sank to the floor together in tight embrace. But the second man came upon them, kicking and clawing; soon all three were battling viciously. Barton wasn't sure whose side the woman was on.

He started to say something to Siewen, but a great feeling of heaviness came over him. His legs collapsed; the impact half-stunned him. He rolled over painfully, and was able to see that nearly everyone else was on the floor also. The heaviness increased.

"This tells us where we are, Barton," Doktor Siewen said, in great strain. "Or where we are not. You know what is this? Artificial gravity, it has to be."

Barton tried to shake the moths out of his brain. "How about just straight acceleration? I mean, on a spaceship thing you could get that, couldn't you?"

"On a spaceship with a room this big," said Siewen, "who could bother to disturb the navigation, only to stop a little squabble in the zoo?" The heaviness increased into blackout . . .

Barton ached all over; someone was shaking him by the shoulder. "Wake up, Barton; wake up." It had to be Doktor Siewen, unless the whole thing had been a bad dream, so Barton opened his eyes. It hadn't been a dream, or else

5

it still was. Standing beside Siewen was a woman, not like any Barton had ever seen. Barton stood up; she was taller than he and very slim.

"Barton, this is Limila," Siewen said. "You can see, she is not the type human we grow on our world." Limila smiled; her teeth were small, and by Barton's standards, too many. She held out a hand for him to shake; it had an extra finger. A glance downward showed a pair of six-toed feet. The nails of both toes and fingers were thick and pointed, clawlike.

"Hello, Barton. Yes?" she said.

"Hello, Limila. Yes." Her hair was odd. It was perfectly good shiny black hair, twisted up into a knot at the crown of her head, but forward of her ears it did not grow. The front hairline began above one ear and went straight up and over to the other; Barton recalled an old movie of Bette Davis playing Queen Elizabeth I. In compensation, at the back it grew solidly down to the base of the neck. Like she's slipped her wig, Barton thought before he got his thoughts back on track. "Where's she from, Doc?"

"We can't yet talk such technical data," Siewen said. "But Limila has been captured a longer time, was in another group with English-speakers, has fantastic talent of linguistics to learn as far as she has."

"Does she—" He turned to Limila. "Do you know what any of this is all about?" Her breasts were wrong. Not in shape, but set very low and wide on the ribcage.

"We are have by the Demu, I think," she said. "No one know what happen then. No one come back." She looked away, her eyes half-closed, apparently losing interest in the discussion.

"What's a Demu?" Barton asked. She didn't answer, and in a moment walked away.

"Now what's wrong with *her?*"

"We were talking before," Siewen said. "You were not awake for a long time, Barton; finally I worried you were not all right. But Limila told me of the Demu. Likely she did not feel to repeat herself.

"The Tilari, Limila's people, have star travel," he continued. "They are not what you call easy to the mark. They trade with other races and have respect from all. But the Demu raid the Tilari or anyone else; they take people and there is the end of it. They come from nowhere and go back the same way."

6

"Hell, somebody must know something about them," Barton growled. He was getting a little tired of being told how invincible the Demu were, because he didn't want to have to believe it.

"They are seldom seen. They have unconsciousness devices, which also derange memory function for a time, and other ways not to be noticed. They could have slept everyone here without the gravity if wanting to; that likely was for threat, to make us to behave better."

"Or maybe just plain sadism," Barton said. "I think I'd like to meet one of them sometime without his magic gadget. Anybody know what they look like?"

"A small ship of them, raiding scout perhaps, crashed on Tilara very long time ago. All were killed. The Tilari just began to study the wreck and the dead ones; then must have come another ship. The wreck and dead ones gone, also all but two Tilari in the study group. The two had gone for food supplies and needed instruments."

"At least somebody lucked out," Barton said. "So what's *their* report?"

"I said, a long time ago, Barton. It is all vague, very vague by now; Limila has only read it in her schooling as a child.

"She says they were roughly human shape and size. Hard like stone to the touch. She thinks they have not the features of face and other things real people have. But the Demu think *they* are the only real people."

"How can anybody know that?"

"Demu picture record, seen by the two Tilari not taken," said Siewen. "With sound-capsules, from which their name Demu is learned. By reports, showed unmistakably Demu in relation to other races as people to animals."

Barton didn't answer; the concept angered him. The phrase "hard like stone" stuck in his mind; he had the impression he'd cracked open quite a few rocks in his time, for one reason or another. His memory was vague but the picture of a fossil fern came to him, and the smell of a campfire. A field trip?

"Anything else Limila knows about them?"

"Legend, folklore, from other peoples made victims. They take you, they use you as domestic animal; maybe eat you."

"Seems like a long haul to the meat market," Barton

7

said. "Wouldn't it be easier to breed their own stock from what they get on the first raid?"

"As I say, Barton: folklore. But the great fear is not of being killed or even eaten. There is a story so old, the race that first told it is extinct. By supernova, long past. This is, the goal of the Demu is to make animals into people."

"I don't get you."

"If I have it, they catch people to try to turn them into Demu."

"Oh, come off it, Doc! How could that be?"

"I don't know; Limila doesn't know. But it is said on many worlds."

"So's a lot of other horse-puckie, I imagine." The subject had no handle he could grasp. He began stretching and bending, working the aches out of his muscles. Doktor Siewen shrugged and said nothing more.

Limila was back. She started to say something, but an excited babble broke out across the room and cut her off in midsentence. Barton wheeled to see what was going on.

The walls were leaking. At intervals, small jets of liquid spurted at a height of about five feet. Barton realized he was deadly thirsty. He wasn't alone; there was a rush. Barton held back for a moment but decided that if the Demu wanted to poison them, the air supply would be simpler.

The water was cool with a slight mineral taste, not unpleasant. Then it changed; the liquid became thicker and milk-colored. Just like Instant Breakfast, Barton thought, except not sweetened. He found he was hungry, too.

The stuff stopped coming before he'd had enough of it, but he could feel relief from the low blood-sugar condition he hadn't consciously noticed. Barton felt a little more as if he might have some sort of chance in this game after all. He realized it was silly to feel that way from a mere shot of nutriment at the whim of his unseen captors. But what the hell . . .

He turned from the wall, looking for Siewen or Limila. The other people of non-Earth origin began to register with him. They hadn't necessarily had surgery or depilation or tattooing, he saw now; they were simply different by nature. Some weren't all that different; some were hard to accept. He decided to work his attitudes out later when he had the time for it. When things weren't so crowded, if ever. What he really wanted to do was sit down with his back to a corner and feel less vulnerable, but his fellow captives shared his preference for using the corners of the room as urinals; they were all in use.

He noticed a discrepancy, and the vagrant thought crossed his mind: That's funny; I don't *feel* constipated. Then he saw Siewen and moved across the room to join him.

Their discussion brought no new information or ideas. Barton got tired of standing or sitting; he lay down and dozed off. Having his back against the wall was better than no shelter at all.

Barton was having a good dream; it got better when he woke up. Limila was all over him. What she had in mind was obvious, and Barton found that he had no objections. But first he pulled them both up sitting, looking at each other; he wanted to see her fully as a person.

Her hair was down and loose; there was a lot more of it than he would have expected. Her features were so lean and delicate as to be almost harsh, but her face had beauty to him, once he was used to its not stopping at the forehead. Her eyes were the color of liquid mercury, with more iris and less white than seemed reasonable. And her lips curved sweetly as she smiled.

He must have looked for longer than he knew, because she said, "Will we now?" Barton didn't answer in words. He found some differences in the way things were angled and the way some muscles worked, but he had no complaints.

Not much later he was startled to find that Limila was on the same friendly terms with Doktor Siewen, but Barton was realist enough not to try to impose his own ideas on a lady he didn't understand more than about 5 percent, if that. In the way he had now, he put everything out of his mind but the moment. In fact, some hours later, he and Limila were exchanging pleasured smiles when he felt the blackness of approaching unconsciousness. There wasn't even time to kiss.

The next time Barton woke, he was alone. The qualities of the room were the same but this one was smaller, about ten feet square. Not exactly ten feet, not exactly three meters, not exactly any measurement Barton was familiar with—and Barton knew he was capable of estimating dimensions quite closely. The gray surfaces, the low ceiling, the temperature, the light with no sources or shadows, the floor and walls you could piss through but not escape through—these were all the same. But the feel of the place was that of a solid planet, not a spaceship. There was nothing more, just Barton, alone in his room. This, he realized, is how to go crazy.

Barton was of no mind to go crazy. He felt he might be a little bit crazy already, but he didn't intend to let it go any further than he could help. He still knew only a little of what he was up against; as a matter of survival he set out to learn more. The effort kept his mind occupied, and he figured that was all to the good.

Over an unmeasured period of time he discovered several things. His solid wastes, infrequent on his present diet, also went through the floor without trace, but not instantaneously; they sank gradually, leaving no residue. The room reserved one corner of itself for these functions; it told Barton so with electrical shocks.

His food and water, neither separate nor appetizing, rose through another area of the floor in the same way, the floor forming itself into a sort of cup or bowl to hold the liquid mush. The intervals between meals were irregular and unpredictable. When Barton got angry at an especially long delay and pissed in the bowl when it appeared, the room left the mess with him for several hours before removing it and providing his next feeding. He didn't foul his food again. Frustrated out of his mind, Barton was, but not of a mood to let himself be stupid.

There wasn't much that he could learn from his limited environment, but he tried. With the constant illumination and irregular feeding schedule, there was no way to tell time. Barton first tried a makeshift count of his own pulse, but aside from the variation with his emotions, he invariably lost track of the thousands. He tried to keep a record of his own waking periods, and had no better luck. The walls and floors would not retain marks. When he tried to lay out hairs or nail bitings on the floor or glue them to the walls with spittle, they simply vanished, usually while he was asleep, though once he saw an attempted marker absorbed into a wall. He shouted and struck at it at the last, which did no good either.

Barton knew he was a little off his head when he began trying to make permanent marks on his own body to keep the one count that meant anything to him: the number of his waking periods. He tried gouging his skin with his fingernails but found his healing rate was accelerated;

he could not produce scars. He tried biting himself and was dissuaded by a series of shocks from the floor. The room allowed him to pluck marker stripes through his body hair, but the process was tedious and the result impermanent. He abandoned the effort and gave himself up to the sulks.

Once in a blank reverie he found himself pulling at his whiskers, and suddenly realized he had had a rough time measurement at hand all along. He pulled one hair from his sprouting beard; the length of it told him he had been caged for about four months, give or take a couple of weeks. His next period of sleep was more relaxed than any since this whole thing had started. Since Before.

Before! Barton hadn't thought of Before, more than fleetingly, since he had wondered what he was doing in the drunk tank. How could he? There was nothing but Here, and Here was so terrible and so frustrating that he couldn't put his attention fully on anything else. And for a time, he hadn't been able to remember very much, anyway.

He woke thinking of Before, though, and wondering about it. His emerging memories were still incomplete. The condition didn't bother him because he didn't recall any better one, except vaguely.

He knew that he had been born in 1950 and was pretty sure he'd been thirty-two at his last birthday. He was an only child, perhaps a little too smart for his own good in the childhood jungle of school, he recalled. Stubborn, somewhat of a loner in his teens. But not much of a rebel at home, or in two years of liberal-arts studies at the local university.

Then the war in Vietnam. He'd panicked and shot a scrawny kid who didn't have a grenade after all, just a small clay jar of oil. Later he'd shot one of his own squadmates who had begun to spray a village with submachine fire; no one could prove it on him for sure, so he didn't get court-martialed. Barton had never told anyone about these things; he'd just lived with them.

He hadn't tried hard drugs, just dew and hash sometimes, so when his hitch was finished he had no trouble getting home and out of the service. But he couldn't get along with his parents anymore. They kept trying to put him back in the little-boy bag and it didn't fit. He knew they loved him but he couldn't take the way they showed it.

Barton went back to college on the G.I. Bill. He wasn't doing well with people, he felt, so he undertook the study of things; he became a physics major. He would have preferred paleontology—he enjoyed fossil-hunting—but there wasn't any money in it and he'd been broke long enough. He was good enough at his studies to graduate with honors. He had about eight to ten dates per school year but got laid once a month by a friendly-mannered professional. As a matter of fact he liked the part-time whore, personally, better than he liked the coeds he dated. Barton felt that he knew honesty when he met it. On the dating scene he hadn't found enough to notice.

After graduation, Barton took a Master's degree and then a job with a company that gave him time to work on his Ph.D. on the side. It seemed to be a good deal, and for the most part, it was. Except for the red tape, which started strong and kept growing.

Just before leaving school, Barton had met a girl who frankly admitted she liked getting laid, and proved it. Her name was Ada Rongen; she was nearly Barton's height, and slim. She had green eyes, long red hair and a crooked nose from having played shinny at the age of ten. Barton proposed on their third date; they were married in time to avoid a fourth one.

For the most part, over the next few years Barton liked his job and his studies and his marriage. He enjoyed his hobby, oil painting. When the package came apart on him, it did so all at once.

The red tape on Barton's job had piled up until it took nearly half of what should have been productive time. He got clobbered in his Ph.D. Orals by a professor whose main gripe seemed to be that Barton had never taken the prof's own pet course. And he found that Ada's liking for getting laid was not exclusively in his favor.

The day he came home from the Orals fiasco she told him she was pregnant. Then she said, "I think you should know; the child is probably not yours."

Barton didn't ask who, how or why. He moved out. From the job, from the school and from Ada. First he told her to go ahead with a divorce; he'd give her any grounds she needed. " . . . and don't say anything. I've never hit a woman in my life and I don't want to spoil my record." She nodded, silenced by the look of the man who had always been gentle to her.

He moved into a walk-up room and concentrated on

his painting. A little of his work began to sell, but mostly he lived on the refund from the company's retirement plan. He picked up, on a part-time basis, with the young salesgirl at the gallery that handled his paintings. And once divorced, he found that without bitterness he could share Ada's eclectic enjoyment of casual sex. They became fairly good friends, in bed and out.

A year or two had gone by like this, a comfortable vegetative time. Painting, drinking with Ada and turning on with Leonie the salesgirl, being lover to each of them in a friendly noncompetitive way. By the time his retirement money ran out he could almost but not quite make a living from the painting. He made up the difference with a part-time scut job at the gallery; Barton's tastes, when he so chose, could be relatively inexpensive. He was drifting and he knew it; what better way to spend the dregs of his youth?

And then somehow, at no specific point he could recall, Barton had been torn away from that placid half-remembered existence. To wake up in a gray, seamless cage.

Thinking back, then, Barton lay supine on the gray floor and for the first time in his new existence masturbated slowly and luxuriously, building his urge almost to the deathwish-point of convulsions before he gave himself release. Then, relaxed, he wondered why in hell he had taken so long to think of such an obvious answer to his tensions. The relaxation carried through all that waking period and into sleep.

For the first time Here, Barton woke almost happy, smiling in reminiscence and anticipation. He ate in no great hurry, voided, thought vaguely and with only faint regret on what he could remember of Before. Then he lay down, arranged himself comfortably and thought of pleasure.

Nothing worked. No thoughts, no touch produced the slightest response. There was no doubt in Barton's mind what had happened. The room had noticed that he had discovered a source of pleasure, and turned it off.

That was the first time Barton tried to find a way to kill himself.

He couldn't; the room wouldn't let him. When he tried to do any real damage such as biting at an artery, the room jarred him out of it with electrical shock or radical variations of the gravity, temperature or air pressure, until he gave up and lay cursing, or sometimes crying.

The room had taken a long time to notice that Barton needed a bath or its equivalent. He was getting pretty stinking; his skin was spotted with inflamed areas and mild infections. Then suddenly he began to receive treatments he really didn't appreciate too much. Barton decided the method was probably ultrasonics.

At any rate, the outer layer of his skin flaked off in patches, and so did much of his hair, quite roughly and unevenly. He didn't have a mirror, but by the feel of himself he knew he looked like bloody hell. Furthermore, his beard "calendar" was shot down.

So when Barton one "morning" woke to find one wall no longer gray but looking like a window, with people or something else looking in at him, he was more angry than curious. At first he paid little attention to the appearance of those outside, although they certainly didn't look especially human. But at that point he didn't give a damn whether school kept or not; he was more concerned with what these beings had done to his own looks and functions than with what *they* might happen to look like. What he wanted was a little action.

He did all the standard things: he shouted, made faces, waved his arms and beat on the window. The people (or something) showed no reaction, except now and then to turn to one another and exchange comments. Or apparently so: he couldn't be sure; there was no sound.

When his mainspring ran down, Barton realized that he had better pay attention. Here was a chance for knowledge; it might not last.

What he saw was a group of robed cowled figures, vaguely human-shaped and apparently human-sized. Of course, he thought, this could be closed-circuit TV and not a window at all; in that case the apparent size wouldn't mean much. But Limila had said the Demu were about the size of humans.

Besides gray robes and hoods, he saw shadowed faces and occasional glimpses of hands that didn't have enough fingers. The faces didn't show him a lot. Heavy hairless brow-ridges hid the sunken eyes. There was no nasal ridge, only close-set nostril-holes a little below the eyes. The lips were deeply serrated—like a zipper without the handle, he thought wryly. The whole effect was rather chitinous, like the body shell of a boiled crab and with the

14

same ivory-tinged-with-red color. If there were ears, the hoods covered them. There was no sign of hair, fur or feathers. Hell, not even scales; he wondered if a snake would seem more alien to him, or less, than these creatures. "Demu?" he thought. "They look like a bunch of overgrown lobsters to me!"

One of them stepped forward and gestured to him. Yes, the hand had only three fingers, plus an oversized thumb set at an odd angle. No fingernails. The gestures carried no meaning to Barton; in return he thumbed his nose at the alien, who conferred with the two others before turning again to repeat the movements.

Barton knew what he wanted, now. He paid no heed to what the other did, but repeated over and over a simple gesture of throwing back a hood and dropping a robe, followed by throwing his arms wide in exhibition. The result was another conference among part of his viewing public. Eventually one of the lobsters stepped close to the window or screen and pushed the hood back, exposing its head.

It was about what Barton had expected. The head and neck looked crustacean; he was sure he was viewing an exoskeletal being. There were no external ears, but slightly flanged earholes not much displaced from the human position. The mouth, when open briefly, showed no teeth and a short stumpy tongue. The skull was slightly broader than deep, Barton thought, but couldn't be sure since the creature did not turn to full profile. The neck was thick and continued the chitinous look. Barton couldn't tell about the hands, when they reached up to replace the hood; perhaps the chitin was more flexible there.

Barton kept making doff-the-robe gestures but the upfront lobster ignored his movements and repeated a gesture of its own, with one hand in front of the middle of its robe. Suddenly Barton realized that the creature was pantomiming masturbation. He spat on the window, went to the far side of the room and curled up facing the wall. But as he did so, he felt unmistakable signs that his sexuality was working. Then, abruptly, it turned off again. He couldn't imagine how the lobsters could control him in that aspect. Some sort of subsonics? Induced brain waves? Hell, *he* didn't know. He tried to think in terms of physics, but the concepts seemed dim and jumbled in his mind. However, he did give some thought to the properties of the exoskeleton in combat.

For one thing, assuming the creatures were approximately his own size and operating in the same gravity field, the outer shell had to be light in weight. It would have great tensile strength and good resistance to compressive loads along a limb segment. But given a little leverage, Barton thought, it should bend and crumple like so much macaroni. He hoped with considerable gusto for a future chance to check his hypothesis; he was still thinking about it when he went to sleep.

Barton was next awakened by a metallic jangling sound, like a gong made of chain mail. The wall was a window again (or TV screen, he reminded himself), with one robed lobster facing him and gesturing. It might have been the same one or it might not; Barton couldn't tell for sure. But from the one-handed gestures and a stirring in Barton's groin, the creature obviously wanted Barton to demonstrate autoeroticism.

Well, the hell with that. He'd done it once and they'd turned him off for it. In return, Barton made throw-off-that-robe motions. If I have to be a solo whore, he thought, I'll get paid for it. In knowing a little more what it's all about. The session ended with no sale when the window turned back into a gray wall. This time they left him turned on, but feeling stubborn, he ignored the possibilities.

The dickering was repeated each waking period. Sometimes there would be only one robed chitinous alien, sometimes several. Occasionally there was one in the background that unlike the rest seemed nervous and twitchy, moving back and forth. Although he couldn't get a good look, it seemed to Barton that the twitchy one didn't have quite the same chitinous sheen as the others, though the features (or lack thereof) were much the same.

Throughout this period of silent bargaining sessions, Barton took a perverse pleasure in refusing himself any sexual release except for the involuntary nocturnal type that occasionally caught up with him. He had thought to huddle up facing away from the window and do it himself, but suddenly realized that all four walls and maybe the floor and ceiling could be one-way windows. Certainly the lobsters had turned him off before he'd seen any wall as other than gray and opaque. The hell with them, Barton felt. At this point, he realized, he might cheerfully have cut off his nose to spite his face, given the proper tools for the job. He almost had to laugh.

And yet Barton felt aggrieved when the silent arguments ended, when the wall stayed gray and no robed lobsters tried to gesture him into doing anything. During his first waking period without such an interview he was subjected to an ultrasonic "bath" of such vigor as to shake nearly every dead cell off him, leaving him not only stone-bald but also tenderly shallow of skin and with thin nails on toes and fingers, not to mention a filling or two that resonated painfully. Barton took this as a display of temper on the part of his personal number-one lobster and set in his mind the goal of someday repaying that entity in kind as best he might. Thereafter the ultrasonics were mild, shaking loose only extraneous matter. Barton theorized that a different lobster had taken charge of his cage.

Going by the length of his regrowing beard, Barton figured it to be nearly a year before he had any further interaction with the outside of the room, other than exchanging food for wastes and an occasional light ultrasonic "bath." Then one "day" he was sitting in a corner staring at the intersection of two walls and the floor, hallucinating. He was hallucinating a great deal at that time; he had found the practice a considerable help to personal peace of mind.

At the moment he was sitting on soft grass at the top of a rounded hill under warm sunlight, facing a slim girl with long red hair. Between them was a cloth laden with a picnic lunch. The girl's nose began to develop a crooked outline; absent-mindedly he thought it straight. They sipped from cold moisture-beaded cans of beer and toasted each other, smiling. A light breeze brought the scent of flowers. He had to straighten her nose again; it wouldn't stay put. He noticed movement far down the hill at the edge of a swamp. Insects, huge yellow-jacketed wasps, were buzzing around a cage. In the cage was a robed hooded lobster that flailed its arms at the wasps. He smiled and watched low-lying smog drift in across the swamp. Then—

He felt a slight "pop" in his ears, as in change of altitude. At first he thought it was part of his hallucination, but on second thought it didn't fit, so gradually he took his attention from inside himself and put it outside, slowly rising and turning from the corner to look at the room overall.

A sort of dome had appeared in the middle of the floor.

17

Yeh; air displacement popped my ears, he thought, and wondered why he bothered trying to explain anything any more.

He watched the dome awhile but it didn't do anything. He was in the process of deciding to find out whether he could pick up his hallucination where he had left off or would have to start over, when the dome disappeared with another ear-pop and left the original flat floor with a woman lying on it. Not an Earth-type woman, but humanoid and female.

Barton remembered Limila. He had seen her for a number of hours, a long time ago—how long? He had largely forgotten her exact differences from women of Earth. But this woman, coming awake, beginning to sit up and shake her head and look around, had to be of the same race. Yes, the extra fingers and toes. The high forehead, Elizabethan hairline straight across the top of the head above the ears. The breasts set so much lower and wider on the ribcage. Then she opened her mouth and snarled at him, and he saw the many small teeth. There had to be at least forty; Limila had about that many.

Barton prepared to make gestures of friendly welcome; he *felt* friendly and welcoming. In truth he felt friendly and welcoming and lustful. Not excessively lustful, because he had developed a method of self-service sex that involved curling up into a ball so that he figured those lobster bastards couldn't see what he was doing without x-rays. He used it sparingly, but often enough to keep some levels of his mind and his prostate gland in reasonable health. So he was not exactly intent on rape when he extended a hand to help his new roommate up off the floor.

She didn't see it that way. She took the hand, pulled on it and launched herself at him in attack. Barton wasn't ready for her; he had not been conducting any real exercise program during his term in the room. In fact he was more flabby and slothful, he suddenly discovered, than he really cared to be.

The woman clamped more than enough of her many teeth onto the ridge of Barton's jawbone below his right ear. One knee missed smashing his crotch, slipping to the outside of his thigh as he twisted. They fell to the floor, he under her. He caught one wrist and felt safe for a moment until her other hand clawed down his forehead; he felt a finger, its nail, digging into his right eye. He panicked

18

then, and screamed; the eye didn't hurt much, but he could feel blood or something worse running down his cheek. He caught the finger, twisted it and could feel it break, but that wasn't much solace. Then the gravity field hit, heavier than he had ever felt it. His ribs creaked and he blacked out. When he woke, he was alone again.

The bitch had got at his eye, all right. It was mostly healed, which didn't surprise him any more, but there was a wavy line pointing from northwest to southeast in anything he saw with his right eye. A wave of despair rolled over him; he felt crippled, mutilated, as though he'd lost an arm or a leg. Barton didn't have much hope for himself, certainly, but the prospect of a permanent ditch in his vision was more embittering than anything that had happened since his sex had first been turned off.

He couldn't blame the woman too much; he had seen some marks on her that probably would not cause her to view a strange man as a guardian angel. But Barton had the distinct idea that there had to be somebody around who should pay up accounts. He almost got rid of the shock in his corner-sitting hallucinations, but it wouldn't quite go away. After a while he let it alone. Over a time his sight slowly returned to normal, but his feelings didn't.

The second time the dome came, Barton happened to be looking at it. There was the flat floor, and then "pop" there was the dome. About fifty pulse beats later, it disappeared. Barton was hard put to describe in his own mind the female creature on the floor, but by comparing some marks he'd seen the first time, he had to admit it was somewhat the same woman who had clawed his eye.

A few minor alterations had been made. The fingers and toes were shorter and scarred at the ends; each end joint with its claw had been lopped off. Half-healed scars ran down the sides of the head at the temples, just forward of the Queen Elizabeth hairline. Barton knew what this might be, but hoped he was wrong. He wasn't; the woman looked up and gave him a blank childlike stare. Then she smiled, and Barton cursed all the lobsters that ever were. How many teeth had Siewen said—forty? Now, none.

The smiling dull-eyed creature climbed into his lap and hugged him. It took some time before Barton could bring himself to let her kiss him. But she was persistent, and Barton had been alone a very long time.

What was left of the woman had very simple tastes.

She loved to eat, off the floor with both hands, which was really the most efficient method. She was quite unhousebroken until the floor conditioned her electrically to use the proper corner most of the time; she cared nothing for cleanliness or appearance.

She was diligently but not urgently horny; after his first lapse Barton fended her off for a time in the interests of what he considered self-respect. But after he once woke to find her straddling him and too late to stop, he gave in and enjoyed it, occasionally. He did keep an eye on the window wall and was prepared to stop at any moment if he saw robed lobsters, but he put out of his mind the possibility that they could watch unseen. After a while he had sex regularly with her, just as though she had been a fully rational intelligent person. After all, she did like it, didn't she?

Sometimes it bothered him that she couldn't talk. Not only his language, but *any* language. He told himself it wasn't his doing, but the telling didn't help much.

He was so unused to paying heed to her bodily functions that he was considerably surprised to realize, eventually, that she had become not merely fat in the gut but alarmingly advanced in pregnancy. Barton simply had not considered the chance of interspecies fertility. She began to have increasing spasms of ill health; Barton's sex life ceased abruptly. He spent much time trying to make signals to the blank wall that had been a window. There were no answers.

Barton sweat up a storm. He knew he couldn't handle what was going to happen in a little while, that he would have been out of his depth delivering a normal easy birth, with full plumbing and antiseptic facilities. He had none of these and the birth was not at all normal, but very difficult. Barton cursed and prayed and got his hands awfully bloody, and the woman-shell was not beyond pain, unfortunately. She screamed and cried as pitifully as though she had had her whole mind with her.

At the last of it, when nothing else could help her, he tried to kill her painlessly in a way the Army had taught him. But the lobsters still knew a trick worth two of that: their gravity gadget. When Barton woke up, it was hard to tell which way he hurt the most. The woman was gone, finally now, and for the last of it he blamed himself.

Barton had given up caring about time passage when

the room gave him the second woman. This one looked like Earth ancestry, very young, just past puberty. Like Limila's fellow citizen, she was toothless, temple-scarred and one joint short of nails on fingers and toes. Barton staggered over to a corner and threw up, without regard to where the plumbing was supposed to be.

He couldn't ignore her, though, because she too was strongly sex-oriented and kept trying to get to him whether he was awake or asleep. There was no way to beat that kind of dedication. So he introduced the girl to sexual juxtapositions that could not result in pregnancy, and for quite a long time he thought he had the situation whipped. But one "morning" he woke to find that he couldn't stop the girl from following the example of her predecessor; she had managed to bring him into a "normal" sex act without waking him until the onrush of climax.

Without thought, with only rage, Barton made one move too quickly to be countered. He swung the hard side of his hand and broke the girl's neck. The gravity field hit him then, and he didn't fight it. All he needed was a time to cry for his dead. But when he woke he felt no grief—only emptiness.

They left him alone for a while, until the beginning of what he recognized as language lessons. When the window began showing sets of visual symbols matched with the first sounds he had heard from outside, he knew what they had in mind. He felt, Barton did, that it was a little late for that crap. He already knew all the important things. And it might be advisable to deny the lobsters the insight into his own mind that they might gain by observing his learning processes. Each time the lessons began, he faced the opposite wall. He was pretty deeply into self-hypnosis, and thus fairly successful in ignoring the sounds.

They turned off his sex again. He learned to hallucinate it so well that he didn't really care; in fact, since his mind could experience it more often than his body could, it was in some ways an improvement. More and more he stayed in his own mental world, emerging for feeding and elimination but for very little else.

They worsened the flavor of his food, which took some doing. After the shock of the first taste, he ate it and pretended enjoyment. When they made it completely unpalatable he substituted a hallucinatory taste for the actual one and wondered why he hadn't thought of that answer before. They put stenches in his air also, to no

21

avail and for the same reason. One thing was obvious to Barton: he might have been a slow learner, but the lobsters weren't such great shakes either. He had to hand them one thing, though—at least they were getting his attention, more than he liked.

They played games with the temperature, air pressure and floor gravity. Barton played games right back at them, with his growing abilities of hallucination and self-hypnosis. The only things that really got to him, he noted grimly, were of a type that couldn't possibly gain his cooperation.

The first was dropping the oxygen content of his room; he couldn't fight that, but it rendered him unconscious. The second was electrical shocks from the floor; with some effort he could put them on his "Ignore" circuit but the muscle spasms left him sore. And the third, once only and probably due to a loss of temper by some lobster or other, was floating him in the air on zero gravity and suddenly slamming him to the floor. It broke his right forearm. He healed rapidly, of course, but the break was not set. It left him with a lumpy arm, and painful. Barton wondered how that would work with an exoskeleton. He took up a regular exercise program for the first time, so as not to waste a chance to find out, if he ever got one. After a time his physical condition became surprisingly good, even by his own standards. He decided that the food must have been nutritious even though its natural taste was more rancid than not.

When Barton's self-propelled hallucinations began getting out of hand, he figured they were experimenting with drugs in his food. He knew with certainty that here was something that could take his high ground away from him. He had to change his tactics, so he decided to watch the lessons. The same drugs that cut into his control of his own mind should also distort his responses and thus anything the lobsters could learn from them. So when the window next began to show a language lesson, he sat and watched it. Of course he fiddled in a little hallucinatory content to keep things interesting.

He noted that the impersonal symbol-sound pairings had been replaced by one or more lobsters holding up the symbols and making the sounds, with gestures. He found that he understood a lot of it almost immediately; perhaps some of the earlier material had been getting through on a subliminal basis while he thought he had been ignoring it.

22

Since he did not *want* to learn lobster language he forced himself to ignore as many as possible of the meanings that came intuitively into his mind at each sound-symbol-gesture showing. And after several depictions of a concept that he was fairly sure meant "friendship," he stood up and deliberately pissed on the window. His act brought the lesson to an abrupt end. The lobsters conferred with each other in something resembling a state of excitement; then two converged on the twitchy one Barton had noticed when the creatures had first shown themselves. At least it looked like the same twitchy lobster; there might be more than one. If I were a lobster and had me in a cage, Barton thought, I might feel a little twitchy myself. Then he chalked that thought off to a natural paranoia and watched the outside action more closely.

The three lobsters were coming closer to the window, the twitchy one in the middle, the other two apparently urging it forward. Sure as hell, Barton thought, that one looked different. Not so much like a lobster; the texture was wrong. But the features were about the same, what he could see of them.

Barton had the feeling of almost recognizing the twitchy softer-looking lobster, when it spoke to him. "Barton! For your own good you must—" The lobster face broke into entirely unlobsterlike spasms and the voice went shrill. "No, DON'T! Let them kill you first! I was once—" And the window turned back to gray wall.

Well. The voice had been in English. The sound quality was distorted abominably, but he'd detected only overtones of any "lobster accent." There had been a hint of familiarity to that voice, and so far as he knew, Barton had never been on speaking terms with a lobster. But he had the feeling that there was something he should be remembering.

Then there were new scents in the air and Barton guessed that the lobsters had hit upon breathing-type drugs to bend his mind. Serve the hardshelled bastards right if they killed him first, he thought for a moment, before he passed out cold.

The problem was that any chemical agent in the food or air that broke Barton's will also dispersed his powers of concentration. After all, those were two looks at the same bag of ego, though Barton had not previously considered the matter in those terms. He had not, he began to realize, considered a lot of things. For one, he hadn't given much thought to why he should be so important to the lobsters, out of the fifty or so people he'd seen in the first cage, maybe two or ten years earlier. It hadn't occurred to him that perhaps the lobsters had stupidly and inefficiently killed most of the rest in their clumsy experimentation, and were getting worried. It seemed a fair guess, though, now that he thought of it.

A different mind than Barton's, he recognized, might have seized upon that possibility and hoped to do some bargaining with it. Barton's mind was stuck on the picture of a mutilated mindless woman forced to die in horrible pain. It was not exactly revenge that held his thinking; it was more on the order of Corrective Annihilation . . . something like a Roman galley slave with a fixation on the extermination of the Caesars. The idea amused him a little, but not much. Idly he wondered what had become of the easygoing fellow he used to be, and decided that that man had died with the Tilaran woman.

Now, though, he thought he knew his one possible chance for escape. He'd figured it out; the logic was flawless. The only problem was that he had no idea whether he could really do it or not.

For a time, then, Barton played an intense and deadly game with the language lessons, a game his would-be teachers could not be equipped to recognize. He would register understanding of one symbol, no comprehension of the next, confusion about another, in a calculated fashion. Today's knowledge was tomorrow's incomprehension, he pretended. His idea was to drive the lobsters as nuts as he suspected *he* was becoming.

It worked for longer than he had expected. The lobsters took long pauses during the lesson sessions, conferred in their tinny little voices, and became so agitated as to reach under their robes and apparently scratch. Barton didn't see how a lobster could get much of a kick out of scratching itself.

The twitchy one didn't show up again in the window. That figured.

During the between-lessons periods Barton had been pushing himself as hard and as far as he could manage it, along the lines of heavy self-hypnosis. The drugs were out of his food and air now that he was "cooperating" with the lessons, and he worked that breathing spell for all it was worth. Because there wouldn't be more than one chance, and while that one might not be worth the effort, what *else* could he do?

When the creatures in the window got tired of his lack of progress and began jarring him again with floor shocks, Barton knew he had to try it. He gave them a little jelly for their bread with his responses to the remainder of that lesson. When the window turned back into gray wall he curled up in the middle of the floor, well away from the latrine and feeding areas, and began willing himself as close to death as he might possibly get back from, and perhaps a little further. Besides hallucination and self-hypnosis and faking, he threw in considerably more true death wish than he would have done if he were still capable of giving a real damn. He knew what he was doing, but it didn't frighten him. The floor would not allow passage of a living organism; therefore Barton had to be effectively dead. That was how he had figured it, what he was betting on. There was no other chance for Barton, none at all.

The sensation of interpenetrating the floor was disturbing beyond anything he could have imagined; he hadn't expected to be able to feel anything. But his will held; he gave no betraying heartbeat. Some ghost at the back of his mind tried to guess how many pounds of his own excrement he was finally following, but the estimate was impossible. He didn't know how many years it had been, let alone his average excretion.

The sudden drop through the air and subsequent impact jarred him. He saw through slit-tight eyelids that he was on the floor of a corridor. At least he had lucked out and missed the plumbing. Only one robed lobster was in sight. It approached, bent over him and reached . . .

In two breaths Barton was alive again. He caught a bruise and a laceration across the face before he had the chance to prove his theory that with the proper leverage, the limbs of an exoskeleton shatter beautifully. When the lobster began to make its characteristic noises, Barton kicked the back of its skull in, holding it against the floor and stomping again and again with his bare heel until the thing crumpled.

At that point, like it or not, he had to stop and take stock. His flirtation with near-death had left him weak, and his soul was equally shaken. Barton's vision was flickering around the edges; he waited until it settled down.

Then he stripped the robe from the lobster-creature and looked at the latter with great care. It wasn't all that impressive, he decided.

All right. The thing was outer-shelled for the most part, but not boilerplate with joints. Instead, the surface went gradually from hardshell to gristle where it needed to bend. The shapes of limb segments were not unlike the endoskeletal human, but of course rigid on the outside. The soles of the feet and palms of hands were the softest and most padded parts of the body. Up the center of the abdomen ran a hand's-width pattern of dots, some concave and some convex. The crotch was devoid of anything Barton might have expected; it was like a branching tree.

Barton didn't take long, seeing what there was to see; it took him longer to decide what to do. Not so very long, though. He searched the robe, found a small cutting implement. He carved a great part of the shell off the front and top of the creature's head, pissed in it to wash out most of the brownish blood, and wiped the thing dry with the tail of the robe. Then he put it on his own head. The eyeholes didn't quite fit, so he took it off and gouged them a little larger. He didn't look at what still lay on the floor. Not yet.

Everything inside him said to put on the robe and hood and move out of there, but Barton knew that first he needed something more on his side. He had no real weapon except his ability to break exoskeletal arms and legs, which did not seem quite enough. So, messy hands or not, he took his dead lobster apart rather thoroughly. He didn't even throw up.

He learned that the creature's main nerve trunks were ventral rather than dorsal, and down its middle found the bonus of a fine sword-shaped "bone" that needed only some lobster foot-cartilage to serve as hilt-wrapping.

Barton decided that time was running out. There was no way to hide his gutted lobster in the narrow corridor, so he left it. He chose his direction simply: the way he could step least in the juices of the corpse. He kept his "sword" and the other cutting tool under his borrowed robe, out of sight.

When Barton met a pair of real live lobsters face to face in one of the corridors, he came close to losing his toilet training. He had no idea what to do. He knew that no one person can stand off an enemy population in its home territory. So he tried to pretend to be a lobster who didn't want to talk to anybody, and it worked. After that experience he merely kept moving and hoped that nobody would cross him. Nobody did; Barton decided that maybe lobsters were too mean even for other lobsters.

After a time, Barton came to the top of an up-ramp and saw the sky. Now he knew that he had been kept underground, for however long it had been. He set out walking, paying no more attention than he could help to the lapse of time since he had last had food or drink.

The sky was spectacular, but Barton couldn't be bothered. There were stars in the daytime, for instance. Barton couldn't have cared less. He needed a place to sleep. He found a clump of odd-looking brush and crawled into it, hungry and thirsty and cold.

The lobster that found Barton and poked him with a stick to wake him was a very unlucky lobster. Barton's sword was entangled in his robe, so he bashed its head in with a fist-sized rock. Then, his hunger and weakness overcoming any remaining scruples, he ate the tender flesh of its forearm, raw. It was something like crab meat, and the best-tasting food he'd had since they caught him. He decided he was beginning to develop a taste for the place. He also decided that he scared himself.

Barton was beginning to believe that he was invincible. When he didn't meet any more lobsters, he was sure of it. He blanked out all idea of how weak and vulnerable he really was, because his mind didn't want to work along those lines. He accepted the knowledge that his hallucinations were no longer entirely separate from his objective experiences, and hadn't been since he didn't know when. There was something about a woman . . .

While he was gnawing at the last of a lobsterish forearm, Barton stumbled onto the outskirts of a field scattered with odd-looking vehicles, dully metallic in hue. Anyone with half sense had to know that a saucerlike object in such a place would be a spaceship, so Barton sprinted for a saucer.

It was bigger than it had looked from a distance, about forty feet in diameter. The bottom surface curved upward; the outer edge was inches higher than he could reach and offered no handhold to jump for. He walked around it, looking for access and finding none. Dammit, there had to be a way into the thing! He stood for a moment, baffled, then began a second and slower circuit, inspecting the surface above him inch by inch.

Ahead, out of sight around the curve of metal, Barton heard a sound of machinery in motion. Carefully he disengaged his bone sword from the robe and advanced, to see a curved ramp descending from an area about midway between edge and center of the saucer shape. He scuttled forward, to be under and behind it as it touched ground. Then he waited. Somebody certainly was in no hurry. His sword hand was sweaty; he wiped it on his robe and discarded his lobster-mask for better vision.

When Barton heard footsteps above he peeked around the edge of the ramp. One robed lobster was descending. Barton waited to see if more would come or if this one would look back and say anything to others in the vehicle. Neither happened; there was only one lobster.

As it stepped off the ramp, the mechanism began to rise, slowly. Barton took three steps forward and swung his sword to belt the lobster across the side of the head as hard as he could. It went down but didn't stay down; it came up facing Barton. Holding the sword hilt in both hands, he lunged to the midsection with his full weight. The thrust bounced off but the creature dropped, holding itself and breathing in ragged gulps. Out of breath himself, Barton let go the sword, turned and jumped to grab the end of the ramp.

The gap was within inches of closing; the thought flashed through his mind that he could lose some fingers. But with his weight on the ramp, it sank again. He didn't wait; as soon as there was clearance he scrambled on and clambered up as fast as he could manage.

At the top was a door. Barton turned its handle and pushed the door open, wishing he hadn't had to leave the sword behind. But he found only an empty corridor. A glance below showed that the lobster wasn't having much luck getting up, so Barton didn't wait to see the ramp all the way closed. He found the way to secure the door from inside, and settled for that.

There were a lot of doors, and presumably compartments behind them. Barton ignored these and stayed on the main corridor. A little later, in a closed windowless room that he also locked from inside, he looked at the control assembly and wondered if it made *any* sense.

There had to be a way to find out, if he could think of it. For starters, there was a projecting lever that swung smoothly in every direction, to no effect. And another that moved only up and down, but nothing happened there either. And a neat rectangle of what seemed to be toggle switches, with one larger turquoise-handled one in the center. Starting at top left and working to the right, like reading an English-language book, Barton gingerly flipped each of the smaller toggle switches up and immediately back down, to see if by momentary activation he could get some clues without necessarily killing himself.

Nothing happened. OK, Barton said to Barton. The swivel bar has to steer this thing, and the up-and-downer has to be the go pedal. Or else I am already dead and just don't know it yet. And these other flips are auxiliary controls. So the big blue devil in the middle has to be where the action starts.

Checking to see that all the toggles were back where he'd started, and the two levers also as near to neutral as he could tell, he flipped the turquoise switch. There came a heavy pervasive hum all around him, then a thin screaming from somewhere else in the place. The scream wasn't steady like the hum; without thinking, Barton left the controls and went looking for it, on the run.

It was a smaller-than-average lobster, about three-quarter scale. Barton caught it trying to unlock the door to outside. Every impulse shrieked at him to kill it, but even now he had a soft spot for small, presumably young creatures, so he tried to subdue it instead. Paradoxically, his weakness prevented him from doing so without injuring it—in the struggle he accidentally broke one of its arms. He dragged it back to the control area, and using its own robes, tied it down into a seat. Still it screamed.

The high piercing sound didn't help Barton's concentration. His sight was flickering again, like an out-of-tune TV set with the picture jiggling to the peaks of the sound track. His ears filled the silences with a dull ringing and once a voice spoke in his head: "Give it up, Barton. You lost." When the control panel began to change into a gray wall he fought himself back from past the brink of panic and proceeded to reason with the small screaming lobster in the only way he could manage.

He persuaded it to stop screaming, and then to stop a kind of whimpering, by giving it a full open-hand slap across the eyes every time it made a noise. After a while it got the point. Barton was glad, because his hand was getting as sore as his sensibilities. So was his throat; he had accompanied every slap with a shout. He was parched thirsty.

His spaceship was still humming. Barton tried his tentative steering and throttle levers but nothing happened. Well, then; back to the rectangle of toggles.

The first few, as he flipped them quickly on and off, did nothing spectacular. The one at the right end of the top row made the whole machine push up at him gently. He flipped it full on, then, and realized the thing had to be airborne. Flying by the seat of his pants, he worked his self-designated throttle and steering levers gingerly, and found that indeed they gave the feelings of acceleration and turning that he had expected. So he went straight up, the best way he knew to keep from hitting anything while he figured things better.

The only trouble was, he still couldn't see out. Also the little lobster was keening again, and he couldn't spare a hand to slap it.

Suddenly Barton was standing under a great golden dome, with deep tones of organ music reverberating around him. He shook his head; this was no time to play around with hallucinations, even pleasant ones. It was hard to get back. He had spent a lot of time perfecting that mental escape from the lobsters' cage, he was beat all out of shape, and the miniature Demu's noise was disrupting his thought patterns badly. He wasn't *used* to noise, dammit!

But he made it, and instead of slapping his small lobster to shut it up he took a deep breath, bracing himself, and hit them both with a heavy-G vertical swerve. It did the job; he had silence. Then he went back to the methodical quick testing of the bank of switches.

He was a long time finding the one that gave him an outside view, and somewhat longer in learning that the toggle switches also twisted to give fine controls such as focus or magnification. It was then that he found he hadn't captured a spaceship after all.

It was nothing but some kind of goddamned air car. There were quite a few more of the same, hanging with him and surrounding him. Barton didn't quite panic, but he did try to make a run for it. It didn't work; they stayed right with him. His mind had not quite decided to run away from home and leave him to manage by himself when he noticed that neither his nor the other airborne vehicles could approach each other too closely; some invisible cushion kept them apart. Barton the ex-physicist thought briefly on the possible ways of obtaining such an effect; then Barton the escaped caged animal took over, wanting only to escape what came at him, or smash it if necessary. He explained the position to his captive lobster several times, but it did not answer, having learned that noise would cause it to be hit, by Barton. It did get up the nerve to say "Whnee," quietly. Barton took this well; he smiled and did not slap the smallish lobster. The exchange might eventually have developed into the first conversation between Barton and a Demu, if he had had the time for it. But of course he didn't.

Barton, though, was only stretched out of shape, not out of commission. He went back to testing the switches that he'd merely flicked before to see that they wouldn't kill him; now he left each one on long enough to see what it controlled. So sooner or later he had to turn on the visual and voice intercom, through which the opposition appeared to have been trying to reach him for quite some time. It was the third switch from the right in the fourth row from the top.

The big lobster in the foreground of the viewscreen broke into excited gestures and loud shrill sounds, so Barton knew the view was two-way. The smaller lobster beside him shrilled back in answer. It was all too loud and too fast for him to follow, but finally it struck him that they were exchanging communication he didn't understand.

He could *not* allow them to talk over his head. That way led back to the cage. Bracing himself so as not to move the controls accidentally, Barton belted the small lobster across the eyes as hard as he could, backhand. It felt like hitting a rock; he hoped he hadn't broken his hand. The creature slumped limply; brownish fluid dripped from one nostril-hole and a corner of its mouth. Barton felt remorse, but only briefly: he didn't have time for it.

The big one on the screen was yammering again; Barton couldn't follow the text. He shook his head impatiently. He knew it was his own stupid fault for not going along better with the language lessons, but he didn't feel like admitting any blame. "You want to talk with ME, you lobster-shelled bastard, you talk MY language!" he shouted. "TALK ENGLISH, or go to hell!"

He repeated this with variations while with half his

mind he jockeyed the air car against the attempts of his escort to herd him in the direction of their choice. The other air cars surrounded him and tried to mass their pressure shields to move Barton the way they wanted him to go, but there weren't enough to hold him and push him at the same time. And he was feeling just stubborn enough to fight anything they wanted him to do: anything at all. Hallucinations nibbled at him, but now he decided they must be effects of the Demu unconsciousness weapon, leaking past the air car's shields. The hypothesis, true or not, made it surprisingly easier to fight the phantoms off. So with something like enjoyment he used his considerable kinesthetic skills to thwart their efforts to herd him. The upshot was that the dozen or so air cars danced around much the same area for quite a while before the next development on the viewscreen. Which was that it spoke his name.

"Barton!" it said. "Thish ish Shiewen. You musht lishen to me!" On the screen was what Barton had come to think of as the twitchy lobster, the one that didn't look quite like the rest. It sounded like a voice he knew, and now he remembered Doktor Siewen. But why would Siewen sound like a comic drunk act?

Barton put the odd pronunciation to the back of his mind and concentrated on the meaning. "Doctor Siewen? I don't believe it. Throw that damn hood back and let me see you." It seemed strange to be *talking* with anyone, anyone at all.

As the hands came up and the hood went back, Barton heard a ghost voice: Doktor Siewen's. "They catch people and turn them into Demu."

They sure as hell did. Without the hair and ears and nose and eyebrows, with the serrated lips over toothless gums and a shortened stumpy tongue, the thing on the screen didn't look much like Siewen except for the chin and cheekbones. But the skull and neck were human-shaped, not lobsterish. The eyelids looked a little odd; Barton decided they'd been trimmed back to get rid of the eyelashes. And a long-forgotten memory reminded him that the sounds of *s* and *z* cannot be made without touching the tongue to teeth or gums at the front of the mouth; otherwise the result is *sh* and *zh*. He put that answer in cold storage, too, trying to absorb the shock.

It wasn't that the creature on the screen was so horrible

in itself; when you've seen one lobster you've seen them all. The obscenity was in knowing what it had been before the Demu had set to work. Barton had thought he hated the lobsters already; he found he hadn't even begun.

"All right; it's you, I guess," he said. "I'm listening; go ahead." Idly he noticed the hands with three fingers and no nails; the jog at the wristline showed that the little finger had been stripped away, all along the palm. He bet himself a few dead lobsters on the condition of Siewen's feet, then shook his head and listened.

"Barton, you musht come back." Barton's mind, back where he wasn't paying too much attention to it, was irritated by the distraction of the distorted sibilants and decided to ignore them. "The young Demu you have is the egg-child of the Director of this research station. Shut off your shield; it is two up and three over from bottom left of your switch panel. The Director offers you full Demu citizen rights."

Barton chuckled; sometimes you draw a good card. "Well now, is that *right?*" Not waiting for an answer because he didn't need one, he went on: "Forget what the Director wants. Forget what the Director offers. If the Director wants his gimpy-arm egg-child back in mostly one piece, the important thing is what *I* want. And for starters, I don't need any company around here. Get this bunch of sheepdogs off my back; I won't talk any more until you do. And get that damned sleep-gadget off my mind, too. I'll wait." By *God,* but it was good to be able to talk back for a change, to have a little bit of personal say-so. He waited, not too impatiently.

Soon the surrounding air cars grouped to his right and departed. The twitchy lobster who had been Doktor Siewen came back to the screen. Barton spoke first.

"Now I want information. Lots of it. How much fuel time do I have in this kite? And look, Siewen, or whatever you are by now—tell him, don't anybody try to shit me about anything. Because, anybody gets tricky, nobody can stop me from using this bucket to kill myself. They know damn well I've been trying to do that for a long time. And there goes the Director's egg-child, whatever that means, right down the spout along with me. You got that straight?"

Siewen nodded, scuttled back to exchange shrill communications with the Director.

You may be the King of the Lobsters, thought Barton,

but to me you're just one damned big overgrown craw-dad!

Siewen came back to face Barton. "It is not fuel, your problem," he said. "Thirst and hunger, yes. You have no food or water, Barton. You must come in; I give you directions. Yes?"

Barton looked at the small comatose lobster beside him, and snorted. After all this time, these creatures still didn't realize what they had on their hands, what they had made of him.

For one thing, they were still trying to lie. Rummaging under his seat, he had found a container of liquid: about two quarts and nearly full. It smelled as if it could be lobster piss and maybe it was, but probably it wouldn't kill him. No point in telling everything he knew, though, Barton thought.

"Where are you, Siewen? I don't mean the location, but what kind of place?"

"It is Director's office, of the research station. Also control area for spaceship landing place just alongside. You can get here easily. Location device, bottom left switch, homes on signal beacon here. Small instrument." Siewen pointed; the thing looked like a portable radio. "Just watch on screen."

"Sure. Are there spaceships there?"

"Yes, several. Different sizes."

Barton told himself to be very, very cautious. "Siewen, has the Director ever been to Earth? Our Earth?"

"Oh yes," Siewen responded. "He was in charge of navigation on expedition picking ourselves up. But first time he or this group ever see humans or Tilari, any of our type humanoid. Some mistakes they made." You can say *that* again, Barton thought. But now he needed more facts, in a hurry.

"What's the smallest ship available that could get from here to Earth? How many does it take to handle such a ship? TELL THEM NOT TO LIE TO ME!"

"There is no cause to lie," Siewen said calmly. "A ship to carry eight is here; it could go twice to Earth and back; one can control it. But you are not to go to Earth, Barton. You are to come here and become a citizen of the Demu. Out of the mercy of the Director and his concern for his egg-child."

Deep in his throat Barton growled, not quite audibly. "We'll see," he said. "Take that robe off, Siewen."

34

"What? Why?"

"Just do it."

He had known all along, Barton thought wearily. He glanced perfunctorily at the feet, long enough to confirm that the little toes had been cut away back through the metatarsals to the heels, and that the toenails were missing. The obliteration of body hair and nipples and navel was no shock, nor was the Demu pattern of abdominal dots. And of course the crotch was like that of a tree, or a lobster.

Siewen must have noticed Barton's gaze; one hand tentatively reached for that juncture, then drew back. "You don't understand," Siewen said. "They didn't know. I said, it was first time this group had to do with humans. Only with other races, not like us. They didn't *know*."

"Sure not," said Barton.

"I don't really mind so, any more," Siewen said hurriedly, "and they don't do that way now. They learned, some from observing you, Barton. Now they retain function and only minimize protrusion. There is one here, done so. I must show."

"Later!" Barton ground out. He didn't want to see any more examples of Demu surgical artistry for a while; his will to live was shaken enough, as it was. "Just tell me one thing, will you? *Why* do they do these things?"

"Hard to understand, for us. But Demu are old race, very old. And for long long time they know of no others, intelligent. They have deep belief, almost instinct, that Demu are the only true *people*. That all others are only animals."

"Well, haven't they learned better than that by *now?* And what does that have to do with—your facelift, and everything?"

"When they meet long ago a race, animals they think, who learn Demu language, it is great shock. Animals being people when only Demu are people. Demu cannot accept. So they—this is only guess by me, you understand, but I think it is very good guess—so they when any animal learns Demu language, make it Demu, best they can. As with me and others. They make mistakes; many die. I am lucky." Barton thought that was a matter of opinion. He didn't bother to say so.

He was still digesting what he had heard when Siewen's voice reminded him that this was no time for philosophizing. He had things to do, fast, before the opposition caught its balance. He couldn't afford to get off the main point.

"Barton!" Siewen began. "You must—"

"LATER! Siewen, get your Director up front with you and translate for us. I'm in a hurry; tell him that; don't either of you try to mess around with me. Now MOVE!"

Barton told them exactly what he wanted. They didn't believe him at first, and he supposed they would have laughed if a lobster knew how to laugh. But he persisted, figuring that he had an ace in the hole.

"Barton," said Siewen, "you are speaking useless. The Director will not give you a spaceship to go to Earth. No one can command the Demu."

"Does the Director want his egg-child back alive, or doesn't he?"

"Wants back, yes," Siewen acknowledged. "But at your price, no. Demu have died before and will die again." I'll drink to that, thought Barton. "Safe return of egg-child buys you life and citizenship among the Demu. No more. I do not want to tell what will be done if you are taken alive and egg-child dead. Now see reason, Barton. You have tried well. You are admired for it, even. But now it is finish. You must come here and accept Director's terms."

"Want to bet?" thought Barton. But he said, "Tell me one more thing, Siewen. Can the Demu regrow lost limbs? Like the lobsters back home?"

"No," said Siewen. "Why ask that?"

"Just curious." Barton paused for a moment, thinking it out. "Siewen, tell the Director that I am getting very hungry." There was a muffled conference on the screen.

"The Director says come here and be fed," Siewen announced. Barton grinned.

"I don't have to," he said softly. "Let me tell you about the last meal I had."

He told them, and the funny part was that Siewen seemed every bit as shocked as the Director. Barton let them chew on the idea a minute before he threw the bomb.

"OK, Siewen, here's how it works. Tell the Director and tell it straight. Either I get the ship to go home in, instructions and all, and the deal gets started right away, or else I have lunch now." He thought about it. "Considering everything, I don't feel especially sadistic. So first I'll just eat the arm I've already broken. I'll leave the screen off, so the Director doesn't have to watch."

Barton hadn't thought a Demu-lobster could get as loud as the Director did then. Eventually Siewen got the floor. It seemed Barton had won his point; he had a good healthy ship for himself. Sure, Mike, thought Barton; just watch out for the curve balls.

Well, he'd known there had to be a handle somewhere in the mess; luckily he'd found it. It had been a one-shot bluff, a game of *schrecklicheit*—because it would have done him no good to carry it out, even if he could have brought himself to do so. But what the Director didn't know wouldn't hurt Barton.

His mind was getting hazy again, ghost-hallucinations flickering around the outskirts. Toothlessly, the Tilari woman was telling him that they were expecting a little bundle from Heaven. He shook his head and tried to concentrate on the essentials.

"OK, Siewen," he said, "I don't need any coordinates to get to you, if I understand this location-blip thing on the screen." Siewen nodded. "Here's what happens," Barton continued. "You and the Director get down by the ship—my ship. Bring your locator gadget with you so I don't have to mess around looking for you when I get there. Everybody else stays away. Any last-minute tricks, I cut the shield and ram us all dead. You got that? Any questions?"

There were several, but Barton simply said "NO" to most of them without paying much attention. He knew what he wanted. There was no point in arguing.

Then Siewen, at the Director's prompting, insisted Barton should see and talk with some other newly made citizens of the Demu, before doing anything so drastic as what he was planning. "The hell with that," said Barton. "Later. Just you two. Nobody else."

It was about an hour that Barton's air car took, cruising to its destination. He saw no signs of habitation; possibly the research station was the only Demu installation on the planet. The little lobster was conscious again and whimpered occasionally, but it looked so apologetic that Barton didn't feel like hitting it, even to maintain the precedent of silence. Anyway, the small sounds weren't joggling his mind as the screaming had done. He sipped on the foul-tasting water and decided it wasn't lobster piss after all, since his small lobster made begging motions toward it, and drank some when he relented and made the offer. Then it opened its mouth and lifted its short tongue. Barton had no idea what the gesture meant, but the creature rewarded his generosity with silence. It was a good trade.

The spaceport, when he reached it, didn't look like much. There were three really big ships, two medium and one small. Upright torpedo shapes, not saucers. The big ones would be the meat wagons, he thought. They had an air of neglect about them.

He set the car to hover a little above and to one side of the small ship, facing a delegation of robed figures at fairly close range. He cranked up magnification on the direct-view display screen, and saw that there were four of them.

"What the hell you think you're doing?" Barton said. "I said *nobody else*."

Siewen shrugged and spread his arms apologetically. "You must see other new Demu citizens," he said. "You said later, but only chance is now. You must know. With me there were mistakes, yes. But these are functional breeders and Demu citizens. As millions of Earth humans will become, and all eventually, when the Demu have arranged. But see——! You will not forget Limila; the other is of Earth." Siewen gestured.

The two figures slipped off their hoods and robes. Barton took for granted the hairless earless noseless heads with serrated lips hiding toothless mouths with shortened tongues. (But oh! the lost lovely curve of Limila's lips!) He didn't expect to see breasts set low on Limila's ribcage, and sure enough, there weren't any. The lobsters scrubbed clean, singlemindedly. Siewen had said that the smooth treelike look of her, where Barton was looking now, still concealed true function: even so, it was one more coal on the fire in Barton's heart and mind.

Then there was the man, an Earthman if Siewen had that part right. Siewen had certainly told truth that the Demu had "minimized protrusion" in the genital area; whether or not the Demu citizen on the screen "retained function" was of only academic interest to Barton. He was trying very hard not to throw up. It's like the old joke about the man who went into the barbershop, he thought. "Bob Peters here?" "No, just shave-and-a-haircut."

"*Siewen!*" he shouted. "I've changed my mind."

"You come now and become Demu citizen?"

"Like bloody hell I do!" Barton, bursting with frustration and hatred, took especial pains not to turn and kill the small lobster beside him. Hell, it probably hadn't even carved up its first human yet.

"Then what is it you mean?" said Siewen.

"I mean we all go on the ship," Barton said. "The two of us here and the four of you there. All together we go in; don't move yet, any of you, or I crash the lot of us."

There was a conference down below. "Not possible," said Siewen. "The Director does not agree."

"In that case," said Barton, "I think it's time I had some lunch. I've changed my mind; I'll leave the screen on so that the Director can observe. I always did like crab salad." And he reached for the dangling broken arm of the small quiet lobster, the Director's egg-child.

Not too much later the Demu spacecraft lifted off, carrying six assorted entities with very little rapport.

The ship's basic control system was roughly the same as the air car's, though with many more control switches. For the moment, all Barton needed was power, navigation and an outside view. He'd worry about the rest of it later, when he had to.

Siewen assured Barton that the Director had given him the correct course toward the region of Earth, and had agreed there would be no pursuit. Barton assured Siewen that the Director damn well better had, if the Director wanted Barton to watch his diet.

A tense truce prevailed, largely because of Barton's policy that he would not put up with the company of fully functional Demu. He had broken one of the Director's arms the moment they were sealed inside the ship, when that worthy had tried to make use of a concealed weapon. Then after a moment's thought, he broke the other one. Subtler methods might have done the job, but Barton had found something that worked, so he stayed with it. He had trouble thinking outside the narrow boundaries of his main goal: freedom. The Director treated Barton with considerable respect, and was fed at intervals by his egg-child, one-handedly.

Barton set and splinted the broken limbs, which was more than the Demu had bothered to do for him in like case. His own forearm still had a permanent jog to it and hurt more often than it didn't.

That wasn't all the hurt in Barton. Limila remembered

him; the Demu hadn't done anything to her mind, that he could detect. He realized, though, that he wasn't much of a judge of minds. Including his own.

She came to him, in the control area which he never left unguarded; when he slept, he sealed it off from the rest of the ship. She told him, in her *sh-zh* lobster accent, that she wanted love with him. She parted her maimed lips and showed the Demu-shortened tongue lifted in what he now knew to be the Demu smile. With the forty teeth gone he could see it quite clearly.

The trouble was that the Demu-Limila still had Limila's shape of skull and chin and cheekbones. The quicksilver-colored huge-irised eyes were as deep as ever, though their shape was subtly marred by the slight cropping of the eyelids. Her arms and legs were graceful if Barton avoided seeing the hands and feet, and aside from breasts and navel and external genitals, the Demu had not altered her superb lithe torso.

Barton closed his eyes to shut out the sight of the Demu-denuded face and head, put his cheek against Limila's and tried to make love with her. It might have worked if he hadn't noticed the ear that should have been against his nose and wasn't. So instead he failed; he failed her. He was crying when he gently put her out of the control area and relocked it, and for a long time after.

Then he went into the main passenger compartment to see if he could keep from killing the Director and his egg-child out of hand; for the moment, he succeeded. It was a success that helped Barton's dwindling self-confidence. He had all he could do to keep himself under control, let alone keeping the ship on course or his fellow-voyagers in hand.

For one thing he was continually bone-tired. The pseudo-death experience had taken more out of him than he'd realized at first. Followed by a period of hectic activity and nervous tension, and now the need for near-constant alertness, it still dragged him down; recovery was so slow as to be undetectable.

His condition made him easy prey to mental lapses. He became accustomed to waking, as often as not, to find himself apparently back in his cage; each time it took minutes to fight his way back to reality. More frightening were occasional hallucinatory lapses in the presence of others: once he found himself on the verge of defending his Ph.D. Orals presentation to the professor who had

40

washed him out, before he realized that the prof couldn't possibly be there; it was the Director who sat before him.

Every sight of Limila burned more deeply into him than the last, into a place where gentleness had once lived. Where now grew something else—something that frightened him.

He didn't let the others see his difficulties any more than he could help, and they were too afraid of him to try to take advantage of his lapses. They were not wrong; Barton was walking death and knew it; he had been for longer than he liked to admit. He kept to himself as much as possible, consonant with the need to keep tabs on his passengers.

Once he looked into a mirror and found he didn't recognize himself. He had no idea how long it had been since he might have been able to do so. He looked at the face in the mirror and decided he didn't like it. But then it wasn't really his own work, he realized when he stopped to think about it. The thought made him feel a little better, but not much.

So it was a long tired haul. The "trip out," as Barton thought of it, must have been either on a faster ship or with a lot of induced hibernation; he had no way of knowing which, if either, was the correct guess.

Limila came to him again, wanting his love. He tried to turn her away; she didn't want to go. "Barton," she said, clinging to him desperately, "I am still Limila. They do all this to me, yes"—she stepped back and gestured at her head, at her body—"but inside I am still ME. I AM!" His eyes blurred with tears, losing the fine outline of skull and cheekbones, of neck and shoulders as she stood before him. Seeing, then, only the lobsterish lack of features, it was easier for him to keep shaking his head speechlessly and back her firmly out the door, locking it after her with a vicious yank that nearly broke the lever.

The next time he saw her she was slumped in a corner looking at the floor. He didn't disturb her trance, but it disturbed *him* a lot.

Hallucinating was a dangerous game to play, for him, now; he knew that. But he thought it might be a solution, with Limila. He invited her into the control area, looked at her and deliberately tried to substitute in his mind her natural appearance.

It worked, and for a few moments he thought it was *really* going to work. But his mind-picture of unmaimed-

Limila shifted and distorted. Against all the force he could bring, it changed into the other Tilaran woman, the one with no nail-joints, the blank stare and the scars at the temples. It writhed and screamed, dying again. Barton screamed too, but he didn't hear most of it. When he fought his way back to reality, the sight of the lobster-faced Limila seemed almost beautiful. But only almost. He could not love it, would never be able to do that.

Limila crouched against the door, terrified. "You must think I'm crazy," Barton said. "I'm sorry. I thought I could fool myself, pretend you were unchanged. It—it didn't work out quite that way. I saw something worse, instead." He knew he couldn't explain further, and said only, "I'm sorry, Limila."

She went away of her own accord, looking back fearfully.

Barton tried to pair her off with the Demu-ized Earthmale who supposedly "retained function." That one was a real enigma; he wouldn't speak to Barton, or to anyone at all except in Demu. Barton couldn't discover his name or anything else about him, except that apparently he had become Demu wholeheartedly in spirit as well as in guise. Barton decided that when it came down to cases he had more respect for Doktor Siewen. Which wasn't saying much.

At any rate the pseudo-Demu wanted nothing to do with Limila, nor she with him. Barton asked Limila about the matter but wasn't sure whether he misunderstood the answer or simply didn't believe it. "He say," Limila told Barton, "it not Demu breeding season now." She gave Barton the view of uplifted-tongue, the Demu smile. "The Tilari do not wait on season, nor you, I think." But she had smiled like a Demu. Of course, Barton reflected, locking himself alone into the control area, it was the only way they had left her to smile. Well, there wasn't any answer; maybe there never had been. Or not lately.

Barton now avoided Limila almost entirely. It was the only thing he could do for either of them. The next time the functional Demu-Earthmale got in his way, Barton without warning knocked him square on his back against the opposite bulkhead and was happily beginning to kick him to death before Limila tried to push between them, shrilling, "NO, NO! WHY? WHY?" Barton had no answer, shrugged and moved away, marveling at his ability to leave the two Demu alive as long as he had.

Actually, not noticing the change much, Barton had become rather fond of the Director's small egg-child. Without knowing its name, or being able to pronounce it, probably, Barton thought of it as female. He called it "Whnee," after the sound of its rather plaintive little cries when uncertain what was wanted of it. It tried to be helpful with the ship's few chores, and Barton came to think of it as a nice-enough kid; too bad she came from such a rotten family. Occasionally it would make the Demu lifted-tongue smile at him, and oddly he found the gesture not at all repulsive, but rather appealing.

Siewen was no trouble; he was only a shell, not a person. He reflected the thought or policy of the One in Charge; once that had been the Director, now it was Barton. Any authority was good enough for that which had once been Doktor Siewen.

The Director was no problem either. Barton simply didn't bother to take the splint-harnesses off his arms, even when they had probably healed. The other Demu-human tried to unstrap the Director once, but Barton caught him and so reacted that neither Whosits nor anyone else tried it again. It took another set of splints; Barton guessed he was in a rut.

But what the hell; it worked, which was more than Barton could say for much of anything else he'd tried lately. The only late effort he liked much was his clothes. He'd hated the Demu robes, which all the others still wore. He had essayed nudity but found it too reminiscent of his captivity. Eventually he had ripped a robe into two pieces: one made a loincloth and the other a short cape that left his arms free. Barton didn't care what it looked like; it was comfortable. He could use all the comfort he could get.

Finally the ship approached Earth's solar system. Barton was going home. Not really, of course. There was nothing for him there. He knew he'd be lucky to get a hearing before being locked up as a public menace. But he had to take the risk, because it was everybody's chance, maybe the only one Earth would ever get. He wasn't looking for a return to normal life. That wasn't in the cards; he'd been playing too long with a 38-card deck. But there was one thing, for sure.

Barton had survived; maybe Earth could survive. He had to give it the chance to try. He was bringing home a

43

fair sample of what Earth was up against: the lobsters, their ship and some of their other works.

The lobsters would be confined and studied; Barton smiled grimly at that prospect. He wondered how long it would take them to get used to the fact that on Earth it's messy to piss on the floor. He might go to see the little one sometimes if anyone would let him; they could say "Whnee" to each other and maybe now and then she'd raise her tongue in the Demu smile.

He couldn't bring himself to worry about what might become of Siewen or Whosits; he had enough worry on his own account. But he hoped someone—someone more capable than he—would take care of Limila. All Barton could do was try to take care of Earth, and maybe of Barton with luck.

The ship could help a lot. It and its weapons would be analyzed and copied, maybe even improved. Human science had been moving fast, the last Barton had heard; no telling how much further it had gone.

Most important, though, was showing Earth what the well-barbered humanoid wouldn't be wearing next season if the Demu had their way, as modeled by Siewen and Limila and Whosits. Barton thought he knew how the people of Earth would react.

They wouldn't like it any better than he did. They might decide to teach the Demu what it meant, to cage a man.

II.

Humpty Dumpty

Barton approached Earth like a boy asking a girl for his first dance. He was dubious of his welcome, both in space and on the ground. Stalling, he took a course that kept the moon between his ship and his destination, while he tried to think his way through the situation.

The alien ship and its occupants were bound to be something of a surprise to the home folks, and it would take time for Barton to get his story across straight. He was braced for that necessity.

What the locals would make of his companions was something else again. It would require a sharp observer, he thought, to tell them apart at first: the Demu, God rot their hypothetical souls, were remorselessly thorough in enforcing conformity of appearance. Barton was hit by a surge of belated relief: maybe he looked like the wrath of God and fresh out of thunderbolts, but at least he still carried all his normal appendages.

The moon approached and was past; Earth was ahead. The blast of a warhead, a megaton at least, caught Barton off guard. The Demu shields blocked heat and other radiation, but the buffet dumped Barton out of his seat and slammed him against a wall, bad arm first. Cursing, he clawed his way back to the controls.

Evasive action was skittering zigzag toward Earth; Barton did it, while fiddling frantically with the communications controls. Not too much chance that Earth and Demu frequencies or modulation systems would match up, but worth trying.

From outside the ship he could hear nothing but incoherent noise. He figured it was probably the same at the other end, but he kept talking anyway.

"This is a captured alien ship. For Chrissakes don't blow it up; it wasn't all that easy to get. God DAMmit!"—as another warhead went off near him—"I said I captured this thing. I stole it; you need it. Lay off the stupid fireworks . . ." and so on. There was no sign that anyone was paying attention.

With artificial gravity, he didn't have to mess around with the gradual approach. Barton guessed that the shield-effect would keep him from getting fried; he hit air in a full dive. He scared himself by the narrow margin he had left when he pulled out level. But at least he was down where nobody could get a clear shot at him, and with enough speed to beat anything local that he knew about.

He was over the Pacific; that was all he could tell about the geography. It was either dawn or sunset; he'd lost orientation after that second blast. Barton bet on dawn because he didn't know how to fly the ship near the surface in the dark. He hoped he was right, because he didn't know how to speak Chinese, either.

Meanwhile he kept saying things like "All I want to do is land this bastard and let somebody look it over. My name is Barton and I used to *live* here." Somebody was hammering on the other side of the control-room door, wanting in. Somebody could go to hell, the way discipline seemed to have done around here. Out in space where he could leave the controls and move around, no one had bothered him this way. Barton decided he'd make a lousy drill sergeant; his teachings didn't seem to stick very well.

A voice came over the comm-gear; someone on the ground (a computer, more likely) had decoded the Demu modulation pattern and matched it. Probably hitting every frequency band in reach, Barton suspected. "Calling the human on the Raider ship," the voice said. "Are you in control of that ship? Come in, please."

"Yeah, yeah," said Barton. "I got the ship; where do I put it?" His relief was so great that the event hardly registered: that this was the first contact he'd had with Earth since the Demu had taken him. How many years had it been? He had no idea.

A nervous laugh came from the other end. "You sound

human enough, all right," the voice said. "Are you alone?"

"Hell no; I brought the Tenth Marines with me, band and all. What did you think, dummy?" Barton caught himself. "Sorry; I'm a little bent out of shape. No, I'm not alone, but I'm in charge. I have two of the Demu—the Raiders, you call them; I guess they've been back here some?—as prisoners. Take it easy on the little one; she's just a kid. Hasn't done anything, that I know of, to have taken out on her. The big one, her old man, was Director of the research station that carved up the other three on here, that used to look like us but don't any more. To him you can do any damn thing you want, except kill him: that's my privilege; don't anybody forget it." Barton caught himself just short of fully raving.

"OK," he said, "will somebody talk me in to land this bucket someplace, please?"

"Are you low on fuel or anything?"

"No." Low on patience, maybe, but he didn't say it.

The voice talked him in. The Demu instruments he knew how to operate, lacking Demu ground-based locator equipment, were no good to him. Local radar spotted his position and course so that he could be told how and when to turn, when to slow down, and what to look for at the designated landing site. He had guessed right on the dawn part; they brought him down somewhere in New Mexico. It was about noon there.

Barton sweat the landing, but the ship turned out to be practically foolproof; he was sure he was overcontrolling, but it touched ground gently. The Demu shield helped, he supposed. He felt the large muscles in his neck and shoulders relax almost explosively, and only then realized how tense he had been.

But maybe this was no time to relax. The outside viewer showed him a lot of tanks and artillery surrounding him at close range, so he was in no hurry to chop the ship's protective field. "What is the hell is all the hardware for?" he asked rather plaintively.

"Well, you must realize we can't take any chances, Barton."

Barton laughed right out loud; he couldn't help it. "Buddy, you're taking chances right now you don't even know about. You don't have any choice, come to that. I can help your odds. And get this: I'm not taking any chances at all. I don't have to; I've done that bit." He

47

thought a minute, aimed a device and briefly activated it.

"That big hunk of gun off to my left," he said. It was the largest of the lot, that he could see. "Tell 'em to point that at me; just to point it. And see what happens."

Barton waited. Nothing happened, because he had used the Demu unconsciousness weapon on that gun crew. He had to make his point, and sometimes it takes a while. Patiently he waited until the voice channel quieted.

"All right," he said finally, "somebody has to trust somebody and I will if you will. Can we can the crap now and get to it?"

"What do you want?" The voice was tense and a little shaky.

"Nothing much. Just get the hardware off me and I'll keep mine off you. There have to be some big wheels out there someplace who want to talk. I want to talk with them, too, because I damn well have news for them. So if they'll come here to this ship I'll come out and meet 'em, and bring my zoo with me. We can talk, and it's perfectly safe for everybody unless some damn fool tries to cross me."

"I don't understand that last part, Barton."

"Be your age." He was dealing with paranoids, he told himself, so he had to fit the part. As though he didn't, already . . . "I push one button and we have a three-hundred-mile crater around here. I'll have the button in my hand." He heaved a sigh of exasperation. "Can we just talk now, instead?"

Barton had no such button. But he knew that sometimes a man has to bluff a little.

He shut off the voice channel: best to quit while he was ahead. Systematically he checked through the control assembly of switches, across and down, deactivating all but standby power to the ship. He was struck, wistfully, by the fact that he'd never learned the function of most of those switches—had never activated them, had never dared. Well, other people could tackle that job now, if things worked out.

Barton looked around the control room of his ship. Hell, it was like leaving home. Not that there was anything he needed or wanted to take along. His snappy two-piece outfit, much smudged, was the lot. Barton turned abruptly and joined the others in the main compartment.

48

There they sat, all in Demu robes. No way of knowing which had hammered on the control-room door at a crucial moment. Barton didn't ask; it made no difference.

"We're on Earth," he said. "We go out now, to meet the people. If you have anything you want to keep with you, bring it. Siewen, Limila: interpret."

Little was said. Siewen shrilled a few lobster phrases to Whosits and the Director. Limila sat looking starkly ahead. Whnee scuttled to her bunk and picked up a few items to tuck into her robe. Barton wondered whether the others were out of brains or merely out of ears. So he repeated himself, only louder.

It took a while, but eventually Barton herded everyone out of the Demu ship to talk to the home folks. He faced a General Parkhurst, a Presidential Assistant Tarleton of the Space Agency and a bevy of news-media types among the trailing retinue. Barton put thumbsdown on the newsies. "Get those bastards out of here," he said. "They never get anything right in their lives, the first time. This is too important to let them fuck it up. Later, maybe, but not right now." But he was too late to stop them from taking pictures of the two Demu and the three pseudo-Demu. Not that it mattered all that much, probably, but it did bother him.

General Parkhurst was a small dapper man; his idea of efficiency was to do everything in a hurry. He took several reels of taped notes in the first hour. Then he departed abruptly while Barton was still trying to explain the difference between the Demu and his other companions. Barton shrugged and didn't miss him much.

The civilian, Tarleton, was a different bucket of clams, a big sloppy slow-talking bear of a man. He asked and he listened and he observed, without trying to tell Barton what to do. Barton had all his passengers shuck their robes and hoods to show themselves, whether they liked it or not.

The Director was apparently quite indifferent to being paraded before an alien species. Of course his upper limbs were still strapped into splint-harnesses, so there wasn't much he could have done about it.

The smaller Demu shrank timidly until Barton patted it on the head and said "Whnee" in a gentle, encouraging tone of voice. Then it displayed its chitinous protrusionless exoskeleton in relative confidence. Barton had un-

splinted its healed arm some time ago, and also Whosits';
he still didn't care to trust the Director that far.

"These are the Demu, the race we're up against," he
said. "The big one ran the show at our zoo, as I said before,
and it's the daddy or mother or something of the little one,
if you can figure out how. She's his egg-child, anyway.
What that means I don't know; they haven't said."

"It might imply more than one method of reproduc-
tion," Tarleton said mildly, talking around the stem of his
unlighted pipe. "Now how about these others?"

"Two of them used to be human males," Barton began.
"The skinny one with nothing between his legs is a Doktor
Siewen; they amputated his spirit too, I think. Whosits
there won't talk anything but Demu, so I don't know his
name; supposedly he's still male, but not much of one by
the looks of him."

Tarleton looked closely at the pertinent parts of Whosits, something Barton preferred not to do. There was a
sort of nubbin; it might still work, at that. Hardly seemed
worth it, though.

"There's no fertility," Tarleton said, "or won't be for
long. Apparently one gonad is left, tucked neatly back
into the abdominal cavity. The Demu must not have
realized that this would produce sterility and eventual
impotence." Whosits' serrated lips twitched but he said
nothing.

"This is Limila," Barton said then. "She's a woman of a
humanoid race much like ours: the Tilari."

"A woman?" Tarleton said slowly.

"Hell yes," Barton said. "Use your eyes; they didn't
cut her butt off." He toned his voice down; he hadn't
meant to shout. "Dammit, she was beautiful, Tarleton.
Different from us, several ways. An extra toe and finger
she had, all around. Forty teeth. Breasts set down low like
so"—he gestured—"forehead clear up here by the ears.
But beautiful. And mostly our kind of people.

"Why for Chrissakes, Tarleton," he said, mind jarred
back to the bloody death of the other Tilari woman, whose
name he'd never known, "they're even interfertile with
us." His jaw locked. "Don't ask me how I know. Not just
yet."

Tarleton didn't ask. Unlike General Parkhurst, he
seemed to sense that at the moment Barton was something like a time bomb coming to term, needing careful,

50

patient defusing. Barton was dimly thankful for the man's presence.

Tarleton motioned the five exhibits to resume their robes, and directed the laying out of food and drink he'd ordered earlier. Apparently he did not see any of the five as human; he hadn't addressed a word to them.

"Can the Demu eat our food?" he asked.

"Damned if I know," Barton answered. "All I ever saw them eat, and all they ever fed me, was liquids and several kinds of wet lumpy glop. If they can't eat our stuff there's plenty of theirs on the ship. Siewen can fetch it."

The Demu ate Earth food all right, chewing with their hard sawtooth lips. But the other three couldn't manage anything except liquids and "glop" foods; their lips looked lobsterlike but chewing was out of the question. So Siewen was sent to the ship for Demu rations.

There was a hassle when the military guard, left by General Parkhurst, didn't want to admit Doktor Siewen. Barton headed for the ship; before the guard could shoot him, Tarleton intervened.

"Get that sonofabitch away from my ship!" Barton exploded. "Who the hell does Parkhurst think he is?"

"Easy now," Tarleton said mildly. "The General naturally tends to think in terms of security. The guard doesn't realize that you, of course, have free access." He motioned the guard away to one side, where he wouldn't bug Barton.

"Any more of this crap," Barton continued, "and Earth can go whistle. We'll see if maybe the Tilari, Limila's people, have a better idea of how to use a ship." Limila cringed; he had no time to wonder why.

"It'll be all right now, Barton," Tarleton said. "Come on; have something to eat. You'll feel better."

And in truth Barton did. He hadn't realized how much he'd missed the smells, tastes and textures of his own planet's foods, all the years he'd spent in a Demu cage.

For the first time, he thought to ask how long it had been. The answer was a little less than eight years. Barton repeated the current date. "What d'ya know?" he said. "I was forty a couple of weeks ago. Could have had a birthday party if I'd known." He grimaced. "Yeah, sure. Some party!" But Tarleton was talking on a radiophone link to someone he addressed as "sir," and only nodded absently.

After lunch a lanky technician insisted on taking fingerprints. He didn't seem too put out that Demu fingers had no recognizable patterns, but was a little upset that no one except Barton had enough fingers to fill all the blanks on his forms. Barton tried to explain that Limila's prints couldn't possibly be on file; the man grinned, and drawled, "Orders, buddy." He was so phlegmatic about it that Barton merely shrugged. Tarleton relaxed visibly.

Whosits' prints were taken by main force while he protested shrilly in lobster language, but the Demu made no such complaints. The Director certainly didn't; Barton had finally unstrapped his arms in honor of his first Earthly meal, and the Director was experiencing freedom of movement for the first time in a long while. Twinges and all, probably. Barton kept an eye on him at first; then he got tired of the necessity and went into the ship. He came out with a small device necessary to the operation of the controls; even if the Director managed to sneak onto the ship, he couldn't get away with it. If the Director had had the sense to do the same thing at the far end of the ride, Barton thought, things could have been rough.

Tarleton was trying to explain what the problem was. Bureaucrats and administrators with the habit of explaining to Barton what the problem was had helped him decide to drop physics and take up painting. But this man seemed like a sensible sort, so Barton decided he'd better listen.

"The problem is," Tarleton said, "that we need to study the ship, and quite near is the best facility for that purpose. Also we need to study the Demu and—er—the others, and a hospital on the East Coast is best for that. In Maryland, as it happens. But," he concluded, "the hell of it is that we need the Demu, the big one at least, on hand here for information about the ship."

"Yeh, and Siewen and Limila to interpret," Barton added.

"Precisely. Any ideas?"

"Well, just offhand, Tarleton, I'd say a medical or life-study lab is a lot easier to move than the stuff it's going to take to check out this ship. And if anything goes wrong, like maybe blowing up the whole schmeer, you

52

want a lot of empty country around. You're not going to find that in Maryland."

Tarleton looked at him obliquely. "Speaking of things blowing up, how about that button in your pocket? The three-hundred-mile-crater button you mentioned earlier?"

Barton grinned sheepishly. "No such animal," he admitted. "All it was, those fogheads had a lot of guns aimed at me and I didn't like it." He was surprised to see the shudder that shook Tarleton; he hadn't realized the man had been so tense under his slow easygoing exterior. "I'm sorry," Barton said. "I'd have said something before, but I forgot all about it."

"That's OK," the big man said. "Let's get to work figuring things out." He ran Barton through the high points of his story again; he got on the phone to D.C. several times. He even questioned Siewen briefly, though it was obvious he would have felt as much at ease interviewing a giant grasshopper.

Then it was time for another meal. Afterward Barton was really and truly pooped out of his mind. It was hard to tell a coherent story, leaving out the hallucinations, and Barton figured he'd better not tell anybody about that part. Not ever.

Some improvised quarters in kit form had arrived by truck and were in process of assembly, but Barton said the hell with that. "We'll sleep on the ship. I'm used to it, and the guards can make sure nobody goes sleepwalking."

Tarleton didn't like the idea too well, so Barton showed him the locking device he'd removed from the ship. "Here, these are the keys to the car. You hold 'em for tonight." He looked the other man in the eyes. "I guess you know what this means: I have to trust you a lot. I wouldn't want anyone else, like that Parkhurst, to get his hands on the gadget. OK?" Tarleton nodded, and Barton shepherded his charges aboard for the night. After eight years or so, that was Barton's first day back on Earth.

The next few days were hectic but inconclusive. Quarters were erected for the research people who were being moved in, as well as for Barton and his entourage. There was a hassle the second day when Limila refused to be quartered anywhere at all away from Barton; they settled in a two-bedroom unit not far from Siewen and Whosits and the two Demu. The latter had a larger unit, built much the same. Except that there was no guard on Barton's quarters.

Portable lab buildings were brought to the site, and truckloads of gear with which to equip them. The ship itself, Barton at the controls, was moved to the vicinity of a complex of buildings about five kilometers away, behind a low range of hills. Fat lot of good that would do, Barton thought, but kept his reservations to himself.

And eventually General Parkhurst trundled his guns and tanks back to the nearby Army base he commanded.

Trickles of response began to come in from the outside world. Barton's fingerprints were verified, and Doktor Siewen's; Whosits' were not on file in any country lending cooperation. Barton hoped no one had wasted much effort looking for Limila's.

Barton got a post-mortem on his own former personal life. His father had died five years ago, and his mother a few months later; he had no siblings or other close relatives. Seven years after his disappearance Barton had been declared legally dead. His ex-wife and her new husband were living well, helped somewhat by his estate, since his paintings had gradually become popular enough to be valuable. His ex-mistress, Leonie, had married and gained four children, plus ten or fifteen pounds of weight for each of them.

Well, it was all pretty much as he'd expected. Par for the course. Barton could find no emotional reaction in himself; it was as though his former life were someone else's—a total stranger's.

Tarleton assured him that while his estate was legally out of reach, a grateful government would see to his financial well-being. Barton would believe that when he saw it, but the keys to the car were in his own pockets again and he hadn't signed anything yet, he reminded himself. He requested a small safe for his bedroom and set his own combination; the keys were secure enough for now.

Idly, once, he guessed at the value of the Demu ship in terms of ransom for the planet Earth. Then he shrugged, and moved a mental decimal point four places to the left. He'd be lucky to get a dime over living expenses and a consultant fee, but no harm in trying. Besides, he wanted to see the chintzy bastards sweat when he hit 'em with the big numbers. Just for kicks; he hadn't had many of those in the past eight years.

Doktor Siewen's middle-aged son and daughter sent their kindest personal regards. They were *so* glad their father was alive and safe, but Barton noticed they didn't offer to visit him or vice versa. He suspected they'd seen those first news pics, before the government had suppressed the story. Siewen didn't seem to notice, or care.

And still there was no word on Whosits. Maybe Siewen had been wrong; maybe Whosits wasn't of Earth origin after all. Well, who cared? Not Barton, for sure!

Tarleton filled him in on what Earth knew of the Demu, the "Raiders."

"The ship that got you was spotted on radar, but nobody believed it. It was too big." Barton gave him an estimate of the size of the larger ships he'd seen at the Demu research station. Tarleton said the radar had shown something a lot bigger. Barton wondered if the protective shield could have bollixed the readings. Tarleton shrugged. "We can check that out when it's time for you to fly this one for us next." That was OK with Barton.

"We have no idea how many people that ship took," Tarleton continued, "because every day, all over the world, people disappear. Some are murdered, some are accidents and suicides, some disappear deliberately. But the best estimate is that the Demu got at least several hundred."

Barton looked surprised. Tarleton raised his eyebrows. "Well, of course," he said, "you saw only the people—including those not of this planet—in your own, er, cage. A ship of the size you indicate could have contained many such.

"The Raiders, the Demu, have been back twice since then." That too was news to Barton, though he'd guessed something of the sort when he first heard the term "Raiders." "Once about four years ago; they must have taken over a thousand that time. And then roughly two years later." Tarleton smiled grimly. "That time we were ready, or thought we were. With the high-G rockets and warheads, like the ones thrown at you when you came in. The Pentagon still claims they got that ship, but judging from the results with yours I'd guess the Demu were merely startled and cautious, and withdrew for the time being.

"Well, with luck and a good analysis of your ship,

55

Barton, we may be in a considerably better position to handle them, next time they turn up."

Barton nodded. That was what he had in mind. For starters.

Research got under way so unobtrusively that Barton hardly noticed how quickly it developed. On the ship and its weapons, on the Demu, on Siewen and Limila and Whosits. And then, as he had known it must, on Barton.

The physical exams were all right. He was organically sound, he was told, and had been living with a lower background-radiation level than Earth's. He took the offer to have his lumpy arm rebroken and set to heal straight; he had it done with a shoulder block rather than a general anesthetic. The cast was light and didn't bother him half as much as the unset break had for so long.

His teeth needed some work. All right; dental care was available at Parkhurst's Army base. Novocaine though, not gas.

He was questioned repeatedly and in detail, by persons and teams of several specialties. Considering that he had to edit a number of important details out of his experiences, he told a fairly straight story. What he omitted was of a personal nature, mostly: the two mutilated women who had successively shared his cage, and some of his stronger reactions both before and after escaping. And of course, any mention of self-hypnosis or hallucination. The only mental irregularities he admitted were the temporary memory-loss effects of the Demu sleep gun.

He had devised, he thought, a fairly credible explanation of his escape: that in the absence of any better idea he'd formed the habit of lying on the food-service area of the floor after meals, and that once, finally, the thing had malfunctioned and let him through.

Everyone bought it, except the psychology boys. Dr. Roderick Skinner, acting head of the branch in the absence of a Dr. Fox, called on Barton one afternoon. Limila was elsewhere, being interviewed. Skinner carried a briefcase, from which he extracted an untidy clipboard. "Barton, I'll tell you frankly that I'm not yet satisfied with the total picture." Barton waved him to a chair.

"Yeh, well, sit down. Be with you in a minute." He went to the kitchen, opened a can of beer. He thought for a moment and decided what the hell, he might as

56

well waste a beer on this clown in the interests of public relations. He didn't ask, but merely brought another one out and handed it to the psychologist. "OK, shoot. What don't you like?"

"That's the trouble, Barton; I'm not certain. Everything *seems* to check, but the data do not quite explain the reported events."

"Well, I've told you everything I can." That much was true, Barton thought; he carefully had not said he'd told everything he remembered. He savored the difference.

"We ran it through the computer, Barton, and we keep getting nulls in the output. Any idea why?"

"Not my line. What's your idea?"

"That there are nulls in the input—in your report. So we're going to have to check for them."

"If you have any new questions, ask away. I've answered the old ones enough times, I think."

"It's not a matter of new questions. It's a matter of confirming your answers to the ones we've already asked."

"You want to look at the Demu research station yourself? Bon voyage, Skinner; it's a long trip."

Skinner's laugh wasn't convincing. "No, we'll do our checking right here, Barton. With you."

"OK; get on with it, then."

"I didn't mean *right* here, actually. The necessary drugs are best administered in the laboratory under controlled conditions."

"*Drugs?*" Controlled conditions—Barton had had enough of those! He went rigid inside. "What the hell are you talking about?"

"A simple hypnotic, Barton. Quite harmless. We think that some crucial memories are hiding out in your subconscious mind, and we must get them out in the open, for analysis."

"Not with hypnotics, you don't. Not on *me*. The Demu—'"

"I'm afraid we have to; you see—"

"You have to *shit*, too, if you eat regular! No dice, Skinner. You take your drugs and—"

"I think you forget who you're talking to!"

"And I think you forgot where you are. You're in *my* place. Get out."

"It won't do you any good to be hostile, Barton. I can have you *brought* in to the labs, you know."

That did it. "Like *this?*" He grabbed Skinner, pulled

him upright, spun him around. The man was yammering; Barton didn't listen. He aimed Skinner at the door. He didn't exactly throw him out or kick him out, either one; it was a combination of both. The door was open but the screen wasn't. Nothing fatal, but messy. "And *stay* out, you son of a bitch!"

Skinner wouldn't be back, but Barton knew he was in the soup, for sure.

He had stalled off all requests to take mental tests, but now he'd blown it. He went looking for Tarleton, trying to think of an excuse to get the man to take the heat off him, but he was in D.C. briefing the President or something. Barton thought again. Dr. Fox, whose minion he had thrown through the screen, was arriving the next day. Barton decided to be one of her first customers, and, next morning, was.

Dr. Arleta Fox was a compact woman in her thirties, with frizzy auburn hair and a face like that of an especially attractive Pekingese. Her smile was friendly but made Barton wonder if he were really out of range of a fast snap. She asked him what the problem was. Well, that was a nice switch.

"Your boy wanted to poke hypnotics into me," Barton said. "I got mad and threw him out."

"Yes, I believe he mentioned that," Dr. Fox said, with considerable understatement. "What's your twistup on hypnotics, Mr. Barton? You know we have to get all the subliminal data you may have—things you saw without noticing that you saw them."

"I had enough different kinds of dope from the lobsters to last me," said Barton. "In my food, in the air: you name it; I had it. I don't need any more. I tried to tell Skinner, but he wouldn't listen."

"He had his orders, Mr. Barton." The smile. Unconsciously, Barton pulled his hand back. "Perhaps that was my mistake. But you see, we have no real psychological data on you at all, more recent than eight years ago before all this happened, so I had no way of knowing there would be a problem." Barton nodded, but said nothing.

"I'll make a bargain with you, Mr. Barton. As I said, we have no recent psychological information on you, whatsoever. If you'll take the standard battery of tests, over the next few days, we'll shelve the question of using hypnotics."

"For how long?" Barton asked.

"Indefinitely. Until you give your consent. Whatever you say."

"Never, then. It's a deal, Doctor. Thanks." Barton stood up.

"Here tomorrow morning at nine sharp, Mr. Barton? We'll provide pencil and paper."

Barton smiled, nodded and went out, surprised to note how heavily he was sweating. Well, he wasn't out of the woods by any means, but maybe he had a chance. At least they couldn't open his mind and see what was there, that not even Barton knew about for sure. He wasn't ready to look at that stuff himself, and he knew it. Meanwhile he didn't want anyone else grabbing a sneak preview.

He caught a ride to the ship. Nothing much doing there: they were still piddling around snipping off bits of materials for analysis. At this rate, Barton thought, the ship was going to look as though it had been gnawed by mice, before the government in its infinite wisdom actually got around to seeing what the damn thing would do.

However, he had one pleasant surprise. Kreugel, Tarleton's crew chief for ship operations, greeted him. "Hey, Mr. Barton! I think we're going to get the handle on the artificial gravity, and that's not more than a jump or two from their space drive."

Barton was flabbergasted. "Now how in hell did you manage *that?*"

"When we learned how to read the circuit diagrams and equipment drawings, it turned out to be awfully close to what the Space Agency labs have been working on for the past three-four years. Close enough that I think we've nearly got it whipped."

"Hey, hold it," said Barton. "*What* circuit diagrams? And how did you learn to read them, anyway?" He felt as though he were in a play and hadn't read the script.

"They're built into the viewscreen circuits." Barton felt like a damn fool; why hadn't *he* dug up any of this stuff, in the months he'd had?

"You wouldn't have found them," Kruegel went on, "because the switches that throw the schematics on the screen won't work when you're under power, without throwing a special cutover switch that doesn't give any indication until you do move the circuit-diagram controls.

You wouldn't have hit the combination by random chance in a long time even if you'd been playing games on the board, and in your shoes I don't imagine you felt much like doing that." Barton's ego pulled its socks up a little.

"So how did you find it?"

"Well, Mr. Barton, you know we've been interrogating Hishtoo, the bigger crawdaddy, with that poor devil Siewen interpreting. Some of our other people are trying to learn the Demu language so we can work faster, but so far they're getting nowhere fast." So the Director's name was Hishtoo; how about that? Or something that sounded like Hishtoo. "Well, when we asked where the devil the tech manuals were for this beast here, he got cagey and wouldn't talk. So Mr. Tarleton put a hammer-lock on him and leaned on it and said something about crab salad, and Hishtoo began talking and just plain wouldn't stop." Barton grinned, not a nice grin. So Tarleton had paid attention to his report—the early version —after all. Crab salad, yet!

"Well, good on Tarleton," was all he said. "Stick with it; you're doing great." He wandered around a little and decided to go back to his quarters. There was no vehicle handy, so he walked it. Sweating in the hot sun felt good, for a change.

Back at the quarters he hesitated, hating to enter. Limila seldom spoke to him lately except in answer to a direct question; her silent withdrawal was hard to take. He supposed she responded to the interrogations of the data-gathering team, or someone would have told him what the problem was. He shrugged and went inside.

He didn't see or hear Limila at first. The tri-V was blaring; he turned the sound low. Then he heard her, in her own bedroom. He opened the door a few inches and saw her as well. Curled into a tight ball in the middle of her bed, she was crying in great racking sobs. After a moment he shook his head, closed the door gently and turned away. There was nothing he could do.

He poured himself the stiffest damn drink he could manage, and watched the stupidities of tri-V. The 3-D picture was new to him, but the content of the medium hadn't improved a bit in eight years, or since he could remember, in fact. If anything, it was getting worse. Or maybe it was he who was getting worse . . .

Barton opened a package of tri-V-advertised prepared food, heated it and ate it. The taste, when he noticed it, was about like that of a well-composted pile of mulch.

Returning to his drink and ignoring the tri-V, Barton ran in his own head the ultimate tri-V commercial he could imagine.

"Buy Mushie-Tushies," it went, "the truly effort-free food! Mushie-Tushies are pre-cooked, pre-chewed, pre-swallowed, pre-digested and pre-excreted! Just heat them up and throw them down the toilet!" Barton finished his drink, turned off the tri-V, and went to his own bed. He caught himself short of slamming the bedroom door; Limila might be asleep. Whether she was or not, the thought of her kept Barton awake another hour, not pleasantly.

Next morning he was at Dr. Fox's office at nine sharp, as agreed. Not one second late; that was his commitment to her. Not more than five seconds early; that was his commitment to himself. Nine sharp, as nearly as he could manage.

Dr. Fox smiled continually. Barton didn't listen closely to what she said or to what he answered; it was small talk and not relevant. Bla-bla-bla, she said in polite tones. Bla-bla-indeed, he answered gravely, equally polite. Maybe it even made some sort of sense.

When she got down to cases, he paid attention. First there would be a simple IQ test. Well, not a simple test, but a test simply for the measurement of his intelligence. OK; he presumed he had some of that left and he didn't mind if they measured it.

The test was part verbal and part written, and all of it no sweat. Barton's memories, which had been suppressed and foggy early in his captivity, and spotty for nearly all of it, had begun coming back more rapidly since his escape. He and Tarleton had discussed the phenomenon early in their acquaintance, in light of the fact that memory suppression was a side-effect of the Demu unconsciousness weapon. The gun crew Barton had zapped when he first arrived had been pretty foggy-minded for several days afterward. And the Demu had used the gadget on Barton a number of times, while they had him.

But now his logic and memory circuits were, so far as he could tell, in reasonably good order. He breezed through the many sections of the test, not giving much of a damn how he came out on it but still giving honest answers when he could settle on any answer at all. And in most cases, he could.

The test was a long one; it was past noon when he finished and time for lunch. He and Dr. Fox said smiling blas-blas at each other while they ate, until she mentioned that next on the agenda was a battery of personality-evaluation tests.

Barton knew what that meant. They would rate him on or off the permissible scales of Aggressive-Submissive, Masculine-Feminine, Dependent-Independent—oh yes, the whole set of categories that he could not possibly fit correctly from where he stood, after nearly eight years in a cage. What it added up to was a rating of Sane-Insane. Barton knew he would flunk.

"And which tests are you using, Doctor?" he asked. She named the series. It was unfamiliar to him, but a book of that title caught his eye, on a shelf not too far out of his reach. I think, thought Barton, it is time I had a bad attack of the clumsies.

"Could I have another cup of coffee?" he asked. Pre-creamed pre-sugared instant crud, but he didn't say so. Dr. Fox poured it for him and handed him the cup. He dropped it, spilling the liquid toward a stack of papers on her desk.

His apparent effort to save the papers pushed them off the edge. He and she both dived to save them; their heads hit squarely. Barton was braced for it, so while the lady got her eyes back in focus and her jaw back up where it belonged, he neatly lifted the book he wanted and tucked it down the front of his trousers. Then he helped her up, helped her pick up the papers and mop up the mess.

"Hey, I *am* sorry, Doctor," he said. "I guess my co-ordination still isn't what it should be." He paused. "You all right? Me, I think I'm getting a headache. You suppose we could put this next one off until tomorrow?"

Dr. Fox hadn't had a chance. Nine sharp? No, you'd better make that one p.m. Bla-bla, smile, see you tomorrow. Barton hoped without malice that she was too woozy to wonder how a man could pilot and land an alien spaceship, who on solid ground couldn't keep from spilling his coffee.

He went directly home. Limila wasn't around; she was probably with the interrogation team. At the moment he felt he could use the absence of personality pressure.

Barton had to beat those goddam tests or they'd have him, for sure; he knew it. Several times since his return to Earth he'd caught himself just short of assaulting someone he found excessively annoying. With intent to commit mayhem. He knew this was not unusual in the overcrowded cultures of Earth; he also knew it was grounds for getting locked up.

Barton had been in a cage for a long time; he was not about to be locked into another one. *That* was what the problem was.

For starters, he took the tests honestly (he'd gambled that sample copies and grading instructions were in the book; they were). The answers he got were about what he had expected; Barton was not safe to have at large, even to himself. Well, he'd have to chance that, the same as he'd been doing for some time. As for other people— well, he figured he'd taken his own chances long enough that it wasn't out of line for others to share them now. He knew no one else would see it that way, though it should be obvious that anyone who did away with the tri-V announcer, for instance, deserved a bonus . . . Oh well.

Looking at the summaries of "preferred" (sane) answers, Barton knew he couldn't possibly memorize enough of the responses to give a reasonable picture of a man with his head on straight; it couldn't be done. But there had to be a way.

The series of tests ran to a total of over 1,300 multiple-choice questions: five choices per question. The odds against him were incalculable. But what about a random approach? Barton looked about the room.

A pair of ornamental dice sat on a low table. Barton took one die in his hand. Six choices: #1 through #5, the answers to any question on the test. #6, leave it blank.

Barton threw the die and marked the result for each of the 107 questions on the first test. Then he turned again to the Evaluations section. Hopeless.

"These results indicate either a fragmented incoherent mind or a highly irresponsible attitude. In either case there is urgent need of custody and therapy." OK, OK, he thought; I've already bagged that idea.

Barton's situation didn't need a drink, but he did. He mixed it about half as heavy as he really wanted it. He sat down in front of the tri-V set, thought about turning it on, then got up and carefully turned the bulky heavy thing around to face directly into the wall. At that point, Limila came in.

As usual she did not speak. Barton had long since quit offering unanswered greetings, though he knew he needed to talk with her and maybe vice versa. In fact she was the only person he knew that he *could* talk to, about a lot of things. But that problem would have to wait.

She got herself some food and took it into her bedroom, softly closing the door behind her. Barton ached, thinking of how she must feel at what had been done to her. But he shrugged it off; he had to, just then. He ranged around the place, looking for something to spark his mind toward a way to beat those damned tests and stay out of a cage. Because he wouldn't go. Not again, he wouldn't.

His eye was caught by the supply of canvases and paints in the far dimmest corner of the room. He'd asked for the materials several days ago but hadn't used them yet. Maybe it was time he did; it struck him that sometimes the hands can tell the mind what it really means.

Barton arranged the easel, the canvas, the palette and brushes, the lights. He hadn't painted for eight years; he had no idea what he was going to do. But he needed to do it; he knew that much. Barton blurred his mind and began. Working, he lost track of time.

A sound behind him brought him out of it. A harsh accusing sound. Barton turned and saw Limila, sawtooth lips squared in an almost-human grimace of horror, blank Demu lack of features throwing the horror back to him. She shook her head, the bald earless skull shining in the overhead light. "No more, Barton," she panted. "No MORE!" She wheeled and disappeared through her bedroom door, slamming it and throwing the bolt against him. As though there were any need for that, he thought sadly.

But what had caused her reaction? Barton looked at his canvas and gasped in shock. What he had painted, what he had doodled while his mind looked the other way, was Limila. Limila the undefiled, as he had first seen her. Several views. Two full-faced, one with closed curved-lip smile and one showing the tiny perfect teeth. A profile highlighting the delicate lean nose and over-the-ears front hairline. A pair of complementing three-quarter studies. Two full-length figures. And each sketch, though lacking in fine detail, was lovingly exact in contour. No wonder Limila could not bear to see them.

Barton turned his ears on. It was about time he did that; the noises from Limila's room were not nice. He took a run at her door, jumped and landed with both heels alongside the door knob. The lock broke; Barton sprawled inside, to see Limila turning and twisting as she hung with her neck in an impromptu noose.

He never knew how he clawed her down from her ad-lib gibbet, though several shredded fingernails took long enough to heal. He gave mouth-to-mouth breathing to the sawtooth lips he had not been able to bring himself to kiss since the Demu had cut their sweet curves into harsh notches. He said her name over and over. And when he saw that she was conscious and could hear him, he said to her, "Don't ever do that again. I need you; do you understand me?" She nodded, weakly.

"Limila," he said, "I don't know yet what we can do about how things are. But I'll work on it. You hear me?"

"You can do nothing. I am as I am." Her eyes were closed. Barton shook her, gently, until she opened them.

"And the Demu had me in a cage for eight years," he said. "I thought my way out of that one, or we wouldn't be here, would we?" She looked at him blankly. "Give me a little time, won't you? To try to find a way out of the cage *we* are in."

The mangled lips twisted in what might have been a smile. Barton blotted it from sight by kissing her smooth forehead. He held her for a moment longer and then said, "Forgive me. For hiding from you, for not paying attention because it hurt to see you. I won't do that any more. You understand?" Her head nodded against his lips. He got up slowly, turned away, stopped at the shattered door. "I'll do *something*."

Barton slept without pills; his dreams were not of horror. And he woke knowing what he had to do next, to stay out of a cage.

At one o'clock he met Dr. Arleta Fox. All of ten seconds early, in fact; under the circumstances Barton felt he could afford to give a little. He put the pilfered book back in place under cover of clumsily dropping his jacket when he hung it up; Barton knew he had to clown it a little and he figured he could get away with that much. Dr. Fox was tolerant.

65

"Don't be nervous, Mr. Barton," she said. "You needn't be. Your intelligence tests show no significant changes from the earlier data in your file. A slight drop of no importance. These tests are so sensitive that what you had for lunch could shift the results by five points, and that's approximately the degree of change we have here." Dr. Fox smiled. By now, Barton's subconscious knew she wasn't really going to bite him; he didn't flinch. "So now," she said brightly, "are we ready for the personality-evaluation series?"

I don't know about you, lady, thought Barton, but *I* sure's hell am. Because now he knew how to beat their system, for a while, at least. All he needed was a little cooperation.

"Sure, I'm ready," he said. "One thing, though. I'm a little nervous today. Could I have a closed room and no interruptions until I'm finished?" He tried to smile disarmingly. It didn't feel much like it, from the inside.

Dr. Fox bought it, at least. "Oh, certainly," she said, and escorted him to a small, comfortable room. With ashtrays and everything.

Ever since Barton had willed himself dead enough to fall through the floor of the Demu cage—all the way home on the ship and ever since—he had, with one exception, stayed clear of self-hypnosis and the hallucinations that had saved him from Demu domination and mutilation. Because he wasn't a captive mind any longer, and a free one can't afford to goof off if it wants to stay free. So Barton had tried to stick with the real world all the way.

But policy must change with circumstances. When Barton sat down to fill out the 1,300-plus questions of the personality-evaluation tests, he shoved his mind into full-hallucinating gear. What he tried to bring into being was the thirty-two-year-old Barton and all his attitudes, before he had been zapped and abducted by the Demu. He knew it was a pretty thin trick but it was the best he had. And it began to work. So be it.

Barton had no idea how long it was taking him to answer all the questions on Dr. Fox's fancy test; he stayed with it until he was finished. Then he snapped out of his earlier-Barton hallucination and paid very close attention to reality. He punched the buzzer; when Dr. Fox answered he told her he had finished and was ready to leave. The time turned out to be late evening; he'd skipped dinner and hadn't even noticed.

"Why don't we have a drink and a bite to eat in the lounge before you go, Mr. Barton?" she asked. Why don't we break open my skull and get it over with, Dr. Fox? But the hell with it; he had to go along, a little.

The lounge wasn't bad; the lighting and music were within his tolerance and Dr. Fox wasn't pushing him about anything. Barton ordered the strongest drink he figured he could get away with under psychological observation. He got a bonus; food service was so slow he had time for a second one. Partway into it he realized he couldn't afford to get smashed, either. But physically and mentally he was floating free, ready to move.

He wasn't surprised when one of the lumpier and more muscular of the young lab techs brought a sheaf of papers to Dr. Fox, whispering in her ear somewhat more than was really courteous. She began to leaf through the stack, skimming.

Barton figured they had him cold, but he wasn't going to make it easy. There was a pot of coffee on the table over a heater; he poured some for Dr. Fox.

For one thing, if he needed to throw the rest of it at Muscles' face it would be quicker if he already had the thing in his hand. So he held onto it for a moment, waiting to see what Dr. Fox would say.

She said it. "Mr. Barton, I can hardly believe these results." Barton wasn't too surprised but there wasn't much he could say. The technician left them. Barton returned the coffee pot to its place.

"Your test results," Dr. Fox continued, "are almost precisely the same as the way you tested eight years ago." She smiled, frowned, scowled and looked blank. It was like a major earthquake on a small scale, thought Barton.

"Our computer read-out," Dr. Fox went on, "allows only one conclusion. It indicates that your capture and imprisonment have inflicted a so-called 'freeze trauma' upon you. You appear to be frozen into your earlier emotional attitudes, without much reference to any happenings since the trauma began."

Well, if you'll believe that, Barton thought, you'll believe anything. But what he said was, "It doesn't feel that way to me, but I guess I can't argue with you experts, and the computer and all." Oddly, he found that he enjoyed skating on thin ice.

"The tests were really very tiring, Dr. Fox," he said. "The food is good but my appetite isn't up to it. I hate to be a poor guest, but if I don't go home and get some sleep about now, I'll probably cork off right here and have to be carted home." Dr. Fox was understanding and obliging; soon Barton was delivered to his quarters. Limila was still awake. Just sitting, looking at the walls.

"I was soon going to bed," she said. "I will now."

"All right," said Barton, "but not in there. In here."

At first Limila expected more than Barton was able to give. He could not make love to her mutilated self, nor did he try. But he could hold her and cherish her; they could give each other warmth. After a while, Limila appeared to understand how it was with them, how it had to be. She cried, but it did not hurt Barton as much as he expected. After a little longer it didn't hurt at all, because it was a different kind of crying. Whatever it was, he succumbed to sleep before he figured it out.

He woke up alone. Well, Limila would be over at the ship, helping with the translating. Tarleton and Kreugel had become wary of having only one translator. Frail and shaky as Siewen was becoming, no one knew how far he could be trusted.

Barton fixed himself breakfast. More real food was coming in lately, to replace the TV-dinner junk that had first been shipped to the site. He broke three eggs into the frying pan, thought a moment and added another. The bread was standard glop-type but not too bad when toasted. There was real coffee.

Idly, Barton wondered what to do next. Dr. Fox was off his back for a time; probably she knew something was fishy, but it would take her a while to get her nerve up to doubt the computer results. He wasn't needed at the ship immediately; someone would have told him. He'd like to get the cast off his arm, lightweight or not, but the doctors had told him not to pester them again for at least another week. It wasn't limiting his activities; it itched, was all.

When in doubt, he decided, take a walk. He'd never been much for gratuitous exercise Before, but now he found he liked to walk when he had the time for it. So he clothed himself and stepped outside. The day was hot and sunny, which was nothing new around here, but he liked it anyway.

His way took him past the quarters of the Demu and the Demu-ized. As he approached them, he wondered how and what little Whnee had been doing lately. At first he had looked in on her occasionally; she'd been pleased to see him, as near as he could tell. Then a couple of times she hadn't been at home; she was being studied by a research team. A little perturbed, he'd checked with Tarleton and been assured that the small Demu would not be harmed. Then Barton had got busy with his own concerns and had had no time for much of anything else.

As he passed the guarded house he saw Whnee looking out a window. He was across the street, but he paused and walked over. The guard said, "Yes, sir?"

"I'm Barton. I see the little Demu is at home today."

"Yes, sir. It and the Freak; he's here all the time, though. The teams gave up on him." That would be Whosits. Well, Barton had given up on Whosits a long time ago.

"How about the young one? They give up on her too?"

"Oh no, sir," the guard answered, "they're pretty happy about that one, the way I hear it. It's just their day off today. Sunday, you know." Barton hadn't known. His work and Tarleton's paid no heed to the weekly calendar, so neither had he.

"I think I'll stop in and see the kid a minute," Barton said. A thought came to him. "Hey, OK if we go out for a little walk?"

"Just a moment, sir. I'll ask it." The guard turned and entered the house, leaving Barton a little puzzled. *Ask* it?

A few minutes later, the guard escorted Whnee outdoors. No robe and hood now: Whnee was wearing a small sunhat, a light loose garment that covered the torso but left the limbs bare, and sandals. The lobster face looked incongruous, but on the whole Barton liked the effect. The standard Demu garb held bad connotations for him, naturally enough.

"Hello, Whnee," he said.

"Hello, Barton. But my name is not Whnee. It is Eeshta."

"You talk English!"

Whnee's—Eehta's—tongue lifted in the Demu smile. "Yes, Barton. They have taught me. I wanted to learn. I wanted to talk with you. Now we can talk."

Barton looked at the small lobsterlike Demu in its absurd but pleasant Earth-type garb. Remembering. How its egg-parent had kept Barton as a caged animal for years. How he had broken this one's arm, slapped it into silence and later, unconsciousness. How he had kidnapped both and brought them to Earth as prisoners. He had treated this small one with kindness or at least with tolerance during the voyage, yes. But still he wondered what he and Whnee, or Eeshta, had in common to discuss. It might be interesting to find out.

"OK," he said. "Want to come for a little walk?" The guard nodded; as the oddly assorted pair turned away, Barton saw the man looking after them.

"I like your outfit," Barton said. "Kind of a change from the old one."

"Yes. That is out of place here, so I changed to this. Dr. Ling chose it." Dr. Ling? Oh, yes; Barton remembered. Female doctor, Chinese ancestry, in charge of the team studying Demu biology.

"Well, it looks fine, Whnee—I mean, Eeshta."

The smile again. "Call me Whnee if you like. Or Eeshta. Either is all right."

"Eeshta. I'll try to remember. Anyway, what-all else have you been learning?"

"Very much. Most important, that you are Demu."

"What?"

"That you are people. Demu is our only *word* for people. We are taught to believe that all others are animals."

"Yeh, I found that out the hard way. Not as hard as some others we know, of course."

"Barton, I am ashamed. For us, who call ourselves Demu. For what we do to others, treating them as animals. Because they do not speak our words. And when they do, we make them like Siewen and Limila and the Freak. I am glad you did not let us do that to you, Barton."

"You call him the Freak?"

"He is. He is one of you but pretends to be one of us. He wears the old clothing. He will not speak his own language. It is our fault, of course. We have broken him."

"Hell; you didn't do it."

70

"But if I had been older, I would have. I believed it was right, also."

"Well, we all do what we have to," Barton said. "I wasn't exactly gentle with you there at first, either. I can't see that I had much choice, but still I'm sorry you had to be hurt."

"So am I," Eeshta said. Barton looked at her sharply, but apparently it was a purely matter-of-fact comment. "Barton, I was so frightened then! Attacked by a vicious animal, I thought. Injured and tied and beaten. Almost I died of fright."

Barton started to say something but thought better of it.

"I first had hope, Barton, when you let me drink. You could have not done that." Eeshta made a grimace Barton hadn't seen before on a Demu. "I am glad I did not know your language then. If I had known you were saying you would eat me alive, I am sure I would have died of hearing it."

"Who—who told you about that?" Barton didn't bother to deny it or say it had been a bluff. It had been, but this was no time to expect her to believe it.

"Siewen," she said, "or Limila. I don't remember now. It is not important." She looked at him. "What is important is that *we* made you do that. I am ashamed." Barton had no answer. Hell, the kid was right, wasn't she? *It?* Nobody had told him the findings, if any, on the Demu, and he'd been too busy to think to ask. Well, it might make a good change of subject; the present one bothered him.

"Eeshta," he said, "what does it mean that you're Hishtoo's egg-child? I mean, is there some other kind of child, with you people?" She paused for a moment, stopped walking. Barton thought it might be time to turn back; they'd come quite a way.

"It seems strange to us, Barton, that you people are male or female. Only one or the other, I mean. We are both, all of us. But not so strongly, to see. That is why we didn't understand, and spoiled Siewen and the Freak." And Limila?

"I will show you," she said, and pulled up her garment, baring the torso. Barton didn't see anything especially noteworthy, only the flexible chitinous body shell, with the little bumps and dimples up the front.

"Look closer, Barton," Eeshta said. "See the small

raised portions, and the indented places? How they make a pattern up the middle of me there, thus-wide?"

He nodded, thinking: "So *that's* what the non-skid tread is all about . . ."

"It is the same on all of us," she said, "so that if any two come together, they fit, each feature." True: the pattern was symmetrical. With two Demu face to face, every bump would meet a dimple. There were about a dozen of each. Barton was too embarrassed to count carefully; it had been a long time since he'd played ". . . and I'll show you mine."

"In breeding season," Eeshta continued, "two adults come facing together and hold. From the concave parts which have the eggs, a substance flows that hardens and maintains the two tightly together but does not block the passages. From the convex parts then come cells to fertilize the eggs. The two Demu are not entirely awake but are in bliss. A day later comes the hard work of breaking loose from each other. Then the eggs are laid, each adult's into his own breeding tank. The hatching and growth cycles are complex, too long to explain now. Only a very few of many survive. Dr. Ling is writing a paper on it, I think."

"I'll try to get around to reading it."

"So for me," Eeshta concluded, "Hishtoo provided the egg, not the other cell."

Yeah, I think I've got it now, Barton thought. Hishtoo's her mommy; at the same time Hishtoo was being some other little Demu's daddy. Or several. And Whnee, or Eeshta, wasn't a "she" at all; the concept didn't apply. Nonetheless Barton continued to think of the young Demu as female.

"Well, thanks for telling me," he said finally. "I think we'd better be heading back now, don't you?" Eeshta was agreeable; they began the return walk. They had gotten well away from the building complex and were in open country; Eeshta seemed to enjoy looking around, observing the terrain. The walk back was mostly silent. Something was nagging at Barton's mind, something about Eeshta. It wouldn't come clear. Maybe more conversation would jog it loose.

"What are you going to be doing next, Eeshta?"

"I want to learn more. Much more. There is a great deal to learn, I think."

"Yeah, I wouldn't be surprised. But then what?" He

really shouldn't push the kid this way, Barton thought. How can a prisoner make plans? But at least Eeshta was only a captive, not a zoo creature and experimental animal as Barton and the others had been.

"If you ever take me back to my people," Eeshta said, "I will be a—a missionary, you call it. I will tell how you are also people and not to be treated as animals or made like Siewen or the Freak."

"That's a worthy cause," Barton said absently. Then it hit him. "Like *who?*"

"Like Siewen or the Freak," she said in puzzlement. *Siewen*. Not "Shiewen."

Barton had become so used to the *sh-zh* lopped-tongue accent of Siewen and Limila that he no longer heard it consciously. So he hadn't noticed until now what had been nagging at him—that Eeshta's pronunciation was perfect.

"Say after me, Eeshta," he said. "Siewen. Shiewen."

"Siewen. Shiewen. Why, Barton?" Then Eeshta gave the Demu smile. "Oh, I see. It's the thing they made for me. Look."

She opened her mouth wide and pointed to its roof. There was a piece of acrylic plastic there, like part of a dental plate. And it made a ridge that Eeshta's short tongue could touch squarely to make the sounds of *s* and *z*.

"Every morning I must spread a paste on it so it stays in place," she said. "The man who made it showed how to do this. A dentist, he is called."

A dentist. Dental plates. Barton, you are the most stupid man in the world.

"We'd better get on back, Eeshta. There are some things I have to do."

They walked faster then, not talking. Barton was in a hurry when he left Eeshta off at her guarded home. He took time, though, to thank the guard for letting her come walking, to gravely thank Eeshta herself for the pleasure of her company and to assure her he'd see her again soon. Eeshta gave him the Demu smile and went indoors.

Barton hotfooted it to his own quarters. As he tried to get Tarleton on the phone, he was thankful that Limila wasn't there. He didn't dare let her know what he had in mind, until he knew more. Tarleton wasn't in his office, and Barton couldn't get through to the ship; those lines were hot most of the time. He flipped a mental coin and decided to stick his neck out; he punched the number of Dr. Arleta Fox, and got her on the third ring. He wasted no time in idle chatter.

"This is Barton. About the medical group here on the project—how are we fixed for plastic surgeons?"

It took a little time. Dr. Fox reached the ship via a priority line. Tarleton checked back to see exactly what Barton had in mind. When Barton told him, he didn't argue.

"I feel stupid as hell," Barton said, "for not thinking of this sooner. The only saving grace is that none of the rest of you bastards did, either." He could say that to Tarleton, because his real respect was no secret to either of them.

"I suppose the reason we didn't—and believe me, Barton, I feel every bit as badly about it as you do—is that we have only seen your companions as they are now."

"Yeah, I guess that's so. But hell, I don't have even that excuse."

"You had your own worries, Barton. Nice that you're working out of them."

Two days later Barton was talking with a plastic surgeon named Raymond Parr, a tall languid-seeming man, in an office not far from Dr. Fox's. They were looking at Barton's paintings of the Limila-that-had-been, alongside some unflattering closeups of Limila as she was now. "What do you think you can do, Doctor?"

Parr was in no hurry. He looked at the pictures and at the paintings. Finally he spoke. "It depends on how far you and the prospective patient are willing to go. I assume from my limited knowledge of this entire project that expense is no object. A great deal more can be done in the way of repairs, these days, than most people think. But there are limits; in some cases these depend on whether it is appearance or function that you have in mind." Dr. Parr raised his eyebrows at Barton as if he'd asked a question; Barton shrugged the ball right back to him.

"All right; let's go down the list systematically. I could add a toe to each foot with a cartilage graft, but it wouldn't bend naturally; same thing with the fingers. I'd advise you to leave all that alone, but it's your choice; it might be worth it on the feet, at that, for better balance.

The nails are gone; if you like, I can recess niches for cosmetic glue-on nails. For social purposes a few well-shaped daubs of nail polish would do nearly as well, and be less difficult and expensive." Barton shook his head with impatience, but he was making notes.

"Well, whatever you choose," the doctor continued. "The navel is no problem; any of my assistants as a routine chore can remodel one or delete it or punch out a new one in a better cosmetic location. As to the simulation of external genitals, it's a simple matter to stretch folds of skin and bond them into place, if you wish. And I assume you'll want the minor abdominal scarification removed."

Too bad that's not all it would take for Siewen or the Freak, Barton thought wryly.

"Plastic insert breasts are common these days," Parr went on, "but a padded bra would do the job nearly as well, unless one of you is a fetishist." Parr never knew how close he was, then, to sudden violence; Barton didn't let his face show what he felt.

Parr paused; it was a habit he had. "I realize the head and face are your major concern, Mr. Barton." Well, about time! "I assume you realize a wig will be needed, along with false eyelashes and stick-on eyebrows." Barton nodded; would this sonofabitch *ever* get to the point? "And dentures, of course." Of course. "The tongue is beyond my skills; amputation of muscular tissue cannot be reversed at this time."

But the face, you fool, you goddam fool; the *face*.

"Our remaining problems," said Parr, "and they are the most important ones, of course, are the nose, the ears and the lips." Barton braced himself.

"I can make her a good nose by use of cartilage grafts, with perhaps a bit of plastic implanting if need be; the skin will stretch and bond to it. I will not guarantee to match your paintings exactly because these things don't work that predictably, but I can promise you a presentable and even a handsome nose."

He hesitated. "Mr. Barton, I couldn't guarantee you a thing about trying to restore the ears. Skin, even grafted skin, won't stretch and bond dependably, around the extensive concave angles that make up much of normal ear structure." Parr sighed. "I suggest you settle for cosmetic prostheses, soft-plastic ear-cups."

Well, if it had to be . . . the wig would cover them, anyway.

The *lips*, now.

"The mouth presents a real problem." Yeh, let me tell you what the problem is. Well, he would in a minute, Barton thought.

"Tissue has been cut away in sawtoothed notches at about a 45-degree angle, nearly a quarter of an inch into both upper and lower lips. The question is whether to cut back to a smooth line or try to divert some of the tissue from the tips of the serrations into the deepest part of the gaps. The one alternative would shorten facial length nearly half an inch; the other might leave wrinkles in the lips, even though we'd use stitchless bonding at the surface layers. In either case we must semi-detach and stretch some mucous membrane of the mouth's inner lining to constitute the outer visible lip tissue when the operation is complete, and this is always chancy. It might not hold, or it might contract and pull the lips inward. The least risky alternative is to cut back all the way and make do with the shortened facial structure." No, Doctor; safer than that is to hang yourself.

There was more discussion; Barton hadn't got it all straight on the first reading, and he needed to have it very straight indeed. He thanked Parr and told him he'd be in touch in a day or two. As an afterthought he asked the doctor to remove the cast from his arm; it came off like peeling a banana. Then Barton left and talked to the dentist, whose name he could never remember for more than five minutes, and to Tarleton, who gave him the full authorization he needed.

Barton was becoming accustomed to having to get authorization for things; it had taken him a while to realize that other people had to have some say-so. But with Tarleton it wasn't so bad.

Then he went home. Limila had dinner hot on the range for him; she herself was eating some kind of damn mush, as usual. Barton could have kicked himself.

"Hi, Limila," he said; she was answering him these days. "We've got some things to talk about."

"Hello, Barton. All right. You eat first, though." Her ragged mouth bent, and Barton realized she was trying to smile. She hadn't given him the Demu lifted-tongue smile since the first night they'd slept together. But only slept . . .

Barton ate, he had developed a good appetite, mostly

for high-protein foods. He wasn't putting on any weight; thank Heaven for small favors.

Then he had to talk. "Limila . . ." he said, and began to tell her slowly and haltingly, starting from where he himself had started with Eeshta's pronunciation aid, all of what he and Dr. Parr had discussed.

He got only a short way into it when Limila started crying and couldn't stop. Barton said a little more, but it didn't help. He caught and held her to him; that didn't help, either. Then he got mad.

"Don't you *want* to get back more to yourself?" he shouted, holding and shaking her by the shoulders. Her soft fingertips with no nails moved on his face; instinctively, she was trying to claw him. His anger vanished; he realized she was fighting the revival of hope, that she couldn't stand to have it and lose it again. Barton could understand; he'd been through it.

He gentled her, gradually. And finally ventured speech again.

"Limila," he whispered, where her ear should have been, "won't you at least listen to what can be done and decide how much of it you want to try?" She nodded against his face.

"But not now, Barton, not tonight. It's too much to accept. I can't." They held each other tightly. But that's as far as it went, even later in bed together.

The next day they could and did talk it out. Barton worked from his notes, in order; it was the only way he could think to do it. Parr had said that even a stiff cartilage toe would help in walking balance, so Limila reluctantly agreed to have both feet chopped open again, if it might help. Not the hands, though; who needs a stiff finger? She did want Barton to find out whether a graft could minimize the unsightly jog at the wrist, where the Demu had stripped away the two fingers. Barton made a note; it was something he hadn't thought to ask.

Emphatically, Limila wanted her belly free of the simulated Demu sex-organ pattern. She didn't care about a navel one way or the other, but Barton thought she should have one so she agreed. Somehow, though, he couldn't bring himself to argue in the matter of external genitalia; it was a little too personal, or something. "Many Tilaran women," she told him, "are circumcised much this same way. It was a beauty fad of some years ago." Barton suddenly realized there was a hell of a lot

77

he didn't know about the Tilari culture. Well, he'd never asked.

Breasts? "I don't know, Barton," she said. "Dead plastic lumps under my skin? But yet they might make my body feel better-balanced again." She cupped her hands, one at each side of the lower edge of her ribcage.

Barton laughed, and gently moved her hands higher. "No, more like this, Limila. You're on Earth now. Haven't you noticed?"

Angrily she pushed his hands away. "I am a Tilari woman, Barton. I will have Tilari breasts or none at all."

"But—" he began. She shook her head, would not listen to him. "Oh well; skip it for now. You and the doc do whatever you decide between the two of you. But—" He wasn't getting anyplace, so finally he did skip it.

She nodded absently at his mention of wigs and so forth. Barton asked if she'd like to have one right away, and maybe the dentures. She shook her head.

"With this face? No, thank you, Barton. I prefer the hood and veil." Limila had added a half veil to the Demu garb, for working with humans, hiding everything but her eyes. Only at home with Barton would she show her face.

She was disappointed that nothing could be done about her tongue, but moderately cheered by Barton's reminder of the prosthesis that had corrected Eeshta's pronunciation. And she was unhappy that Dr. Parr felt he could not rebuild her ears.

"I suppose you had better have him provide the plastic ones," she said. "I do not know if you would have noticed, but my directional hearing is almost absent. The cups of the ears serve that function." Barton kicked himself again for having taken so long to think of doing anything about Limila's difficulties. Oh sure; he'd had his own problems, as Tarleton had pointed out. But was that excuse really good enough?

Her first real enthusiasm was for Parr's confidence in his ability to recreate her nose. "Oh, Barton! That will be so wonderful. I *hate* this face, and that is a thing I hate most about it. But what about . . . ?" She touched her lips.

In a quiet voice he told her the two choices Parr had given.

She had to think about them. "If he tries to spread tissue to fill these in," she said, touching a finger to one of the harsh notches, "the result may be lumpy?" Barton nodded. "Or he must cut back, so they will be shorter."

"Yes."

"Second choice is preferable, I think," she said. "But I can talk about it more with Dr. Parr, what he thinks chances are in each case."

They left it at that. Limila was already late at the ship, engrossed in their discussion, neither had noticed the time. "Come on; I'll walk you over to the motor pool," he said. Limila put on her robe, hood, veil and sandals, found her notecase. They set out.

Jeeps were available, but no driver. Barton hadn't driven a car in eight years; it seemed like a good time to practice. He didn't have a driver's license, but he hadn't had one for the Demu spaceship, either.

The controls were different from the ones he'd known, but he figured them out without much difficulty. He and Limila arrived at the ship safely, without even a close call. They found Tarleton fuming quietly and pretending not to.

"We've hit some snags here," he said, giving them only a bare nod as greeting. "Siewen can't make head or tail of the astrogational data. Limila, your people have interstellar travel; maybe you can do better with it."

"I picked up a little of it on the trip back," said Barton. "Want me to sit in?"

"Later, maybe. Glad you came out, though; I have an item or two for you. Why don't you go on into the ship and let Kreugel fill you in? I'll be along as soon as we get this other on the road." He and Limila walked to the nearby prefab as Barton climbed into the ship.

Kreugel had blueprints and circuit drawings spread over most of the control room. "Hi, Barton," he said. "Good to see you." They shook hands.

"How's it coming?"

"Not bad, not bad at all. The theory boys are handing us some pretty weird answers, though. For instance, how long are the Demu supposed to have had space travel?"

"Oh, since about the time our ancestors left the forests and started using antelope bones for clubs, I'd guess. Why?"

"That's about what I thought," said Kreugel. "Then tell me how come, Barton—tell me how come in all that time they never improved their space drive?"

"How do you know they didn't?"

"Well, we don't, really. But we think so. The thing is that the drive the Agency was working on—given a couple of clues from this ship—turned out to be a better, more efficient drive than the one the Demu have."

"Couldn't that be coincidence, or luck? If true?"

"Maybe. But now again, once the Agency got their drive working—"

"They *have* it working?"

"Yes, as of last Friday," Kreugel said, grinning. "Anyway, from nothing but static test runs, the boys came up with about sixteen different ideas for further improvements. Now what does that tell you, Barton?"

"It doesn't tell me the Demu are stupid, if that's what you mean. They are in some ways, such as their cultural inertia, but that little Eeshta is nobody's dummy."

"Not stupid, Barton. Just not inventive. You see it now?"

"I'm not sure, Kreugel. You tell me."

"The guess is that the Demu didn't invent this drive in the first place. They got it from somebody else, somehow, and just plain copied it. The same with the other stuff: the leaky no-splash floors, the sleep gun, the protective shield and all the rest of it. All it would take, Barton, would be the capture of one ship, plus a reasonable level of technology and a lot of patience. I'm told we could have done it ourselves as early as—well, whenever semiconductor application was first being developed."

"Late 1940s," Barton recalled. "Well, it's an interesting idea, but what's so important about it?"

"It means that we can build ships that outclass the Demu—and that maybe they can't improve theirs without a model to copy."

"Hmm, maybe so," said Barton. "I wouldn't bet too big a bundle on it, though."

Tarleton came in. "Hi. How far along are you?"

"Just that somebody thinks the Demu are copycats, not inventors, and stole their antigravity and everything," said Barton. "I'm not totally sold, but it could be. What else is there?"

"Not too much. But before you leave I'd like you to check Limila's interpretation of the astrogational data. She's pretty sure she's right, but you're the one who worked with it." Barton nodded, waiting for Tarleton to continue. Kreugel waved them off and went back to his blueprints. The two men moved out into the other compartment.

"Kreugel tell you the Agency has its own drive working?"

"Yeah, and improved six ways from Sunday over this one, he says. No kidding?"

"Fact," said Tarleton. "The lab people are going out of their minds with the possibilities. Apparently they were only a couple of jumps from the whole antigravity thing already. They have to admit that those jumps weren't in the direction they were trying to go; they'd been on a wrong track. But they claim it would have been a matter of only a few months. They could be right; those lads don't spend too much time in blind alleys."

"So what's next?" Barton was getting bored with the Agency's ego trip.

"Well, they've cobbled together this one ship, a sort of breadboard model, to experiment with. Washington is in a hurry to settle on an adequate design and get into production: the old argument between 'Get it on the road *now*' and 'Give us a little more time so we can make it better!' You know."

"Afraid I can't help you much on that," Barton grinned. "I learned a long time ago to keep my neck out of policy arguments."

"Maybe so, but I want your advice on the auxiliary hardware. Just how far do you think we should go in duplicating what the Demu carry?"

Barton shook his head impatiently. "I don't know all that much about it, Tarleton. We don't need their fancy floors; plumbing's simpler. Or the no-source lighting; it's nice to have no shadows on your control console but not necessary. I imagine those two items would be a big part of the cost problem, so skip 'em.

"When it comes to weapons, maybe I brought you the wrong ship. The bigger ones may have stuff we don't even know about, and you can bet that Hishtoo won't be telling us anything he doesn't have to. This crate has the unconsciousness weapon—the sleep gun, you call it—and the shield. Personally, I don't even know what the shield will handle and what it won't. But if there's more offense or defense on here, I never found it."

"Yes, I thought that would be about the size of it. Nobody else found anything more in the way of weapons, either. But we still haven't eliminated the possibility of

81

another of those tricky 'Enable' switches like the one for the circuit diagrams. It's a slow cautious process, checking out all the combos on that control board.

"Anyway, they're testing the shield, all right. Took a pilot model out into space on a rocket shuttle, with all sorts of test objects and instruments and telemetering equipment inside. Now they're throwing everything at it but the kitchen sink."

"Any useful results?"

"So far, the sumbidge will take anything *we* know how to throw, except for coherent radiation. That goes through it like a knife through cheese."

Barton laughed. "So we just take a big-daddy laser . . ."

"So big it takes up the whole central axis of one of our new ships . . ."

"And ZAP! Well, I hope it works."

"That makes a crowd of us. But we still have a problem."

"Let me tell you what the problem is," thought Barton. But the other man didn't say it.

"How effective is the shield against the sleep gun or vice versa?" he asked. "That's not a simple question. It's a matter of the power to the gun and the power to the shield, the distance, and the time of exposure."

"So what the hell? Test it."

"On whom, Barton? We've already used it to knock Hishtoo out once, to make sure it would work on the Demu as it does on humans. We don't dare take a chance on scrambling his memories much; we *need* the hardshelled bastard, for what information we can worm out of him."

Well, by God, there *was* a problem. It would take a lot of testing to get the necessary answers, and the sleep gun played hell with memory. Who was going to volunteer for a case of amnesia? Not Barton, for sure; he'd had that bit, and still he wasn't sure all his mental nuts and bolts were back in the right bins.

"Yeh, you've got a point. Lemme think a minute . . ."

There had to be answers; Barton thought of one. Some men and women were trapped in cages, permanently.

"The hopelessly insane, Tarleton. It's their memories that have them tied up in knots. The sleep gun might even cure a few. If it doesn't, they haven't lost a hell of a lot, have they?"

Tarleton looked dubious. "Pragmatically it makes

sense, but we'll play hell trying to get authorization. A lot of people would holler bloody murder, you know."

"Federal booby hatch," said Barton. "That big one near D.C. The Agency can slap Security on the whole bucket."

"You give harsh answers, don't you? Well, it can't hurt to try, I guess. Thanks." Barton was beginning to make motions preliminary to leaving. "Oh, don't forget to check Limila on the astrogation; OK? And in a few days we'll want you to take some student pilots up in this ship. Also in the new Agency model, to show them how it goes and give us an operational comparison."

"Hell, any of your trainees could fly this thing right now."

"Yes, but they haven't done it. You have." Barton shrugged an OK, and left. Outside, he realized he hadn't said goodbye to Kreugel. Oh well; the man probably wouldn't want to be interrupted again anyway.

Over at the prefab he checked Limila's interpretation of the data necessary to travel from Star A to Star B. As he had expected, she had it right. He noticed that Hishtoo seemed distinctly wary of him; that reaction didn't hurt Barton's feelings. Siewen didn't say much, but seeing him gave Barton an idea: maybe, before working on Limila, Dr. Parr could use a trial run.

Limila wasn't needed for the rest of the day, so Barton took her with him in the jeep. He enjoyed testing its performance and handling over the bumpy dirt road, now that he had the hang of it. First he stopped by Dr. Parr's office to make sure the doctor could see Limila that afternoon. Then he and she went home for lunch and a shower; the day was hot. There was a note in the mailbox; Dr. Fox wanted to see Barton.

Dr. Parr had priority; they went to his office immediately after lunch. Although he had seen the pictures, the doctor was visibly shocked when Limila doffed the veil and hood. He hid it well but fooled no one. Quickly, though, he put his professional manner together and carefully examined Limila's head and face, hands and feet. He didn't ask her to disrobe; Barton remembered that Parr considered the problems of the torso to be minor.

"Your description and pictures were accurate, Barton," he said. "I see no reason to change the prognoses I gave you earlier. Does she wish to proceed?"

"Hell, Doctor; ask her. She's right here in front of you, brains and all." Parr colored.

"I'm sorry, madam," he said; Barton didn't bother to correct him about Limila's marital status. "It is only that . . ."

"I know," said Limila. "I cannot ever get used to it, either. That is why I hope you can help me." Her eyes filled with tears. Parr was obviously shaken.

Barton cut in to display Limila's wrists and ask if anything could be done about the jog where the fingers had been cut back.

"Either plastic sponge or cartilage could be used to fill out a smoother line," Parr said. "Cartilage would be best but we will be using quite a lot of that elsewhere; the supply is not unlimited."

"Well, however it works out," said Barton. "Look, I think I'll leave you two to work out the details. The lady shrink wants me again. See you at home, later, Limila. See you too, Doctor, and thanks." Handshake, pat her shoulder, and out.

Dr. Arleta Fox welcomed him smilingly. He noticed that her dark-red hair had been shortened a little and tamed a lot; it was nowhere near as frizzy as before. She wasn't a bad-looking little woman, Barton thought, if you liked strong jaws and didn't mind the implication of tenacity.

"We'd like to do some nonverbal tests today, Mr. Barton." You mean "you," lady; "we" don't want to do anything of the sort. But he smiled and nodded; the two of them exchanged polite bla-bla-blas on the way to the testing room.

The ceiling was low and gray, and Barton's guard went up. This woman had been reading the reports on him, *really* reading them.

But the tests weren't too bad. First there were a number of color-filled sheets of paper bearing abstract patterns. He was supposed to choose which he liked best, and least, out of a dozen or so groups of five each. Inevitably he was drawn to the gaudiest, most violent combinations and bored by the pastels; naturally he announced the opposite choices. Dr. Fox looked dubious, but didn't say anything.

Then came the good old Rorschach ink blots: "Tell me what you see in these, and tell me a story about each one, if you can, please."

Barton saw a mutilated woman dying in mindless pain.

"This is a little boy in a Hallowe'en mask. He is going out trick-or-treating."

He saw two grotesque entities ready to lock in mortal combat. "A boy and a girl are having a picnic, out in the country." The room was air-conditioned, but he was sweating worse than he'd done outdoors in the heat. Dr. Fox paid no apparent heed.

Barton saw a group of pseudo-lobsters who had once been human beings. "I get the impression of a family of baby rabbits. I guess my imagination is throwing in the ears; they sure aren't in the picture, are they?" He hoped it looked like a smile, what his face was doing on the outside. Because that had been too close.

Finally it was over and he could leave, smiling and bla-blaing with Arleta Fox. In another job, he felt, he could have liked her.

When he got home, Limila was fixing dinner. She appeared happier than he'd ever seen her, though with an undertone of anxiety.

But "Later, Barton; eat first," she said when he asked. For a girl who had never seen Earthly foodstuffs until recently, he thought (not for the first time) that she was developing into one helluva good country-style cook.

Idly he noticed a row of scratches down her right arm. Not so idly, he saw that some were red and swollen. "What's all that?"

Testing for allergy reactions to antibiotics, it turned out. Dr. Parr had no wish to resort to full-asepsis surgery if he could help it; bacteria abound, and mutate. And he wanted to begin operations the next afternoon, if possible. Starting with Siewen.

Barton nearly had to laugh when Limila told him of the Great Breast Controversy. Parr hadn't quite understood Limila's differences from Earth-human; he'd been flabbergasted when she told him where she wanted her surrogate breasts implanted. "Then he refused," she told Barton. "He said he cannot rebuild an anatomy he doesn't know. So we decided none at all, for this time. He thinks I will change my mind . . ."

But there was more, Barton could tell. And for once, he *did* want to hear what the problem was. He was a long time getting it out of her. Finally in bed, in the dark, holding each other like two small children afraid of the bogeyman, she said it.

"The pain, Barton. The pain again. I am afraid."

"Well, sure," he said, "these things hurt some, as they heal up. But it's not all that bad. I mean, it's sure as hell worth it, isn't it?"

"No, I mean the cutting, the stretching, the binding together, all of that. It was very bad before, Barton, with the Demu. Why should it be easier now?"

He sat upright, dislodging her from his embrace. "For Chrissakes! Didn't the Demu put you to sleep for all that butchering? Or even give you a shot or pill to kill the pain?"

They hadn't. The sleep gun? "They never use it again on one they have decided to make Demu. With much use, effects on memory become permanent." Barton cringed, thinking what she must have endured.

"But you don't think *we* do surgery that way? You have surgeons on Tilara; what do they use to control pain?"

"There is a drug; pain becomes ecstasy. I think you do not have it here."

"If we have, it's probably illegal. We use anesthetics; you go to sleep, and wake up when it's all over. Didn't Parr say anything?"

"No."

"Did you ask him?"

"About pain, I ask. No trouble, he said; we do it with a general. I say no. Such a foolish idea!"

"Huh? I don't get you. Run that one through again."

"A general? Like the man Parkhurst? What could he do?"

Barton broke up; he couldn't help it. Grabbing Limila and hugging her fiercely, he laughed so hard that tears came. He hadn't laughed like that in over eight years. Then he explained, gently, the difference between a general officer and a general anesthetic. When she understood, Limila managed a small laugh of her own. It was tentative, tremulous, but in the right direction. "It'll be all right," he said. "Really, it will."

He held her close until she was asleep. For a time he had little luck getting himself to sleep. He was thinking how much respect, even more than he had accorded her, Limila deserved for what she had gone through. Or Siewen, for that matter. Or even Whosits.

Next morning Barton was to take Dr. Parr to the ship, as well as Limila. At the motor pool, no one hassled him for permission about anything; they assumed he had it.

From Parr's office he called the dentist; might as well have impressions made for plates as soon as possible. The height factor could be measured as soon as lip surgery was complete, but Parr had said the mouth would then be too tender for impression work.

At the ship, Tarleton was in a hurried mood. Compared to the slow bearlike man Barton had first met, he was practically a streak of lightning. "Barton," he said at once, "the new ship, up at Seattle, is ready for comparison testing; Boeing really pushed it to meet the contract. Tomorrow we take this one up there. All right?"

Barton shook his head, not in negation but to get his bearings. Yes; all right. "OK, Tarleton; I'm ready if you are. But I want you to meet Dr. Parr, the surgeon who is going to do the job on Limila and the rest. I hope it doesn't bust your program any, but he needs Siewen and Limila for a while, starting this afternoon."

Tarleton started to swell and possibly burst like the frog in the fable, but he too shook his head and considered his priorities. "How long?" he asked. "Will I have access to them for questions if I need them?" Barton turned to Dr. Parr for the answers.

"Not for the first three days, Mr. Tarleton. Even with the newer drugs, it takes that long to reduce the swelling; it used to take weeks." He paused. "Will that be satisfactory?"

Tarleton started to speak. Then he looked at Limila, her mangled face hidden by the hood and veil. He looked at Siewen, too. "Hell, I guess I can spare three days. Considering everything. After all, I'll be busy up north that long, before I can leave Barton on his own."

It was settled. Tarleton wanted to run Hishtoo through one last intensive grilling session before he turned Siewen and Limila over to Parr. To pass the time, waiting, Barton took the latter into the ship for a guided tour and some chat with Kreugel. There wasn't much that was news to Barton, but he liked Kreugel and didn't mind hearing again what obviously interested Parr. The only new facts were the initial results of testing the sleep gun versus the shield: as expected, given the maximum of power to both, you were safe behind the shield unless you were too close to the gun for too long. The parameters were still being evaluated, but the limits had been determined. Barton didn't ask about the effects on the test subjects. He didn't really want to know.

Toward lunchtime, he and Parr bade goodbye to Kreugel and went to the prefab, to pick up Limila and Siewen. No one had asked Siewen whether he wanted to be remodeled or not; Barton because it never entered his mind, and no one else because this was Barton's personal project. Siewen had heard the proposal discussed and hadn't said anything one way or the other, but then he never did, except to answer questions. Not any more.

In the prefab were Tarleton, Limila, Hishtoo, Siewen and two people Barton knew by sight but not by name. Assistants of some kind. He nodded to all.

"You have it about wrapped up for now, Tarleton?" he asked. The place was tense: Tarleton was obviously displeased, Limila stood in an apologetic stance. Siewen looked as if he weren't there at all, and Hishtoo looked defiant.

"What's the problem?" said Barton, and mentally kicked himself for saying it that way.

"Oh, Hishtoo's up on his high horse." Tarleton sounded weary. "He's just realized we're going to take this game back onto his own home grounds, and he doesn't like the idea."

Hishtoo suddenly shrilled a rapid burst of lobsterese. "He says," Limila interpreted, "that we animals had best not dare disturb the homes of the Demu."

"Well now, is that right?" said Barton. He knew he looked nasty; he knew he sounded nasty. Above all, he knew that he couldn't afford to show it, not before Tarleton, of all people. But he couldn't help himself. He walked up to Hishtoo, face to face. "To you I'm an animal?" he said softly. "To me, you're crab salad!"

Hishtoo cringed and turned away. "I'll be damned," Tarleton said in a hushed voice. "That hardshell understands more English than he lets on." He turned to Barton. "When I said that to him I was twisting his arm and shouting. But you said it just like 'Pass the bread' and it got to him."

"Not quite," said Barton, knowing he shouldn't. "More like 'Pass the crab salad.'" Tarleton looked at him, but said nothing more except the usual so-longs. Barton herded Parr and Siewen out to the jeep, Limila following. He agreed to meet Tarleton in the morning, and drove off.

Lunch at the Barton-Limila residence was on the awkward side. Doktor Siewen was being as nonexistent as possible. Limila's reluctance to show her face to anyone except Barton was eased somewhat because Parr had already examined it, but her discomfort was apparent. Parr's appetite was scanty for a man of his size; the reasons were obvious. Barton ate like a horse and complimented Limila on her cooking; it was one of his days to be contrary (though the food *was* good).

Next stop, he announced, was the dentist. No, come to think of it, first they would drop by and pick up Whosits; Barton hadn't seen him for weeks and hadn't missed him, but the Freak would also benefit by a set of dentures, so that he wouldn't have to subsist on mushy gloop all his life. So what the hell . . .

The guards at the door of the unit housing Siewen, Whosits and the two Demu accepted Barton's authorization readily enough. Eeshta was pleased to see Barton; he expressed his own pleasure at seeing her. Whosits was something else again. He didn't want to go anywhere. Barton and Parr took him out the hard way but not very; Whosits was so flabby as to be wholly ineffectual.

The dentist was noticeably jolted by the looks of his patients, but he took Limila's and Siewen's dental-plate impressions with reasonable aplomb. Whosits made a problem of himself; he refused to open his mouth. Dr. Parr explained the purpose of the project, but Whosits paid no heed. Barton took over then, not gently. Whosits not only opened his mouth but then also kept it closed—on the second try—for the proper length of time to produce a usable impression. Meanwhile Parr was explaining how he was going to help Whosits look presentable once more in human society. He was working with a tough audience.

As soon as the hardened impression was removed, Whosits reared back and spoke words. Actual human words, the first Barton had ever heard from him.

"Nein; nein! Ich bin Demu! DEMU; Hören Sie?"

Barton shook out his rusty knowledge of German and tried to talk with the creature, but that was all Whosits would say. "Oh, the hell with it," Barton said finally. "If this nut wants to stay a lobster, why argue with him?" Parr said nothing. He did not object when Barton dumped the Freak back at his own guarded quarters, before the rest of the group went on to Parr's office and improvised operating room.

(Later, through hush-hush channels, Whosits' fingerprints turned out to be those of one Ernst Heimbach, missing from East Berlin for about five years. Barton suggested, "Why don't we dump him back where he belongs?" but Tarleton said, "Hell, if we did, they'd blame his condition on *us*." The old Cold War had softened into almost-free trade, considerable real cooperation and very little risk of hot war, Barton learned, but somehow the propaganda part continued as idiotic and irritating as ever.)

Parr summoned a couple of nurses to take charge of Limila and Siewen for the preliminaries; Barton was about to become superfluous. He took Limila in his arms, pushed her hood back enough to kiss her forehead. "I'll see you in a few days," he said, "when I get back from Seattle." She nodded but said nothing. "Look now. I'd be around with you if I could; you know that. But Tarleton wants those test runs in a hurry and I'm tagged for it. You'll be all right; Parr is *good*. And I'll see you, soon as I can."

"All right, Barton," she said, finally. "I hope then you can like what you see." She turned abruptly and followed a nurse out of the office, not looking back. Siewen and the other nurse trailed after.

Barton looked at Parr. "I know you'll do what you can."

"I'll try to do better than that, Barton. You know? The hardest thing to realize in this case—please don't take offense—is that I should be seeing her as a woman to *restore*. Forgive me, but I've been seeing a *something* to be turned into a woman."

Barton sighed, not angry. "Yes, Doctor; I know how it must be for you." They shook hands. "However it works out, be kind to her."

Barton went home to be alone with himself and his memories. It wasn't fun. He skipped dinner and got drunk. Not too drunk; he went to bed at a reasonable hour. Alone, and missing Limila more than he would have thought possible.

Knowing that Tarleton, next morning, would be like a cat on a hot stove, Barton got up early. He breakfasted quickly and with his packed suitcase was at the ship a few minutes ahead of the other man. Three of the four student-pilots were there before him; the fourth arrived almost on Tarleton's heels.

Tarleton cut into the exchange of greetings. "All right,

we're here. Let's get on board and stash our luggage."
They did so quickly, and followed Barton into the control area.

The room normally seated two. Tarleton had had four more seats installed for training purposes. Even though these were small, bucket-type shells, the seating was cramped. But they all wedged in; no one complained. Well, they'd better not have, with Tarleton on edge as he was.

Barton explained the major controls. "I won't bother running you through the whole switch panel because ours are different, they tell me; our people left out a lot of things on here that we won't really be needing, so as to get into production sooner.

"The principles will be the same. Start out with all the small toggles off and your guidance lever *here* and go-pedal *here*, both in neutral; then you apply power with this blue jobbie in the middle." He knew they'd heard the instructions before but it didn't hurt to tell them again, and at the same time reinforce his own knowledge. "All right, here's your outside viewscreen and here's your 'Drive on' switch," pointing them out, throwing them and remembering how in the Demu aircar he'd discovered them in reverse order. What a panic *that* had been. "Artificial gravity, indoors here, set to hold at one-G. Now we're hot to trot; here goes nothing." And he took the ship up.

He took it straight up at maximum lift, because he wanted them to realize immediately the kind of power they'd be handling. At an altitude of about one thousand kilometers he made the tightest right-angle turn the ship would manage, pointing out the rather incredible G-forces that, because of the artificial gravity field, they were *not* feeling. Then he slowed to roughly orbital-drift speed, put the major controls to neutral, and clambered out of the pilot's seat.

"OK, I want each of you to play around with this can for a while, out here where it's safe. You first, Kranz." Kranz climbed gingerly into Barton's pilot chair; Barton squeezed into the empty one. "For now," Barton continued, "we work only with the two drive-control levers; leave all the little toggles alone unless I tell you different. And don't use more than half power. Just play loose in this general volume of space. OK?"

Each man had about a half-hour of practice, mostly

experimenting on his own with only an occasional suggestion from Barton. Kranz started cautiously and gradually built up his confidence. Slobodna, the next man, did the opposite, applying all his allowed half power immediately in violent maneuvers, losing orientation and scaring himself. But then, after a few minutes of more cautiously feeling out the controls, he too achieved a degree of mastery over them. The other two, Jones and Dupree, began with medium-power settings and modest acrobatics; each progressed to as proficient a handling of the craft as could be expected in so short a time. Barton was satisfied with the lot of them.

"OK, Dupree; that's fine," he said. "I might as well get back in the saddle now, and take us down. My gut says it must be nearly time for lunch."

"Just a minute." It was Tarleton.

"What's the problem? Aren't you hungry yet?"

"Damn it, Barton! Don't you think *I* want a turn at driving this kiddie car?"

Barton laughed; hell, he should have thought of that. "OK, Tarleton, she's all yours."

Tarleton was a model of caution and precision. He never applied the maximum-agreed power nor made violent rolls or turns. He returned the ship quite closely to his starting point and to drift speed before turning it over to Barton.

"Thanks, Barton. I just wanted to fly a spaceship once in my life. You realize that once the program is under way, an unqualified guy like me won't have a chance."

"Hell, you can fly any ship *I* have any say-so about, any time you want." Tarleton was silent; finally Barton realized why. He, Barton, probably wasn't going to *have* any say-so about these things much longer, is what it meant. Well, maybe. People had had that kind of attitude about Barton before. Like the Demu, for instance. Barton filed the whole bit for future reference. After all, it wasn't as though he'd failed to provide for the contingency.

"OK, gang," he said. "I'm going to haul her down like a real bat, so you can see how she hits air. Then I'll ease her back, just above SST traffic levels, and go in quiet from there." He chuckled. "It's going to be fun trying our own ship; from what I hear, it has considerably more legs on it than this baby has."

He took her down like a real bat indeed; his passengers, including Tarleton, were noticeably shaken. Barton chuckled to himself, thinking how they might have reacted to his first atmospheric entrance, when he'd guessed wrong and nearly joined the Submarine Service before he pulled out of his dive. He decided not to mention that occasion.

He flipped a jury-rigged switch for the special channel to Boeing Field; Control gave him the OK to drop in on a straight vertical. He made a good landing because the Demu shield allowed no other kind. He wondered if, later, everyone shouldn't learn to land without the shield, just in case.

Barton had heard that it always rained in Seattle, but the six of them stepped out to face a sunny day. Claeburn, the Space Agency's liaison man, apologized for the unusual heat wave—all of 80 degrees. After New Mexico it felt like a cool pleasant early-morning. In fact, the time was a little after noon; they had lunch at a nearby restaurant. Claeburn suggested the company cafeteria but Tarleton wanted a drink with his lunch, and insisted. Barton was damn glad; he wanted one too. He was appalled at the size of the luncheon check picked up by Claeburn. Inflation hadn't slowed down.

After a briefing so lengthy that the drinks had had plenty of time to wear off, Barton put the prototype, Earth's first starship, through its paces. It carried about 50 percent greater acceleration than the Demu version, nearly as much advantage on tight turns, and an interlock that would not allow hard maneuvering to overload and blow the ship's internal gravity field. Barton hadn't known, and was surprised enough to say so, that such a danger existed on the Demu ship; apparently he had been wildly lucky not to exceed the limit. Especially, he thought, on his first reentry to Earth. He felt uncomfortable, having his ignorance exposed. He felt it put more chinks in his image than he really needed.

The revised controls were no problem. There were about two-thirds as many toggles as in the Demu ship—larger, more widely spaced, and each clearly labeled. Claeburn had run them through the list of functions, anyway; it couldn't hurt. Barton could see that pilot training was going to be a real snap, especially after the four trainees, Tarleton and even Claeburn had given the new ship a workout. The procedure was like that of the morning tryouts, but faster and smoother. And more comfortable: the seats weren't so crowded. Barton felt that they were definitely making progress.

Over dinner, just the two of them, Tarleton explained the Agency's plans. "Tomorrow and the next day, you take those four men up and wring them out on navigation, test procedures and trouble-shooting; stuff like that. Pilot practice is incidental at this stage, but they'll be getting it, anyway. Mainly, though, you're training the next generation of instructors."

"Jeez," Barton protested, "I don't know any more about testing and trouble-shooting than they do."

"But they think you do," Tarleton answered. "Here are the books; you and I can go over them tonight. I've skimmed them; they're well put together, easy to follow. All you have to do is keep two jumps ahead of those four guys for the next few days. Then you come on back south in the Demu ship and they're on their own."

"But why me?" Barton was sincerely puzzled. "Why not the guys who *wrote* the books?"

"Because you are the one man on Earth who has actually piloted an interstellar trip. I know and you know how much luck you needed, but you have no idea how much the simple fact means to the Agency. They think you're Superman. It's simpler to let them keep thinking so, because then when you pass your students as trained they'll figure some of it rubbed off. You see?"

Barton saw. He saw, moreover, how maybe it gave him a handle on something he wanted, something he was utterly damn well going to have.

"Tarleton," he said, "if I'm all that important, how about letting me in on the Top-Hush? I mean, we're building ships and training pilots. What are we going to do with them?"

Tarleton was quiet for a time. "All right, Barton," he said finally. "I guess you deserve to know. Most of it, anyway.

"We're having forty ships built, all about the same as the one we flew today, but more advanced. You noticed ours is somewhat bigger than the Demu ship, to carry the more powerful drive. The hulls and loose hardware have been in production since the second week after you got home. I've put in the OK to go ahead and standardize on the drive units as-is, based on our tests today; the theory boys can incorporate later improvements into our second fleet, and so on. And what we're going to do should be obvious. We're going after the Demu."

"We?" said Barton, very quietly.

"Well, not you or I personally, of course. After all—"

"The hell you say!" Barton hadn't meant to put it like that, but there it was. "Me personally! Very definitely, me personally. Who the hell's fight do they think this is, anyway?"

"Well, I know how you must feel, of course, but you can't really expect the Agency and the military to let an outsider into the act, can you?"

"I can," said Barton. "I can and I do. You think I can't?" Slowly, deliberately, he pushed the stack of training books off the table; they landed on the floor in disarray. He looked Tarleton in the eyes, both of them suddenly quiet.

"You want me to pick those books up, Tarleton?"

After a while, Tarleton nodded slowly. Barton picked up the books, dusted them off, stacked them neatly. "All right, Barton, you've made your point. I'll do the best I can for you."

"You'll get me one of those ships. In charge of it."

"I'll try."

"You'll *do* it." He leaned forward across the table. "Listen, Tarleton, I can do a lot more for you, than be some sort of lousy figurehead. You say we're going after the Demu. Just like that?"

"Just like that."

"That's stupid. You know how big they are? I don't either, for sure, but I do know a little, from what Limila learned. I told it, but maybe nobody paid attention.

"They inhabit—that's *inhabit*—about a dozen planets. To our one. On top of that they have 'farm planets' with a few Demu supervising populations of ready-made Demu like Limila and Whosits—but of many races, not only humanoid. They have those poor bastards brainwashed into altering their own children to the Demu style of looks. Then they have research stations like the one I was at, the one that had never seen humanoids before. There were six ships at that station alone, until I stole one. Three of them hadn't been used for a while, by the looks of them, but they were there. And you're going after the Demu with a lousy forty ships?"

"What else can we do?"

"Unite and conquer, for Chrissakes! Limila's people,

the Tilari, have star travel. All they don't have is the shield against the sleep gun, or any idea how to find the Demu. We can give them both."

"Well, yes," said Tarleton. "I'll put through a memo upstairs in the Agency, on that idea. You give me the location of the Tilari planets and—"

"Limila will give you that stuff when the expedition is in space, no sooner. Christ on a crutch, you think I trust a bunch of Agency wheels to keep the faith for you? No sale. I'll go ahead with this training jazz, on your word to go to bat for me. But the Agency gets the scoop on the Tilari—and how to find the other races they know who'll want to get into the act and could help a lot—you get all that when we're on our way, not before." He wasn't bluffing. He'd talked the matter over with Limila; she was in full agreement with him.

"It might work, Barton." Tarleton spoke slowly. "But how do you know the Agency couldn't get the information directly from Hishtoo?"

"If Limila doesn't feel like interpreting for you? How much do you trust Siewen's abilities any more? Even if Hishtoo just happened to be feeling cooperative, which I doubt. Think about it."

Tarleton, from the looks of him, did think about it. "I think you've got us boxed, Barton. And you know something? I'm glad of it. Because as you say, it *is* your fight." Barton looked at him and felt he could trust the big man. He purely hoped so.

The training went about as planned. On Barton's fourth day at Seattle, after seeing Tarleton off to New Mexico by SST, he was riding supercargo observing one of his first four students instructing a new batch of trainees. Three days later he decided the program had become self-sustaining as scheduled, and packed his suitcase. He had lunch with Claeburn and the four original trainees, enjoying this goodbye scene a lot more than he had expected. About an hour later he lifted the Demu ship off for New Mexico.

Just for the hell of it he got clearance to go by way of Luna. He cruised slowly back and forth above the surface at eyeball range, seeing the manmade installations and the undisturbed areas that had thrilled him on TV in his younger days, when the first landings had been made. With a sigh for that younger self, Barton turned back to Earth.

It took him a little time to locate New Mexico and get talked in, but eventually he found the proper spot and set the ship down. Tarleton had left the site for the day. Barton got a ride to his quarters. He called Parr and got no answer, so he had a shower before preparing a pre-packaged dinner and eating it. The package was nationally advertised over tri-V and tasted like it, but Barton hardly noticed. He was too busy being lonesome.

He called Parr again; for a wonder he got him on the first try. He could, Parr told him, see Limila the next day. In fact, the timing was good; the bandages were to be removed tomorrow. Maybe she could use Barton's presence in support. Barton tried to ask detailed questions but was brushed off. "Come see for yourself," was how Parr put it. Barton growled his thanks and hung up.

He was still restless; tomorrow was a long time away. There had been a day-old note in the mailbox: Arleta Fox was in urgent need of his company. Barton was in no hurry for that interview. He supposed he'd have to give the lady one more session of brainpicking at least, before he got the hell off Earth again. But the later the better. He was too close to making it, to take any more chances than he could help.

Now in the early evening, he decided to walk off his tensions, out in the clear air. He thought to look in on Eeshta, realizing that he hadn't had a real visit with her since the time she'd given him the clue to Limila's plight. Limila! It was going to be a long night.

The guard was unfamiliar but recognized Barton's name. "Do you want to go in, sir?" he asked.

"See if she'd like to come out for a little walk," Barton said. "We'll be back before dark. It's OK with Tarleton." The guard nodded and went inside.

Sooner than Barton expected, the guard came back with Eeshta. She was wearing a small cap and a short sleeveless robe, and sandals. Looking more acclimated all the time, Barton thought. He was surprised at the glow of real pleasure he felt at seeing her. "Hello, Eeshta," he said. "How's it going with you?"

She Demu-smiled at him. "I am happier now, Barton." she said. They strolled westward into the after-sunset light. "I learn much about your people. They are so different. Not only from ours, but from each other. It is very new and very challenging, to try to understand. I try to tell Hishtoo, my egg-parent, but he does not want to hear. He says I am becoming an animal." She hissed—the equivalent, Barton knew, of a sigh. "Perhaps one day he will be willing to learn." Barton decided he wouldn't bet much of a bundle on that possibility.

"How's the Freak doing, these days?" he said.

"Heimbach? I do not know. They took him away several days ago. I have not seen him since." Barton was faintly surprised that Eeshta knew Whosits' real name.

"Who took him?" Not that Barton cared, particularly, but it was something to say, to keep her talking.

"The man Tarleton and others I do not know." Tarleton hadn't *said* anything . . . Well, what did it matter?

"What else are you learning, Eeshta? Anything you especially enjoy?"

"Oh, yes, Barton! Your music. It is so different from ours. Some of it, I am told, is out of my range of hearing. But it seems I hear parts you do not. I think if I stay here, music will be my study and work. I like it so very much."

Barton was no music buff himself, but he asked Eeshta about her favorite composers and performers. He didn't give a damn what they discussed; he simply wanted the young Demu to feel comfortable with him. He realized he might still be feeling guilt for having roughed her up so much at first acquaintance. But the way it felt to Barton, he liked the kid, was all.

As the conversation hit a lull, it struck him that Eeshta might not know what she and her little speech-prosthesis had done, inadvertently, for Limila. So, as best he could, he tried to explain what had happened, what was being done.

"They make her as she was? It seems not to be possible. But so good, if true."

"Well, not exactly the way she was," Barton admitted, "but a lot closer. Some things, like the teeth, will be artificial. But for the most part we hope she'll look pretty much like the original model, or at least a close relative.

"The doctor is doing some work on Siewen, too," he added. "What he can."

"Poor Siewen," Eeshta said. "Some things are not possible for him, too late. And Heimbach?"

"The Freak wouldn't have any part of it, not even teeth. I guess he *likes* eating mush all the time."

"I feel badly, Barton. For Heimbach, for Siewen and Limila, for all the dead ones where we made worse mistakes. But now for Limila, and some for Siewen, I can feel better. For helping, even not knowing I helped."

"Well, you know now, Eeshta. And we're grateful to you, believe me."

"Of that, I can be glad."

The short twilight was ending. Barton took Eeshta's hand; they jogged back toward her quarters, laughing as they ran out of breath from the unaccustomed exercise. At least Barton was laughing; Eeshta's mouth was doing something he couldn't make out in the dim light, but he felt she shared his mood. Then they were home.

Her home, at least, such as it was. He started to say goodnight but Eeshta spoke first. "Barton," she said, "soon you go seeking the Demu, my people? I have heard it. It is supposed to be secret from me. But many do not believe I understand your speech. They speak where I hear, though they should not."

Barton nodded. "Yes, we have to visit the Demu at home. You can see that."

"I must go with you."

"You want to go home? Yes; sure you would. But this trip won't be too safe, you know. You'd better wait awhile."

"No, *now*, Barton," said Eeshta. "I know; you will fight. With the ships. You must. Demu will not talk with what they think animals. You will force them. But I must be there, when first there is talk."

Barton didn't argue; she was right. But would Tarleton agree?

"I'll see what I can do, Eeshta." His arms acted without his volition. It was only after Eeshta had entered her quarters, and he was walking away toward his own, that Barton thought, "Well, I'll be go to hell if I didn't *hug* that hard-shelled little crittur!" Somehow it didn't bother him any.

Barton barged into his own quarters, shucked his shirt and shoes, and poured himself a hefty slug of bourbon. He looked, and carefully poured half of it back into the bottle. He sat, and sipped, and thought a lot. He went to bed early, and slept much better than he had expected.

Dr. Parr the next morning, tall, languid and about to get a flat nose if he didn't take Barton off the hook pretty soon, was in no hurry. "The patients will be with us shortly," he said. "Meanwhile let me explain some of the problems." Yeh, let me tell you what the problem is.

The trouble was that Parr told it in medicalese, which might as well have been Greek. Finally Barton had had it. "Goddammit, Doc! Did it work, or not?"

"See for yourself." Parr pushed a button on his desk; shortly, three wheelchair patients were brought in. Three?

All were wearing loose hospital-type bathrobes. Two were bald; the third had a towel around its head, bandages covering its face, and five toes on each foot. That one had to be Limila, but Barton knew Parr was going to run the show his own way. So he took a deep breath, and hoped for more patience than he could reasonably expect to have on tap.

The first chair carried a tall skinny guy who didn't look especially familiar. A little, maybe, but not much. "Say hello to Mr. Barton," said Parr.

"Hello, Barton. I am Siewen; remember?"

It wasn't, really, but there were lips and a nose, and dentures that beat the Demu accent. The ears, Barton supposed, were plastic. But what the hell.

"Hello, Doktor Siewen," Barton said. "How do you feel?" Feeling very unrealistic, himself. How long could he keep up this charade? How long could Limila?

"Much better, thank you," said Siewen. "It is good to be able to chew food again. And to pronounce correctly." Well, good on you, Buster, Barton thought, turning to the second wheelchair. The man was no one Barton remembered.

"Who's this?" he asked Parr.

"Heimbach, of course."

"I thought he wouldn't play ball."

"Mr. Tarleton requisitioned him for tests of the Demu shield versus the sleep gun. After the third test, Herr Heimbach rediscovered the desire to be human rather than Demu." Dr. Parr grinned. "As it happens, I was able to improve things somewhat, that are not visible through the bathrobe." Barton thought he should probably feel glad for Heimbach, but he couldn't seem to find time for it.

He shook his head, hard. The formal touch, he supposed, was required.

"That's fine, Doctor," he said. "It has been interesting seeing your success with Doktor Siewen and Herr Heimbach. May we excuse them now, please?"

Parr nodded. The two were wheeled out. Barton was left alone with Dr. Parr and Limila. He walked over to her, and for the first time she looked up at him. Then she stood, and was in Barton's arms. For a moment they only held each other. Then, unsatisfactorily through the gap in the bandages, he kissed her, very gently.

The rest of it still took a while. Dr. Parr fussed about the unprofessional aspects of the reunion until Barton told him, not politely, to get on with it. Then the bandages came off, along with the towel. Not the robe, though.

The nose and lips were not quite the originals; Barton had known better than to expect perfection, though the nose was very close to it. But below the bare scalp and the fake brows and lashes was a human face. Barton found it comely and knew he could find it lovely, given the chance. The few hairline scars had already begun to fade; they would not be noticeable. He looked at Limila's new lips and was thankful for the existence of Dr. Parr, for they were close to what he had remembered. Only a little shorter.

Limila wasn't happy with the dentures; they were comfortable enough, and effective, but she wanted her full forty teeth, not merely the human twenty-eight. But she was glad to have the little ridge, so that she no longer talked like a comic drunk; Barton figured she'd settle for the rest of it eventually. He noticed that she hadn't yet bothered with simulated nails on toes or fingers, though recesses had been made for them.

The soft plastic ear-cups, part plug-in and part glue-on, were so realistic that Barton first thought they were real. Then he noticed they were cooler to the touch than real ears. Well, he could live with them if she could.

He wasn't going to ask about anything under the bathrobe, but she told him anyway. No breasts; from a quick study of dress styles she was resigned to wearing Earth-type falsies in company, but bedammt if she'd have them implanted permanently on her Tilari body. All right . . .

She confessed that she had allowed Parr to restore the appearance of external genitals, as well as the navel. "When I found it really didn't hurt," she said, "it might as well be as much the way you would like, as could be done."

Barton hugged and kissed her a lot longer than Parr appreciated, before he allowed the doctor to throw him out. He went home with more of a load off his mind than

101

he had expected, and hardly noticed what his pre-packaged lunch didn't taste like.

In the afternoon he took a jeep and went shopping in the nearest medium-sized town, about eighty kilometers to the southwest. He had dinner there, and drove back in the evening. That night he slept without chemical aids of any kind.

The next morning, up early, it took Barton so long to reach Dr. Parr's office, by phone, that he could have walked there and saved time. He was told that he could not see Limila again immediately; Parr was running final postoperative checks on her. *But,* if he would come over around three in the afternoon, Parr finally got across through Barton's protests, he could probably bring Limila home. If the tests turned out all right. Barton thanked him sheepishly and hung up.

He decided to visit the ship; he had nothing else he wanted to do. As he started out the door, the phone rang. It was Dr. Fox.

"I'd like to see you this morning, Mr. Barton."

"Well, I was just going out to the ship."

"I spoke to Mr. Tarleton, there, and he tells me he won't be needing you today. So why don't you come here instead? Nine o'clock?" He had to agree, he guessed, so he did.

Seated across the desk from Arleta Fox, Barton wondered at the tenacity with which this small woman dug for the worms in the undersoil of his mind. She was smiling but he didn't trust it.

After the usual perfunctory chatter, she said, "I understand that Dr. Parr's corrective surgery on your companions has been remarkably successful."

Barton nodded.

"Do you suppose the woman—Limila?—might consent to taking a few evaluative tests now?" Limila had refused anything of the sort, earlier, and the Agency (meaning Tarleton) didn't see that it had any right or authority to try to coerce her.

"I don't know; I'll ask her, if you like. But what do you expect to learn that she hasn't already told the biological and cultural teams?"

"Why, a million things! She's the first person we've met of a whole new race. If we're going to have contact with them, and I assume we are, we need to know something of what they are like psychologically, as individuals."

"Do you think she'll be typical, after what she's been through?" Then he could have kicked himself. Why remind the doctor that Barton had been through a few atypical experiences himself?

"Given a little time to stabilize, now that her appearance has been restored, I think she can give us a valid picture of what the Tilari are like. I wish she had been willing to cooperate before; the comparison would be very informative. Well, at least I can extrapolate after retesting Siewen and Heimbach."

"You've tested them?" He shook his head incredulously. "What did you find out?" Yes, lady, let's talk about somebody else, everybody else. Anybody but Barton.

"Doktor Siewen, as you probably know, seems to be devoid of normal motivations. It remains to be seen whether his change in appearance will reactivate him to any significant extent. I had little time to work with Heimbach between his reversion to human speech and the beginning of the surgery by Dr. Parr; he is a very confused man. I realize that he was semi-amnesiac for a time from the results of the so-called sleep gun, but my feeling is that Heimbach has a very weak ego." She paused. "Quite different from yourself, for instance, Mr. Barton. Quite, quite different."

"Oh, hey, Doctor," Barton stammered. "Am I all that much of an egomaniac, in your book?" Watch it, Barton; *watch it!*

"A strong ego is not the same thing as egotism, Mr. Barton. I mean that unlike Heimbach you have a strong, even a fierce sense of your own individuality; it is of central importance to you. And you have a very powerful will to survive."

"That's what the tests say?" So he hadn't fooled her much, after all.

"I didn't need the tests to tell me that; your report of the eight years with the Demu was enough. The tests, in fact, have been unsatisfactory because they do *not* show me the man who could do what you obviously did."

Barton felt that he was in over his head. "Well, we all know a person can do more than he thinks he can, when he has to. Maybe it's just that I was under a lot of stress

there, and back home here I can let down and relax."
Like hell he could!

"Possibly. Another thought is that due to repeated exposure to the Demu sleep gun you still may have been partly amnesiac when you first took the personality tests."

"But I took the IQ tests at the same time; just before, actually. And you said they read about the same as what was already on file for me."

"Well, as I say, I'm not sure yet. So that is why I'd like you to retake the personality test series now, Mr. Barton, if you would."

When in doubt, stall! "I really wouldn't have time for all that today, Doctor. Early this afternoon I'm supposed to pick Limila up at Dr. Parr's; he thinks she can come home now."

"I didn't mean the entire series, Mr. Barton," she said. "A few key sections: a couple of hours at most. And it's only nine-thirty . . ."

He was hooked. He knew he couldn't get away with hallucinating his younger self again to answer all the questions; for one thing it would look fishy if he asked for full privacy a second time. Well, maybe he could hallucinate a little of it now and then, without her noticing. Throw a modicum of confusion into the works. Unless she were more devious than he suspected—and he suspected one hell of a lot, where Arleta Fox was concerned —by now he had her fooled into thinking he was sane, safe to be at large. All he needed to do, probably, was soft-pedal himself on the parts he couldn't hallucinate.

She brought out the test forms—Form B, so his answers from last time would have done him no good even if he could have remembered them—and he sat down. He wasn't directly under her eagle eye, but she could look him over any time she wished, while he couldn't look to see if *she* were looking without being conspicuous about it.

He did the first few questions straight, then tried to dredge the younger Barton up to answer the next few. *He couldn't do it.* Whether it was her presence or whether he'd simply lost the knack, he didn't know. He hadn't practiced self-hypnosis since his escape, maybe that was the answer. But one way or another, he was stuck with his present self and its attitudes, to cope with a lot of tricky questions.

All right; the hell with it. Tarleton needed the help of

the Tilari and other races. He couldn't get it without Limila's cooperation; in effect, that meant Barton's. Even if this lady does catch me out, he thought, she still works for Tarleton. He kept telling himself that, trying to believe it.

Finally he was done. Sweat from his armpits ran down his sides. He took the finished sheets to Arleta Fox, who did not look up until he laid the papers before her.

"All completed, Mr. Barton?"

"Best I can do, Doctor."

She pressed a button: a girl came in to take the test sheets. Presumably for scoring: no reason the doc should do all that routine stuff. The girl had gone before Barton realized he hadn't noticed what she looked like—whether she was pretty or not. That wasn't like him.

"Would you like a cup of coffee before you go, Mr. Barton? I would have offered you some before, but I didn't want to interrupt your concentration."

"Yeh, sure; thanks." He sat across from her. He didn't want coffee; he wanted a drink, and to get out of here. But best to play along, just now.

The girl returned, bringing coffee. This time Barton noticed that she was slim and pretty, with blond hair cut considerably shorter than he would have preferred. Well, at least she could grow it if she wanted to, he thought with a pang, thinking how nice it would be if Limila had the same option.

"Do you have any idea when the expedition is leaving, Mr. Barton?"

Barton looked at her. Not the old security-leak ploy, for Chrissakes!

"Oh, we all know about it. But you don't have to tell me anything Mr. Tarleton told you not to. I merely wanted to get some idea of when I should cut off research and turn in my reports. They always tell me, officially, about twenty-four hours ahead of deadline. Then I don't get any sleep for a while until the reports are completed."

"Always?"

"I do research for a lot of things, Mr. Barton. This does happen to be the first interstellar expedition I've prepped for; yes." It was a wry smile, the one she gave him then.

"I don't really know, Doctor," he said. "I was up at Seattle for a week, got back yesterday afternoon. No; day before, it was. Anyway, I haven't seen Tarleton since he left Seattle, and the last I heard there was no firm date set. Or if there was, he didn't tell me."

"You don't need to sound so defensive, Mr. Barton; I believe you. More coffee?"

"No, thanks; I'd better be going. Thanks, though." He got up, they said goodbyes and he left. He wished that either he didn't feel so much like liking Arleta Fox or that he had less cause to be wary of her. His feeling for her was not sexual. Oh, he considered her attractive enough; Barton had no prejudice against small sturdy women. But what grabbed him about her was the compact tidy bulldog mind that the fierce little jaw so strongly implied. Too bad it made her such a danger to him.

Barton didn't feel like heating another frozen lunch, to eat alone. He got a jeep from the motor pool and drove out to the ship area. He caught Tarleton and Kreugel on their way to the new cafeteria. It had been established in a big hurry when Tarleton got tired of bringing his own lunch in a paper bag.

"Wait up for another hungry man, will you?" Barton called, and they did.

Inside, they went through the line and soon were sitting with laden trays. Barton didn't talk much. He was thinking of how to ask for what he wanted. Tarleton was telling Kreugel that the first ship of the Earth-built fleet would be here for testing tomorrow or the next day. Kreugel would be installing the central-axis laser weaponry.

Then Tarleton noticed Barton's silence. "What are you chewing on, over there?"

"Beef Stroganoff, it says on the menu. And a couple of questions."

"I thought the Stroganoff was pretty good, myself. Shoot the questions."

"OK," said Barton. "First, do you have any kind of proposed takeoff date yet?"

"For the fleet? Sure."

"Do I qualify to know it?"

"You're specifically authorized, I'm happy to say. Just four weeks from now, Saturday the 12th, with a possible week's slippage. OK?"

"That's pretty fast, isn't it?"

"Things get done fast on crash-priority," Tarleton said. "I haven't been just standing around here cracking whips, Barton. As soon as any item, any part of the ships is

106

cleared for production, I start it through the line. For instance, a lot of the drive components were firm several weeks ago. I goofed on a couple and had to have them done over again when new improvements were suggested, but the waste was minor for a job of this magnitude. Before I left Seattle I put the go-ahead on the last remaining components. Production and testing is seven days a week, twenty-four hours a day: overtime and bonuses for the working troops all the way down the line. My guess is, two-to-one we don't need that extra week. OK?"

"Damn good, Tarleton. You really know how to run a railroad." He hesitated. "Now I want to ask a favor."

"Ask ahead," said Tarleton. "You have a couple coming, assuming they're reasonable."

"OK. I expect you want Limila to check over whatever your amateur translators have been getting from Hishtoo lately. And maybe you'd like me to sit in at first while your boys check out our first production-line ship. Right?"

"Yes," Tarleton agreed, "I did have those things in mind. So what's the favor?"

"Limila comes home this afternoon, I think," Barton said. "She and I can work with you tomorrow and the next day, no sweat—one or two more if you need it. But then—Tarleton, I want to take her on vacation. Show her the country; be a couple of tourists. Get lost from here —see the sights and meet the people. She needs it, you know, if she's going to be able to give her people any idea of what we're really like. I mean, a project site doesn't give much of a true picture, does it?"

Tarleton was silent for a moment. Barton could sense the wheels going around, in that brain he had learned to respect more than a little. "Dammit, Barton," he said finally, "you're right. I should have thought of that. I guess I'm too wound up in production schedules. Fair enough; you and Limila hit here bright and early tomorrow, and I won't keep you a day longer than I have to. You'd better see the Finance Office today if you can, and put in for expense money for your tour. Those people can't put a stamp on a letter in less than forty-eight hours." Barton grinned; he knew about that.

Kreugel hadn't said much but he shook hands and said "Good luck" when Barton stood up to go. "Remind me to show you how our zap-gun works when you get back."

"Yeh, I want to see that. OK, be seeing y'all."

Barton did stop at the Finance Office on his way home; he had plenty of time. A Mr. Will Groundley was querulous and resentful that Barton should want anything outside the routine. Barton's patience lasted quick, as the saying goes.

"Look," he said, "call Tarleton. He'll tell you yes or no, and then you do it or you don't. But don't quote me any more goddam regulations, Groundley. We both know you can find something in your books to let you do anything you want, or keep you from doing anything you don't want. So get off the pot. Either you have the money here for me tomorrow, or Tarleton will find me somebody who will."

He didn't wait for an answer; one more word might have exceeded the limits of his control. He walked out and went home. For a change there were no notes in his mailbox. That was nice.

Before heading for Dr. Parr's, Barton unwrapped the results of his yesterday's shopping trip. Jeez, he hoped Limila would like them. He ran his fingers through the one he liked best . . .

Parr was not as infuriatingly languid as usual. He seemed embarrassed, instead. "Good afternoon, Mr. Barton," he said, "I'm happy to tell you that Limila checked out 100 percent; I can discharge her unconditionally. She'll be with us in a few minutes." Parr smiled; it took him a while to do it. "Would you like some coffee while we wait?" Might as well; Barton did his nod. A young orderly brought coffee; they sipped it, bla-bla-ing politely. I was a bla-bla for the Space Agency, Barton thought.

Then Limila came in, carrying a small suitcase. She wore a sort of turban with earrings pendant from her plastic lobes, a loose-fitting short chemise with contours that indicated Earth-positioned falsies, and half-calf suede boots. It wasn't the greatest ensemble Barton had ever seen in his life, but she moved well in it and his heart sang.

"I can come home now, Barton," she said, "but first I must thank Dr. Parr for what he has done." She turned to Parr. "Doctor," she began, but choked on it. She tried once more. "Doctor. You have made me a person who wants to live, again."

Parr wasn't used to raw emotion; Barton saw him

trying not to react to it. Barton took him off the hook; he pulled out one of the wigs from his shopping trip.

"Here, Limila," he said, "take that thing off your head for a minute, and try this on."

The hair was long, black and glossy; there was a lot of it. The forehead was in the high range for Earth, but of course nowhere near the over-the-ears Tilaran hairline.

And Limila didn't like it at all. "Barton! This is not me. This is one of *your* women. I do not have hair growing so far forward. You must remember that?"

"It's the highest-foreheaded wig I could find. And it looks *good* on you."

"*No!* I am Tilari!" She tore it away, threw it against the wall.

Barton had had enough. He caught her by the shoulders, taking great care not to grip her as hard as his impulse demanded.

"Now *look!*" he said. "You are on Earth, not on Tilara. You're wearing plastic Earth tits, aren't you?" She looked at him, blankly.

"Tits?"

"*Breasts,* dammit!" Barton relaxed his grip. Limila nodded slowly.

"All right," he continued. "So while you're here you wear the local-style scalp fixtures, too. So that you can mix with people without them staring at you all the time. When we get to Tilara you can do it your way. In fact I'll get a special wig made for you, as soon as I can.

"But meanwhile, Limila," Barton said in a harsher tone than he intended, "you pick that wig up and dust it off and put it on your head, and we will go home."

Nobody said anything. Limila followed Barton's instructions. The wig looked a little mussed, but not badly. Dr. Parr wore a pained expression, as if he desperately needed to visit the toilet but was too polite to say so.

He looked even more as though he'd never make it when Limila went to him and kissed him strongly, before letting Barton lead her away.

In the jeep, Barton couldn't think of anything to say; he was too taken with Limila's new appearance as seen in his peripheral vision. He was embarrassed to look at her directly too much or too often. In fact, he was just plain embarrassed, a feeling that was strange to him. He was glad when they reached their quarters and the ride was over.

He parked the jeep and walked with Limila into the house. Then he asked her.

"The doc's a pretty good guy, huh? Naturally you're grateful to him."

"Oh, of course," she said. "And I had not made love for so long, either."

Before or after the bandages came off? Barton didn't ask; any question would be the wrong one. Tilara was not Earth, he told himself. But now he saw why Dr. Parr had been so uncharacteristically embarrassed.

Limila was happy, bubbling. She found things Barton hadn't known were in the freezer, and prepared the best dinner he'd had in a long while. She showed him, from the suitcase, two more dresses. Dr. Parr's nurse had helped her order them. She drank with him, bathed with him, and eventually went to bed with him.

First, though, she asked, "Barton, do you want me to wear the wig to bed?" She had it in her hand.

"Suit yourself," he said. "Whatever you want."

"Without it I do not repel you?"

"Hell no!" said Barton. "Look, Limila: one time I was going with a girl who did fashion modeling work. She was quite a doll—long blond hair and a face like an angel with a body to match. One night I went to pick her up for a date, and damned if she wasn't shaved as bald as you are right now. This nut of a fashion designer had her do it, to get some publicity for one of his shows.

"Well, it startled the hell out of me. She wore a wig on our date, of course, but she took it off for bed because she didn't want it mussed up. At first it was odd as hell seeing her with no hair, but after a while I took it for granted; it was still her, wasn't it?" He chuckled. "In fact it looked better on her than the crew-cut stage when she grew it out again."

"But I thought that was part of why you couldn't . . ."

Barton shook his head. "No, Limila; that wasn't it. It was what they had done to your face. I'm sorry I could never see past that, but I couldn't."

"Do you like my face now?" she asked. "It is not as before, really."

"I like it," he said. "It's not exactly as I remember you; no. But it's close enough that it could be, almost. It is you, Limila.

"Limila!" he whispered against her cheek, and that

110

•was enough talk. Barton didn't get as much sleep that night as he was used to, but he didn't miss it.

Before he went to sleep, it struck him that this was the first sex of any kind that he'd had since leaving the Demu research station. He had not been able to bring himself to love the Demu-ized Limila, and yet her presence, her accusing presence, had inhibited him from seeking other women. Well, how about that! Until freed from it, he'd had no idea how heavy upon him had been the burden of Limila's disfigurement. He sighed, yawned, and drowsed off into relaxed slumber.

Limila was nervous, next morning. "At the ship, Barton, what will they think? I am all new. Almost I want to hide, to wear the veil."

Barton laughed, then sobered. "Don't worry about a thing. They'll stare, sure. Why not? You're worth looking at, you know."

"And before, I was not."

Barton went to her. "I'm sorry. It's just that now you're *you* again." Then he smiled, and it was all right.

She took as much time choosing between three dresses as if they had been thirty, but finally chose a white smock. Carefully she donned and brushed the wig, applied tinted polish to the glue-on fingernails she was wearing for the first time. Barton could see that they were not going to be "bright and early" as Tarleton had specified, but he controlled his impatience.

Eventually they were ready to leave. Barton drove faster than usual and made up some of the time; they were about ten minutes late. Tarleton was waiting, pacing back and forth alongside his car.

"Well, *there* you are!" he said. "I've been—" Then he saw Limila, and stopped. "Great day in the morning!" He reddened. "I mean, uh—how do you feel, Limila?"

"Like a person, like myself again. It is not exact, no. And much you see is artificial. But I see me in a mirror and want to be alive, not dead. For that I thank you who authorized that it could happen, as well as Barton and Dr. Parr." She went to him; before he knew what was happening she pulled his head down to hers and kissed him soundly. "You see? I do thank you."

"You're—you're certainly welcome." He was redder than ever. "Look, are we going to stand around out here all day? We've got work to do."

111

Inside were only Hishtoo and a guard. Doktor Siewen was still under Parr's care; old flesh heals slowly. The guard was new; to him, Limila was a pretty woman, not a phenomenon. Hishtoo's response was something else; he came forward, stared at her closely and burst into outraged-sounding babble.

Limila laughed. Tarleton looked at her in wonder. Obviously, Barton thought, he'd never heard her laugh before. It did make a nice change of pace.

"He is furious with me," she said. "He says he found me worthy to be Demu, had me made Demu with great effort. Now I waste it and choose to be animal again. He scrapes his hands clean of me."

"He's breaking my heart," said Barton. "I weep big tears."

"Tell him," said Tarleton, "to can the clatter. There's work to do. And that goes for us, too." So they got down to the laborious business of asking questions, of cross-checking the answers they could not trust, against previous results. Hishtoo lied about half the time but his memory was not perfect; he could be caught in inconsistencies. These weren't thrown back at him; that wasn't the idea. But by careful checking, the facts slowly emerged. It was a tedious process, but it was the only game in town. Eeshta, unfortunately, had no technical training.

Barton spent only a short time with them; his main business was with Kreugel, and the ship.

Barton and Limila worked hard for Tarleton that day, the next and part of a third, before his requirements were met. At lunch that day he told them they were cleared to go touring, vacationing.

"Fine business," said Barton. "Is the 12th still on for takeoff?"

"Looks like it," Tarleton said. "Why don't you figure on getting back here by the 10th? In time to check with me and maybe confer a little, that day?"

"Fine by me. Look, would you run through the money thing again?"

The government had reimbursed Barton, by act of Congress, for the value of his lost estate. In fairness he should have received the amount as of the time he had been declared legally dead. But some deskbound nitpicker, by dint of an obscure regulation, had managed to fob him off with the lesser sum that had existed at the time of his disappearance, before the vogue for his paintings. When he heard, Barton said a few four-letter words and shrugged it off. He'd long since forgotten his earlier idea of soaking the government a real bundle for the Demu ship.

He was on an adequate though not lavish salary, and there was provision for expenses when he was off the project site and out into the world; that part had been explained to him earlier, but he'd been preoccupied with other matters and hadn't paid much attention. On the Seattle trip, accommodations had been provided; Barton had spent nothing but a little pocket money. So Tarleton patiently went over it again.

"Your expense-account setup is a modification of the old per-diem system. You draw a flat $200 a day ordinarily. Any week your expenses run over $1,400 you either swallow the loss or turn in complete receipts if you want to pick up the difference. Up to you. If you're planning to hit any really plush resorts I advise you to collect the receipts. I've put in a special voucher for Limila to get $100 a day. Previously she's been on the books as a temporary ward of the government. You can draw the full advance at the Finance Office this afternoon."

He grinned. "I heard about Groundley trying to give you the runaround yesterday. That was one too many; he's been a nuisance before, and I'd been looking for an excuse to fix his wagon. He's been reassigned to the filing section, so if they can't find your file you'll know why."

Barton and Limila thanked Tarleton, shook hands with him and Kreugel and went home, with a no-problems stopover at the Finance Office. Barton sincerely appreciated Groundley's absence . . .

They made love, packed luggage. Barton exchanged the motor-pool jeep for the rental car he had arranged to have delivered, and they were off and away. Limila was wearing the shortest of the three wigs Barton had bought. It was a short-cut, smooth-cap effect. All were black; Barton couldn't imagine her any other way. It remained to be seen whether she would have a different idea.

She didn't seem to have, when they reached the town and shop where Barton had made his earlier purchases. Mrs. Aranson, the owner, was startled when Barton removed Limila's wig. He borrowed a piece of chalk and drew the Tilaran hairline on her scalp, correcting it to her eventual satisfaction. Mrs. Aranson made sketches, took careful measurements and jotted them on the paper.

"Black and long, like the longest of the three I bought the other day," Barton specified. "And send it here." He gave the lady their address at the project. "How soon do you suppose we could have it? I'll pay extra for speed, because after the 10th of next month is too late."

"There will be no difficulty meeting that date, and no need for extra payment. But with these contours—rather unusual, you must admit—I'll have to design the piece to be held by adhesive at front and back. Will that method be satisfactory?" Limila nodded; she seemed totally unruffled. Mrs. Aranson obviously wanted to ask more questions, but could find no way to do so without breaching her calm professional courtesy.

Barton took her off the hook. "The role in question," he said, not lying, really, "is that of a lady of an alien race, from another planet." Mrs. Aranson smiled. These actors and actresses; they'd do anything!

Back outside, Limila was in a sunny mood. "Thank you, Barton. Now when we come to Tilara I will have other teeth made, also, with the full forty." She looked at him, put her hand on his arm. "But if you like me better as an Earthwoman, then when we are alone I can wear Earth teeth and Earth hair. And Earth *tits!*" Barton broke up laughing.

"Honey, you wear just any little ol' thing you damn please! Or not . . . "

His comment reminded Limila that her wardrobe left something to be desired in the matter of quantity. She shopped rapidly, but it was an hour later when Barton paid the clerk and they were ready to drive on.

They had gone about fifty kilometers further across the high desert plateau when Barton realized he'd forgotten to say goodbye to Eeshta, or to put it to Tarleton that she should accompany the expedition. He made a mental note.

They stopped for the night fairly early. Barton spotted an attractive motel, shortly after they left their narrow two-lane road for an Interstate freeway. After quick showers, they headed for the motel's restaurant.

"We have twenty-two days free and clear," Barton told Limila over dinner, "not counting today or the day we're supposed to get back. Suppose I pick up some maps at the service station. I can tell you what kinds of

114

country we have around here in various directions, and you decide what you'd most like to see."

"That would be nice, Barton," she said. "Can we be among some of your forests, and mountains? And see the ocean?"

"I wouldn't be surprised. Would you like a liqueur with your coffee?" She would. Then they returned to their room, passing the motel pool. In the room, Limila sighed.

"Anything wrong?" Barton asked.

"I would so much like to swim," she said. "I have not swum since Tilara." He started to say go right ahead, and then saw what the problem was. Limila's padded bra wasn't made to fool anyone, under the current styles of swimsuits. Not that many of the swimmers had been wearing suits.

"Excuse me a minute," he said, and went to the manager's office. He noted on the way that the poolside sign quoted a ten-o'clock closing time, and that no one could see into the pool area if the gates were closed. He estimated that by ten it would be getting chilly; they were still in plateau country.

For money in hand the manager was quite willing to close the pool two hours early and turn the gate key over to Barton for the rest of the evening. The expression on Limila's face when he told her (he didn't mention the cost) made it well worth while.

Waiting, Barton put his mental note about Eeshta into written form and mailed it off to Tarleton. Then he and Limila swam nude together until the chill chased them indoors, though they'd tried a little mutual warmth in the water. It was fun, but more under the heading of pleasurable gymnastics than true passion.

Three weeks together. Forests and mountains and the ocean; yes. Motels and hotels and ethnic restaurants and miniature $5 hamburgers at drive-ins. New Mexico, Arizona, California, a brief journey into Mexico. All the way up the California coast and further to Oregon and Washington. A quick visit to Canada. East into the Rockies, and then south again, back toward the project. Love in the morning, in the afternoon before dinner, and again late at night; nearly every day was like that. Barton knew he was forty but he felt more like twenty. They spent their three weeks' expense money in the first two and forgot to keep receipts; what the hell, Barton's

115

checkbook had his "estate" and accumulated salary to draw on. And once he got off Earth again, he had no idea whether he could or would ever come back. Meanwhile he was having the best three weeks he could remember, ever.

Limila wasn't complaining, either. She *liked* what she saw of Earth, its people and its scenery. Some things must have been greatly different from Tilaran ways; they seemed to puzzle her mightily. Barton tried to explain; she appeared satisfied, usually, with his attempts. Occasionally he asked her about equivalent Tilaran customs, but she shook her head. "You must see; I could not tell you so that you would know." OK; he'd settle for that.

Barton was surprised that no one seemed to notice that Limila's hands were each short a finger by Earth standards. He watched her a lot, the second and third day, and finally saw what she was doing. She had a way of using the fewest fingers possible when eating, say; she'd tuck one or two under, out of sight. Barton didn't ask whether the action was deliberate or unconscious; it worked, didn't it? Barton was all for anything that worked; he always had been. He decided that Parr's cartilage graft, to eliminate the jog at the wrist, also helped conceal the difference.

The first week their free time had stretched endlessly ahead; the second week he put the deadline out of his mind; during the third it rushed upon him like a juggernaut. He ignored it as much as he could. But the night they stopped at a little town in southern Colorado, he was right on schedule. They would reach the project site on the afternoon of Thursday, the 10th, as Tarleton had requested. Part of Barton's mind was damned good at keeping schedules, he decided, even when he didn't want to.

After dinner Barton took the car down the street, to replenish its fuel cells. When he got back, Limila had maps spread across her bed. She looked up at him. "I have been looking to see all the places we have been. May I keep these maps, please?"

"Sure; of course. Whatever you want. Why?"

"You have a lovely world, Barton. I would like these to remember it."

"Oh hell!" he said. "I should have been taking color pics; we could have, easily enough. I didn't think of it.

116

Hey, look: I can order up a bunch of tourist slides for you."

"For me, no need, Barton. Tilarans have full visual recall; we use photographs only to transmit information to one who has not seen personally. Some pictures to show other Tilarans would be nice, yes. I use the maps merely to focus memory on a given sight." Barton made a note to get the pics, anyway.

"Barton?"

"Yes?"

"I have liked Earth; it has been good to me. I wonder if you will like Tilara. It is beautiful, too, but differently. And our ways are very different, you know." Barton didn't know much of anything, he felt, but he'd long since done a lot of guessing.

It was their last night of freedom, of total privacy. Nostalgia for what they had had together made it sweet. Just before sleep they held each other gently. Limila cried and Barton wanted to, and both knew why. For now it was over.

It was a long drive next day but Barton pushed the car, driving faster than he usually did. They arrived at the project early in the afternoon. The mailbox had its quota of messages: Dr. Fox wanted to see Barton; Dr. Parr wanted to see Limila for final routine checkups; Tarleton wanted to see both of them. Somebody was obviously going to have to take seconds.

There was also a box from the wig shop. Limila set it aside, for the time being.

They were unpacking. "Fox can wait," said Barton. "In fact I'd like to dodge her completely, if I could get away with it. Tell you what; let's run over to see Parr. I'll wait; it shouldn't take long. Then we can go and chin with Tarleton."

"No," Limila said, "you drop me at Dr. Parr's and go meet with Tarleton." Barton started to ask a question, but didn't. A special goodbye for lucky Dr. Parr. Well, dammit, the man had earned anything she wanted to give him. And Limila was not of Earth. If that's what she wanted, so be it.

"OK," he said, "I understand."

"Barton," she said, and kissed him. They didn't get away just then, after all.

So he caught Tarleton at the midafternoon coffee break. "Nice trip?"

"Great, Tarleton. Thanks for the vacation; I needed it. Now how do we stand?"

"I hope you're not superstitious, Barton. We've had to allow one day of slippage; Up-Day is Sunday the 13th. It was two days for a while but we caught up one of them."

"Will all the ships come here first? I see only six out there now."

"Four more come here; there'll be four groups of ten each. I couldn't tell you before—it was Top Clam—but the groups are leaving from different bases: here, Seattle, Houston and someplace in Russia they won't tell us for sure."

"Russia? You're kidding me, Tarleton." But Tarleton wasn't. Early in the game the Agency had realized that forty ships were more than the U.S.-Canadian complex could produce within any reasonable time limit. So under top secrecy, Tarleton's superiors had gotten permission to deal quietly, behind the scenes, first with their country's out-of-hemisphere allies, then with the "neutrals" and finally with their nominal antagonists. The result, Barton was surprised to learn, was that the First Demu Expedition would consist of seventeen U.S. ships, seven from the USSR, three each from Britain and Western Germany, and two each from Japan, France, Australia, China and the Greater Central African Republic. Several other countries had pledged at least one ship to the second fleet, given the data and the additional time.

"How in hell did everybody manage *that*, Tarleton?"

"How in hell did you manage to get your ship from the Demu?"

Barton grinned and shook his head. "OK, I get the message.

"Now then. How about me? Personally. Do I get a ship or don't I?"

"You do, in a way."

"What is that supposed to mean? I *told* you—"

"Easy, Barton. You get a ship. But there's been an unexpected development. Of all people, *I* ended up in command of the whole damn fleet!" He grinned. "Some of the military shit green when they heard about that, I shouldn't wonder."

"But what about my ship? Is it or isn't it?"

118

"It is. Except that you'll have your boss—that's me—riding with you. And maybe looking over your shoulder sometimes."

"Hell's bells. Given the choice, do you think I want to ride with anyone else?" Well, it was a compliment of sorts. Barton poured them both some more coffee. The other man looked ready to go back to work, and Barton had more on his mind.

"Who else rides with us?" he asked. "Limila has to, or no deal. How about Eeshta? Did you get my note about that? And who else?"

"One at a time, Barton; OK?" Barton shrugged. "The ships are built to carry twelve but we're crewing them with ten, all but ours; it rides full. The idea is that if we lose a ship but not all the people, we'll have someplace to put the survivors. You see?

"Standard crew is four qualified pilots, two communications techs and four weaponry artists. Everybody doubles in brass for the other chores. Sound reasonable?"

"OK so far. Now come on with it. What does the Easter bunny have for *me?*"

"All right. You get Limila and Eeshta and you have to put up with me and with Hishtoo. Don't argue; we're going to *need* Hishtoo, somewhere along the line. You know it, if you stop to think for a minute instead of looking stubborn.

"That leaves seven slots. You and three of them will be pilots. I and one other will be communicators. You'll be one short on weapons people. And all of us a little overstretched, guarding Hishtoo during part of our offwatch time."

Barton thought a minute. "Let me tell you what the problem isn't. Limila is your other communicator, or maybe Eeshta is and Limila is a gunner; we can figure that part out later; it's a long haul. And I see no reason to guard Hishtoo."

Tarleton looked skeptical, so Barton told him. "Nobody guarded him on the trip back here, did they?"

"But he had casts on both arms, or splints, or something."

"Any reason he can't have them on again?" Barton asked. Tarleton looked shocked. "I wouldn't even have to break his arms this time, though I don't mind a bit if you're dead set on realism. Well?" Tarleton still looked

119

shocked; Barton laughed. "I'm *kidding,* man. Hell, all we need to do is keep him locked up."

"I see your point. The Agency figures to give Hishtoo free run of the ship, using some of our manpower to watch him. We may as well not bother their heads about our improved version."

"OK, Tarleton; it's a deal."

Tarleton looked embarrassed. "There's one more thing. I'm sorry, but Dr. Fox went over my head. Her professional standing is such that I can't overrule her in her own specialty."

Barton's guts went cold. "What's to overrule, specifically?"

"She has a red tab on your card and she won't lift it until you take one more test run with her. I hadn't thought we had any problem there, but she seems to have a real bee in her bonnet. Believe me, I'd have squashed this if I could. I need you and Limila both; you've convinced me. And I wouldn't really expect Limila to want to come along if you were grounded."

"No," said Barton. "If that happens, I'll tell you what else will."

Tarleton waited.

"You and the fleet will go looking for the Demu, all by yourselves. You could take Eeshta along by force, I suppose, and Hishtoo of course. But if you took Limila that way she'd never help you find her people. *Or* the Demu. Don't try it."

"I have no such intention. In fact"—Tarleton looked a little sheepish—"I'm going to give you the keys to the car, if that'll make you feel any better. Do you remember that first day, when you handed them over to me?"

Barton remembered. Well, he had picked the right man. "Thanks, Tarleton," he said. "I'll take the keys now, if you don't mind." He got them.

Tarleton wanted to talk some more, trying to give reassurance, but finally recognized Barton's preoccupation and let him go. Still driving the rental car, Barton went home. There was another note from Dr. Fox, this one marked "Urgent." Limila was steaming in a hot bathtub. Dinner was simmering on the stove; it smelled good. Barton fixed a drink for himself and thought about a small woman with a bulldog mind, and about ships, and cages.

Limila came into the room, wearing a short robe and

the Tilari wig. She stood before him, waiting for his reaction. Her look was anxious.

A line came to Barton, out of a comic strip from his childhood. "Funny," he said, smiling, "how a pretty girl looks good in anything she happens to throw on." Then she was in his lap, and the problem, if there had been one, was over.

During and after dinner he brought her up to date. "But why do you fear this Dr. Fox?" she asked. "What can she do?"

"She can put me back in a cage, Limila. She has the authority. She can look in my mind and decide that I belong in one, and I'm afraid she will."

"But that is foolish, Barton." He shook his head. He knew that in the back of his mind was something that shouldn't be allowed to run loose. But it would, anyway, as long as he was alive. Determinedly he changed the subject and made it stick.

That night when they made love it was with an air of desperation, and sadness.

The next morning they were cheerful enough, at breakfast and when Barton drove Limila to the ship for briefing. On the way, Barton turned the rental car in to the motor pool and took a jeep in exchange. He and Limila talked, but of nothing in particular. They had a habit of doing that sometimes, he kept telling himself.

Tarleton must have been watching for them; he met them just outside the prefab where Limila usually worked.

"Hi, Barton," he said. "Limila, we have a problem here. Either Hishtoo or Siewen, or both of them, may be getting cutesie with us. And the question is too important to take chances. Come on and we'll run them through it again."

"Maybe I could—" Barton began.

"You go see Fox; she's kicking up a storm," Tarleton said. Then, over his shoulder, "See you later," as he escorted Limila into the building.

"Yeh," Barton said to nobody, "ol' Indispensable Barton. They just couldn't get along without me." The funny thing was that the incident truly depressed him; he hadn't thought he was quite so touchy.

Well, he might as well go see Fox. It was starting out to be a lousy day; why spoil it? Moodily he drove off in the jeep, kicking up great bursts of dust by gunning it through the more powdery parts of the bumpy road.

Home again, he decided he needed a shower to cool off. He changed into fresh clothes to replace those he'd dusted up so thoroughly, horsing around with the jeep on the way in. He tried to call Dr. Fox and let her know he was on his way. He couldn't get through; the local phone exchange was having one of its own bad days, which were frequent lately. So he set out, unannounced and unenthusiastic.

Barton found himself driving jerkily, and knew the tension was getting to him. He was so close to his goal—so *close*. He felt as though the raw ends of his nerves had grown out through his skin. Normal sensations became almost pain. Everything *jarred*. He forced himself to breathe slowly and deeply, trying to relax, as he parked the jeep and walked to Dr. Fox's office.

Arleta Fox greeted him pleasantly enough. "Do sit down, Mr. Barton. This is Dr. Schermerhorn, our new intern." She gestured toward a bullet-headed young man with a short, scraggly beard. He and Barton shook hands, mumbled greetings, sat.

"I'll be with you in a moment; let me refresh my memory first. This is the latest computer read-out on your overall test series. A quick skim, only, if you don't mind." And what, Barton wondered, if he *did* mind? He recognized the thought as pointless.

Covertly, he appraised Schermerhorn. Intern? He looked more like muscle to Barton; he had the size and weight. Well, we'll see, thought Barton. He hoped he was wrong.

Sooner than he would have preferred, Dr. Fox got around to him. "Mr. Barton," she began, "I'd like to ask your cooperation in a few more experiments. Brief ones, I assure you." Barton saw her seeing his face freeze, but she smiled and waved a hand as if to mitigate something. "You must understand," she said, "that our basic purpose is to gain some comprehension of the Demu mind, so as to know what our race faces in the future."

"How does *my* head help you with that? You have two for-real Demu, and three people who were bent pretty far in that direction. Plus the ship."

"The study of the ship is in good hands. It is not my province; I deal with living minds. In this case I have very few to deal with, and some are of little use.

122

"You know as well as I that Siewen is reduced to something of a pushbutton mechanism. His data and logic are intact, but in a sense there is no one home to operate them. He answers questions literal-mindedly, ignoring connotations.

"Heimbach is so disoriented as to be useless not only to me but to himself. Having no access to his earlier records, I cannot tell whether his condition is a result of his treatment at the hands of the Demu, or whether he has always been an incapable personality."

Well, she had those two pegged right, Barton thought. And himself?

"I have had no opportunity to study the woman Limila. I do not like to begrudge you your vacation tour, but I'm afraid I do. Because it eliminated my only opportunity to learn about the mind of the Tilari race. There is no point in trying to perform such a study in only a day or two, I'm sure you'll agree.

"Of the two Demu, we can get only the grossest of behavioral data from the adult. The younger one, on the other hand, is so eager to learn that she is rapidly becoming more like one of us than one of her own race, which we need so desperately to understand."

"Yeah, the kid has come a long way in a hurry," Barton said. "I noticed that."

"So that leaves you, Barton." Well, at long last, she had dropped that goddam phony "Mister." "You see why you're so important to us? You're the only one who went through the entire ordeal and came out fully human." (Want to bet?) "They didn't cut you up physically or break your spirit. You are the one who escaped and brought us back the whole package. And I think perhaps you may be the most important part of that package."

"I think you're reading too much into the fact that once in a while somebody does luck out. You already have my head on your computer tapes, along with the story and all my knee-jerk reflexes. What more can you get from me that you don't already have? In my honest opinion, I think you're looking for something that isn't there." He wished with all his heart that he could afford to *have* an honest opinion.

She looked at him, long and hard. "Damn you, Barton! I've analyzed the tapes from that simpleminded computer, and I don't believe the 'freeze trauma' theory any more than you do. I *wish* you would allow questioning under hypnotics. Oh, you needn't worry; I promised not to use them without your consent, and I won't. But you're keeping things back. Not on purpose, probably. But you have valuable data that you won't give me. You can't, because you won't look at it yourself!"

Entirely too close for comfort, lady. Oddly, as Arleta Fox became a greater and greater threat to him, his reluctant liking for her increased. Of course, it was not as though he could let his feelings make any difference to anything.

"I don't know about all that," he stalled. "You could be right; how would I know?" With an effort, he smiled at her. "All right; you must have something you want to try, to get at whatever you think I know that you don't. Or you wouldn't be bothering now, would you? So what's the pitch, Doc?"

"Nothing to worry about, Mr. Barton." *Oh*-oh! Back to the phony deal; watch out. "A few further nonverbal experiments. That is, not written tests; I may ask some questions, of course. May we have your cooperation, Mr. Barton?"

Well, what *could* he say? He nodded.

"Dr. Schermerhorn," she said, "would you show Mr. Barton to Lab B? I'll be along in a minute, as soon as I abstract the notes I'll need, from the file here."

Schermerhorn, doctor or muscle, whichever, politely showed Barton through a maze of corridors to a door marked "Laboratory B." He fumbled a key ring out of his pocket and found the key that fit. Out of the corner of his eye, Barton noticed Arleta Fox briskly rounding a hall corner to join them.

Schermerhorn opened the door, and gestured for Barton to precede him. Barton moved, still watching Dr. Fox over his shoulder. Then he looked at the room he was entering.

The ceiling was low and gray. The room was empty, barren, about ten feet square with no other visible openings. The opposite wall lighted; he saw the outline of a robed, hooded figure.

Eight years hit Barton like a maul. Adrenalin shock staggered him; he lurched, recovered. Almost in one motion he turned and grabbed the doorframe, kicked at the door Schermerhorn was closing. The door swung back.

Barton was on his way out. On his way out of the Demu research station and stopping for nothing.

Schermerhorn was too big, too strong to mess around with; Barton braced a foot against the edge of the doorframe and launched himself. His head caught Schermerhorn square in the face. Barton landed in the middle of the corridor, on all fours; Schermerhorn sprawled on his back against the opposite wall, blood spurting between the fingers held to his face. Instant nose job, thought Barton, getting up. Well, things were tough all over. And the ceiling back there was low and gray.

Schermerhorn tried to sit up. Barton kicked him under the ear; he fell back again. Behind him, Barton heard a noise. He looked around, and suddenly was back on Earth. It wasn't much of an improvement.

Incredibly, Arleta Fox was still coming toward him. *"Wait,* Barton!" He shook his head impatiently; there was no time to waste, talking with a dead woman. He moved toward her, flexing the hand on which he'd landed much too hard.

Finally she had the sense to back away. "No, Barton! It's all right! That was the test!" Yes, I know, Doctor, and now here come the results. Sorry. But you could be worse off. You could be in a gray cage.

She had stopped backing now, but was still talking. Never shut off a source of information while it might still be of use. There wasn't that much hurry.

"Barton, let me explain, *please!"* Oh hell; why not? Barton stopped, but not before he was within reach of her.

"What's to explain?" he said, dead-voiced. "You caught me out, didn't you? Just the way you wanted." The trouble was that he didn't *want* to kill her. She was small like Whnee—no, Eeshta—and female, as he had come to think of Eeshta. And she hadn't harmed him, herself; she had the potential, was all. Suddenly Barton knew that he would not, *could* not hurt this woman. But he mustn't let her know. The hostage principle had got him loose from the Demu; maybe it would keep him out of a cage here, too. If he worked it right . . .

She was still talking; he tried to tune in. ". . . what we needed to know, Barton. Don't you see?"

"Sorry; I missed that. Say again?"

"We knew you were obsessed with something that was blocking communication. We had to find out what it was.

125

It was obvious that you had flummoxed the other tests, but I don't know how and I don't care." She paused. "Well, I do, really, but that can wait. Anyway, we set up this room, as you had described it, and brought you here. That was *it*. You see?"

"Yeh, I see. You found out what I couldn't let you find out. That Barton isn't safe to be running around loose. But here's how it is. Barton is going to run around loose anyway. As long as he is alive, that is." The trouble now was that whatever she might say, he couldn't afford to trust it.

"So right here is where you quit talking and start listening."

He hadn't misjudged her tenacity. She was still trying to talk after he stuffed her mouth full of his handkerchief and tied her gauzy scarf around her face to hold it. She tried to claw the scarf away; he used her belt to tie her hands behind her back. She kicked at him with her high heels; he faced her away from him and gave her a solid knee square in her compact rump, hard enough that her eyes were running tears when he turned her around again.

"Now lookit, Dr. Fox," he said—gently, considering the panic that racked him—"you just behave yourself for a couple of hours until I get me loose out of here, and you can sleep in your own comfy bed tonight and forget all about it."

He looked over to Schermerhorn, who had managed, barely, to sit up. "You, there! If you want to kill this lady, all you have to do is to get on the phone or ring the alarms. If you want to see her alive some more, just rinse your nose and don't do any one more damn thing until she tells you so in person. You got that?" The man nodded, but Barton didn't trust him. There was an easy answer; the door to Laboratory B opened only from the outside. Schermerhorn, with a little help, went inside. Then Barton began steering Arleta Fox down the corridor, hoping he remembered his way out of the place.

He did even better, by luck. He came upon a side exit that opened directly onto the parking lot. In the jeep he fastened the woman's seatbelt and drove away, planning as he went. There had to be a chance or two left.

First he stopped by his and Limila's quarters, locking Dr. Fox in a closet for safekeeping. He packed a couple of suitcases and a grocery bag. He called Limila at the project site.

"Don't say anything, Limila; just listen," he said. "I'll be out there in less than half an hour. Watch for me; I'll be in the jeep. I'll go directly aboard the Demu ship, with all we'll need for a head start. Get loose from whatever is happening and join me *fast,* because then I have to take off in a hurry. You got it?"

"Yes, Barton. But why?"

"They caught me out, Limila. I have no choice. Are you with me?"

"Yes, Barton. Of course."

"Then watch for me, Limila. And be ready to move fast." He retrieved Arleta Fox, led her to the jeep and buckled her in. He set out for the Demu ship. It had served him once . . .

Approaching the ship area, Barton was on the lookout for a possible reception committee. There was none; no one was close enough to notice anything unusual as he hurried Dr. Fox aboard the ship. Relieved to find it unattended, he took her to the control room. It was the best place to keep her, he figured, until Limila arrived.

Almost at once, Limila joined them. He hugged her briefly, then turned to the doctor. "OK, lady, you can go now." He removed her gag, turned and knelt to fumble with her wrist bonds.

"I *won't* go!" She spun to face him, looking down at him for once.

"Now, look! You're free, you're loose, you're safe. Get your ass *out.*" He reached for her; she backed away. "I *won't.*"

The hell with it. Barton stood, grabbed her, retrieved the handkerchief and scarf, and replaced the gag. She scored one good bite on his thumb.

"All right, if you want the Grand Tour you can have it. Here, Limila; hold her, will you?"

It was time, past time, to seal the ship. He did so, returned to the control console and sat down. He inserted the "car keys" assembly.

It didn't work. It just plain didn't *work.*

Well, they had him. Nothing he could do, and no point in taking it out on Arleta Fox, though it had to be her doing. He would have to run on Earth, not in space, was all. But he'd give them one hell of a run, Barton would.

The viewscreen lit: Tarleton's face appeared. Barton

hadn't noticed that the ship's switch was on. It didn't matter. What mattered was that his talk with Limila had been bugged. That figured.

"You sonofabitch! You said you were giving me this way out if I needed it!"

"Barton, I was overruled. I gave you the keys to the car. Somebody went over my head and had your drive disabled some other way. I'm sorry; I wouldn't have okayed that."

"Yeh, sorry. I guess you wouldn't. OK, the Agency keeps the ship. I can't carry it off in my pocket."

"Or anything else. A lot of guards showed up here a minute ago, and I'm afraid they have you surrounded. So come on out, why don't you, and talk it over? We can figure out something."

Barton looked at the sleep-gun controls. No, they couldn't have been dumb enough to leave those operational. Of course it wouldn't hurt to try the thing if they went to rush him.

What else did he have on his side? Nothing but a woman he didn't want to hurt, and in fact couldn't. The bluff didn't seem worth pulling.

"How about a head start in the jeep, Tarleton? A lousy half-hour, for services rendered?"

"It's out of my hands, Barton. You'd better come out."

The hell you say. Barton said goodbye to himself. He pulled Limila to him and kissed her. Not long; there'd never be long enough. Then he let her go.

"Well, so long, Tarleton," he said. "You were a good guy; luck with the Demu." You have an easier touch than I do, maybe, he thought. Seeing a bare, gray room.

"What the hell do you think you're going to do?" said Tarleton.

"Barton!" Limila cried. "Do not go. You cannot!"

"No," said Barton, "I guess I can't, from here. No place. So I might as well listen to Dr. Fox now, for I don't intend ever to listen to her from inside a cage." He cut the viewscreen and activated the Demu shield. He stood, and removed the gag and bonds from Dr. Arleta Fox.

"So speak up, Doc."

Wearily, he waited for her to tell him what the problem was. His mind blurred.

". . . very ironic, really," she was saying. ". . . in a cage, yes, all those years. Naturally you would do anything—nearly anything—to avoid such a trap again.

"The terrible irony, Barton, has been that your mind is sound as a rock but you wouldn't believe it. Your one great phobia, of course, was being caged. That was the only aspect out of normal range, and understandably.

"So you cheated on the early tests"—she sighed—"and I suppose I'll never know how you did it. At that point you probably were *not* safe to run loose, as you put it. But at the same time you were too valuable to lock up."

Barton's head, he thought, was not only running loose; it was baying at the full moon. He wished to hell somebody would say something that made sense.

"It ever occur to anybody to level with me?"

"How could we? We didn't *know,* because you hid your real self so well." He had to admit she had a point there. Not that it mattered much, now.

"Besides, you wouldn't have listened. It had been too long since you had been able to trust anyone, since you had *had* anyone you could trust." And was there anyone now? Yes—Limila. But what could she do?

"Barton, you came home broken, like Humpty Dumpty. And gradually you have put yourself together again. No one else could have done it for you."

All the king's horses. That didn't make sense, either. Humpty Dumpty was an egg. If Barton was an egg, he was a very bad one.

"I don't know what you're talking about. Maybe you do, but I don't."

"You do, Barton. Think about it: In spite of your hatred, your quite natural hatred for the Demu, you took pity on Eeshta and then befriended her. You stood by Limila when you literally couldn't stand the sight of her —I'm sorry, Limila, but I *have* to make him see—and it was largely your doing that she is as she is now. You—"

Barton shook his head. She'd made it sound good for a minute, but he couldn't buy it. "I threw Skinner through the screen door. Closed."

"That was early on, and he was a nincompoop, besides. But yes, Barton; at that time, before I'd met you, you were one small hesitation away from custodial care. *My* hesitation."

"But—! Aside from guarding your mental privacy, you *were* cooperative. You worked with Tarleton and Kreugel; you worked hard. You trained pilots and in-

129

structors. You proposed a plan to bring other races together to help us against the Demu menace. You insisted against all odds upon going back to face that menace again, personally. And when you thought I was the worst possible threat to you—"

Well, she'd had to get to it sooner or later. Now, at last, she was making sense. "Yeh; I busted your muscle boy's face, and kidnapped you."

"He's not a muscle boy; he really is an intern. It was his own fault. I warned him to be careful. But either he didn't take you seriously, or you were simply too fast for him."

"What difference does it make?" Barton was tired, very tired. "I blew it, the whole bit. Let's get it over with. I'm not going back in any cage, is all. Not alive."

For a small woman, Dr. Fox heaved a very large exasperated sigh. "Barton, it is time you stopped being so singleminded. As I said . . . when you thought me the worst possible threat to you, *you still would not hurt me!* Is that the reaction of a man who isn't safe to run loose?"

"I kicked your ass pretty hard, there." Why were they talking so *reasonably?*

"Oh, that! I've fallen harder, at the skating rink!" Her gaze dropped. "Well, almost . . ." Abruptly, she turned to Limila. "Is there any way, do you think, to change the mind of this stubborn man of yours?"

"I do not know, Dr. Fox, but *I* believe you."

She had turned against him! Now they had him almost in a cage, and Limila was on *their* side.

There was nothing left. He had to get out. Where to go? No matter; there had to be a place. Smash Arleta Fox and go!

But she—she was small, and female. He didn't know . . . The walls, it seemed to him, were turning gray.

"Limila!" the woman said. "Help me. Quickly!"

One at each side, holding him, they kept Barton from falling as his knees began to buckle. He shook his head, tried to speak but could not. It was Dr. Fox who spoke.

"Barton, can't you believe that I mean you no harm?"

He heard her as from a great distance, but he felt her pressed as closely to him on one side as Limila was on the other. And now his legs supported him again. His arms came to life; he held both women, fiercely. He looked at the walls, and they were not gray. Not gray at all.

"Shit!" he said. "Barton, you always *were* the dumbest man in the world!"

Neither woman contradicted him.

Two days later, right on schedule, the First Expedition lifted for Tilara. Barton had had Limila give Tarleton the necessary coordinates over the viewscreen before they left the Demu ship, as soon as Arleta Fox had announced all-clear and sent the guards home.

Barton found himself regretting that Dr. Fox couldn't have come along with the fleet. It was a damned shame, he thought, that he'd wasted his opportunity to get better acquainted with that tough little bulldog mind of hers.

She was a winner, that one. And Barton always liked a winner.

The Learning of Eeshta

———◆———

Author's note: the astute reader will notice
that in this short story I have taken certain
liberties with the order of some events that occur
in "Cage a Man" and "The Proud Enemy."

—F.M.B.

The young person is surrounded by the animals. In this room on their planet Earth—a strange room, all plane surfaces and right angles—Eeshta is their captive. One of them has taken its robe and hood; under the odd discrete lighting sources, the smooth exoskeleton shines ivory tinged with red. Eeshta is one of the Demu and eggborn; the symmetry of its head is broken only by the eyes and their brow ridges, the nostril openings and serrated chewing-lips below, and the slightly flanged earholes.

The heads of the animals are marred by fleshy and fibrous growths. Although their general shape is acceptable—head and body, arms and legs—they do not have correct appearance. None but eggborn Demu have correct appearance without aid. When captured animals learn to speak as Demu and thus earn citizenship, they are given whatever aid is needed.

But now it is Demu who are captive—the young Eeshta, its egg-parent Hishtoo, and three not eggborn. Taken by an escaped animal named Barton, they are brought in Hishtoo's ship from the Demu planet Ashura to Earth. Although its arm was broken in the struggle of capture, Eeshta no longer fears Barton, for Barton encased the arm for healing and offered no further injury during the long journey.

Eeshta fears these others; it does not know what they want of it, except to learn to speak with them. Demu do not speak with animals or in the tongue of animals. Hishtoo has told it thus, and the young person respects the word of its egg-parent. After a time the animals cease their attempts.

One enters who is Demu but not eggborn. It is of the type that grows young inside itself; before its citizenship it bore on its chest the growths by which such persons nourish young.

To correct the appearance of such a one requires much aid. Knives and other instruments eliminate the growths on head and face, remove the teeth, notch lips, and shorten tongue to proper proportion. Chest and crotch are pared to smooth and sightly contours. Fingers and toes are rendered clawless, and if necessary, the number at each extremity is reduced to the proper four. And on the abdomen the single useless depression is replaced by a pattern simulating concave oviducts and their matching convexities that produce cells to fulfill the eggs. This is how deserving animals are honored for their intelligence. It has always been the way.

The one who enters is called Limila; on Ashura its appearance was made correct. It wears proper robe and hood but has added a cloth that covers all the face except the eyes. It did not do so on the ship, during the trip to Earth.

It approaches. "It is that you do not speak, Eeshta, and that you should."

"It is that you, Limila, not eggborn, speak with animals. I do not."

"It is that you are foolish. On this world you can now speak only with Hishtoo or with me, or the other two who are made Demu. Much is to be learned here, and you learn nothing."

"You may learn, and tell me in our own speech."

Limila nods. "That for the present we do it so. Also, I ask questions and you answer. Later we speak more of this."

"It is as you say, but that I have my robe and hood." The garb is returned; the questions begin. An animal speaks to Limila, who asks the question. When the young person answers, Limila speaks to the animal. Eeshta's fear is soon dead of boredom, as it waits while things are said that it does not understand. It finds itself trying to understand, and quickly changes its thought.

"It is," says Limila, "that we would know of your age."

"That I am nearly three fingers, of four, toward end of growth." Eeshta waits while Limila and the animal speak.

"It is that your duration may be counted in revolutions of your planet around its star."

"We do not count it so. And Ashura, where Barton escapes and takes our ship, is not my planet. The revolutions of my own planet, while we are on Ashura, are not known to me."

Finally the speaking ends. Eeshta is taken to its place and, with Hishtoo and the others, fed. While eating, it does not speak with any, nor wish to.

"She's a hard-shelled little devil, isn't she, Limila?" Annette Ling smiled across the table; then her delicate Oriental features moved in a slight frown. "In more ways than one. Not as bad as Hishtoo, though. That one wouldn't talk at all."

"He talks, Doctor Ling, when Barton asks through me or Siewen to learn of the ship, to build others. Hishtoo fears Barton, and with reason." She shook her head under the hood. "They are not he and she, of course; each is both. I have listened too much to Barton—and I suppose it is natural to assign gender in terms of size."

"Yes. You know, I'd like to meet this Barton of yours."

Within the concealment of hood and veil, Limila shook her head again. "Not mine, not now. He allows me to live with him, but cannot bring himself to . . . touch me."

For a moment, embarrassed, Annette did not speak. She brushed fingers through her short black hair. "Uh—why does Hishtoo fear him?"

"You have not heard? How he forced the ship from Hishtoo, to bring us here? He was without food, but had Eeshta captive. He threatened to begin eating her alive."

Doctor Ling gasped. "Would he have . . . ?"

"I do not know; I have not asked. But once aboard the ship, he broke both Hishtoo's arms so Hishtoo could do no mischief. And when Barton says to Hishtoo, 'crab salad,' Hishtoo answers any question I ask."

Annette Ling's laugh was shaky. "I'm not so sure I want to meet the man, after all."

"You must remember, he had been seven years—more than that—in a Demu cage. The ship was his only chance of escape. And he had no other way to restrain Hishtoo safely, short of killing him."

"Yes. Yes, I can understand that. And he rescued you and the other two?"

"We were there, at the ship. Although Barton had refused to learn Demu speech, Hishtoo offered him citizenship as an inducement to return Eeshta safely, and surrender. We were supposed to be . . . exhibits, to persuade him. Hishtoo did not understand Barton very well."

"I should say not." Annette paused. "Limila, do you feel that Eeshta will cooperate more fully, eventually? To counter the Demu threat, the raiding and kidnapping, we *must* know more about them. Eeshta is the only window we have any chance of opening; it would help a great deal if we could speak with her directly." She raised a hand against an unvoiced protest. "I don't mean to say—*your* help has been invaluable. But still . . ."

Behind the veil she saw maimed lips move in a kind of smile. "Yes, Doctor. As Eeshta would say, I am not eggborn. For more than six years, after what was done, I lived as Demu. But even yet, I know them only from outside." Her hands, together, clasped and unclasped. "And Eeshta? I do not know. The Demu never speak another's language. It may be that they cannot learn as we do. We can only continue to try."

"Yes, and hope for success." A knock sounded. "Come in." A boy entered with coffee and a snack plate. Annette moved papers to clear space on the table. "Thank you," she said. He smiled, set down the tray, and left the room.

"I'll pour, Limila. Cream? Sugar?"

Her cup prepared, Limila raised it. She held it before her veil a moment, then set it down. "Thank you, but I do not want any, after all. I must go now."

"Limila! We're going to be working together a long time, probably. Can't you—?"

"You have seen me." The voice was flat, wooden. "In the pictures, at least. Do you wonder that I hide myself?"

A small five-fingered hand shot out to grasp one that

138

now had only four. "Oh, damn all! I do tend to forget that anything is important, except my work. But I feel I know *you* only from outside, and—well, it was a long session; you should have some coffee and a bite to eat. I'll go out, if you wish. I'm *sorry*, Limila. Forgive me?"

Limila shrugged. "You have not harmed me; it was done before. And if you wish to see me, I can bear it if you can. When we are alone . . . " She removed the veil and pushed back the hood.

For long seconds, seeing what had been a woman's face, Annette Ling could not speak. "Yes," she said at last. "When we are alone. Thank you, Limila." She busied herself, leafing through her notes.

"Now I'd like you to look at the questions my team has prepared for us to ask Eeshta tomorrow. Do you think perhaps . . . ?"

As they talked, Limila sipped coffee and ate small bits of cheese and wafers. Without teeth it was a slow process.

The young person has eaten. It sits with its egg-parent Hishtoo and the two Demu not eggborn. They are of the type that does not grow its young inside but supplies cells to fulfill the eggs. Siewen, the frail one, supplies no more such cells. It is one of the first of its kind to be made Demu, and live; there was not knowledge that to provide correct appearance to its legs-juncture would render it useless for breeding. Like Limila, it speaks with animals, but only in response. Here among Demu it does not speak.

The other has taken the Demu name Shestin and does not speak with animals. It has been given citizenship later when more is known of its kind. Its appearance where its legs join is not fully correct. Protrusion has been minimized but not entirely eliminated; this one, it is hoped, retains ability to fulfill eggs. It shows no signs of wishing to do so. On the ship it did not speak to Barton. Barton called it Whosits. Those who bring food call it The Freak.

Hishtoo addresses its egg-child. "It is that you speak with animals?"

"I speak with Limila, who speaks with animals. I do as you."

"It is that I should not. But the animal Barton—"

"It is that first you do not speak with Limila in presence of animals. But when Barton makes the sound 'crab salad,' then you speak. I do not know that sound."

From Doktor Siewen comes a harsh cackling.

"It is," says Hishtoo, "that your mind is not waking when Barton first makes that sound. Then, if I do not give the ship to it, it eats you. On the ship it destroys use of my arms. And the animal Barton eats me now if I do not speak of the ship with Limila and Siewen. But I speak much of no truth."

"It is that if Barton finds you speak not truth, Hishtoo . . ."

"It is that we have no certain way of safety. That the worlds must know the Demu and become Demu. Barton eats me before I allow it to eat our race."

The young person pauses, thinking of what it knows. "It is that Barton harms me also when we meet, but not again. I do not know when it says to eat me, for, as you say, my mind is not waking. It is that the animal puts its hand to my head and makes a soft sound when I have pain and want no more."

"It is that you forget, Eeshta, that it is an animal and of no assured mind. You forget no animal is Demu. Barton has not our speech, nor correct appearance."

"You say much truth, Hishtoo. I think on your saying." The young person thinks of what it knows, and of what it does not know.

Limila waited. When Barton arrived, his dinner would not take long to prepare. He did not need her to cook for him; he could manage well enough on packaged meals. But he had brought what was left of her away from the Demu; she had no one else, and felt he deserved some payment for suffering her monstrous presence. So she did what she could, though she found it ever more difficult to talk with him.

A groundcar stopped outside; Barton's footsteps approached, and he entered. "Hi, Limila. You have a good day?" He sounded as though he were reciting a set speech.

"Well enough, I suppose. Are you hungry, Barton?"

He looked at her, then away again. When they were alone she did not wear the veil; it was no use. On the ship he had seen her too long without it.

"In a little while—any time you're ready. Right now I

140

need a beer." He made busy at the refrigerator, then sat near her.

"Hishtoo's lying, you know," he said. "At least half the time, maybe more. That big lobster is nobody's fool."

"You have charged him with lying?"

Impatiently, Barton shook his head. "Wrong approach. Let him think he's getting away with it. For now, at least. No, we just keep asking questions, sometimes the same ones from a different angle. He'll slip up; he already has. We'll transcribe the tapes and cross-check; feed it to the computers. Nobody can lie consistently over the long haul. The parts of his story that don't stay put, we can throw out. Where it hangs together, it's probably fact. And sooner or later we'll figure out how the Demu ship works."

"And the Demu mind, Barton?"

He looked at her, his expression unguarded for a moment, as though she still had a face. "That's the hard part, isn't it? What *you're* doing. We need force, sure—ships, and all—to stop the raids. But we need to know about them, too, and the little one's the key. How you coming with her, by now?"

"It is hard to be certain. She answers questions, but obliquely."

"Comes by it naturally, I expect; her egg-daddy's a liar by the clock. Too bad—I've gotten to like the kid, but she sure as hell comes from a rotten family."

Explanation was too difficult; she served dinner instead. Barton ate silently, saying only, "Hey, pretty good there," after the first bites. When he finished, he said, "You want to watch the Trivia or anything?"

"The Tri-V? No, Barton."

"Yeh; well, maybe I'll read awhile."

"Yes, Barton." But she needed to talk. "Barton?"

"Yeh? Something?" He seemed interested, so she plunged ahead.

"Barton, how did you know not to learn Demu language?"

"Huh? Oh—well, I didn't. I mean, I didn't know . . . what happened, if you did. It was just, they pushed me around so long, before they tried the talky-talk, that by then I was too stubborn to do *anything* I thought they wanted. There's a lot happened that I never told you . . ."

And a lot, she thought, that I can never tell anyone. "I wish I had been stubborn, Barton. But I was alone and did not want to be alone, and I did not guess that harm could come from learning."

She stood and went to him. Once more, she thought, and then not again. She took his hand. "Barton? I—"

He clasped her to him but turned his face away. She heard him curse, his voice thick. Then he said, more quietly, "I wish I could, Limila. I wish . . ." He released her. "Oh, hell! I'm going to bed."

She went to her own room. This is not life, she thought; I am not living. I need to work yet awhile for others, and then I can stop.

The thought comforted her more than any had in a long time.

The young person sits with Limila and the animal Ling. The fourth of the second four of questionings begins. Against its will, Eeshta understands more each time, of animal speech, but as Hishtoo has said to do, it pretends ignorance.

Also, it understands some meanings of Ling's face movements. The downward-together pull of the small dark growths above the eyes means the animal is dissatisfied. The young person has known this meaning earlier, for on the ship Barton often made the sign—but never the upcurving of incorrectly smooth mouth, meaning pleasure, that Ling makes. Eeshta has made the Demu sign of pleased feeling, mouth opened slightly to show the tongue uplifted, but Ling does not understand until Limila explains in animal words. Then, to Eeshta, Ling lifts its own tongue, so incorrectly long.

Eeshta is certain Ling comes to understand some Demu speech, also. It sometimes speaks before Limila repeats Eeshta's saying fully. On Ashura, perhaps Ling would soon be worthy of being given citizenship and correct appearance . . . though Eeshta is surprised to find that with familiarity the animal's deformities are less offensive and seem almost natural.

Now Ling speaks directly to Eeshta but in its own animal speech. "Eeshta, do you know what I say? You do know, don't you?"

"Limila, it is that Ling speaks. That you tell its saying in our tongue."

"It is that I hear you," says Ling, "that you hear me, also. That we forbind and enfeel." The last has no meaning; Ling is not yet worthy of correct appearance.

"It is that I am pleased that Ling attempts Demu speech, Limila. That it may continue to do so."

Ling turns to Limila. "I didn't get that last." Limila repeats Eeshta's words in Demu and then in animal tongue.

"I *know* you understand me," says Ling. "Why won't you answer? Limila? *Why?*"

The young person shakes its head; animal gestures demean less than animal words.

"The Demu see no view but their own, Annette. We can only keep trying."

"Yes. But not today, Limila; the hell with it." And to Eeshta: "It is that you go to your place, that another time we speak in both our tongues."

"Limila, it is that I go to my place."

As the young person leaves the room it hears Ling say, "Sometimes I think Barton had the right idea the first time."

The young person sits with Hishtoo. Across the room Siewen looks at nothing, while Shestin very softly speaks an old Demu chant it has learned. Outside, on guard so that all must stay in, is the animal that speaks much with upcurved mouth when it takes Eeshta to and from its place here. Eeshta thinks upon a matter.

"Hishtoo, when Barton crushes our armshells, it is that there is much pain."

"That the animal gives us pain, we remember."

"Is it that there is much pain in the giving of correct appearance?"

"Much pain and loss of body liquid. It is done over many days, or animals die of becoming Demu. When Barton and the others are taken, none on Ashura had experience. We lose many as we learn. Siewen is one of the first to live, and Limila. It is that each for a time is near to death."

"That I find it not good, Hishtoo, to give such pain."

"It is that the pain is not from us, Eeshta, but from being animal without correct appearance. That animals may become Demu, we do what is proper."

"Is it that the pain is soon gone?"

"As correct appearance heals, pain goes. And we learn a thing, Eeshta. On each day of correction we give the greatest pain first, so that often the mind becomes not awake and does not feel more of what is done."

"That I am pleased you give no pain without need."

A sound is heard. Siewen is crouched over, holding itself. Its shoulders shake and it makes harsh rasping sounds with its breath. Eeshta moves to bend and see under its hood. Its face below the eyes is wet.

"Siewen," says the young person, "is it that the food today is not good to you?"

The animal of the upcurved mouth closes the door of the room behind Eeshta and remains outside. The times of questioning now count nearly to two fours of fours. Ling sits behind the squarish thing that is always covered with papers. Limila sits to one side; it no longer hides its face, and has thrown back its hood. Its smoothed head is deeper and less wide than is quite correct, but the shell of it is inside and difficult to reshape. Attempts to make such changes cause dying, and so are now abandoned on Ashura.

The young person moves a seat closer to the others, and sits. "It is that you ask and I answer," it says. "That I would now ask."

Limila would speak, but Ling waves a hand and says, its mouth curving: "All right, Eeshta, we'll make a deal. Ask anything you want—*in English*—and we'll answer. What do you say?"

"That I do not use your speech, that I must not. Hishtoo—"

Ling waves the hand again. "Forget Hishtoo for a minute. We've been asking questions, playing by your rules. If you wish to ask in turn, you'll have to play by ours for a change."

Eeshta considers. Already it speaks with an animal, though in Demu tongue. And what it would ask, it needs to know. There is no need to inform Hishtoo . . .

"Then tell me what you really want to know from me. And why."

Ling nods. "We want to know about you, about your people. How they think, and why they do what they do."

"What we do? What is it that we do?"

Limila brings its hands near its face, its two fours of fingers pointing stiffly toward itself. *"This!"* It touches here and there on its head and body, and its extremities. "And this, and this, and this!"

"It is only that you are given correct appearance,

144

Limila." Startled, the young person uses its own speech but is not rebuked.

"But why?" Limila's voice is high and harsh with strain. "Do you know what it is to be cut and sewn, and to have no face?"

"I know you had pain, yes."

"Pain? I saw others die and envied their luck. The flesh was bad enough, and the teeth. But"—it indicates the jog at the base of its hand—"the disjointing of bones! And here!" It points to the nostril openings. "There was bone. A saw, and the chisels. After the first of it I could not see, for the blood. Pain? You do not know of pain, Eeshta. Why, how, can you possibly do such things?"

"But, so you could be Demu and not animal. And now that is a long time past. You healed, and are Demu and have no more pain."

"*No pain?*" Limila's breathing is harsh and rapid. "Eeshta—Eeshta, how would you like to have your arms cut off?"

At first frightened, after a moment the young person realizes there is no threat. "I would not; no one would. But why . . . ?"

"Suppose you met a race of super-Demu with no arms. They give you correct appearance by removing yours. How would you feel?"

"But without arms, how could they?"

"Damn your stupid little soul to Barton's hell, they'd *bite* them off!" In awkward haste, Limila pulls its robe from itself, crumples it, flings it against a wall. Unlike its conduct, its appearance is most correct for one not egg-born.

"Annette?" says Limila. "Would you show yourself completely?" Ling looks for a moment at Limila, then removes its own garb. The two stand together. Ling's appearance is not at all correct, but in it Eeshta can see a kind of symmetry.

"Look!" With one hand Limila touches Ling, and with the other, the same portion of itself. "This!" The mouth, the growth above it that is partly bone, the flaps at the sides of the head, and at top and back the fiber called hair.

"This!" The lumps on the chest, the changes at the extremities, the fiber-covered protrusions where legs begin. "This! This! *This!*"

It pauses, breathing heavily. "These things are all part

of her. They were part of me, too, until you—your people —took them from me. My face was myself. Now I have no self."

"But you are Demu, Limila."

"Am I? No. I am not eggborn; I cannot in breeding season lock to another bearing eggs and at the same time fulfilling that other's. I cannot go to Sisshain once to visit and perhaps a second time to become—or if not, no shame to the eggs."

"No shame to the eggs," Eeshta responded.

"I cannot even truly have correct appearance. I am not Demu, Eeshta. I am only something that was once a woman, who can no longer be a woman or even a person, from what the Demu have done to me. Because of that I am of no use, even to myself."

The young person is confused. "But the Demu mean no harm, only good. Not to take, but to give. It has always been our way, when we can, to help animals. I am sorry, Limila, that even though not eggborn, you can find no pride in being Demu."

"Pride? *Pride?*" Limila shakes its head. "Eeshta, you work very hard at not understanding me. Barton, I suppose, would call it a racial trait. Let me try again. Eeshta, would you prefer to live, or to die?"

"To live, of course, Limila. To live."

"Yes? Why?"

"Because—because alive I can do and learn. Dying ends all of it."

Limila still stands, feet apart. Its legs shake, but it does not seem to notice the shaking.

"Yes. You are right, Eeshta. Dying ends all of it. But for me it is all ended now. It ended under your knives, on Ashura. And I would rather die than live as I am."

"No, Limila—!"

"If I did not feel I were needed here for a time yet, I would die tonight."

"But how is that? Have you a sickness?"

No Demu mouth ever moves as Limila's serrated lips move now. "Not the kind you mean. My sickness is only that I would take a knife, and let out all my blood, so as to die."

The young person resists belief. "But that is—no one does so except those twice-come to Sisshain, who would become but do not become—no shame to the eggs."

"No shame . . . " Limila murmurs. "You are beginning

146

to understand. I cannot become, as you would, because I am not eggborn. And I cannot become in my own way, because of—because of having been given correct appearance. This is what you do to me and others. This is what must be stopped. This is why we need to know of you. Not to hurt you. But to stop your hurting us!"

The young person is troubled. "Can you not still become, Limila, in your own way?"

"My way? I have no face; I have no self. There is no one left who can become. I would have—Barton would have been my most needful person—and he cannot stand the sight of me. I cannot stand the sight of what is left, either. It is not Limila. I am inside, but no one can see me, and I can no longer see myself."

All that Eeshta knows collapses; nothing is left but to believe. "But then," it cries, "Hishtoo is *wrong*. We, the *Demu,* are wrong. For to give such hurt—it cannot be correct." It hardly notices that it speaks in the tongue of animals.

It goes to Limila and holds that tall person in its arms as though for breeding—although Eeshta is one of four fingers short of breeding age, and Limila not eggborn. And the feeling is not of eggs, or of fulfilling eggs.

"Limila, it is that I help you, that I learn in both our tongues. That I try to tell Hishtoo, though I think Hishtoo does not listen or understand. That when you go to our worlds, I go, also, and tell what you say, so that it is known.

"Whatever else, Limila, it is good that Barton brings me here."

Barton got home late; the Tri-V was off and the lights were dim. "Hi! Anybody home?"

"Yes." The voice came from the kitchen. "I am here, Barton."

She sat on one chair, leaning back with her feet on another. The drink she sipped was dark between the ice cubes; the bottle on the table was bourbon. She wore no robe or hood; for a moment he saw her as she once had been. The light was dim, and the slim body almost the same—but the moment passed, and again she was faceless.

"Had to work late." He rummaged in the refrigerator, found a beer, and opened it. "A breakthrough on the Demu space drive, if Hishtoo slipped as bad as we think

he did. So I ate in that crackerbox cafeteria, by the ship."
He sat, and swallowed beer from the bottle. "How'd it go
with you, today?"

"We broke through, also, Barton. The young Demu has
decided to cooperate." She sipped slowly at her glass.

"No kidding? You cracked the shell? That's great! Hey,
how did you get through to her?"

"Personal talk, Barton. Exchange of reminiscences,
among all of us there."

"Yeh? I'll bet you did most of it, Limila. Didn't you?"

"I was of some help; the matter is not important." But
the ring of her voice belied the words. "At any rate, it
has agreed to learn and exchange information, to reduce
the conflict that must be."

He wanted to go to her, but then she would expect
more than he could give. "Well, that's great. I'm glad the
kid's shaping up."

"Yes. We should make much better progress now."

"Good. Hey, you look tired. Rough day, really, wasn't
it?"

Her maimed lips lifted into a ragged curve. "It's all
right, Barton," she said.

"I'll live."

The Proud Enemy

To Clarion West—
and the
Expository Lump

Barton took the ship straight up.

A million kilometers out from Earth, with Luna in quadrature, he cut power and coasted Ship One into solar orbit. The rest of his command, Ships Two through Ten, were not far behind. The other three squadrons, following, showed on the screen as groups of dots.

Beside Barton the big, bearlike man chuckled. "Hurry up and wait, is it? That was quite a takeoff."

"I figured you'd want your command ship first at rendezvous, Tarleton. So I got us here."

"I wasn't complaining. I've ridden with you before—remember?"

Barton grinned. "Yeh, I know." He glanced at the screen. "They're coming up pretty good. You want to talk them into formation?"

Tarleton nodded—even the fleet commander had to wear two hats; his second one was communications. He activated the board and began coaching squadrons and individual ships into a dish-shaped formation, curving back from Ship One as center.

"Spread your group a little, Slowboat. Our drive wakes may be harmless below light speed, but let's don't get into bad habits. Right?"

"Right," said Slobodna, and Squadron Two dispersed slightly.

Tarleton smiled and turned back to his second-in-command. "Well, Barton, there they are. The first starships Earth ever built, and all ready to go. Do they look as good to you as they do to me?"

"From here? Better." Barton shivered, remembering how close it had been—whether he'd ride this ship or stay home, in a cage. And the years he'd been caged by the alien Demu . . . well, that was what the fleet was all about. "Do we move it now?" he said.

"It's all yours."

Barton punched coordinates into the fleet's linked computers, took a deep breath, and stabbed a finger at the activating button. As one, the forty ships accelerated.

"Next stop, Tilara. Anything more we need, before the all-ships briefing?" Tarleton shook his head. "Okay." To the woman sitting behind him, Barton said, "Limila, you want to get the others in here now?"

"All right, Barton."

"You'd better take ap Fenn or maybe Scalsa with you, to bring Hishtoo. Just in case that big lobster is still on his high horse."

"You think Hishtoo would harm me while you are on this ship? But, very well; I will ask Scalsa's aid." Briefly, before leaving, she touched Barton's cheek.

As the control-room door closed behind her, Tarleton said, "That's some woman you have there."

"Yeh. I noticed."

"What I meant is, that if she's any sample of the Tilaran race, we *need* them as allies."

"I told you that before."

"Relax, will you, Barton? We're in space now—the first time any of us have ever left the solar system under our own power. Or had the chance to meet other races . . . . "

"Except as Demu captives! Yeh, I know. Let it go, huh?"

Behind them the door opened; the crew of Ship One entered, along with the two Demu escorted by Limila. Vito Scalsa came last and closed the door. The group—three men, five women, and two Demu—stood as if uncertain what to do next.

Tarleton didn't say anything, so Barton did. "Okay, it's time for the bossman to talk to the troops. Let's the rest of us get to the sides, out of center stage." He stood and motioned the others to either side, bringing Limila and the two Demu to stand with him. "All yours, Tarleton."

Tarleton pushed buttons. On the large screen at the

front of the room appeared a segmented, composite picture; each of the forty ships' control rooms was shown in miniature. The circuit was multipled; here and there Barton saw people waving hellos to others they recognized on their own screens.

Tarleton cut it short. "All right, we can chatter later; it's toll-free." The picture became still. "I'm Tarleton, commanding this fleet. I came into the job by way of being presidential assistant to the United States Space Agency and then in charge of getting the ships built. So it's new to me, and I expect I'm going to need all the cooperation I can get." The smiling, hand-waving miniatures on the screen looked fully cooperative to Barton; he nodded in satisfaction as Tarleton turned to him.

"Now I want you to meet Barton, second-in-command. You've heard of him—his escape from the Demu in their ship that he brought back to us, along with three other prisoners and the two Demu here." He motioned to the smaller man. "Okay, you take it."

With deliberate confidence, Barton moved front and center. "I'm Barton. In a way, it's my fault you're here. Some of you I don't know, but we'll be getting better acquainted, over this gadget.

"Most of you have the background. But this was a hurry-up job—there were some last-minute people brought in. So I'll skim through it a little." He paused, thinking of where to start, how to keep it short. "We're riding a souped-up version of the Demu space drive—the Labs improved a lot on the one I swiped. Besides their own weapons—the Shield and the sleep-gun—we have the only thing we could find that will punch through the Shield. High-powered lasers. They may have more stuff; we don't know.

"Maybe you noticed the empty space at the front of your ships. That's on purpose. Before we tackle the Demu, we're going to visit some other folks; we need all the help we can get. And if they have any weapons we can use, we'll have the room to mount them."

Making speeches, Barton reflected, wasn't his specialty. What next? Oh, yes—exhibit the two Demu. He motioned for them to join him.

"These are Demu. The big one in the robe and hood —that's their standard-issue clothing—is Hishtoo. He was in charge of the raid that grabbed me, and others, off Earth. And he ran the research station where I . . . spent nearly eight years in a cage." He could say it now, but still not easily . . . .

"The little one is Eeshta, Hishtoo's egg-child. I'll explain that part later." Eeshta wore a short smock, and a cap like that of a baseball player.

"They're exoskeletal," he said. "Invertebrate. Take a look." He made a sign for the two to disrobe. Eeshta complied readily but Hishtoo refused. That figured. Barton saw no reason to force the issue; one was enough. So Eeshta's chitinous form was displayed for the fleet's enlightenment.

Some of the viewers appeared shocked by the serrated lips, the lack of nose or ears, the smooth featureless crotch. With a vague feeling that Eeshta might be embarrassed, Barton gently patted the hairless skull.

"Don't think of the Demu as monsters," he said. "They evolved in their own way, that's all. Those lips are rockhard; they chew with them. Open your mouth, please, Eeshta . . . see? No teeth—and notice the short tongue." Eeshta lifted it. "That's how they smile." The smile was turned to Barton and he responded, human-style.

"They're short one finger and toe all around, by our standards. That's all right—the Tilari, the first race we're going to meet, normally have six of each.

"I generally think of Eeshta as 'she,' but each Demu is both male and female. I don't know whether you can make out, over the screen, this pattern of little dots up the middle of the abdomen—but that's why you don't see anything where you expected to. They lay eggs, tiny ones that mature in breeding tanks. That's all I know about that side of it."

Shrugging tension out of his shoulders, he took a deep breath. "None of these differences make them monsters, or even enemies. They're our enemies for one reason only —because they're firmly convinced, as a race, that the Demu are the only true *people*—that all the rest of us are merely animals.

"So they raid and take captives—and when an 'animal' learns their language, they do their best to make it look like a Demu. With knives, they do that. Most of you have seen pictures of the results, I think.

"And *that*," said Barton, "is what we plan to bring to a screeching halt!" Return-volume on the screen was turned low, but the sound of cheering was clear enough. Barton waited for quiet.

154

"They can be taught better," he said. "They can learn. Eeshta, for instance, has already come around to our way of thinking, on that point. Egg-daddy there is another story—to Hishtoo we're still animals, and uppity types at that.

"The Demu aren't going to change their minds easily. Before we can get them to listen to us—well, we're probably going to have to whip their hard-shelled butts." He turned to Tarleton, but the big man waved for him to continue.

"We can't do it alone," Barton said. "They're too many for us. That's why we're going after some help first." He beckoned Limila into the field of view. "This woman is of the Tilari, the first race we seek as allies. And if she's at all typical, they'll be damned good ones.

"The Demu worked her over—as I said, you've seen the pictures. One fine plastic surgeon is the reason you wouldn't recognize her from them."

Limila smiled. The restored curve of her lips parted to reveal teeth fashioned in a dental laboratory. No one would know by looking, thought Barton, that her nose owed its shape to a cartilage graft—or that the ears were soft-plastic prostheses.

She wore her Tilari-fashioned wig with its high Elizabeth-I hairline showing smooth scalp forward of her ears. The long black hair was swept up and displayed how Tilari are hirsute solidly to the base of the neck, behind.

Barton didn't feel like mentioning the breasts the Demu had taken from her, nor that the Earth-style plastic substitutes under her dress sat more than ten centimeters higher, on her rib cage, than the Tilaran norm.

"I am glad of being here," she said. "Tilara will give you welcome, as Earth gave to me."

"Limila's people," said Barton, "have suffered Demu raids for a very long time. Because of the sleep-gun there could be no detection or defense. But several hundred years ago, a Demu scout ship crashed. The crew was killed, and the Tilari had a quick chance to get a little information. Not much—the Demu came in and got the ship—and most of the study group, too.

"But the survivors had some good pictures. Limila has seen copies, and she confirms that the Demu ship we took is almost identical to the crashed scout." Barton's smile was grim. "We took pains to make our ships look a little

155

different . . . so that the Tilari don't try to blow us out of their sky before we have a chance to get acquainted."

He turned to Tarleton. "Anything else, for this go-round?"

"Just the slide show; I'll take that."

"Jeez—and I was trying *not* to be long-winded!"

"You did fine." With relief, Barton moved aside, hugging Limila with one arm and briefly squeezing Eeshta's shoulder. Hishtoo stood woodenly; without ceremony, Barton grabbed a handful of robe and jerked the Demu off-stage.

Tarleton pushed buttons. On the screen appeared a stellar map—a spiral arm joining the edge of the galaxy's main body. He moved forward, until he could reach the screen with a pointer.

"Here's Earth," he began. "A long way out, you notice. Now our first stop is *here*—about a hundred and sixty light-years down the Arm, and close to the middle of it, laterally. We can't see the Tilari stars from Earth—too much other stuff in the way. Other people we want to see are roughly *here*, and *here*.

"*Here* is the Demu research station, where Barton and Limila were. Close to three hundred light-years, and toward the outside edge of the Arm. The major Demu planets are about *here*—down a bit more, and back toward the middle again. All of this is transposed from the Demu charts—it should be fairly accurate. We had a little trouble finding some of the reference points, but nothing to worry about."

"No worry," said Barton. "When we ring the doorbell, they'll answer."

With a brief grin, Tarleton stepped back from the screen and laid the pointer down. "Keep in mind," he said, "that while to us these distances are vast, they cover only a segment of our spiral Arm. Compared to the galaxy itself, they are insignificant. I think we need that perspective.

"One more thing. Beyond the Demu suns, toward the galaxy proper, lies a volume of space entirely devoid of habitable planets. The charts end there. I don't know anything more about it, except that we won't have to worry about any neighbors on the *other* side of the Demu.

"I think that's all for now. Maintain acceleration at half-max. Go ahead with ship and squadron training programs, and if you have any questions, *ask*." He cut the screen circuits.

"You did okay yourself," said Barton. "But are you sure they have translators on the Russian ships, and the Chinese—?"

"And the French, and German, and Japanese and Central African. Hell yes, Barton."

Impatient with himself, Barton shook his head. "It's just—all this got put together in such a fucking *hurry*. A lot of it, I wasn't in on; I keep worrying maybe we forgot something. Okay—that's your department and you're good at it; I'll try to quit jogging your elbow.

"So now we have a minute," he said, "let's go over it again—how we handle this command routine."

The discussion was short . . . .

The way it worked in practice was that Barton ran the fleet. Tarleton rarely gave orders; when he did, it was Barton who relayed them. With the three "hats" he wore— ship commander, senior squadron commander, and the fleet's El Segundo—it all seemed reasonable enough.

Especially to Barton.

The first time he took the bit in his teeth was when he found a list, taped alongside the comm-board, of the names of the forty ships and their commanders. He took it to Tarleton.

"Look—we can't use this thing. If we're ever in a hurry we won't have time to look up names—and damned if I'm going to try to memorize the lot. Half of them I can't pronounce anyway."

"You have a better idea?" Tarleton's voice was mild. When the fleet was nearing completion he had been tense, harried; once in space, he had again become the easygoing, bearlike man that Barton had first known.

"The ships are numbered—what more do we need? And the commanders know who they are; we don't have to tell them. When I call a ship or a squadron I'm talking to the guy in charge, no matter who answers the phone. Okay?"

"That's fine with me. But when you announce the procedure, could you put it a little more tactfully? Some of the national contingents—particularly the smaller ones —are sort of proud of their ships' names."

Barton thought it over and nodded. All ten ships of his squadron were U.S.-built—and seven of "Slowboat's" command, which also included three from West Germany. Tamirov, the Russian, had seven of his own, two Central African and one French. Estelle Cummings commanded her three British ships, two each from Japan, China, and Australia, plus the second French vessel. The French hadn't wanted their forces split, but neither had anyone else—the decision had been made by drawing lots. Certainly, Barton realized, national prides could be touchy.

When he went on the screen he stated, truly, that his procedures were designed for fast tactical operation. "But so that we all get used to it," he said, "let's stick to just the numbers for all our official communications." As far as he could tell, no one objected to the simplification.

As the ship-days passed, Barton handed on further information when he happened to think of it. It was not that he took his responsibilities casually, but merely that he had had no time, previously, to organize what he knew.

Tarleton seldom used the viewscreen circuits except in his special capacity of expert on the ship's weaponry. It was he who explained the alarms that integrated incident energy, time and distance to warn if a vessel's Shield were seriously threatened by a Demu sleep-gun. He demonstrated the adjustments for obtaining optimum rise curves in pulsing the mammoth lasers that occupied each ship's central axis. And especially, he was a stickler in his insistence that every Shield be kept in perfect balance at all times.

Barton was glad to be spared these chores. For one thing, he wanted more time with Limila than he could usually manage.

It was not merely that they were lovers, though they were—and had been, since the restoring of Limila's face. But also they spent much time in talk—exchanging the questions and answers for which there had been no opportunity on Earth.

And Barton was learning the Tilaran language. Others were, too, of course—but he wanted to know it in depth, with all the nuances he could absorb. It was a musical tongue, rich in intonations that conveyed the subtleties. Barton made progress, but slowly.

Back on Earth, when Tarleton showed him the Space Agency's assignments of ship's quarters, Barton had reacted violently. "Hishtoo and Eeshta," Tarleton said, "will be in Six, which locks from the outside. Eeshta doesn't need locking up, of course, but we don't want

Hishtoo getting into any mischief." Barton nodded. "Cabin One, directly behind the control room, is yours and mine. Limila can room with Myra Hake, my assistant comm-tech, and two of the other women can—"

"What in hell do you think you're *talking* about?" Barton demanded. "What kind of silly-ass game *is* this? Limila rooms with me, and you know it!"

Tarleton laughed. He hadn't laughed for a long time, probably—now it rolled out of him, loud growling belly laughter, until he sat wheezing. "All right, Barton," he said, finally, "I'm sorry—but I couldn't resist that." He waved a hand to fend off Barton's indignation. "This, I should have said, is the Agency's *official* assignment of quarters."

Barton had to grin. "You're a sadistic bastard, you know that?"

"Sure I am." Tarleton wiped his eyes. "But look— why do you think the ships *have* double compartments, when a pair of dormitories would have been cheaper? Because we do have mixed crews, and I don't have any silly-ass ideas—as you put it—that they're all monks and nuns. So I said to myself, why not make things comfort-able and congenial, for whoever wants them that way?" He looked squarely at Barton. "All right?"

Barton nodded, and left. As he had intended all along, he moved his and Limila's gear into Compartment Two. At first, the living arrangements of the rest of the crew were monastic, but soon Tarleton was sharing Number One with Myra Hake, a tall, sandy-haired woman of con-siderable energy and competence. A few days later, Bar-ton noticed that Myra had been replaced by one of his copilots, a short, sturdy brunette named Alene Grover.

Other cabin exchanges occurred; Barton didn't keep track—it was none of his business. Eventually it struck him that with five men and five women sharing five com-partments, the Agency had *had* to be kidding. Or else Tarleton had been. Barton decided not to ask which . . . .

He did ask, one day, whether the other crews were evenly divided by gender.

"No," said Tarleton. "For our own ships, I tried to swing that, but somebody got into the aptitude-rating files and went over my head with some last-minute reassign-ments. So we have a few six-four combinations, both ways."

Barton frowned. "Six-four? Oh, yeh—I forgot. We're

159

the only ship running full; the others only carry ten each."
He laughed. "Well, it gives them room for a little incompatibility."

"That's true. Anyway—for the rest, the British have one seven-to-three imbalance; I don't know why. The French and Germans are balanced but I don't have information about the Russians—their rosters list only last names and initials. And I can't make heads or tails of the African and Chinese names."

"Ignorant Yankee!" Barton grinned as he said it. "Me, too. But—how do you figure a seven-to-three setup is going to work out?"

"Flexibly, I hope. I gave one order on the subject—verbally—to the effect that individual morale is top priority. Because we may be out here a long time."

"Yeh. Well, Tarleton, I hope it works. We have enough to worry about, without personal problems."

"Yeah. Just keep your fingers crossed."

The pressure of training kept most personnel too busy to worry overmuch about their libidos. The crash program on Earth had been limited to the bare bones of necessary knowledge; these now needed fleshing out in practice. Piloting and navigation, communications, weaponry and ship maintenance—there was always plenty of work. And only in space were airlock-and-suit drills meaningful. The captured Demu ship had had no suits or airlock, but it was assumed that their raiding and fighting ships would be so equipped.

The logistics of shipboard life could not be neglected—for instance, somebody had to cook. Ship One was lucky—or perhaps, Barton thought, Tarleton had stacked the deck—three competent cooks were aboard. Terike ap Fenn, the big weaponsman, was the best of the lot, though Limila ran him a close second. Barton, who could boil water without burning it if he read the directions carefully, was properly grateful.

He was not merely grateful for Limila's other achievements; he was thoroughly impressed. He had expected her to pull her weight on the comm-board, and perhaps do standby duty at Weapons. She had become not merely adequate but expert at both specialties and was well on her way to becoming a middling-fair pilot. And Barton had already known she could cook . . . .

It struck him that if she were representative of the Tilari, the hoped-for alliance might wind up with Earth

160

playing second fiddle. The idea didn't bother him much—
he didn't care who led the parade, so long as *someone* did
a good job of it. But it was a damned good thing, Barton
thought, that there were no politicians along on this junket!

They were five weeks out, about a third of the way to
Tilara, when the first rabbit came out of the hat. Myra
Hake, now sharing Cabin Number Four with one of the
pilots, had a problem. Tarleton was catching some overdue sleep, so she posed it to Barton and Limila, who had
the duty in Control.

"I've missed my damned period, is what!" she said.
"And with ten months to go on a one-year contraceptive
implant, that should be impossible."

Barton had no answers, so he kept silent. Limila sat
quietly for a moment, looking thoughtful, then said, "I
have an idea. Can you spare me here, Barton, for the rest
of this watch?" He nodded. "Myra, come to our compartment, please. I must ask questions, that I may seek a
valid solution."

Barton wanted to ask a couple of questions himself,
but this wasn't the time for it; he had his own routine to
follow. But after he had drilled Vito Scalsa in ship maneuvers and Terike ap Fenn in weapons control, his watch
was done. He joined Limila in Compartment Two.

"So what's with Myra? Did you find out?"

"I can't yet be sure, Barton. But I think that in your
women this cycle is related to the lunar tide of Earth. Not
so rigid as clockwork, but somewhat akin. Here, our artificial gravity is constant—with the clock absent, the response may fail. Or so I think it."

"If you're right, what can be done about it?"

"I have done it, Barton. There must be time, before we
see if the problem is solved. I must ask if others are in like
case.

"But, with help from an expert computer person—a
Miss Chindra of Ship Thirty-four—I have set our gravity
fields to pretend the variations from your sun and moon.
Not entirely accurate—I chose the phases as they have
progressed since our departure, the best that Chindra and
I could remember. It will have to do; we will see if this
corrects."

Suddenly, Barton realized he might have a problem of
his own. Well, partly his own . . . . He wondered how to

161

ask, because no matter what he said at this late date, he was going to sound pretty stupid.

"Look, Limila—maybe I was locked up too long, away from everything—because it only struck me, just now. But I mean—*you* never have, since we . . . I mean, are you pregnant? Or did the Demu . . . ? You can't be *past* it . . . are you?"

She shook her head; he was certain she repressed a chuckle. "No, Barton, to all questions. The answer is more simple. That cycle is not of Tilaran women. With us, ovulation is voluntary act; only thus can placenta form. On Tilara are no accidental conceptions."

"But—the woman in the cage!" Long since, he had told her of the Tilaran woman, scarred in mind and body by the Demu—how, never guessing that their species might be interfertile, he had succumbed to both their urges and unwittingly brought her to agonizing death in futile, abortive childbirth. The telling—of his desperate, unskilled efforts to help, while the Demu stayed hid behind their blind, gray walls and let the woman die—it had not absolved his inadvertent guilt, but the sharing helped him to bear it. Now Limila touched his face.

"But they took away her control of her mind," she said, "so of course she would ovulate, of instinct. Barton! It is not a thing you could have known."

"Yeh, I know," he said. "But I wish to hell I *could* have."

"Of course you do . . ." And in the ancient, timeless way, she soothed him.

Later, Barton looked in on the control room. He found Tarleton talking on a four-way hookup, to the other squadron commanders. "Sit in, will you, Barton? We're having an argument about how the drive works."

"Sure—hi, everybody. But what's the problem? Slowboat knows it backwards and forwards, and his doctorate in physics is a lot newer and shinier than my near miss at that brass ring."

"He explained it, all right," said Tarleton. "The trouble is, the rest of us don't speak Higher Math." On the screen, Slobodna grinned. "And the one time I heard you talking about it in plain language, the parts I understood seemed to make sense."

Barton shrugged. "I feel a little like Newton trying to tell Einstein, but okay." He sat; against regulations, he set his coffee cup on the ledge below the comm-board. "Here's how I got it from one of the Bell Labs people when he was drunk enough to talk English. . . .

"The main drive field gets positive traction, on some aspect of space-time that we can't measure or even detect in any other way. The only way we know it's there is that the thing works."

A voice came from the screen. "Tamirov here. A question: we are above light speed. Where is relativity, time dilation, mass increase?"

"Well, that's the other part of the drive. Ordinarily, when something approaches light speed, what happens is—well, you know about time being at right angles to space?"

"Mathematically, yes," said Estelle Cummings. "But I've never been able to visualize it."

"Join the club," said Barton. "But now cut your idea of space to one dimension—your direction of motion—and think of time as perpendicular to *that*. Okay?" Cummings' long, heavy blonde hair rippled with her nod.

"All right. Your time is always at right angles to *your* space—and everyone else's is to theirs, if you follow me. But at high speeds, Einstein says, your space vector begins swinging off at an angle, toward everybody else's time vector. And vice versa—your time gets mixed into their *space*. You see?"

"I see where you're heading," said Slobodna. "But you're not there yet."

"Okay," Barton said, "you're still going in the same direction in space, of course, but it's *as if* you were shooting at an angle and wasting most of your thrust off to one side. And at light speed itself, ordinarily it'd be like pushing altogether sideways, with no forward thrust at all. Because your space-and-time vectors would have swung all out of kilter with the velocity.

"So the second part of the drive holds those vectors in line where they belong; that's all. It takes power, sure—but the load is linear with speed; we can handle it. And so we don't get any mass increase. The only effect we notice, above light speed, is that our drive wakes—they still propagate at "c"—become deadly as hell, at close range.

"Did I get it about right, Slowboat?"

"I have to admit it sounds a little funny, Barton, but it

fits the math." Cummings and Tamirov nodded agreement; Barton hoped they weren't merely being polite.

"If anyone else is as hungry as I am," said Tarleton, "I move we adjourn." No one objected, so he waved a hand in signoff and cut the circuits. "Ready for lunch, Barton?"

"For me it's dinner, but I'm with you. I'll just check to see if maybe Limila's hungry, too, and join you in a few minutes."

He got sidetracked. Outside the control room stood Eeshta. From appearances, the small Demu had been waiting a long time and was prepared to wait even longer.

"Eeshta! What are you doing here?"

"Waiting. Barton, we must talk."

"Sure, sure—I haven't seen enough of you lately, anyway. Just a minute; let's see . . ." Behind Compartment Number Three was a small lounge, intended to keep card games and bull sessions from getting underfoot in the galley. Like many another good intention, this one hadn't worked—coffee went with cards, and a sticky table was small price for it. So, as usual, the lounge was vacant. They entered and sat.

"Okay, Eeshta. What's it all about?"

"Barton, I worry for my egg-parent. And if not for him, then for you."

"Hishtoo getting cabin fever? Isn't someone bringing him out to walk around awhile every day?" Barton thought of the years he had been caged at Hishtoo's research station. No daily walks for Barton—and food that oozed up through the floor. Hishtoo should have it so good. . . .

"He comes out, yes. But his mind, no. I fear; he says strangely to me—not real, sometimes, I think. But if real —*if* real—I fear even more. For you, Barton, and for Earth."

"Hishtoo's laying on threats, or something?" Barton considered the idea. "Maybe you'd better tell me about it."

"Threats? Closely to that, yes. You know what he said, on first hearing of this fleet."

Barton laughed, not long or with humor. "Yeh. That we animals had best not disturb the homes of the Demu. But hell, Eeshta—you know we're not on any war of extermination. We're simply out to convince your people that

164

we are people, too, so lay off the zoo bit and the fancy surgery."

"I know, Barton, and am of agreement. It was not right to cage you, to cut and change Limila and Siewen and the Freak. So many others, too—it is good, I think, that you did not see."

"I saw a couple—no, skip that. But what else about Hishtoo?"

"If he says what is real, no an imagining of his own wishes, then I fear—and you should fear."

"Just what does he say?" Questioning the young Demu about its parent, Barton felt like some kind of Gestapo agent—but what choice did he have?

"He says of Demu history, long long past. How from a far place we came—whether from deep in this galaxy or even from another, is not clear. But Demu came where we are, and wiped away any who would not have us there."

"You mean, if the natives weren't friendly, they got clobbered? Eeshta, we're not exactly primitives, to be overawed by a little technology."

"Not like that, Barton—a *terrible* war! Not in small space, a few planets only. It was from outside our place that the Demu were attacked. That outside was wiped away; it does not exist."

Yes, he thought! Down the Arm from Demu country, the space with no habitable planets. God Almighty! It could be! And if it were, what the hell was he heading the fleet into? What might he be doing to Earth?

But wait a minute—was this interpretation for real, or a fantasy of Hishtoo's? "Eeshta, is this the first you've heard of that war? And if so, how come?"

"I have been—am—too young to be told fully of Demu glory. So Hishtoo says. It would be at an older time. But now he tells me, so you will know." Mentally, Barton shrugged off his Gestapo uniform; without it, he felt a lot better.

"There's more to it, Eeshta, isn't there?"

"So much more; your speech does not hold it all. But I will try." She looked up and to one side; she began to sway rhythmically. Her voice became a chant . . . .

> *"The Demu come from far—*
> *The Demu come, and live—*
> *The eggs grow, the worlds know the Demu.*

165

> *Others know the Demu—*
> *The animals who had this place,*
> *Who now make space for Demu."*

Her voice was thick; Barton had never heard it so. "And what happened, Eeshta?" In a hushed tone, he asked it.

> *"The ships that come—they say,*
> *Proud Demu, be you gone—*
> *In our space is no place for Demu.*
> *Others came before you—*
> *Now none remain to call us foe,*
> *And so shall go the Demu!"*

Barton muttered to himself, "I'll bet *that* went over like a lead kite!" Eeshta stiffened; the swaying became more rapid, and her voice raised in pitch:

> *"The others went, the Demu stay—*
> *The Great Race dead, or gone away—*
> *Its heritage is Demu.*
> *Never go the Demu!"*

Eeshta's eyes closed tightly.

> *"The war will be, the Demu know,*
> *And worlds will go, for animals*
> *May not command the Demu.*
> *The Demu rise—the eggs must grow,*
> *The worlds must know the Demu.*
> *Though worlds are gone, the Demu stay—*
> *Ever grow the Demu—*
> *Ever . . . grow the . . ."*

". . . Demu." Barton whispered it. Eeshta shuddered and crumpled forward, hands covering her face. Barton moved quickly to put his arms around the small creature. "Are you all right?"

After a moment, a nod. "Yes, Barton. But it is a strong thing that Hishtoo tells. Real, or not real."

"How real do you think it is?"

"To him, I think, all. And to me, almost, in the telling of it. The true danger I do not know. But it is for you to be very careful, Barton, because I do *not* know."

"Yeh. Thanks—I'll keep it in mind." What to do with her, now? She shouldn't go back to her quarters just yet, and maybe catch another load from Hishtoo; she wasn't up to it. "Hey," he said, "how'd you like to take a tour at the comm-board? Myra Hake's on watch—she says you're coming along really well. Want to sit in with her for a while?"

"Yes, Barton. A change of thought is good."

"Okay, fine." Then a phrase from Eeshta's chant caught his attention. "Wait a minute—what was it?—that part about the Great Race. Do you know what that means?"

"No, Barton." Shaking of head. "When it was said, I asked, but Hishtoo would say no more. He was startled, I think, by what he spoke. For to him there could be no Great Race—no people, even—other than the Demu. There is a children's rhyme, but—no, I do not remember."

He had to leave it at that.

Entering the control room, he turned Eeshta over to Myra Hake. "See you later," he said impartially to both, and left for his own quarters. He was thinking he'd damned well better take some lessons from Eeshta— Demu language lessons.

He found Limila napping but not difficult to wake. She was hungry, too.

Tarleton's meal had also been delayed; the three ate together. The big man looked gloomy, so Barton didn't mention his own new bag of troubles. Instead, guessing that he was due to get another one unloaded on him, he ate silently—preferring to enjoy the meal and ease digestion. Hishtoo's thing could wait—whatever it was, it wouldn't erupt until they approached Demu territory.

What did bother him was that for a time, listening to Eeshta's chant, he had caught himself wishing he were on *their* side.

Could that be the real weapon?

Finally, over coffee, Tarleton told them what was on his mind. "It's ap Fenn—he has it up for Myra again and won't take no for an answer. And she's quite happy with your pilot—what's his name?"

"Cheng," said Barton. "Cheng Ai. But who's ap Fenn with now? And why can't he be satisfied with her for a while?" He considered what he knew of Terike ap Fenn— a large, lowering bruiser who was the ship's best weaponsman as well as its best cook. Why couldn't competent people carry their competence over into their personal lives? Wryly, he conceded that the question might sometimes apply to himself.

"The past couple of weeks," Tarleton said, "he's been with that little matchstick blonde—Helaise Renzel. One thing he doesn't like is that with both of them in Weapons, they're on different watch schedules. But I nosed around a little, and found that he's the one who's initiated *all* the recent cabin changes. If ap Fenn isn't a problem, he's certainly working on it."

"You mean his grass is always greener on the other side?"

"Something like that—and he's making waves. Barton, can you do something about it before we have ourselves some real trouble?"

Barton felt his stubborn streak rise. "What's wrong with you doing it? You're the admiral, with the scrambled eggs on your hat." Looking sheepish, Tarleton spluttered.

Limila put her hand on Barton's arm. "No, Barton. This is for you to do." He looked at her. "Tarleton is a fine man," she said, "but he might not in your place have succeeded in bringing the Demu ship and all of us to Earth." She turned now to Tarleton. "You must understand, I mean no offense. But you are one who looks long at all parts of a question. And sometimes only one side allows survival. Barton of all people understands this, in instinct. He—"

"—Sometimes does it the hard way," Barton finished. "All right; I'll talk to ap Fenn." He looked at Tarleton, but the other man stared silently down at his coffee. "I can't guarantee he'll wind up fit for duty. Do we have any problem about that?" Without looking up, Tarleton shook his head.

By forethought, Barton gave his dinner time to settle before looking in on ap Fenn. He found the man at home in Compartment Three, on pouting terms with his roommate. Barton felt that Tarleton's term "matchstick blonde" was unfair; Helaise Renzel was slim, but delicately curved and—to Barton—attractive.

Nonetheless his request for her to leave was brusque and only marginally courteous. Barton wasn't looking forward to the encounter; he wanted the side issues out of the way. But his move allowed ap Fenn to take the offensive.

The man had remained seated. "What the hell are you butting in here for, Barton? I know you're the big cheese, but these are *my* quarters."

"Yours?" Barton moved a chair slightly, and sat.

"That's right. Now, what do you want here?"

"I thought the cabin was yours and Helaise's, jointly."

"It has been. But I have other arrangements in prospect, *if* you don't mind."

"Maybe I do," said Barton—watching the other man, taking his measure. "But it's not what *I* mind. The way I get it, you want to trade Helaise in for Myra, who is settled in with Cheng. None of the other three are willing to change, but you're trying to bull it through anyway."

Terike ap Fenn glowered. "Yes, I am. I lived long enough in the Service, in a mustn't-touch situation. Now things have changed—we get to live the way we want to. So don't try to stop me from doing it, because you can't."

Barton kept his tone casual. "The hell you say, ap Fenn. The hell you do say."

By Barton's standards, ap Fenn was terribly slow on the draw. Barton watched him make up his mind to rise and annihilate, watched him start to carry out his decision.

Barton didn't give him a chance; given ap Fenn's size and weight, he couldn't afford to. Taking a solid grip on the arms of his chair, he swung both feet up and planted them full force in ap Fenn's face. Too bad there wasn't a dentist on the ship, he thought, as he rose wearily to stand over his late foe. And he wondered what else in the way of first aid would be needed.

Ironically, Myra Hake was Ship One's medical technician. After stuffing and taping the nose, she dutifully plugged several dislodged teeth back into the unconscious man's bleeding gums. "But," she confided, "I'll be surprised if more than two of those will actually reroot."

She gave Barton a long, close look. "Did you have to be *that* rough?"

When it came to long, close looks, Barton knew he was second to few. "No, of course not," he said, finally. "I could have waited until he or Cheng killed the other. Or Helaise got her pride hurt bad enough to do something really stupid. And then I could have punished whoever was first out of bounds.

"The way I did it, I went to the guy causing all the trouble and asked him to stop. He thought he'd beat my head in but he wasn't fast enough, and lost some teeth. If you think I liked having to do it that way, you're out of your tree.

"You still want to second-guess me, Myra?"

Finally she shook her head. Her attempted smile was feeble, but Barton was convinced that she meant it. "No, Barton. And thanks. Sooner or later he might have killed Cheng—and I happen to love Cheng."

"Well, *I* happen to think that makes Cheng a very lucky guy." He grinned. "You know I'm safely taken, so I guess it's okay to say that in my book you're one whole lot of fine lady."

She nodded. "Why, thanks, Barton." He turned to leave. "Oh, I almost forgot. Tell Limila for me that her trick worked, with the gravity." Barton scowled, puzzled. "I mean, my clock's running again just fine." Glad of a little good news for a change, he grinned again and left her.

When he went to the galley for coffee, he found Tarleton and Limila waiting for him. "How did it go with ap Fenn?" Tarleton asked.

Barton didn't like the question. "Ask him yourself." He set down the empty coffee cup and got out a beer instead.

"What's the trouble? Something you don't think I should know?" Barton shook his head. Eventually, Tarleton would find out for himself—meanwhile, why bother with it? That was all.

But he wasn't to be rid of the subject. Liese Anajek and Vito Scalsa, of Compartment Five, joined them. The dark, wiry Scalsa, who was shaping up into a grade-A pilot, didn't say much. Liese, a small, rounded, birdlike girl from Indonesia, couldn't hide her curiosity. Oddly, she didn't look as if she could swat a fly, let alone handle Weapons. But she was good at her job.

"I hear you had to crumb Terike, Barton," she began. "Wow! Teeth all over the deck! What was it, anyway? Girl trouble?" Barton nodded; he didn't want to talk, but no point in denying the facts.

"He's certainly been the rounds," said Liese. "First Alene, then Myra, then me, then Helaise—and now he's after Myra again. I can't figure him out—did he go

170

through the list on a trial basis and then make up his mind, or is he just a butterfly at heart, ever flitting from flower to flower?"

"It doesn't matter," said Barton. "He's taken his last flit."

"How do you know?" the girl asked.

"Because everybody else is satisfied where they are. It took a while, yes. But look at you two, for instance. You're practically spot-welded."

Liese broke into laughter. Barton stood; the change of pace gave him a good opening to leave the group.

"Just a minute," said Tarleton. "Look—I don't want you to think I was criticizing. I wasn't. It was my job and you did it for me, so how you did it was up to you.

"But now I'm worried. Ap Fenn is a proud man, even a vain one. What if he tries to get back at you?"

Barton shrugged. "I'll think of something."

"Well, whatever it takes, you have my backing. He's good at his job, but on this expedition you're worth ten of him. So even if you have to . . . I mean, Limila's good on weapons, too."

"Oh, hell, Tarleton! I'll go talk to the guy, when he's out of shock. He gives me any trouble a little bluff can't cure, and he'll get a change of roommates, all right." Barton grinned, not nicely. "I'll move him into the ice-box—Cabin Six—with Hishtoo."

Finally, he got away from the uncomfortable conversation. At least, Limila hadn't asked any questions.

Cheng had the pilot watch. Barton put him through some training exercises, although these had now become ritual rather than necessity. The man was embarrassed and grateful about the ap Fenn incident, and kept trying to thank Barton, but Barton wouldn't let the discussion leave the mechanics of the control panel. As he left, he clapped Cheng on the shoulder. "Just let it lie; I'll take it as read." Cheng smiled in obvious relief.

In Number Three he found a tense, frightened Helaise ministering to ap Fenn, who growled in surly mumbles through swollen lips. Barton's presence obviously increased her discomfort, but she said nothing beyond a noncommittal greeting.

"Helaise," he said. Then, "Well, ap Fenn, where do we stand?"

Ap Fenn scowled but refused to speak.

Helaise turned on Barton. "How could you *do* that to him?"

"It wasn't easy. Ap Fenn! I asked a question. Speak up."

"Maybe next time you won't be so lucky." The words were muttered.

Explosively, Barton released an exasperated sigh. "*Next* time? Man, this expedition is no schoolyard—it's a life-or-death matter, for the human race. I can't—and I won't—be bothered, worrying about some muscle boy with a childish grudge. Yes, that means you! Now hear me, ap Fenn—and hear me well.

"If there is anything like a 'next time' with you, you know what happens? I'll tell you—you will damn well get out and *walk.*"

Ap Fenn snorted, then winced at what the pressure did to his damaged nose. "I imagine Tarleton will have something to say about that."

"Hell yes, he will. He'll wave to you and say 'Bon voyage!', is what. You think I'm stupid enough to try to bypass Tarleton's authority? Well, I'm not."

Ap Fenn still didn't answer; Barton decided to rub it in a little. "As a matter of fact," he said, slowly and with relish, "when I came here earlier today, I had full authority to use my own judgment about you. No limits. Because by circumstance—I won't say merit—I'm more valuable to this expedition than you are. I suggest you keep that in mind."

Time to throw the man a bone, deserved or not? "On the other hand, you're right—I *was* lucky. I'd hate to tackle you even-steven. If I'd figured you to get so hostile, I'd have brought a sidearm to equalize things." Pure soothing soap, that; big as ap Fenn was, and quick at weapons control, he had little skill at personal combat.

"Now why don't we drop it? You're good at your job and we can use you. But forget about swapping roomies any more, because everyone else is settled and satisfied. If you aren't"—enough carrot, time again for the stick—"you can swap bunks with Eeshta, and move in with Hishtoo." That should do it.

"Come on, Helaise; the Shield is due for a balance check. You haven't been through those procedures lately." Until ap Fenn had time to cool off, he wanted her out of that room. . . .

At the door they met Limila, carrying a tray of dishes steaming hot from the galley. "I will stay with him awhile," she said.

Barton and Helaise went to the rear of the ship and check-marked their way through the Shield-maintenance routine. It went slowly, because she wanted to talk. Well, Barton figured, she might as well get it off her chest.

"Terike is not a bad man," she said.

"So how come a good man wants to throw you out?"

"He's greedy, like a little boy—he's been repressed. Now he is breaking loose, and can't stop grabbing for the next goodie on the Christmas tree."

Barton had to chuckle. "Before this came up, did he treat you okay?"

She nodded. "Yes, mostly. He's not very sensitive to anyone else's feelings, but he does try. Even now, it's not that he means to hurt me—but suddenly he has this big urge for Myra, and simply can't see anything else. Or anyone . . ."

"Childish, is what. How the hell did such an unstable character ever get past the screening tests?"

"He has an uncle, high up in the Agency." Silently, Barton used some high-up obscenities with regard to all politicians.

When the tests and adjustments were finished, he commended Helaise on her work and they went forward to their separate cabins. Barton found that Limila had not yet returned to Number Two; he washed up and lay back for a relaxing doze. When he heard a knock, he thought he'd forgotten and locked the door, and got up to admit Limila. But it was Helaise who stood in the doorway.

"Anything wrong?"

She seemed flustered. "I—she—I mean—Barton, I have nowhere else to go."

"Ap Fenn throw you out? Well, we'll see about that!"

"No, Barton. She—Limila—is with Terike. She told me to come here. Didn't you know?"

"I will stay with him awhile," Limila had said. Barton had thought, sure, stay long enough to feed him—but apparently she had meant considerably more. He felt empty. He couldn't be angry—not at Limila—but suddenly he wanted to take Helaise like a bull, a tiger, a force of total destruction.

He didn't, of course. He took her, and she him, because each needed the other. But very gently.

When Limila came in, they awoke. She looked as though she had been beaten in such a way as to leave no marks.

"Please go to Terike, Helaise," she said—and would say no more until the girl had gone. Then she looked at Barton. "I thought I was doing a right thing."

Barton was stumped. Finally, "Maybe you'd better tell me about it."

Limila sat facing him. "On Tilara, there is a way a woman may stop a killing matter between her man and another. It is not law, only custom. But if she goes to the other man with a gift of food and herself, for that time, and is accepted, that man has agreed to end the matter."

"How about her own man?" Barton's growl was deeper than he intended it.

"He must accept the truce or the woman kills herself. Thus the custom is not lightly followed, nor broken."

Well, I should think not, thought Barton. His anger—no, resentment—at Limila was replaced with a kind of awe.

"So what happened?" His voice was quiet, and he knew he must not touch her—not yet.

"At first—I should have realized—Terike could not understand. He did not believe I meant it. Then he became excited, eager. But when I removed my clothing, he—he could not do anything, after all.

"And then he laughed, a laugh to hurt me. And he said I am to tell you that you are quite welcome to your plastic bitch."

For a moment, Barton was like a statue. "I see," he said. Without hurry, he got up and dressed.

"Barton—what are you going to do?"

"Nothing much," he said. "Just kill Terike ap Fenn a little bit."

"No! You cannot!"

"The hell I can't. I have Tarleton's express permission."

"But that was for the good of the ship—not for only a personal matter."

"He said I could use my own judgment. Well, I've used it."

"Barton, you must not. Or if you kill him, I must kill me."

He turned on her. "This isn't Tilara; the custom doesn't apply! And besides, the sonofabitch *didn't* accept you."

"He tried to do so; it is not his fault that I do not have breasts."

He was beaten and he knew it, but still he tried. "*Why* do you want him alive?"

"Except that Helaise needs him, I do not care if he lives or dies. It is you, Barton, who must not do this killing, for this reason."

Barton slumped as if she had let the air out of him. "All right, Limila—you win. Ap Fenn lives unless he actually attacks me—and I won't goad him into it. But I am going now, to tell him something."

"I may go with you, Barton?"

"No."

At Number Three, Helaise answered his knock. Barton pushed in, patted her cheek, and spoke directly to ap Fenn. "I got your message." The man said nothing, only glared.

"Maybe I didn't get it quite straight; maybe you'd like to repeat it." Still no answer. "Let me ask you—did you understand the terms of Limila's offer?"

"I think so, yes."

"Then you know why you're still alive." Ap Fenn tried a smirk; it was not convincing. "All right—by Tilaran custom, this matter between us is at an end. I so agree." Ap Fenn *did* smirk.

"But," said Barton, "any further move by you—even one word—and it's a brand new ball game. In fairness, I have to tell you that." And he left.

Limila asked for, and got, a verbatim report. Big-eyed, she nodded. "You have beaten him—you have freed me from the consequences of my act. Barton . . . I I am very glad that you will never be my enemy."

For a few days Barton was edgy about the incident, but nothing more happened. He and ap Fenn spoke only in line of duty, but that was nothing new—they'd never had much in common. Barton had enough work to

175

keep him busy, so eventually he relaxed and—mostly —forgot about it.

Except that he didn't trust Terike ap Fenn behind his back, and never would.

The next time he found Eeshta on comm-watch, he proposed the matter that had been on his mind since their last meeting.

"You wish to speak Demu, Barton?"

"Yes, Eeshta—for when we meet your people. Will you come to my quarters when you're off watch? After you've eaten and rested, of course." Eeshta was agreeable.

Limila spoke Demu, but Barton wanted to work both with her, the linguist, and with Eeshta, the native-tongued. He progressed more rapidly than he had expected, and decided he must have absorbed more than he'd realized of what the Demu had tried to teach him in captivity. Then, he had refused to learn out of sheer stubbornness and resentment—and because he wanted to keep his own mind a mystery to his captors.

Only later had he learned that the refusal was all that had kept his anatomy safe from the drastic surgery the Demu practiced on "animals" who learned their jailers' speech.

Barton couldn't match the high-pitched Demu intonations, but he mastered the hissing sibilants well, to Limila's and even Eeshta's satisfaction. And as the fleet neared the end of the first leg of its journey, he decided to give his new accomplishment the acid test. Eeshta accompanied him to Compartment Six; they entered. Sitting, the older Demu looked at them in silence.

"I greet you, Hishtoo," said Barton. "It is that we now may speak."

Hishtoo stood, then turned away. "I greet you, Hishtoo," Barton said again. "Is it that we shall speak together?"

Still facing away, Hishtoo spoke; the hood muffled the Demu's voice. "It is that you are not Demu, but animal. It is that Hishtoo does not speak with animals."

Nothing that Barton—or Eeshta—could say, made any apparent dent in Hishtoo's obstinacy. Eventually, Barton shrugged and gave it up. He had his answer, anyway—his speech had been understood, all right. It would do. . . .

The fleet, slowing and tightening its formation, approached Tilara without challenge, more closely than anyone had expected. But finally the hail came. Tarleton had comm-watch; since his fluency in Tilaran was minimal, he put out the squawk for Barton and Limila to come take the call.

Limila had briefed Tarleton, from her layman's understanding, on Tilaran communications frequencies and modulation systems. She had done well; the controls required very little adjustment to bring a clear picture and voice over the viewscreen.

Barton gestured for Limila to take over—if need be, he could supply answers to questions concerning Earth. Automatically he transposed her Tilaran idioms into their English equivalents.

"To the Tilaran ships, greetings," she said. "To you speaks a woman of Tilara—once taken by the Demu, now returned here by people of Earth. It is their ships you see—they who seek your aid and offer theirs to you.

"In especial is this man beside me. He is Barton, who took me from the Demu of his own force and without help. He is become to me my most needful person and is to be granted that respect by all, though he is not Tilaran." Barton began to feel embarrassed.

"I ensure," said Limila, "that we of these ships, that number three twelves and four, are of friendship, of help—of hope to end the Demu terror. Our weapons are for use only against your enemies, who are also ours. In your kindness, give us the neednesses to come to rest on Tilara, where all may share knowledge and grow to share effort—that the Demu take us no more.

"Did I say it right, Barton?" she whispered.

"Hell, I couldn't have done it better myself." And that, he thought, was pure truth!

The Tilaran speaker proceeded to give landing instructions. Limila translated for Scalsa, the pilot, and Myra Hake relayed the information to the fleet. "Looks like everything's under control," said Barton. "Let's go have us a drink, Tarleton." The other nodded, and the two men repaired to the galley where Barton opened a cold beer. Tarleton poured coffee for himself.

"What, in particular, do you want me to do while we're here?" Barton asked.

The big man paused, then said, "Just about what you would anyway, I guess. Hang with me in conferences, to bolster my lousy grasp of the language. Back Limila up, where she may be a little shaky on facts about Earth. We have to impress on these people that we need help, that it's a hurry-up operation, and that we're all-out to help them, too. And get all the social data you can—so our troops don't go around dropping bricks."

Barton nodded. "Fine—that's about what I thought. Now, how much local exposure do you want Hishtoo and Eeshta to get?"

"How much do you think is wise?"

"For the general public," Barton said, "let's keep it purely on the viewscreen. I'd hate to see some bunch go hysterical and mob them—especially Eeshta. I couldn't chance her with an unselected audience, if you see what I mean."

"I do see." Tarleton hesitated. "Uh—another point. How are you and ap Fenn getting along?"

"He's alive, isn't he?" Barton's voice was flat. "What more do you want?"

"I've . . . never quite understood that situation. Barton —while we're down on Tilara, would you prefer that we trade him off to some other ship?"

Barton needed no time to consider the proposal—he had a mental picture of ap Fenn, safely out of Barton's reach, indulging childish spite by discussing Limila. But he answered mildly. "No—I'd rather have him where I can keep an eye on him. I mean, guess what could happen if he tried his tricks on a crew that wasn't braced for him." Tarleton looked doubtful, but did not press the point.

Guidance to Tilara, and the subsequent landing, proceeded smoothly. Back in the control room for the landing approach, Barton was first impressed by Tilaran architecture—except as a last resort, it seldom used straight lines or solid colors. Conic sections were favorites, especially the ellipse and parabola, and colors blended smoothly from one shade to another. Tilarans were not slaves to symmetry—one side of a building might be convex paraboloid and the other concave elliptical. The effect, Barton noted with approval, always seemed to come out right. Belatedly he noticed the plentiful growth of treelike foliage, but had no time to pick out details before Ship One touched down.

A few minutes later, four hundred humans—including one Tilaran and two Demu—had landed on Tilara.

"There'll be a short delay," said Tarleton, "before the reception committee shows up. Time for a quick briefing." For the first time since liftoff, he was unmistakably taking charge. Back in his own element, thought Barton—well, good enough.

The big man signed to Barton and Limila. "For this first meeting," he said, "I think six of us is about right. You two, of course, and the other three squadron commanders." Limila whispered something to Barton that he didn't quite catch, and left them. Tarleton turned to Myra Hake at the comm-board. "Hook up the squadron honchos for me, would you?" Then, to Barton, "You give them the drill, right?" Barton nodded.

Myra flipped toggles and made low-voiced requests. Soon the picture split into four quarters: Barton saw himself, Slobodna, Tamirov, and Cummings.

"Hi, Slowboat—Tammy—Estelle. We're all elected to go out with the boss and meet the new neighbors, so gussy-up and come on over. I don't have the full landing layout, but Ship One is some place in the middle—shouldn't be too hard to find. Any questions?" The two men shook their heads and cut screens. Slobodna had been one of Barton's first pilot trainees on Earth, and the Russian was Slowboat's own prize pupil—they wouldn't have questions, Barton reflected.

Estelle Cummings was still on. "Uniform of the day?" she asked.

Barton studied her image on the screen—the strong features framed by her long, blonde hair. He had never met the tall, big-boned woman, didn't know quite what to make of her. She pushed the fall of hair back from one side of her face. Beside her stood her husband, Max, a surgeon. He was shorter than his wife, but from what Barton had heard, they made a good team—no pecking order. He brought his mind back to business.

"Uniform, Estelle? Whatever you like. I don't think our hosts are the type to be picky." She nodded and switched off, as Limila returned, having changed to a short, loose robe.

"I've had my fingers crossed for that ship," said Tarleton.

"Cummings'? How so?"

"That's the one I mentioned, with the seven-to-three ratio—seven men to three women. With one of the women married—and the ship's captain and squadron commander, at that—things could have gotten messy."

"What arrangement did they come up with, do you know?"

"I haven't asked," said Tarleton. "As long as it works for them, it's really none of my business." And that, Barton reflected, was one of the things that made Tarleton a good man to work for.

Myra Hake turned from the viewscreen, which now showed the area near the ship's lowered access ramp. "It's time for you to go out, I think. Company's coming."

The three disembarked. Breathing deeply of the air of her home planet, Limila pointed ahead, where the Tilaran delegation approached. The long, straight wig was brushed back to hang free behind her. The loose robe, in shades of pale blue-green, disguised the shape of her body, but a gust of breeze showed Barton that she'd altered the harness of her padded bra. The false breasts now sat lower and wider, approximating the natural Tilaran location. He hid a grin.

The other three squadron commanders converged to meet them; all six walked toward the nine Tilarans who waited a few yards distant. Barton noticed that Tilarans did not come in blond; hair was black like Limila's or dark brown with reddish tinges.

Of the nine, there could be no doubt which was in charge. He was not the tallest, nor more richly dressed, nor did he carry himself with arrogance. But while he looked squarely at the visiting group, the other Tilaran men and two women looked mostly to him.

He stepped forward. So did Tarleton, bringing Limila with him.

"I am Vertan," the Tilaran said. "There exists a number to distinguish me, if need be, from other Vertans. You are as if invited here; feel yourselves home-born of Tilara. Now I have said too long, before giving a new friend turn to say."

"I am Tarleton," said the big man, slowly. His accent, Barton realized, was really bad. "I do not say your

180

speech well. So if it may be, Limila, our first Tilaran friend, says for me." He reached to shake Vertan's hand, appeared to realize that the gesture meant nothing to the Tilaran, and started to retract the movement. But after a moment's pause, Vertan reached out and clasped Tarleton's hand with his own.

"This is how you meet?" Vertan motioned to his retinue, and a handshaking free-for-all ensued. Before it was over, Barton was sure he'd shaken hands with one of the women at least three times.

When order returned, Tarleton—speaking through Limila—outlined the Earth fleet's background and purpose. Limila translated both ways directly, omitting such frills as "he says." Barton observed that Vertan's occasional questions were very much to the point.

After a time the Tilaran raised a hand and began to recapitulate what he had been told. "You wish us of Tilara," Limila relayed, "and such others as are of like interest, to join you in forcing issue to the Demu." Tarleton nodded.

"You have and will share the Demu sleeping-weapon, their Shield against that weapon and others, and your own uniform-radiation device that penetrates the Shield." Another nod.

"Have you other weapons?"

"Not on this fleet. Everything else we tried, the Shield stops."

"Some of our own weapons might be of help. Do you want?"

"Sure, of course. Anything that can crack the Shield."

"But we cannot know until we meet the Demu."

"How's that?"

"The sleeping-weapon. On our ships that survive Demu contact and are not taken, no one can remember the happening of battle—that our weapons were used or had effect."

Sure, Barton recalled—the memory-blanking. With heavy exposure, the damage could be extensive, even permanent. Nice trick . . . .

"Can't hurt to take them along," Tarleton said. "Just in case."

For the first time, Barton cut in. "You're missing the point."

"So?" Tarleton didn't sound disturbed.

"Like back home. We float up a Shielded hulk, loaded

with instruments, and cut loose at it with everything these folks have. Then we know."

Limila looked at Tarleton. He nodded, and she repeated Barton's proposal in Tilaran. Vertan smiled, and half-bowed toward Barton.

"We can proceed so." He looked at Barton more closely. "You are he who took the Demu ship?" Limila did not translate.

"Yes, with much fortune."

"Then you of all be home-born among us." Barton couldn't think of an answer, so he tried the half-bow in return. Judging by Vertan's smile, Barton had made adequate response.

"Next of importance." Limila was relaying again. "Two other peoples, of friendship to Tilara, are also of possibility to join against the Demu. These are the Larka-Te and the Filjar. You meet them in an early time—some here on Tilara. Their weapons are as ours, for we share.

"Others of acquaintance to us would aid but have not the way." Tarleton asked for a repeat, and learned that several other races had the willingness to help, but not the resources.

"I think we're agreed, then," said Tarleton. "Can we set up a schedule of conferences and arrange a place for them?"

"At soonest. I will inform direct to your ship."

Barton decided that the party was about to break up, but first Limila stepped forward to speak quietly with Vertan. After a moment, he embraced her. In low tones they spoke further, then separated, both smiling. But when Limila returned to Barton's side, he saw tears in her eyes.

Barton had bet on a final orgy of handshaking, and he won. Then after brief "so long"s to Slobodna, Tamirov, and Cummings, the walk back to the ship was silent. Far off, among buildings edging the spaceport, Barton had his first clear look at Tilaran trees. The foliage appeared feathery, with more yellow to its green than most Earthly vegetation. The breeze brought a light flowerlike fragrance, though he saw no recognizable blooms.

Inside the ship, Tarleton said, "See you at dinner? About an hour?" and left the other two. In Compartment Two, Barton and Limila doffed clothing. He had been right—she had lengthened the bra straps so that the pads now sat low and wide on her rib cage. She looked at him, but he made no comment.

He made drinks and gave her one; they sat relaxing. Finally, he said, "You know Vertan before?"

"I knew of him; we had not met. He is one of great respect."

"I noticed, and I agree—he's a man, in anybody's league."

Limila smiled. "You want to know of what we spoke, that you did not hear?"

"Sure, if it's any of my business." Well, she'd saved *him* from asking. . . .

"We spoke of teeth, Barton—of teeth and of *tits*. Soon I shall smile to you with forty teeth, again. And perhaps, though it is not yet certain, I no longer will need to wear dead padding. Vertan is to set a meeting of me with Tilaran surgical experts, and in a day or two I will know."

A couple of hours' talking in Tilaran, Barton thought, certainly brought back her native turn of phrase in a hurry. Not that he minded, so long as he knew what she meant. . . .

"That's fine with me, honey—whatever you want."

And at dinner, they and Tarleton were agreed that the fleet's first day on Tilara showed considerable promise.

Conferences—planning sessions—began the next day. A Tilaran ground car delivered Barton and Tarleton to a building at the edge of the spaceport, indented into a grove of the feathery trees. Its shape was a simple parabolic ellipsoid. Inside, the surface blended smoothly from copper-colored at floor level to shining silver at the top.

The first order of business—exchange of technical information—went slowly at first, as the two groups became accustomed to each other's modes of thought. Top priority was the project for testing the weapons of the Tilari—and their allies—against the Demu Shield. But the longer they talked about it, the more complicated it became.

Barton found himself becoming impatient. He felt his boss was too easygoing, too willing to allow the discussions to get onto side tangents. While the squadron lead-ers and other specialists continued to talk, he drew Tarleton aside.

"Look—we're wasting time. They're talking projectile systems; we already know the Shield will stop those. Hell, it stood up against our fusion warheads, didn't it?"

"True," said Tarleton. "But we can't really tell our new allies, can we, that most of their arsenal is effectively a pile of junk?"

"We don't have to. But can't we zero-in first on the possibles, and let 'em test the other stuff later? You've listened to the pitch, same as I have—they have just three things that might work. I want to set it up to test those first, so we'll know what the hell—if anything—we have going for us."

"Three? Did I miss one?"

"Okay." Barton held up his index finger. "One. The Tilari twin-ion beam, that converges when it hits solid matter, and induces kiloamps of high-freq current in the target. And they have that in a handgun model, believe it or not. I think that gizmo should be number one on our list."

"All right, I agree. What else?"

Barton now had two fingers extended. "The plasma-gun. Whose is that? I didn't get all the spiel. . . ."

"A Filjar development—and that's the one I missed; I didn't understand the explanation."

"Me either, in detail," said Barton. "But what I did get is, it throws a sort of souped-up ball lightning—a plasma that's stable until it touches something. Then it unstables in one hell of a hurry, focused toward the point of contact. Only drawback is that comparatively, it's a little slow."

"But will it penetrate the Shield?"

"Jesus Christ! That's what we want to *find out!*"

Tarleton shook his head. "Sorry. Trying to think in Tilaran, all day, has me a little confused."

"Yeh—me, too. Don't worry; we'll get used to it."

"I hope so. All right, then. Your third candidate?"

Barton had forgotten his finger-counting routine. "The Larka-Te high-drive torpedoes."

"I thought so, from the way you looked when they were being described. But that's a projectile system, isn't it?"

"Not quite," Barton said. "It starts that way, all drive

and warhead, so it goes like a bat. In fact, the drive *is* the warhead, if I have that right.

"But why it might work is that when it hits and the drive begins to blow, it blows in a coherent wave front. And while the front end is blowing, there's a matter of picoseconds when the back end is still pushing. So I think it's worth a try."

"All right, Barton. We'll arrange to put those three at the head of the line, for testing, and not worry about how long it takes to check out the rest."

"Good enough. One other thing, though. So far, we haven't talked about when we land and have to get out of the ships, in Demu territory. It's a safe bet the Demu have the sleep-gun in portable size—and maybe individual, one-man Shields. We don't, and we should. Hell, we haven't even worked up hand lasers."

"I know, Barton. Look—this was discussed on Earth. The decision, was, that rather than delay the fleet, we wait to develop personal hardware until we saw what our allies might have to offer."

"All right—so here we are and here *they* are. When do we get to it? Just in case the Tilaran ion beam doesn't fill the bill?"

"Well, I suppose now is as good a time as any."

Barton was satisfied; the two men rejoined the group. Tactfully, as always, Tarleton arranged the agenda so as to test the three "possibles" first, and initiated a project to work on development of personal Shields and weapons.

By the end of the second day, a firm schedule had been set. Slobodna would have a Shielded instrument package—complete with telemetry—in orbit the following day, with three more in reserve in case of too-vigorous success against the first one.

On that cheerful note, Vertan issued an invitation. "Our work is well. Now, also at leisure should we meet." In other words, Barton translated, come to the party. He was right. Two evenings hence—come prepared to relax.

One thing bothered him. The Earth group had met no members of other races present on Tilara—nor were any such to be present at this first social occasion. The next time he and Limila were alone together, he asked her, "How come the apartheid?"

"It is difficult," she said, "for persons of any race to accustom to other races, at first, even without facing several differing kinds immediately. You will meet the others later.

"But now—here is what you must tell your people, of the customs of Tilara."

Barton listened, then shook his head. "They'll never believe it," he said. "*You* tell 'em." And he stuck to that.

The problem was the casual, friendly Tilaran attitude toward sex, considered as a social grace. He should not, Barton realized, be surprised—from their first meeting, Limila had made it clear that the ideal of sexual monogamy did not dominate Tilaran culture, even superficially. But now he found that he had not understood the extent of the difference . . . .

On social occasions, Tilarans wore loose robes—for the specific purpose of facilitating intimate advances. One might, Barton learned, be intimately fondled at first meeting, if the other person were attracted. Consent was not mandatory—Tilarans took "no" for an answer, with good grace.

But there was a form—a protocol—to it, that he found hard to understand, and despaired that most of fleet personnel would *ever* understand.

The first thing he did was to make sure that Terike ap Fenn wasn't on the list to go to the party. The second was, he insisted that Limila repeat her briefing lecture at least twice. And still he had his doubts.

A few more than fifty Earthfolk attended the function —one from each ship, plus a few extra. At first, Barton was nervous as hell—too nervous to pay due heed to the lush decor of the place. He sipped a tart, greenish wine and hardly tasted it, preoccupied with wondering how he should react if groped under his Tilaran robe. After a while, when nothing happened, he began to feel aggrieved—how could he protect his virtue if no one propositioned him?

He turned to whisper to Limila, to make a joke of his unease, and saw her leaving the room—accompanied. Beside him was another Tilaran woman, obviously young, whose long, reddish brown hair was coiled into a single curl falling forward over a bare shoulder.

She spoke. "Limila meets the one who long ago, before the Demu took her, was her most needful person. Is it not happy for them?"

Barton couldn't have said "yes" if someone had offered him a drink. Sure, it was all right by Tilaran custom, but . . . Then, showing her small Tilaran teeth in a smile, she reached under his robe.

"I am Iivajj. Might you be with me now, Barton? Limila has said you may not wish to, but that it is fitting to ask."

When in Rome, thought Barton, and allowed her to take his hand and lead him away. And when they were alone, Iivajj met him not casually but as though she had loved him all her lifetime. Barton was shaken; he felt unworthy, but did his best—hoping that best would be good enough—to be to Iivajj as she was to him.

She seemed to have no complaints or reservations. And later, her good-byes to him were warm and happy.

He decided to ask Limila no questions. He didn't have to—next day, back at the ship, she told him the answers anyway.

"Barton, it was so good to be again with Tevann. I am glad you did not mind and that you were with the little Iivajj. So young, she is, but of good thought." Well, yes, Barton mused—that, at the very least.

"Limila," he said. "That is how it is, with all your people?"

"Yes, of course. You know that, Barton—you pretend you don't, but you do, and have for long. With conscious control of ovulation, and lack of sexual diseases you have on Earth, why should it be otherwise?"

"But—I would have expected things to be sort of —oh, casual, I guess. Just for fun. And there was certainly nothing casual about Iivajj."

"Nor about you with her, Barton, I would think. Freedom is not a thing to be taken lightly. But now—is there more you wish to ask, that you also know already?"

Barton thought. "No, I guess not. Except just one thing—am I still your most needful person?"

"Always, Barton. *Always.* You gave me back my life, and before that, you helped me through the time when I was not alive. That was then—and now it is as we say, simply that you are my most needful person." She drew a shuddering breath. "Am I yours?"

"Do you have to ask that?" It turned out she didn't, really.

Apparently no one from the fleet had blown any gaffs, for Tarleton was now invited—solo—to meet representatives of other races who were on visiting terms. Over dinner, he gave Barton and Limila his impressions.

"You'll have to see the Larka-Te, to believe them. They're impressive—not especially tall, but slim and elegant. They make you feel they're something special —and it's not anything they do on purpose. It's just the way they are.

"The Filjar remind me, a little, of myself in a fur coat. Big and lumbering. But Vertan says they're not easy to push around." Well, thought Barton—neither was Tarleton, for that matter.

"The big question mark is the Ormthu. They're new to the Tilarans—made contact only a few months ago. There is one Ormthan on this planet—I repeat, *one*— unsupported by any troops or weaponry, and treated with utmost respect. I don't know when I'll get to meet him; Vertan wasn't sure. But if I didn't misunderstand —and I may have—the Ormthu long since came to peaceable terms with the Demu, on the grounds that if you're tough enough, you get left alone. So apparently they're neutral, where the Demu are concerned. We'll have to find out more about that—if and when we ever meet the Ormthan."

"Tevann has seen it once, briefly," Limila said. "In rest, like a large pink egg, but with ability to shape itself as it wishes. A head, eyes, mouth, arms—all form at need, and retract when need is gone."

"Like an intelligent amoeba?" Tarleton asked.

"I think, yes. But warm to touch, it is told, and not wet."

Barton shook his head. "I guess it takes all kinds. But look, Limila—you must have seen Larka-Te, and Filjar, too. Can you tell us more about them?"

"On Tilara, before, I was seldom where they go—I saw them only a few times, and at distance. But with the Demu were several of each, taken as we. Along with other peoples not known to me."

"Did I see them? I don't remember any."

"No, Barton. These were taken earlier, by another

ship. And I did not see them whole, but only after the Demu had changed them. Quite different."

"I'll bet." The thought of Demu surgery gave Barton's voice a harsh edge.

"In some ways not so terrible as for Earth people or Tilarans," she said. "The Larka-Te produce not live birth, but eggs—like your birds. No breasts or outside sex—so not as damaged as your people or ours, except face and hands and feet—and hair, of course." A strand of her wig twisted between thumb and finger.

"Yeh," said Barton. "And how about the Filjar?"

"You would have to see. Size, bulk of Filjar is of large part fur and loose folds of skin. Slow movement is not of bulk, but slower racial characteristic of nervous system. But Filjar minds are fast and keen.

"Filjar with fur removed, loose skin cut away and made tight, are strange to see. The ones I saw did not adjust—they set their minds and, of purpose, died. And they had not lost sex, even—when not of use, it retracts, so Demu did not notice and remove."

"Bully for them." The comment was a conversation stopper and Barton knew it—but what else was there to say? "Well, I guess we all have things to do—right?" Barton didn't, but he left the table and set out to look for something.

In the control room he found Vertan, the Tilaran, in discussion with Vito Scalsa. Both were having difficulty with the language barrier; Barton volunteered to interpret.

"What we're working on," said Scalsa, "is coordination and timing. Flight plans—all that."

Barton knew what the problem was. The Tilaran space drive was similar to that of the Demu, but less efficient—it could match the Earth ships in top velocity but not in acceleration, either line-of-flight or turning. The difficulty was in planning departure times and routings so that all would arrive at rendezvous in Demu territory near-simultaneously.

"When we think we know agreement," Vertan said, "we find we have, one or other, failed to make all numbers of same kind." Tilaran duodecimal numbering had confused matters before—Barton was surprised that no one had come up with an overall solution. He thought about it—why, hell, it was simple!

"Scalsa, you're good on the computer. Why don't you

program the tin beast to run all calculations parallel—decimal and duodecimal, both? Tag your input data whichever it is, and run comparison-conversion checks on your double readouts to catch any glitches. Won't that do it?" Switching to Tilaran, he repeated the proposal to Vertan.

Scalsa grinned. "Sure, it'll do it. *I* should have thought of that." He frowned. "You know why I didn't?" Barton waited. "Because I had the idea I was here to take orders, same as back on Earth, working for the Agency."

"Well, from now on you're here to think, too, Scalsa." Barton saw he had been too abrupt, and added, "No blame—I know how it is." He spoke briefly to Vertan—putting him and Scalsa on their own again—and left them.

He found Limila, in their compartment, packing a suitcase. *What the hell?* She looked up from the dress she had folded neatly, and smiled. "Hello, Barton."

"Yeh, hello. What's going on? You moving out or something?"

"For a time, yes." She stood, came to him and embraced. "I told you—I am to have Tilari teeth again. Perhaps even breasts, of a sort. And for that—to find out—I must go to a surgical place, what you call a hospital. Only a few days—and then we know, Barton, how I am to appear in life for all our time. You do not object?"

Barton's anxieties collapsed—god*damn* my paranoid instincts, he thought. He held her close. "Sure not. Can I come to see you?"

"I would think so. I will ask. Barton . . . ?"

"Yes."

"Good. I will have to change clothes, anyway."

Next day the prospect of meeting Larka-Te and Filjar helped take Barton's mind off Limila's absence. Over breakfast, Tarleton gave him additonal briefing.

"Don't smile at the Larka-Te, any more than you can help—it confuses them." Barton felt himself looking puzzled. "Among themselves," Tarleton continued, "they converse with facial expressions nearly as much as with words—and mostly with variations, or modes, as they call them, of the smile."

"How do they manage talking over a voice circuit?"

"They don't. The Larka-Te never bothered to invent

voice-only communications. Until they had a workable picture-phone, they made do with writing—including a sort of hieroglyphics for the accompanying smile modes. Used as punctuation, no less."

Barton thought he saw the problem, now. "So if we smile, they think we mean something we don't?"

"Precisely. A Larka-Te may say 'welcome,' and be smiling in anything from the 'my dwelling is yours' mode to the 'I have waited long for vengeance' mode. Reduced to nothing but words in a foreign language, they have a hard time of it. The ones here on Tilara have had a lot of practice—but still, try to hold it down on the grins."

"I'll keep it in mind," Barton said. "By the way, are they all men? No Larka-Te women?"

"I have no idea—they haven't said. They all dress alike, and the names don't tell me a thing—any more than the Filjar names do."

"Yeh—how about our furry friends? Anything in particular to watch out for, there?"

"Nothing special, except don't try to be in a hurry. You won't have to worry about facial expressions—with all that fur, they don't really have any. And again, I have no idea which ones might be male or female. All that loose skin and bulky fur doesn't tell you much."

"They don't wear clothes?"

"Just a sort of utility harness, with pockets and such. Several different kinds—according to rank, maybe, or job function—I don't know."

"They don't sound too interesting, somehow."

"Don't sell them short, Barton. They wouldn't be on the same team with the Tilari if they didn't have something on the ball."

"Yeh, I guess so. You ready to go?"

A few preparations later, they left the ship. As usual, a Tilaran driver waited in a silent, oddly shaped ground car, to take them the kilometer or so to the conference building. At the end of the ride, Barton thanked her. She smiled in reply.

Inside, with about half a dozen each of Larka-Te and Filjar added to the usual group, the building seemed crowded—but Barton found that the feeling didn't last long. During the introductions he was somewhat bemused, wondering how the Larka-Te managed to be so impressive.

They were not tall—the tallest matched Barton's own height, which was average for Earth. But there was a lean, proud look to them—hawklike, almost, yet not predatory. Barton caught the name of the first one—Corval—and missed the rest. It was par for the course; he'd never been good at names.

There were no discernible sex differences. All the Larka-Te wore snug, bulgeless tunics, brightly colored, reaching to midthigh. Each had short, light-reddish hair; in the front it fell to cover perhaps half the forehead. Like a crew cut growing out, thought Barton—or maybe it was like fur and grew no longer. Or then again, possibly the Larka-Te were conformists. Nonetheless, Barton could not ignore the impact of their lean, intense faces.

Tarleton was saying the right words; Barton had only to nod. Then he saw Corval smiling at him, and realized he had let his own face slip. Quickly, he pulled it back to solemnity.

"You have heard, then." Corval spoke in Tilaran. Barton signed assent. "Be not of care, Barton—we know you do not share that means of communion, that your face does not mean what it says." Somehow, Corval's nonsmile was most expressive. "Do you know what your face said?"

"I'm afraid not. Nothing of discourtesy, I hope."

Corval curved his lips in a way that could mean nothing but delight. "It said, 'May I help to produce your next egg?' Not that such is possible. . . ."

Oh, Christ! What to say? "You're not—you don't produce eggs, yourself?"

"No. But even if so, one of your race could not assist —no more than the Filjar or Tilari. Our seed does not mix and act. But I say this—even without your knowing, your face said a thing of kindness. Be us friends now, Barton."

"Yes." Either humanoids took naturally to handshaking or Corval had run into the custom before—Barton reached out instinctively, and there was no delay. These egg-laying characters, he decided, *were* impressive—he could like them.

Now the Filjar came forward—taller than Barton but not so tall as the Tilari, they loomed huge in sheer breadth. He reminded himself that the appearance of bulk was illusory. And from the colored harnesses—

leather?—no two alike, depended pouches and implements.

The Filjar, too, shook hands. Firmly but not painfully, heavy, blunt claws pressed Barton's skin. The last of the delegation—Kimchuk, if Barton had the name right—stayed by him.

"Pleased to be with you, to find Demu at last." The Filjar spoke in a slow, tenor monotone. Tarleton had been right; no expression showed through the sleek, dark-brown fur. Except for the eyes—Tarleton hadn't mentioned those. They were large and deep—not bearlike at all, Barton thought—more like deer.

"And we are pleased to have you," he said. "Tilari tell us, Filjar are worthy friends."

Momentarily, Kimchuk inclined its head to one side. "Tilari tell the same of Earthani." Earthani? As good a name as any, thought Barton. Kimchuk spoke again. "You are Barton? Taker of ship from Demu?" Barton nodded. "Our songs will tell of you, of that taking."

"I had much fortune, Kimchuk." Barton was embarrassed; he could never be comfortable in a hero suit. "Tell of that, too."

Kimchuk made a high-pitched snort and clapped a hand to Barton's shoulder. Startled, Barton decided the sound had to be laughter.

"Fortune that prevails against Demu is fortune made of purpose. But our songs will be of Barton who is, not of some storied god who treads stars."

"Then one day I hope to hear your songs." He had struck the right note; Kimchuk clasped his shoulder again.

The assembly was preparing to settle down to business; the two moved to join it. First was Slobodna's report—the verdict was in, on the three major weapons systems. Barton listened with interest. Slobodna spoke in English, pausing for Tamirov to translate into the common language, Tilaran.

"First, the Tilaran twin-ion beam—it punches through the Shield and is effective after penetration. Traverse, to follow a moving target, is rapid enough for our needs, and—at close range—so is propagation speed. Against the Shield, effective range is roughly three hundred kilometers. Beyond that distance, the Shield produces instability in the beam and shorts it out. On unshielded objects the range is three to four times as great."

There was a pause while Tamirov ran conversions of number systems and units of measurement.

"Range varies," Slobodna continued, "as the square root of applied power. We can get some advantage by beefing up the power source, but not much—we'll run into space and weight limitations."

Tarleton stood. "Okay, let's take a breather while the specialists make a horseback guess—keeping time limits in mind—of the optimum power increase we should go for. All right?"

"Just a minute," said Barton. "Slowboat, what's the range of the handgun model?"

Slobodna conferred with Vertan, then said, "It hasn't been tested in space, or against the Shield. In atmosphere it breaks down at about a hundred meters."

"Then we need the hand lasers, and we need them bad." Tarleton nodded, and the two men sought refreshments.

Coffee and its alien equivalents were served; the racial groups tasted each others' beverages with differing reactions. Earthmen and Tilarans had previously traded samples—largely with appreciation—of coffee and the tart, bubbling Tilaran *klieta*. Now Barton tried a cup, given to him by Corval, of a pale, lukewarm liquid that seemed to have no taste while he sipped it, but afterward produced in his mouth a warm, tangy glow. Corval's reaction to coffee seemed noncommittal; he did not ask for seconds.

Kimchuk started to offer Barton a shallow dish filled with a thick gray substance that looked like mud soup, but seeing the Larka-Te beverage in his hand, said, "No, wait another time. The two are not well together." Barton took a rain check—it was time to get back to the agenda, anyway.

As they sat down, he said to Tarleton, "I just thought of something. Remind me to bring it up when Slowboat's finished."

"Next," said Slobodna, as cups were cleared away, "we tried the Filjar plasma-ball projector. Within its limits, it can't be stopped—it not only penetrates the Shield; it destroys it and keeps going. But it's slow—much slower than ship speeds. And once launched, there's no way to alter its course.

"So we recommend that the plasma-gun be installed on all ships, but reserved for use at close quarters."

"How about a land-going, portable model?" asked Barton.

"It won't work in atmosphere. The instant the plasma emerged, it would blow."

Slobodna's conference with the Filjar was brief, dealing only with the mechanics of installing the weapon on Earth ships.

"The Larka-Te high-drive torpedo," he next began, "cracks the Shield only within a certain range of relative velocities. Too fast or too slow, and it blows harmlessly. But within a considerable range"—he read off the numbers and waited while Tamirov converted them—"the torps penetrate, and smash whatever is inside. To get those results, we used up all four of our clay pigeons and two more that we haywired from spare parts. But by tomorrow we'll have a couple more ready, to check out the other systems.

"We're not entirely sure why the velocity hangup, but we *think* it's the way the torp itself blows, from front to back. So at some speeds the reaction front stays in contact longer, with the Shield interface, and breaks it down.

"But we know how to make best use of this weapon. Add limiting circuits to the spotter and firing equipment, so that the torp won't go if the relative speeds aren't right. It won't be difficult; Scalsa was running computer simulations on it, this morning." Then, to Tarleton, "Anything else I should cover?"

"You hit all the bases just fine. But Barton has something he wants to bring up."

Slobodna stepped down and Barton took the floor, signing for Tamirov to interpret. "One thing I'm not sure is clear to everybody. It just struck me a few minutes ago. That is, you've all lost ships to the Demu, so we can expect they have all these weapons also. Which means we have to plan offensive *and* defensive tactics based on the properties of the ion beam, the plasma-gun, and the torps. Our one edge is the laser—and that's only true until the Demu capture one and have time to copy it."

The nods that answered Barton were thoughtful and sober.

Lunch-break came. Slobodna's team conferred with the Larka-Te; elsewhere Barton heard discussion of his own latest point.

Barton found Tilaran food sufficiently different from Earth's to be intriguing, yet similar enough to make his digestion feel at home. Four sat together. Tarleton and

Corval spoke slowly, making heavy weather of Tarleton's accented Tilaran. Barton and Kimchuk ate in silence, which was fine with Barton; he felt pooped.

Kimchuk excused himself for a few moments and returned with two dishes; he offered one to Barton. Unfortunately, the stuff not only looked like mud soup—it also tasted like it. But under the attentive gaze of large Filjar eyes, Barton dutifully ate the thick mess. What the hell—it wouldn't kill him!

And then he felt a slow relaxation, a welling of reserve energies. The knots in his mind untied themselves —he was at peace, yet alert. In his thought patterns, nagging discrepancies fitted themselves together, in harmony.

It wasn't, he thought, like the hit from a drink or a joint. His head hadn't speeded up, slowed down, nor lost itself in contemplation. Except for the removal of a lot of niggling, extraneous pressures, he was exactly the same Barton he had been five minutes earlier. He turned to face Kimchuk directly.

"Whatever that may be, it is of good."

"We find it so," the Filjar replied. "On a day of effort, the release given by the *dreif* adds to what may be done well." For a moment, Kimchuk was silent. "For that day, once is all—for help or harm, more would do nothing. You feel so?"

"Yes." Barton felt—knew—that sleep would be necessary to reset the mind's mechanisms, before the substance could act again. He found it strange to know such a thing by intuition or instinct, but he did not doubt it. Nor was he surprised to see a similar dish at Tarleton's place, and at Slobodna's.

Combined-fleet logistics occupied the afternoon session. Tarleton, proposing a tentative plan, put Scalsa's double-track computer readouts to good use. Again Tamirov interpreted.

The point was that taking the whole Earth-Tilaran fleet to Larka and then to Filj, to pick up the contingents from those planets, was the slow way and the hard way. Tarleton had a better idea.

"Once we're ready," he said, "it makes sense to disperse—and assemble later, down-Arm, in striking distance of the major Demu planets. First we iron out the weapons problems, and the organizational stuff. Then, with the planning done and only the hard work left to do, we can start setting schedules.

"At that point, one of our squadrons—I had yours in mind, Slowboat—can accompany Larka-Te ships to Larka, and help there in any way that is needed. Such as design modifications of Larkan ships to carry the laser, and so forth.

"At the same time, your squadron, Tamirov, can be doing the same drill with the Filjar. Cummings, your group stays here and comes to rendezvous with the Tilari ships. All right so far?" There were no complaints.

"Meanwhile, as soon as Squadron One is rigged with as many new—to us—weapons systems as it can use, it takes a high-grav trip to Larka and to Filj. Mostly just to say hello and confirm schedules. By then, some will already be heading for rendezvous. On that, we're still working out the timing."

Vertan rose. "And have all heard and understood choice of meeting point?"

Barton caught a nudge in the ribs. "This is your baby," Tarleton muttered. "You explain it."

Barton stood. "Flash the map, will you, Tam?" On the wall, distorted only slightly by the curvature, appeared a section of the galactic Arm. Tilari, Larka-Te, Filjar, and Demu areas glowed in different colors. Barton walked closer to the wall, and pointed to a blinking spot of light, near a patch of deep black.

"Here's rendezvous," he said. "Just short of Demu territory, and hidden from their guard planets by this dust cloud." He spoke through Tamirov; his reasonably fluent Tilaran was not, he felt, up to precise technical description. "We hope to synchronize well enough to meet and barge out all together before they spot us—and close enough that, from then on, acceleration differences won't be much of a problem.

"We want to converge on their major world, Demmon, before they have any chance to gather and meet us. If we can take that planet as hostage, we figure they won't dare force a fight—they'll have to talk instead, and that's what we're after." Well, the hostage principle had got him free from the Demu. There were worse means —especially if the bluff worked.

"At least, that's the plan, unless someone comes up with something better." He paused. "Questions?" There were several, but none he couldn't answer.

197

Slobodna took charge again; the discussion concerned ways of installing Earth's "big-daddy laser" in ships not designed to leave the central axis vacant for it. The problem was not simple. Slobodna suggested parallel-tube construction outside the main hull. A Tilaran expert countered with the proposal of a folded-path generator to be mounted at front-center of each ship. People brought out calculating machines, textbooks, and charts—and the argument was on. Barton decided they were doing fine without him, and relaxed.

Corval approached and sat beside him. "You Earthani decide what is to be done."

Barton remembered not to smile. "Not of our need, Corval. We say what *may* be done. Perhaps someone—you, Vertan—says a better thing. We speak together—it is the better thing, all agreed, that we do."

"I am not of complaint," said the Larka-Te. "It is good that one says, this we will do. It is good that another says, it can be better, and is heard. When I say that you decide, I say it as a needed thing you do, that is of good."

Not a gripe, then, but a compliment—Barton kept his sigh of relief *sotto voce*. "It is of good that Larka-Te and Earthani have minds together." As Corval rose and moved away, his nonsmile gave Barton a warm feeling.

But, Filjar supermud or no, Barton was pooped. He sat silently, half-listening, until Tarleton approached him. "I think we're about wound up. Ready to go?"

"You never spoke a truer word."

Hands shaken to completion, the two escaped. Outside in the ground car, the young Tilaran woman waited. Barton hoped she hadn't waited all day, then decided that Limila's people would not so waste an individual. Maybe, he thought, he'd spent too much time in the Army. Or in the Demu cage. . . .

As they approached the ship, Tarleton spoke. "What do you think?"

Barton wasn't sure what he thought, because he wasn't sure what Tarleton meant. He turned to look at the bigger man, and saw in his face only expectancy.

Then he knew. "I think," he said, "I like the new neighbors."

It was close to dinner time, but Barton didn't go into the ship. He let Tarleton off there and asked to be taken to Limila, at the Tilaran "surgical place." Despite his sketchy description the woman nodded, and drove toward the far end of the spaceport. Soon they were off the bare field, moving among trees and buildings.

There was little traffic—only a few other cars—and Barton realized he knew practically nothing about the Tilaran economy or way of life. This was the rush hour?

There were no streets. Buildings were placed seemingly at random, interspersed with trees and shrubbery. In the open spaces the ground cover looked a little like moss and a little less like grass; its greenness was quite Earthlike. The car's soft, bulky tires left no marks.

The building, when they reached it, didn't look, to Barton, much like a hospital. It was not large—about the size of a two-story, ten-room house—and was irregularly convex with, here and there, dished concave sections. Some of the latter were tinted windows; others were opaque. The Tilaran flair for shading colors was evident. A broken corner near the entrance showed Barton that the color—at that point a pale blue-green—was not any kind of paint; it went solidly through the material. His artist's curiosity was roused—he decided to ask later about the techniques. Meanwhile, his interest lay inside.

He arranged for the driver to leave him and return later, after she had eaten. The time period, if Barton's grasp of Tilaran chronometry were at all accurate, was about an hour.

He left the car and entered the building. He found no registration desk or information counter—in what appeared to be a combined bedroom and living room, a male Tilaran sat, reading. As Barton entered, the man looked up but said nothing.

"I would meet with the woman Limila," said Barton. "She is here?"

The Tilaran nodded, stood, and led the way along a curved, narrow corridor. They passed three doors. At the fourth he stopped, nodded again, turned, and went back the way they had come.

Barton knocked on the door. The material was somewhat elastic; his knock made hardly any sound. He lifted the handle and opened the door. The room was much like the first one he'd seen. And Limila, sitting in profile to him, was also reading.

For a moment, making no move to draw her attention, he looked. The long wig, tumbled loose over the shoulders of a turquoise robe, hid part of her face—but the lines of brow and nose, of cheekbone and mouth, caught at him.

"Limila. . . ."

"Barton!" Tossing the hair back with a quick move of her head, she rose. He moved to embrace her, but she put a palm against his chest. "Hold me, yes—but greatly gentle." All right—he could do that, and did.

When they had kissed long enough, he asked, "What's the matter?"

"I show." She opened the robe. Low on her ribcage, where once her wide-set breasts had been, were two palm-sized bandages. Barton's eyebrows asked his wordless question.

"It is cut to explore—to see what is there yet, of use to restore what the Demu took. As well as may be done." She smiled. "Not a bad hurt, this, except when touched, pressed."

"That's good." Barton recalled that the Tilari had not developed anesthesia. "But there is a drug," Limila had told him—"pain turns to ecstasy." When the drug wore off, though, he supposed the situation would be a little rough.

"What—uh, what was found?"

"I am not yet told. Tomorrow I will learn. But, Barton . . ." Her expression became intense.

"Yes? What is it?"

"Teeth, Barton. Is it important to you, that sometimes I have Earth teeth?"

"I don't get it. What—?"

"There is a way now, a new way, that teeth might again grow of me." As she described what she had been told, Barton recognized it. ". . . From another, a dead child, perhaps—that part from which grows a tooth, implanted. . . ." Dentists on Earth had transplanted toothbuds before Barton was born. He didn't know why the practice had never become widely spread—whether there were bugs in the process or if it was merely too expensive.

"And so I would have Tilaran teeth, in size and number. Would that disturb you?"

He almost laughed—then he realized she was serious. "Good Lord, *no!* Hell, get sixty, if you want." She hesitated, then smiled.

"For a time, while they grow, I will be with none."

True; dentures over sprouting tooth-buds would be not only painful but unusable. She shrugged. "But, so it was before."

Barton thought of another problem. Demu cosmetic surgery included shortening tongues to Demu standards —in speech, the sounds "s" and "z" became "sh" and "zh." Limila's denture had a transverse ridge the shortened tongue could reach, for better pronunciation. But when he asked, she had the answer.

"I thought to inquire. It is all right; surgery can provide."

Careful to avoid the bandaged areas, Barton hugged her. "Anything—*anything* that helps you feel more like yourself—well, don't worry about me. Just go ahead. Okay?" He wished she would not go to such lengths to defer to him, but he knew why she did it. He had taken her from the Demu, and on Earth—when it was alien to her, and she to other eyes only a mutilated monstrosity —he had been her one anchor of stability. But Barton didn't want to be her lord-and-master. "Most needful person" suited him a lot better. . . .

They talked further; he brought her up to date on the latest conference results. Then they kissed again, and he left. As he passed, the male Tilaran looked up and nodded.

Outside, car and driver waited as agreed. The end of twilight was near; the clear air bore pleasant, unfamiliar fragrances. Barton enjoyed the ride, and at the ship, bade the woman a cheerful good night.

It had been a long day. Although he knew there was much he and Tarleton could discuss profitably, he had a quick snack, retired to Compartment Two, and went to bed early, for a change.

For the next two days he did not see Limila—he was told that she was not to be disturbed, and that was that. Knowing his own tendency to stubbornness, Barton surprised himself by accepting the restriction without protest.

Work kept him busy. The job of fitting new weapons into the nose sections of the Earth ships turned into a real jigsaw puzzle. Many drawings and scale mockups were tried and discarded before the first sample installation began. It worked, largely because Corval, the Larka-Te, had a genius for spatial configurations and an unorthodox way of tackling them. Barton's admiration grew; he could appreciate the results but could not follow the process by which Corval reached them.

As soon as the prototype was complete, Tarleton put it to use in training his weapons personnel on their new equipment.

Fitting the alien ships with lasers was more difficult. The Tilaran folded-path model could not handle the power required; effective range would be less than half that of the Earth version. Slobodna's outside-tube idea, though unwieldy, was adopted—except by Corval. On his own ship, the Larka-Te removed everything forward of the drive unit, along the central axis, relocating the uprooted items helter-skelter. To Barton, the result looked like Riot Night in the gasworks—but it worked.

The next time Barton saw Slobodna, he asked him about the hand weapons. ". . . And any luck on the personal Shields?"

"The hand lasers and sleep-guns look good; Vertan's ready to start production. The Shields—well, they *work* fine, but the generator is too heavy to carry in combat. We're trying a new approach, and, at the least, we can rig the present model on motorized carts, to cover men in small groups."

Barton frowned, then nodded. "Yeh, that's an idea. Well, stay with it, huh, Slowboat?"

"Right. Hey, you know that one each Larka-Te and Filjar ship headed home this morning, to start things moving from that end?"

Barton had heard; he nodded. Moving on to his next job, he found himself wondering at everyone's calm assurance that Larka-Te and Filjar fleets could and would be organized on such short notice. But then, he reflected, Earth had reacted in a hurry when he alone brought a Demu ship and news of the threat. And these races had known the Demu longer than Earth had . . . .

Inside the conference building, Barton poured himself a mug of *klieta* and leafed through the latest planning sheets. Integration was setting in, he saw—Corval would leave his own redesigned ship to ride with Slobodna when Squadron Two lifted for Larka; Kimchuk would accompany Tamirov to Filj.

Logically, he supposed, Vertan would have joined Tarleton on Ship One—but the presence of the two Demu left no vacant quarters, and Barton himself would have complained to high Heaven at the prospect of losing a trained crew member. So, instead, Vertan would join Estelle Cummings in the lead ship of Squadron Four. Well, Barton told himself, nothing ever fits *all* the pigeon-holes.

He noted that there would be further interchange of personnel for liaison purposes. The details were still being run through the conference mill. And he had read enough, for that day.

On Ship One, sitting at dinner with Tarleton, he realized that it had been two days since he had seen Limila. All the days were long days now; Barton felt his age as he hadn't since he was eighteen and discovered the fine art of staying up all night. He said so.

"Well," said Tarleton, "tonight you'd better rest up a little extra. Another party tomorrow night—it's the weekend."

Barton had never figured out the Tilaran "week"—for one thing, it was not of fixed length. The weekend concept was simple enough, though—party time.

"Yeh, wow," he said. "Okay—I'll get braced for it."

"Get braced for more than that."

"Oh? What else?"

"Tomorrow I am allowed to meet the Ormthan."

"The joker in the deck? The strange cat who walks by himself?"

"Yes, all of that. And I've insisted that you meet him with me."

"Thanks—I think. Anything special we're supposed to know?"

"Only that the Ormthu are worthy of respect."

"Yeh. You run into anybody around here, so far, who isn't?"

"No—but I get the distinct impression that this one is something special."

"Okay." Barton grinned. "I'll wipe my feet on the mat and try to remember not to spit on the floor."

"If I didn't know you better, I'd worry. I mean, worry *more*."

"Why worry? The critters are neutral, aren't they?"

"That's what I'm afraid of." Gulping the last of his coffee, the big man rose. "See you tomorrow."

"Sure thing—if they don't call it off." Tired, Barton sat awhile, brooding, before he too called it quits for the day.

He was lonesome in Compartment Two, but eventually he managed to get to sleep.

Next morning, as he and Tarleton were finishing breakfast, Vertan entered. Liese Anajek, escorting him, said, "Another customer. Or did the cook quit?"

Vertan smiled. "I am of thanks, but have eaten."

"Have some coffee, then," said Tarleton, and poured it. "An unexpected pleasure, Vertan. A little last-minute briefing?"

"Of pertinence to the Ormthan, yes. To say again the limits of our knowledge." Tarleton signed for the Tilaran to proceed.

"Half a year ago, as has been said, we first knew such a race to exist. The Ormthan ship appeared—our warning devices did not tell its coming—its landing was of complete surprise. Immediately the one creature, and no other, left the ship. It brought with it several cased belongings, but had no clothing or arms. So we knew not to fear, for it showed trust and thus asked our own."

"It knew your language, right?" said Barton. "So it knew something about you already."

"Yes. It said it had come to make our peoples of acquaintance. Our person of command at that time, a woman of the name Jilaar, gave it welcome. Groundcars were brought to carry it and its cases. When the cars were of a distance from the ship, it lifted and was gone. Again our instruments gave no sign—but by eye its path was seen to be of care to avoid harm to our own craft, in air and above."

"Dumped the baby on your doorstep and vamoosed," said Barton. "And what have you learned from the Ormthan, to now?"

"For the most, that it is of friendship—and, when it knows us of sufficiency, would commerce with us. That it is long agreed that Ormthans and Demu do not meet, for help or harm. That its name—or perhaps title—is Ormthol. That it seeks always to know, and thus asks many questions. But the larger part is what we do *not* know."

"What kind of things?" Barton said. "Remember—I have heard very little of what you say now."

"Of Ormthan numbers or power, we know nothing. Of the place of its home worlds, Ormthol says only that we will know when the knowing is of need. It speaks not of its customs or interests, only of our own. Yet we cannot be of doubt that it is of good intent."

Barton could. He was, he knew, no longer the paranoid who had first escaped the Demu, but doubting the unproven was still one of his strong points. He said nothing, but made a few mental notes.

Finally, realizing that Vertan had no more to say unasked, he said, "Is there anything special, in meeting with the Ormthan, that we should say or do?—or *not* say or do?"

"No more than among ourselves. It acts and speaks in courtesy. One matter of difference, perhaps—be not of offense if you ask and are not given answer."

"And what if we choose not to answer some of *its* questions?"

Vertan looked startled, as if he hadn't thought of that possibility. Barton wondered if Tilara had any pastime that resembled the game of poker.

"We had not considered of doing so," the Tilaran said. He smiled. "The result might be of interest." Tarleton raised an eyebrow; Barton shrugged.

Before leaving the ship, they showed Vertan the progress of weapons installations. He showed keen interest, and said, "Tilara has thanks that such ships as this are of our friends, not of our enemies."

"The friendship of Tilara honors us," said Barton in Tilaran, "as does that of the Larka-Te and Filjar."

"What we do," said Tarleton, "we do together—all of us." Barton noticed that his accent had improved—but still had a long way to go. And as for going, it was now time . . .

The Tilaran woman drove them to a building that surprised Barton—it was the first he had seen on Tilara that utilized straight lines and plane surfaces. A five-sided pyramid, perhaps twenty meters in diameter and ten in height, truncated at a shallow angle, it was all of one color —an iridescent golden brown.

"The structure," said Vertan, "was made by us to the Ormthan's asking. We find it of a strange seeming."

Barton nodded. It wasn't that the building was ugly, he thought—but surrounded by the subtle curves and shadings of Tilaran architecture, it had a decided impact on the neighborhood.

The three left the car, and Vertan led the way through

rows of feathery bushes. At the door, a trapezoidal inset, the Tilaran placed his palm flatly against it. After a moment it slid to one side, and they entered.

The ceiling was low and gray—for seconds, Barton fought his instincts back from the edge of violence as the Demu cage, nearly eight years of it, screamed in his skull. He caught himself—he grabbed his mind by the back of the neck, shook it hard, and made it function.

All right: *one*, it could be coincidence. And *two*, maybe this Ormthan was one tricky son-of-a-bitch—so watch out. Barton took his head out of combat gear—but kept one mental foot on the clutch . . .

He estimated the room—oddly shaped, with area out of proportion to its height—to cover more than half the ground floor of the building. The lighting came from web-like configurations of luminous spots, dotting all surfaces. Except for a few large cushions grouped loosely at its center, the room was bare. Barton walked to the nearest cushion and sat. The others followed him but remained standing.

A little to his right, a rounded pink object formed from its upper surface a head-shaped protrusion—and opened two blue eyes, then a mouth. "Earthani, and Vertan, be welcome."

The hell of it was the thing spoke in English. Accordingly, Barton raised his mental sights.

He waited, but neither Tarleton nor Vertan made answer. All right, then—Barton felt the excitement of challenge—he would play it by ear, his own way.

"Our thanks," he said. "I am Barton, of Earth. You are Ormthol?" The head resembled an impressionistic sculpture—aside from eyes and mouth, only hints, vague contours of other features existed. The effect, Barton decided, was not unpleasant.

"I am Ormthol, here to learn and speak for the Ormthu as you speak and seek to learn for the Earthani. Shall we inquire together, Barton of Earth? What would you know? I shall ask much, for to learning there is no end."

Barton thought—hell, either the blob knew its English or it didn't. "Is Ormthol your personal name or your job description?"

"The question surprises. I had not considered the concept—with us there is a joining, not a difference between the two thoughts. And which thought does Barton serve?"

206

No doubt about it; the alien was quick. "Barton applies to me, not to what I do. I've done a lot of different things. Right now I work for Mister Tarleton here. He's in command of our ships and I run the show when he's busy." It struck him that he had never before called Tarleton "Mister". . . .

"Earth has not previously traveled ships to visit others. What does Earth seek?"

There was only one answer. "The Demu."

"And with the Demu, what does Earth wish?"

"We wish"—oh, the hell with diplomacy!—"an end to raiding, an end to carving people into imitation lobsters. Live and let live."

"Your view is admirable. Likely, the Demu will not share it."

"Ormthol, what do you know of the Demu?" Tarleton was motioning for caution, but Barton shook his head—it was time to shit or get off the pot.

"Much," said the Ormthan, "that would aid you, but that it is long promised we do not say to any. Ask, though —ask and ask, for it may be that you find questions I am permitted to answer."

"I take it you're not really great buddies with the Demu?"

"Long ago our races met, competed, and reached limited accord. A major factor of our agreement is that we do not have contact." The blue eyes closed; the mouth disappeared. The pseudohead became a vague, blind sculpture. The Demu hadn't lost a lot, thought Barton, by agreeing to leave this race alone—they'd play hell trying to carve a pink egg into lobster form.

The Ormthan wasn't helping much, but Barton couldn't afford to let the talk end. If Tarleton had handed him the ball, he'd better run with it. "What *does* your agreement allow? What can you tell us?"

Eyes and mouth reappeared. "Not what you need to know. That matter is sealed—you must learn it, if indeed you do, as did the Ormthu."

"The hard way, you mean."

"You state things aptly. But your askings are less apt."

Rack your stupid brains, Barton—it's your move, nobody else's. Rummaging through his pockets he pulled out a print of a star map, showing the segment of spiral Arm between Earth and the planet-bare space below the Demu. He pointed to the Demu sector.

"Is that accurate? Is that where we must come to terms with the Demu?"

The Ormthan gazed, and extruded a thin tendril; its tip moved on the star map. "I may say as much as this. The major Demu planet is here, as you show it. But *here*"— the tendril moved—"on this planet, was accord reached between Ormthu and Demu. Not elsewhere."

"And you think that's important?" No answer. "All right, you do." He looked more closely at the map. "The planet is in that dust cloud? Hey, Tarleton—that's the cloud we plan to rendezvous at, out of sight of the Demu guard planets!" The big man nodded, but said nothing.

"Not *in* dust cloud—the planet and its sun sit indented in a clear pocket of space, seen only from one view—*so*." A little toward the inside of the Arm, from Tilara, Barton noticed—and directly opposite to the side of the cloud that faced the rest of Demu territory.

"You say that's where we should go, then? Can you say why?"

"Only that something there is to the Demu of great importance. What it is, I do not know entirely and could not say in any case. But one who sees, it is said, cannot fail to know its importance. And you will go as you choose, not as I direct you—for I do not."

"Right. We'll think about it." That dust cloud—the pocket—would be one bad place for the fleet to get caught in a trap, Barton thought. Especially if the Demu saw them coming . . . .

But it was a lead, a start. Another thought: "Do you know what weapons the Demu have, besides their Shield and sleep-gun—and weapons copied from the Tilari and others?"

"On such matters, I am not informed."

Well, so much for that. Barton hitched up his guts— here came the big one. "The blank space—the belt without habitable planets—on the other side of the Demu . . . they say they made it, in war. Did they?"

Without shoulders, the Ormthan managed to shrug. "We do not know. The Demu, know you, were here before us, in this reach of the galaxy. And so also was the dead space.

"It has been thought that if the Demu could do so, we the Ormthu would have suffered it. Yet we live, and thrill of life and learning."

Barton started to answer, but with a pseudoarm the

208

Ormthan waved him to silence. "The Demu are a puzzle we long ago agreed, reluctantly, to leave unsolved. You wish a solution—the Ormthu, who by nature speak as with one mind, share your wish. But whether you reach truce with the Demu, overcome them with your weapons, or cease to exist and your worlds also, I cannot see. What my next-day holds is clear from what my this-day produces. But what your next-days hold, I do not see. Go with the joy of learning."

No booze, no coffee, tea, or dancing-girls—time to split, thought Barton. No way to shake hands without a pseudopod showing, and be-damned if he'd reach first. As he'd thought earlier—the hell with diplomacy. Not that the creature had been unhelpful . . . .

One thing he had to ask. "About the ceiling . . . . "

"You admire it?"

"It is neither high nor colorful. Is there a reason?"

"You came to ask of the Demu. Within bounds, the surroundings were made appropriate." Barton couldn't be sure whether he saw the hint of a smile on the disappearing mouth, but he was sure of one thing—the Ormthan had a sense of humor—and his mind relaxed.

On their way out, he thought of another question, but waited until they were back in the groundcar. Then, "Tarleton—Vertan—all the time we were in there—how come neither of you said one goddamned word?"

Vertan looked blank. Tarleton frowned, then said, "I'm not sure. Every time I felt like speaking up, suddenly I *didn't*. Does that make sense?"

"Maybe," said Barton. "You know—I think that Ormthol is *really* one strange cat." No one answered him.

They arrived at the conference building in time for lunch. Barton greeted Slobodna. "How's it going, Slowboat?"

"Fine as frog fur. The prototype of the lightweight-model personal Shield has a few bugs in it, but we're working on them. For a fact, planning and implementation are getting to be almost routine—I wouldn't have believed it."

"That's because we're dealing with some truly high-grade people," said Tarleton.

"Yeah, I'd noticed. Hey—you and Barton try some of this sticky soup here. It looks like an unhatched rubber boot, but wait 'til you taste it."

Barton had found the mixture of Tilari, Larka-Te, Filjar, and "Earthani" cuisine to be quite an adventure. He had been faced with a few items he couldn't stomach, even under the amused gaze of the person whose favorite dish it was. But for the most part he'd enjoyed the new tastes and textures. And the "sticky soup"—"It tastes as good as it looks bad. I'm having seconds." The taste seemed familiar—but he couldn't place it.

"You enjoy?" It was Kimchuk, the Filjar.

"Truly. It is of Filj?"

"Of Treka, another Filjar world. A ship came this day from Treka. We requested of it the *ouilan* for you and all here to share. We are pleased it is to Earthani taste."

"Very much so, Kimchuk. Our thanks." The Filjar tipped its head to one side in its characteristic gesture, touched Barton's shoulder, and moved away.

Tarleton, who had been talking with Corval, the Larka-Te, approached. "Barton, the whole thing is running on tracks, for now. Why don't you and I skip the afternoon session and go back to the ship? Vertan and Corval agree we're not needed. And we have a couple of things to talk about."

"Okay with me," said Barton. They made their good-byes.

The Tilaran woman brought the car; the ride to the ship was silent. Walking up the ramp, Tarleton said, "My quarters; okay?"

Alene Grover, who shared those quarters, was present when they entered. Because they had been on different watch schedules for most of the trip, Barton was not well acquainted with the sturdy, bushy-haired woman. Now, he paid heed to her.

"Hi, Alene."

She smiled, a slow smile that showed only the tips of large, white teeth. "Hello, Barton." She pushed back the heavy, black hair that had fallen forward across one cheek. "Must be a strategy meet, to get you two back here this time of day. Should I leave?"

Barton grinned. "Not on my account. Ask the boss." He waited while the two embraced, kissed, and disengaged.

"No—it's nothing Top Hush," said Tarleton. "Let's sit down. Anybody want a drink?"

Barton sat. "You think I'll need one?" he said. "Well,

that white-green Tilaran wine makes nice sipping, if you have some chilled. But what's the discussion?"

Tarleton brought out a cold bottle and frosted glasses. "It's not a big thing—merely the party tonight."

"What about it?"

"We're *all* invited."

"Well, what's wrong with . . . ? Oh, yeh; I see. Who's watching the store, right?"

"Too right. I'm certain we could safely leave the ships unguarded, but still . . . ."

"Yeh." Barton thought. "It's not our way, that's all. Instinct, or custom—but we 'Earthani' leave somebody in charge. At all times—no exceptions."

He swallowed wine. "Well, hell—can't we just tell 'em that? The Tilari don't strike me as fanatics; I expect they'll put up with our little foibles. If they even notice—you think they'll take a head count or something?"

"Not really," said Tarleton, "but I wanted your opinion. All right—how far do we follow our custom? Every ship?"

Barton shook his head. "Not necessarily. Hell, they lock from inside, and the locks can be put on remote to the squadron command ships. For real security, if you like, add a ten-way viewscreen hookup."

"Sounds good. You set it up, will you?"

"Sure. But I'll leave it up to each squadron—Slow-boat and Tammy and Cummings—to decide between one-man watch or one per ship. Okay?"

"Yes, that's probably best. We don't want to discourage initiative."

Barton scowled. "Well—in one area we do. This ship."

"I . . ." Tarleton paused. "Spell it out, will you?"

"Well, there's Hishtoo, of course. We can't just leave him locked up, because the hard-shelled morphodite needs a little regular exercise, as well as meals. So somebody has to be here, big enough to handle him if he gets any bright ideas.

"Eeshta certainly doesn't qualify—and even if she did, it would be unfair to strain her loyalties that way, between us and her egg-daddy. So we need one more, here on this ship."

"Any suggestions?" Tarleton topped-up glasses all around; the wine was moving slowly, but obviously with appreciation.

"One guess." Barton's voice came out flat and harsh. "You think I'm turning ap Fenn loose aground?"

"Aren't you being a little hard on that one? He's been behaving himself."

"You're damned right he has. He knows what happens if he doesn't." Barton grimaced; it still hurt, what the man had said to Limila—and hadn't paid for. He made a gesture, pushing with his hand. "All right, I do have a personal thing there. But that's not why I want him kept aboard. I don't trust the sonofabitch out in company, is all."

"That's good enough," said Tarleton. "Tell him he has the duty tonight."

"No—you tell him. From me, he'd be sure it *was* personal—from you, maybe he'll take it as just part of the job."

"As you say. But you set up the rest of it, won't you?"

"Sure—might's well do it right now. See you . . . . "

Tarleton's smile and gesture were vague, as though his thoughts were elsewhere. Alene Grover sat straight, and said, "Barton—we'll see you at the festive brawl tonight?"

"Sure thing." He left—next stop, the control area. His own thoughts, now, were of Eeshta. It was hard on the kid, being cooped up on the ship so much, getting out only for short, accompanied walks. But there was no help for it . . . .

As it happened, when he entered the control room, Eeshta had the comm-watch. "Hi," he said. "Everything okay?"

"It is well, Barton, though today there is little to do."

"We can fix that. How about a squadron-command hookup?" When Eeshta had arranged the connections, he passed along the agreed security instructions and had them read back to him for confirmation. With that task completed and the screen cleared, he had begun to coach Eeshta on putting a call through to Limila—not an easy job through the Earth-Tilaran communications interface—when he was interrupted.

"You really are a grudge-holding bastard, aren't you?" It was Terike ap Fenn. Barton turned and looked at him —yes, the man was riding an adrenaline high, for sure.

Barton paused before answering, then spoke softly. "Yes, maybe I am. But what does that have to do with anything?"

"Everybody else gets off this damned ship, and I don't! Are you trying to tell me that's not deliberate?"

"I'm not trying to tell you anything—I don't have to. You take orders, mister!"

Ap Fenn's face reddened. "The great god Barton! You know something? I've half a mind to break you in two, right here!"

Thinking it wouldn't be right to give this dumb clown what he was asking for, Barton restrained both his rage and his smile. "Stay with the other half, ap Fenn. It's better for your health. And now I think—"

"Don't tell me what you think! I may have to take orders from you, but I don't have to listen to what you *think*. If my uncle were here—"

And that did it. *"Shut up!"* Barton shifted his voice down a few gears. "Get out of here. You've been told what to do. Not by me—by Tarleton. Go do it." He was down to a gravelly monotone. "Now. You hear me? *Now*."

Full of breath, ap Fenn exhaled explosively, wheeled, and made his exit.

So much for that, thought Barton. One more such scene and by God he *would* put ap Fenn in with Hishtoo. If pushed, Tarleton would buy it . . .

Myra Hake and Cheng Ai, the rest of the duty watch, had listened without comment. Now, in a subdued tone, Myra said, "Sometimes he's a little hard to take, isn't he?"

"No," said Barton. "Not hard to take. Hard to leave alone."

He gave up the idea of calling Limila. In his present mood it would do no good for either of them. Instead, he went to his quarters, Compartment Two. It was lonely there.

Leaving the ship for the gala occasion, Barton decided that he still wasn't in one of his better moods. Only one groundcar was at hand. He and Tarleton, Alene Grover, Myra and Cheng boarded it—the rest would have to wait until a second car arrived. The Tilaran driver assured them that one would soon be there.

The ride was short; the destination was new to Barton —a building considerably larger than the site of the earlier party. It would have to be, he thought, to accommodate nearly four hundred from Earth and probably several times as many Tilarans—and others.

Inside, under a high-domed ceiling, artificial clouds of vapor, lit by constantly moving beams of colored light, drifted above the crowd.

"Pretty spectacular," said Alene. Tarleton murmured agreement. Absently, Barton nodded. As they moved through the assemblage, his gaze scanned everyone he passed.

"Looking for someone?" said Tarleton. Barton gave a start, then grinned. Of course he was, though he hadn't realized it—Iivajj. *"So young she is, but of good thought."* Oh, knock it off, Barton told himself—you old tomcat . . . .

They came upon a wine-laden table—one of many—surrounded by a group of Tilarans, with a sprinkling of Larka-Te. It was time for refreshment and discussion. Barton tried to follow the conversation, making polite noises and hoping they were the right ones. His gaze wandered.

He saw a Tilaran woman move close to Cheng Ai. He could not see what happened but he could guess, for Cheng first looked startled, then smiled, and shook his head. Smiling also, she patted his cheek and moved away. Cheng and Myra whispered to each other—her expression was questioning, his was smiling disclaimer. He'd give a pretty, Barton decided, to have heard *that* exchange. When in Rome. . . .

He found himself in a conversational vacuum of his own making, and drifted away from the group—solitary among the hundreds. His glass was full—his attention was diffused and free-floating. When he recognized someone he exchanged greetings, then moved on.

A Tilaran greeted him by name. The man's face seemed familiar, but Barton couldn't place it. "I am of regret," he said, "not to recall your name."

"We are only now of direct acquaintance. I am Tevann —Limila may have said of me."

Tevann—he who had once been Limila's most needful person. No wonder Barton hadn't recognized him; he had seen him only once, a brief glimpse. "Yes, of course," he said, "and that it was good to be with you again. It is of pleasure to know you." On the males, Barton had decided, the Tilaran hairline resembled a beardless Shakespeare rather than Elizabeth I. Like all Tilarans, Tevann was tall and lean. Barton found his air of vitality attractive; he liked the man.

"I would speak of Limila," said Tevann. "You Earthani are of different ways between men and women—our ways may be of disturbance to you?"

Barton shook his head and smiled. "For a time, perhaps. Now I am of understanding for Limila's joy and your sharing of it. She has said you once were her most needful person—for that, I am of respect for you."

In silence, they sipped wine together. Barton had learned that the Tilari did not drink toasts, as such—instead, after an appreciated statement, the listener drank lightly, without comment. The pause was brief.

"Persons may change," said Tevann. "The one most needful may become of less need—and another, in her place, of more. Always, such changes, of agreement between all. But had Limila not been taken by Demu, I am of the thought that Tevann and Limila would not have changed."

Barton braced himself. "Your want is of Limila—to return to you?"

Tevann clasped Barton's wrist gently, then released it. "No, Barton—that is not a thought of what may be. What I say is this—that Limila was of such need to me, and I to her, that it is of good, that you and she are now each so needful of each other."

"I am not yet of understanding—only of willingness to hear."

"She and I were of such closeness that our life was of one house together—a thing of rareness among us. She had a son of me. Then our friend Renade implored that his first child be of Limila, and we were of agreement. Then followed, a daughter, of me. I am of great fondness for the young of Limila, of Renade and me. Even now that they are of full growth and finding persons needful of themselves."

"You speak, though, of Limila." Barton was absorbing the news that Limila was the mother of three—and had never mentioned it. But he was still waiting for the kicker . . . .

"Yes—I would say of Limila. When I knew she was taken, I was of despair. For long and long, I was of no interest for any other, in her place—and when one came to my acquaintance, I was of blankness and could not see."

"Yes," said Barton, "I can understand."

Tevann smiled. "Then, as it will, a time happened that I saw, and knew Uelein, who is not of your acquaintance.

215

And now for long we have been most needful, each to the other."

"I am of joy for you—for you and Uelein. I would be, if I may, of her acquaintance. But—what more of Limila?"

"That when you came here—when Limila came here —again I was of despair. For I had promised Limila of all time, and now I had promised Uelein also. And though —as you are of knowledge—a Tilaran can be many things to another, only one can be most needful."

"Many peoples are of that feeling." Still, Barton waited for the other shoe to drop.

"When, on viewscreen, I saw and heard Limila, I was of shock."

"Yeh—the Enoch Arden bit." Tevann looked a question; Barton shook his head and signed for the other to continue.

"Then when she spoke of you—that you are her most needful person—Barton, my mind was of peace. Then I could be with her—we could be of joy!"

The pause, Barton felt, deserved a little silent wine-sipping—so he did, greatly relieved to know what the problem was. "That you have told me these things, Tevann, is of good. I am of thanks to you."

The Tilaran smiled, touched Barton's hand, and turned away. Barton stood a moment, wondering if he had lost anything in the translation. No—it made sense— and he was pleased to find that Limila's former most-needful person was someone he liked thoroughly.

Again drifting through the crowd, Barton felt detached. He was not drunk; his mind was clear. Limila was right, he thought—no one could handle the impact of too many alien concepts all at once—there was a disorienting effect. Okay, he told himself—simmer down, now . . . .

His glass was empty and he was thirsty. Ahead, in a dim corner, he saw a group gathered around a table. Approaching, he nodded to persons half-seen in the dimness and filled his glass. The wine was cool and tart; he rolled the first sip on his tongue before swallowing.

Turning away, he was met; someone pressed against him. "I ask of pardon," he said, and sought to move.

The person was shorter than he, so not Tilaran surely. "Try English, Barton." He bent to look more closely; thick, springy hair brushed his cheek.

"Alene?" he said. "You get lost, or something?"

"No, Barton." And under his robe, he felt her hand move.

"Hey, now . . ."

"Tilara grows on one, don't you find?" Her voice was soft.

"Yeh—sure. But you and Tarleton . . . ?"

"On the ship, yes. But at a Tilaran party? The customs of the country, Barton—I have *carte blanche*. Do you?"

"I guess so . . . yes—sure. But why me?"

"I want to know you, Barton. When we were first on the ship, before Tarleton and I were together, I told him I wanted to know the man who started all this—and he knew what I meant. He thought about it a minute, as though I'd asked a question, and then said yes, it was all right."

Barton laughed. "You mean, he gave you permission?"

"Not exactly. He was worried it might hurt one of us, and then decided it wouldn't. He was *concerned*, Barton."

"Good of him. But then, he's a good man."

"Yes. You see that little door, over there? Is that a place where we could—?

They went, and they did. And for all her brash exterior, Barton found great sweetness to Alene Grover.

From outside the quiet little room came unquiet sounds. Barton raised his head; for a moment he listened. He kissed Alene fiercely, in lieu of taking longer about it, and got them both robed before opening the door. Outside, the sounds were clearer. No doubt about it, he thought—it's a hassle somewhere. What the hell could be going on? He pointed his senses toward trying to find out, gripping one of Alene's hands to keep her with him.

He pushed through milling groups that seemed, themselves, to have no purpose of action. Ahead, the crowd parted momentarily; he saw Tarleton moving through a large doorway to the left.

"Come on, Alene," he said, and tried to move faster. Then he saw she was hobbling, her feet only half into her shoes. He bent, pulled the shoes off, and handed them to her. "Now come *on!*"

Several Tilarans, doing nothing in particular but blocking Barton's way, were bunched against the door.

He needed both hands, and released Alene's. "Follow as close as you can."

"Yes, Barton, I'll be all right. This doesn't look dangerous."

"Of pardon, of passage, of need to progress! Gangway! Party through! Lady with a baby!" One language was as good as another, as Barton bulled his way through the clutter and reached the door. Inside, he paused to get his bearings.

At the near side of a milling group, Tarleton was arguing with Vertan; he gripped the Tilaran by the shoulders and pushed him away. Turning, he saw Barton, and said, "If he won't help, the hell with him!"

"What's needed?"

"A doctor. It's bad. He—"

"Squawkbox over there, isn't it? Alene! Holler for Max Cummings, will you? And now, Tarleton—what's the goddamn *problem?*"

"Ap Fenn."

"But he's on the ship!"

"He was. He isn't. He's over there bleeding to death."

"Oh, *shit!*" Barton took a deep breath. "All right—what did that silly sonofabitch do *now?* And what's he doing *here?*"

Tarleton gestured toward a corner; a Tilaran woman huddled there, crying. Her heavy, pointed fingernails were smeared with blood.

"*She* did it?" Tarleton nodded, and Barton moved toward her.

"Aren't you going to have a look at ap Fenn?"

Barton turned. "If you think first aid has priority, *you* do it. Two races are more important than any one man." He went to the woman and crouched to speak with her. After a time, she answered. "It was not of purpose," she said, "not of purpose. . . ."

It took a while to get it straight; Barton tried to be patient, and eventually she became more coherent.

"As you know, we touch, of question to be with the other. When the Earthani touched me, the touch was not of my liking, and I answered that I was not of that wish. You must know—"

"Yes," said Barton. "Choice is of both. But then?"

"He was of force to me—of pain. I could not understand—we are not of that way; it is not known to us. And when I knew his intent—"

"You clawed the living hell out of him." He rephrased the remark in Tilaran. "You were of need that he stop. You were of hurt to him, but the hurt was not of your purpose."

"You are of understanding. So it was."

Since no one else volunteered, Barton said the things necessary to take the woman off the hook of the situation. As he rose to rejoin Tarleton, Max Cummings entered, and Barton forgot the woman entirely. He followed the surgeon across the large room and had his first look at what had befallen Terike ap Fenn.

He didn't like it, and didn't look twice. He waited long minutes until Cummings completed his work before he asked any questions.

Cummings looked mild and wispy; he didn't talk that way. "Well, I saved his balls—he may end up sterile, but they'll keep, I think. Anyway, no one deserves to perpetuate his genes if he's stupid enough to try to force a Tilaran woman."

"Or any woman," said Barton.

"There is that. Next—he retains his damaged left eye, but it may not be much use to him. And there are possible internal injuries—a bad bruise under the sternum, perhaps from a kick—without laboratory facilities, I can't be certain." Cummings shrugged. "Unfortunately, that's the best I can do."

"Under the circumstances you're doing just fine. And thanks. Now, if you'll pardon me"—he turned to Tarleton—"what I'm sweating is how the bastard got here in the first place."

Tarleton shook his head. "I don't know."

"You don't *know*? Why the hell not?"

"We can't contact the ship."

"And we're still pooping around, *here*?" In reflex he reached a hand out toward Tarleton, then pulled it back. "I don't believe this—it has to be a bad joke." The hand clenched into a fist. "Let's *move*."

"I've asked for a car. Wait a minute—here comes Vertan."

The Tilaran approached. "I have called. A vehicle will be of your service, shortly."

"Yeh, thanks," said Barton. "And while we're waiting —Vertan, what's this about your refusing to help? Remember, Tarleton?—you said that, when I got here. What happened?"

"When the shouting started," said Tarleton, "Vertan and I went to see what was up. When we saw, I asked him to get help. He refused—that's all."

"The hell you say." Then, "Vertan, why is it you would not be of help to an Earthani in need of that help? Is this how you are of friendship?"

"Barton—were you not told of his act?"

"Yeh—he got rough. I mean, he was of force to the woman. If he lives, there will be punishment. Of your jail, or ours?"

"I do not know of jail. But why must he live?"

Barton considered what he had heard. "Vertan— what is the Tilaran way, with those who violate your laws?"

"We are of reason, of persuasion, that all be of good actions. If a person will not, and all cannot be of safety from that person, the matter is of death. But first there is talk and agreement."

"Your custom is of greater harshness than ours. But of this man's act, where was talk and agreement?"

"The woman said he was of force; she showed the marks. No more was needed—all were of agreement."

"I don't exactly remember being asked for *my* vote."

"You were not of presence." Vertan turned aside as another Tilaran spoke to him, then said, "Your car is now of readiness."

"All right," said Tarleton. "Thank you. Later, Vertan, we will speak of this matter."

The Tilaran inclined his head as the two men left. Tarleton beckoned to Slobodna. "You heard most of that, Slowboat?"

"Enough, I think. I've alerted the ships, as you said. And appointed some folks to pass the word that we leave the party early—and all together. When do you want me to pull the chain?"

"Hmm—stay near a squawkbox, or have someone on it who can find you in a hurry. Barton or I will give you the office, either over the box or by messenger."

"You think we're in a jam?"

"I don't know. Not in danger, I think, but maybe on our own, from here out."

"I hope not," said Slobodna. "I've come to like these folks."

"Me too," said Barton. "But have we come to *know* them?"

"That's the question, all right," Tarleton said. "Well, there's the car—let's go. See you, Slowboat. And stay on top of it. Right?"

"Will do." Slobodna turned back to the group inside, as the other two entered the car.

To Barton, the ride to the ship was interminable. Neither man spoke—what was there to say?

The ship was supposed to be buttoned up. It wasn't— it was wide open, the main ramp down and the airlock door ajar. Barton won the sprint to the ramp. Peripherally, he saw the other man turn aside, into shadows. No matter—he charged into the ship, nerves keyed high in readiness for the unknown.

Empty—all compartments, the lounges, and galley. No need to explore the drive room—its seal was intact. The control room was locked from inside, and his pounding on the door brought no response. He heard a sound of thin crying—but it came from the airlock. On the double, he went there.

Just inside, he met Tarleton, half-supporting, half-carrying Helaise Renzel—it was she who cried, standing crouched, blonde hair plastered wetly across one side of her face. Her mouth gaped squarely, in agony.

Barton spoke first. "Hishtoo has the ship! How the hell can we break into the control room?"

Tarleton shook his head. "Hishtoo has a ship, but not this one. Helaise saw. She's hurt—get Slowboat on the box and have Cummings out here five minutes ago. Tell him who's injured, and how."

Then Barton saw her arm, bent horribly between elbow and wrist, with a sharp end of bone showing through the torn skin.

Above the break, deep, saw-toothed lacerations oozed blood. *Hishtoo—he's paying me back, all right!*

Barton activated the compartment's screen; sooner than he expected, he reached Slobodna's man at the party. *Some party!* He relayed Tarleton's orders and signed off.

On Tarleton's bed Helaise huddled, moaning; beads of sweat rolled down her cheeks and forehead. Like a mother elephant, the big man fussed over her, not daring to touch. But all his concern wasn't helping anything.

All right; Barton knew how to reduce a fracture. He'd learned the trick in the Army, the hard way, and Renzel's frail arm should be easier than an infantryman's muscular leg. The jagged end of bone would carry bacteria into the wound, but that's what antibiotics were for—and he needed this woman in shape to tell her story. Some pain-killer would have helped, but he didn't know where Myra kept the stuff.

So he talked Tarleton into position for helping, and applied traction to the crumpled arm. It straightened; Helaise screamed once, then bit her lip; blood ran. When he thought he had it right, he said to Tarleton, "Can you hold it right there?" At the man's nod, Barton got up and poured a jolt of his boss's best bourbon. Helaise wasn't in shock, near as he could tell, so the stuff should help. And when she sipped it, her color began to come back. As an afterthought he gave Tarleton a taste also, then took one himself before giving Helaise the last of it.

"Now we're bourbon-brothers," he said, "so you can tell us what happened. Like how come you stayed here, and not ap Fenn."

The tale was short but ugly. After his defeat at Barton's hands—or, rather, feet—ap Fenn kept Helaise afraid of him and more afraid to complain. When he saw that everyone who knew he was assigned to ship duty had left in the first car, he made Helaise back his story, to the rest, that she had the duty and he could leave with them. At the party he figured to avoid Barton and anyone else who knew him for AWOL. " . . . and if you did see him, what could you do about it, in public?"

Fear, not loyalty to ap Fenn, had kept Helaise from calling to warn Tarleton and the rest. "And I still fear Terike. What will happen to me when he comes back?"

"Nothing," said Barton. "Because he'll be locked in Compartment Six. Which brings up a point—Hishtoo. What happened there?"

She had taken food to the Demu, and he'd knocked the tray aside and grabbed her. Barton nodded. "Must have known you were the only one of us aboard; that hardshell always knew more English than he let on. Then what?"

"Eeshta tried to help me; he knocked her down. Her mouth ran blood but she got up and ran, crying out, 'I will not let him take the ship to Sisshain!' Hishtoo dropped me and went after her, but she slammed the control room door in his face. He shouted something after her—in Demu, I think."

"So that's who's in there," Tarleton said.

"Who else?" said Barton. "Once you said Hishtoo didn't have this ship—and that's the next job I mentioned, how to get to her. She's hurt, or in shock; that's why she didn't answer your calls."

Barton shook his head. "All right, Helaise. The rest of it?" She'd tried to run but she was half-stunned. Hishtoo caught her, and slammed her forearm against his knee until the bones gave.

"Then he bit me—horribly—and I heard him speak in English."

"Crab salad," Barton muttered.

"How did you know that?" She tried to sit up, and failed.

"Hishtoo has a long memory. I said that to him a couple of times, when the break was on the other arm. *His.* But, anyway. Then what, Helaise? Did Hishtoo have a weapon?"

He hadn't. He'd dragged Renzel out of the ship, across the spaceport. A car passed; to avoid its lights, Hishtoo pushed the woman one way as he fell the other. She could still run, and found hiding in shadows under another ship. "He couldn't find me. I lay there a long time." And eventually she saw the Demu climb the ramp into a Tilaran ship; a few minutes later, that ship lifted. Then she walked, and sometimes crawled, trying to seek her way back. But when Tarleton found her, she didn't recognize where she was.

Barton nodded. "That covers it. And that *blows* it. Hishtoo's off to tell all good Demu that now is the time to put down the upstart animals." He felt his lips stretch over his teeth and knew he wasn't smiling. "Tarleton, we can forget the surprise party. The birthday boy is going to be damned well braced for it."

"We can't sit on this," Barton said. Again he punched for a circuit to the party building, and this time asked for Vertan. Soon, on the screen the Tilaran appeared.

Barton spoke first. "Hishtoo has escaped, taking a ship of the Tilari. He goes, we think, to a place of the name Sisshain. Is its location of your knowledge?"

"No, Barton. Of Demu planets, we know only from the maps you show us. Except for Demmon, their major world, we know not of names. But now—what is to do? And of what mischance did the Demu escape?"

Irritated, Barton shook his head. Post-mortems

223

wouldn't put Hishtoo back in Compartment Six. But maybe he'd better soothe the Tilaran. "It was ap Fenn—the man who was of force to the woman. He put his duty here on a woman, who was not of strength to contain Hishtoo. She is injured and of great pain. As for now, Vertan—can you send a ship after Hishtoo? Your pilots must be of greater skill than he, in your own ships."

"Of what hour was his departure?"

Barton thought. "The time is not of certainty—only that it preceded discovery of ap Fenn with the woman."

"Then effectively he is beyond detection range, since we know not of his direction. And it was your part to keep the Demu of no harm to us."

The entry-request light blinked—Cummings, probably. Barton let his resentment flare. "If you are only of futility and recrimination, Vertan, the matter is not of immediacy. We will speak of it later." He cut the screen.

"A little rough, weren't you?" Tarleton's voice was edged. "Are you trying to cancel the alliance?"

"Oh, bullshit! I'm tired of people bitching from the cheap seats. First, Vertan wouldn't help with ap Fenn—now all he can say is that Hishtoo was *our* problem. Where the hell was his own security, that let Hishtoo get away with his ship?" He shook his head. "Skip it—I think Cummings wants in."

"One thing, first. You're the one, Barton, who said that two races are more important than any one man. Have you changed your mind?"

In midstride, Barton paused. "No—no, I haven't. It's just that I'm beginning to wonder if one of those races is going to pull its weight, after all." Tarleton did not answer.

Barton half-walked, half-ran to the main airlock. Cummings was there, all right, and the doctor wasted no words. "The man is dead. Where's the woman?"

"Follow me. Ap Fenn died, huh? Not much loss, maybe, but it still bugs me that the Tilari wouldn't help."

"They couldn't have saved him. After all—without hospital facilities—and there wasn't time to move him—I didn't quite manage that myself. The things you saw looked bad, but the real damage was internal. Ruptured spleen—internal hemorrhage. The Tilarans don't know our anatomy well enough to have handled that in the emergency situation." Well, maybe not—but Barton was still angry. It was the principle of the thing, he grumbled to nobody.

In Compartment One, Tarleton showed signs of strain. Holding constant tension for any length of time, Barton realized, was a fast way to get tired. "Want me to take over for a while," he asked, "until Dr. Cummings has it under wraps?"

"No. A little longer won't kill me."

"Okay—then I'll get on the control-room problem."

"Try the screen from the galley, Barton. It's usually left on 'Open' from the control end."

"Okay. Hey, fill Slowboat in, will you, when you get a hand free? I got sore there, and forgot. Besides being in a hurry to answer the door."

"Right." With a motion of the head, Tarleton waved him off. As Cummings began inspection of Helaise's arm, Barton left. He decided he could do without the next few minutes in Compartment One, anyway.

In the galley he first poured a cup of coffee. It was old, strong, and rank—it tasted like Barton felt. He flipped the switch that put the control room on the screen. Tarleton's hunch paid off; the screen lit.

Eeshta was there, all right—he could see her, slumped in the copilot's seat—hat off, head down, hands over her earholes—unmoving. But sitting up like that, she couldn't be dead, or unconscious. In shock, he thought—but why, and how?

"Eeshta," he said. "Eeshta—this is Barton. Eeshta, it's Barton. Are you all right?" Dumb question—obviously she wasn't all right. "What's wrong, Eeshta? It's Barton—let me in. Get up and open the door, Eeshta. Whatever's wrong, open the door—let me in to help you. It's all right, Eeshta—nobody blames you for anything. It's all right—let me help you."

Over and over, repeating and varying, Barton pleaded with the young Demu. But except for an occasional flinching movement, Eeshta made no response. Barton kept trying, but he felt he was running out of steam. Finally he paused, silent—and saw Eeshta begin to tremble, a tremor that built until it shook the small form.

"*Whnee?*" Without thought he said it, the first sound Eeshta had ever uttered to him in communication. Shrill and plaintive, he made it. And suddenly the small Demu was on its feet, facing him.

"He cursed my eggs," Eeshta said, one slow syllable after another. *"Hishtoo cursed my eggs!"*

Not immediately, but soon, Eeshta unlocked the door. Disregarding the question of whether his action suited the exoskeletal Demu instincts, Barton gave way to his own and cuddled the small, unhappy creature. Sounds of Demu distress mingled with his "there, there" and "It's all right" and "Okay now—nothing to worry about." Barton began to feel a little foolish, but gradually the kid was calming down.

When Eeshta was quiet, he asked, "Can you tell me about it?"

"Barton—Hishtoo cursed my eggs. My own egg-parent!"

"Well, how did it happen? Mind you—I don't think it really counts."

"It does! I defied him—and all of Demu pride. So he cursed me . . ."

"First, he broke loose—right? And grabbed Helaise?"

"Yes, Barton. He said we take this ship, and Helaise as prisoner, to Sisshain. There we copy your new weapon that we do not have—and wipe you from our sight."

"I see. And then, Eeshta?"

"I find that although I am Demu, I must not let him do what he says. I try to turn Helaise free; Hishtoo with terrible force throws me to a wall. But I am not dead—bleeding, yes, but living. I win to here and lock him away from me. But his curse follows—as the door closes, I hear it.

"Barton, that curse can kill. Why am I not dead? Hearing it, I want to be dead—I belong dead. So why do I still live?"

The idea required careful handling—witch doctors, Barton knew, could kill by the victim's faith in their powers.

"Eeshta," he said, "do you believe all the things that Hishtoo believes?"

"Barton, you know I do not—did I so, there would be no disagreement . . . and no curse. I would be whole, not filled with the death that is soon to come."

"You're missing the point, youngster. Curses—and believe me, I'm an expert on curses—only work between people who believe the same things."

"Can such a thing be true?"

226

"It's a fact. Really—it's been proven, on Earth. Now, you no longer believe as Hishtoo does—right?"

"That is right, Barton—yes."

"So Hishtoo, any more, can't put a curse on you and make it work." Barton had a touch of inspiration. "And of course you can't put a curse on Hishtoo, either. You see?—it wouldn't work at all."

After a long silence, Eeshta nodded. "I see, now. Thank you for explaining—I could have died of my own ignorance, could I not?" Her tongue lifted in the Demu smile. "Barton, you are good to me."

"Then, is everything okay now?"

"Almost, I think—though it will take time for me to know fully, what you say. But there is still one thing."

"What is that?"

"I am very hungry."

"Hell, so am I. Let's go!"

In the galley, after washing Eeshta's face, Barton decided to try a little culinary bluffing. Ordinarily he limited his "cooking" to the heating of Frozen Freddies, but he felt like taking a flyer. As a boy, on camping trips, he'd scrambled a few eggs without disaster—the Tilaran soft-shelled variety couldn't be too different . . .

He did not say "eggs" out loud—not to Eeshta—he merely scrambled them, threw in bits of green pepper and a dollop of Worcestershire sauce, and hoped for the best. As they ate, he thought: Barton, actually you are one hell of a good cook. On your better days . . .

"Still hungry, Eeshta?"

"No, Barton. I am satisfied."

"Good. Me, too. A little coffee?—I made a fresh pot."

"I would like that." Barton poured for two. No side-arms—they both drank it black. And now he set out the star map he had brought from the control room.

"Eeshta—can you find Sisshain on this map?"

"What is it, that you would do?"

"I don't know yet. Nothing, maybe. Or if the place is important, try to get there before Hishtoo."

Eeshta shook its head. "How could you? He is so far ahead."

"This ship is faster than the one Hishtoo took. We could do it."

"And kill, then, my egg-parent?"

"I wouldn't think so—no *reason* to, that I can see. Get

227

there before him if we can, yes. But killing isn't what we want. As you know. We want to meet your people before they're prepared to fight, and not *have* to fight them. But Hishtoo, if he gets there first, could warn them—and then there would be war, and killing.

"So—on this map, can you locate Sisshain?"

Eeshta puzzled over the map, drew a finger across it. "I think here, Barton. Far from my early home or from where you were, or from the centers of Demu power. But somehow, in our heritage, important. It may be the world of our beginning."

Eeshta's finger jerked back, away from the map. "I should not tell you—or *all* Demu may curse my eggs!"

Barton sighed. "Eeshta—you have agreed with our purpose—that Demu should not capture other peoples and mutilate them—that such things should be stopped. But they *won't* be stopped, unless you help me. Eeshta, where is Sisshain?"

Tentatively, then firmly, Eeshta's finger touched the map. Barton felt relief—he'd thought he had it right the first time, but it never hurt to make sure! "Good. Thank you, Eeshta."

And it was the hole card—the planet the Ormthan had mentioned. For its sun sat in a pocket of a dust cloud, approachable from only one direction.

"More coffee, Eeshta?" Barton was thinking that he hoped the small Demu wouldn't be hurt by whatever happened. Remembering Eeshta's chant, he added a few hopes for Earth's welfare.

"Barton. What do you do now?"

"I don't know yet. We had our plans—I suppose you've heard them; they were no secret. We hoped we could just turn up and show our muscle and say 'let's talk.' But now that Hishtoo has escaped, I'm afraid that won't work. Probably our best bet is to get to Sisshain ahead of him, if we can.

"There are other problems—ap Fenn is dead, for one thing. And the Tilari . . . well, we'll figure that out later." He stood. "Shall we see how it's going with Helaise?"

In Compartment One the scene looked cozy enough. A slim, plastic dressing covered the broken arm, but Helaise held her drink—by eye, much milder than the one Barton had given her earlier—in her other hand. Her hair was brushed back into relative neatness.

From his big easychair, Tarleton asked, "Is Eeshta all right?"

"She'll do," said Barton. "Here, sit down, Eeshta." He remained standing. "Did you get hold of Slowboat?"

"Yes. He called back."

"What's the scoop there?"

"Everybody's cooled down—apologies and condolences all around. I told him to use his own judgment—no need to break up the party until some of the other contingents begin to leave—but for all our people to be careful with the polites."

"Good enough."

"Yes. Now, how about you, Barton? You have anything new?"

"We know where Sisshain is—where Hishtoo's going. It's the world the Ormthan told of."

Tarleton frowned. "But why would he go there? That's not where the Demu keep most of their muscles. I'd expect him to hit for Demmon or for one of the guard planets, at least."

"I purely don't know, Tarleton. Any ideas, Eeshta?"

"It may be that Sisshain is the place where decisions are made."

Barton nodded. "That figures. Tarleton!—we have to get there first." Over the big man's protest, he said, "Not the whole fleet, but a strike force."

Tarleton's expression changed. "Of course. How many ships?"

"That's your decision. You're strategy; I'm tactics. I'd settle for one Earth ship, as long as I'm on it." He reached to the mini-bar and poured himself a slug of his host's bourbon. "Cheers, Tarleton."

He turned to the woman, resting now but still pale. "You feeling better, Helaise?"

"Lots. Thanks to Max's little needle. And he's leaving me some ampoules, for when it starts hurting again." She sounded a little punchy, Barton thought, but not bad. Now she frowned. "One thing: What about Terike's body? Do they have cemeteries here? Or cremation, or what? I mean—he wasn't the best man I ever knew, but still he should have some of the good things said over him."

"I'm afraid that won't be possible," said Cummings. "Tilara has different customs. The body was taken to be used in agriculture."

"Oh, no!" Her voice broke in a sob. "How *could* they?" Tarleton tried to comfort her, but she cried all the harder.

"Helaise!" said Barton. "*Let* the body help grow turnips, or whatever. You want good things said, we'll say them. Over your memories of the good side of Terike ap Fenn. That's what's important."

"How can *you* say that? You hated him!"

"A little, yes. And for cause. Not to want him dead, though; I don't like that any better than you do. And I still have a bone to pick with the Tilari, that they were willing to let him die without trying to help. That's how I feel, Helaise."

Slowly, she nodded. "All right; I guess you mean it."

Barton rose and moved toward the door. "Just a minute," said Tarleton. "We're not through here."

"Oh? Okay, shoot."

"You're still working for me, I think. While that's true, I don't want you picking any bones with the Tilari. Comments?"

Barton thought it over. "Yeh, comments. You sit back so much, sometimes I forget who's running the show. And that's no complaint; I *like* having a free hand. But if you don't want me taking over too much, it's about *time* you spoke up."

"I'm doing it. Mostly I have no complaints, either; you run a good fleet. But policy's my bag. You stay out of it."

For a moment, surprise at the challenge kept Barton silent. Then, "Right; we each have our own job. All right —outside of regular operations I won't say Word One to Vertan, without your okay."

"Good enough. And when it comes to fleet operations I'm not putting any wraps on you. You understand that, don't you?"

"I'm not with the fleet any more; remember? I'm on the hit force, to Sisshain." Tarleton's brows raised, but he said nothing.

Helaise was dozing; her outburst had drained her energies. "She might as well be in bed," said Max Cummings. Tarleton shrugged, lifted her gently and carried her to Compartment Three.

"I would be with her," said Eeshta. "If she wakes, needing something, I could bring it." The young Demu brought a few things from Six and settled in as night nurse, showing no signs of planning to sleep immediately. Cummings said good night and left the ship.

"All right," said Tarleton then. "Let's talk strike force. When do you want to leave?"

No arguments? Good enough. "About three hours ago. No—a couple of days, to get the hardware together. And I need to see Limila first. . . ."

"Sure. The hardware, I'll expedite. You think about the makeup of your strike team; we can settle it tomorrow. Right now, I want a look at that map." They took the map into the control room, where Barton spread it across the operations desk.

He pointed out Tilara, the major Demu worlds and their guard planets, and the dust cloud, with the pocket facing away from Demu space. Deep in the pocket, one star held lone sway. Tarleton put a finger to it. "That's the one the Ormthan mentioned?"

"Good memory. As I recall, it was a single mention."

"When that one talked, I listened." Then Tarleton proposed that instead of going straight for the cloud, Barton should first get that obstacle between him and the Demu guard worlds. Less risk of detection that way, he said. Of course the detour would add to Hishtoo's lead, but as Barton said, Hishtoo was limited to light-speed communications just like everybody else, and would have no chance to alert any other Demu worlds. While it would be best to catch Hishtoo in space, the real need was to prevent any ship leaving to take word *from* Sisshain. "Assuming he does go there," Tarleton added. "And if he gets there first, what's your plan?"

"Depends on what we find. Maybe sit down and look around—or hang loose upstairs and hold the line until the fleet arrives."

"Sounds reasonable." Tarleton yawned. "Barton, I've about had it for tonight. Excuse me?"

"Sure. See you." But before Barton could leave, the entrance alarm blinked and sounded.

"Must be the troops coming in," said Barton. "I'll get it."

Tarleton sighed. "I'd better stay and hear if there's any news. In the galley?"

"Right." Barton walked to the main airlock. Awaiting entrance was no crew member, but Vertan. Barton spoke his name, nothing more.

"Barton. I may enter?" Barton waved him in, and led the way to the galley. "I am of regret," the Tilaran said, "for the hurt to our friendship. Of the man ap Fenn, that you and we were of ignorance to the ways of the other. Cummings has told me that our help would not have been of use. But had I known how you feel of such matters, I would have been of willingness.

"Of the Demu's escape—I was, in speaking, of shock and surprise, and am now of apology. Part of the fault is of ourselves, that the Demu could take our ship. Shall we both be of forgiveness, Barton?"

Hell—his promise to Tarleton surely didn't cover the acceptance of olive branches! "Be it so, Vertan. And again of friendship." Pausing at the galley's open door, they shook hands.

"Be of welcome, Vertan," said Tarleton. Then in English, "I gather we're all buddies again?" Barton nodded. "Coffee, perhaps?"

"It is of pleasure," said Vertan. "Is not 'buddies' of friendship? I am now, from study, of some skill in your language. Shall we speak in it?"

"If you like." Tarleton did so. "I'm still not too good in yours, I admit. And what is your thought here, tonight?"

"First was to repair friendship. I think—I hope—that is done. Then, to exchange facts and discuss the plans— the changes of plan—we must put before the group to-morrow. You have thought on this already, perhaps?"

"Yes," said Tarleton. "We know where Hishtoo is going. Barton will take a small force and try to get there first. The fleet will follow as soon as possible. Barton?"

The latter had stood. "Go ahead with the fill-in," he said. "I'll get the map. And I have a few questions my-self."

A few minutes later the three were tracing routes and estimating time-distance factors. "It is not a certainty," said Vertan, "that you can overtake Hishtoo. With two or three days' lead, a very good pilot and navigator could negate your advantage in acceleration, between here and Sisshain. Do you know whether Hishtoo is so skilled?"

"He's traveled plenty," said Barton, "and in charge of a ship, at that—it was his raider that picked me up on Earth. But whether he was the brains or just the brass, I don't know." He paused. "I just thought of something.

232

Your ships' controls work a lot different from ours, or from the Demu's—and that could hamper Hishtoo."

"But the Demu have captured Tilari ships, in the past," said Tarleton. "I wonder what the chances are, that he might be familiar with your control systems . . . ."

"We had best," the Tilaran said, "assume the most dangerous possibility."

"Right," said Barton. "And there's where I have questions."

He didn't like the answers. Hishtoo's ship carried a laser, installation complete except for the power leads—and a full set of instruction manuals. Barton had seen those manuals; they were good, very graphic. Hishtoo wouldn't have any language problem.

"Well, gentlemen," he said, "that puts knobs on it. Hishtoo *has* to be stopped on Sisshain—if not sooner."

He asked further. Vertan could supply the stolen ship's drive-wake patterns, for detection and identification in space, but not until the next day; that particular computer file was not attended at night. All right; Barton asked about Hishtoo's fuel supply, and other weapons the Demu might have, both ship's and personal. None from Ship One, he knew; in port, handguns stayed locked up. "And I assume your ship was empty."

Briefly, before he answered, the Tilaran's face twisted; Barton wondered at the look of it, for the news wasn't all that bad. Hishtoo had enough fuel to reach Sisshain *or* another Demu world—Demmon, say—but not to go first to one and then another. He probably had two ion-beam handguns, but in space, what good were they?

The ship's nose carried one large ion-beam projector, a plasma gun that had been intermittently malfunctioning, so maybe it was working and maybe not, and only one of the two high-drive torpedoes it would normally carry; the other had been used in testing and not yet replaced.

"We did get a few breaks, then," said Barton. "Anything else?"

"Yes," said Vertan. "The part I do not like to say— or think about. The ship Hishtoo took—it was not empty."

"You mean he killed some of your people?"

"Or worse, that he did not." Face contorted, Vertan shook his head. "Two were on board. In charge, a man named Gerain. And visiting him, his most needful person. Her name is Iivajj—a person well loved by those who know her."

Iivajj! *"So young she is, but of good thought."*

"I know her," Barton said. "Damn it all! Hishtoo does *learn."*

"What do you mean?" Tarleton spoke. "What's wrong? I mean, I know it's bad, but what—?"

Barton felt old. "The hostage principle, is what. Same as when I used Eeshta against Hishtoo, to bluff my way onto the Demu ship I took to Earth. If I catch up to Hishtoo, he breaks Iivajj's arm, gets on the screen to me and says 'crab salad.' The only difference is, Hishtoo won't be bluffing. You saw what he did to Helaise."

"Then he has achieved immunity?" Vertan.

"You mean we're stymied?" Tarleton.

"Hell, no." Barton shook his head. "But it's hard. And I'll be breaking my promise to Eeshta, too."

"You lost me, Barton. Maybe you can spell it out?"

"What Hishtoo doesn't realize, the big hard-shelled copycat, is that the stakes are too big now. With me it was Eeshta's life against letting me board the Demu ship. I was stretched all out of shape and Hishtoo had a gun; not a bad bet, in his view. And even if I got on the ship, what could I do with it? Where he missed was, you cage a man like an animal long enough, what comes out *is* an animal. When he pulled the gun, he learned that."

"I follow you," said Tarleton. "But what about now?"

"Like I said; he's made the stakes too big, especially now that he's got a laser. *No* two people's lives—" Barton's teeth gritted. "He won't eat anybody alive—but I'll have to gun the ship. If I can." He shuddered. "That's where Eeshta comes in. When she fingered Sisshain for me, the idea was that I had no intention of killing Hishtoo."

"Will you tell her?"

"I *have* to! If we ever make talk-contact with the Demu, Eeshta's the key to all of it. With somebody in that spot, you don't fake. Besides, on straight merit, the kid deserves the truth."

"And if she turns against us?" said Vertan.

"If we have to do things without her, the hard way, better we know it now."

"What you must do, Barton, is very hard," Vertan said. "Bad enough, for me, will be the telling that Gerain and Iivajj are as dead. At least, can you do so, dead swiftly and without pain."

The Tilaran stood, saying he must leave and declining

234

the offer of a spare compartment for sleeping. "My most needful person waits, and I would not disappoint her." So the two men escorted the Tilaran offship to his groundcar, shook hands, and watched him drive away.

"How'd you make it up so quick?" Tarleton asked.

"He said he was sorry and I believed him. Instant peace pipe."

"Yes? Well, good. For a while there, I was worried."

Barton saw lights approaching. "Two cars, there. The crew?"

"I'm afraid so." Tarleton shrugged. "Not looking forward to reciting the whole situation again, for them."

"Hell, I'll do it, if you want." But Tarleton shooed him away, saying that one of them had to be able to think in the morning, and sloshed full of coffee, the big man couldn't sleep, anyway. So Barton went aboard, and was asleep before any returning footsteps may have sounded outside his door.

He woke refreshed; the load on his mind had settled, some. He dressed and headed for the galley passing the control room he saw Cheng asleep. Well, any of the alarms would wake him, fast.

No one else was up; Barton was stuck with his own cooking. Well, what was wrong with scrambled eggs again, and some toast? Figuring that he wouldn't be alone very long, he made a large pot of coffee and cooked for several.

Heavy-eyed, but looking cheerful, Alene Grover was his first customer. She leaned to hug him; her hair brushed his cheek. "Tarleton's still with the dead. I didn't try to wake him."

"Good job you didn't. He can use the sleep."

"Yes. Any of those eggs have my name on them?"

"Help yourself."

She did, and sat across from him. "Hell about Terike, isn't it? I can't say I liked him—I was his first roommate here, you know, and it wasn't the greatest relationship I've ever had—but he had his good points.

"I guess he was pretty badly out of line with the local girl last night. But I can't see that he deserved to die for it."

"By these people's lights, he did. But in case you hadn't heard, they didn't kill him, even by inaction—it was an internal injury that Cummings couldn't spot until too late. And on the woman's part, it was self-defense. As to ap

235

Fenn, I agree with you. I won't miss him personally, but I didn't want him dead. Tarleton fill you in on all the rest of it?"

"Quite a lot, yes. Oh, those poor Tilarans!"

He wasn't up to this. "Is it all right with you, Alene, if we don't discuss them just now?"

"Yes, Barton." For a time, they ate in silence. "Barton?"

"Yes?"

"Last night, being with you—I liked it. I'm glad we did."

"So am I, Alene."

"Barton, do you suppose . . . ? Can we, sometimes?"

"Not on the ship. Not unless the rules—our customs—change a lot."

Her eyes widened. "And if they did?"

"If they did, agreed by all—hell, yes! Did you need to ask, Alene?"

"Maybe not—but I liked hearing the answer."

"You smile nice, but you have egg on your face. Literally, I mean."

She laughed and used her napkin. "When it comes to romance, Barton, you're in a class by yourself." But as she patted his cheek and left, she was still smiling.

Barton had begun to think he had run out of customers, when Eeshta came in to the galley. Her chitinous face could show no sign of fatigue or refreshment, but she moved well. "Good morning, Barton."

"Morning, Eeshta. You get enough sleep? Breakfast there in the cooker, still hot." He set up more toast.

"Thank you—I am rested, as is Helaise. Is there enough food for us both?"

There was. Eeshta dished up two plates and put them on a tray. Barton distributed the toast when it appeared, and added two cups of coffee. "Can I deliver this, or would Helaise rather be left alone?"

"She would see you, I think. She asked my help in composing her appearance." So he poured one more cup of coffee and they set out, Barton moving carefully to avoid spilling anything.

In Three, Helaise Renzel lay gracefully arranged, propped by pillows, hair shining-smooth, smile relaxed. A slight puffiness around the eyes gave the only sign of inner disquiet. Barton greeted her. She seemed to want to apol-

ogize for something, but he said, "Eat first; talk later."
With her left hand, she managed the fork well enough.
When the food was done, and Eeshta had gone for more
coffee, Barton said, "All right. What's on your mind?"

The gist of it was that Helaise had done everything
wrong, that the whole mess was her fault and no one
else's. Listening, Barton shook his head, and waited his
chance to reply. When it came, he pointed out that it
took everybody in a situation, to make it happen. "You,
me, Terike, the woman he tried to rape, the two Tilarans
who weren't paying enough attention to ship's security—
Hishtoo, even Eeshta. You realize that back in 1982 if
I'd been someplace else instead of where the Demu
grabbed me from, most likely none of us would be here!"
He shook his head. "Assigning blame, Helaise, is the
world's most futile pastime. So drop it."

Mouth working, fingers twisting in her hair, she nodded.
"Yes—it's like bragging, isn't it? '*I* did it.' All right; I
won't, again."

Eeshta returned with the coffee, explaining that she'd
had to wait while a new batch was made. "Fresh is better,
anyway," Barton said. "Thanks." But he'd had enough,
really, and drank only about half the cup before he rose
to leave.

As he stood, Helaise said, "Did you mean it, that all
of us who knew Terike will say the good things about
him, together?" He nodded, and she said, "I'm glad; he
should have that. There was a great deal wrong about
him, but not everything."

Barton shook his head. "There's a great deal wrong
about most of us. Some have better luck coping with it, is
all." He turned to Eeshta. "Could you come with me a
little while?" He wasn't looking forward to his talk with
the small Demu, but might as well get it over with.

Your place or mine, he thought, then led Eeshta to
Cabin Two. As they entered, Limila's absence hit him
afresh. He motioned Eeshta to sit, and sat also.

"Eeshta, I have to tell you something—something bad."

The small person sat straight, primly. "Hishtoo is
dead?"

"No—no—but I told you, remember, that I don't want
to kill him. That is still true. But I said I had no reason to
do so—and that is no longer true."

"What has changed, Barton?"

He told her of the Tilaran prisoners, and how he thought Hishtoo would use them, and why. And what he, Barton, would have to do about it. Eeshta made no protests, indulged no hysterics; her questions were simple and logical. There was something, Barton thought, to be said for the Demu mind—it had definite possibilities.

"The trouble is," he concluded, "that I *can't* give him what he wants. You know that."

"Yes, Barton." Eeshta paused. "I have thought of when we met, and you used me to take the ship. Now that I know more of you, I think you won, over Hishtoo, with a lie. For I do not think you would have killed me—even then, and desperate as you were."

Barton's breath left him with a great shudder. "Yes, Eeshta. You're right."

"But why did you not tell me this before?"

"I didn't think you'd believe me. I thought it would sound like a cop-out."

"I see. Barton, you have the pride of a Demu. That is both good and bad."

"Yeh. Thanks . . . I think. But the problem is, Hishtoo *won't* be bluffing. So no matter what I said before, Eeshta, right now I don't see any way out of killing the lot of them."

"Barton, why do you tell me this?"

"Because if we're going to work together, when we meet your people, we have to be honest with each other. I don't think you ever lie to me, and I mustn't lie to you. Understand?"

"Yes. I believe I do. And it is true, I do not lie. Barton, I hope you need not kill my egg-parent—and I believe your saying, that you have no wish to kill. But as things are, if you must, then you must. And I have no choice but to accept that need."

Barton gave a relieved sigh. "You're all right, you know that?"

"Yes, I am in good health, and not overly troubled. Shall I now see to Helaise?"

"Yes. Good idea." Eeshta left him shaking his head. Would he *ever* stop underestimating that young, alien mind?

In the control room, where Myra Hake had the duty, again Barton had to talk through all that had happened, and what to expect next. He was getting tired of the replays, but could find no way to skip them. Eventually he got the answer he was after, which was that Myra and Cheng would be willing to go with the strike force.

The rehash stirred his own resentments, though, and he aired them: not only had ap Fenn endangered the alliance with the Tilari, he had also enabled Hishtoo's escape, *with* a laser, and blowing any possible advantage of surprise. "If he were here alive, right now, I'd be hard put to keep from breaking his stupid neck for him!"

Myra nodded. "I can see that. But was it all his fault?"

A sudden realization obscured her words—the gut-level knowledge that ap Fenn's insult to Limila had been avenged, forever. Somehow, the thought made Barton feel petty; he shook his head, and said, "That goddamned politician, Terike's uncle. Using Agency pressure to pass an unstable man through the screening test. He—"

It still didn't work. "Assigning blame," he'd told Helaise, "is the world's most futile pastime." And what was *he* doing, now?

"Skip it, Myra. We all do what we think we have to, and sometimes we don't know our ass from third base."

Before she could answer, the screen lit, and Tarleton said, "Barton. Join me in the galley and help wake up my brains?"

"Sure." The screen blanked. "See you, Myra."

Tarleton had the map spread, its corners held down by dishes. Down-Arm from Tilara appeared a new dark nebula—a coffee stain. Barton grinned. "Watch it with the stellar geography."

"Oh? Yes—it doesn't wipe off very well. Here, sit down." Facing the map upside down, Barton sat. Watching his boss pick at the remains of his breakfast, Barton decided it must have started out as a good-sized meal. Tarleton looked up, and said, "Have you thought about what you'll need for the Sisshain mission?"

"Depends. What do we expect to run into, there? How many alternatives can we plan for?" The two men talked it out. If the Demu at Sisshain beat off the strike force, or if Hishtoo changed his mind and went somewhere else, instead—either way, a ship would have to retreat. And report to the combined fleets in transit. "But that means," Barton said, leaning forward, "the strike force can't leave until you set the fleet's schedule. Or else no ship coming from Sisshain could possibly make rendezvous."

Not so, Tarleton claimed. He was updating fleet liftoff, and since pinpoint rendezvous was out of the question, Scalsa was programming for " . . . a space-time corridor, whatever that is. Does it sound workable?"

Barton shifted his mind back, to his studies toward a doctorate in physics. "Sure. Flexible, prearranged parameters. Parallel input to the tin brains on all ships; shouldn't diverge too much, in the length of time we'll be out of contact. Just so you keep schedule."

"We will." Any ships not ready, Tarleton said, would be left behind to form a second contingent, with its own, later rendezvous "corridor." He sipped dregs from his coffee cup. "Now—how many ships do *you* want?"

Barton had thought about that. Now he said, "Three, I make it. One to land, if possible." Tarleton's eyebrows rose. "Well, how else do we find the thing the Ormthan mentioned, the thing of importance?" The big man nodded. "One ship to stand off, the way you said, and stoolie back to the fleet, maybe. And a third, just in case, for the hell of it. Okay?"

Tarleton kept trying to get liquid from his cup; no luck. "All right; which ships, and what personnel?"

Barton grabbed the cup. "If you want to pickle your kidneys some more, let me get you a refill." That done, he sat again. "The other two ships, and their people, just pick me good ones. For myself, I'd like *this* ship; I know its quirks by now, and that could be handy in the clinches. Personnel, though . . . " He wanted people he knew, but obviously he couldn't swipe all of Tarleton's top hands. Scalsa, for instance—the fleet needed him worse than Barton did. And Liese Anajek stayed with Scalsa, of course.

Barton started with the obvious. "Eeshta has to come; in a way, this is first contact. I want Cheng and Myra, and they're willing, so there's one pilot and one communicator. I can double in weapons if I have to, and Limila's trained herself in all three jobs. But I suppose we should have one full-time weapons man with no other job on his mind."

"Or hers. How about Helaise? Her arm won't be a problem long." While Barton tried to decide why he didn't like the idea, Tarleton said, "Aren't you running awfully shorthanded?"

"No. It's my ship that lands, if any do, and on the ground, numbers won't count. Not the difference between six, and ten or twelve." About Renzel, he made up his mind. "I'll talk to Helaise; if she's willing, find me one more good hand to equalize the watch loads, and we're in."

Tarleton's cup was empty again; he looked at it as though he had caught it cheating at cards. "A pilot who can shoot, that would be?"

"Right. Now, then—two things I want, if there's time for them." First was a "side gun"; Corval had suggested putting a gyromagnetic valve between the exciter and the laser's delivery system, and running an auxiliary system ". . . to exit between the main airlock and the viewscreen above it. Side-shot capability, with traverse. On my ship, anyway. Can you do it in time?"

"Shouldn't be a problem; we have plenty of spares. But your tube has to go right through the middle of Compartment Three."

"With a short crew, who cares? Now I've got one for Vertan. Originally, if we landed on Sisshain it would be for an official confab, after convincing the Demu that it was best to talk. Now it's a whole new ball game—maybe a sneaky one."

"Barton, you drive someone crazy! What's your point?"

"Remember how I got out of the Demu research station?"

"Masquerading as a Demu, you mean?"

Barton nodded. "That's the ticket. And it might come in handy on Sisshain—but I don't especially want to carve up a Demu to get the mask. So maybe the Tilaran plastics industry could whomp us up a few, and some four-digit gloves." He held up one hand, little finger and ring finger together. "And footgear. Eeshta can model for them. We'll need robes and hoods, too—and this has to be one fast job of work."

"I'll call Vertan before I head for the conference building. As soon as we're done here."

"Far as I'm concerned," said Barton, "that's right now."

"Good enough. What are you going to do next?"

"Go see Limila."

It wasn't that simple. Myra put his call through, but Limila was elsewhere, undergoing treatment; late in the afternoon, Barton could see her. Barton had no luck getting further information from the Tilaran woman at the other end. She might, he felt, have been trained in any Earth hospital he knew.

Well, should he hit the conference scene with Tarleton? No—first, talk with Helaise. In Three, he found Eeshta starting to take the invalid's lunch tray back to the galley. The young Demu paused, and said to him, "I have thought more on what you said of Hishtoo and his curse. Peace grows in my mind."

"Good for you. Any time you want to talk some more, so do I." Eeshta left; he turned to Helaise. "If you feel as good as you look, I may have a job for you. I'm taking three ships after Hishtoo, hotfoot. You want to be my chief gun girl?" He saw her hesitating. "On my ship the roster is Cheng, Myra, Limila, Eeshta, you if you agree, me, and some fella Tarleton picks out of the records."

She counted fingers. "Rather a short crew, isn't it?" He repeated what he'd told Tarleton, and she said, "Then why the new man? Oh, I see!" She laughed. "Company for poor little Helaise." Barton spluttered, and she said, "Well, whoever he is, he won't have a very hard act to follow. And I can't say I was looking forward to being a fifth wheel around here." Eeshta returned; she opened a beer for Barton and put a few in the cool-box. Helaise sighed. "I'd thought of transferring to a ship with imbalance between men and women, with sharing rather than pairing."

"Is that what you want, then?"

Before she could answer, Eeshta spoke. "I do not understand. So much concern as to who is with whom—and all the time. With the Demu it is not thus. There is a season, and beforehand it is agreed which twos shall be formed. The time comes, and it is done and over, until the cycle returns and the eggs again ripen."

"Different peoples, different ways," said Barton. And I'll bet, he thought, that there's no such thing as a Demu soap opera! "It's no wonder you don't understand us, Eeshta. To tell the truth, sometimes we don't understand ourselves all that well." He turned back to Renzel. "You still have a job offer, Helaise."

"Can I think it over? See whether Max thinks I'll be fit enough in time, and then let you know?"

"By tomorrow?" She nodded. "Sure; fine. Well, I'd better get moving. No rest for the wicked. See you, Helaise—Eeshta."

He went looking for Tarleton, didn't find him in the control room or galley, so went to Compartment One. Alene Grover answered his knock and question. "He's gone to the conference. Said for you to come along if you got bored, but no need. Care to come in and sit a spell, Barton?"

We're on the ship, he told himself—we shouldn't. But he went in, anyway, and sat and talked for a while, making no advances at all. He wasn't sure whether he was relieved or disappointed when Grover made none, either, but after a time he excused himself and went to Cabin Two. He was lying down, half dozing, when Tarleton paged him from the galley.

The boss was drinking coffee again, this time with Liese Anajek. "That stuff'll kill you," Barton growled, and opened a beer before joining them. "So what's the scoop from today's big confab?"

"About what you'd expect," said Tarleton, "or maybe a little better. The hand weapons—you'll have them. The personal Shields—well, it's *hoped* they'll be ready— enough for strike-force personnel, anyway—day after tomorrow when you lift. If not—do you wait, or go without them?"

"It's up to me?" Tarleton nodded. "We go without them."

"Yes. I couldn't make that an order—but I didn't figure I'd have to."

"What else?" Barton felt his guts grinding into action gear. *By God, finally it begins!*

"Your Demu disguises—no problem. Vertan says they have a lightweight variable-stiffness plastic that's perfect for the job. Eeshta models for them this afternoon; she'll only be needed for an hour or less. You'll have the stuff in time."

"Good. I'll tell Eeshta."

"I already have." Barton blinked. "We've updated the fleet schedule," Tarleton continued. "Scalsa's already feeding route-and-timing data to the Tilarans and our own squadron commanders."

"I won't even *see* Vito until the strike force leaves," Liese said, mock-pouting, "unless I disguise myself as a computer tape." Considering her rounded little form, Barton suppressed the obvious comment.

Instead he asked, "When's the new liftoff?"

"It's a staggered operation. One of Slowboat's ships left today for Larka, and one of Tammy's for Filj, to set it up. Our contingent here leaves ten days after you do."

Barton shook his head. "How the hell do you figure on making rendezvous if Scalsa's still working out the timing?"

"He's got enough of it. We moved the meeting spot up closer. Where's the map?—oh well, it's just up-Arm from the coffee stain.

"The ships that left today have that data—the place, timing, and approach velocities. On rendezvous—which will be a little strung out, I grant you—we can distribute the rest of the trip schedule that he's working on now."

"Yeh," Barton said, "it could work. What's your estimated attendance?"

"You mean, how many make the deadline? Better than eighty percent, we think."

"Murphy's Law says different."

"I allowed for that. The initial estimates were more optimistic, by quite a lot. I took a fudge factor, then doubled it."

Barton grinned. "In that case, I buy it. Your guesstimates were generally good when we were putting our own fleet together. It's just our friends-and-neighbors that had me worried."

Tarleton looked at him, hard. "Are you still carrying a chip—about ap Fenn, or anything?"

Barton shook his head. "No—I don't think so. It's just that—that incident showed me, we don't know as much about these people as we might think."

"I think we know enough. If you don't agree, maybe we'd better ask some questions fast. Any ideas? Or just general misgivings?"

Barton thought about it. "One idea, maybe. Have we ever clarified with everybody what happens after we win? *If* we win?"

"But that's obvious, isn't it?" said Liese Anajek. "The Demu stop raiding."

"Right—as far as it goes," said Barton. "But after ap Fenn, it struck me—maybe our friends have some further ideas. Like revenge. Hell—before I got to know Eeshta, I used to think that way myself. And these people have been victimized for centuries, not just a few years. It might be they won't be satisfied to let it go at a cease-fire."

Tarleton's face showed concern. "I hadn't thought of that—but I will. Barton, tomorrow morning I'll put Vertan on the griddle—in a subtle way, of course—and find out what his thinking is, and that of the Filjar and Larka-Te, about what happens afterward."

Barton laughed.

"What's so funny?" said Liese Anajek.

"You have to see it from where I sit. Here we are, about to tackle the invincible Demu—and worrying about *their* welfare!"

Leaving the galley for the control room, Barton tried again to reach Limila. He encountered, via screen, the same taciturn Tilaran woman. Limila was there, yes. No, she was not available to come to the screen. No, nothing was wrong. Yes, Barton could visit her. Yes, it would be permitted that they dine together. Yes, Limila would be informed.

Barton thanked the woman, thanked Myra for setting up the call, asked her to promote a groundcar for him, and left for Compartment Two to bathe and change. On his way, he stuck his head into the galley.

"Dining out tonight, Tarleton," he said. "Back sometime this evening."

"Oh? Anyone I know?"

"Yeh. Limila."

"Oh—fine—give her our best, won't you?"

"Sure thing." And he was off, Barton was—to get all duded up to go see his best girl. Four days can be a long time.

He drew the same driver; she understood quickly where he wanted to go. At destination, unsure of reaching her duty station via the Tilaran communication system, he asked that she return in approximately two hours.

He entered the building and found the first room empty, so he followed the corridor to its fourth door and knocked. Limila's voice answered, "Be of welcome." He opened the door.

"Barton! It has been so long." Sitting in bed, propped up with pillows, she held out her arms. He didn't keep her waiting.

But, "Careful," she said, as he started to tighten his embrace. "Under the robe, I am connected to things. With tubes, pipes." She smiled then, and held the smile until he noticed that her teeth were now smaller, and more numerous.

245

"Pete's sakes! They've grown Tilaran teeth for you already?"

"Oh, no—these, too, are manufactured. But the part against the gum is made soft, so that I may wear them even while the new teeth grow. Except for a short time, perhaps, I shall not have to eat glop food again."

"And what else—?"

She waved him to silence, and to a chair beside the bed. "No, Barton—tell me first of *your* progress. When does the fleet depart? Do all the problems find solutions?

"And you, Barton—in my absence, have you moped, or sensibly taken consolation with the little Iivajj?"

Stunned, Barton said, "Has no one told you *anything*?"

"Told me what, Barton?" The smile was gone. "No, nothing. Tell me now."

"I don't know where to start—it's bad, most of it. Oh, the work on the fleet itself is going well, but—" He began with the party—ap Fenn's French leave, the attempted rape, and the man's death from it.

"Against her wish?" Limila shook her head. "He is as well dead. But there is more—?"

He told of Hishtoo's escape, and the parts Helaise and Eeshta had played. ". . . And that ship has a laser; we *can't* let the Demu have it, to copy. But that's not the worst." And haltingly, he explained the plight of the Tilaran hostages.

"Oh, no, Barton—not Iivajj! And poor Gerain, too. But what can you do?" So he told her of the strike force and its limited hopes.

"Day after tomorrow, we leave. We had to wait until the new weapons are installed—plus a few other things we need—I'll explain later. With our greater acceleration factor, we still have a good chance to catch Hishtoo before he reaches Sisshain."

"Sisshain?"

"That's where he told Eeshta he was going—and it's the jackpot planet, the one in the dust cloud, that the Ormthan mentioned. But when—if—we do catch him. . . .

"It's bad, Limila—very bad. He won't surrender—not to animals. He'll try to use Iivajj and Gerain for leverage—'crab salad'—remember? And I can't let that happen, or give in, either. I'll have to kill—kill the ship, and all of them. Kill *Iivajj!*"

She took his hand and squeezed it, gently. "Barton.

Don't you think Iivajj—and Gerain—would prefer that? Even if Hishtoo were not to rend their flesh. They have seen the pictures—what was done to me, to Siewen and the Freak. Iivajj is young; to suffer that would break her mind. No, Barton. I know you would save them if you could. But if not, the death is better."

He found he was gripping her hand brutally, and loosed his grasp. "Yes—you're right; I know that. But still . . . ."

"You will do what you can. As always, Barton." Gently, he kissed her.

"Okay," he said. "For now, enough about *my* worries. But"—he gestured toward her robe, where it bulged strangely—"what's all this? About you being hooked up to plumbing. Is something wrong?"

"No—nothing. Oh, I must tell you—all that has happened—I almost forgot. It is the tits, Barton. They are *real!*"

Barton looked askance at the bulges. "*That* big?"

She laughed. "No, that is the machinery. So that my body accepts them." Biochemical jargon wasn't Limila's strong point in English, nor Barton's in any language, so the explanation took a time. But he did gather, immediately, that the new breasts were transplants.

"She was climbing, and fell from a height and did not live. She was young, Barton—very young, so they are quite small. I have asked will they grow to the size of my age; none can say. But I do not care. It matters only that they will be real upon me." Then her face showed sadness. "But even so, Barton, I would not have them if I could choose her to be alive instead."

"I know." Briefly, before asking further, he hugged her.

Barton knew about transplants—how the body's own immune reactions rejected foreign tissue. Unfamiliar enzymes were treated as hostile invaders and repelled. On Earth, the suppression of immune reactions worked as a stopgap method, but seldom permanently.

The Tilarans, if he had it right, removed the offending enzymes from the blood as it returned from the new tissue, so that the defensive mechanism was not alerted. At the same time, Limila's blood was gradually shifting the enzyme balance of the transplants until it would be compatible with her own.

"And soon," she said, "I can be free of the tubes and machines."

"How soon?"

"Five days, they say—maybe six. Why?—Oh—"

"Yes. How much of a job is it to disconnect the plumbing? Because the strike force lifts—*has* to lift—in two days." The muscles of his face twisted his expression into harsh lines. "Will I have to leave you behind?"

She frowned slightly, thinking. "No. I was told, when I asked of what marks would be left on me. At the start, you know, it was thought to put dead matter into me, for appearance only. I said no. Then was proposed the pulling of fat layer and skin, tying it from inside so as to protrude convincingly, but lacking the sensations that once were there. I was ready to agree. But when the girl fell and died, I was offered these of her. And so I asked what it would mean."

"And?" Why, Barton wondered, did he have to love a woman who took so long to get to the goddamn *point?*

"Oh—the tubing, yes. It is not difficult. It is to be pulled, when the time comes, gently and slowly. I am told the pain will not be great. As it leaves me, there will be some blood, but not of danger. The bandaging will be as of small cuts. No, Barton—I am not to have to stay behind."

His sigh of relief was more evident than he would have wished. "That's good. I wouldn't have liked to do that."

"Nor I, Barton. As it is, I have been from you too long."

He looked at her. "Yeh. Well—after you're unhooked from those tubes—"

A sound at the door interrupted them—something between a knock and a scratch. "Be of welcome," Limila said.

A woman entered—the one Barton had met on the screen, who granted information like pulling teeth. He smiled at her; after all, what the hell . . . ?

"It is of time for feeding," she said. "Are both of pleasure to eat here?"

"It is of best convenience," said Limila. The woman brought a wheeled cart, laden with covered dishes, and left with Limila's thanks. Barton realized he'd been hungry for some time.

They seldom talked during meals, and did not now. As he finished, Barton looked at his watch. Unadapted to the longer Tilaran day, it was of little use to him off the ship—except to measure specific intervals, as now. But he noticed that his Tilaran driver was due to return soon.

"Barton—was it a good meal?" He realized he had hardly noticed.

"Good, yes. But I was thinking too much of other things to appreciate it as it deserved."

"Yes—I saw. You do that too much. More than you should."

"I know," he said. "Maybe later, when there's not so damned much to worry about—oh well. Look—when can you come back to the ship?"

"I will ask. Tomorrow, if it may be, would be best."

"It would." He looked at her. "Limila—I wish you were free of all that hardware. Well, it won't be too long . . . . I guess I'd better go outside now. The driver should be back with the car pretty soon."

He bent to kiss her. When he would stop, she held him.

"Barton? As we ate, I, too, thought of other things. And I think that if I were to move so as to lie this way, and you were to—no, more here to the right of me. Shall we see, now . . . ?

"Barton, see the opening in this cover, over where it grows to me? Reach, touch the tip of your finger inside. They say the nerves are to heal together, but I do not— Barton! I feel your touch! Barton, it will be as it was!"

"Barton?" she said, when again it was time for talk. His hand cupped the back of her head; she reached and pulled it in an involuntary caress over her scalp, free of the Tilaran-styled wig that lay to one side. "I could have had that girl's hair, too—or the skin that would grow it. Should I have?"

"Huh?" The caress ceased to be involuntary.

"It was offered. It is in preservation, should we return here and I choose. But I wished to know your feelings, and could not reach you, so I said no, for this time. Was I wrong?"

"Hell, I don't know. But you shouldn't have waited on me, Limila. Do what *you* want to do."

"Perhaps I did." Starting at the bridge of the nose she ran her own fingertips up her forehead and, without pause, over the smoothness of her head. "I would choose your wish, Barton, because I am of two minds. Sometimes, in this matter, I have felt bereft—more so, even, than of breasts. But at other times it is of much enjoyment that I may clean my hair but not have it wet on me for so long, so inconvenient."

Barton laughed. "Well—as long as you're satisfied, for now! We'll be back here, you know." He suppressed the thought that the Demu might have something to say about that. "You can make up your mind then—okay?"

"Yes, Barton. And now I see you look again at your wrist; you must go. Once more kiss?" They did. "If I am not to the ship tomorrow, then my message, saying the reason, will be."

"All right. Good night, Limila."

He went outside; the car was waiting. Somehow, a great load was off his mind—and he hadn't even managed to tell Limila about Alene and himself. Well, he knew she wouldn't get fashed . . .

Riding back to the ship he was more relaxed—mind and body—than he had been for a long time.

She is good for me, he thought—very good for me.

Back at the ship, he found Tarleton in the galley. Had the man ever left it in the past few hours? Barton decided not to ask.

With the big man was a bigger one, a stranger, who rose and introduced himself before Tarleton could do so.

"Mister Barton, I think? I am Abdul Muhammed, perhaps to join your ship. I am trained as a pilot, and in weaponry." The man stood more than two meters tall; Barton estimated that he grossed perhaps 120 kilograms. His handclasp, obviously restrained, was still stronger than most.

"Glad to know you. Barton's all you need, though."

"How is that?" A half-smile showed white teeth against his blue-black skin.

"I mean, you can skip the 'Mister.'"

"Ah, yes—I understand. You do not need titles. I will remember."

"Abdul is the top weapons man in Squadron Three," said Tarleton. "When I asked for him, Tamirov practically sang the 'Volga Boatman' with string accompaniment."

Abdul laughed. "If you are not joking, please let me continue to believe that you are. Tamirov is a fine commander—but I have heard him sing."

I like this guy already, thought Barton. "Hey, sit down, everybody," he said. "I need a beer. Anybody else?" Abdul held up a finger; Tarleton pointed to his perpetual coffee cup. Barton did the honors, and sat with them.

"How's Limila?" Tarleton asked.

"Fine." Barton grinned. "Some new developments—tell you later—but she's okay to go with the strike force."

Abdul spoke. "Limila—she is the Tilaran woman, the former Demu prisoner?"

"Yes," said Barton, "and now my most needful person." Deliberately, he used the Tilaran phrase.

"I see." For a moment the black man was silent. "The Greater Central African Republic saw fit to put only men into space. My own most needful person, as you put it, tends our two children in a pleasant house amid a grove of fruit trees. I hope to meet her there again. But even more, Barton, I hope she is spared what came to your woman. That is why I am here."

Barton made up his mind. "Glad to have you, Abdul—you just signed on." The handshake wasn't so bad, he found, once he was braced for it.

As the three exchanged information, and Barton and his boss confirmed plans, the shank of the evening went fast. Everything was on the money except the personal Shields; their readiness was still up for grabs.

Barton excused himself and went to bed early. Limila's absence did not haunt him now; instead he felt her past and future presence.

Next morning he found Tarleton in the galley ahead of him. "You live here?" Barton asked. "Or do you go home to sleep?"

"Both, maybe. Barton, I've made up my mind—this is your ship, for the strike force. There are only four of us left on here, who aren't going, and the other ships are carrying ten each with two spare bunks. So I'm taking over Ship Two—it's one of several that carry command-type comm-gear—by bumping a couple of its people to other ships. We'll be riding full, in Two."

"Okay—fine. How's my side gun coming?"

"It'll be ready—on all three ships."

"Even better. You picked the other two, then?"

"Yes. One of Slowboat's and one of Estelle's. The commanders will be at the conference today."

"Sounds good." Barton moved to where Eeshta was running a miniature food-production line. "Morning, Eeshta. Got a couple batches of scrambled? I'm hungry. And maybe a little toast and some sausages."

"Of course, Barton. The sausage is not quite prepared, but soon."

251

"Fine," he said. "How's Helaise doing?"

"Her arm heals and its fever lowers. But now her mind fevers, I think—and she will not say what disturbs it. Though I have asked." She filled a plate to his order and handed it to him.

"Okay, thanks—I'll check on it." Back at the table, he relayed the conversation to Tarleton. "Should I follow this up?"

"No; I'll do it. Today is strike-force day at the conference building—it's more your potato than mine. I'll give you my notes from yesterday. Try to remember to write down any important developments—all right?"

"Sure." Barton ate silently. Then, dabbing up the last morsel, he said, "You picked me a good one, in Abdul Muhammed. I'd trust that man to back me up, no matter what."

"My opinion exactly. With his intelligence, I don't understand why he's not commanding a ship, at least."

Barton shrugged. "Politics, probably—it usually is. Look at ap Fenn."

Tarleton said nothing.

"All right," said Barton. "Scrub that—sorry I brought it up. Now, about today's agenda—fill me in a little, will you?"

Tarleton did so, and Barton left for the conference with more in his head and notebook than he expected he could keep straight. But he would try . . . .

Entering the conference building, he was met by Slobodna, accompanied by a short, sandy-haired man. Barton felt he should recognize the latter, but couldn't place him. "Hi, Slowboat."

"Morning, Barton. You remember Kranz?"

"Oh, sure I do, now." Other than Barton, Kranz had been the first man—and Slobodna the second—to fly the captured Demu ship. But that had been months earlier; Barton hadn't seen the man since. "How are you?" They shook hands.

"Just fine, Barton. My ship got the nod to go with you on the strike force. I hope you're not superstitious—it's Ship Thirteen."

Barton laughed. "The only unlucky numbers I know are the ones that lose at roulette—and I don't play roulette."

"Me neither." Kranz looked toward the entrance. "Hey, I think we're about to meet our other sidekicks."

Estelle Cummings approached; a dark, thin man escorted her. "Gentlemen," she said, "I should like to introduce to you, Captain Lombard of Ship Thirty-four. He joins you with my highest recommendation."

They exchanged names and handshakes all around. "Let's stick together pretty much," Barton said, "so we all get the same info and don't have to pass it around later. Okay? I know we won't get too much chance to confab on our own plans, but Tarleton's asked for a skull session this evening on Ship One, if that's agreeable."

It was. Referring to Tarleton's notebook, Barton checked on each ship's current state of preparation. Progress was good; he decided that these people knew how to work fast under pressure. He was almost through the list when the conference was called to order. "Okay—we'll get the rest of it at the first break."

Vertan spoke; he gave a brief status summary and assigned troubleshooters to a few problem areas. Slobodna reported on weapons, including Barton's side gun. "The weapons group can discuss this at the break, and decide how many ships it is feasible to convert." He did not mention the individual Shields; Barton made a note to ask him later.

Scalsa described, as simply as possible, the complex arrangements for rendezvous between the various groups. "Don't bother to write this down," he said. "We're feeding it to each ship's computers; you can get a readout on your own boards." He related the contingency plans—for a later rendezvous of ships that couldn't meet the accelerated deadline, and for the possible meeting with part or all of the strike force returning from Sisshain. The concept of a time-space corridor for rendezvous confused several. Not Corval, though—when Scalsa ran into difficulties explaining it, the Larka-Te took over for him.

Then it was break-time. Vertan joined Barton's group and was introduced all around. "It is good to have you back, Barton." He spoke in English. "Is all well now, with you and your ship?"

"As well as circumstances allow—yes, progress marches. The strike force—I guess that's next on the agenda, but we leave on schedule, late tomorrow. Far as I know, we'll have everything we need—everything we've *thought* of, that is—except maybe the personal Shields. Oh, yeh—how about our Instant Demu kits?"

"Those are to be delivered to your ship this morning."

"Good. That was a fast job, Vertan—thanks."

"They are well executed. The young Demu cooperated well. I . . . I spoke with it, Barton. And behind that bony mask I found a young person that I could easily befriend. I had not expected such a thing."

Barton hid a grin. "Yeh—the kid grows on you, doesn't she?"

"She? But I thought—"

"Oh, sure—they're bisexual—but our language doesn't allow for that very well. And Eeshta being small, I—and most of us, I guess—tend to think of her *as* her."

Vertan nodded. "I can understand. And—it does give hope, the young one's attitude. . . ."

"Yes—but it's the adults we have to worry about. We never made any kind of dent in Hishtoo's hard shell—his mental one, I mean."

"No. But some of our own people, and allies, are as rigid. Many resist Tarleton's saying that the Demu are to be stopped only, and not punished. They consent because they must, but deep in their beings they do not agree."

"Trouble, you think?"

"None, I would hope—but the balance may be fragile."

"I'll tell the boss." A nagging worry surfaced in his mind. "How come we haven't seen Corval or Kimchuk today—or any of their people—to talk with? Are they bugged with us? Offended, I mean?"

Vertan shook his head. "No, Barton. It is that you have had trouble. As is their custom, they leave you to recover from it, and signify your recovery by approaching them."

"Oh? Interesting—and useful to know. But if you see them first, tell them our trouble is past and their company is welcome. All right?"

"I will do so. And now I see my assistant beckoning. Will you permit my departure?" Smiling, Barton nodded.

He turned to Slobodna. "I notice you didn't mention the one-man Shields in your weapons roundup. Will we have them?"

The other man frowned. "I wish I could tell you. The team's working like crazy, but there's an instability in one of the phasing circuits. It didn't show up until we applied heavy stress, testing, and they haven't located it yet because the damned thing is intermittent. You know how *that* is."

"Yeh, I know. So—what do we do?"

"Pray, maybe. Meanwhile we've delivered two of the earlier model, on the self-propelled carts. They're stable, and good for protecting a group in the open. Some of the lightweights haven't shown the flaw yet, but it seems to be unpredictable. If we don't get a solid solution, do you want to take a chance on the ones that haven't failed, or just skip it?"

Barton didn't have to think twice. "Take the chance. One thing—you're testing under maximum sustained attack. If we get into that kind of bind, we're already in big trouble."

"Okay. But we'll keep plugging, right up to the last minute, before we give up and hand you that option."

"Good enough, Slowboat. Oops—looks like I'm being paged."

It was, indeed, Barton's turn at the podium. First, he thanked all for their concern with the Earthani's troubles, and reassured them that he was once again accessible to his friends. Then, unsure of how much Tarleton had told of the strike-force plans, he gave a fast roundup, including contingencies. "And I guess that covers it," he said. "Questions?"

Tamirov interpreted for a Filjar. "Why go we to Sisshain, and not to Demmon where Demu power is massed?"

"Because Hishtoo goes to Sisshain. And because on that planet is something of importance to the Demu—more so than the ships and weapons of the Demmon sector."

And what is this thing? I do not know. How do you know its importance? I was told. By whom? I may not say. Are we, then, to go in ignorance? Yes—as we ourselves go; there is no choice, if we are to go at all.

The emphasis on Barton's final remark ended that line of questioning.

Next, a Tilaran asked why the Demu, if beaten, were not to be punished. Barton inhaled deeply.

"We know of one race, only, that achieved agreement that the Demu do not molest it. That agreement has worked. It did not include punishment. We follow a successful precedent. If we were to try to punish, the result might be not peace, but endless war."

The questioner persisted, but Barton shook his head and would not answer. Finally, he said, "Come with us, or do not. In either case it will be as I have said." As he left the podium, he thought: not exactly my day for tact.

Lunchtime. Barton chose a bowl of *ouilan*, the Trekan "sticky soup," and was surprised that the limited supply of such a delicacy had not been exhausted. With it he took a cup of Tilaran *klieta;* the two flavors blended well.

As before, his group sat alone. But as Barton sipped the last of the *klieta*, Kimchuck approached, a shallow bowl in each furry hand.

"*Dreif*, Barton?" Barton nodded, and smiled his thanks. "Effort of talk shows effect on you. The *dreif* will restore." This time the mud-soup look and taste didn't bother Barton; he took it gladly, and soon felt the characteristic relaxed alertness.

"Thanks, Kimchuk. Say—I don't suppose we could get a little of that to take along? With the strike force, I mean?"

The Filjar tipped its head to one side, and back again. "Would be glad, Barton. But cannot."

"Oh?"

"*Dreif* must be new. In a day it changes and is of harm, not to be eaten. Making *dreif* is secret skill; I do not know. Among Filjar here, only one does."

"I see. Well, thanks anyway, Kimchuk." Too bad, he thought—that's a great little booster shot you've got there. The Filjar clasped Barton's shoulder and left to rejoin its own group.

The conference reconvened, analyzing in detail the morning's results. Barton followed the talk until it began to repeat Tarleton's notes from the previous day, so closely as to make little difference.

It wasn't exactly repetition, he decided. It was dissection of problems down to the level of individual tasks—a level that Tarleton had to leave to others. Barton listened with half an ear and let most of his mind wander. Some of its wanderings were less pleasant than others—Iivajj and Gerain, for instance . . . .

At the next break, Corval came to offer Barton a cup of the Larka-Te beverage that was first tasteless, then all aftertaste. He started to accept, then remembered. "Thanks, Corval, but I'd better not. I had some *dreif* from

Kimchuk, at lunch—and he says the two do not go well together."

"He is right," said Corval. "Very well—it will not be of waste." The Larka-Te was smiling in one mode that Barton had learned to recognize without mistake.

"I see your smile and am of gladness," he said. "Tell me, Corval—of what are we in agreement?"

"Of the Demu, of punishment." The smile changed to one Barton could not interpret. After a moment, Corval put it into words. "Do we punish an animal of predation, even though it kill our young? No. We prevent—if we cannot otherwise, we kill it. Punishment is not of relevance.

"We go to prevent the Demu. It may be some must be killed that the rest agree of prevention. But once agreed, what point of putting hurt to Demu for hurt given *by* Demu?"

Slowly Barton nodded. "I'm glad you agree, Corval. But do you speak for all Larka-Te?"

"For most. And those who are not of agreement will be of obedience."

"That's good to know. I am of thanks, Corval, that you have told me."

The break was over. As the final session began, a Tilaran came to Barton. "Your ship would be of speech to you." Barton followed the man to a viewscreen. It was Tarleton calling.

"If they're down to the small stuff," he said, "why don't you come on back to the ship? Pass the notebook to Slowboat, and remind the strike group that we meet here tonight for a recap. Okay?" Barton nodded; the screen went blank.

He briefed Slobodna and took his leave. Outside, the car waited; obviously, Tarleton had known he'd be ready to return. He greeted the woman driver, got into the car, and sat back to watch the scenery.

The feathery trees were less yellow now; the green of foliage showed, in some cases, a purplish tinge. It came to him that he had no idea of Tilara's seasons—except that he was pretty sure the current one was not winter.

He'd have to remember and ask Limila . . . .

Entering the ship, he saw and heard no one. By habit, he went first to look in the galley.

He froze. *"Hishtoo!"* The robe and hood, the lobster

257

face—figure too large to be Eeshta. But—Hishtoo? The surging adrenaline, buffered by Kimchuk's *dreif,* began to subside.

"All right—what the hell is this?"

The creature's laugh was soft. "Realistic, isn't it, Barton? I *thought* you'd be pleased." The voice was a woman's.

For no reason, Barton was disgusted with himself. He took a beer from the cool-box and sat across the table from the disguised prankster.

"You're right—it's a damned good job. But Halloween's over now; take off your head and let's see who's inside."

The hood was thrown back; the gloves came off. The mask wasn't so easy—"Help me, Barton"—it was like pulling off a rubber boot. Then, there was Helaise Renzel, grinning through the tangled blonde hair that fell to veil her face.

"Well. Nice to see you out and around, Helaise. That first look, though—it just about had me back in diapers. Whose idea?"

"Oh, mine. I modeled it for the others, and then decided to stay in costume and give you a personal preview." Her hands were busy, disentangling her hair, smoothing back the strands as they came loose from the mass.

"Where is everybody?"

"Various places. Everyone seemed to have something to do, or maybe think about—I don't know. So I just stayed here and waited for you."

"Anything wrong?" The cast wasn't hampering her movements, he noticed, and thought: That's good.

"No—no, nothing's wrong." She wasn't looking at him.

"Good." He swallowed the last of his beer, rose, and got another. "Well. Have you decided—has Max Cummings said—whether you're coming with the strike force?"

Head down, fingers working through the last tangles of her hair, she said, "Max cleared me, all right. But I'm not going; I'm staying. Alene will join you instead." With her hair now in fair order, she dropped her hands to her lap and looked up at him.

"Alene? I don't think I get it. Explain?"

The hair was still good for a spectacular toss of the head. "It's simple. I've moved in with Tarleton."

"You've *what?*"

"Moved in with Tarleton. In Compartment One, on

258

Ship One, with *man* Number One. Do you mind, Barton?"

Jesus Christ!—was there no end to the supply of kooks? Sure as hell, he thought, she saw her move as a power play. Well, maybe it was contagious—she'd been with ap Fenn quite a while . . .

"No," he said. "I don't mind—I don't mind at all. It's none of my business, except that I still need a weapons man for the strike force. But one thing I'm curious about."

"Yes?" Her air of disinterest struck Barton as overdone.

"I've worked for Tarleton a long time—a lot longer than you have. He has a lot of good qualities. And I'm wondering—which of these attracted you the most?"

Eyes bright, mouth stretched past smile into grimace, she answered. "He's *big*, Barton! Not just tall—he's Number One! I had to live with Terike—a large man who was small inside. *You* beat the living hell out of him—and I couldn't have you, except once. And then I couldn't even have poor goddamned Terike, because he died."

"Are these the good things you wanted said over his memory?"

"Damn you, Barton!" She almost screamed it. "All right—it *was* a corny idea, wasn't it?" She shook her head, hair swinging. "No, not that, I guess—it's more that whatever good there was to say, I've already said it, when the hurt of his death was fresh and I felt guilty for it. Does that make sense?"

"I guess so. All right—consider the ceremony cancelled. And now what?"

"And now I have Tarleton—Number One. And I'm going to keep him."

How had she managed it? No matter—she had. "Well. My best wishes, Helaise. And keep one thing in mind, will you?"

"What's that?"

"Tarleton *is* Number One. Don't forget it. Treat him that way."

She looked away. "Yes, Barton—I know." Then she met his eyes. "If you want to speak with Alene—about going on the strike force, or anything—she's in my old compartment. It's torn up a lot, installing your spare laser —but she's there."

"Yes. I see. Thanks. Perhaps I'll look in on her a little later." He thought briefly. "Tell Tarleton I'll see him after dinner." If Limila wasn't back yet, Barton was of a mood

259

to eat alone, in Two. He'd had enough company for a while.

In Two, no Limila—Barton bathed and changed, found himself hungry. Back at the galley he found Helaise gone; Cheng Ai was loading a tray with two thaw-and-heat dinners to carry out.

Cheng smiled at him. "It's not very good, but it's quick."

"Yeh, I know. I'm probably having the same." He wanted to say something to Cheng—but what? "Hey. You and Myra ready to plunge with the strike force tomorrow?"

The man nodded. "Oh, yes. We would come in any case, since you asked for us. But we talked it over, Myra and I, and decided we are glad to be asked—to be relied on in such an important matter."

"You both earned it—I just hope you never regret it."

"We'll take our chances, the same as you will, Barton."

"Your dinners are getting cold, Cheng. See you. . . ."

Barton was tired of the frozen stuff but too lazy to try anything more ambitious. He brought out a package, thought a moment. On the intercom circuit, he punched for Cabin Three.

"Yes?" It was Alene, all right.

"Barton. Speaking from the galley, and hungry. How about you?"

"Oh . . . ." A few moments of silence. "Thanks—but I don't feel like joining a group just now. Later, maybe."

"I was thinking of heating a couple of Frozen Freddies. If you can't use company, I could hand yours in to you, and leave. Okay?"

"Well . . . yes. And thanks, Barton."

"My pleasure. And signing out—I go to heat the meat."

The process was rapid. Soon, with a tray in each hand, he used a knee to knock at Alene's door.

He had expected more of a mess from the laser installation. There was only a hole in the hullside paneling, and a line of bracket mountings hanging from the ceiling.

"I'd like to join you for dinner," he said, "but I'll leave, if you'd rather."

Pause. Then, "Oh, come on in—I don't *mean* to be a surly hermit. And thanks again, for stirring me up to eat."

Alene was another silent eater, this time at least. With

260

side glances he appraised her appearance, trying to guess her state of mind—it could be important.

If she had been crying, it didn't show. The black, crinkly hair told him nothing—it was bushed out no more than usual, and no less. Funny, he thought, how it felt so much softer than it looked.

He eked out his last bites of food so that they finished the meal in a dead heat. Then they looked at each other.

"Coffee or anything?" he said. "I'll get it."

"If you'll settle for beer, it's in the box. I could use one."

Barton did the honors and sat again. "Welcome to the strike force, Alene. If you really mean it, that you want to go. For my part, I couldn't ask for anyone better."

She shook her head and did not speak.

"You don't want to, after all?"

"Oh, *that*—sure I do. I wanted to, before, but I couldn't—because of Tarleton having to be with the main fleet. And now—well, now I can. It's just that. . . ."

"Alene—what in hell happened? I think you have to tell it, and if you're riding with me, I have to know your mind."

"Yes, Barton—all right. The plain fact is that Helaise needs him more than I do. I love him—have loved him —but I can control my needs. Helaise can't—in some ways she was a fitting match for Terike.

"Tarleton went this morning, to see what was troubling her. When he came back, Barton, he looked—*old*. And he said he would have to take her to him, instead of me. That he would *have* to."

Barton growled in his throat. "The trouble with Tarleton is, he's never learned that sometimes somebody just needs a good swift kick in the ass."

She laughed. "I like you, Barton—I really like you. You expressed my own thought, exactly. But as you say, Tarleton couldn't do the kicking."

"It does take a certain amount of training."

"Yes. But you know what really hurts?" He shook his head. "It's that I could have shared, and so could Tarleton. But *she* wouldn't—so we all have to do what the little cripple wants, so as not to hurt her little *feelings*. Barton, I could kill her!"

"So be my guest." Alene, he thought, was getting healthier by the minute.

"Oh, stop it! I couldn't, really—I don't want her dead.

261

I just want to stomp her silly little pointed blonde head into the *dirt*." She drew a deep breath. "Figuratively, of course—or maybe a little more than that. Barton, I'm talking gibberish—stop me."

"You're doing fine, for now. What else, about Helaise?"

"She's so aggressively a one-man woman." Seeing Barton's raised eyebrows, she tried again. "Correction. She insists on having a one-woman man. Better?"

"Not that, either." Remembering what Helaise had said the previous day, he shook his head. "Since— Hishtoo—her attitudes have been swinging like a pendulum gone crazy. But in this case, I think, it's not the man she can't share—it's the status. And maybe more than that, really. Her pride has taken a lot of lumps on this ship, you know.

"But let's forget the sociology—how do *you* feel? Are you prepared for the strike-force situation, just three ships all on our own—and you, all on *your* own? Are you, Alene?"

Long, she looked at him. "I was that bad, with you? I hadn't thought so. Well, then—damn you to hell, Barton! Alene Grover can make it on her own—any time, any place, and in any company! Satisfied?"

"Very much so." He reached for her hand; she pulled it away. "One thing, though—I wasn't rejecting you—I value you very much. My point is that when the ship— or you—needs to act decisively, I might not be around. I could get clobbered, you know, just like anybody. So, what's important is, can you cut it on your own?" Silence. "Well, can you?"

And now her tears flowed. Through them, blinking, she tried to look Barton eye-to-eye. "I can! You know something? You're as hard-shelled as Hishtoo!" She wiped at her eyes. "Now will you get your ass out of here, so a lady can do a little genteel crying?"

Barton left. Sometimes, he thought, a guy can make a guess and come up lucky.

In the galley he found Tarleton with Myra Hake. "Barton," the man said, "Helaise said she's told you about . . . the changes. I—"

"She told me. And I spoke with Alene. I don't need to talk about it any more, unless you do. I think Alene will do fine on the strike team. Glad to have her."

"Yes. Well, that's good." Tarleton frowned. "You're

right—no point in talking. Maybe I just wanted you to tell me I'm doing the right thing."

"Maybe."

"I see. All right—our strike meeting is due in a couple of hours. Here, I guess—more room for everybody.

"Oh—Limila's back. Came aboard a few minutes ago. I didn't know where you were. She said to tell you she'd be in Two—and hungry."

"Thanks." Barton punched the intercom for Two. Limila, it turned out, would settle for thaw-and-heat food. He set about preparing it. Tarleton rose and left the galley.

"You can be pretty hard on people, can't you?" said Myra.

Barton turned to her. "What the hell was I supposed to say—that I think he's done ginger-peachy fine? I don't. And Tarleton's a big boy now—he has a right to his own mistakes. But I don't have to pat him on the back for them." He looked closely at her. "Did *you?*"

"A little, I guess. I couldn't exactly put my heart in it."

"Then why bother? You think he can't tell the difference?"

"I don't know. Probably. Your food's ready, Barton."

"Thanks." Leaving with it, he said, "Cheer up, Myra. Tarleton'll be okay. Especially after tomorrow, when we're gone from here."

She only nodded.

In Two, Barton set Limila's dinner down and embraced her, careful of the two ungainly lumps that bulged her robe.

"Welcome home, lady!" They sat, chairs facing across the small pull-down table.

"You are not hungry, Barton?"

"I've eaten."

"Something more is wrong? It seemed so, when I spoke to Tarleton, but no one would say, so I did not ask."

As she ate, he told her, keeping it brief. "It's a mess, but nothing fatal."

Limila shook her head. "Poor Helaise—trying to *be*, through another."

"Poor Helaise, hell! How about poor Alene? She's the one that got the dirty end of the stick."

Limila chewed and swallowed a final mouthful. "No. Helaise forces herself upon a man who takes her because of pity. If she had been willing to share—but no. Tarleton will try to be good to her—through the hate that will grow as he misses Alene, he will try. But—"

"You're underestimating the boss-man." He poured coffee. "Helaise caught him on his soft side, yes. But five gets you ten that if he sees it won't work, he'll have her off his ship before the fleet lifts. And save her face when he does it, too."

"It may be you are right—I hope you are. But—you say of Alene?"

"She'll make it all right. We talked—she's hurt, but she's tough."

Limila smiled. "Certainly she has a rare chance. The new man, Abdul—I met him—is he not beautiful? And of a good mind—even the few words I had of him showed me that. He will be welcome among us."

"That's for sure. He impresses the hell out of me, and I don't mean just his size."

"But if—I wanted to say, Barton—if Alene should need of you, I would gladly have it so."

He smiled and took her hand. "I know you would. Maybe you will." Hell's bells—he still hadn't told her! "Uh—in fact, you already have—at the party, when ap Fenn was getting himself killed."

Knowing full well that he couldn't possibly be in the doghouse, still Barton felt relief at the way Limila smiled, then.

The intercom sounded; Barton answered it.

"Cheng here. Company's coming. Meeting starts in about ten minutes."

"Thanks. See you then," said Barton. He and Limila dressed and went to the galley. The group assembled rapidly: Tarleton and Helaise, Cheng and Myra, Vito and Liese, Abdul, Alene, and Eeshta.

Kranz was the first off-ship arrival; with him were a heavy-set woman and a boy who looked about seventeen: Inge Larssen and Clancy Ferris, respectively.

"If you want any hot-pilot work," said Kranz, "Inge's your girl. Clance's reflexes are equally good, but he sticks to weapons." At first glance, the two hadn't impressed Barton much; he looked at them with new appreciation.

Captain Lombard, Estelle Cummings' nominee, arrived during the introductory chatter. The girl who accompanied him was small and dark, slim in her bright sari. In any other context, Barton would have guessed her to be no more than twelve years old. Her forehead bore a red caste mark, and when momentarily she faced away, Barton saw that her black braid of hair reached to the bend of her knee.

"Miss Chindra," said Lombard. "Absolutely top-drawer in communications—and Chin also makes computers jump through hoops." Yes—Barton remembered now. Limila had mentioned this one. It did look as though the strike force would be carrying some top talent.

Tarleton spread the star map on a table and started the show. It was old stuff to Barton—he followed it with the top of his head, made comments as indicated, and at the same time pursued more personal lines of thought. *Should* he have patted Tarleton's ego a little? After all, the man had charge of the combined fleets—his stability was essential. Barton thought about it, and found no answers.

Helaise, he thought, acted the queen bee to perfection. She said little, but somehow Barton was reminded of some newly favored king's mistress—fresh from slopping hogs and determined not to show it. But what had evoked this side of her, that had not shown itself during all the preceding months?

He saw her mouth twist slightly, in reaction to something Tarleton said. What was it?—something about Hishtoo. And then, to Barton, the whole problem, all the pieces, fell neatly into place. *Of course* . . . .

Hishtoo—the strike team was going after Hishtoo. And after what had happened to her, getting anywhere near that big lobster—or any other—was the *last* thing Helaise wanted. So—how to wiggle off the strike team with her pride intact? Simple enough—she had tied herself to the one man who *had* to stay with the fleet.

It was too bad, he thought—it was a lot more than her arm that Hishtoo had broken. He hoped she wasn't counting on the command ship as a guarded haven of safety in case of battle—for if she was, she didn't know her new man very well.

But he revised his earlier opinion—it wasn't a good hard kick she needed. Helaise was in need of repairs—

and, Barton thought, unlikely to get them. Helaise Renzel, casualty . . . .

No point, he decided, in saying anything to Tarleton—either the man would figure it out for himself or he wouldn't. And a dollop of fear wasn't such a bad thing, objectively, in someone holding down the weapons job.

The discussion wound toward a weary close. Equipment, supplies, timing, goals, tactics, methods, contingencies—all were belabored at length. Finally, Tarleton said, "I think we've covered it. Any further suggestions?"

"I move the meeting adjourn," said Barton. He stood, knowing that if he had timed it right, others would follow suit. As usual with him, it worked. Taking Limila's hand, he said a few good nights and gave a general handwave to the rest. "Good show, Tarleton. See you in the morning." He took Tarleton's nod as permission to leave.

Back in Cabin Two, he asked Limila, "What do you think? Is it solid?"

"Don't you know, Barton?"

"I have my opinion. I want yours, too."

"Yes. So I thought. It is, I think, of enough good."

"I think so, too—but thanks for the double-check."

To Barton, the next day moved too fast for him to follow, and yet endured forever. He talked with Tarleton, with Scalsa, with Alene—and it seemed as though he had never known them, had perhaps newly met them. The talk was wooden—as was his own mind, this day.

Tarleton, Helaise, Vito Scalsa, and Liese Anajek were moving their belongings to Ship Two. Barton hated goodbyes—he said them early and briefly, and caught a car to the conference building.

When he found Slobodna, he wasted no time on formalities. "How's with the Shields, man?"

"I'm afraid we honestly don't know." Slobodna's voice sounded sheepish but his face wasn't built for it. "We *think* we have it whipped—but there isn't time to test heavy, to make sure. We're making the indicated modification on all the units, including the eight that didn't fail. You get those—use at your own risk. I'm sorry as hell, Barton—I hoped we'd do better."

Barton poked a gentle fist at the man's arm. "You did your best, Slowboat—we'll ride with that."

Leaving Slobodna to his work, Barton talked with Vertan for a time. The Tilaran seemed in need of reassurance—Barton gave it, with confidence that he had to manufacture for the occasion.

He spoke with Corval and with Kimchuk, gravely exchanging pledges of trust and friendship. He meant every word, but no word rang true to him.

Vertan drew him aside. "The Ormthan is here, and would be of speech with you!" And in a curtained alcove at one side of the building, Barton again met the pink egg with the head on it.

"Barton of Earth."

"None other, Ormthol. Would you wish me well?"

"All of that—and victory. But what of afterward? For the Demu?"

"As with you, Ormthol—live and let live. *If* we win. But I hope we can have contact with them, afterward."

"For what purpose?"

"You've heard of the young Demu with us? From that one, we think the race can learn to outgrow its ways."

"I have heard, yes, Barton—and have been greatly interested. If you did not require that one for the meeting with its elders, I would ask that you lend me its company. For the Demu are an unsolved puzzle, and always I would learn."

"Yeh. Well—later, maybe, with luck. Anything else on your mind?"

The Ormthan vibrated, shook. Laughter, thought Barton. Probably. "Your pardon—it is the question. On my mind, you ask, is there anything else? Much and always, Barton. It is a racial trait, a major one—our preoccupation with the joy of learning."

"Yes—all right. Now—a question, maybe?"

"Whether or not I may answer, you are free to ask."

"On Sisshain—the Demu thing of importance. You said something like, one who sees it cannot fail to recognize its importance."

"You remember well my saying."

"Okay. Now—can it be recognized from a distance?"

"You will know it from afar, I am told."

"How?"

"I was not told that."

It was time, Barton felt, to get the hell out. He said the formalities—including thanks—and left, with the nagging thought that anyone with good sense would have asked better questions.

Before leaving the building he went through the rigmarole with Vertan also. Marking time before departure, nothing seemed entirely real to him.

At the ship it was the same. Tarleton, Helaise, Vito, and Liese—all characters in a play. Only when they left did he turn to Limila and find a thread of credence.

"When do we lift?" he asked.

"Not long now, Barton. The others have grouped to the control room. Shall we join them?"

Alene Grover sat in the master pilot's seat. "Do you want to take it, Barton?"

"No, you go ahead—I'll sit here." Beside Limila.

"All right. I'll lift with the signal."

She did. The strike force was on its way.

For eight days the ships drove, not toward Sisshain but toward the line that put Sisshain and its dust cloud between them and the major Demu sector. Optimum angle of approach to that line, for least time to Sisshain, had been computed by Vito Scalsa.

Once in space, Barton found himself free of his pre-departure disorientation—everything was real again. Getting himself into gear, he checked the angle-approach problem with "Chin"—Miss Chindra, on Ship Thirty-four—and was not surprised that she checked Scalsa within one second of arc. He told her so.

"His calculations," she said, "were from Tilara. Mine had to consider distance already traveled, and the course change to avoid incoming ships as we left the Tilaran system."

"Thank you." Barton matched the gravity of her speech and face.

The first day, Barton and Limila moved into Cabin One. The change had nothing to do with status—One had command-comm facilities and Two did not. The omission had sometimes been inconvenient, and Barton was glad to be rid of it.

Alene Grover took Compartment Two. Cheng and Myra retained Four, and Eeshta stayed in Six—but now without benefit of the outside lock. Abdul Muhammed was in Five—the tube of Barton's side gun crossed Three at a height that made that room unusable even for Eeshta, let alone Abdul. Barton was surprised at how soon Three became filled with everyone's excess belongings.

As the strike force accelerated, ship-to-shore communications suffered—the time lag grew, and signals weakened. Long before light speed was reached, the three ships would be cut off from Tilara. When Tarleton called, late in the second day, it was obvious that there could be no further contact.

"I guess this is it, for now," the man said. "Barton—how does it look?"

"I think we have a winning combo on here. No weak links." Immediately, Barton regretted the implicit slap at Helaise. Nothing to do about it, though—anything he said would make it worse. He waited through the transmission lag.

"Yes—good," Tarleton said. "Well, the fleet will follow, on schedule. Looks as if the number of slowpokes, the second wave, will just about match the original fudge factor."

"Before you doubled it, you mean—not bad, not bad at all. Well, after rendezvous, just be on the lookout for any of us heading back from Sisshain like a bat outa hell—in case we run into something we hadn't figured on."

Another wait. "I know. We've set up a think-tank to brainstorm possibilities we may have missed. Well, Barton, you know the priorities—that helps our guessing a lot, and"—a noise surge smothered the next few words—"very likely, with luck."

"We're losing signal," said Barton. "So long—see you, some place."

At first he thought the circuit was dead. Then came "—Hear much of—too far, I—and good—" There was nothing more. Barton cut the screen.

Well, now he was on his own, for sure. The feeling was not unpleasant.

Once, only, Barton checked Abdul Muhammed through piloting and weapons drills—the man was superbly proficient in both; he displayed an intuitive talent for predicting the variations of Barton's simulated problems. Suspecting a touch of E.S.P.—which would be of no help in real battle at spatial distances—Barton tested the man against computer-generated situations. The results were equally good; E.S.P. was not a factor. Abdul, Barton decided, was simply one hell of a good man at the controls of ship or weapons.

"You certainly don't need any more training that I could give, Abdul. Just practice when you feel like it. Okay?"

"When on watch and not otherwise busy, it is my habit to work against problems—random series—from the computer. I would like to continue to do so."

"Oh, sure—fine." Barton thought of something. "Tell me—does the computer ever win?"

"Of course, Barton—I do not restrict its parameters. Sometimes it almost appears to become angry, and by sheer force it—what do you say?—wipes me out."

Barton laughed. "Well—if you can make the computer throw in its reserves, you're doing all right." And after a little more routine chatter, he left Abdul to his hobby.

He went below and made maintenance checks on the drive's tuning and the Shield balance. Returning, he found the entire crew in the galley, with the viewscreen on relay from control. They were playing the familiar game of "What's going to happen?" Barton poured himself some coffee, and sat in.

The alternatives were solid enough: Hishtoo would go to Sisshain or he wouldn't; Ship One would catch him first, or not. At Sisshain they could either handle what they met or would have to run for help. And the permutations of these choices were finite.

" . . . unless," said Barton, "we're overlooking a joker in the deck." He turned to Eeshta. "What do you think?"

"I know little of Sisshain, Barton, but I know the Demu. You wish to speak with them, and I would like to believe that they will listen. But I think there will be much death, and I grieve, that it must be a cause of it. Even though, having seen what I have seen, I know that my people, the Demu, do wrong, and must change. No matter what happens to me, if against all Demu will and pride, you force that change."

Barton frowned. "I don't think I understand you."

The small creature sighed. "When all is over, if I live, I must submit myself to Demu judgment, for what I do now. To Hishtoo—or if he is dead, to another. And if I am told to die—"

"Forget it, Eeshta! I won't let you do any such thing."

"Barton—though I have come to know you and feel well of your people, yet I am *Demu*, and know what my actions mean. I am pleased that you value my life—

but even so, I will do what is required of me." Standing now, Eeshta left the galley.

Limila held Barton's arm or he would have followed. She said, "Do not fight her thought now. But think upon it."

Frowning again, he shook his head. "Yeh—the Demu mind. She's our window on it. But I won't let her sacrifice herself. . . ."

"Nor I," said Limila. "But no point, now, to argue. Our part is to save our effort for the occasion, if it comes."

"Yes." Gently, careful for the apparatus she still wore, he hugged her. And decided to keep his mouth shut.

After a pause, Abdul looked at his watch and announced that he was going back to control, to make a data check in real time for the upcoming course change. As he left, Cheng stood, and drew Myra up also. Saying, "Time to go. I'm due on watch in an hour." Well, Barton thought, it made sense if you listened right.

Alene said, "There goes a good pair. I never understood why Myra and Tarleton didn't mesh, before he and I—well, it doesn't matter, does it?"

Without thinking, Barton said, "How do you like Abdul?"

Alene's face went blank. "I don't seem to exist." She rose. "Will you excuse me?"

Left alone with Limila, Barton said, "The famous Barton tact strikes again. Mind telling me what I did wrong this time?"

Limila shook her head. "There is a difficulty between them, it would seem. But I had not known, either." And that was that.

On the eighth day they changed course. To minimize time lag the ships grouped closely; from Thirty-four, Chindra gave the coordinates. On the mark, all three ships shifted thrust vectors; straight ahead now, though not yet visible, lay the dust cloud. "Good job," said Barton, to Abdul—and, by screen, to the other two pilots.

Inge Larssen grinned. "We do our best." On Thirty-four, Lombard touched an eyebrow in casual salute, and behind him Miss Chindra shyly raised a hand. Barton smiled and waved back to all of them, then signed to Eeshta to cut the screen.

It was time for Cheng to relieve Abdul of the watch. Barton waited while Cheng, straight-faced, confirmed the course he'd watched Abdul lay. The formalities done, Abdul turned to leave. Barton followed. "Got a few minutes? Like to talk with you."

"Surely. Will you join me in Compartment Five?"

A good host, Abdul produced cold beer. As the two sat, Barton decided he was getting used to the other's great size. Trying to think of a good lead-in, he said, "How are you settling in, on here? Any problems? I mean, confusion about different customs, anything like that?"

Like a god blessing his worshipers, Abdul Muhammed smiled. "In general, I have been made to feel very much at home; you have good people here. But yes, I am often puzzled. I observe, though, and think—and in most cases I come to understand."

"Most, huh? Anything puzzling you right now?"

Face blank, the god Abdul became an enigmatic Buddha. "Yes. Alene Grover. I believe she wishes to cohabit with me."

I've heard of worse problems, Barton thought, but he waited, and Abdul said, "She is a fine woman. But I may not do such a thing."

Barton sighed. "I expect she'll live. You told her yet?"

"I find the prospect difficult. Barton, I would explain to you. Another beer, perhaps?"

"Sure. Thanks." Barton settled back, into listening mode.

"It is not," said Abdul, "that I am a Puritan; I do not find the concept valid. My people's sexual customs, originally quite ritualized, underwent many changes during and after the rebellions. Including a period of recoil to a brand of Puritanism much the same as that accepted in your own country for so long." He smiled again. "You see, I am historically cognizant."

"You are, that. But then what's the problem?"

"On its ships, my country sent only men. So my wife has said that while I may have no woman, she will have no man. My words cannot reach Earth, to tell her she might be more free. So in fairness, I may not accept Alene Grover. Do you understand?"

"Yeh." Shit oh dear—people could sure find ways to make things tough on themselves! "Like me to say anything for you, to Alene? Get you off the hook?" A little horrified, Barton found himself *volunteering*, of all things.

"If you would. Only that I act from duty, not from choice."

"Okay. Next chance I get, I'll do that."

The next day, Myra detected a star-drive wake. "Either it's an old one," she said, "or else we're getting only the fringe of it. But in the latter case, it could be Hishtoo."

"Too faint to identify?" Barton asked.

"Yes. Most of the pattern detail is blurred."

"How far ahead of us, do you think?"

She shook her head; the sandy bangs needed trimming. "Indeterminate—no data, or not enough. If the courses converge, we'll learn more."

"Good enough. Stay on it, and log everything."

"I will. I already have. Barton—sometimes I wonder why you don't try to tie my shoes for me!"

He looked at her. "I'm sorry, Myra. I guess sometimes I fall into the delusion that I'm doing all the thinking on this boat. I know better, too."

She frowned. "No. I was wrong, Barton. I forgot that while I'm doing my job, you have to try to do everybody's."

Barton grinned. "One way or another. As long as it works."

After dinner that evening, back in Cabin One, Limila announced, "Barton—the machinery—I think it is time to rid me of it."

Barton was familiar with the look of the bulky enzymic filters that hid the transplanted breasts—a lot of metal and plastic, was all, with tiny colored lights flickering out information he didn't understand.

"You sure this stuff is ready to come off?"

"It is as I was told it would be. The lights say it—that the tissues have become the same, and I can have my own tits again. Though they will be small."

She had told him before, but he wanted to be sure he did it right. Yes . . . pull the tubes out slowly, gently. Dab the blood away and spray the small wounds with Tilaran anti-infectant. Apply the bandages. Simple enough . . .

Limila gave no sign of pain but Barton was nervous, anyway. The tubes were longer than he expected. The gush of blood each time startled him, though it was small and brief. The bandages covered tiny incisions at the bottom of each breast. He was surprised to see no other scars.

"It is around the tip, at the color change, and so not apparent. The skin was lifted and stretched much, to accomplish." She half-sighed, half-laughed. "Do you mind, that they are so small?"

Truly, he hadn't noticed. Now he looked, and spoke the truth. "They're just fine, Limila. Whether they grow more, or not. As long as you like them."

She looked at him with silver eyes. "Barton, I will not forget. You have loved me without them. And now, love me with them. We can be less gentle, if we like."

The drive trail—Hishtoo's or another's—departed from the strike team's course. Barton considered following the spoor, but decided there wasn't enough evidence in favor. During the next few days, the detectors gave no sign.

Barton hadn't exactly avoided Alene Grover but he hadn't sought her company, either. Then one day the two were alone in the galley.

He eyeballed her. "How's it with you, Alene?"

"Not bad for a loner. I told you I could make it." She looked good—the brash, bushy hair, the strength in her smile—eyes clear, not puffy.

"I should tell you something. Privately. Your place?" She nodded.

In Two they sat facing, over beers. "You were saying, Barton?"

He told her what Abdul Muhammed had said. Her smile was rueful. "I'd figured it had to be something like that. I knew the big gorgeous joker *liked* me, all right. And I like him—I still do. He's good, that one." She sighed, then exaggerated it. "I *would* get stuck with a monastic. On the other hand, why the hell am I—are any of us—so damned hung up on sex, anyway?"

"Well," said Barton, "the way they designed these ships, there wasn't room for a volleyball court. So we make do. . . ."

Eyes narrowed, she met his gaze. "Barton, if you try to offer me a charity fuck—I will kick you square in the balls!"

"Who, me?" Barton rearranged his thinking. "Wouldn't

dream of it—you're not the type. You want to know—I liked everything a lot, with us. I like *you*. But no charity. I don't happen to be a charitable man."

She had leaned forward so that her hair hid her eyes. Now she raised her head. "All right, Barton—I guess I asked for that. I like you, too. But if you ever want me again, you're going to have to ask—and ask damned *nice!*"

He gauged the risk and laughed, right in the face of her vulnerability. "That's fine, Alene," he said. "Maybe I will."

He left before she could find an answer. But she was smiling.

They had entered Scalsa's "corridor"—where a returning ship might need to rendezvous with the fleet. Barton saw to it that numerous landmark sights were taken—if he had to meet somebody in a hurry, he wanted to know the neighborhood.

A week later the detectors caught another sniff—fresher, and pointing toward the area of Sisshain—quite possibly Hishtoo. Barton called a viewscreen conference.

"We've got a nibble. Time to go maximum acceleration."

An hour later, Limila—on comm—called him back to control. "The other ships, Barton—they fall behind." Sure enough, Ship One was visibly pulling away from Thirty-four, which in turn was building a slighter lead over Thirteen.

"I suppose there were bound to be small differences," he said. Then he laughed. "Know what? I'm betting that Tarleton looked at the test-flight results of all our seventeen U.S. ships, and picked the one with the longest legs."

"But what do we do?" she asked.

"Set up the three-way again, will you, please?"

As soon as Limila had Kranz and Lombard on the screen, Barton said, "Here's where we split up, it looks like. I have to follow this trail at max. Lombard, you ease back just enough not to lose Kranz—okay?"

Kranz said, "I warned you about Thirteen, didn't I?"

"No problem," said Barton. "If it had been the fastest, Tarleton would probably have made it number One.

"All right—we'll still be in talk range for a while, in case there's anything to say. When we lose touch—well, you know the plans. Good luck."

By Barton's next "morning," Ship One had opened a sizable lead over the other two. The current rate of separation was nearly one light-second per hour, and increasing.

The "trail" was stronger—Eeshta, who had the comm-watch, showed Barton the numerical readouts. "They're getting stronger, *faster*," he said. "I wonder what the curve is." He began to punch the data into the computer input.

"I've done that," said Abdul, from the pilot's seat, "but of course you may wish to recheck." Barton shook his head and hit "Cancel."

"It's an exponential, Barton. Of low order, but still indicating a good rate of overhaul."

"Good. Eeshta, are we getting good enough definition yet, to try to match detection patterns? These readings, against the pattern Vertan gave us for Hishtoo's ship?"

"I do not know, Barton. No one has shown me how to do that." Mistake number "leventy-leven," Barton thought. *When do we run into the one that kills us?*

"Hmm—I've seen Myra do it, on a dry run. Let's see if I can remember how it goes." He turned the detectors, ranged for max gain allowable by the noise level, and switched the pattern onto the screen. It was clear, and reasonably steady. "Strong enough, all right." Then he punched the computer code for Hishtoo's pattern and fed that, also, to the screen.

Visual gibberish. "Well, either it isn't Hishtoo, or else I wasn't watching close enough when Myra did it."

"Myra remembered to put both feeds through parallel chopper circuits, and alternate the phases," said Myra. "It works better that way."

"Oh, hi! Didn't see you come in. Okay—would you take over, and show *all* of us how to do it right?"

"Sure. You have it all, except—here, the chopper, to alternate the two feeds." On the screen appeared a fast, steady blinking. "Now, just run the computer signal slowly around the phase circle—that's right. If the blinking stops—"

A clear pattern showed. It wavered, as Barton overran the setting, then steadied. He took a deep breath. "It looks as if we have the right party, friends."

"It does indeed," said Abdul. "Myra, can you—"

"I'm doing it. Just give me a minute." Her hands were all over the board; Barton couldn't begin to follow her actions, but he saw her repeating some steps and guessed she was rechecking. She turned to him. "We've cut his original lead by better than half. But we're also slightly more than halfway to Sisshain. See, here on the readout? It's going to be close."

"I—" he began.

She cut him off. "I want to confirm these figures with Chindra while we're still within range, and get from her an optimum turnover point based on max accel and decel all the way. Sorry, Barton—you were going to say?"

"You just said it, Myra; I'll get out of here and let you do your job. Coming, Eeshta? You were relieved five minutes ago."

"I will stay, Barton. Perhaps, Myra, you will later have time to show me things I have not learned, and should know to perform my watch correctly?"

"Sure, Eeshta. Why don't you sit here, alongside me?"

Cheng arrived to relieve Abdul, so Barton had company on his way to the galley. They found Limila and Alene chatting over the remains of breakfast. Barton said his hellos.

"Hi, Barton. Hello, Abdul," said Alene. "Excuse me." She drained her cup, rose, and left the galley.

Barton raised eyebrows to Limila. "Anything wrong?"

"No new thing."

"Oh. Well—have you heard the news? Of course not —we just got here with it. That ship up ahead—it's Hishtoo, all right, and on course for Sisshain. And we're catching up—maybe fast enough, maybe not." He gave her the numbers of it. "Say, why don't you go tell Alene? It might cheer her up."

"Firsthand news is better, Barton—you tell her. Abdul can keep me company—if you're not busy, Abdul?"

"No, not at all. This is a time to relax. And there are many more questions I would ask, about Tilara."

"Okay," said Barton, "I'll get out from underfoot."

Alene answered his knock. "Come on in, I guess. What's up?"

He told her.

"Well," she said, "at least now we can see some action ahead. I suppose that calls for a celebration. All I have is beer, I'm afraid."

"Not quite all, Alene." He reached out. First she tried to pull back; then she let him hold her. He made no further move, until she kissed him. And then, gently, she pushed him away.

"That wasn't charity, Barton; I can tell. But, no, thanks." Puzzled, he waited, until she said, "You know, I don't need sex, as such. I love it, mind you, but I don't *need* it, physically, the way men seem to. I never have to—well, never mind. . . ."

For a few seconds, she frowned. "What I've always needed was to be *close* to a man, and I guess I've never known any other way to get that closeness. Am I contradicting myself?"

"No, I don't think so. Uh—you said something about beer?"

"Oh, sure." She got out one for each of them, and sat. "What I'm trying to say is, you told me I had to stand on my own feet. I've been working at it, and now I think I can."

Barton picked his words. "You don't need to be so close, now?"

Her bushy hair swung with the headshake. "Not as much, no. And what I *do* need—" She laughed. "You *do* give a nice hug, Barton. I like you. But the fact that you're the only game in town is a lousy excuse for going to bed with you. Even though I liked it, when we did."

Barton swallowed a lump of ego, and said, "So did I—but I think you're right about the rest of it."

She smiled, showing the large white teeth. "I've learned to need less in the way of emotional support, and to get what I do need in other ways. In fact, it's time I broke the habit of sulking at Abdul." Shrug. "Not *his* fault."

Well, now. Barton tried to keep his sigh of relief under wraps. "That's good; I know it's bothered him some. One other thing, though—and this is *not* a pass at you. Alene, it's all right to need people a little more, sometimes. We all do."

"Sure; I know. And I—" A knock interrupted her.

Barton got the door; Myra was there. "You weren't anywhere else, so you had to be here." She handed him a readout strip. "These are Chindra's figures for turnover, arrival at Sisshain, and our chances of catching Hishtoo first. I ran a set, too, and there's not enough difference to matter."

"Rough it out, will you, Myra? I'll read this later."

"Sure." Accepting a beer from Alene, the tall woman

sat. "Figure turnover in about forty-nine hours, toward the middle of day-33. From then, thirty-one days to Sisshain at max decel, and nearly thirty to the most optimistic guess at catching Hishtoo."

"That long?" Barton had hoped for better.

"We've been close to max all along, you know. Now, then—we're starting to lose signal with the other ships. Anything you want to say, or ask, before we do?"

He thought. "Well, if you haven't already, and you probably have, get me *their* arrival guesstimates for Sisshain."

Myra grinned at him. "I don't have them yet, but I did ask. Any minute now . . . "

"Good on you. Well, give them the usual best wishes, and all."

"I will." She stood. "Back to work. Alene, thanks for the beer."

"Pleasure. Come again." Behind Myra Hake the door closed, leaving silence.

Barton broke it. "Anybody around here hungry, besides me?"

Grover stood to face him. "I am. Soon as you try me with that hug again, once." He did; then the meeting adjourned for lunch.

Cheng and Eeshta had the watch; appetites satisfied, the other five stayed talking in the galley. The question at hand was Limila's: Now that they had Hishtoo spotted, could the Demu detect Ship One, also?

Barton knew the answers, so he didn't listen too closely to Abdul's explanation. First, Hishtoo couldn't "see" anything through the turmoil of his own drive wake. Second, on accel a ship's wake—the gravitic ripples, ionization, magnetic turbulence, unstable particles—all of it propagated rearward. And at light speed, at that, so that even on decel, with Ship One's wake shooting out ahead, Hishtoo couldn't spot it until he dropped below "c."

Myra frowned. "Then could one ship sneak up through another's wake and pull a surprise attack?" And when Abdul told her that above light-speed, the wake itself would destroy the attacking ship, she wanted to know how, on decel, they could pass through their *own* wake.

"Our drive fields are more intense than their product,"

279

Abdul said, "so they deflect it to the sides. But—" His raised hand anticipated the next question. " . . . not the wake of another ship, because it cannot be of exactly the same pattern."

But why didn't the Shield protect at *any* speed, Limila asked, and this time Cheng fielded the question. "The Shield's built to work in normal space, not in a drive wake. There, the Shield's own collapse would destroy the ship within it."

"Then the drive itself is a weapon!"

"It could be," said Barton. "Except, in practice it'd be damned hard to get into position to use it."

"But, Barton—if we overtake Hishtoo in deceleration?"

He thought, nodded. "Yes; approach on a parallel path to keep our own view clear, then swing over. But—it's a killing weapon, Limila. No other way."

Hand to mouth, she gasped. "Oh! Iivajj and Gerain—I had forgotten them." She stood and fled, but failed to reach the door before her tears flowed.

Barton's vocabulary, then, did him little credit. Alene Grover patted his hand. "That makes two of us."

The gathering broke up. In Control, Barton ran a number of simulations based on Chindra's tapes—Hishtoo's choices of turnover points, the Demu's consequent decel rates. It still came out a tossup.

He prowled the ship. Eeshta was in Six, door closed. Barton wanted to talk to the youngster—but not in his present mood. He took a test kit from Three and ran a full series of maintenance checks that weren't due for another week. Only when he had pooped himself thoroughly did he return the kit and approach Compartment One.

At least it wasn't locked; he entered quietly. Limila was asleep. Barton tiptoed across the room; as quietly as possible—the bourbon only gurgled, but the ice rattled—he made a drink. Then he sat in the half-dark, thinking.

When he made a second drink, the tinkle of ice was answered. "Barton?"

"None other. You feeling better?"

"I am, yes. And a little hungry."

So—she will be all right now.

As the days passed, tension grew. Turnover came on schedule; Ship One, on max decel toward Sisshain, still closed slowly on Hishtoo. The readouts varied; some indicated that the Demu would be overtaken in space; others showed him grounding with impunity.

"He does not keep constant deceleration," Abdul said. "He may be changing it, cut-and-try as you say, as his own computers show his course overrunning or falling short."

"Maybe that's where he's weak," said Barton. "If he's never had to make a speed run before, he's having to figure it out the hard way. That could help us."

When Barton told how it had gone between him and Alene, Limila looked thoughtful. "She knows, of course, that I would not begrudge. She was with you, once, when I could not be. So now that she has no other . . ."

Barton quoted Alene on the subject of lousy excuses. "No, honey; it's nothing to do with restrictive morals or anything. This is strictly her own mind. Declaring independence, I think."

He wasn't sure he'd made it clear, but Limila nodded. "Then that is good." She went silent, and looked sidelong at him. "New subject, as you sometimes say. I have progress to show. Look and feel, both." One hand extracted her Tilaran-styled dentures; she opened her mouth. Barton looked; sure enough, here and there, the tips of new teeth showed. And his hesitant finger traced the ridges of bumps that hadn't parted yet. Seemed straight enough, he thought, the whole set of alignments.

He nodded, and waited while she put her mouth back together. Then he said, "Any trouble yet, teeth interfering with the plates?"

She shook her head. "Oh, no—and not for a time yet. As I said, the flexible elastic lining—there will be, I was told, only a brief period of real inconvenience. And it is much too soon for that."

"Well, good. Glad to see that things are working so well." *They better had, too*—because Barton purely had no idea how to handle the problems of a teething adult. He hoped he wouldn't have to.

On day-50, seventeen days after turnover and fourteen short of Sisshain, Barton took the last half of Myra Hake's watch. "I have stuff to run through Tinhead, so I may as well take the duty, too. Go get drunk, huh?"

She shook the bangs away from her eyes, and smiled.

"Well, not exactly. But maybe Cheng and I will take a few practice swings." She left with a light step. Barton exchanged greetings with Abdul, who was holding down pilot watch, and set to work.

An hour later he had all the answers he was going to get, and turned to Abdul. "The beast still can't tell me whether we catch Hishtoo. Well, I'll try it again tomorrow."

Abdul's reply, he didn't expect. "It is good that you have solved the problem of Alene Grover."

Well, the serve's in your court, Barton. Return it. "How's that?"

"As in the olden days, with my people. When the mate of friend or brother was quite naturally entitled to comfort and support, approved by all. It is good to see the ways of my ancestors found worthy by others." Abdul cleared his throat. "Had it not been for my agreement with my wife, I myself would have been glad to cherish Alene. For she is a splendid person, is she not?"

"Right," Barton growled. "But don't tell me; tell *her*."

"Did you not tell her for me? My regrets?"

Exasperated, Barton gave a snort. "Not the same thing. Abdul, don't you have some common sense to go with your brains and good looks?"

After a pause, Abdul Muhammed smiled. "Your words are harsh, but your face is not. But very well. It will be difficult to speak so to Alene, but at the first opportunity I will do so."

"First opportunity in *private*. Just the two of you."

"Oh? Very well; you know your own people best, I suppose."

Somehow the conversation had gotten totally off track. Barton thought, and said, "You've got one thing wrong, Abdul. All I did with Alene was talk. The rest of it, that she can get along without any of us, she figured out all by herself."

Down, down the galactic Arm. Barton felt a malaise of no apparent cause. He recognized it, though—it was the same unease that had plagued him throughout his years at the Demu research station. Then, he had thought it the natural result of being caged like an animal. Apparently, there was more to it, than that . . .

He spoke of it to Limila. "Oh, yes," she said. "It is known to us. You see, Barton . . . "

He understood most of what she said. He knew that spiral arms are spiral because in the nature of things, outer orbits are slower than inner orbits. So what she was telling him, he decided, was that he was uncomfortable, "down here," because with respect to angular momentum, his moment of inertia didn't feel at home.

That discussion sparked another. In her explanation, Limila quoted Tevann, and now Barton remembered the talk he had had with Tevann—how many days ago?

And how to ask—to change the subject? But she was his most needful person, and he wanted to know.

"Limila," he said, "I just recalled something Tevann told me."

"Yes, Barton?"

"About your children. You had never mentioned them. Why didn't we see them? Or did you?"

"But no. They live far from where we were. One is on Chaleen, another of our worlds. All are grown—two have children of their own, Tevann tells me. But there was not time to arrange travel and visits, Barton—you must know that. Tevann promised to send messages, to tell them I am alive. More must wait for our return." She looked at him thoughtfully. "But why, Barton, if you were puzzled, did you not ask before?"

He didn't answer; he was too busy thinking. She'd handed him more than he had asked for—that was for sure. Limila a grandmother? Well, what was wrong with that? He knew Earthwomen who'd achieved that status by the age of thirty-five, or less. But now he was curious about something else.

"Limila—how old are you?"

"In your years? Your numbers? I must think." She frowned. "Oh . . . not greatly more than eighty. I would guess."

"*Eighty?* But you're a young woman. With us, eighty is—*old.*"

"With us, too, of nature, Barton. But with the treatments to stabilize metabolism, we live long and are young for long. It is strange we have not talked before of these things, but I thought—you do not have such treatments on Earth?"

"No." I will grow old, thought Barton—and she will not.

"When we return to Tilara," she said, "you must have the treatments."

"Yes—maybe." If they worked, for Earthani. Barton blue-funked. He didn't know why Limila's revelations bothered him so much, but they sure as hell did.

Nearly a week it took him, to shake off the effects and regain—mostly—his normal spirits.

Down the Arm. Day-60—on the screen showed three dots of light. Two of them—close together and slowly closing—rapidly approached the more-distant third: Sisshain.

"It's still a tossup," Barton said.

"What's his estimated lead now?" said Alene.

"Only about a light-minute, maybe a little over. But our rate of approach is dropping off, damn it! On decel, our exponential curve has a negative exponent."

"Barton, look!" said Eeshta. "What is happening?"

The Hishtoo dot now maintained constant distance from its pursuer.

"He's speeded up!" Alene.

"Reduced decel, you mean," said Barton. "But why?"

Abdul had entered unnoticed; now he spoke. "He has dropped below light speed, and now detects us. I will obtain a readout of the exact time and coordinates. What can be done?"

"Two can play." Barton's grin was tight. "Back off decel, Alene. Back off until we start closing again."

"But what if—? Barton, we'll overrun Sisshain!"

"Do it. If we overrun, so does Hishtoo—he can't land, either. And he can't keep too much speed, or he won't be able to turn inside the limits of the dust cloud. We have the bulge on him in turning radius, too." He slammed a fist into his other palm. "If only the other ships were in talk range!"

Of them all, Abdul showed no excitement. "What would you wish to do?"

Barton wheeled from the board, faced him. "We could chase Hishtoo to the limit where we could land and he couldn't. Then the others could bag him."

"They might, anyway," said Alene. "But you're forgetting something."

Barton exhaled, shrugged. "I wouldn't be surprised—it happens all the time. Now what?"

"According to Vertan, once Hishtoo is this close to Sisshain, he doesn't have the fuel to go anywhere *else*."

"Grover, I love you!" In jubilation, he hugged her. "Go get 'em, kid!"

"He pulls away more rapidly," said Abdul. "How——?"

"He's made turnover again," Barton said. "Match him, Alene! Not turnover—just slack hell out of your decel." Again, the two dots approached each other.

"You have *all* forgotten something," said Eeshta. "Hishtoo need not land. He need only speak with Sisshain, and perhaps more ships will rise from there, to warn the Demmon sector, than you can intercept."

"If I catch up with him, he won't be speaking to anybody!"

"But," said Abdul, "I thought you did not wish to kill the hostages. Of course, if it is necessary . . . . "

"Burning off his antenna systems won't kill anybody."

"Barton," said Alene, "he's slowing again. Fast!"

"Another turnover? Wants us to overrun him, meet and pass too fast for any action. Or else he passed light speed, lost us again, and panicked. Whatever—just match him, is all."

She tried, but Hishtoo reversed his action, and then again. And with each move, the Demu increased either the distance or the relative velocity between the ships.

"This method—matching his moves after the fact— will not be effective," said Abdul. "He has the initiative; he is acting, while we can only react, too late."

"I never said he was stupid," said Barton. "You got any suggestions?"

"May I take the pilot's seat? What I have in mind is easier to do than to explain. No reflection, Alene Grover, on your abilities. Under a great disadvantage, you have done well."

"No offense at all, Abdul. I'm a good jet-jock if I do say so, but you can make that computer do tricks I never heard of." They changed places; as he watched the screen, Abdul began running simulations.

"You guessed then, Alene. I too am limited to reacting to received data—but I am responding not to Hishtoo's moves as shown directly on the screen, but to a computer prediction, in real time, of his response to my *next* change, on the basis of his earlier actions.

"I will lose ground—rather, I *did* lose ground—you see it, here?—on the first move, for it had to be made arbitrarily, to establish a baseline. But now we are working with a converging series and should soon begin to gain appreciably."

And it worked, Barton saw—sure as hell, it worked. First slowly, then more rapidly, Abdul recouped from Hishtoo his advantages of distance and speed-differential. The dot that showed the Demu's ship darted frantically.

"He now makes changes at random, I believe," said Abdul. "That method will not help him—his actions cancel each other, and the computer can work with trends as well as with individual moves." The dot subsided to a slow, steady drift.

"He's not doing *anything*," Alene said. "What's happened?"

Abdul consulted the screen, checked a tape readout. "He has established a constant deceleration that will bring him to rest at Sisshain. I will set course to intercept at soonest."

"I don't understand," said Alene. "Has he given up?"

Barton shook his head. "He hasn't quit—not Hishtoo. It's just that he can't do it with his ship, so now he'll do it with the hostages." His face took on the feel of weathered rock. "Or so he thinks. I'm sorry, Eeshta— sorry for all of them, and for us."

Eeshta spoke. "When do we come to meet with Hishtoo?"

"If he makes no change—" said Abdul. "—Wait, let me try a variation." For nearly two silent minutes he ran calculations. "We both are off the original course, and thus at a lower velocity than before, toward Sisshain itself. His present—and optimum—deceleration is now considerably less than our own capability. Barton— may I suggest?"

"May? Hell, it's an order!"

"What? Oh, I see." Abdul's smile was broad. "Very well—on straight deceleration we would reach Hishtoo in approximately thirty hours. At that time he may be within communication range to Sisshain. I presume we do not wish that to occur."

"Abdul—if you don't get on with it, I'm going to climb you like a tree, stand on your shoulders, and punch you in the nose!"

"Abdul Muhammed laughed. "Yes. Then I propose something we could not have done earlier, with our higher direct velocity—that we make turnover and accelerate for a time, then reverse again to pass Hishtoo while still exceeding light speed—and finally, apply maximum deceleration until Hishtoo catches *us*."

After a moment, Barton whooped. "You'll *blind-side* him! He'll know we've passed him but not until after the fact, and then he won't know *where* the hell we are—until we knock to collect for the charity drive. Abdul—did anyone ever tell you you're a genius?"

"Oh, yes. But always that I would never make anything of it."

"Oh? How come?"

"My scholarship to University was athletic. It was predicted that my brain would be scrambled in playing rugby, or perhaps soccer."

Except for Eeshta and Limila, everyone laughed. In the room, tension diminished.

"Okay then," said Barton, "when *is* the party? For Hishtoo . . . "

"In slightly over six hours. If we gather here at 2100, ship's time, there will be ample time for preparation."

"Okay—good enough. Alene, if Hishtoo changes so much as his socks, call me. Correction—call Abdul; I'd only be the middleman, anyway."

"Right. And I'll pass the word to Cheng when he takes the watch—in case you don't see him first."

"Good enough," said Barton. He and Abdul left for the galley, leaving Alene and Eeshta to finish the shank-end of their watch. Certainly, thought Barton, it had been an eventful one.

They found Cheng and Myra dawdling sleepily over a prewatch brunch. "Hey," said Barton, "you missed the show—starring Hishtoo, as Houdini the escape artist."

"Hishtoo? What happened?" Suddenly both were wide awake.

"You tell 'em, Abdul—I'm pooped. See you all later." Feeling only mild hunger, Barton found a slice of cheese to munch, on his way to Compartment One.

Limila was awake, dressed and fed—ready to share beer and information. Barton gave her a full report. The news excited her. At the end she smiled for a moment, then shuddered.

"Mostly it is good, Barton—that we can perhaps stop Hishtoo from rousing Demu power against us. But now we must face—oh, the poor, young Iivajj!"

"I'll do everything I can—you know that. Limila,

would you rather stay away tonight? It might be ugly."

"After seeing me, Barton, as I came from the Demu—
how can you say that anything else is ugly?" She shook
her head; the motion rippled the long Tilaran wig. "No—
I must be there, and see. If only to know, to say to the
other needful ones of Iivajj and Gerain, how it was that
they must die, and how well they undertook the death."

"Assuming we get back ourselves."

"I have no fear that we will not." She looked at him
squarely. "Barton, I do not entirely understand the
Earthani theological construct called Hell. But if it
were to exist, and you were to be taken there, I would
have no doubt of your return." She paused. "Have I
said, I wonder, what I wished to say?"

He could only hug her, and he did. The rest would
have to wait.

At 2100 hours, the seven gathered in Control. Eeshta
sat farthest from the screen. Barton went to her.

"Eeshta, perhaps you shouldn't be here. You don't
have to be."

"I must, yes. Barton, I know what may happen. But I
do what I do because it is right. And I will not hide away
from what may come of it." Eeshta's gaze was steady,
eye to eye. "Do not ask me to, Barton. I am Demu."

"I know," he said. "That's the hell of it."

"What do you mean?"

"The more I know you, Eeshta, the more I see the
good side of your people. But I can't let that stop me, stop
us all. The Demu have got to be made to let other people
alone."

"Yes, Barton, I know—or I would not be here as I
am."

"Yes. Well, I hope . . . I hope it goes better than I
think it will." He left her and took his place. Abdul—
who else?—as pilot, with Myra Hake on comm—leaving
the weapons seat to Barton. For if killing were to be
done by his decision, he was not going to delegate the
dirty work.

On the screen Hishtoo's ship grew from a dot to a tiny
silhouette, seen from the rear and at an angle. The passing maneuver had gone well; now both ships, decelerating,
dropped tail-first toward distant Sisshain. But Ship One,
ahead, was slowing harder, allowing Hishtoo to overtake.
And the Demu could neither see Ship One nor know of

its proximity. If Demu could sweat, Barton decided, Hishtoo should be sweating quarts.

"Getting close, Abdul," he said. "About time to pop out through his wake—much closer and it could shake us up pretty good, even at these speeds. When we come out of it, tilt and try to give me a dead-bead on his nose, all the way in."

"As well as I may," said Abdul. "He will move when he detects us."

"Maybe—we'll see. Just try to keep the laser on target, if you can. Too bad the forward delivery system can't traverse." He grinned tightly. "So stay loose for quick alternatives, just in case."

"You have other plans?" said Abdul.

"Yeh. The sleep-gun's on, for one—in case we crack his Shield good, we've got him. Watch it now—here comes the wake."

Out of that hazard, Abdul's closing of the last few hundred kilometers was rapid. "When do you wish—?" he began, but Barton waved him off. Hishtoo had spotted Ship One and was changing deceleration—and perhaps course; Barton couldn't tell for sure.

He had to think fast. If he had the ship turned to bring the sidearm laser to bear, Hishtoo would be out of range in seconds. The chance wasn't good enough. But Abdul was having trouble keeping any part of Hishtoo's ship in Barton's sights, let alone the nose of it.

Barton activated the Tilaran ion beam; it had limited traverse—and the range was close. Where the beam touched Hishtoo's Shield, a golden glow appeared. Barton heard hull plates creak, forward, under the stress of the sweep-magnets.

And at the nose of Hishtoo's ship a flower of blue fire bloomed; where his antenna systems had been, twisted stubs remained. Barton drew deep breath and leaned back in his seat.

"Get him on the screen, Myra. Tilaran frequencies."

"With his antenna gone?"

"Do it. This close, he'll hear us—maybe not good, but good enough. Move us in closer, Abdul—ready to dodge if he goes to point at us. And go in on a spiral—I've got another target in mind. . . ."

Ship One was still "behind" Hishtoo; the spiral brought Barton the view he wanted. Briefly, Hishtoo's side-mounted laser tube showed, dead-center. Barton's own laser drove through the other's Shield and cut a great swatch from the side of that tube. He didn't know whether the weapon was permanently disabled—but the odds, he thought, were improving.

The picture on the screen was streaked and wavering, but good enough for Barton's purposes. In the foreground he saw Hishtoo—by nature, the exoskeletal face showed no expression. Behind him were two bound figures—Iivajj and Gerain. From what Barton could see, blurring and shifting, Hishtoo had not harmed them—yet. But Barton knew why the Demu had the two with him, on display, so to speak.

Time to say hello—"It is that I greet you, Hishtoo," Barton said in Demu. "May we speak now?"

The voice was distorted, too, but Barton could make it out. "It is that Hishtoo does not speak with animals. I will speak with my egg-child."

Wih no further prompting, Esehta came forward. "Hishtoo, it is that these are not animals, but Demu. You are to speak with them."

"Is it that you are without sight, Eeshta? You see they are not Demu—that they have not correct appearance. As these with me are not Demu, but animals. But it is that they will learn, Eeshta, and on Sisshain, become Demu."

"Whnee!" Barton recognized. Eeshta's call of distress. Eeshta switched to Tilaran. "Iivajj! Gerain! Do not learn of Hishtoo's speech—do *not!* Or he will do of you as was done of Limila—and Siewen, and the Freak. You saw—you would be as dead." Eeshta turned away and staggered; Limila caught her. "Limila, I am sorry. But it was needed, to say it."

"You were right to say it. I *was* as dead."

Barton had been trying to get back to Hishtoo, now he could. "Hishtoo, it is that I want of you the two Tilarans, who are Gerain and Iivajj. I will have them. We have protective coverings for moving between ships—"

"It is that you have nothing, animal. I proceed to Sisshain and you do not hinder. Or it is as you have said to me—crab salad." And he lifted Iivajj's forearm to his chitinous, serrated mouth.

"Hishtoo!" Barton's shout was urgent. "It is that your first bite is your last. I kill you, Hishtoo, if you draw her blood."

Hishtoo gave a pulsed hiss, the Demu laugh. "Kill me, kill all," he said. "It is that I think you do not."

"But it is that I do." Then, in Tilaran—"Gerain—Iivajj, my dear—I am of grief. In moments you may be dead, of my doing. It is of need greater than your lives, or of ours here. Be, if you can, of understanding, of acceptance. And—"

"Barton!" It was Ivajj. "I know—I understand enough. And so does Gerain. So do of need—and be of peace."

Hishtoo pushed her aside. "Why is it that you kill, animal? To kill your own—why do you?"

"It is that you give me them, Hishtoo, and I do not kill. You, or anyone."

"It is that I give you nothing, animal."

Say that word a few more times, Barton thought, and I'll show you what it means. But he said, "It is that you give me only their safety, Hishtoo—your saying that you will not cut and change them. Give that, and I do not kill."

Hishtoo did not answer in words—on the monitor screen came a burst of light. "Swing us right, Abdul!" Without thought, Barton's hands moved—switch laser output, traverse, activate! The ship rocked and shuddered with impact.

"What was that, Barton?" Limila.

"The—" A wave of blackness hit him.

*

"What—?"

"I—" And another wave.

*

"Barton!" And another . . .

*

"Abdul—!"

*

"—Get us—

*

"—away!" The ship lurched.

*

The surges of blackout grew less and finally ceased. Alene was first to speak. "What the hell was *that?*"

Barton shook his head, clearing it. "First, the Larka-Te high-drive torpedo. I tried for it with the side-gun—don't know if I even touched it—those things are *fast*. More likely, the propagation-speeds didn't match right for Hishtoo, and the Shield took care of it.

"But it got the Shield, too, sort of. See that meter—oscillating? The Shield's out of balance, blinking on and off. And every time it blinked off, Hishtoo's sleep-gun got through. Nothing we could do but get the hell out, before he could get his ion beam on us."

He turned to Abdul. "Good job, man—you can drive *my* kiddie-car, any time you want." Then, "How's our position now?"

Abdul shook his head. "He's ahead of us again. I'm sorry—if possible, I would have done differently. But the recurrent unconsciousness would not allow connected thinking. My hand was on the power control—I could only push it, applying maximum deceleration. Another choice would have been preferable."

"Don't feel bad about it," said Alene. "You got us out, didn't you?"

"She's right," said Barton. "And under those circumstances, it took some doing.

"Now, then—with Hishtoo ahead of us, *we're* the ones blinded by our own wake." He thought. "Tilt us, Abdul. Our wake-cone spreads about five degrees from center. Tilt us—oh, make it ten."

Abdul looked puzzled, but his hands moved on the board. Then he smiled. "I see, Barton—a side-vector to take us out of our existing wake, and enough tilt to see past the edge of our new one and locate Hishtoo again."

"Right." Several minutes passed. Then: "There he is!"

"Can we catch him?" said Alene.

"I doubt it," Barton said. "But it wouldn't do us any good if we did—not until we rebalance the Shield. He'd just knock us out again. All we can do is follow, and get to Sisshain as soon as possible." Abdul reset the course.

"But then," said Limila, "why does he not attack? As we did, from the blind side?"

"Several reasons, maybe. Weapons. He's used his only torp. If he tested the Filjar plasma-gun, he may have found that it's still unreliable. And I think I got his laser. That would leave him just the ion beam and the sleep-gun. We've got him outgunned—and he can't *know* our Shield's fucked-up.

"Mainly, though, he doesn't have to fight now. He can beat us to Sisshain, so why take chances?" Barton rubbed his throat. "Would somebody - kindly get me a beer?"

"Sure," said Cheng. "Anybody else?" Limila took the comm so that Myra could go with him; the two soon returned with beer, coffee, *klieta,* and a tray of assorted snacks.

"As long as we're allowing goodies in Control," said Myra, "let's do it right." No one made any objection.

Barton found he had no appetite. Limila, relieved of comm duty, came to him. "Do not feel badly, Barton. You did of your best, to save them—and they know it."

"Yeh. Close, but no cigar—not good enough, Limila. But you're right—no point in brooding about it. Let's go fix that damn Shield."

Barton found the job more difficult than he had expected. Normal realignment procedures failed; the result was still unstable.

The group had scattered, leaving Cheng and Myra on watch. Barton went to Five—maybe Abdul could help.

"Yes," said Abdul, "I worked in repair of units damaged in our testing at Tilara. I will see what I can do."

Only two were needed in the work, and Limila was tired; Barton sent her off to rest. It was a long job—before Abdul had any results to announce, Barton also felt fatigue.

"There are, of course, damaged components," Abdul said, finally. "It is the 'lock' circuit that is most severely affected. For the rest, I think, I can compensate."

The question was whether Ship One stocked all the right spare parts. Although the Shield couldn't possibly be needed for another day or two, and both men were overdue for sleep, neither was willing to stop work until they knew exactly what they were up against. So first they checked inventory on computer readout, and then went to root through the parts-bins physically. And a good thing, Barton decided, that they did follow through; records showed a spare exciter for the lock circuit, but the damned thing wasn't there!

While Barton was trying to work up enough energy to swear, Abdul said, "If I may disable one of the Larka-Te torpedoes, we can manage." The torpedoes, he went on to say, contained a very similar circuit package; all he'd have to improvise was the connectors, a mounting, and a phase-shift network. To Barton it didn't sound that easy, but if Abdul thought it was, why argue? And in any case, two torpedoes plus the Shield beat hell out of three and no Shield. Though Abdul said the robbed torpedo could still be fired as a solid missile—and maybe a dummy could come in handy, sometime.

So Barton okayed the idea, and headed back to Compartment One. He went in as quietly as he could, but Limila woke anyway. "Barton? You are still up?" She stretched. "Oh, I am so refreshed!"

Barton wasn't. But he knew the look of her, and be damned if he'd turn his woman down twice in one day.

Short of sleep, he was up before ship's-noon, feeling reasonably energetic but somewhat less than clear of mind. Limila was gone; he didn't find her in the galley, either, when he stopped by for coffee and took it up to Control. There, Alene and Eeshta had the watch; Barton sat alongside them. "Morning. Any news?"

"Not to speak of," said Alene. "Abdul and Limila are running around with circuitry coming out of their ears, if that helps."

"It had better. Without the Shield, we're in mucho tough."

Alene nodded. Eeshta said, "Barton. May I speak?"

"Huh? Sure, of course; any time. You know that."

"Then I would say this—that while I am glad Hishtoo is not dead, and the others, still you should have killed, Barton—while you could yet do so. Am I wrong to say it?"

Barton gripped the small Demu's bare, horny-carapaced shoulder. "No—not wrong, Eeshta. But you see— I didn't want to pull the trigger until I had to—on Iivajj and Gerain, or even on Hishtoo. And then while we were still arguing, he shot off the torp—and school was out."

"Yes, Barton—I saw. I could have told you what he would do. But I thought you knew."

He laughed briefly. "Maybe I did know—maybe I just got fat and sassy, and thought I could match whatever move he made. Anyway, it doesn't matter, Eeshta—except that they're still alive, and so are we. All that's changed is, now we have to do it—whatever we do—at Sisshain."

"Yes, Barton." Eeshta's head bowed, then straightened. "So that you know not again to relax vigilance against Hishtoo—that is all."

"I won't, Eeshta. And thank you."

"May I be relieved of watch for a moment? I would have *klieta,* if you permit."

"Sure thing. I'll hold it down."

When Eeshta was gone, Alene said, "You know something, Barton? That kid scares me."

"That right?" He paused, thinking. "I see what you mean—but it's not fear, Alene; it's awe. How she could come so far, so fast. All by herself, and after one hell of a bad start. The first time I met her . . . well, skip that; just take my word for it, she had no reason to love the Earthani.

"And yet, after only a few months on Earth, on her own hook she decided that when it comes to the Demu treatment of captives, we are right and her own people are wrong. To the point that she's willing to die for what she thinks."

"I know, Barton—that's what I mean. She scares me."

"Well, there's worse ways to be scared. And . . . oh, hey—Abdul! How's it going?"

"Very well, Barton. The modifications consumed much time, but after I have eaten, another hour—two, it might be—and the Shield will again be complete. Then only realignment remains—a brief task, as you know."

"Need any help?"

"Not immediately—Limila is doing all that is needed. Later, perhaps. If so, I will ask."

"Fine; do that." Abdul left them. "Anything else happening, Alene, in the way of progress?"

She shook her head. "Every now and then we tilt and take a look. Hishtoo's still on constant-decel for Sisshain. We're catching up a little, but not enough to count."

"Yeh—that figures. What's the latest guess as to when he lands? And when we do?" Eeshta returned with her *klieta.* Barton rose and turned the comm back to her, and Eeshta made the lifted-tongue Demu smile.

"The latest," said Alene, "looks like just under three days, for Hishtoo. Us?—we'll be close enough to watch his landing on visual, I think—maybe just a matter of being minutes behind. Oh, Barton—have you looked outside yet, today?"

"No. What's to see?"

"Show him, Eeshta." The young Demu turned switches; Barton watched the screen as Eeshta slowly panned the view through a full circle.

The change was that in the lower portion, no stars showed.

"I get it," Barton said. "We're entering the dust cloud —the pocket in it, I mean."

"Right," said Alene. "Pretty soon there won't be anything to see except a few stars directly behind us."

"And Sisshain ahead," said Eeshta. Her tone was hushed. Barton sympathized—he felt a little subdued himself.

He stood. "I think I'm enough awake, now, to eat breakfast." He waved a hand and left.

He found the galley empty, and set about scrambling eggs and making toast. He ate slowly, thinking ahead— to Sisshain. Guessing in a vacuum, he decided, was getting him nowhere fast—he went to check on Abdul's progress.

In the drive room, Abdul and Limila were working quietly, exchanging only a few words now and then. Barton watched silently for a few minutes, then spoke.

"Things coming along all right? Need any help?"

Limila looked up. "Good morning, Barton. Yes, it is well. A short time now, Abdul says, until we may test and realign."

Abdul finished the set of connections he was making, before he, too, looked up at Barton. "She is correct. Unless further damage has escaped my notice, it is only a matter of tedious assembly until the Shield is again complete, prepared for testing."

"So we'll know pretty soon—that's fine. Need another set of hands?"

Abdul shook his head. "No, I think not. Unless you are tired, Limila?"

"No, I am of good energy. I shall be hungry again, though, when the circuits are complete, before the testing."

"I, too," said Abdul. "At that point, we will pause."

"Okay, then—I'll get out of here and let you get on with it."

Barton returned to the galley and brooded over a cup

of *klieta,* alone. This damned waiting, he thought, was enough to stretch a man *all* out of shape.

The morning passed, and lunchtime, and the testing of the Shield. Abdul found and replaced another damaged component that might cause instability under stress. By midafternoon the Shield was as good as new. The jury-rigged assembly from the torpedo looked to Barton like a plumber's nightmare—but if Abdul vouched for it, Barton was satisfied.

Deeper into the mouth of the dust cloud. That day—and the next, and the next—dragged interminably. The seven spoke less and laughed seldom, each caught in his or her web of tension. There was no bad temper, no irritability—it wasn't that kind of tenseness. It was, thought Barton, like bleeding to death, one drop at a time. And about two-thirds done with it. . . .

Day-64: the day that would see Ship One landed on Sisshain, or—or *what?* A riddled hulk? A ship in dire retreat from Demu force? Barton wished he knew. But at least now, by God, they were getting down to cases!

He didn't bother with breakfast, but took a pot of coffee along to Control. Soon he had a full crew; Cheng and Myra had been relieved from their "night" watch but made no move to leave. Alene was pilot, Limila on comm, and Abdul sat at the weapons position. Barton prowled, unable to sit for long.

"How close?" he said. "When does Hishtoo land?" They were slowed to a fraction of light-speed; the ship's wake, streaming ahead, was only a tenuous obstacle to viewing or detection.

"Very close," said Limila. "Soon—less than an hour. He has passed the star—Sisshain's primary that is off the left side of our present view. As soon, we will pass it. He is inside the orbit of Sisshain, thus approaches its daylit side."

"That's a help," Barton growled, "unless he swings wide and orbits when he gets close. How far behind him are we?"

"The prediction," said Abdul, "based on present courses, speeds, and decelerations, is that we land twenty-five minutes after Hishtoo. The margin of error is five minutes, plus or minus. If we are not prevented or deterred, of course."

"Of course." Barton paused by the seat he wasn't using, to sip cold coffee. "Any more ships spotted? Or other signs of activity?"

"It is yet too far," said Limila, "to note details of Sisshain—even under high magnification. But our picture becomes clearer; soon we can see much more."

"Yeh—good. Excuse me a minute." He was carrying too much coffee, both in his nerves and elsewhere. A few minutes later he returned to Control—this time with a hastily assembled sandwich and a cup of *klieta*—and sat.

"Nothing new?"

"Not yet," said Alene. The waiting continued, with little talk.

On the screen, Sisshain grew. Limila ran the magnification up, and slowly scanned the visible hemisphere. Suddenly, Barton sat erect.

"Back it up, and to the left a little—there!" He stood, moved to view the screen at closer range. "Just what the hell is *that?*"

Whatever it was—the needle-like glint visible at such distance—it was big. "There is no way to judge scale," said Abdul, "but if I may venture a very loose estimate, the object is at least a kilometer in height—quite possibly, more."

"And Hishtoo's headed for it," said Alene. "Close to it, at least."

"I think," said Barton, "we just hit the jackpot. The Ormthan said, one who sees the thing cannot fail to know of its importance. Limila—don't lose Hishtoo, of course, but any time you get a chance, give us more detail on that thing. And its surroundings—the terrain could be a big factor."

"Yes, Barton. The shadows are deceptive, but the object appears to rise from the side of a mountain, about halfway of its height."

Barton squinted. "That's more than I can make out, from here. How tall a mountain, would you say?"

"I do not know yet—not outstandingly so, I would think. I—oh, now I see a thing here. The shadows—look! The tops of mountain and object are nearly at a level."

Barton looked. "Yeh—I think you're right. If the

298

angle isn't fooling us. Okay—now, how's Hishtoo doing?"

The view swung. Hishtoo was approaching atmosphere. For a fugitive, Barton thought, his approach was conservative. Which reminded him . . . .

"Alene," he said, "let's change seats. I'm relieving you."

She looked at him, startled. "But why, Barton? Am I goofing?"

"Not a bit of it, Alene—you're doing fine. I'm taking her down, is all. Got some ideas, and wouldn't be able to say 'em fast enough to do any good, in a pinch. Okay?" He smiled at her, and after a moment she smiled back and let him take over.

Barton checked his control settings, flexed both hands. "Show me Hishtoo again." The screen shifted. "Yeh, I see. Now the surface behind him . . . hey, beautiful picture! Look—the whole mountain is covered with trees —no landing, there." The screen again brought Hishtoo's ship into sharp focus.

"Clear space," said Alene, "off to the side of the picture. Not a very big one."

"Yes," Barton said, "and looks like he's dropping toward it. No other ships, that I can see. No buildings— nothing. Camouflaged, maybe?" He shook his head; no point in guessing. "A couple of items in a hurry, people. Limila—that monolith." The screen showed it briefly. Closer now, it glowed with rippling iridescence, polychromatic, stippled with random markings.

"Some show," said Barton. "Limila, on the way in I'm going to make a pass at that thing. I want cameras and instruments on it, recording.

"Abdul. If we make it down, I intend to land as close to Hishtoo as I can. Switch the laser to side-arm—now. And as soon as you get the chance, burn the hell out of his drive generators. You know where they are, close enough—slash around a little extra, to make sure." He frowned. "Oh, yeh—put the sleep-gun on, too. Now. Full strength, spherical distribution. And leave it on, after landing—just in case they got infantry."

"Barton?" said Limila. "Why disable Hishtoo's drive? He has no fuel left, to leave Sisshain."

"He could get some. And why let him hop around any further *on* Sisshain?"

299

"Yes—I see. Look, Barton!—Hishtoo is landing. And it is where we thought."

Sure enough; the stolen ship had come to rest. Briefly, the view expanded to show both clearing and mountain —ship and shining, flickering monolith. God!—that thing was *huge.*

"Okay—it's visiting hours!" Barton's hands moved; he heard gasps as the screen showed wheel and swoop, Sisshain's surface expanding and sliding across their field of view.

The mad slide went on, and on—twenty minutes, Abdul had said? Or was it forever?

Barton was taking her down like a bat out of hell. Well, he'd done it before. . . .

The giant needle, shimmering—*"Get it!"* he shouted. Trees almost close enough to touch, passing so rapidly as to blur into dull-green carpet. Sisshain swung to the side and vanished—one glimpse of Hishtoo's ship—as Barton pointed his straight up, then at tilt to kill lateral momentum, then up again.

Seconds short of touchdown, Barton's controls went dead; the ship fell at an angle. The Shield absorbed most of the impact; Ship One rocked dangerously and then settled upright, between Hishtoo's ship on one side and sheer ocher cliffs rising on the other.

Barton looked around. "Use that goddamn laser!" Abdul unfroze and obeyed; Hishtoo's ship would not lift soon again.

"Okay, we're down," said Barton. "But that last part wasn't my idea."

He flipped switches, checked instruments. "Well," he said finally, "it looks as if Hishtoo isn't the only one who's grounded. The Demu had a weapon we didn't know about—probably in the Washington Monument up there. Because some way, I don't know how, our drive has gone dead as a mackerel."

The outside view-scan showed no one, Demu or otherwise, within its range.

"Too bad," said Barton. "We might have got lucky and caught somebody in the sleep-field. It's still on, isn't it, Abdul?" The man nodded.

"Well then—I guess I go calling on Hishtoo. I'll need—"

"You may look, Barton," said Limila, "and with care, of course. But I think that ship is empty. For a moment as we came here, I saw—here, it is recorded, I think."

She ran the tape into the screen circuits. Reduced to slow motion the flash of view, lightning-fast as it had been, stretched into seconds. Speed and magnification blurred the picture, but one thing was clear. On the opposite side of Hishtoo's ship, the main airlock was open, its ramp down. "They are gone, you see."

"Maybe," said Barton, "maybe not—could be a mousetrap, a setup. I'll have a look, anyway."

"And I with you, Barton," said Limila. "You do not go alone."

"But—" He saw there was no use arguing. "All right."

"And I, Barton," said Eeshta. "I too must go."

He turned to her. "*No*—and that's flat. We need you for later, when we meet your people and—I hope—talk with them. You can't be risked in some dumb shoot-out, at this stage."

"And can you?" But Eeshta shrugged in resignation. "Very well—it will be as you say."

"All right—now here's what we do—"

A cloverlike growth carpeted the ground. It did not show footprints; if Hishtoo was gone, there would be no tracking him. Circling one to either side, Barton and Limila approached the other ship. To their right, Alene Grover moved toward a pile of boulders—to take cover and then, if necessary, give it. On the ground beside Ship One, Cheng and Myra waited in reserve. If there were no fight, they would begin a search, circling outside of view-screen range—for Hishtoo, his hostages, or anything else of interest.

All five wore the nonguaranteed portable Shields and carried sleep-guns—redundant, in view of the ship's sleep-field—and either ion beam or laser handguns. No breathing gear: Demu presence meant the atmosphere was suitable.

On Ship One, Abdul Muhammed—carrying the new title of second-in-command—was left at the weapons board and Eeshta at the comm-board.

Out of the corner of his eye, Barton saw Alene reach her position. All right—time to move in. He gestured to Limila and she returned it; then they moved forward and the bulk of the crippled ship came between them. Rounding it, Barton stayed close to the hulk—remembering another time, another ship.

The ramp was down, all right. He saw it and Limila, rounding the ship from the other side, almost at the same time. They exchanged signals—he to approach, she to move past and cover the airlock at the top of the ramp.

Nothing barred him from walking up the ramp and into the ship—nothing at all. It was too easy. On the ground, Barton found a dead branch of wood, thick as his arm and over a meter long. He picked it up and threw it at the ramp. At the impact, the ramp snapped shut, up into the body of the ship. Fragments of wood fell. Then, slowly, the ramp lowered again.

Mousetrap wasn't a bad guess at all, thought Barton—Hishtoo must have really souped the hell out of those motor circuits. He saw smoke drifting from the airlock, and on a hunch, threw another piece of wood. Nothing happened—a one-shot trap, now burned out.

"Limila? I'm going in. If you don't hear anything that sounds like trouble, come on up in about five minutes. If you do hear trouble, play it from out here—and get help."

"I will do as I think best. But most likely as you say."

Cautiously but not slowly, Barton climbed the ramp. At the airlock he paused and listened. From inside, no sounds came; he entered. After a quick inspection he returned and beckoned to Limila.

"There is nothing here," she said after further exploration, "to show that Hishtoo or Iivajj were ever on this ship. Gerain, yes—a few belongings that are of a male Tilaran. Nothing more."

"At least there's no sign that Hishtoo hurt them any. All right—we might as well get out of here and back to the ship."

Outside, Barton waved for Alene to join them; together they trudged back to Ship One. "Where's Cheng and Myra?" Barton asked.

Alene answered. "I gave them the high-sign to start search, as soon as you came back out the first time. Was that all right?"

"Fine," said Barton. "Let's go on in and button it up. We'll set the screen to watch for them—a perimeter watch."

The two scouts were beyond view-range, Barton discovered when he reached Control. Eeshta had last seen them going behind a low range of hills at perhaps a kilometer's distance. An hour later, after the reconnaissance of Hishtoo's ship had been discussed thoroughly, the two reappeared in line-of-sight, moving slowly and showing fatigue.

"They look as hungry as I feel," said Alene. "I'm going to cook up some stuff. Anyone who's chicken to try a Grover Special, never before tasted by man or beast, raise your hands—and cook your own dinner!" No hand raised. "All right, you're not chicken—you're just lazy." She exited toward the galley.

When the entrance alarm sounded, the screen showed Myra and Cheng waiting. Soon the two entered Control.

"I'm bushed," said Myra. "It's been too long since I walked so much. But one thing's certain—our sleep-field didn't catch anything, unless you want to count a few small furry creatures."

"Perhaps I should turn it off for a time," said Abdul, "and allow those a chance for escape."

"Sure," Barton said. "Set it to go on again if anything big—people-size—trips the alarm."

Before he could ask more questions, Alene called dinnertime. "Here's trays made up for whoever has the watch. Everybody else dish up for yourselves, in the galley." Abdul and Eeshta stayed on duty; the rest adjourned.

Barton decided not to ask what Alene had put into dinner; it tasted better than it looked. He did have another question, though.

"Cheng? Myra? You *sure* we don't have any sleeping beauties around here?"

"Quite sure," said Myra. "We scouted to the perimeter of the field."

"You *what?* Now that's a good trick. How do you know?"

"We thought about it," said Cheng, "and tested. Starting at the viewscreen perimeter we went out on a gradual spiral—"

"Not to miss anything," said Myra.

"And finding nothing," Cheng continued, "we decided to test the extent of the field in atmosphere. It was not difficult. One of us would switch the Shield of the other off, then on again."

"Either a quick blackout, or not," Myra said. "We took turns."

"God*damn* it!" said Barton. "Didn't anybody tell you, you could lose a chunk of memory that way?"

"We used only very brief—momentary—exposures," said Cheng. "We notice no ill effects."

"I hope you're right. But—you *sure* you didn't miss any live corpses? I mean, you covered a lot of territory."

"We're pretty sure," said Myra Hake. "One person, given time to hide, we might have missed. Those three together, caught by surprise, we could *not* have missed. You see the difference?"

Barton saw. He agreed, and congratulated the two on a good job well done. ". . . but the next time you want to go fucking around with the sleep-zapper—or anything else you're not briefed on—for Christ's sake, *ask* first!"

Grave-faced, the two agreed. Barton didn't believe a word of it. But either they could take care of themselves or they couldn't, and his bet was that they could.

The main thing was what to do next—and that was his decision, no one else's.

There was only one possible answer. "Tomorrow morning," he said, "some of us are going up the mountain to see the totem pole. Dressed like locals.

"Be thinking about it."

Barton and Limila, next morning, were the last to assemble in the galley. Alene was serving breakfast; Cheng and Eeshta were packing marching rations into belt pouches, to be worn under the Demu robes.

"A bunch of early birds," said Barton, and noted that the replies were cheerful. He took a cup of coffee and sat.

"Hungry?" said Alene. He nodded, and she set a tray before him.

"Fast service. Thanks."

"Barton," said Abdul, "I have information about the drive."

"You got it working?"

"No, I cannot. But I know what has happened."

"Damage permanent?" Barton said.

"Again, no. But it is not a matter of repair. Focused on this ship is a beam of incident energy that neutralizes and cancels the wave forms of our exciter output, so that it cannot activate the generator fields."

"Through the Shield, it does that?"

"Yes, Barton. Like the laser, this beam is coherent radiation, but of dimensions that penetrate our hull without damage to it. I tried a method of evading the effects, but my effort was fruitless."

"What was it?"

"I changed the exciter frequency slightly—there is a workable range each side of peak tuning, without much loss of efficiency. But the Demu device followed my adjustments exactly."

"In other words," Barton said, slowly, "we're stuck here until we can get to their gadget and turn it off."

"It would seem so."

Barton had another thought. "They'd have conked us at high altitude, if they could have. And you know—I bet they tried. It's a damned good thing we came in fast, and took that side swoop at the monolith—that's probably what threw them off. Otherwise, we could have been splattered over a couple of acres, Shield or no Shield."

"Jesus!" he said. "Abdul—make a tape, warning off Thirteen and Thirty-four, so they don't try to land. Beam it straight up, thirty-degree spread, max power, and leave it running—loop tape. Okay?"

"Yes, Barton—immediately. Is there anything else I should do?"

Barton thought. "Yes. Can you rig a good loud alarm to sound off if the interference stops and the drive goes operative again?"

"Easily. But why—? Oh, I see."

"Yeh. So that whoever's available can lift this baby the hell out of here—fast. Waste fuel like crazy by going all-out max, and stay low and flat until Cleopatra's Needle is below the horizon. Everybody got that?"

"But, Barton," said Limila, "what of those who are not on the ship at such a time? Are they to be left?"

"No. The ship comes back later, of course. Comes back the same way—low and fast and sneaky—and makes a sidewise pass at the monolith with enough speed so that if the drive goes dead, you can *coast* out of range, to safety."

"That range would be a matter of estimate," said Abdul.

"Hell, yes—the game doesn't come with any guarantees on it."

"I know. Very well, I will arrange the tape and the alarm."

305

"Okay—and good work, Abdul, finding out what the problem is."

At another table, Myra and Limila were sorting the Demu-disguise components by sizes. "Barton," said Limila, "you have not spoken of who is to go, and who to stay at the ship."

"I know. I've been thinking about it." He, Limila and Eeshta had to go, for sure. Anyone else? And if so, who?

He could afford no weak links—not, he thought, that any of his people could be called weak. But Cheng and Myra—who could hardly be assigned separately—were not weapons-oriented, despite their precautionary training. Nor did they speak Demu.

Abdul was a true artist with weapons—never mind that Barton's landing had momentarily paralyzed him—and a man Barton would like to have backing him in hostile country. He spoke very little Demu but had picked up a limited listening vocabulary.

Alene, now . . . Barton appreciated a sort of native ferocity he detected in her—but she was impulsive. Could he risk her in a deadly situation that might call for subtlety as the key to survival?

He decided. "You and I, Limila—we go, of course. And Eeshta—and, I think, Abdul."

A series of hisses startled him—Demu-fashion, Eeshta was laughing. "Did I say something funny, Eeshta?" Barton's voice was mild; he was puzzled, not irritated. "If I'm making a mistake, please correct me."

"It is Abdul, Barton."

"You don't think he's a good choice?"

"In all but size, Barton, he would be admirable. But no Demu is so very large, nor even closely to it. Limila, I would say, is near to the greatest height believable as Demu."

Barton had sat straight; now he leaned back in his chair. "Thanks, Eeshta. I guess if it weren't for you I'd have pulled a real blooper. Maybe you'd better keep tabs on me, and sing out if you catch me doing anything else stupid."

"Very well, Barton. But it was not stupid—you could not know."

"Yeh. But—" He thought, I could have *asked,* damn it! Am I to kill us all, yet, with my single-minded lack of vision? Abruptly, he chose his course.

"Just the three of us, then. The rest stay."

"Wait a minute," Alene protested. "What about me? You know you need another gun—at the least."

He answered in Demu. "It is that you know not the tongue of the land."

"What did you say?"

"You don't talk the local lingo. We couldn't communicate in the presence of Demu. If you forgot, in a bind, and said even a few words in English, we'd all be up the spout. I'm sorry—in a different situation, there's damned few people I'd rather have backing me."

"I'd be careful," she began. Then, "No—you're right. Grover's tough and Grover's smart—I think you'll grant me that—but Grover's mouth does have one of the lightest trigger-pulls known to modern man. I hate to admit it, Barton, but you're right." Her eyelids lifted; reflected light flashed from widened eyes. "But it's not just because I'm a woman! My father's even worse!"

He laughed—he had to laugh. After a moment, so did she.

"Well," he said, "it's Halloween, kiddies—time to get dressed up for trick-or-treat. Incidentally—everyone who's staying home—if you wander around outside, go costumed. That way, if you're seen from a distance you won't set off any flares." He frowned. "I should have thought of that before we went out yesterday, but as usual I was in too damned much of a hurry to think at all."

"Barton," said Limila, "I do not like this mood—blaming yourself, calling yourself stupid. It is no mood in which to start an enterprise such as we now undertake." She looked at him. "I would see you alone."

In Compartment One, Barton expected a lecture. He was agreeably surprised.

Under the dark blue sky, the day was sunny, the air cool. Inside the headpiece, though, Barton felt smothered —the Tilaran plastic was somewhat pervious to air, but not enough for comfort.

His eyelids burned. Around the eyeholes the plastic was thin and flexible, adhering to the lids in a perfect match under the lowering brow ridges. But another unforeseen difficulty had arisen—in any adequate light, the eyelashes were a dead giveaway that whatever Barton might be, he was not Demu. So, one by one, Limila had plucked them out, and now the lids were sore and swollen. Limila, of course, lacked lashes—the Demu had removed them permanently. She merely removed the false lashes she usually wore.

The robes and hoods were bulky and awkward, but Barton had worn such garb before and soon adjusted his stride to move more easily. At his belt, under the robe, he carried food pouch and water bag, his Shield generator, and a small two-way radio set to ship's frequencies. Under one arm was holstered a sleep-gun—under the other, a hand laser. Limila carried a Tilaran ion-beam weapon; Eeshta was unarmed.

The four-digited gloves bothered Barton a little— the two smaller fingers confined in one tube, and the loss, as with any glove, of tactile sensation. The footwear, Barton thought, was the best of it. Simulating bare Demu feet, the outline was mittenlike—the great toe separate, the rest together in a casing marked and indented to indicate three nailless toes. The heavy soles gave good protection and sure footing.

On inspection, before leaving the ship, consensus had been that Barton and Limila were nearly as convincing as Eeshta herself.

Still puzzled about Hishtoo's reason for coming to Sisshain, Barton reopened the question as they walked.

"Truly, I cannot say," said Eeshta. "As I have told you, Sisshain is of such importance to the Demu that it is both duty and privilege for the fortunate among us to come here at some time in their lives."

"Yes. Abdul's people once had a similar custom."

"He has said—the place, Mecca. But as to Sisshain— Hishtoo my egg-parent traveled here, in his younger days. He has spoken of it to me, but not greatly, as I am too young to be told of such importances. Also my other parent, Tashin, was here."

"Did they come here together?" Limila asked.

"No. At the times of their visits, they did not know each other. Nor do they now, except casually. The Demu do not carry the intimacies of breeding into their later personal lives. Each keeps ties with the lives of its own egg-children, nothing more."

"Ann Landers would starve to death," Barton muttered. "You didn't have contact with your other parent?"

"Tashin? I have met Tashin. Long ago Hishtoo and I visited him at his home in Shestri, on Demmon—when we lived on that planet. Tashin greeted me civilly and wished me well."

This isn't getting us anywhere, thought Barton, and let the subject drop.

At the end of their first hour of walking, first in sun and then shaded by trees, they had seen no one, nor signs of any. Occasionally some small brown animal, furry and plump, scuttled across the ground to take refuge in a tree. The three were climbing now, a gradual rise—if not the foot of the mountain itself, then close to it.

The thick growth of trees looked unfamiliar to Barton, but not alien—mottled grayish brown bark, straight sturdy trunks that branched above, leaves like dark evergreen but wider and thicker. Pulpy-looking, Barton thought, but a fallen leaf picked from the ground was tough and springy to his touch. Barton found its pungent, spicy smell rather pleasant.

Gradually the slope increased. The climb was tiring; their pace slowed. Barton called a rest stop. "We're on the mountain now, all right. Snack time, if you want to."

"How much farther, do you think, Barton?"

"No way of knowing, Limila, until these trees thin out a little—or we walk smack into the thing. We've been going straight up-slope, near as I can manage it, so we shouldn't miss by much." He turned to Eeshta. "You tired?"

"Not badly, Barton. I grew for the most part on Demmon, where gravity pulls more strongly, before going to Ashura."

"To where?"

"Ashura—the planet of the research station, where you were."

Barton laughed. "You know, that's funny—I never thought to ask the name of the place."

"I thought you knew. The questioning teams, on Earth, asked me such things."

"I guess I had my head into too much other stuff, then." He rose. "Okay—everybody ready to move on?" Snacks were finished; the three sipped water and resumed the climb.

As they proceeded, the forest grew less thickly. The change was not great—Barton remembered that the mountain was tree-covered to its peak—but now he could see that they were on a ridge with sides that dropped away more steeply as it rose. It vexed him, for the ridge slanted about ten degrees to the right of his chosen course, but he had to follow it—the alternative was a steep descent and steeper climb to regain lost altitude.

Where the ridge ended, the major mass ahead rose sharply from a talus slope of broken rock. "Must we climb that?" Limila said.

"Not here. We'll follow along the lower edge, as far as we can. To the left—the ridge brought us quite a bit the other way, and it looks like it might not be quite as steep above, over there. And at least there's no trees directly above us, for a while. Maybe . . . . "

Picking their way along the tumbled fringe of the talus, they continued. Now Sisshain's sun was hot; sweat flowed under Barton's robe. Reaching a point at which the ridge began to drop off steeply, they had to leave it, and began to clamber up and along the loose rock.

On the treacherous footing, progress was slow. Barton cautioned the others, and saw to it that no one was ever directly in line below another. He paused frequently, not only to rest but to squint, uphill and at an angle against the sun, through binoculars Limila had carried.

The side of the talus petered out at the edge of a bare wash—a gully—that cut almost directly up-slope. Standing at that edge, Barton looked up—and saw the monolith.

"Holy Christ!" Showing at the immediate left of the gully's top was what he guessed to be the upper third of the thing. "If that's what I think it is—!

"Let's get to moving."

Climbing the gully took the party into afternoon, but until they reached the top, they made no midday meal. Above them, the mountain—forested once more—rose less steeply. And from their vantage point they could see, above the trees, almost the whole of the dazzling, iridescent tower.

Now Barton would speak. "It's a ship! It has to be the biggest goddamned granddaddy-starship ever built; it can't be anything else. I wonder who. . . ."

"Who but the Demu, Barton?" said Eeshta. "Now I understand."

"Understand what, Eeshta?"

"From things Hishtoo said, Barton, and from talk among the young as I was growing. We are not told, so we fasten onto chance hints and make ideas—theo-

ries. We believed—and thought the grown believed also
—that Sisshain is our home world, the source of all
Demu.

"When Hishtoo said to me, on the ship before Tilara,
'the Demu came,' I thought it was from Sisshain he
meant, to the other worlds. Remember, Barton—when
I told you what he said?"

Barton remembered—Eeshta's chant. His spine prickled.

"But now you think differently?" He knew what she
would say.

She did. "Sisshain is not our origin. This is the kind of
ship that brought the Demu *to* Sisshain. It may be the
ship—one of the ships—that burned away the worlds.
Further down the Arm, where none are now to be
found."

Slowly, Barton nodded. "Yes—it might be, at that.
Certainly, you're not related to what we've seen of the
local fauna. But take a look through these binoculars—
they adjust, like this. Then you too, Limila."

They looked. "See?" he said. "That baby's been out of
commission—or at least, not used—for a long time.
See those gouges? Deep ones. The cameras blurred that
detail when I made the pass at it, landing—we were just
plain going too fast—but some of those marks must be a
meter deep, or more. And notice how the colors, and the
way they flicker, go all the way into the metal, if it is
metal. Hell, it has to be—or something just as tough.
From here, I don't see any holes that go through the
hull—I wonder how thick it really is.

"See the vegetation growing in some of the dents? It
doesn't look like much, from here, but some of those are
good-sized trees. Lower down, the ship's covered with
vines, something like ivy. It grows almost halfway up—
how many centuries would that take?

"Most of all, look at the *little* marks. Erosion patterns
—erosion patterns in metal. We're looking at a *lot* of
time."

Eeshta looked at him. "You say, then, the ship is
dead."

"Not dead. *Something* around here has enough
whammy to lay a field on us at several kilometers that
kills our own drive. So, not dead—but not flown for a
long, long time. Maybe not in shape to fly. Or maybe
kept idle for some reason we don't know.

311

"Yet," he added. "Well—I don't know about everybody else, but I'm hungry."

"Yes," said Limila. "We had forgotten of our lunch, had we not?"

They ate; afterward, Barton waited another half-hour before resuming the march. They were getting close now; he wanted everyone well-rested. For one thing, a place —a thing—like this couldn't be deserted. He found himself tensed, waiting for the other shoe to drop.

Less than an hour later, they found the trail. Only a foot-trail—from below it came up at their left, crossing Barton's course at a slight angle. He stopped, looked at it.

Limila spoke. "Shall we follow it, Barton? Or stay clear, with perhaps less chance of being seen?"

"We follow it. We're supposed to be Demu—remember? This gives us our first chance to start acting in character."

The footing was easier, too.

The trail rose, skirted steep rises and crossed a narrow stream, the first they'd encountered. "Most of the steady runoff must go to one side or the other, of the way we came up," Barton said. "Shall we see if the local water's fit to drink?" He knelt and scooped with both hands together, smelling the first dip and tasting the second. "Not as cold as I'd like—or expect—but not bad. Not bad at all."

Belatedly, he wondered about the possibility of infectious organisms. But what the hell, he thought—the Demu had fed and watered him for eight years, and he hadn't died of it. With no apparent qualms, the others drank also.

To the left, a brightness flashed upward. Seconds later, thunder rolled. After a moment, Barton spoke.

"Well, there went a ship."

"Ours, could it be?" said Limila.

"Not a chance—wrong direction from here. No— Hishtoo has convinced somebody to get the word to Demmon in a big hurry."

"Thirteen and Thirty-four may intercept it."

"And maybe not," Barton said. "Well—nothing we can do from here, except keep going." Again they began walking.

Not much later, rounding a tree-covered hill Barton saw two things: less than half a kilometer ahead, the great ship, all of it—and preceding his party, at perhaps a tenth of that distance, a group of four robed Demu.

"Barton," said Limila, "what shall we do?"

"Start speaking Demu, for one thing," he said. "In a minute, that is. Eeshta—I just thought of something." *At the last minute again, damn it.* "We should have names, shouldn't we? Limila and I, I mean. What would be suitable?"

The lifted-tongue smile. "Names? I must think." Silence, then a nod. "Oh, yes. You, I think, are Bashta. And you"—to Limila—"are Linish."

"But do not give names until asked. You remember?"

Barton nodded. He had tried to take a crash course in Demu manners and customs, but somehow there had never been time for much of it. He had resigned himself to relying, in the clutch, on Eeshta's and Limila's knowledge.

"All right—thanks. From now on, there's nobody here but us Demu."

At first, Barton kept a steady distance behind the party ahead. Then as the trail took a slight angle past a clump of trees, he saw a group of robed figures near a door in the base of the titanic structure. They appeared to converse; then some disappeared into the opening, into the ship. Odds on, he thought, the gatekeepers just passed in a squad of pilgrims.

He quickened his pace, gaining on the four ahead. Limila caught his robe, looking at him with an unspoken question.

"It is," he said, "that these before us are received soon by those near the portal. That we listen to what is said."

"It is not to be so easy, surely? Simply to enter! It is certain that they must guard."

"It is certain that they guard for animals, for Earthani and Tilari. But do they guard for Demu?"

She nodded in agreement, and along with Eeshta, matched Barton's faster pace.

He timed it to come up behind the four almost as they reached the reception committee—hoping to hell that in doing so he was committing no breach of unknown etiquette. He—all three—stopped a short distance behind, but well within hearing range.

Of the waiting group, Barton bet himself that the one with the gold-edged hood had to be the kingfish. That one spoke.

"It is that the Keeper of the Heritage would know, who visits and who would become?" The question had the rhythmic sound of a ritual chant.

One of the four moved forward. "It is that I, who am twice here, would become. These with me visit." The response sounded equally ritualistic.

"You who visit, see no more the one who brought you." Another receptionist led the three away, into the ship. Barton watched and listened closely. "You who would become, may you become as you wish." A small cloth bag was handed to the one addressed. "This is to use by those who do not become, no shame to their eggs."

The recipient dipped head and torso without bending, and in tow of another guide entered the ship. Too bad, thought Barton, that there hadn't been more ahead of him, to deplete the greeting contingent a little better. For now it was his turn.

Since neither Limila nor Eeshta stepped forward, Barton took the lead, and waited for his cue.

"It is that the Keeper of the Heritage would know, who visits and who would become?"

"It is that we three visit." Barton tried to match his questioner's cadence.

"But it is that none visit, not brought by one who is twice here. All know it."

"It is that I am twice here." *Shit, I blew it already!* Now what?

"Then it is that you are named here." Barton took a moment to figure that one. Oh, yes—let's check your membership card . . . .

"Tashin." Out of the blue he said it—and good-bye, Bashta, whoever you were . . . .

"Tashin?" The Demu mumbled into a device dimly seen under its hood, and waited. "It is, say our records, that Tashin is not living." Limila's gasp was barely audible.

"It is that records may err," said Barton. "The records say I am not here, but it is that I am here."

"It is that you are here, Tashin." Gold Hood dipped head and body, upright. "Then it is that you are twice here. You are here to become, not to visit. It is so."

"It is so." Barton wished he knew what the hell was going on.

"Why is it that Tashin, who wishes to become, says that he visits?"

Because my head was on backward! "It is that as

314

records may err, so may persons. Tashin, who would become, thinks of much, and says in error. It is that Tashin would become."

The rigamarole was back on track. "You who visit, see no more the one who brought you." A robed figure led Eeshta and Limila inside . . . and there was nothing Barton could do about it.

"You who would become, may you become as you wish." The cloth bag; Barton took it. "This is to use by those who do not become, no shame to their eggs."

Barton remembered to do the erect curtsey before following his own guide to the great ship. Only then did he venture to feel the cloth bag, to determine the outlines of the object within.

It was a knife in there—a sharply pointed, two-edged dagger.

Inside the ship Barton paused, stunned. Seeing his guide hesitate, he programmed himself to follow automatically. But his mind rocked, bombarded by the total impact of the place.

It wasn't the flood of colors, which flashed and changed and flowed along every surface. It wasn't the thunderous music—or what would have been music, to anyone who heard mostly in the subsonic range. He thought: but the Demu's hearing extends *above* ours, not below. It wasn't the strange scents of the air, or its shimmer . . . .

Barton had once attended a showing of Escher's works—M. C. Escher, the man who drew in more than three dimensions, who twisted space so that one man walked on a surface that was another's vertical wall, and each validly oriented to the viewer's perspective. And more—Barton had been amazed and delighted by the exhibit. But now he found himself *in* an Escherlike environment—one little figure among many, madly juxtaposed.

And which way *was* up? Shimmering air and vast distances diluted the reality of what he saw. But surely, there—at the farthest reach of vision—six Demu walked in single file, taking their slanting course up a vertical wall.

He looked up, and was shocked—where was the top of what he could see? Two hundred meters above? Five hundred? The great ship was much taller, but still . . . .

And the space was half-empty, half-filled with spirals

and ribbons, floating circles, moving shapes that interlocked and moved apart again. Barton's attention was caught by a meter-wide ribbon, probably metal, that stretched like a twisted length of crepe paper almost vertically from the floor to a vanishing point high above, where other objects hid it. Perhaps twenty meters above him, a Demu walked sure-footedly down its spiraled course—while on the ribbon's other side, another, upward bound, passed the first—each unseeing and oblivious of the other, each body extending nearly horizontal from the double footpath.

Savagely, Barton shook his head. All right, he said to himself, so they have artificial gravity on any individual surface they damn well please. Quit acting like a country boy at the nudies, and *watch it!*

Still following the Demu guide, he looked around, trying to find Limila and Eeshta. Impossible—robes and hoods, shimmering air, shifting lights and colors—well, it all helped his own disguise, too, for what that was worth.

After about twenty minutes his guided path approached the center of the place. There, something new was added—on the floor were two circles, each nearly two meters in diameter and the same distance apart. One was brightly opalescent, the other a deep, throbbing redpurple. Demu moved onto the lighter one and rose vertically, visibly unsupported. From above, others drifted down onto the darker one. Beats the hell, Barton thought, out of waiting for elevators.

Barton was led to the opalescent up-circle. If I could think of anything better to do, he thought, I'd do it. But he couldn't—he followed his leader, who gave the preceding Demu about three meters' vertical head start before entering the circle. Noting, Barton did the same.

As he began to rise he heard a cry: *"Eeshta!"* The voice was Hishtoo's, and if Barton could have jumped down he would have done so, even from the height he'd reached before the voice registered. But if there was a way to move out of the path of the lift force, he didn't know it. All he could do was realize how thoroughly he had managed to trap the lot of them.

He rose and rose—above the open volume, into space divided by levels. He looked up and saw Demu entering and leaving the lift—the way to leave, he saw, was to reach an arm toward one of the large metal rings that bordered the lift-space at each level. Barton quit cursing his ignorance—down below, where he had wanted out, there were no such rings. He was on the express, and no help for it. Forever and a little longer, he rose.

Above, his guide whistled a signal. Not exactly a whistle, but close. Barton looked up again; the top of the shaft was near. By choice, he did not look down— not even to see if Hishtoo were following.

The guide reached toward a ring, drifted to it and grasped it, and stepped out onto solidity. Moments later, Barton did the same. Then—only then—he looked down.

He couldn't see the bottom, only rising figures in diminishing perspective. None were looking up; if Hishtoo was among them, Barton couldn't identify him.

The guide touched his robed arm, and he straightened and looked around. A Demu approached and entered the down-shaft, paying Barton no special attention. The lighting was steady here, a pale yellow with occasional bursts of orange, and the music was faint.

Barton was led along a corridor that was out of Escher by Dali. It was not long; Barton guessed that they might be near the pointed top of the great ship, where space would be limited. The only door, at the end of the corridor, was black and featureless—shocking, by contrast, in its very simplicity. The guide reached toward it and pushed; it moved only enough to indicate that it was not locked.

"It is," said the Demu, "that here, in the place of becoming, you become—or do not. I am become; now I bring others who would." It gestured toward Barton's cloth bag. "For those who do not become, no shame to the eggs. It is said—I go."

Barton entered the room and closed the door—there was no lock. Slipping the bag and its knife inside his belt, he turned and looked around the room.

The lighting was steady and adequate, but not brilliant—the sourceless light he remembered from the cage on Ashura, and the Demu ship. There were none of the color effects he'd seen below.

The room, though large, was simple—black floor, gray walls, white ceiling. And the room contained nothing but the pictures on its walls and the pedestaled statues that crowded its floor. Puzzled, Barton began an inspection tour of the strangest art gallery he'd ever seen.

Demu were portrayed repeatedly, though subtly different from the way Barton knew them, and never clothed. But the predominant life form shown, among several others, was one Barton had never seen nor ever imagined. It had too many arms and legs, too many eyes. It was not spiderlike—it was simply a large humanoid with too many arms and legs, too many eyes.

Barton looked, and looked. And then—he *saw*.

He took out the two-way radio, hoping to God that the great ship's hull was pervious to its special type of emission.

"Ship One! Barton to Ship One!"

"Ship One here—Abdul speaking. What—?"

"First things first—*tape this!*" Quickly he told what he had seen, was seeing—and what it meant.

"Got it, Abdul? . . . Okay, put it on the beam for Thirteen and Thirty-four, along with the landing warning. But coded, under seal. And the following instructions . . ."

Abdul read it back; then there was a brief, silent pause. "It's going out now. But not with the landing warning—Thirteen and Thirty-four arrived this morning; they are overhead, in synchronous orbit. Do you wish one or both to pursue the escaped Demu ship?"

"No. I think we win or lose it, right here."

"Very well. Barton—I assume you are all right?"

"Remains to be seen—so far, I'm unharmed and undetected. Limila and Eeshta, though—we got separated, earlier—a ritual thing, takes too long to explain." He shook his head; *that* line of thought could freeze his mind. "Anything new at your end?"

"Approximately an hour ago, more than one hundred Demu approached, from the direction opposite to you."

"Armed how?"

"Hand weapons only, except for a self-propelled unit ridden by one Demu."

"Portable Shield maybe, like our bigger ones?"

"No, Barton. The vehicle passed the perimeter of our sleep-field; the driver fell off, and it stopped. Approximately half the Demu also entered the field and dropped; the other half have been busy, trying to retrieve them. Some have fired their hand weapons at the ship,

318

but without effect. Naturally, we are alert for a major attack, with larger weapons or by ships."

"Five gets you ten, it won't happen."

"Why do you think that?"

"Just like Hishtoo five days ago, Abdul. First, it's dangerous, and second, they don't need to. Or so they think . . ."

"I see. Is there anything further you wish me to do now?"

"Well . . . no point in giving your Demu there any more amnesia than we have to, I guess. You might pull the field in until they start to wake up. Then if they pull back, ease it up to max. If they try to keep coming, though, sock it to full strength and the hell with them."

"Very well. I will do so, making certain they have no chance to reach their larger weapon. And—"

"Oh-oh! I've got company." The knock at the door came slow and heavy. "I'll leave the channel open, this end. Don't be heard from there unless I ask you a question. Barton out."

He replaced the radio at his belt, activated his personal Shield. He took the sleep-gun in his right hand, concealed under the robe. With his left, he opened the door—not widely, only enough to see, and to be seen.

The Demu who had knocked moved to the side of the corridor and back along it, past the group that faced Barton a few meters distant.

Foremost stood Hishtoo, his hand weapon trained on Barton. The design was unfamiliar; Barton hoped it was the sleeper, not the ion gun or something he didn't know about. Behind Hishtoo was Limila, unmasked and hood thrown back—under her disguise, she had not worn the wig. Beside her, Eeshta stood, and—Barton's heart leaped —Gerain and Iivajj, apparently unharmed. Behind the lot of them were five armed Demu.

"It is Barton?" said Hishtoo. "It is that you look Demu, yes, as Limila does when I find her with Eeshta. But inside is Barton."

At least Hishtoo was talking, not shooting—up to now.

"It is that you are not to be there, Barton. You are not to become, for it is that only Demu become, and you are not Demu, but animal. It is that you are to be Demu soon, as Limila again, and these others when they learn. But still not to become, for you are not egg-born. So it is that you are not to be where you are." Hishtoo beckoned with his weapon. Why hadn't he used it? And what was it, anyway?

Suddenly, Barton knew—the important parts, anyway. If it was the ion gun, Hishtoo couldn't fire it into the place of becoming—whatever that meant, and Barton was beginning to have some ideas on the subject. Ergo, for the time being, Barton stayed right where he was.

And the sleep-gun? "After they decide to make a person Demu," Limila had said, "they do not use it on that person."

Well, now . . . *but don't get overconfident, you dumb bastard!*

"It is that you are wrong, Hishtoo. It is that I *am* become, Demu or no."

"It is not so! It is that you are not Demu—and you are not twice here!"

Twice here! "But it is that *you* are twice here, Hishtoo. You are to become. It is that you are to enter now, and become!"

"It is not that I become. I have not that which is to be used by those who do not become . . . . "

". . . no shame to their eggs," Barton finished. He drew out the cloth bag. "It is that I have that for you, Hishtoo." He held it out. To the group behind, he spoke the first benison, in the chantlike pattern he had heard earlier. Whether or not it strictly applied, it should affect Hishtoo.

"You who visit, see no more the one who brought you."

And then, to Hishtoo, "You who would become, may you become, as you wish." Again he held out the bag. "This is to use by those who do not become, no shame to their eggs."

Hishtoo moved forward, then stopped.

"No shame to their eggs," Barton repeated. Hishtoo's hands fumbled as he tucked the weapon away. Like a sleepwalker he came forward and took the bag. Barton opened the door to admit him, then closed it, the two of them alone in the place of becoming.

Fascinated, Barton watched as step by slow step, Hishtoo moved to view a statue, then another, then a painting. Clearly the Demu had, for the moment, forgotten Barton's existence.

But not for long. Jaws working, Hishtoo turned on

him. The gun was out again, the covered knife fallen to the floor. "No! *No!* It is not true—it cannot be! The Demu were never—" He couldn't say it. "You—it is that I curse—I curse—" The hand and arm began to shake; he dropped the weapon. But when he reached, it was for the bag—the knife.

He didn't find it. Slowly, Hishtoo crumpled to the floor and curled into a tight ball. His breathing was slow and ragged; he no longer tried to move.

Well, thought Barton, what the hell—the fetal position would be about the same in an egg, wouldn't it?

His guess had been right. But now—could he make it stick?

"Barton to Ship One. Abdul? You heard most of that —no, don't answer—here's what's important. Hishtoo took a good look at the Demu family tree and went into catatonic shock, it looks like. Barton out."

All right, back to the door. Funny, he thought—even in a crisis, the Demu could not breach their own sanctuary. Or maybe they were merely waiting for proper authority—he'd better take a look outside.

Proper authority was there, all right. This one's hood had no mere gold edge; robe and hood were solidly gold-colored.

Barton spoke first. "It is that Hishtoo, who would become, lies without move or speech. It is not by me, but by his seeing in this place. It is that some now might enter and help—some who are to be here."

"It is that I am to be there," said Gold Hood, "as you are not. But you are there, though you do not become, being not egg-born. It is that I enter now." Barton stood aside to allow it.

"And I!" cried Eeshta.

"No," the Demu said, turning in the doorway. "It is not that you are to be here."

"It is that I am to be with Hishtoo, who is in need of help."

"It is that you are not twice here, nor grown to proper age. It is that you are to obey."

"But Hishtoo . . . !"

"It is that Hishtoo needs no help, that it is with Hishtoo as with all who first enter here. Hishtoo becomes, or uses that which is needed—the only choice of all who

321

would become. It is that you, the young, remain outside the place of becoming and be silent."

"No." Eeshta advanced. "I am once here; I do not come twice. It is that I enter now, to become or not." In a quandary, Barton followed his hunch and let her in, blocking the other's attempt to bar her.

For long seconds, Eeshta looked around the room. The young Demu drew in a great gasp. Then, unmistakably, came the pulsed hiss of Demu laughter. "Oh, Barton! Poor Hishtoo!" No longer laughing, she shook her head. "I am right to help him—without help he cannot see this and still live."

"You understand it?"

"I think so, yes—enough. Later, perhaps, I will feel its meaning more strongly. But now I must see to Hishtoo." She went to him, sat and took the tightly clamped head in her lap.

"It is now for us to talk?" said Gold Robe. "It is that I am he who takes the name Sholur, Keeper of the Heritage. You are Barton who are here though you should not be. It is that we decide now, what is proper to do. Most proper is for you to be made Demu."

"No," said Barton. "Most proper is for me to be as I am, and the others, also, outside this place. Most proper is that no more be made Demu who are not egg-born." He gestured toward the room at large. "It is, Sholur, Keeper of the Heritage, that I know the meaning of all this. It is that I know what your people do not—but which they may be told, all of them, if things are not most proper in my view."

"It is that you are here, and can tell nothing to the Demu people."

"It is that I am here, but my voice is free from here." He pulled out the two-way radio. "Barton to Ship One. Abdul—listen carefully. I'm going to ask you a question in Demu. Answer likewise. And say it loud and clear— you have an audience.

"Is it," he said, "that what I tell of the Demu place of becoming is told to ships outside the Demu reach?"

"It is," said Abdul, haltingly but clearly, "that those ships know what you say of that place. It is that they tell it further or not, as you wish and as you say."

"Then it is that as I say before, I say again. For these things not to be told, it is that I and ours be free to re-

322

turn to our ship, unharmed. That the ship be made free to depart unmolested. That the Demu ship, going to Demmon to rouse for war, be returned—or that another follow, to change the message to peace. That there be no war. That the Demu no longer take captives to make them Demu. That—" He knew Abdul wasn't getting more than half of it, but Sholur was—and he'd already told Abdul, in English. He added a few more touches, then signed off.

"All that, you ask?" said Sholur.

"All."

"It is that the others, when they see here as you do, ask less."

"It is the Ormthu you mean?"

"You know them?"

"On Tilara, we meet one."

"It tells you—? But they agree *not*."

"No," said Barton. "What I see here, I see for myself, with no telling from the Ormthan." True, he thought —as far as it went. . . .

"Then it is as you say—no more Earthani to become Demu."

"Nor the others."

"Tilari, Filjar, Larka-Te?" Barton nodded. "Tlengin? Eroci?" Again the nod—he'd never heard of the last two, but what the hell.

"Nobody," he said.

"It is that the Ormthu do not ask so much."

"We are not the Ormthu; they speak not for us, nor we for them."

"It is that you are not allied?"

"We know them little. We are not in conflict."

"It is that your terms are difficult, you who take the name Barton—but that the Demu are without choice but to agree."

"It is that I am pleased, Sholur, for the Earthani and others."

"Then it is that I go outside this place of becoming, to say what is needed. That our ship returns, or if not, another is to follow and correct. All the things you say, that are of now-doing. That no others are to be made Demu, cannot be told to all in one saying, for many are not near to listen."

"Yes, it is understood."

"Then I go, and return soon—for it is that there is more to say between us."

"It is that I stay and await you, Sholur." As the Demu reached the door, Barton had another thought. "It is also that the three Tilari are to be here with me now."

"It is that they are not Demu. They—"

"It is that they are needed by me, that they enter as you leave. That all things taken from them are returned."

"It is as you say." Sholur departed without further word. Barton looked to Eeshta, still cradling Hishtoo's head in her lap.

"You heard all that?" Eeshta nodded. "How's Hishtoo?"

"He relaxes slowly, gradually. He will wake, but not soon."

"And then what?"

"If I were not here he would surely kill himself. But I know what to say."

"You do?"

"Surely. I heard, as you did, what is said here. I heard what you said to Hishtoo, to bring him to enter this place. So when he wakes, and can hear me and perhaps understand, I shall say to him, 'Hishtoo, there is no shame to your eggs.' "

"But he—" I will never, thought Barton, understand this small creature.

"He cursed mine, yes. But you explained to me why his curse was futile—I do not believe as he does. What I say, though, Hishtoo will believe—to his good."

"I hope you're right. I—" The door opened; Limila entered, with Iivajj and Gerain. Both women embraced Barton; he was hard put to free a hand to shake Gerain's.

"You all right, everybody?" he said.

"Yes," said Limila. Then she saw Eeshta, and Hishtoo. "But—what has happened? How—?" She looked around the room, first casually and then intently. "Oh . . . ? Yes—I think I see."

"I wouldn't be surprised," said Barton. "But later, honey. Help me off with the headpiece, will you? The Keeper of the Heritage—Sholur, his name is—will be back here pretty soon. He and I have to talk for a spell, to iron out the peace treaty a little better. And then we all go back to Ship One."

When Sholur entered, his first words were: "It is that we leave this place and talk in another."

"Barton," said Limila, "do you think it is safe?"

"It is," Eeshta said. "The Demu do not break their word."

"But, Hishtoo . . . ?"

"No," said Barton, "Hishtoo never broke his word to us; he never gave it. He didn't pretend to be a Friendly; he was an honest Hostile all the way. Let's go."

Barton and Gerain carried Hishtoo as the group followed Sholur first to the drop-shaft, then down eight levels—Barton almost missed the exit ring—and along another corridor to a yellow-lighted room, furnished with couch-sized cushions.

"It is that we eat," said Sholur, "and talk. It is also that you sleep here when that is your wish."

Two Demu brought food. The stuff resembled the "glop" Barton had eaten during his years of captivity. It was served in bowls that each had a serrated half-spout at one side, for Demu mouths to sip from. Barton tried it—it tasted better than he remembered from Ashura, but he wished that politeness would allow him to dig into his marching rations instead.

The talk afterward took longer than Barton had expected. He found himself yawning—well, it had been a long, hard day.

"It is," said Sholur, "that now you wish to sleep. That which is left to say, we talk when you wake." The Keeper of the Heritage rose and left them.

Barton checked the door. "Well, it's not locked," he said. "That's good, I guess." He relieved himself over the gray quarter-circle at one corner of the yellow floor. As in the Demu cage or on the Demu ship, the stream vanished without splash or trace. Good thing, he thought, that no one present was overly burdened with modesty —Demu plumbing wasn't built to allow for it.

He reported again to Ship One—that all was well . . . so far.

He found no way to dim the lighting—all right, he'd pull the hood over his head. The air was cooler than he liked; he snuggled close to Limila and soon dozed. When he half-woke to feel warmth against him on the other side, he opened his eyes long enough to see two more hooded figures huddled with them. He went back to sleep without bothering to ask which was which.

Two hours after breakfast, Barton and Sholur shook hands over a complete set of peace terms. If they weren't truly complete, Barton hoped he'd left the proper loopholes for later changes. He was surprised, then, when Sholur offered him—alone—a guided tour of the great ship. Naturally he accepted.

From another corridor on the level of the place-of-becoming, they entered the control area—or rather, its bottom level—it occupied eight, and had its own pair of lift/drop-tubes.

At the top level the hull was transparent—from inside, at least. It had the same refractive index as air—no distortion—but the film of dust on the outside gave Barton an estimate of its thickness: nearly five meters.

He counted sixteen control positions, similar to the one on the Demu ship he had captured but each larger and more complex. And this, he thought, was merely the top concentration of control—the lower levels were filled with lesser installations.

He sat at one position, and Sholur at another, beside him. The seat-panel configuration was out-of-scale for both of them; Barton had to stretch to reach a knob he guessed to be the focus control for a monitor screen. His guess was right; the picture sharpened, and showed Ship One from above and at an angle. The range was close; Barton scanned the ship's surroundings and saw no "sleeping beauties." So the Demu had retreated when Adbul gave them the chance. Good . . . .

His seat was comfortable enough, though subtly wrong for his physique, but it extended to both sides of him with troughlike depressions angling steeply forward. He nodded—of course!

Sholur reached toward a switch and said, "It is that I make your ship again alive."

"Wait!" Barton got out his two-way radio. "Ship One! Barton here! Come in, please!"

"Ship One—Abdul speaking. Barton, is there trouble?"

"No trouble. It's just that we're about to take the damper off your drive, and I forgot to rescind the order to take off. But that's no longer necessary."

"I see." Barton nodded and Sholur moved a switch.

"You should be live now, Abdul. How is it?"

"The drive is operative."

"Good enough. Stay tuned. Barton out."

Sholur turned to him. "It is that I show you, if you wish, the extent of what we visit next." Barton nodded, and on Sholur's screen appeared a line drawing, in silhouette and cross section, of a torpedo shape. Barton realized he was seeing a simplified schematic of the great ship.

When he had oriented himself, he saw that more than a third of the ship was dug into the mountainside—its total length was nearer to two kilometers than one. Everything below the level at which he had entered was devoted to drive and power. And—weapons? He looked at the upper segment and saw empty spaces. And wondered what had been removed, and when . . . how long ago?

"Why is it, Sholur, that you show me all this?"

"It is that one who takes power should know what he has taken."

"It is that I thank you, Sholur."

They left the control section, dropped into the vast sense-numbing space Barton had first entered, and then went below, among the looming hulks that were the great ship's drive.

The ship—as a ship—was dead all right. Here and there, at what Barton intuitively deduced were crucial points, rows of units were interrupted by gaps—empty spaces with nothing plugged into their exposed, complicated connectors.

He knew enough of the Demu drive, original or modified, to see that single or duplexed components of those versions were here multiplexed into feedback systems. From where he stood, he knew he could rough-out a design that would jump Ship One's performance a magnitude—maybe two. Not that Ship One's hull could contain the layout. . . .

He had seen enough—all that he could handle in one bite. Bemused, he paused to translate, "Let's go back upstairs now, Sholur," into Demu.

"It will be all right, Barton," said Eeshta. They were in the yellow room, all Barton's group; Sholur had left to arrange transport to Ship One. "I must stay and care for

327

Hishtoo. But I am provided a communicator; I can call you at any time."

Barton looked at the device and flipped its largest switch. The screen flickered, lit, and showed Myra Hake. She said, "Yes, Barton? I thought this was Eeshta's channel."

"It is. Just checking. See you pretty soon." He cut the circuit. "Okay, Eeshta—but call me any time you need to—you hear?" Eeshta nodded. Barton put his arm around the small shoulders, squeezing hard for a moment before he released his grip.

Sholur entered. "It is that now you go to your ship."

"Yes," said Barton. "That we do not delay." He and Limila, Gerain and Iivajj gathered their accessories and followed Sholur—not to ground level but a staging area on their own level, where an aircar waited. A white-robed Demu sat at the controls. The four entered.

"It is that I may not leave here," said Sholur, "but that this one knows where you go now. And it is that if Eeshta says you would talk with me, I come to do so, as soon as I may."

"Sholur, it is that I thank you for your help. But that I do not understand entirely why that help comes so freely."

For a moment Sholur did not speak. Then, "Barton, whom I find where you are not to be—it is that perhaps you may succeed where the Keepers of the Heritage do not." Sholur turned away, and the aircar left the great ship.

At first the flight path was level; then it dropped to follow the contour of the mountain. Interested, Barton looked down to see if he could locate landmarks of the previous day's trek. He caught a glimpse of the slanting ridge and the talus slope at its head, and then the aircar swooped at treetop level and landed beside Ship One. The group disembarked; Barton turned back.

"It is that you fly with skill," he said to the pilot.

The Demu looked at him, then spoke. "It is that Sholur, Keeper of the Heritage, tells me to bring you here in safety. It is that if he did not, you are dead among the stones of the mountain—and I with you, gladly." The aircar lifted.

His laugh, Barton realized, was shaky; it didn't quite

make it. "Well, the troops don't always agree with the generals, do they? Let's get the hell into the ship."

Barton called the conference in the galley, with view-screen and alarms on relay from Control. He opened a beer and sat.

A sound like thunder made the ship vibrate. "There goes Sholur's envoy to Demmon, to call off the war," he said.

"But can it get there before the other?" asked Limila.

"Doesn't matter. The messenger on the first ship was only that. This time he sent his personal number-two fella. You can tell he's Number Two by the white edges on his gold burnoose.

"Sholur's something on the order of a priest-king; what he says, goes. We won't have any trouble—or not much. Now let's all bring each other up to date. Abdul?"

"Nothing significant has occurred here since we last spoke. But I have a question. Now that our drive is operable, do you plan to rendezvous with the fleet?"

"No, we'll wait here, for Tarleton. He should run into the relay beams pretty soon, from Thirteen and Thirty-four, so he'll know what the score is. I'd like to see his face when he finds out the fleet has an educational mission on its hands instead of a war to fight. After the first jolt I expect he'll be a happy man!"

"I should *think* so," said Myra Hake. Then, "Barton? Is it true that most of the Demu who try to 'become' kill themselves when they come out of shock?"

"The attrition rate is something awful—nearly ninety percent. Sholur says the percentage is improving, that someday the Demu will be able to face the truth without mass suicides. But the Keepers think in terms of thousands of years—and we can't wait that long to have the raiding stopped.

"It's ironic, really. The Demu outgun us—even the combined fleets—so badly I hate to think about it. But the poor hard-shelled bastards are hopelessly vulnerable to one simple thing—the truth."

"Look, Barton," said Alene Grover. "Maybe everybody else gets it—you've talked all around it—but I'm still in the dark. What's your *gimmick?*"

"Abdul hasn't told you?"

"I have told no one," said Abdul Muhammed. "The information I sent out was locked and coded, as you in-

329

structed, to Tarleton's private cipher. I couldn't decode that tape myself."

"So except for those of us who were in there, you're the only one who knows?"

"And soon, of course, Tarleton."

"Right. Well, this info *is* Top Sphinx—it has to be, because it could destroy the Demu as a race and a lot of people would like to do just that. But I think everybody on this ship has earned the right to know it. Just remember—not only you don't tell it, you don't even admit you *heard* it. Okay?

"All right. I took some pictures in there. Look at them, Alene—Myra, Cheng." He handed them out. "See the big fellas, with the extra arms and legs? Well, they were the Great Race, and that ship was theirs. The Demu just copied it, partially."

"You can be sure of that?" said Abdul.

"The seats in the control room are built for people with four legs. Good enough?" Abdul nodded, and Barton continued. "It must be hell to have to live in the shadow of something like that. The Demu chose not to. Instead, they wiped the Great Race out of the official version of Demu history. Then they overreacted, and began teaching their young that the Demu are the only true people, that all other races are merely animals."

"This Great Race—" said Alene. "What happened to it?"

"Even the Keepers don't know that one. There was a war, against somebody or something. During it, the Great Race cleared the lower Arm of habitable planets. Then they just . . . disappeared."

"I still don't see the problem," Alene said. "Okay—so a long time ago there was somebody a lot bigger. So what?"

"Not just bigger, Alene—look at the pictures. The Demu you see there aren't the same as the ones we know. Maybe they weren't even intelligent, originally—maybe the Great Race changed them genetically. If that's true, all this surgical changing of other races began as imitation—as playing at being the Great Race themselves.

"But that's not all of it. If you look closely, you can't miss it. To the Great Race, the Demu were not only animals—they were *pets!*

"That is the knowledge that kills ninety percent of the Demu who face it."

"Jesus H. Christ on a crutch!" said Alene Grover.

His ninth day on Sisshain, Barton was standing watch alone when Ship Thirteen relayed a call from Tarleton. The picture was fuzzy but the voice came through clearly.

"Hello, Barton! I've studied all the material you sent up. You win a pretty good war, don't you?" The big man laughed. "Well, I don't mind if your name beats mine out, in the history books."

"Mine's easier to spell," said Barton, deadpan. "Hey, you sure got here pretty soon."

"Still about thirty-six hours out. That's *our* fleet—when nobody met us in Scalsa's corridor, I decided we'd better come at max, with the others arriving when they got here."

Barton squinted at the picture. Besides Tarleton, he recognized Vito Scalsa and Liese Anajek; the rest were strangers.

"How's Helaise?" he said.

"Fine, the last I saw her," said Tarleton. "She stayed on Tilara."

"I see," lied Barton.

"Yes. By the way, how come you're alone? Where's everybody else?"

"Mostly over at the great ship—studying it like crazy. Alene's in the galley, though. Want to talk to her?"

"Uh—yes. If you would . . . . "

Barton paged the galley and Alene came to Control. "Hello, Tarleton," she said.

"Alene." The big man paused. "I'm alone now, and . . . . "

She frowned and started to turn away, then swung back to face the screen. "I'll think about it. Okay?"

"Yes. Of course." Alene Grover about-faced and stalked out. Tarleton tried to smile. "I suppose I can't blame her."

"No," said Barton, "I suppose you can't." Tarleton didn't answer, so Barton said, "Now then—can we get on with it? We're finding enough problems to last you maybe twenty years. Even moonlighting. . . ."

" 'Twas the night before liftoff, and all through Ship One . . ."

"Barton," said Alene Grover, "you couldn't carry a tune in a bucket."

Barton grinned. "Another thing I can't do is worry about it. But if you don't appreciate my golden voice . . . . " He opened a beer and sat, considering the events of the past eight days. Once landed, Tarleton had made a lot of decisions in a hurry.

The combined fleets were preparing to disperse on various missions, carrying Sholur's spokesmen to take the "peace treaty" to other Demu planets; Ship One's job was to return and inform Tilara. Iivajj and Gerain had Cabin Six, since Eeshta was to stay on Sisshain with the slowly recovering Hishtoo. He had neither become nor died; a new factor had entered into Demu ritual. Or perhaps, thought Barton, in a way Hishtoo *had* become.

Eeshta would not be alone. Tarleton's ship, Estelle Cummings' and one ship of each allied race were staying, to set up a joint embassy. It should work out, thought Barton.

"Abdul—you have enough data on the great ship?"

"In so short a time? Hardly, Barton. But enough for now. As I have said, the ship is dead only in that it was deliberately disabled—I am certain—by the Great Race. It could be lifted within five years, perhaps less."

Barton sat straight. "Nobody heard that! Except to us here, that ship is dead! Tarleton agrees."

Abdul shook his head, protesting.

"No, Abdul! With the political mess on Earth, do you want to see *any* of those idiots get control of that kind of power? In fact," he said, "it's going to be tricky enough as it is, keeping the existing fleet out of politics. But that's Tarleton's problem—we help as we can, is all."

"I am convinced," said Abdul. "The ship is dead."

"Maybe not for always. Someday, under allied jurisdiction . . . . " He stood. "I don't know about anybody else, but I'm pooped.

"We lift off early, tomorrow—and since I set her down, I'll take her up. So good night, all."

In Compartment One, when the door closed them into privacy, Limila said, "Barton? I would ask you something."

"Go ahead."

"There is a thing I have not done for many years— that tonight, here on Sisshain, I would do." Her eyes were silver-irised wide, her smile unsteady. He remembered

332

—what had been done to her, all that had passed between them.

"Sure, honey—what is it?"

"I would ovulate. Barton—do you approve?"

Finding no words, he nodded.

"Then—will we, now?"

Next morning, Alene Grover came to breakfast carrying a duffle bag.

"That's a pretty big lunch bag, isn't it?" said Barton.

"I'm moving to Ship Two. I mean—I don't have to
ask, do I? You can spare me, here."

"Sure, if you want. Going back to Tarleton?"

She shrugged one shoulder. "I don't know yet. But if
I leave with you, I won't have the choice."

Barton looked at her. "That makes sense. Anyway,
Alene—whatever you decide, best of luck."

"I know." She hoisted the duffle bag. "I guess I don't
need breakfast after all. Kiss good-bye?" Barton gave it,
and she walked away.

In Control, Ship One's complement watched Tarleton
on the screen, giving his parting instructions. "I guess
that's about all, Barton," he said. "Have a good trip—
and say hello."

"Will do. Over and out." He cut the screen.

Barton took the ship straight up.

End of the Line

I.

Tilara

Until the three approaching spaceships closed in to box Barton's own Ship One, he was glad to see them. Obviously Earth-built, they had to be part of the second fleet, and it was about time they showed up! Ever since he'd made turnover, forty-three days out from Sisshain, he'd halfway expected to spot the backup fleet. But not until now, two days short of Tilara and almost within talk-distance of that world, had any of it appeared.

When the hailing came, Abdul Muhammed had the watch; the outsized Central African paged Barton immediately. Barton was in Compartment One, talking with the Tilaran woman Limila, his "most needful person" in the Tilaran way of putting it. Both of them went to the control room, hotfoot style. Barton caught his breath. "What's up, Abdul?"

The black giant gestured toward the viewscreen, and Barton saw three ships in delta formation, nearing fast. "They called, Barton—well, one of them did so—and identified themselves. Ship Sixty-five and two others from Squadron Three of the second fleet. I identified us in return, and they asked to speak to Admiral Tarleton." Abdul smiled. "I said he is not aboard."

Admiral, huh? Tarleton, now on Sisshain in charge of working out the kinks in the Demu peace treaty, commanded the first fleet, all right. But nobody, except Barton now and then in a joking way, had ever called him "admiral." "What else did you say?"

"That you command this ship and that I would call you. In the meantime I have kept the voice channel shut down." A buzzer sounded. "I would guess they are becoming impatient."

Myra Hake had the comm panel; Barton nodded to her, and the tall, sandy-haired woman shook the bangs away from her eyes and made competent motions. The screen's view split, the three ships smaller in their remaining half and two men looking out of the other. One of them, the heavyset one, said, "You're Barton? Second in command of the first fleet?" Barton nodded, and the speaker turned to his wispy-looking blond associate. "He's the one. That takes care of a lot." Then, back to Barton: "Start from the beginning and bring us up to date. Recording."

From the beginning, huh? From when Barton had been snatched off Earth by the exoskeletal Demu and caged for eight years and escaped and brought a Demu ship back to Earth? And the first Earth fleet, forty ships under Tarleton's command, had set out from Earth to Tilara and allied with the people of that world, and with the Larka-Te and Filjar? And Barton taking a strike force to chase Hishtoo the Demu to Sisshain, and there finding the secret that forced the Demu to stop raiding, and stop carving other humanoids into the likeness of featureless Demu? Not hardly; this officious-sounding Chubby Boy had to know the first parts, or he wouldn't be here. But "beginning," to Barton, meant all of that.

He said, though, "You'll have it already, up to where I took off after Hishtoo and his two Tilaran hostages. We did save them, by the way; Gerain and Iivajj are aboard here. And then Tarleton followed with the combined allied fleets." He cleared his throat. "Everything after that is in my report, which will reach you through channels in due time." Barton hated to make reports at the best of times, and he'd sweat blood over this one, because he had to leave out the secret of Demu psychological vulnerability so that no revenge-minded group could wipe the Demu out. He'd left out the mystery of the vanished Great Race that had left the great ship moldering on Sisshain. And particularly he'd omitted any suggestion that that huge monolith could be put into working shape in a relatively brief time. But on the whole, he thought, it read plausibly.

"Report, hell," said Fatso. "Give me a summary, to

338

pass back to the admiral right away. That's one reason we're out here."

"And why else, I wonder?" said Limila.

She said it softly, but the man on the screen must have heard. Red-faced, he said, "To stand outpost against a Demu attack; what did you think? In case the first fleet lost the war. So tell me what happened."

Well, why not? "It won't take long," Barton said. "The war's over before it started; we won it, hands down. On the Demu world Sisshain, Tarleton's in the saddle. But he's running an embassy, more, not an army of occupation. The main job is to spread word to other Demu planets that the raiding is over and done with. Takes a lot of coordination, but that was always one of Tarleton's strong points." He paused. The heavy man's expression puzzled him. "Anything else?"

"That's not much detail, but—all right; thanks, Barton. We'll pass it on in. And right, now, you get an escort to Tilara. Just feel snug as a bug in a rug."

That half of the picture blanked; the view of the three ships expanded to fill the screen. As they matched velocity with Ship One, Barton saw that these newer ships were larger than his by half, and had nearly the same edge in acceleration. Their central laser delivery tubes were bigger, too, which probably meant more power. And now that he noticed, around each center lay three peripheral muzzles. As the ships closed to box Ship One in, he had a good clear view.

And wondered, why he being himself "took care of a lot."

He'd taken it easy, Barton had, on the run from Sisshain back to Tilara. Going the other way, chasing Hishtoo to stop that Demu from spreading warning of the first fleet's approach, he'd run Ship One close to max acceleration most of the way, and part of it full out. He was no expert on space drives; he'd stolen one from the Demu and thus given Earth interstellar capability, but all he really knew about them was what he could understand of what the Lab boys told him, plugged into his somewhat obsolete studies in physics. And he'd never quite made his Ph.D., at that.

But he did know that things wear out, so returning from Sisshain he'd kept accel and decel at no more than half of max. Since elapsed time for a given distance was a reciprocal square-root function of applied force, the trip hadn't taken all that much longer. Sixty-four days on the way out; coming back, maybe ninety. With the pressure off, he hadn't bothered to keep close track, once turnover was calculated and achieved.

It had been an odd trip in more than one way. Limila was pregnant and teething at the same time. The pregnancy was still early, not bothering her to any noticeable extent, and the teething was the eruption of tooth buds planted by Tilaran surgeons to replace the forty teeth the Demu had taken from her when they had her captive. The flexible linings of the Tilaran dentures still accommodated the half-grown teeth, well enough. Maybe it was only Barton's imagination that made his tall, lithe woman seem a little strange now and then. Well, if she wasn't entitled to a bit of oddness after all *she'd* been through, then who was?

He did wish she'd make up her mind, though, whether to take the scalp transplant available on Tilara when they got there, or stay with the Tilaran-styled wig to cover her Demu-inflicted baldness. It wasn't that Barton cared, either way; he merely wished that Limila would decide, so she could quit stewing about it. She looked fine to him right now; it no longer jarred him at all, that forward of the ears the Tilaran scalp is bare by nature.

It didn't bother him, either, that her transplanted breasts showed little if any sign of growing. They had come from a young girl, killed in a fall while rock-climbing, and the Tilaran surgeons had no idea whether they would grow to mature contours. Well, Limila didn't seem to sweat it much, and no doubt her bustline would develop as her pregnancy did.

It was the nearness of Limila's home planet, Barton thought, that set him musing on her possible problems. Not a good time for it, really; he might have a few of his own to chew on. He looked around the control room. Cheng Ai, the other pilot, who shared Cabin Four with Myra Hake, had come in; in low tones, Abdul Muhammed was bringing him up to date. Noticing Barton's gaze on him, Abdul paused, and said, "There is something, Barton?"

"Yeh. Let's pool what we noticed about those ships out there, best we can remember."

"I taped the view," Myra Hake said. "Run it on the

340

aux screen?" Barton nodded, and again the three ships showed, closing in.

Barton pointed out the added laser outputs, and Cheng said, "I'm not sure, but to me the gasketing around the three extras, on each ship, looks like pivot mountings. Which means traverse capability."

"Flex feeds from the exciter," said Barton. "Tricky job, but I can see how it could be done." The tape ended, and Myra began it again. "Now, then, what else do they have, or not?"

No hatches, Abdul pointed out, for the Larka-Te high-drive torpedoes. No sets of nodes, Limila said, to emit the Tilaran twin ion beam. "And the spitter for the Filjari plasma gun," said Cheng, "isn't there, either."

"Right." Barton had made the same observations, but it never paid, he felt, to do all the talking. Now was his turn. "Except for the extra lasers, they're equipped the same as we were when we got here. The Demu sleep-gun and the Shield against it don't use outside equipment, but of course they'd have both."

Limila touched his shoulder. "Why do you ask all this? These ships are of Earth, are they not? So—"

Barton shook his head. "Not sure. Something about Fat Boy's manner, on the screen, maybe. But doesn't it strike anybody else as a little strange that those ships haven't been modified to add any of our allies' weapons?"

Before anyone could answer, the comm-panel alarm sounded and its screen lit.

The picture wavered, the colors were off by hundreds of Angstroms; still the face looked somehow familiar. "That's a Tilaran frequency, not fleet," said Myra Hake. But the party on the screen was no Tilaran.

The face was compact: no Tilaran leanness there, and a strong jaw. The hair was apparently curly and quite short; the contour of it bulked out only far enough to make a smooth line with the ears, and at the front it grew to frame an Earth-style forehead.

Barton motioned. "Open to answer on the other half of that pair of downside freqs, Myra. We're some distant, still, but—"

"I already did." Barton had to grin; he was *always* telling this woman something, slightly after the fact.

"Good." Yes, the Send light was on. He said, "Barton, speaking for Ship One, answering Tilaran call. Come in, Tilara." He repeated it a few times; when he saw the face on the screen change expression, he shut up.

"Hello, Barton. It's good to see you. Don't you recognize me?" He knew the smile, all right; when he'd first met this woman his instincts said the smile was prelude to being bitten. And the crisp, calm voice cinched the identification—attenuation and distortion notwithstanding.

"Doctor Fox!" He almost shouted it. "Doctor Arleta Bulldog Fox! What in all the hells are *you* doing here?"

He was glad to see her—overjoyed, in fact. No matter that for months, back on Earth when he'd first returned from Demu captivity as a mental basket case, she'd been the worst threat to his chance to go out again and take the fight to the Demu. And to his very freedom, for that matter, she being the boss psychologist and he the reluctant subject. But they'd worked that out—the hard way, for both of them—and parted friends, more or less. Now, coming toward Tilara into what looked to be a very iffy situation, with no "i" dotted and no "t" crossed, Barton said, "Doc, you're the best news I've had all day."

Up to now, he'd waited through the distance timelags without impatience. This time he got nervous, until the small woman said, "I'm afraid you won't say that, in a minute." She leaned forward, closer to the pickup module; now Barton could see that she'd aged a little. Not much, though; the vigor he liked about her still showed. She said, "Get away from those ships, Barton. Don't land where they tell you to."

Not land on Tilara? He had to; hell, he didn't have fuel to go anywhere else, unless it was damned close, and he didn't know where such a haven might be. For the moment he put aside the fact that he couldn't escape the second fleet's ships, anyway, and asked if she had any ideas about where he might go. She didn't. So then he asked, "Why shouldn't I go in and land, just like I'm told?"

He saw her head shake. "I don't know, really. The admiral's close-mouthed in a way; he doesn't ever tell a full story. But he can't help dropping broad hints. And the hint I got, Barton, is that you are in very real trouble."

It didn't make sense, so Barton began trying to sort it out. For starters, a few facts about the second Earth fleet, and how long had it been here, and how come it didn't

seem to have any weapons it hadn't started with, and—
Barton did ask a lot of questions, then.

The answers didn't help much, but he kept trying. The
second fleet had landed on Tilara more than sixty days
ago. The landing would have been earlier except that the
admiral overruled his chief navigator on the timing of
turnover, so as not to interfere with the admiral's birthday
celebration. "He said not to tell him what could or couldn't
be done. One of his favorite lines is that executives decide
and that subordinates carry out those decisions." But the
way it went, most of the second fleet reached Tilara with
too much big-Vee and overran the planet and had to decel and come back to it, quite a bit behind sked. One
squadron commander had refused to follow orders and
had landed on time. When the rest of the fleet arrived,
finally, that commander was court-martialed for insubor-
dination and might have been executed if he hadn't escaped and hid out among the Tilaran community.

"That was Dupree," Fox said. "I don't know where he
is, because it's better if I don't, in case I get picked up by
ap Fenn's troops."

Jesus H. Caruso! Barton didn't know where to start
asking. Three questions she'd handed him, all at once.
He started with the easy one, and yes, Dr. Arleta Fox
had jumped ship. "When I heard a rumor that he might
even put you under arrest, all my misgivings came together, and I went to ground." She gave a shaky laugh.
"Literally and figuratively. Off the ship, *and* into hiding.
It's not as sordid as one might think, Barton. I'm staying
in the household of your friend Vertan, and it's really
quite luxurious."

Barton shook his head as if he wanted to get rid of his
ears. Vertan? Vertan was the highest-ranking Tilaran that
Barton's group had dealt with, when the first fleet had
stopped over on Tilara. If Vertan was siding with Doctor
Fox . . . Again he went with the easiest question he had
left. "Dupree, you said. That's Armand Dupree, maybe?"
That man had been one of the first four, after Barton
himself, to fly the original captured Demu starship under
Barton's instruction. *No* Johnnie-come-after should have
court-martial clout over Armand Dupree; the man was
totally sound, dependable.

But Fox said, "He's the one, yes. He was right all the
way, of course, and his performance proved it. But on the

sixty ships of the second fleet, all five squadrons of it, being right is of little importance. What counts is being on the right side of Admiral Karsen ap Fenn."

Well, he'd known it was coming, ever since she first said the name. Barton chose his words. "Terike ap Fenn, who came out from Earth on this ship, would be his nephew?" Terike ap Fenn, the big lout who had caused a lot of trouble on Ship One. Barton had had to clobber him once; then the man had gone AWOL off the ship and tried to force a Tilaran woman, and got his stupid self killed for it. And allowed Hishtoo to get away to Sisshain in a Tilaran ship, complete with hostages. Old story to Barton, old and sour—but still he had to ask.

"That's the one, yes," said Arleta Fox. "And the admiral's still fuming about it, since he heard. That, Barton, is one reason I became very worried, and left the spaceport to hide with Vertan."

Silent, Barton thought. So here we are. Terike ap Fenn's uncle, the big cheese at the Space Agency, and a political appointee at that. In charge of Earth's second fleet? Sure's hell it looked rancid, to Barton. All he said was, "Fox? How secure are your communications there?"

She blinked, and the miniature bulldog jaw tightened. "There shouldn't be much risk, Barton. Ap Fenn won't have anything to do with Tilarans—the 'Tillies,' he calls them. He doesn't even have anyone learning the language here." The bulldog smile came. *"I'm* learning it, since I left Ship Forty-one."

"So you think nobody's eavesdropping. I'd like to believe that." Barton shrugged. "It doesn't matter. We're back in Lab B, Doctor Fox." From her expression, she didn't remember the time she'd tested him past his limits and suffered more than a little bit from his explosive reaction. So he reminded her. "Anybody that's not on my side, Doc, takes what comes." And he wished he could back up that confident-sounding reassurance. But she was his ally, and it always pays to give your friends a little boost.

She didn't answer in kind. She said, "There is nothing on Tilara that can withstand ap Fenn's sixty ships. He has absolute power." Barton only nodded. And eventually she said, "There is one thing, Barton. I don't really mind your calling me 'Doc,' or even 'Bulldog.' But my name is Arleta, and my friends call me Arlie."

Barton thought about it; his mouth twitched into a grin or maybe a real smile. "Okay, Arlie," he said. "Keep in touch."

"Oh, I shall, of course." On the blurred screen he saw her nod. "But I wasn't finished yet; I have some more information you might be able to use. And besides, it's *good* to talk with someone who's outside of this mess."

Outside it? Maybe not for long. Barton said, "Let's hear the news. And how do you like Tilara so far?"

Incredibly, the boss-lady psychologist giggled. "You've been here; you know the local customs. Can you imagine what it was like, Barton, to attend a Tilaran party with no advance briefing?"

Barton could; by effort, he kept a straight face while Doctor Arleta Fox described her experience. " . . . reached up under that short Mickey Mouse robe they had us all wearing, and put his hand on me, all the time speaking with utmost courtesy—Barton, I have never been so totally dumbfounded in my entire life! I knew the language a little already. He was saying, 'If you are of the wish to be with me, I am of that wish, also.' And *feeling* me."

"It can be a jar, yeh," Barton said. "But that's Tilara for you. So what did you do? Not slap the guy, I hope."

"Of course not! What do you think I am? A prude?"

Barton decided he'd better not ask any further on that. He said, "You mentioned more news."

Somehow, Fox looked disappointed. She said, "That party, I think, is where things went bad between the admiral and the Tilarans. He showed up the next morning with a black eye and a gashed cheek, and since then he hasn't given the local authorities the time of day if he could help it. I think perhaps he misjudged the situation and made a wrong move. And Karsen ap Fenn is not a forgiving man."

"I can imagine," Barton said, and thought, that the men of the ap Fenn family sure played hell when they ran up against free-minded women. "So from there, what's happened?"

Colors on the screen were still wrong; Doctor Fox's face went to a darker green. "I didn't get back to the ship the next day," she said, "so I missed his conference, with all officers above the grade of lieutenant-commander. But the decision, I understand, was to stay on Tilara until word came from the first fleet." Barton saw the woman shrug. "That's the extent of my knowledge," she said. "Except that the admiral has a new mistress now. Somebody your fleet left behind on Tilara. After the party, he moved her in. A skinny blonde, I'm told; I haven't seen her."

Barton had, but not lately. All he said was, "Thanks, Arlie. Like we were saying, let's keep this channel open, and talk later."

They signed off, and Barton thought. The blonde had to be Helaise Renzel, and he'd consider her later. *Power plays, again!* And he got the idea that while Tarleton had got the first fleet out before the military could lay hooks on it, the second flotilla hadn't been so lucky. *All officers above the grade of lieutenant-commander?* Well, so it went. On Tilara, Karsen ap Fenn had a real live hierarchy going.

No way to cope with it, certainly, from out here. If at all. Barton turned his mind to the present moment, which was where it usually worked best, anyway. And opened the floor to debate.

"The thing is," said Barton, "I don't have any answers. There's not enough to go on." They still sat in the control room. The other two Tilarans had joined the group—lean, grave Gerain and his most needful person, the young woman Iivajj. Ship One had a full quorum. At the moment, the quorum was eating.

"Unless you wish it, Barton," Limila said, "you need not submit yourself to the mercies of this self-styled admiral." Against the light in her eyes shone silver. "As we have discussed—"

"Yeh, I know." They'd discussed it, all right. If he threw Ship One on max decel, briefly, and then flipped over and attacked? Laser, ion beam, plasma gun, and three high-drive torpedoes, against three ships? Maybe it could work. "But don't forget, one of our torpedoes is a dummy, nothing but a solid projectile." Because Abdul had had to pull the guts out of it, after the abortive space fight with Hishtoo on the way to Sisshain, to put the ship's Shield back in working order against the sleep-gun. Barton didn't go through that part again; they all knew it.

"That's not the problem," he said now. "What is, is that we don't *know* we're in that kind of trouble, to justify an attack."

"I would tend," said Abdul Muhammed, "to give great

credence to the warnings of Doctor Arleta Fox. And yet . . . "

"Sure," Barton said. "If we do, and we're all wrong, where are we? Even if I can stop those ships without anybody getting killed, we're all traitors until proven different." He slumped, straightened, and tried to shrug tensions out of his shoulders. "And the other thing is, *then* where could we get to?"

"Chaleen," said Limila. "The Tilaran world where lives my eldest son, mine and Tevann's. On the charts I can locate it, well enough for computer guidance." She pushed her wig's long black hair away from her face. "If we do not spend too much more fuel in slowing, we have sufficient to reach Chaleen."

In a way, Barton wished she hadn't offered him the option. It would be simpler to dive into one situation and hack it out, win or lose, than to have to choose between so many alternatives.

He thought about it. Should he have Myra call Ship Sixty-five again, to see if he could get any clues from what Fatty or Skinny said? He didn't think there'd be much. Should he try to get through to the second fleet down on Tilara, and maybe talk with the admiral his very own self? No; that wouldn't work, because normal ships' communications wouldn't reach out this far, through atmosphere, except for fancy channel arrangements he didn't have. Doctor Fox had to be using special, more powerful, ground-based gear. So he couldn't do any of that, very well.

Barton made up his mind. He didn't ask anybody's advice—not again, he didn't—he simply made his decision. "We'll go with these ships," he said, "and when we get down on Tilara, we'll see."

Nobody seemed to like the idea any better than Barton did himself, but nobody squawked, either. When Barton and Limila got away to Compartment One, he said, "What do you think?"

She shook her head. "I do not want to think. You have done that."

So maybe he was right and maybe he was wrong. Now was a different time. Undressed and in bed, he tried to forget about everybody else, and Limila seemed to feel the same way. One thing: the small transplant-breasts might grow or might not, but sure as hell their tips were connected to the hot line. Limila rejoiced early, and after a while Barton caught up with her; they laughed together.

Then she turned to him. "Barton. There is danger. No?"

"Sure. You knew that. Didn't you?"

Her hand stroked his chest, her hand that was missing two fingers the Demu had cut away. "Always, Barton, since the Demu took me, there is danger. But you took me back, and made me alive again. And so I trust you." She sighed. "Tell me of the danger."

Barton didn't know why he felt embarrassed. He said, "To you, there shouldn't be any; I can't say, for certain. We're setting down on your home world and you should be *in*, free and clear." He moved to put a kiss where he wanted to; a wriggle rewarded him. But the question still stood. He said, "Arlie—Arleta Fox—says I'm in trouble with the big cheese. I don't know why, yet. But I expect I'll find out pretty soon. One thing, Limila—I don't trust anyone named ap Fenn, as far as I can throw him."

Limila settled for that answer, and they snuggled in to sleep.

The three escort ships, next day, would have been sitting ducks for any attack Barton might have wanted to make. He didn't think much of the second fleet's orientation toward combat training. But like a good little sheep, Barton kept Ship One in the middle of his escort formation, approaching Tilara.

Limila, on the comm, detected no coherent signals from the planet—not even in scramble, which presumably the admiral would use in talking with Barton's escort.

Boredom with jitters was the worst kind. Too full of coffee, tired of pacing, not ready for a slug of bourbon so early in his day, Barton asked Limila for a channel to Ship Sixty-five.

Almost immediately, as if someone on that ship had been poised and waiting for a call, the answer came. On the screen, the skinny blond man appeared. "Light-commander Vannick here. Can I help you?" *Huh?* Oh, sure; now Barton remembered. Short for lieutenant, of the colonel or commander persuasion.

He leaned over toward the screen. "Barton here, Vannick. Feeling like a chat, is all. News from Earth, maybe. And how did it go with the second fleet, on the way out?"

Vannick looked wispy, but his voice wasn't. "About the same as any new group, I suppose. Some problems; nothing too serious." The news from Earth dealt mostly with political and entertainment figures that meant nothing to Barton; in his last sojourn on Earth, less than a year, after nearly eight years of Demu captivity, he hadn't bothered to plug himself into the media versions of current events. He nodded through the recital, hoping he managed to look polite, until he found a hook to ask about the fleet again. General stuff . . .

Now that Vannick was warmed up a little, he talked more freely. The second fleet was Ships Forty-one through One-hundred, divided into five squadrons. The admiral had wanted to re-number everything from scratch so he could have the number One, but the Space Agency wouldn't go for it, so he took One-hundred instead. "The Big Hundred, he insists we call it, though of course, it's the same size as all the rest."

"What's the admiral like, to work for?" Barton thought he knew already, but a few sidelights couldn't hurt.

Vannick's mouth twitched. He looked back over his shoulder and then, maybe without meaning to, shook his head. "Just fine. A little demanding, but that's the way a fleet commander should be." Uh-huh; sure. Letting the matter pass, Barton asked who was running the five squadrons. He recognized only two of the names; Jones was another of the original four he'd trained on the Demu ship, and when Vannick came to Dupree's name, he paused. "I forgot. Dupree was insubordinate and got busted. Grounded, in fact. Kaczca, his exec, got the promotion."

Over the screen came the sound of a door closing. Vannick looked behind him again as the tubby man came forward. "What the hell's going on, Vannick? Who told you to chat it up with these people?" He looked into the screen. "Sorry, Barton. But we do have our orders."

I'll bet you do. "I set up the call," he said. "It's not Vannick's fault, uh—?" He raised his eyebrows.

"Gellatly," said the fat man. "Captain Gellatly." With a hard "g," and accent on the second syllable. Now Gellatly frowned. "By the way, Barton, what's your rank? So we can do these things right, from now on."

Barton was a long time out of the Army, and he hadn't cared for it all that much the first time. He shook his head. "Tarleton's fleet doesn't use military ranks. Just job titles."

The other man grinned. "Things change. We have to be able to fit you into the T/O or the admiral won't like it."

"*Your* admiral. I still work for Tarleton." He shouldn't argue, Barton knew, but Gellatly really raised his stubborns for him.

"And Tarleton works for Admiral ap Fenn. That's in the orders he brought; he read us the non-secret parts." Gellatly squinted, then made a nod. "You have your own ship, Barton, so I guess that makes you a captain. For now, anyway." Carefully, Barton tried to show no reaction to some implications of the last phrase. Gellatly raised a finger. "I outrank you, though, because my rank dates back to Earth, and yours is just being assigned. So now—" He grinned again. "We know where we stand, don't we?"

"I doubt it." Barton waited until the grin went away. "If we're talking rank, what's a squadron commander? Or fleet exec? Because in the first fleet, I'm both of those." He thought back, trying to remember the jargon. "On detached service, at the moment."

"Now wait a minute!" Barton did so. Gellatly bit his lip. "Well, commodores command the squadrons. And there isn't exactly any exec, with us, so—"

"There is with us. Arbitrarily, I'd say that in your fleet's terms, I'm a vice-admiral." Navy rank wasn't his specialty, but it sounded good, Barton thought. "Which means that until further notice, I outrank everybody here, except the admiral."

Gellatly reached for his comm panel; the screen went silent, and as the picture faded to blankness, Barton saw the two men gesturing at each other.

"Not so bad," said Barton, turning away. "For the moment, not bad at all."

Others had come in unnoticed while he was concentrating on the screen. Now Abdul Muhammed nodded. "Yes, you have stymied the Gellatly person. But you realize, Barton, that your new rank lasts only until Admiral ap Fenn thinks to take it away."

"Sure I do." Barton smiled. "But he can't do that, while I'm still in duty status, without a court-martial. Which needs the presence of the accused. I'm not planning on showing up."

"But that's desertion, isn't it?" said Myra Hake. "And how—?"

"The how part," Barton said, "I don't know yet, and

I admit it needs some thought. But the point is that this rank business keeps Gellatly off my back until we land. And if we do get loose, I don't give two hoots in hell what Karsen ap Fenn calls it."

"Barton?" Limila spoke. "Are you making tunes in darkness?"

"Whistling in the dark, you mean? Maybe; it could be. But there's still a lot of facts we don't have, which leaves room for some of them to be on our side." He wasn't really feeling all that confident, but he knew that if he shared his misgivings, his crew would be more likely to freeze up in the idea department. And he needed all the good ideas he could get.

Limila still thought they should zap the escort service and head for the world Chaleen; Barton had checked the coordinates she gave him, and Ship One had enough fuel to ground there safely. The trouble was that even if a surprise attack worked, and got them away clean, the odds were that somebody would get killed. The new, larger ships were built to carry up to twenty people, as compared to twelve for the first fleet; Barton remembered the plans, from Earth. "Maybe sixty on those three ships, if they're riding full." It wasn't that Barton wouldn't kill if he had to, he explained to a group that knew that much already, but rather that he didn't see the need, just yet. "And most of the men and women on those ships are just doing their jobs, nothing more. The admiral is their boss and they don't know me from Adam's off ox. So—" The discussion went a time more, before Limila shrugged and ceded the point, saying that she hoped Barton would not have to regret his forbearance.

"Right," he said. "I'll have a slice of that, too."

"And what," she said, "will you do to obtain it?"

"Try to call Arlie Fox, for starters. She's our window to what's happening on Tilara, and maybe by now I have enough info to ask better questions."

But when Myra Hake got through on the channel Doctor Fox had specified, it was the Tilaran, Vertan, who answered.

"Barton! To see you again is of good. These new Earthani who come—in particular, their person of command—to deal with them is not of pleasure. But now that you are again of presence—" Vertan rattled on; Barton hadn't used the Tilaran language in conversation for so long that he kept missing things and having to ask for repeats, but after a while he caught on again. And when Vertan seemed to have unwound sufficiently for the time being, Barton asked after Arleta Fox.

She wasn't there; she'd gone to an eating place near the spaceport, to meet with her major contact in the fleet. Barton gathered that the contact wasn't sure of security on the channels he used in talking from his ship. And that contact turned out to be Commodore Jones, the first of Barton's pilot trainees back on Earth. Barton hadn't seen the man since, but working with Fox, he had to be one of the good guys in the white hats.

Tilaran was still mixing him up a little, so Barton switched to English for his next questions. Vertan answered, "This man Jones, his position is shaky. He questioned the admiral's landing order, and carried his protest too far, perhaps." The Tilaran's extended forehead wrinkled above the eyebrows. "This Admiral ap Fenn—he is kin to the ap Fenn who—?"

Barton nodded. "Worse than that. He's the mush-head who got Terike ap Fenn into the space service and onto my ship. But what's it about Jones and the admiral's landing orders?" It could matter.

And when Vertan explained, Barton decided that it did matter. He asked two more questions. Had ap Fenn done anything at all about interchange of technologies and equipment on Tilara? And could a spare ground car or two be left at the edge of the spaceport, on the side nearest the building where Earthani and Tilarans had first held conferences?

Barton liked both answers. As he and Vertan exchanged signoffs and ended the call, for the first time he thought he might have an angle on the situation. Not much, but maybe a little.

Hungry now, Barton headed for the galley. Cheng and Myra had the watch; the others followed Barton and asked questions. But until he was fed, he stayed contrary and wouldn't answer. Well, it was more than that; before he said anything, Barton wanted to be sure he knew what he was talking about. Meanwhile, after the first minutes, everybody shut up and let him eat. It was no gourmet treat; Ship One was mostly down to reconstituted rations.

There was still real coffee, though; now Barton sipped it. He looked around at all the group and said, "I think we're going to be all right. *If* Vertan knows what he's talking about."

He still wouldn't answer questions. "About the gimmick, we'll have to wait and see; either it works or it doesn't. I want everybody thinking ahead."

"And to what, Barton?" Limila said. "Unless you tell us—"

He hitched upright in his seat. "Okay; this part's more for you, anyway. And for Gerain and Iivajj." He looked at the other two Tilarans. "Suppose it comes down to it, we're on the ground and we run for it. I'm not sure that's how it'll have to go, but let's say, for now. All right—how do we keep hid out, best?"

Answers differed. The three Tilarans, in a city of their own people, could easily disappear beyond the ability of ap Fenn's people to discover them. For the others, there were problems.

With the front quarter of her hair shaved off and the rest darkened, wearing a loose robe that hid how high her breasts rode on her torso, Myra Hake could pass for Tilaran. No native of the planet was as short and stocky as Barton, but maybe ap Fenn's people wouldn't know that. Surely, though, they'd know that Cheng Ai and Abdul Muhammed couldn't possibly be Tilaran, no matter what cosmetic disguises they might try.

Myra frowned. "Barton, I don't see why you think all this may be necessary to try. The admiral hasn't *done* anything yet."

Barton didn't see, either; he just felt. "You want to trust an ap Fenn again? I don't want to have to." He gestured. "Yeh—I know we don't have real evidence. But Arleta Fox said to stay loose from Karsen ap Fenn, and when that little bulldog gets a hunch, I don't scoff. Maybe I'm borrowing trouble. If I am, it'll be easy enough to scrub the precautions." He leaned forward. "So now let's get down to the nuts and bolts."

The next day, called out of bed to the control room and stuck with a cup of stale coffee from the bottom of an old pot, Barton had misgivings. On the screen, the image suffering a little from relay through Ship Sixty-five, he got his first look at Admiral Karsen ap Fenn. A loud-talking man, the admiral was. "You're Barton; is that right?" It was, so Barton nodded. He wasn't enough awake to talk much; he sipped more of the lousy coffee, and tried to get his brains together enough to cope, here.

"Well, then. You will land, as ordered, and surrender yourself for trial."

Even half-awake, Barton thought, he'd know better than to spring a line like that on somebody who still had command of an armed ship. But all he said was, "Trial? For what?"

"For complicity in the murder of my nephew, Terike ap Fenn." While Barton was trying to absorb that one, the admiral continued. "You, and all aboard with you, will answer for that crime."

Barton shook his head. No point in trying to argue the dubious merits of the case, as such; ap Fenn had made up his alleged mind, and that was that. But the others with him on Ship One—he said, "This isn't the same crew that was on board when your nephew . . ."—he didn't say, your *stupid* nephew— ". . . got himself killed. And the killing didn't happen on this ship, and the Tilaran woman who did it got a local verdict of self-defense. So—"

"I know a whitewash when I see one!" If the colors on the screen were anything like true, ap Fenn's face went purple. "And I won't put up with it. You, and all those with you, will report to me for trial. Soon as possible after you've landed."

"Under what jurisdiction? Who's to be the judge?" He already knew the answer to that one, Barton thought, but he asked, anyway.

And he was right. "*I* am!" said Admiral Karsen ap Fenn. "And don't give me a lot of bosh as to who's guilty and who isn't. You all were. And that included Tarleton. When I get my hands on that man—and I will, once these infernally slow natives manage to refuel the fleet—"

Barton's own hand was on the switch, reaching to cut the circuit and end this insane dialogue. But before he did so, he said, "I believe I understand your position, Admiral. And your orders. When we meet in person we can talk it over, more."

He hit the switch; the screen went dark.

"He is evil, Barton. *Evil*." Limila's silver-irised eyes were wide; her mouth moved as though to spit something out.

Myra Hake slammed a fist against her thigh. "I have

354

to agree, and I didn't think I even *believed* in evil, as such. But that man—"

Abdul Muhammed made as if to speak, then looked at Barton, and didn't. Barton said, "I don't like him pretty much, either. And he's one hell of a threat to us all. But let's skip evil." They looked at him, and he said, "Is a five-year-old child evil?"

"That one," said Abdul, "is by no means a child."

"The hell he isn't." Barton slammed his own fist down, too hard against the edge of the comm-panel, making him wince. "He and his nephew both. They *act* like itty-bitty kids. They want what they want, right now, and if they don't get it, they raise hell with everybody. Tantrums." Trying to think what to say next, Barton felt his face contorting, and made an effort to relax it. "No. The only thing evil about this whole pile of crap is that childish people are able to get into positions of power." He shrugged. "And that's politics, and always has been and always will be."

When nobody answered, Barton said, "I was hoping we wouldn't all have to run. If it turns out we *can* run. But I'm not leaving anybody on here to take the brunt of that idiot's frustration, in case the rest of us made it away. And to hide out right, a little disguise is in order. So let's get to work."

Myra Hake said, "You mean it's Halloween, Barton?"

"That's right. Once we land, there wouldn't be time to get all duded up, except for last-minute makeup work. And even that part we could experiment with a little, now."

With something to work on, Barton felt more good than not. He said, "Okay. Let's start putting some costumes together, and do the stuff with the razors and the hair dye, and see what the makeup will do and what it won't." His smile felt more relaxed than he would have expected. "Once we do this stuff, though, our viewscreen picture is out of order, on the transmit side. Keep that in mind."

Barton didn't have much of a suntan these days, but still it took quite a bit of Myra's makeup to match the shaved forward patch of his scalp to his forehead and the rest of his face. He wasn't the only one who had problems; Myra had it easy, going to Tilaran appearance herself, but trying to use makeup so that Cheng's eyes would look other than Oriental, she cussed a lot. And no matter what kind of stuff Limila used to try to cover Abdul's ebon complexion, he never came out looking much better than boiled potato. And that, Barton reflected, was one of the *good* efforts.

Finally he called a halt. "Good as we're going to get, I think. And let's not use all the gunk up now; tomorrow is when we need it." He looked at the robes Gerain and Iivajj had put together. "Those'll do, I think. Cheng and I, we have to wear lift-shoes for tall. Abdul, anytime we're in public as a group, you stay in the middle and hunch down a lot with your knees bent. I know it won't be comfortable. . . ."

"From practicing," Abdul said, "I am assured of that. But I will manage." He shrugged. "If not, I assume we shall be armed."

If they got caught, the tall man meant. Barton said, "Let's not think that way. If we expect trouble—"

"Barton," said Limila, "you are one who *always* expects trouble. Which, I feel, is the reason you generally surmount it."

She had him, there. Barton said, "Maybe. This time, though, our best chance is to keep our heads down. So let's do that. Now pack up everything you'd want to carry along, and set it out handy."

Nobody argued. Barton scrubbed up and left the group. He had time for a nap, when his own brief packing was finished, and before he faced the situation on Tilara, he figured he could use one.

Limila woke him. For a moment he thought she might have something better in mind, and reached to her. But she smiled and brushed his hand aside. "No, Barton; there is not time. Ap Fenn is shouting into the control room. And does he not resemble, a great deal, his nephew Terike? In appearance, as well as in mind."

Barton hadn't thought about it, or noticed, much, when he'd first seen the admiral. Now while he washed up, crapped fast, and dressed, he put a think on it. Asking Limila to bring along some fruit juice and coffee from the galley, he headed up the ship and reached the control area. He pointed to himself and to the screen; Cheng signed "Out at first!" to him and he knew no picture was leaving Ship One. So, looking critically at the screen's image of Karsen ap Fenn, Barton sat down to the comm panel.

"Ahoy, Admiral. Barton here." Just for the hell of it, that "ahoy."

"How do I know that?" Big scowl from the admiral. "Put your picture through; I'm not in the habit of talking to a blank screen."

"We got a systems failure," said Barton. "Or so I'm told. So no pic, from here. You need to keep things even, I suppose you could turn yours off." While he watched ap Fenn, now seeing how the jutting brow ridges matched those of dead Terike, how the heavy jaw lay muffled by this man's jowls. And how the petulant mouth sat much the same. Limila was right; uncle and nephew were certainly cut from the one loaf. But now it was time to listen, so he did.

"Malfunctions are the fault of personnel," said the admiral. "You don't seem to be too expert in personnel management. But let that go; I called about something else. My instructions to you."

"Of course," said Barton. Well, maybe he could learn something. "Details, you mean?"

Details it was. After the first sentence or two, Barton didn't listen closely because he wasn't planning to follow ap Fenn's directions, anyway. They were all about how and when and where Barton would present himself and his entire shipload of friends to trial by ap Fenn. That wasn't going to happen; win or lose, it wouldn't. So why listen? What he did, then, was wait for a noticeable pause.

When it came, Barton said, "This trial you're calling— I guess you're doing it without lawyers and all that. Which makes sense, maybe. But one thing, Admiral. Somebody has to be able to say what really happened, and looks to me as if the main witness you have on hand is *me*. So who is it that's saying I helped kill Terike?"

The only way Barton could describe ap Fenn's grin, then, was skunky. The man gestured to someone behind him, out of the screen's range. He said, "My nephew's widow will testify. That should suffice."

And sure as hell, the slim blonde who walked into picture range and looked into a blank screen at that end was Helaise Renzel.

All right. Barton tried to make his brains move fast. Helaise had had bad times. Beat up now and then by

357

Terike ap Fenn when they were roomies, savaged by Hishtoo the Demu when he made his escape to Sisshain, taken on by Tarleton when she worked on his sympathy, and then—well, Barton didn't *know* how it had happened that Helaise had been left behind when Tarleton took the first fleet down the galactic Arm, to meet Barton at Sisshain. He didn't know, and in the ordinary case he couldn't afford to care. But now—he said, carefully, "Hi, Helaise. You're looking good. How you feeling?"

He remembered her queen-bee look, that she'd developed when she latched onto Tarleton, and that's the one she gave him now. "Oh, quite well, thank you, Barton. And how do *you* feel?"

"Confused, you want to know." Exasperated, Barton tried to let his breath come out without making a lot of noise about it. "I mean, what's this shit about me killing Terike? You know damn well I had nothing to do with it. Nobody else on this ship, either." Breathing in, he didn't do so well at quiet, any better than out. "Helaise—what do you think you're trying to *pull?*"

Her composure began to slip; Barton knew her well enough to note the signs. But he saw her brace herself before he could say more, and he knew he'd lost the joust. "You're only talking about what you did and what you didn't, Barton. There are moral responsibilities, too. You never allowed Terike to learn Tilaran customs at first hand. So he went out unprepared—"

"The silly son-of-a-bitch went out AWOL and you know it!" And tried to rape a Tilaran woman, and she went ape and killed him for it. Not on purpose, she didn't, but it happened. "He—"

"That's enough, Barton," said Karsen ap Fenn. "I've recorded this little dialogue. At the trial, I think it will suffice."

Feeling the way his face must look, for a moment Barton wanted ap Fenn to see him. But that was silly. He said, still trying to avoid a total break with Earth's authority, "When I stand at any kind of trial, Tarleton ought to be here. He's been my boss, ever since I brought the Demu ship to Earth and got us into space at all. I think—"

"But what you think doesn't matter," said the admiral. "I'm in charge. I'll make the decisions. Land, and report to me."

The two-word reply that came to mind, Barton swallowed. While he tried to think of something else, Helaise

358

Renzel said, "I might be able to help you, Barton. I'll come visit you, when you're down here, and we can talk."

Come visit? Meaning, Barton would be in a cage, to be visited by people who weren't locked up. He looked at her supercilious smile. "Helaise?"

"Yes, Barton?"

"Why don't you go piss up a rope?" He cut the circuit.

Turning around to face his people, who blessedly hadn't tried to cut in and help him, Barton tried to put a smile on his sweaty face. "I know. I didn't work that too good. It may not matter."

Abdul Muhammed had switched the main screen to a downside view; now he racked it up toward high-mag, and said, "The port we near, Barton, where the fleet sat before—dayside approaches it, and we should land not long after local noon there. I am trying to get us a clear view, but cannot as yet obtain clear definition of the details."

It was the port, all right, on the screen. And as Abdul said, there wasn't much to be seen yet. Barton said, "When the sun hits it, we'll get a good angle from visible light. How soon?"

Abdul's answer gave Barton time to go have breakfast and some fresh coffee. Limila and Cheng joined him, but he didn't feel like talking. When they got back up to the control room, Barton carrying a final cup of coffee, the screen showed dawn sunshine making needle-points of light across the port. "Just grazing the ships' noses," he said. "You get a count on them?"

"I make it fifty-three," said Cheng, squinting. "Barton —has the size of the landing area been increased?"

Gauging by the positions of two buildings he could recognize, Barton shook his head. Looking puzzled, Cheng said, "Then except for that small space at the center of the landing formation, those ships are spaced about as tight as they could be set down safely—or lift off again. With the repulsion of the Shields, I don't see how—" Then his eyes widened.

But before he could speak, over the intership circuit came Gellatly's voice. "Are you there, Barton?"

Myra's grin was impish. "Vice-Admiral Barton will be with you in a moment. Picture's out, though; sorry." And she didn't bother to put Gellatly's picture on the aux screen, either.

"You have downview, still, don't you?" The man sounded worried.

Setting his cup down, Barton leaned across to the comm-panel. "Barton here. Yes, our reception's okay. Just a glitch in the transmit side. Easy to fix, probably, when there's time for it."

"Yes. When you're down, we'll see to it." *That's nice.* Gellatly cleared his throat. "Here are your landing instructions. You will set down in the middle of the central open area, my other two ships to follow and land at each side of you. As you've probably noticed, it is necessary to land with Shields off. I will be leaving you in a few minutes, to put Sixty-five into synchronous orbit directly over the port. Do you understand the situation?"

Sure; I'm boxed. "Yes, I do. One change, though; your ships land just ahead of me, not behind." Over the man's protest, Barton said, "Your drive blasts, on those new ships, are bigger than mine. Takes more accuracy to avoid damage to the ships you land beside. I know my pilot; I don't know yours."

In the pause, it sounded like Vannick's voice in the background, arguing with his commander. Barton caught only a few words. Then Gellatly said, "Very well; it makes no real difference. That's all, then. Gellatly, out."

"Roger dodger. Barton, likewise." Myra cut the circuit. Barton turned to wave a hand against a flood of questions. "Thing was, there, I wouldn't put it past ap Fenn to have those ships give us a bath in drive blast. Save him a lot of trouble. Now, then—"

"But you're letting them put us in the middle of the whole fleet!" Standing now, hands on hips, Myra looked exasperated. "If we ducked over to the edge, at least we'd have a *chance* to run."

"We're landing right where I want to be," Barton said. "Abdul, have you done sitdowns with the Shield off?" The big man nodded. "That's good, because I haven't. Well—" Remembering Sisshain. "Not exactly. So you take us in; all right?"

"And what will you do, Barton?" Limila asked.

"Oh, I'll just sit down out of the way, over at one of the weapons positions." He wasn't sure why he didn't tell them all, straight out, what he had in mind. Maybe a feeling that it would be bad luck to say it.

She kept looking at him. "I think I know what you are going to do."

360

Barton gazed at the woman he loved more than anyone he'd ever known. "I wouldn't be surprised."

His words seemed to quiet the others. For long minutes they sat, then, while Abdul Muhammed guided Ship One downward, between the paths of the two escort ships that now kept a slight lead. They hit air gently, without much buffeting. And then, carefully, precisely, only seconds after ap Fenn's ships touched down, Abdul landed the ship in the narrow space that Karsen ap Fenn had assigned.

That's when Barton hit the sleep-gun switch.

When they all saw the indicator come on, there were gasps. Barton stood up, talking. "All right. The sleeper's on max power, hemispherical distribution. I'll set it to turn off about twenty minutes after we leave here; we really don't want the amnesia effect to make the whole second fleet into a pack of zombies." He raised his voice to override interruption. "Get the travel kits you packed and assemble at the airlock. The individual Shields are in the locker beside it. When everybody's there, buzz me here and I'll come a-running." They weren't moving. Well, there wasn't that much hurry, now, so he said, "Questions? Fast ones."

The answers were easy. No, ap Fenn's people wouldn't have individual Shields of their own, due to the admiral's penchant for apartheid with the locals. "So there won't be anyone shooting at us." But what if some of the *ships* had their Shields on?

Limila laughed, then, so he nodded for her to answer. "The closeness of these ships, at ap Fenn's orders. If they began activating their Shields, the repulsive forces—" She brought her hands together, then spread her arms violently. "Poof! Like rows of dominoes, ships would fall."

That seemed to be it, for now. "Okay, we move it," Barton said. "Let's just hope Vertan left a groundcar where he said he would."

Sooner than Barton expected, Abdul called to give him the go-ahead. He set the timer on the sleep-gun, went to the airlock and shucked into his own portable Shield harness, and when the lock opened, waved the group down the ramp ahead of him. For a moment he paused, then decided that if he tried to leave Ship One sealed against ap Fenn's people, the admiral would have them blast their way in. He patted the hull. "Good luck, ol' trooper." And he followed the rest down to Tilaran soil.

Spooky, it was, walking through a jungle of standing ships, with no sign or sound of life except the occasional man or woman sprawled unconscious where the sleepfield had found them. All Earth types, Barton noted: no Tilari, let alone Larka-Te or Filjari. Then, nearly to the edge of the port by now, another correlation came to mind. The men's insignia of rank varied a lot more than the women's. The latter seemed to be mostly noncoms or very junior officers. And they were greatly outnumbered, in the sample he was seeing. Barton frowned. In Tarleton's fleet, Estelle Cummings ran a damn good squadron. In ap Fenn's, he guessed, she probably wouldn't even rate her own ship.

Preoccupied, he started when Myra Hake nudged him; he glanced up to see what she wanted. They both looked pretty funny, he guessed, shaved frontally bald and plastered with makeup to hide the paleness, but her plain features still carried dignity. "We could do it differently, Barton. Why not just unload the carcasses off one of these ships, and take it? You or Abdul could fake past that Gellatly without much trouble, I expect."

He thought back. "I guess you weren't there, Myra. Ap Fenn let it slip that he was having a problem getting the fleet refueled." For seconds, he laughed. "I wouldn't be surprised but what the slowdown began when Arleta Fox jumped ship. I didn't ask, though."

She nodded. "It wasn't that I thought you miss many bets, Barton. But the idea came, and I had to check it."

"Sure. And always do that. Because like anybody else, I do miss some bets." The more he knew this tall woman, the better he liked her.

Nearing the port's edge, they passed the last of ap Fenn's ships. Barton looked; a little to the left of where he expected to, he saw two empty groundcars. One wasn't empty, though; when they reached it, they found Doctor Arleta Fox slumped inside.

"Oh, hell!" Barton said. "Well, let's get out of here, quick. Who drives? I suppose I could figure out the controls if I had to, but let's go with the experts. Iivajj? Gerain?" Both Tilarans signed assent, and each took driver's position in the respective cars. "Next question. Where to? Vertan's place?"

"For a first stop, yes," Limila said. "I know where it is, and so do Gerain and Iivajj. But it is not a place we can stay."

They piled into the two cars and moved off in caravan. Barton sat with Arleta Fox's head in his lap and watched for signs of awakening. He said, "Sure, I know, Limila. Not that I'd expect Vertan to be inhospitable, but that's where ap Fenn might look first."

Tilaran architecture fascinated Barton, and Vertan's diggings were a prime example: no straight lines, but a smooth vari-colored blend of parabolic cross-sections like a statue of a tall skinny armadillo, ranging from pale blue around the lower sides to a deep copper shade along the dorsal ridge. And at the larger end, an abrupt edge framing a concave face that rippled in iridescent silver. From the outside, no windows showed, but Barton knew that various areas would be transparent when viewed from inside. The entrance was in the concave face, of course, and there the two Tilarans brought the ground-cars to rest.

Arleta Fox was moving a little, making small breathy noises, but nowhere near awake yet. Abdul helped Barton get her out of the car, and moved to pick her up and carry her. It would have made sense for the huge man to do the carrying, but Barton smiled and said, "Thanks, but it's my job. The doc and I go back quite a way." By the time they all got indoors, Barton could feel the woman's weight growing by the step. But they were led to a spacious room, where Barton could lay his burden onto a curving couch of sorts, before he ran short enough of breath that anybody could have heard him. Still seeing no sign of returning consciousness, Barton stood up.

Vertan wasn't there; whether the welcoming Tilarans, chattering six ways from Sunday with Limila and Gerain and Iivajj, were family or servants, Barton had no idea. He touched Limila's elbow, and she turned to him. "These folks know what the scoop is?"

"Yes, Barton. Vertan has informed them. He was to be here soon, but now that is not likely."

"Why not?"

"Because he went to the Big Hundred, to confer with ap Fenn."

Well, when you play your cards too close to the vest,

363

somebody's going to bet into the wrong hand. Barton sighed, then relaxed. If he owed Vertan an apology, he'd give it when the time came. For now, the drill was that everybody could go to guest rooms and clean up, and all, and for after that, Barton had heard food mentioned.

One of the Tilaran women, thinner than average and with boldly strong features, was some kind of medic. "Reshane," Limila said. "She will watch over the awakening of Doctor Fox." So Barton thanked Reshane, then followed Limila to their temporary quarters. He was glad to shuck the pack he'd been carrying, and was even more pleased to share a hot spray bath with Limila, and then part of a flagon of the pale green Tilaran wine he'd come to like, during the time Tarleton's fleet had been on this planet.

With ap Fenn's first mousetrap sprung harmlessly, Barton felt relaxed enough to be a little horny, but there wasn't time before the call for lunch, so he and Limila settled on a rain check.

He ate with good appetite; in fact, everybody seemed to. Tilaran cuisine tended to be spicy in a very delicate sort of way, and that was something else Barton had learned to like. During the meal he tried to figure out who was who among the hosting Tilarans, but all he found out was that Vertan's most needful person was away visiting another family member, and did not share Vertan's residence full-time in any case. Well, he knew that the Tilaran equivalent of marriage seldom included total cohabitation. Sometimes, but not often. After a time of listening he was fairly sure that two of those present were adult children of Vertan or of Vertan's absent "spouse" or possibly of both; beyond that understanding, he didn't push it. And when Barton had had about as much of the lunch situation as he really needed, the woman Reshane came in and beckoned to him.

"The small Earthani is of waking, and would see you."

She led him to, and let him into, a small concave-surfaced room that was mostly shades of pink with sparkling blue highlights, and left him. He found Arleta Fox sitting up, holding a beaker of the tart, bubbling Tilaran beverage, *klieta*. As he went to sit facing her, on a puff-stool that wasn't as wobbly as it looked, she gazed up at him. "It's good to see you, Barton. But what happened?

I went to the port with Vertan, and waited for you in the car. And woke up here. I—"

"Easy, Doc—Arlie, I mean." He sipped from his large goblet of the green wine, then set it down beside him. "It went this way." He told it as short as he could make it, then said, "Until we got downstairs I wasn't sure, myself, just how to play it. So no chance to warn you or anybody, even if I trusted channel security. Vertan caught it worse, I'm afraid. He was having a chat with the admiral, on the Big Hundred." He frowned. "And I hope he's not in trouble."

Serious of face, Fox pushed fingers through her frizz of hair. Seen up close, it was really cut a lot shorter than Barton was used to, on her. Fingers couldn't quite hide in it. The woman said, "Vertan's safe enough. He has pressure on ap Fenn, not the other way around." The bulldog smile. "When Vertan began to distrust the admiral, he clamped down on refueling the second fleet. He'll give the go-ahead when he feels reassured, and not before."

"Then Vertan should be back pretty soon, here?"

"I'd think so." She changed the subject, asking Barton for details of how he'd sidetracked the Demu "war" so it didn't happen. He told her, omitting the parts that had to be kept secret, and when she spotted a hole in the explanation and asked directly for answers, he shrugged and said, "Sorry, but that's really Top Clam. I mean, Tarleton could authorize telling you, but I can't."

After a moment, she nodded. "All right; I'll respect that. Now, then—" She leaned toward him. "Let's talk about Tilara."

It took Barton a moment to get the drift, but of all things she was looking *flirty*. He got his wineglass up in front of him and said, "You mean the party you went to, and got surprised how Tilarans talk body-Braille?"

Sitting back again, Fox laughed. "Barton, relax. It's *views* I want to exchange with you—the ways this totally different culture struck us at first—not belly rubbing." His embarrassment must have shown, for she laughed. "I adjusted to Tilaran ways rapidly, Barton, and that party was only the first of several." She paused. "How old do you think I am?"

He shook his head. "That's a game I never play; you can't win."

She blinked. "Not bad thinking; not bad at all. Well, I'm closing on thirty-five." Nearly seven years younger than Barton; he'd have guessed the difference less, so good thing he hadn't. She said, "I gave up on virginity at sixteen, and on any idea of celibacy at twenty-two. But in my line of work, security and all, I had to be quite cautious about my liaisons and never allowed them to develop into affairs." He must have been staring; she shook her head. "I've never seriously considered marriage."

Puzzled, he felt himself frowning. "I must be missing something. What makes this my business? I mean, not that you're—"

For an instant she looked mad as hell; then she relaxed. "Barton, will you quit taking everything *personally?* The point is, here on Tilara I could drop all that silly jockeying and enjoy myself. Security, meaning the admiral, doesn't care beans what happens offship. Except the refueling operation, of course. So—" Her stretch, then, made her small body look more voluptuous than Barton would have believed. "Well, I had my little flings, would you imagine it, and now I'm settled down for a time."

"Sounds great." He didn't have to ask; she'd tell him.

She did. "Vertan's oldest son, Tchorda."

"Settled down, you say. In most needful person status?"

She shook her head. "Only as a temporary thing. He's taken, that way, and that's included in our understanding. But she's off-planet and won't be back for a while. So, until then—"

"You're not planning to stay on Tilara, though."

"I don't know. Maybe until Tarleton returns here. Certainly I'm not going back to ap Fenn's little empire."

"Makes sense." He would have said more, but the room's door opened. Outside, back from it, stood Vertan. He threw off his robe and tossed it to one side, out of sight, and walked in naked.

"I believe," he said, "that Admiral Karsen ap Fenn arranged that my garment carry an eye-ear, a tracer device. Without its presence, we can talk to better effect." He closed the door.

Barton ignored the outstretched hand. "Just a minute." Holding a fold of his robe up to hide his face, he opened the door and went outside the room. Vertan's robe lay on the floor; with his free hand, Barton felt around its hem, and found a lump that didn't belong there, with a tiny "eye" protruding. A metal ornament on a shelf looked sturdy enough; with it, Barton pounded the lump until he could feel only loose fragments through the cloth. The ornament showed no damage; he replaced it and went back into the room. "I killed the thing, Vertan. Simpler that way. *Now* let's shake hands."

And now, joining the rest of Barton's gang, they could talk, too. First order of business was to settle on a better hideout, and soon. While ap Fenn's people couldn't just barge in on Vertan without going through some formalities, Barton gathered, Vertan couldn't stall the admiral off indefinitely. Limila asked and got permission to make a call. The voice-view terminal was in another room; when she came back, she said, "I have spoken with Tevann. His guest-space building is empty now, and can accommodate most of us. If this is all right, Barton?"

Tevann—Limila's most needful person, years ago, before the Demu had taken her. But now with someone else; Tevann had told Barton the name, when they met once at a party, but Barton couldn't remember. "Sure," he said. "If we're welcome, that's fine."

"Good," she said. "This is in another town, not far from here, and adjoining a smaller, auxiliary spaceport."

Vertan added some information. Tarleton's fleet hadn't quite taken over all of the main port, but still a lesser one had been opened, to handle the overflow. Ap Fenn insisted on sole usage, so all other space traffic now went to the auxiliary.

"I wonder what happens if the big ship comes?" said Arleta Fox, then put a hand to cover her mouth, and shook her head. "Cancel that. I'm not even supposed to know, let alone say."

"You've already spilled, Arlie, that there is something." Barton said it quietly. Because he knew she didn't mean the great ship on Sisshain. Because there was no way she could have heard of it. So he said, "You're off the Agency payroll now, ever since you jumped ship. So what's the setup?"

She really didn't know all that much about it, Barton decided after a while. But the Agency had another project on the boards, begun a little before Tarleton's fleet left Earth, and as usual the left hand wasn't giving the right hand the time of day. "It's a big ship, though," she said. "I saw the assembly building—just a huge box to hide it. And it's supposed to be a new principle, a drive that's tremendously faster than your ships, or ap Fenn's."

New principle? From having talked with the lab boys,

Barton doubted it. Still, though, somebody might have come up with the idea of multiplexing units, the way he'd seen on the ship the Great Race had left to grow ivy all over it, at Sisshain. "Well—" He shrugged. "We'll worry about that when we see it." But his smile thanked her, while mentally he filed the info for future reference.

Gerain was fidgeting; now he spoke. "It is not of need that Iivajj and I should hide; this ap Fenn is of no knowledge of us." True enough; the two Tilarans weren't even in Tarleton's records, let alone ap Fenn's. And since they were ship's people, Vertan made a call and arranged to assign them to a Tilaran ship at the aux port, and for a groundcar to pick them up within the hour.

Barton took a vote of the Earthani; it confirmed his own disinclination to accept Vertan's offer to put all of them on a Tilaran ship and get them safely away. "Tarleton's going to be coming back here sometime. And he'll be walking into a trap. Somebody has to hang around and warn him, and try to help. The way you did, Arlie, for *us*." Vertan looked doleful, but he had to accept the logic of it. Certainly, he admitted, he himself was not equipped to play strategy and tactics among Earthani factions.

Barton said, "How long you think you can stall ap Fenn on the refueling? Sure's hell we don't want him going to Sisshain. But he must have a few ships fueled, for patrols, like Gellatly's."

And then he found he hadn't known much about fuel logistics on Tilara. The thing was that production was geared to the normal rate of interstellar traffic. "Perhaps four or five twelves of ships in a year," Vertan said, "though increasing, of course." Tarleton's fleet of forty had laid quite an overload on the system, put the whole caboodle on round-the-clock overtime and wiped out the reserve stockpile. Then with the second fleet expected, the higher rate of production had been maintained. But even with the best of will and intention, ap Fenn wouldn't be refueled yet. And the way things were, Tilara wasn't busting its butt to speed the job up. "While we would be of joy to see ap Fenn go," Vertan added, "we do not wish him to be of access to our friend Tarleton."

So it was a delay game, the best that Vertan could play without really knowing the rules. "Yeh; thanks," Barton said. He looked around the group. What else needed deciding in a hurry? How about Arleta Fox? He pointed to her. "If we figure ap Fenn to get a look-in here, you want to hide out with the rest of us, so's not to catch a court-martial?"

She hesitated, then said, "Thanks, Barton, but I don't believe I will." The bulldog smile. "You see, I'm one of the few people in the second fleet that he couldn't pin down with a military rank. Oh, there's 'equivalent rank,' of course—" She shrugged. "You can't dodge that, or no one would know where you're supposed to sit in the galley."

"Where you *sit?*" Barton found it hard to believe, but obviously she wasn't kidding. "You're still a civilian, though?"

The woman nodded. "So I think I'll simply call in my resignation from the Agency. I'll be a little feisty about it, nitpicking about the exact termination date, and the transfer of accumulated benefits I probably can't collect in any case." Now she grinned. "That's merely a matter of good offense being the best defense. Keep him arguing about *my* demands, so he won't have time to push at me with his own grievances."

Barton had to smile. "You're good; you know that?" He shook his head. "You ever stop to think maybe you're in the wrong business?"

"No. But perhaps you are. Basically, we're both psychologists—even though I have the formal training, and you don't."

Whether she was right or not, Barton gave up the argument.

The car came to take Gerain and Iivajj; Barton felt a little sad, remembering how the young woman had approached him at his first Tilaran party, and the joy he'd found with her. "So young," Limila had said of Iivajj later, "but of good thought." And then she and Gerain taken hostage by Hishtoo, and Barton thinking he'd probably have to kill them—but that had worked out all right. In point of fact, he'd wound up rescuing the two of them.

Now, he thought, as he and Limila exchanged hugs with the two departing Tilarans, he'd probably never see Iivajj again. So he savored her final kiss, then touched his tongue to a tear at the corner of her eye. His own eyes weren't all that dry, either, he noticed. "Iivajj," he said, "I value you; I am of thanks to have known you. Be of happiness together, you and Gerain."

And when they had gone, Limila said to him, "It is a pity, Barton, that you and Iivajj stayed apart all the way from Sisshain. You need not have."

He squeezed her shoulder. "I know. Wouldn't have felt right, though. I mean, we were running an Earthani ship, not Tilaran." Not that anybody would have made any fuss, but still and all . . .

Limila shrugged. "It was of your choice, Barton. Yes."

Not until dark was the Ship One group moved from Vertan's home. Barton wore his Shield harness, since it wouldn't fit easily into his pack; he didn't ask how anyone else dealt with the problem.

There were two groundcars, being loaded. Vertan drove one; Barton and Limila and Abdul Muhammed got in with him, Barton in front alongside the driver, because he wanted a look at where they went. The other driver was, Barton now knew, Vertan's son Tchorda. Beside him sat Arleta Fox—along just for the ride, Barton guessed. Behind him, Myra Hake and Cheng Ai took seats. In the dim light, Vertan waved back to his son, and then the two cars moved out.

The absence of regular roads or streets on Tilara, as far as he'd seen, still puzzled Barton. Now again he tried to figure how Vertan picked his car's way across verdant groundcover, between buildings spaced with no regularity, and still knew where he was going. The cars weren't moving all that slowly, either, and the Tilaran excuse for headlights kept Barton squinting. But he could hear the soft, bulky tires making swishing noises against the ground; for sure, they wouldn't be tearing up the local turf.

He was beginning to relax and quit trying to figure things out, when three cars came up at an angle to block Vertan off, and slid to a stop that had to raise some hell with the underfoot.

Barton turned to Vertan, in time to see the driver slump down, no hands to the controls, and lie over against the door.

The car was headed for the blocking cars, a building, and a tree, in that order. And for the moment, Barton couldn't reach the controls, which he knew only vaguely. He tried to pull Vertan out of the way, but that job

370

took him a time. While he was still at it, the car, slowing gently, swerved to miss first the cars, then the building, and stopped short of the tree.

"What the hell?" He had Vertan out of the way now, and settled in to see if he could find the go-pedal on this buggy.

"There are safety features, Barton." From behind him, Limila's voice. "Not infallible, but sometimes helpful. As now."

"Yeh, sure; thanks." People were getting out of the cars up ahead. They had guns. Sleep-guns for sure, because what else had knocked Vertan out? Barton didn't even remember turning his Shield on, when he decided to wear it, but he must've, or why wasn't he dropped flat like Vertan? And for sure, Limila had hers turned on.

From the cars ahead, eight or ten people charged out. Barton fumbled for his own hand version of the sleep-gun, found it, and dropped the lot of them.

"All right; who's awake?" Out of the car now, Barton was in a hurry to get back in and get moving. Everyone in their second car was out like pow; no help there. Barton looked around and saw a tall figure. "Abdul? You had your Shield on?"

"It seemed a reasonable precaution, Barton."

"Yeh. Yeh, good. I don't suppose you know how to drive one of these things?"

"As it happened, when I was here before, in Tamirov's squadron, I enjoyed some of my spare time in learning that skill. So—"

"So follow me." But first he had to help Abdul wrestle the limp figures in the second car, enough out of the way to give Abdul the driver's seat. Then Barton went back to the other car and got in.

Limila climbed in beside him. He said, "I think I know most of this, from watching as a passenger, but tell me the main handles."

She did, but then said, "I could accomplish this. Why must you?"

"Because you might not push hard enough." Maybe he was wrong; he couldn't know; Barton shook his head. "Navigate for me, please?"

She did, and quickly Barton learned the functions of the controls he really needed. Following Limila's guidance—and she was very good at telling him without the

371

aid of gestures he couldn't have seen—Barton ran the caravan considerably faster than Vertan had done. After a time they left all buildings behind and ran through open country. From the shadowy look of the hills to either side, Barton figured he might be missing a lot of good scenery. But for right now, he couldn't afford to worry about it. Not much chance that ap Fenn might have a second team after him, chasing tracers Barton didn't know about— but if that chance happened, Barton wanted to be all braced for it.

When it didn't happen, when the two cars reached what Limila pointed out as sanctuary, Barton realized he'd probably wasted a lot of adrenaline. Well, there was a lot of that going around.

Tevann, welcoming the group, was as courteous as ever. Just as skinny and handsome, too, Barton thought. But if Tevann and Limila wanted, Barton wouldn't begrudge. He exchanged embrace with the Tilaran, briefly as local custom dictated, then watched while Tevann and Limila took a bit longer about the hugging, before Tevann drew back and said, "Is it of importance that these cars be not seen here?"

Vertan was awake by now, and didn't look or sound too woozy. He said, "Of importance, perhaps not. Of probability, though, a difference can ensue. One of danger." Looking as tired as Barton had ever seen him, Vertan smiled. "That we be of haste, removing the two vehicles to the holdings of myself, may be of best choice."

Your language says it funny, but you said it good. Barton moved up to handshake the Tilaran. "Thanks, Vertan, for everything. You're right; get your cars back, so's ap Fenn won't guess too much."

"Your thought is of merit." So Vertan left in one car. His son Tchorda, with Arleta Fox beside him, followed in the other. Leaving the four Earthani, along with Limila, to accept Tevann's hospitality. Shrugging tension from his shoulder muscles, Barton followed the group indoors.

First came food and drink; then the contingent from Ship One was escorted to quarters in the guest building. Leaving them, Tevann said, "Tomorrow we may be of more speech. For tonight, enough."

Barton couldn't argue with that sentiment, and next morning over breakfast he was in a chatty mood. While he and Limila were bringing Tevann up to date concerning the expedition to Sisshain, a Tilaran woman joined the group. Tevann stood, so the others did, also, as he said, "I would have you be of acquaintance with Uelein, my most needful person." He gave her their names in turn, and she shook hands with each—except for Limila. Those two embraced; obviously they knew each other.

Everyone sat. Tevann poured *klieta* for Uelein; the rest continued eating. Barton studied the woman. She was shorter than average for Tilara, not much over Barton's own height, and slim even for her own race. Like Iivajj, she was one of the minority of Tilarans whose hair was a dark reddish-brown rather than black, and unlike the majority, she wore it cut short. It looked, he thought, like fur.

Limila had backtracked the story a little, repeating in short form what Uelein had missed. Barton's attention roamed, and was brought back when Limila spoke his name. "Huh?"

"I asked you, Barton, if today will be all right for us to go to the medical place. I told you—on the ship, remember?—that when we returned here, we would have to see as to the treatments for you, to stabilize metabolism and postpone aging."

"I—I'd forgotten all about that." And he had. In the shock of learning that Limila had lived perhaps eighty Earth-years and, due to Tilaran medical science, was still physically youthful, Barton's mind had more or less crawled in a hole and pulled it in after him. Now he spoke his fear. "They may not work on Earthani the way they do for you people." He shook his head. "I don't know—"

She gripped his shoulder and shook it. "But we must go and find out! Barton, you are not one to hide from risk."

While he was wondering why he couldn't find an answer, Myra Hake said, "Postpone aging? What's this about?"

Barton shrugged. "It gave me a jolt, I'll tell you. Limila, here—" He gestured. "You wouldn't believe her chronological age if I wrote it in my own blood; the Tilarans have some sort of longevity treatments. Limila says they might work for us, too. In fact, she only mentioned them by accident, because she assumed we probably had the same thing." Talking about it made his mind work again;

he turned to Limila. "All right; I suppose today's as good a day as any to see what we can find out."

"Hold up a minute." Cheng leaned forward. "Taking your word that such treatments exist, how far does it go? Have you thought ahead?"

Barton wasn't sure what he meant, but Limila said, "Why, of course you and Myra, and Abdul, must have the same opportunity. And—"

"*And,* yes," said Cheng. "I—"

Abdul broke in. "For myself, I shall abstain from any such course, until my wife back on Earth can share it with me. I have no wish to stay young while she does not."

"It's not just us," Cheng said. "If something like this hits Earth, what happens to the very delicate population balance?"

For seconds, everybody talked at once. Then Barton held up a hand and got some quiet. "This problem's going to take some thinking, and I admit *I* haven't done any, yet." Now he thought, and said, "Add an arbitrary fifty years, say, to the average lifespan on Earth, and for the first fifty years, the ghost of Malthus is going to have a field day. After that, the death rate catches up again and things drift back to present normal. And there's ways to minimize the bulge. Maybe tie fertility restrictions to artificial longevity—make it an earned privilege, not a right." The overwhelming complications confused his line of thought; he shook his head then, and said only, "Some thinking, I said? A lot of it! But there's time for that, as long as the word doesn't get out into the rumor factory. And mainly, we don't know yet whether the Tilaran processes even *work* for our species."

Cheng nodded. "Ordinarily I take a dim view of the elitist concept of keeping secrets for the good of those left ignorant, but this makes twice this year that I'm forced to accept it as the lesser evil." Looking at Barton, whose eyebrows had raised, he said, "The other? The great ship, on Sisshain, of course."

"Oh, sure." Barton nodded agreement.

"Very well," Limila said. "Barton, can we leave here, do you think, within the hour?" Again he nodded. "Then I will call and arrange a meeting for us, at the medical place."

Limila drove the car; she knew where they were going

374

and Barton didn't, and now there was no need for combat-style driving. She left the scattered settlement that contained Tevann's residence, and Barton soon realized they were headed back to the city adjoining the main spaceport. When she pulled up and parked beside a building, Barton looked at it and recognized it; this was where Limila had gained her transplanted breasts.

The place still didn't look like a hospital, to Barton—an irregularly convex structure with concave sections dished in here and there, roughly two stories high, and finished in colors shading from pale blue-green near the entrance to a fluorescent orange at the top of the side he could see. As they left the car and walked into the building, a broken corner to one side caught his attention and triggered memory. Same building, all right.

And inside, first what looked like a combined bedroom and living room, rather than any sort of lobby. And the curved narrow corridor, and the somewhat elastic door that took a good hard knock to make any sound. From inside it, someone said, "Be of entrance." And they went in.

Doctors are doctors, Barton decided, no matter where you find them. These two Tilarans, a man and a woman wearing smooth, green, tight-fitting jumpsuits of a sort, quizzed Limila as if Barton were deaf, mute, and incapable of understanding. Well, the last part was close to true; their terminology was new to him and there was no point in butting in and trying to learn it in a hurry.

So he kept his mouth shut and did what they told him. He stripped, was scrubbed from the neck down with something that turned out to be a depilatory—among other things, probably—and submitted to the taking of a lot of samples from his goose-pimpled body. The place, he thought, could have used a little warming.

He was handed a pill and swallowed it, and went onto a calm, euphoric high that felt better than anything he'd ever got from black hash in Nam. Each touch of needle or scalpel made a delightful tingling that radiated from the spot in ripples that closed together in the middle of his head and left him shuddering with joy. One corner of his mind remembered that Tilara didn't have anesthesia. "There is a drug," Limila had told him long ago, back on Earth. "Pain becomes ecstasy." It sure as hell did.

He tried to keep track of what samples were taken, not all of them painful in any case. Blood, saliva, perspiration, semen, lymph, urine, spinal fluid, skin tissue, a snip of muscle, fluid from his left eyeball, the involuntary tears that came from his frantic fear (drug or no drug) when they messed with his eye, wipings from his nose, from his ears. Something happening at the back of his thigh as he lay face down, and from the sound of it, the sample was probably bone marrow. A probing at his rear, and he couldn't figure why they'd need to sample his feces. *But be my guest.* Then some twinges, here and there, that gave him no idea at all as to what was being extracted.

Then they were done with him; he was taken to another room and put to bed, flat on his back. The drug was wearing off, but he felt only minor pains from their invasions of his body. Limila leaned over him and said, "Until tomorrow at this time you must lie as still as you find possible. Otherwise, you may suffer very bad headaches, at the least. I will sit with you, as much as I may, to remind you to avoid movement. But now, try to rest."

A whole damn *day*, stuck flat on his back with no advance warning? Why, he'd go *nuts*. He was still thinking that way, a little outraged, when he realized he was about to go to sleep.

When he woke, he was given his breakfast to drink through a bent plastic straw. In the food they must have put a lesser version of the drug, because Barton lay cheerfully groggy for what had to be quite a few hours. Sometimes, when he opened his eyes, Limila was there; sometimes it was a Tilaran he didn't know. When he woke with his head working more or less, though, Limila greeted him. "You are feeling better, Barton? Now it will be all right for you to move, for us to return to Tevann's."

Return to Tevann's? Just like that? Barton blinked once. "They figure the treatment won't work on me; right?"

Limila shook her head. "That is not the situation."

"Then what is? Don't I get a report?"

She told him, and then they went back to Tevann's place.

"Here's how it is," said Barton, across the raised pool

that set in the middle of the foot-well, a few decimeters below eye level. Around the perimeter of padded floor that served for seating, Myra and Cheng looked at him intensely, Abdul Muhammed with an air of total calm. Tevann looked mildly interested, and Uelein as well. Limila, of course, already knew what he'd say, and could correct him if he got it wrong. The colorful little creatures sporting in the pool, Tilaran equivalent of fish, would hardly care. Barton took another sip of a local distillation that came close to being bourbon but didn't quite make it, and said his piece.

"All they guarantee," he said, "is that if I try this option it won't kill me. Going to take them a while, I'm told, to tailor the various stuffs to my individual metabolism. They have to do that with their own people, even, and this has to be trickier."

"And you don't know," said Cheng, "if it will extend your life?"

"*They* don't know," Barton said. "We can try it, they say, and either way I'll live, not lose anything. But it's a pisser."

"How so?" said Myra Hake.

"Whether it works or not, you suffer a lot, for a few weeks. Limila hadn't mentioned that part, before." He shrugged. "Well, no reason why she should. Nothing much comes for free."

"And when would you know," said Abdul, "whether or not the treatment has been effective? In the sense of increased longevity?"

"If over the next ten years," Limila said, "Barton has not aged appreciably, then we might assume some benefit from treatment."

Myra said, "Barton—are you going to try it? Be the guinea pig?"

He laughed, not for long. "Sure. Because guinea pig, that's exactly right. Somebody has to, regardless of how we work out the implications for Earth. And I seem to be the only one in the crowd whose most needful person is going to outlive him by maybe fifty years if he *doesn't* come up with some kind of miracle."

"And the rest of us wait ten years, still aging," said Cheng Ai, "until we see whether the gimmick works on you?"

Myra Hake reached an arm around Cheng's head and

pulled him over to her. "Of course not, you dear idiot. Three guinea pigs are better than one."

The waiting period, Barton thought, before learning whether Tilari techniques could extend Earthani lifespan, took a lot of pressure off the worries about overpopulated Earth. "So long as we keep this whole bundle under Top Clam," he said. Nobody disagreed. Cheng and Myra went to the main port area and underwent the same discomforts Barton had endured. Myra brought back a supply of the depilatory stuff, for use in maintaining the Tilaran front hairline on herself and Barton and Cheng and Abdul, just in case the disguise might really fool anybody. Barton was pleased; he was tired of trying to cover shaving stubble with makeup, even though sunlamp treatment had given the bared scalp areas about the same color as everybody's original foreheads. Barton still thought their attempts to fake Tilaran appearance looked pretty silly, but it was the only game in town, so why argue?

Anyway, his body gave evidence that the effect wasn't permanent.

Vertan came once to visit, and reported that without Tilaran permission, Karsen ap Fenn had put squads of armed Marines to patrolling the main port city. "They are likely of search for all of you," he said. "I am by no means of consent that he do these things, but as yet—"

"You don't want to start an open fight with the son-of-a-bitch," said Barton, and Vertan nodded. Barton thought a moment, and said, "Do you know what he's done about our ship? If anything?"

Invested it with armed Marines, the answer came. What else? Barton frowned. "But is he doing anything about the extra weapons?" Not a chance that ap Fenn's people on their own could replicate the twin-ion beam or the plasma gun or the high-drive torpedoes, but . . .

"He has not asked of our aid," said Vertan. "And should he, he will not be of receipt of it. Though to refuse him might be of awkwardness."

"Yeh," Barton said. "Awkward. But just hang in awkward, Vertan, if that's what it takes."

If Tarleton would only get back here!

But Tarleton didn't, nor did any ships from the first fleet. Ap Fenn fumed, Barton was told, under the slow niggling process of refueling as set by Vertan. Tiring of secondhand reports, Barton once drove to the main port's city and prowled the port himself, feeling that his Tilaran disguise must stand out like a clown suit. But no one challenged him, and indeed he saw Karsen ap Fenn himself within quiet-hello range, and the man glanced briefly at him and turned away and walked on. For a moment Barton was insanely tempted to go after the admiral and do his Tilaran impersonation on some sort of interview format: "I am of the public bureau for information, of disseminating current facts, and I would like to . . . " But then he shrugged and dropped the idea. *Don't be stupid.* So he watched ap Fenn, well guarded by armed personnel, move away.

At "home," at the residence of Tevann and sometimes of Uelein, Barton tried to relax and enjoy life. He wasn't good at waiting; he never had been, which was one reason the eight years in the Demu cage had made him a little hard to get along with, by the time he escaped. He knew all about that, Barton did. It didn't help much.

He had figured that Limila would spend some nighttimes with Tevann, her most needful person in the old days before her capture, and he was right. Tilaran sexual protocol pretty well put it up to him and Uelein, to tidy up the edges; he knew that. But while he liked the woman well enough, and she also seemed friendly, Barton felt no urge or need for intimacy with her. Uelein was sure enough a nice lady, but they didn't *know* each other, any.

That lack hadn't always stopped Barton, though. One evening, left on his own again, he borrowed a car and drove down to the nearby auxiliary spaceport. Where Iivajj and Gerain had been placed in jobs on a Tilaran starship. He found the ship, and found welcome.

They—Gerain and Iivajj and several crewmates—were eating. Barton was fed; he accepted *klieta* and some local booze that had good clout but no flavor pattern that quite fit what his tastebuds recognized. For now, though, it would do.

And then Iivajj bade him rise and steered him to a quiet cabin, and made drinks for them both and sat facing him and took his hand.

"Barton—it has been a long time. I am now of gladness."

Suddenly it was the same as their first meeting. Iivajj still wore her dark red hair in a heavy curl that came

379

forward over her left shoulder. Her lips still parted in a smile of welcome. *When in Rome*—Barton sighed, and went to her without reserve, and found that he hadn't forgotten one sweet thing about her, nor remembered anything incorrectly, either.

Afterward, before he drove home, they fed him well again, too.

Even with the flexible linings of the Tilaran dentures, Limila's new teeth were stretching her jaw muscles. But on their own, those teeth hadn't sprouted quite far enough to work with any real comfort. Put that annoyance together with the developing pregnancy, and Barton could see why Limila was a little touchy, sometimes. So when she said she was heading in to the main port's medical center again, he felt relief and didn't ask questions.

She came back with her head bandaged and no wig would have covered the bulk of it. "The scalp of that girl is implanted on me, Barton. I will again, as before the Demu, grow hair that I cannot wash and hang somewhere, conveniently, until it dries."

First time, this was, that she hadn't *asked* him about making changes in the things the Demu had done to her. So he grappled onto her with a hug, and said, "That's good. We'll see how it goes." Well, they each had their vulnerable spots. Barton's could wait.

As before, with the breasts, Limila's bandages also held protruding bits of apparatus, dotted with small flashing indicator lights. The trick, Barton knew, was to filter the blood entering and leaving the transplant, removing the enzymic factors that would otherwise cause rejection, until Limila's blood shifted the balance and no more filtering was necessary. The indicators had been designed to face forward, so she could use a mirror to check the state of affairs, and Barton was glad of that much, because either he wasn't good at understanding the complex sequence and its changes, or else she was no great shakes at explaining it. At any rate, Limila seemed satisfied by the progress the lights showed.

The tests on Cheng and Myra gave the Tilaran medics enough info, Barton learned, to go ahead and develop longevity treatments for Earthani. With only Barton's samples to work from, there had been questions as to what differences were individual to him and which were inter-species constants. But three people gave the Tilarans a baseline, so to speak, a way to define the parameters of treated and untreated Tilarans and Earthani on a clear-cut basis of "A is to B as C is to D." Which meant, Barton decided, that at least they weren't flying as blind as they had been.

Again, enzymes were an important key. It wasn't enough to introduce modified ones into the body; the trick was to convince the body, from then on, to produce the modified variety. And the process, Barton heard with foreboding, could kick up all sorts of painful hell for the patient. Well, he'd try to be braced for it. Especially since the ecstasy drug would interact and foul up the results, maybe, so it couldn't be used.

Finally, Limila discarded the flex-lined Tilaran dentures; they were stretching her face past the point at which her lips could close naturally. The abrupt shortening seemed odd at first, but that, too, would go away to some extent, and meanwhile Barton pretended not to notice.

One day Vertan came to announce that a Tilaran ship, from Sisshain, had arrived. It was at the aux port, having been turned away from the main one where its captain had expected to land. But the exchange between ship and ground had alerted Karsen ap Fenn, and the admiral wanted to put the crew on the griddle. Or so Barton stated it. Then he said, "You going to let him? You don't have to, you know."

Vertan spread his hands. "I will let him speak to the captain, in my own official place of work. And I have told her that she is not to give this man any of the confidential reports she has from Tarleton. Progress of events, only, in dealing with the Demu, she will relate to ap Fenn."

Confidential reports, huh? Barton was curious. But the packets were labeled restricted, Vertan said, to channels that did not include Barton. "And do *you* get to see them?" Barton said. Vertan signed a negative. Barton thought about it, and nodded. "How about you and I go talk with this captain, first?"

"That," said Vertan, "was to have been my next suggestion."

Barton hadn't been on Tilaran ships much; the layout differed quite a bit. He and Vertan had come alone; a crewman met them at the boarding ramp and took them to captain's quarters. The woman who greeted them, Barton thought, had to be as old as the hills, because her face had deep lines and her hairline had thinned and receded considerably. Of course, if he didn't know Limila was Earth-eighty, he'd have pegged this one at maybe sixty. But as it was . . .

In hoarse, gruff tones, but obviously intending to sound pleasant, the woman introduced herself. "Etraig, Captain, at your service. It is of pleasure, your presence here, Vertan. And Barton—we had not, before, been of meeting." Barton shook her hand, Vertan embraced with her, and she offered them seats and *klieta*. Once settled, she said, "You would be of knowledge?"

"I would." Barton asked, and she answered straightforwardly enough. On Sisshain, things were going to plan. Allied ships paired with Demu escorts had been sent to the various Demu worlds, to announce the end of Demu raiding and the start of peace. Only from the two nearest planets had word come back, but on those the treaty had been accepted. Well, Barton thought—when Sholur, Keeper of the Heritage, laid down the law to Demu, they heeded.

While Barton was trying to think what to ask next, Etraig said, "A recorded message for you, Barton, I have of the young Demu, Eeshta. Whose egg-parent, Hishtoo, is largely of recovery."

"Eeshta? No kidding? I've wondered how the youngster was doing." Well, a couple of times he'd wondered, between other worries, so it wasn't quite a lie. But now Barton found himself eager to hear what young Eeshta had to say to him. "Etraig, will your equipment here handle the recording?"

"It will. But if the message is of confidence . . . ?"

He thought quickly. "Couldn't be. Not anything that you and Vertan can't hear, Vertan trusting you as I know he does."

So she put the capsule into a recess, pressed switches and turned a dial. Then the high, clear voice came. "Hello, Barton. I am Eeshta, speaking. I hope all goes well with you." Then came a pause, and the sound of the pulsed hiss that was Demu laughter, before Eeshta spoke again. And this time, in the Demu language. "Barton, it is that Tarleton worries. That although no trouble comes

382

from my people, since agreement, Tarleton would hear word from you or from Earth. It is that the second Earth fleet of ships is overdue, in his reckoning, that this frets him." Pause again. "Barton, it is not that I laugh at Tarleton's worry, I should reassure; only that I laugh at others hearing this, who perhaps should not, and cannot, know what I say to you." And yet another pause, while Barton gave the kid some points for smart. Then: "It is that Tarleton would know from you what occurs on Tilara—and if possible to say, on Earth." A click came, and Barton recalled that sometimes that sound came with the lifted-tongue gesture that was the Demu smile. And then in English: "That is all, Barton. I am well, and Hishtoo improves with slow sureness. It is certain that he will be able to allow himself to live, and he has not called a non-Demu an animal for some days now. Since shortly after you departed Sisshain, in fact.

"Barton, I hope I will see you again; the Demu owe you much, and perhaps only I and Sholur appreciate how much, yet. And I nearly forgot—I bear Sholur's greetings, also. And now, from Eeshta to Barton, good-bye." The recording clicked to an end.

Before he said anything, Barton thought. Then he nodded, and spoke. "The part you didn't get, folks, was in Demu. Actually, it concerned something I already had in mind: we need to get word to Tarleton, down-Arm on Sisshain, of the situation here." Well, he'd mentioned it before, to Vertan, but somehow never got any real answers.

Now he got one. Twice, Vertan had dispatched ships from the aux port, for Sisshain. The first one, ap Fenn's patrols had hailed and turned back. The second had made a run for it and been overhauled, holed but not seriously disabled by the Earthani laser, stopped and boarded, brought back under escort.

"Why the hell didn't you *say* something?"

"I felt the problem was of Tilara, of myself to solve; not of you. But I have become of willingness to ask your advice."

Barton frowned. "You could've raised hell with ap Fenn for firing on your ship. You didn't, so that means you want to avoid open conflict at any price." He shook his head. "Given a couple-three ships to work decoy for each other, I'd guarantee to break at least one past the patrol ships. But if the admiral has even one ship fueled for a long chase, it'd catch us."

Vertan didn't look happy. "So there is no chance to warn Tarleton?"

Barton shook his head. Silently, he was lying. There was a chance, all right. But it would mean knocking the ships of the second fleet over like so many dominoes, and there had to be a way to circumvent one megalomaniac without doing *that* much damage.

Etraig and her first officer, a younger man whose name Barton didn't quite catch, hosted Barton and Vertan a meal. Then it was time to get back to Tevann's place, and after the usual thanks and felicitations, Vertan drove them there, and left for his duties at the main port. Indoors, Barton returned Limila's greeting kiss and then called council and told the Ship One people what he'd learned. They didn't like it any better than he did.

Myra Hake reached to tug the bangs she no longer had. "You mean, Terike's ass of an uncle has Tilara bottled up?"

"Sounds that way," said Cheng Ai. "Unless, as Barton said, we land a ship in the middle of the second fleet with the Shield on, and wreck things a great deal more than we'd really like."

Abdul Muhammed spoke. "There is another possibility."

"Yeh?" Barton leaned forward, then sat back. The big man would tell it in his own way, as he got around to it. "What?"

"Inhibitor," Abdul said. "It was developed to keep fuel stable for long storage in ground tanks, and must be electrolyzed out before the fuel is usable. If the Tilarans do not know of it, I can give Vertan the basic information needed to make the substance. Then in the normal refueling process he can introduce it into ap Fenn's ships, and—"

"One moment," said Limila. "We are speaking of how much time?"

Abdul shrugged. "Well, several months, I would think. But—"

"Then you must speak to Vertan about this idea," she said. "But meanwhile—and in terms of time, there is no conflict here—Barton and Myra and Cheng will undergo the longevity treatments."

Well, Barton thought, he hadn't really expected a reprieve.

Limila's pregnancy was bulging a little. Her teeth hadn't quite grown to full length; the discrepancy bothered her. And her transplanted scalp itched where she couldn't scratch it. So when it was time for Barton and Myra and Cheng to go in for the attempt at longevity treatments, she begged off from driving them.

All right; Barton had been over the route a few times. Turn right where the valley forked, and cut off short of the main spaceport; from there he could find his way easily enough. He repeated the directions to Limila; she kissed him and sent the lot of them on their way.

Under the pale blue sky, with Tilara's sun warming through thin high cloud, Barton drove the car. A little apprehensive, he didn't feel much like talking. Myra and Cheng, together in the seat behind him, spoke low-toned; he could hear no words so they didn't distract him.

Barton's mind went into daydream-mode and his driving went onto automatic. When he saw the building they wanted, he was surprised to be there so soon. He parked the car and they went inside.

An hour later he lay trussed up in harnesses and tubing, with a variety of needles and syringes plugged into improbable parts of his anatomy. Again he was bald from the neck down, but that was the least of the changes—now he saw his blood leave his chest, go into something that looked like a food blender, and return, all via tubes of more than a centimeter's thickness. The trouble was, the returning blood wasn't exactly what he considered to be the right color. And coming into him, it felt *cold*.

The needles inserted into his major joints—hips to ankles, shoulders to wrists—were electrical. On some of them he could guess the frequencies, pretty close, just from being "bitten" a lot in his undergrad physics labs. The piece of metal in his neck, though, and the one entering his abdomen just under the sternum—those were low-freq, and gradually built within him a nauseous ache, and overwhelming fatigue. For a time he wasn't sure whether he was going to throw up or go to sleep, first. He didn't throw up.

Waking was no better. He hurt and ached and felt sick, or maybe poisoned, and had no energy. He didn't get fed, because his nourishment came directly into his veins, they told him. His mind moved upstairs out of the way, where it didn't have to pay so much attention to the things that made his body convulse, wracking in spasms. Barton hadn't had the dry heaves since the morning after he drank half a fifth of Southern Comfort when he was in junior college, but compared to what he had now, the earlier version seemed easy. He began to think he might be learning what a friend's sister must have felt like, shrinking and slowly dying while chemotherapy failed to stop the carcinoma that had eluded the radical surgery. When nausea is the whole world, not a hell of a lot else can really matter.

There came a time when Barton wanted out, out of all of it. So that sometimes he cursed the stubborn thing within him, that wouldn't let him give up, ever. But then he realized that *he* was that thing. So there was no escape, at all.

At first—how many days later?—he didn't recognize the woman leaning down to face him. He knew, vaguely, that she'd been here before, and often. But she couldn't be anyone he knew, because none of the women in his college classes had foreheads that reached back to the ears. He couldn't understand anything she said, either.

Later—though he had no concept of time—some of her words came clearer to him, and he remembered a few things, and tried to speak. But this woman, he knew, couldn't be Limila, because Limila was either bald or wore a wig, and this person had a faint shadow of dark fuzz on her head, growing in the Tilaran pattern. Not, therefore, Limila. The hell with it; Barton turned away and settled into fretful sleep.

Then one day he woke without nausea; he felt weak, but not sick. On a hunch, he looked and saw that the low-frequency electrode was gone from his belly; he didn't feel the ache-inducing stimulus at his neck, either. And when Limila walked in, this time he knew her. Her scalp carried more than a centimeter of new hair, so if Tilarans grew the stuff at the same rate as Earthani, Barton figured he must have been in Limbo just about an Earth-month.

Careful to avoid the plumbing, she sat on the edge of his bed. Her bulge was prominent now; Barton couldn't remember whether Earthwomen, when they began expanding, did it in such a hurry.

She leaned across and kissed him. "Barton—you are past the worst part now?" He nodded. "Only a few days more, and you can come away from this place."

"That's good." His voice came out sounding like an old man's. "How's Cheng and Myra?"

"They have had less difficulty than you. Because they are younger, perhaps. Two days ago I took both to Tevann's home. They are weak, of course, and have lost much weight, as you have. But recovery should not take any great time. Nor for you, either."

Barton had his doubts about that last part, but all he could do was wait and see. "Anything been happening, I should know?"

"Yes, Barton. And not good." Two ships from Tarleton's fleet had returned, several days apart. The first had landed as directed, and ap Fenn's Marines had taken the crew into custody. The captain of the second ship had asked to talk to his opposite number on the first, or to Barton. When ap Fenn denied the request and repeated the landing orders, that skipper told the admiral where to go, and tried to make a run for it. Ap Fenn's faster, more heavily weaponed escort ships blew him out of space. "And that was the end of Ship Thirty-four and our friend Captain Lombard."

"Lombard!" Ship Thirty-four, one of the two that had gone with Barton on the strike force to Sisshain. And his mind formed the picture of a small Hindu woman, black braid reaching her knees, who looked to be twelve years old—Miss Chindra, the genius-grade computer expert on Lombard's ship. "That maniac—that *murderer*, ap Fenn! I'll—" He found himself trying to sit up, but his outburst threw him into a fit of coughing and he lay back, Limila's hands trying to hold him quiet. "All right; I'll be good."

"Barton, you must not excite yourself at this time."

"Sure not." But he felt his jaw muscles clamp; relaxing them took a conscious effort. Rage shook him, and grief; without warning he found himself sobbing so hard it hurt him in the guts. Limila held him, and after a time he could stop.

"Is it all right now, Barton?"

He shook his head. "It never will be. Not while ap Fenn's alive." The admiral had been hunting them, had he? From now, it was a new ball game. Once on his feet, and back in some kind of working shape, Barton was going to be the hunter.

He didn't know how, just yet, but he'd think of something.

Five days later, Limila came to take him to Tevann's. Barton said his good-byes to the Tilaran doctors and all the staff members he could find on short notice, and walked his slow, fragile way to the car outside. Riding through mist and a light drizzle, with hazy sunlight still making the day brighter than not, he kept silent. On arrival, he got a boisterous welcome; his shipmates and their hosts came outside as soon as the car stopped, and all talked at once as they accommodated themselves to his pace, going in. Lunch was accompanied by quite a lot of wine. Barton wasn't used to the stuff lately, so afterward he took a nap. He hadn't spoiled everybody's fun by making the slightest mention of Karsen ap Fenn.

Later that day, and from then on, Barton applied himself to getting some strength back. He'd lost more than ten kilos of weight, and a lot of it had to be muscle. So, having to start more slowly than he'd like or would have believed, he undertook a program of exercise and rest and diet. He ate more than he wanted, and worked himself to the point of nausea and near to collapse.

He didn't keep track of the days, only of his own progress. And for now, he said nothing to anyone, of his intentions toward the admiral. When he had some kind of good plan was time enough.

Finding a way to kill ap Fenn wasn't the hard part; the trouble was that Barton wanted to kill *only* ap Fenn, not a whole ship or maybe half the second fleet. So he couldn't simply lie his way into control of a Tilaran ship, and put a Larka-Te high-drive torpedo into the Big Hundred. That's the way ap Fenn would have done it, likely, in Barton's shoes—but that was precisely why Barton wanted the man dead.

So it took some thinking, Barton's project did. Well, he had plenty of time for it. But time continued to pass, and no notably good ideas came to mind, even when he'd fought his body back to its normal strength and alertness, and maybe a little better. By Barton's best guess, he'd passed his forty-second birthday sometime during the hospitalized period when he didn't know one day from another and couldn't care, so he didn't really expect Olympic-grade athletic prowess from himself. But he was determined to get into reasonably good shape, and he did.

The morning he completed a five-kilo run without dropping into a walk or getting a disabling stitch in his side, he decided it was time to talk in council. He was panting when he made that decision; his lungs felt like fire and his legs ached, but still he felt *good*. Because now his body would do what he told it to.

At the end of lunch, all having eaten together, he sprung it. "I'm calling council. Maybe you've wondered why I never said anything about ap Fenn's killing Ship Thirty-four. I've wondered why you didn't, either, but it's good you didn't. I wasn't ready; now I am. Not that anybody else is stuck with what *I* want."

"I had told them immediately," Limila said, "that you want the man's death. No one disagrees, to any significant extent. But all consented that the matter lie until you yourself propose it for discussion. Which you have now done."

"Everybody two jumps ahead of me, huh?" The idea rated a smile; he gave it. "Well, I don't have any real plan yet. All I've figured out is what would do the job, that I *can't* do." He told them, and saw agreement all around. "I think we need to know how everybody feels, before trying to plan."

Gripping hands, Myra and Cheng looked at each other; then she spoke. "You know we're pretty much against violence, Cheng and I; that's one thing that attracted us to each other. We've had weapons training, though; we're death on targets." Her mouth made a twist, then straightened. "But I *liked* Chin—she was as sweet as she was smart and pretty. Killing her was an abomination! So I *think* I could pull trigger on ap Fenn." She sighed. "But ahead of time, I can't be sure. I guess that's not good enough."

"It's fine," said Barton, "long as I know. You're willing to help other ways, though?" She nodded; so did Cheng. "Then we'll just plan things so that pulling triggers isn't part of your jobs."

Limila started to say something; his pointing finger stopped her. "You're too pregnant for combat, and that's that."

"Combat, yes," she said, "but not for target practice. And basically that is what a sniper does." Now Barton, trying to speak, was the one overridden. "In your planning, you will include that possibility. If only for a diversion, to aid the primary assailant."

While Barton was trying to think of an answer, Abdul Muhammed spoke. "Before the Central African Republic was formed, a part of it was a separate country called Uganda." Sure; Barton knew of it. He nodded. "For a time it was ruled by a madman; he killed at random and by whim. A plot was formed against him; one of my uncles, in that country for business reasons, became a part of it. His role was as Limila has said, to create a diversion—in his case, at the crucial moment to appear to run amok with a machete." Abdul's smile was wry. "Amok is not indigenous to that area, but the conspirators felt the simulation would be effective, nonetheless."

Myra Hake gasped. "But what *happened?*"

Abdul shrugged. "The plot failed; the tyrant survived and the plotters did not. But none of this was my uncle's fault; he did his part, I am told, to perfection. And took six guards with him, into death."

Barton frowned. "You're saying something. But what?"

"That in case of need, I like to think I would be as good a man as my uncle was."

Barton wouldn't go for the idea; he was adamant. "We're not going to have any sacrifice hitters, any kamikazes. If we can't exterminate ap Fenn without unacceptable risk to our people, we won't try it at all. Nobody takes any worse chances than I'll take for myself—and that's final."

Limila brushed a hand at her new hair, still too short to make use of a comb. "And how far do you intend to risk yourself?"

Barton looked at her. He'd always been honest with this woman, and this was no time to stop. "To tell you the truth, I haven't quite figured that out yet. Except that when I try to guess the odds, I'll never put ap Fenn's death ahead of my own life, if I can help it."

Now Limila's expression relaxed. "So that you do not lose sight of that criterion, Barton, I am satisfied."

Nothing was settled, but Barton needed an after-lunch nap, anyway. He wasn't sleeping too well at night, not in long stretches, so he eked his rest out with brief daytime dozes and the change seemed to work pretty well for him. He was getting up, putting on his exercise clothes for an afternoon workout, when Limila came in and said there was a call for him. "It is Arleta Fox."

When he went to the terminal, he found he had sound but no picture, incoming. He touched the switch that would delete his own image at the distant end, then decided the hell with that.

"Barton here. Who's calling?" Would Limila know the doctor's voice?

A quick laugh came. "It's your little bulldog friend, Barton. Arlie, speaking. I have someone who wants to get in touch with you."

Barton considered. Well, nothing to do but ask. "Like who?"

"Armand Dupree. And perhaps I need a hidey-hole, too. If I do, is there one available?"

He thought about it. Well, Tevann had been willing to put up Gerain and Iivajj, if they'd needed it. "Yes, I think so. But what's up, makes you think you're in that kind of a jam?"

Pause; then he heard the faint sound of a sigh. "Have you heard that Karsen ap Fenn had one of our own ships blown to dust? One of Tarleton's, I mean?"

"I've heard, yes." For now, that's all he wanted to say.

"The captain of that ship was a good friend of Armand Dupree. Armand made a plan, a risky one, to try to kill the admiral. I wouldn't say that Armand was totally stable when he heard about what happened to Ship Thirty-four."

"Which speaks well of him," said Barton. "What happened, though?" He listened, while she told it the long way. It wasn't that Fox was a sloppy thinker, Barton thought. Not hardly. But the teller of a story always puts in stuff that's important to him or her, that doesn't mean doodly to the hearer, who wants the bones of it.

What it boiled down to was that Armand Dupree had sent word asking ap Fenn for a review of his case, and had been admitted to the admiral's presence under all sorts of supposed mutual safeguards. It sounded pretty kamikaze to Barton, but he shut up and listened.

He wasn't clear, the way she said it, how Dupree managed to smuggle the gun in. But he did, somehow, and ap Fenn moved too fast and got away alive, and then Dupree shot his own way out of the trap planned for him. The part that made Barton laugh was that ap Fenn wouldn't be sitting down comfortably for a time, except on one side. That Dupree had killed some flunkies, getting away, Barton didn't find funny at all.

Not much to say, really. "Arlie. You think you're on a secure line now?"

"It's a bootleg. Ap Fenn tapped my residence phone, so I haven't been using it for anything important."

"You know this, how?" In a few words, she convinced him, so he said, "You know you have to get here without a tail on you, or not at all. Can you do it?"

"I think so." He heard her clear her throat. "No, I'm sure I can. It may take a day or two. All right?"

"Sure. And—Dupree comes with you, you say?"

"I won't seek shelter for myself, without him."

"Right. We'll expect you both, then." Barton cut the circuit. Sure enough, he was beginning to collect the right kind of people.

Two days, it took; then Fox and Dupree arrived. Barton recalled this one of his first four pilot trainees on the original Demu ship as a slim, dapper man who looked alert and wore a hairline mustache. The dapper part still fit, and the alertness and the mustache, but the short man had gone podgy since Barton last saw him. He moved well, though, jumping down from the groundcar and stalking over to shake Barton's hand. He said, "This is your base? I thank you for offering shelter. We must compare plans; I have several."

Barton didn't ask, plans for what, because he knew. He said, "I hope you have better ones than I do. But in case nothing fast works, we do have a slow one going." For Abdul Muhammed's scheme, to add "inhibitor" to the fuel tanks of ap Fenn's fleet, was proceeding. Trouble was, Barton kept in mind, that the results wouldn't happen in any kind of hurry. For now, he said no more, and escorted the two guests indoors.

It was mid-afternoon and he should have been exercising, by his own self-set schedule, but it seemed to be conference time, so Barton went along with that. He sat as chairman by habit and because no one else ever seemed to want the job. After all the introductions, and explanations back and forth, Barton cut in.

"I think the question before the house is the termination of Karsen ap Fenn. The chair is open to suggestions."

The trouble was, nobody had any good ones. Armand

Dupree had used up one of the best ideas—the apostate pleading for a new hearing and forgiveness—without success. "No," Barton said. "He wouldn't bite on that again, or anything like it."

Tevann, not at all bloodthirsty on his own account, but sympathetic to his friends' grievances, suggested some kind of public celebration. "Of the most deplorable, to pervert festivities so, but if such is the only way to bring the monster from hiding . . . "

Doctor Fox reminded Tevann that ap Fenn scorned Tilara and its people and all its works. "He wouldn't bother to attend."

Barton thought back. "He might, if we worked it right." Everybody was looking at him, so he continued. "What pissed him off around here, I think, was a Tilaran woman telling him to get lost. And making it stick." He said, "Suppose part of the services is a beauty contest, sort of, and ap Fenn is the prime judge, and he gets the winner he picks."

Uelein gestured negation. *"No* woman would consent. Not to anyone not of choice, and to this man, none at all."

The syntax was a little funny, but Barton caught the meaning. Before he could speak, though, Limila said, "There is no thought that any woman will be of submission to ap Fenn. The prospect of such development, though, will be of lure to bring him from hiding."

But it wouldn't work; Barton knew that much. It was too simple. There had to be more to it, before ap Fenn would bite and be hooked. He tried to think; at first his mind wouldn't give him anything useful, and then it did. He raised his voice to cut through the quiet cross-talk. "Tevann? I know you don't have government in the same sense as we do. But could Vertan, for instance, fake it to be of speech for this world?" Tevann gestured assent, and Barton moved his thinking along the rails. He said, "What if ap Fenn gets hints that besides the beauty contest, he's going to be asked by a high-ranking Tilaran to take over this planet as some kind of viceroy or proconsul, governing for Earth?"

"Barton, I had not thought you were of madness," said Tevann.

"And he is not," said Limila. "But ap Fenn is."

The hassle straightened out, and Barton was able to get his third line into the proposal—that Vertan would ask amnesty for Ship One's crew, Armand Dupree, and Arleta Fox if she needed it by now. "As a *condition*," Barton said, "to granting him viceregal status."

Myra snorted. "He'd never agree."

"I don't expect him to. The idea is to give him something to haggle over, to fix his attention. Then—"

Arleta Fox gasped. "You mean you don't know, Barton?"

"Don't know what?"

"While you were in that hospital, doing whatever it was." That's right; she hadn't been told yet. Barton made a mental note, as she said, "Armand and you, specifically, are on the proscribed list. Ap Fenn doesn't merely want you; now he wants you dead or alive. And preferably dead, the rumor says."

Cheng cleared his throat. "Simply dead? Without trial?" Fox nodded, and Cheng said, "It shouldn't make any difference; we already knew he planned to frame Barton in a kangaroo court. But *this!* Barton, I'm abandoning my dedication to non-violence for the duration. If you need any triggers pulled, I'll take one."

"That goes for me, too," said Myra Hake.

"Thanks." For a moment, Barton felt all choked up. And suddenly he had second thoughts. "You realize, don't you, that regardless of the rights and wrongs of this whole mess, once you're identifiably involved with the execution of this brass-bound murderer, you're outlawed from Earth forever?"

"And you, Barton?" Softly, Limila said it.

"Me?" He shrugged. "I don't need Earth; I don't live there any more. When the fleet lifted—Tarleton's, I mean —I figured right then that I was seeing the last of Earth." He was almost sure he meant what he said.

Limila went to call Vertan, wanting to catch him before he left his place of work because channels there were less likely to be tapped, and present the group's plan to him. Because if Vertan wouldn't go along with it, back to the old drawing board. Barton wandered into another room and got himself a glass of the pale green wine, and came back to find Arleta Fox and Myra Hake in conference. Arlie had one hand to her forehead; she squinted at a mirror held in the other.

"I don't think it'll work," said Myra. "Even if we fix you bald in front, the rest of your hair looks like no

Tilaran's ever did. Then there's the height problem . . . "

No lean-faced Tilaran looked like a cute bulldog, either, but Barton, eavesdropping, kept his mouth shut, as Doctor Fox said, "I could wear Limila's wig; she's not using it any more. And high-lift shoes. It's not as though I had to fool real Tilarans. Just ap Fenn's ignorant troops."

Now Barton joined them. "You sure the admiral hasn't managed to buy himself a few Tilaran finks?"

Looking around to him, Arleta took her hand away from her forehead. "I'm sure you think I'm silly, too, even considering trying to pass for Tilaran." A quick laugh. "Well, maybe I am. But I don't *want* to stay holed up, unable to visit the towns." She shook her head. "I think I'll try the disguise, anyway, and see how it looks. If only to give me something to do." A shrug.

"Your question, though. No Tilarans are working for ap Fenn, except officially and aboveboard, such as Fleet Liaison. As for official cooperation with his insane vendetta—well, when he sends copies of his edicts around, and of course in English rather than in Tilaran, Vertan posts his copies on the dart board in the lounge. And I understand that the other recipients react about the same way."

"Yeh; if I'd thought, I suppose I should've guessed that. I mean, what's ap Fenn got to offer that any Tilaran *wants?*"

"That's it, of course," said Myra Hake. "He's shown no interest in these people, nothing but contempt for them. Calls them 'Tillies,' all that. Everything that Earth had to offer in a military way, they already have, from you and Tarleton."

She frowned. "I can't imagine how he can be so stupid as to ignore the weapons that our fleet got from our allies."

"What I can't imagine," said Barton, "is the stupidity that put that bastard in charge of the second fleet."

Before Vertan made a decision, Limila reported, he wanted to consider the group's plan thoroughly. A conference was in order, but it would be at least three days before Vertan would be free to come and attend. Barton shrugged. "Well, that gives us time to kick the details around a little better, ourselves."

He stood. "But right now, my lunch has settled down

pretty good. I think I'll go out and stretch my muscles some more."

Dupree went with him; the short man had decided that he needed to get back into better condition himself. "That's what defeated me when I tried for ap Fenn," he said. "Because I still felt good—and moved well, I thought—I hadn't realized how the extra kilos would slow me down when I couldn't afford it." He made a one-sided smile. "Since that fiasco, needless to say, I have put myself on a considerably more restricted diet."

Dupree had quite a bit of youth on Barton, but when they began running, he couldn't keep up for long. Panting, he waved a hand and said, "Go at your own pace." And Barton did. Going up a rise, skirting a grove of feathery, purple-tinged trees, Barton dropped into a jog. Past the grove he saw Cheng and Myra practicing on Barton's improvised target range; as he passed, Arleta Fox came to join them. Was everybody turning soldier? Barton wondered. Well, a little over-enthusiasm couldn't hurt.

Running had become painless enough, now, that it left his mind free for other thoughts. Odd, that since learning of the slaughter of Ship Thirty-four, of Captain Lombard and Miss Chindra and the other eight or ten he'd never known, Barton had had no qualms at all about eradicating Karsen ap Fenn. He had simply thought of method, not justification. But one question lay not only open, but almost unasked: *What happens afterward?*

It was time he put some thought to that question.

For one thing, Barton knew nothing at all about the person or persons in line to succeed ap Fenn. Maybe Vertan could give him a clue, or Arlie Fox; he'd have to ask. But the answers to such questions were out of his control, anyway, so meanwhile he might's well look at his possibilities, objectively. If there was any such thing as being objective, in a mess like this . . .

One. Go to ground on Tilara and stay hid out, keeping a communication line to Vertan in case Tarleton got back or someone came from Earth, who might be approachable. Tilara was a planet, not a small town; if Barton's people wanted to hide from Earth's authority, Earth's authority could go whistle. Especially since Barton, bringer of the means to stop the terror of Demu raids, was sort of a hero on Tilara. And ap Fenn was quite the opposite. But still, the idea didn't appeal. Hiding out was all right when you had to, but Barton had a hunch that he could get tired of it in a hurry. In fact, he already had. Because after a while, what would he *do* with himself?

Two. Get Vertan to let him (and his) have a Tilaran ship, maybe Captain Etraig's, that he and Vertan had visited. Now that Barton thought about the problem, he didn't think he'd need any other ships for decoys, to get past the second fleet's patrol. The thing was, starships lifted straight up because any other way wasted one hell of a lot of fuel. So that's what everybody expected and was braced for. But if all he wanted to do was, say, get to Chaleen—and he remembered those coordinates—he could lift and cut low and be halfway around the planet, plowing air all the way, and then turn upstairs and lift in any direction he chose. Hidden by the planet itself when he made his move, he'd be long gone before the patrol ships could get a fix on his drive wake. And then they couldn't be sure of anything, because Vertan hadn't given ap Fenn the file data on drive wake detection patterns for Tilaran ships. And wouldn't. Barton could escape, all right.

To Chaleen. And there again, what would he find to *do?*

Three. Go for broke. If they got ap Fenn, there'd be confusion like all hell wouldn't have. Plan on it, use it. Have part of the troops ready to infiltrate the port, and when the balloon went up, the rest to join them, and take one of ap Fenn's own ships. The Big Hundred itself, maybe, with whatever aura of authority it might still carry, on its own. There was no inhibitor in that one yet, and they could refuel at the aux port. And then—

Three-A. Go to Sisshain? Dump the problem on Tarleton? Not really. Tarleton didn't need that kind of mess, on top of his own job. Having to choose between friend and official duty. No.

Three-B. Go to Earth. Lay the whole thing on the line, start to finish. Barton shook his head. He didn't trust politicians that much; somebody had put ap Fenn in charge. The somebody wasn't about to like being told how big a mistake that had been.

Three-C. Go to Chaleen, or some place like it. But he'd already been through that one.

Four. And there wasn't any. Barton shook his head

and put his mind on hold. Because it wasn't communicating very well.

Briefly he tried a *Four* that had him calling from the control room of the Big Hundred and assuming the admiralty in his own right. Then again he shook his head. This wasn't a Tri-V show.

And then came a thought that stopped Barton in his tracks. Nothing to do with the problem he'd been chewing on. Just a complete change of plans, was all.

He'd worked up a good enough sweat for now, anyway, so Barton went indoors and sluiced it off with a spray-bath. Then he looked for Limila, and found her lying down but not asleep. "Does your body continue to improve, Barton?"

"So-so. I think I've pretty well leveled off. Just a matter of staying in shape, from now on." He sat down on the bed beside her. "Limila, why didn't you tell me that ap Fenn's after my head now?"

Her eyes widened. "But I did; don't you remember? At the medical place. And then you had forgotten, so I told you again."

After a moment, he got it. "I had lucid spells earlier, and you thought I was registering?" Hesitantly, she nodded. "Well, I forgot the second time, too." She started to speak, but he put a finger to her lips. "It doesn't matter; no harm done. Anyway, I've had a new idea." He told her, and at first she was dubious, pointing out dangers, but finally she agreed.

"If you can do this, Barton, it will be much better."

"Yeh; I think so, too. It was only that when we heard about the slaughter, of Lombard and Chin and the rest, I couldn't think of anything but the one way to do something about it."

She stroked his body, still damp from bathing. "Then it is a good thing that there was no way for you to act immediately."

A shudder of relief took him; he hadn't realized the strain until he came free of it. Then he had a different reaction. "Limila? Would you like—?" It had been quite a while, now.

She smiled. "If we are careful; yes." So, quite gently, spoon-fashion to avoid pressure on her, they made love.

Myra and Cheng were off somewhere together, Barton

learned, exploring the hills that edged this side of the settlement. Tevann had driven Abdul to the aux port; apparently the home computer-terminal wasn't programmed for something he was trying to calculate, so he hoped to visit Gerain and Iivajj and use the facilities on their ship. Barton got these data from Arlie Fox, through a closed door behind which she and Uelein were closeted. *Well, all right. I'll tell 'em later.*

As it happened, the whole group was never together all at once until the afternoon that Vertan showed up. So, since Barton didn't feel like repeating himself, until that meeting he sat on his idea and hoped it would hatch something.

Vertan looked tired, and his expression was anxious, as Barton and Dupree did most of the talking about the proposed festival, and Barton kept waiting for a handle for introducing his revised plans. The "beauty contest" part baffled Vertan. For one thing, the Tilaran said, it was inconceivable to humiliate a group of persons of either sex by a public verdict that one of them was the most attractive. And for another, even if normal courtesy were to be sacrificed at this crisis point, how could ap Fenn or anyone else evaluate a woman's attractiveness without having sex with her? Which, assuming a reasonably sized slate of candidates, who would require considerable persuasion to participate in such a grotesque ritual even though it was only a farce for show, would entail several days of scheduling. And—

"Hold it!" Barton shook his head. "Your logic makes my head swim—and I agree with it, now that you point these things out. But ap Fenn's *used* to beauty pageants on a look-don't-touch basis, so we just add a hint that Tilaran custom gives the judge some privileges with the winner he chooses, and—" Vertan tried to protest, but Barton kept talking. *"Of course* it won't happen. It's all a fake, remember? To get ap Fenn out in the open."

"To kill him, yes." Vertan nodded. "Very well; proceed."

"Kill him?" Barton pretended surprise. "I don't have the faintest intention of killing Karsen ap Fenn."

He knew there'd be a hubbub then, and in point of fact he rather enjoyed it. When eventually he got the floor back, he said, "All right, so I should have told you

399

sooner. But everybody was ramping around here and there, so I thought I'd wait and spring it in full council."

"I am a patient man," said Abdul Muhammed, "but—"

"All right," Barton said. "This idea hit me out of the blue, the other day. We can destroy the son-of-a-bitch, as he is now, without killing him. By the amnesia effect of the Demu sleep-gun. I don't know how much exposure it takes, but—"

Then the yelling caught up to him, and it felt as though Abdul Muhammed would pound his back right out through his front. Cheng was shaking him by the shoulder, and Myra's kiss tasted of tears. "Barton, you're beautiful!"

He grinned. "I've never denied it."

Now they got down to cases. Vertan said he'd need two weeks to set up the festival. Barton had to ask how many days that was, because the Tilaran week was not of fixed length. Sixteen, it came out. Okay, then—the fun and games would take place in the area just off the main spaceport, and a temporary pavilion to handle the size of crowd they wanted could go up in plenty of time. So far, so good.

All right; that's where they wanted ap Fenn. Now, how about the bait to get him there? Honor? Glory? Power? It had to be believable. "Don't forget loot," said Barton, and in that comment they found the answer. Ap Fenn had choked off Tilara's interstellar trade; he allowed ships to land, but not to lift off again. "So we name him Chief Customs Officer or Lord Protector of the Port, or something, and give him a cut of the customs duties."

Then he had to explain to Vertan, for Tilara had no such things. "So we offer him a cut of the customs duties you don't have," Barton said. "There's a technical name for it. Bribery." And even if they didn't get ap Fenn, as planned, the gimmick would allow trade to move again.

Now it came down to who was supposed to do what to whom, and where. Barton still liked the idea of trying to take one of ap Fenn's ships—the Big Hundred, by preference—and logically that job went to people who couldn't fake it well as Tilarans. "So, Vertan—can somebody filch us uniforms from this fleet, to fit Cheng and Abdul?" Dupree still had his, Barton knew. Vertan

400

said it would be easier to have Dupree's copied, and that made sense, because something in Abdul's size would be hard to find.

The remaining crux, of course, was getting to ap Fenn, and nobody could think of any better bet than the "beauty contest." "The main thing there," said Barton, "is that we set up our own rules and format. For instance—"

It was Strike Force country again, and that was Barton's territory. Myra and Arlie Fox and himself were all the primary troops he had. "And I," Limila insisted; he couldn't budge her.

"All right." He made a nod to her. "And here's how we use us. All robed-up ceremonially, as chaperones for a group of contestants. I don't know how Tilaran we'll look, but we can try."

Following the group into the newly erected pavilion, Barton thought that Arleta Fox looked like no Tilaran he'd ever seen. Of course, she didn't look much like her own self, either. Behind the artificial baldness above her forehead, she wore Limila's Tilaran-styled wig. She teetered on high-lift shoes of at least two decimeters. Under her robe, false breast-bulges set low and wide in the correct Tilaran location masked any sign of her own smaller mammaries. Myra Hake wore a similar harness, and her sandy hair was dyed black. Limila had a wig in the reddish-brown shade, and makeup altered her complexion to match it. Barton didn't want to think what *he* looked like; he'd never worn drag before in his life.

Vertan had done a good job, he had to admit, setting up the pavilion—an unroofed auditorium that held, at Barton's quick estimate, about five thousand people. A little over that—"three twelves-third," Vertan had said. Enough people to confuse the issue when the crunch came, anyway; that was what mattered. And looking out of the seclusion booth, about halfway back on the left side, Barton saw that Vertan had packed the house, all right.

From where Barton stood, the place looked nice. The walls and minor partitions were done in tones ranging from blue-green to green-yellow—not exactly chartreuse —with random sparkles here and there. The seating looked comfortable and the crowd was quiet. All right; pretty soon the show would get on the road.

A little time, it had taken, to explain to the "beauty contest" candidates that once they'd played their decoy roles, they were to get out of the way, period. "To be not of harm, to be of safey," Barton had said, then finally shut up and let Limila tell it, wondering if Vertan hadn't leveled truly with these women, or if he simply hadn't known how to make the situation clear.

There were thirty-two of them, and if it hadn't been for the high hairlines and low-set breasts, any one could have been a finalist at Atlantic City or wherever such contests were held nowadays, in Barton's home country. Most with black hair, a few with dark reddish-brown, and two in between. All much the same height, standing even with Limila as she gave her explanation. When they seemed to understand, she nodded at Barton and he responded in kind.

His robe didn't hang right; he hitched at it, then reached to make sure he hadn't jarred his own wig out of position. But he couldn't, really, in normal movement; the thing was glued solidly, around the edges, because its alignment was crucial. Barton fingered the improvised remote trigger of the device hidden in the up-piled hair, and reflexively touched the robe over his own false breasts that contained the backup power pack.

Movement caught his eye. Up front at the rostrum, Vertan and four other Tilarans came onstage. And from the other side, ap Fenn entered, with a full squad of armed Marines.

Well, nobody ever said it was going to be easy.

The first part went well enough, Barton thought. Ap Fenn looked surly but was obviously taken by Vertan's carefully worded offer of legalized graft at the spaceports. Then Vertan threw the kicker, to engage the admiral's attention as fully as possible, about amnesty for Ship One. Except Barton. They'd decided that nobody should try to say any good word for rotten ol' Barton, because Karsen ap Fenn wouldn't go for it in any case, and would simply back off from the whole pitch. But the others: "They are, honored Admiral, of innocence and of regret. They would be of reconciliation, if the admiral is of forgiveness."

And the son-of-a-bitch is buying it! Ap Fenn said words agreeing, and moved to shake Vertan's hand on the deal. Barton hadn't truly followed what the interpreter had said, realizing that Vertan was using that skilled person to give him thinking time between exchanges. But he had to agree that Vertan had picked one capable woman.

Then came a couple of nonce-events, to pass time. Ap Fenn was asked to preside, in an honorary capacity, over the presentation of awards that Barton figured were probably invented for the occasion. It took a time, and Barton used it to sneak off and take a leak, so he wouldn't be caught short in the pinch.

And then Vertan took the floor again. He looked serious, and Barton wished he wouldn't do that. But Barton knew that Tilara had, in its culture, nothing that resembled the game of poker.

The beauty candidates came in four clutches of eight each, and Barton's idea was that third in line would have the best chance of catching ap Fenn's people off base. "They have time to get bored, plenty. But the *last* set, they start getting alert again."

So out of the seclusion booth, when their appointed time came, filed the eight Tilaran women and their four escorts. Barton had Arleta Fox in the middle, more or less, so that if she had trouble with her balance on the high clogs, it wouldn't show much. At first he fretted, but she did better than he expected, so he relaxed on that and worried where it counted more. They walked on up.

Ap Fenn's squad of Marines stood close-spaced behind the admiral. The beauty-contingent ritual was that two women at a time came to pose before ap Fenn while the pair's chaperone knelt behind and between them. So when Barton knelt, the sleep-gun in his wig had a good clear shot. First he made sure of ap Fenn, then raised his head a little and moved it from side to side until the Marines dropped.

Barton was beginning to get to his feet when the nasty chatter of automatic-rate projectile fire came from behind him.

Limila screamed, a shout of outrage; he saw her grab her guts and fall down. By instinct, like back in Nam, he reached for weapons he didn't have and dropped to roll under the slugs that screeched past him. But turning, and then sitting up and the hell with it, he remembered where he was, and why. And used his trigger.

Several hundred Tilarans went down when his sleep-gun hit them. But so did ap Fenn's butchers, at the back of the pavilion. Barton stood up. He started to move toward Limila, when something huge cast a shadow over the whole place. He looked up and saw a ship that didn't belong with anything he recognized. Damn it, there wasn't *time* for anything new, here. But the sheer bulk of the thing held him fixed. He saw it dip toward the port, hesitate—dust clouds flew up, from the impact of that ship's fields—and then it lifted again, and moved across his view.

Toward where? Barton shook his head; he'd figure that out, later.

Now he went to Limila. Her head shook violently; Myra was holding her, and said, "We have to get out of here; I can carry her."

"No," said Barton. "I can do it."

"You stupid son-of-a-bitch, Barton!" Myra screamed it. "If you carry Limila, who's going to tote the admiral?"

And then Barton came back to something like normal. "Yeh, sure." It wasn't, he thought, as though he had all his brains working. He looked at Limila, and her color wasn't too bad. He scrunched down and moved things around and got Karsen ap Fenn up into a fireman's carry, and said, "Which way, Myra?" Because Barton was in shock, he knew, and had lost track of his head.

Myra steered him out of the pavilion and got them started across the port. "If Abdul and the others have the Big Hundred for us—" Well, thought Barton, *maybe* it made sense.

No such luck, though. Abdul helped them aboard the ship that ap Fenn had dubbed the Big Hundred, but the place was only a temporary shelter, not a way to go anywhere. Dumping the admiral into a chair, Barton listened. The fuel tanks were saturated with Abdul's inhibitor, after all, and for now the ship was dead.

Its crew wasn't, though. "We were lucky enough," said Abdul, "to get aboard without provoking combat. And once inside, our possession of individual Shields against the sleep-gun made it relatively simple to take the ship without inflicting casualties."

"Yeh, sure," said Barton. "Any chance they got a medic on here?"

"Ap Fenn's personal doctor," Abdul said. "He is not yet awake."

"Soon as you can, get him up. Limila needs help, and fast." Barton turned away.

Abdul Muhammed said, "You leave her now? What is more important?"

And Barton nearly hit the big man. Fuming, raging, so angry that almost he forgot the *needs* of what was happening, he caught himself, and said, "Get that doc on Limila, Abdul. Soon as possible, like I said. No *point* in me sitting by her; I can't do shit. What I can do is frag Karsen ap Fenn's mind back to kindergarten. And that's going to take some time, and I'd better get at it."

Abdul blinked, and nodded. "Yes. I see." And from the look of the man, Barton lost whatever resentment he'd had.

Barton didn't ask aid, though; again he got ap Fenn up over into a carry, and took him to captain's digs and dumped him onto the bed. He heard someone following him, and turned and looked, and saw Arleta Fox. She'd scuttled the high-lift shoes; she was walking in good order. She said, "Once you regress him, maybe I can help."

Barton nodded; then he set to work. He slapped ap Fenn awake and asked questions. The answers didn't satisfy him; the admiral still remembered who Barton was, and that they were on Tilara. Barton hit him with ten minutes of the Demu sleep-gun, waited a time, and used his hands to bring the man awake again. Some while later they had a third session, leaving ap Fenn's cheeks red and swollen by the time he woke. It wasn't that Barton enjoyed slapping the hell out of a zombie, but he had no better way to make the son-of-a-bitch come alive.

This time, ap Fenn didn't know Barton from Adam's off ox. Leaning closer, Barton said, "Where are you? What's your job?"

In a plaintive tone, ap Fenn said, "The Space Agency —I'm highly placed there, you know. What kind of whorehouse is this, that beats up influential customers?" He blinked, and for all that Barton could tell, maybe he was even thinking. "I tell you—call me transportation home, and tomorrow I'll send you a bonus, for luck."

"Sure. You do that." For his own luck, though, Barton gave ap Fenn two more zap-sessions with a waking interlude between, so that when he was done, the admiral seemed to speak as an ambitious and somewhat idealistic young man of about the age of twenty.

Pooped out of his mind, Barton turned to Arleta Fox. He hadn't been noticing that she was there, but now he did.

She said, "This base is going crazy; the control room is flooded with security calls." Looking very strange with her Tilaran wig off, she said, "We need the admiral to speak for us."

"But he can't. He doesn't exist now."

"I know," she said. "But wake him up and help me get this pill down him, and then we'll see if I know enough about hypnosis."

With Fox's prompting, the confused young man (he even looked younger) who had been the admiral, took his Marines off their Alert status. It wouldn't help all that much, but Barton wasn't so ungrateful as to say so; Fox looked too happy.

The troubles were that he was scared spitless about Limila, and that once they left the fuel-dead Big Hundred, Barton had no idea where to go. Not knowing who ap Fenn's successors were, or how long it would take them to catch on, didn't help, either.

When Arleta put ap Fenn through a routine that got some Tilaran medics onto the ship, Barton relaxed a little. But not much. They were still in a hole, and Barton saw no easy way out. If there was one, right now he was too punchy to think of it.

Having ap Fenn declare amnesty—reading it off a paper would be simpler than coaching him—would look just a bit too fishy. Might throw in a reasonable amount of confusion, though, which would help. And, of course, he had the man himself, his physical presence, to use as a hostage. Barton looked across to the groggy amnesiac, and saw nothing left to hate.

Ap Fenn smiled, a little shakily, and spoke: "I'm not certain why I'm here, sir. Is there something I should be doing?"

"Just rest, for now. Arlie, can you cope here?" She nodded, and Barton left the quarters and went to the galley, now used as an improvised infirmary. Limila was out flat on one table, two Tilarans working over her. The stranger standing to one side had to be ap Fenn's doctor. Barton nodded to Abdul Muhammed, who stood guard with a sleep-gun, and went to the other man.

"What's her condition?"

The man blinked pale blue eyes. He was thin, and would have been taller than Barton if he hadn't been noticeably stooped. He said, "I didn't have time to find out. I stopped the bleeding, and I don't think she'd lost enough blood to need a transfusion; then *they* arrived. Which is just as well, since Tilaran anatomy seems to differ somewhat from ours of Earth. Uh—pardon me, but is the woman a relative, madam?"

Barton wanted to laugh, but once begun, he was afraid he might not be able to stop. He'd forgotten that he was still in Tilaran drag; now he took off his robe and falsies, rolled down the legs of his jumpsuit, and peeled the wig off. "I'm Barton. Pardon the glad rags; I guess they've done their job." Because that disguise was tied to the zapping of the admiral, before one big lot of witnesses. He couldn't use it again, to effect.

The doctor stared, then put his hand out. "Sven Barstadt. I don't know why I'm being polite to the one who killed Admiral ap Fenn. We are creatures of custom, aren't we?"

The handshake ended. Barton said, "He's not dead. But he's not the admiral any longer, either. He may need some special care." Barton knew he was talking to keep himself busy while he waited. He knew he couldn't interrupt the Tilaran medics; though he itched to know if Limila was all right, he forced himself to stay away.

Barstadt smoothed back his sparse, fair hair. "What, exactly, have you done to him? I mean, he's still my patient, and—"

"Nothing, physically. Just wiped his mind for him, with the Demu sleep-gun. What talks out of his face, now, is a sort of pleasant young guy, actually. Maybe smart, too, when the pills wear off, but a little groggy at the moment."

Barstadt began to answer, but one of the Tilarans turned and beckoned. Barton followed the doctor, and was surprised when the Tilaran spoke in English. "You did your part well, Earthani. And the woman will live, and should recover quite soon. But there was no possibility of saving the child; it had died already."

Without memory of leaving the galley, Barton found himself at the airlock, starting down the ramp. He didn't know where he was going, or why; all he felt was the urge to *move*.

But there, halfway up the ramp and climbing, he saw Helaise Renzel. Her mouth and eyes went wide, and she turned, but he reached her before she could either scream or flee, and dragged her up and inside. He closed the airlock, and now uncovered her mouth. "Hello, Helaise."

"Barton! What are you doing here? And when did you go bald in front? I—" Voice high-pitched, she was chattering.

"Why are you afraid of me, Helaise?" Now he had something to think about, to take his mind off . . . "Why?"

"I didn't really mean it, Barton. We were a little drunk, Karsen and I, and I was *joking*. I thought if I exaggerated, he'd see how silly he was being. But he took it seriously, and the next thing I knew, he was on the intercom, and they blew that ship apart, and you and Dupree were on the dead-or-alive list. I—" As she saw his face change, she went pale; her knuckles went to her mouth. "You— you didn't know, did you? Until just now . . . "

Through the red haze in his mind, Barton watched her. "Then it was you, did it." Her head bobbed like a puppet's.

"But I didn't mean—"

"You never do. You never did." For long seconds, Barton fought with his own muscles. "Go to your admiral— he's in quarters—and stay there. You give Arleta Fox any trouble and I'll feed you your arms." Slowly she turned away. First her walk was shaky; then she ran. Barton took a deep breath.

His record was still clear. He'd never hit a woman in his life. Except the one he'd had to kill, of course, on Ashura in the Demu cage.

He found Limila partially awake, but she didn't know where she was, or why, because the ecstasy drug hadn't worn off fully. There was no reason for Barton to tell her anything just now, so he didn't. Cheng brought him a Marine captain's uniform that fit him more than not, and Myra clipped his scalp bare to suit the role. The visored cap was too tight, but what the hell? Barton wasn't up to running the show, so somebody had to; he'd go along with it. Cheng and Abdul and Myra seemed to be doing pretty well.

"Ap Fenn's exec," Myra said, "is one Hennessy. The doctor told me. Hennessy's part Polynesian; ap Fenn isn't, but his nephew Terike was, so maybe there's a connection. But the thing about Hennessy is, he follows orders; he follows the book."

Barton's mind came to life, a little. "Try the amnesty ploy?" So, to please the nice lady who was taking care of him, Karsen ap Fenn on all-ships broadcast read the amnesty announcement that Abdul Muhammed composed. After that, ap Fenn called for a Tilaran ambulance and gave it full clearance in and out of the port. Again he read from written text; nobody wanted him having to improvise.

He didn't know at the time that he'd be riding along himself, with Limila and Barton and Cheng and Myra and Abdul and Dupree and Arlie Fox, but when it happened that way, he made no complaint.

Before they left, Barton had brief words with Helaise Renzel. He didn't figure she'd be raising any alarms, because what he told her, in some detail, was exactly how he'd kill her if she did. And if he didn't know whether he was bluffing, how could she?

They didn't need to use their hostage, to get away, and once through the hills to the residence of Tevann, no one could think of any particular use for ap Fenn, here out of his command context. "Might's well send him back," said Barton, so the Tilaran driver was instructed to return the man to the main port. "God knows what they'll make of him there, but he might turn into a good officer."

They went inside. Tevann wasn't there; Uelein said that Vertan had called several times and sounded urgent. Once Limila was made comfortable—she seemed stable now, and was dozing again—Barton hitched up his thinking and put a call through to the designation Vertan had left. When the screen lit, Vertan's agitation was obvious. Barton calmed him a little by assuring him that they'd pulled the job off and got away clean. About Limila, he said nothing.

"So," he wound it up, "what other problems have we got, now?"

"It is the large ship," Vertan said. "The one that came

over us today and could not land at the main port." It had gone to the aux port instead, he reported, and its captain had cited priorities that brought refueling and other loading immediately, ahead of everybody else there. Of course, no other ship had clearance to lift. This one, it seemed, did.

"How soon?" Two days, three, perhaps—Vertan could not be sure.

"But it came here from Earth," he said, "in less than half the time required by your fleet, or even ap Fenn's. And its captain appears to know things that have occurred on Earth *since* he left it."

"Is that right? Okay—thanks, Vertan. We'll be in touch." The screen went dead, and again Barton thought: *Is that right?*

Barton knew he needed a good night's sleep, but was surprised to wake and find that apparently he'd got it. At first he felt pretty good; then he remembered what had happened to Limila. But that loss no longer hit him like a hammer; he knew sadness, was all. The problem was, how was she going to feel? She was asleep, in a separate bed now, so he didn't have to ask her right away.

He went through the house and found Cheng pouring from a fresh pot of *klieta;* the man poured another cup, and Barton sat. "Hennessy revoked the amnesty," Cheng said. "On you, anyway; he didn't mention Dupree."

"I guess he caught on," said Barton. Well, he hadn't really expected Renzel to keep her mouth shut, totally. "Hennessy's acting on his own, is he? Not bothering with ap Fenn for a figurehead?"

"The admiral sits to one side and smiles, or looks nervous. Hennessy does the talking. He doesn't sound especially vindictive, though, Barton. More like a man who's plugging away, trying to follow the rules as he knows them."

"Book soldier, yeh. That's what Myra quoted, too. From the doc." He shrugged. "Doesn't matter; if he's after my ass, I have to keep it out of his reach, is all." So what else was new? Barton decided that was a good question, really, so he asked it.

"Nothing more, officially," Cheng said. Barton knew that Tevann's screen terminal taped official announcements automatically; they carried coding to trigger the equipment. Now Cheng frowned. "Hennessy's trying to make a deal, Vertan told Tevann. He's found out that his ships are being tanked with inhibited fuel."

Probably, Barton thought, by trying to lift one off. He said, "What kind of deal?"

A fairly limited one, it turned out to be. Hennessy claimed to have no urge, as ap Fenn had had, to go after Tarleton in any punitive way. He did want some ships available to move, though—to Sisshain to gather information, to Earth with reports, for instance. And again unlike ap Fenn, Hennessy wanted contact with Earth's other allies, such as the Filjari and Larka-Te. "So he wants some ships ready to go."

"So, what's he offering?"

"To lift the embargo on Tilara. To discontinue the blockade."

And that idea, Barton thought, had some interesting possibilities.

Limila refused to speak or hear of their lost child. On the second day she insisted on trying to get up. Barton wouldn't let her, and they were having quite a row about it when the Tilaran doctor arrived. To Barton's surprise, the man sided with Limila. When Barton protested that nobody could take a gutshot and be in shape to walk, so soon, the doctor said, "You do not know the Tilaran metabolism. And this woman has taken the longevity treatments. Further, consider that it is *her* body; she may risk it as she chooses."

So, against Barton's wish, he watched Limila stand and then, pale lips clamped to thinness, walk. She didn't walk good and she couldn't stand straight, yet, but she did move. When she had done several turns around the room, and sat again, she took a deep breath that came out in a ragged sigh. "I will live, Barton. Oh, yes; I will live. And perhaps someday I will even enjoy it, again."

Hennessy certainly seemed to waste a lot of time thinking about Barton's crew from Ship One. The official afternoon screencast—Barton caught it live—carried the announcement that Abdul Muhammed and Myra Hake and Cheng Ai were restored to the fleet's good graces and should come collect their back pay. Arleta Fox's job was still open and she was urged to return to it. Armand Dupree couldn't be restored to prior status, considering he'd actually tried to pot the admiral. But even so, bygones

411

were bygones and he, too, had some back pay coming. Or so, without ever once mentioning Barton's name, Hennessy proclaimed.

Barton had hit the tape button, and later, showing the spiel to the group, he watched the reactions. At the end: "What do you think?"

"If it's not a shuck," said Myra Hake, "we can't afford to take the chance, anyway. Cheng and I have been talking." She made a throwing-away gesture. "I mean, what do we need Earth for? As you said once, Barton—we don't live there now."

"So what is it you figure to do?"

Get on one of the Tilaran ships, was the answer. Go visit the Filjari or the Larka-Te, or maybe one of the peoples they'd never met but only heard about, like the Tlengin or Eroci. "And there's an Ormthan at Filjar now, the rumor goes."

Ormthan? How long now, since Barton had thought of that protean amoeboid oracle, who had given him the hint to the Demu weakness that avoided war with those proud adversaries? Now he said, "Ormthan! The one here—is it still here? Maybe—"

Tevann shook his head. "Still of presence, yes. But shut away, of its own doing. Ap Fenn went there, and—"

Tevann told it and Barton listened. Vertan had escorted the admiral into the Ormthan's presence. The ceiling, that time, had not been low and gray, but arched and shining. But after ap Fenn had opened the discussion with a couple of arbitrary, conversation-stopping demands, the admiral had gone silent, and red in the face. And then the Ormthan had dismissed the two of them, and as soon as they were outside again, a shimmering dome—almost transparent, but not quite—had appeared. From what Tevann said now, it sounded to Barton as if the Ormthan's dome made the Demu Shield look like a plastic bag. And the dome was still there; nothing entered or came out, either one.

Barton considered the matter, and said, "I expect there's a patrol of Marines there?" Tevann nodded. "Then let's forget it." Barton cleared his throat. "So what does everybody want to try?"

Myra and Cheng had said their joint piece. Abdul Muhammed would stay on Tilara because he wanted to get back to Earth, to his wife and children in their tree-shaded villa. Armand Dupree said, "I'm best off berthing

412

on a Tilaran ship, too, I think. I like the people, and I'm coming to know the language, and I'm a good pilot in anybody's league. So I would think to manage, once away from here."

Arleta Fox hadn't said anything. Barton turned to her now. She certainly didn't look her best—head bald in front and clipped to stubble for the rest of it, ears jutting to each side of the bulldog jaw—but Barton liked her. "What *you* have in mind, Arlie?"

Her level gaze came right back at him. "I seem to have joined your team, Barton. Unless and until you make a choice I can't abide, is it all right if I tag along?"

Like a stone image, Limila had sat. But now she reached and took Arleta's hand, and squeezed it. "Be of welcome, Arlie."

It was too late to run over to the aux port, but not too late to call and set up the visit, for tomorrow. Iivajj said that if the blockade lifted, she was sure the ship she and Gerain were on could use an extra hand or two, and the ship next toward the control building wasn't full, either. Beyond that, she would ask.

Barton cut the screen and turned back to the group. "Well, looks as if we can find offworld berths, given we need 'em." He felt like needing a drink, but before he went to get it, he said, "Tomorrow we go over there, and maybe split up forever. So right now I think we deserve a little party. Just in case."

They had it, and everybody seemed to have fun, more than not. But Barton couldn't keep from wondering: What was *he* going to do?

Barton thought, next day, that Limila should stay home and rest. But she said she would go to see her shipmates off—Iivajj and Gerain, as well as Cheng and Myra —even though the ships themselves might not be leaving immediately. Barton hadn't decided to go or not, but when she did, he did. Arleta said the same.

"I will give my farewells here," said Abdul Muhammed. And he kissed Myra and bear-hugged Cheng and shook the hand of Armand Dupree. "May you all find shelter under the great tree." He smiled. "That is a religious concept of my ancestors. While I do not believe it literally, the thought still has comfort."

Barton, from the driver's seat, waved a hand and then

moved the car out. The route to the port was easy enough, and he found the ship they wanted first, with no trouble. Iivajj met the group at the airlock, and Captain Etraig offered Tilaran wine while she quizzed Cheng and Myra about their qualifications. Then she made a call to a nearby ship, and Barton was surprised at how fast Dupree had himself a new job. The short man stood, and reached to shake Barton's hand. "I wouldn't have thought," he said, "when you and Tarleton took me up to try out on your Demu ship, that I'd end up this way. But I expect that I'll enjoy it."

"Just goes to show," said Barton. "Good luck, Dupree."

After the man left, it was obvious that Etraig wanted to start briefing Myra and Cheng on what their new duties would be. So Barton made polites and helped Limila up, and they all said their so-longs. Myra almost spoiled it, by saying, "What are *you* going to do, Barton? I'm worried."

But he said, "Get on a ship like this one, maybe. And likely see you." So the moment passed, and finally he and Fox and Limila made slow going down the ramp and stood on bare Tilaran ground. Twilight was ending; in moments, the darkness deepened.

Then they got in the car and he put his mind to retracing their course back out of the aux port. He missed a turn, and found that ahead lay the huge ship from Earth. Well, all right. He said, "Long as we're this close, let's have a look at that thing. I mean, I'm wearing the right costume to be entitled."

He wore the Marine uniform Cheng had shanghaied for him—but with the insignia of rank turned upside-down in the way that meant he was off duty. So, in theory, nobody should bother him.

He drove quite near the new ship, before he saw a painted perimeter line and decided it was best to stop without crossing it. Looking up, he sighed. "That thing is *big*."

"Yes," said Limila. If she had any interest at all, her tone of voice didn't carry it. But when Barton said he wanted to take a closer look, and got out, he found that she and Arlie had followed him. She shouldn't do this walking, he thought. But he couldn't argue with her, so they walked, slowly at her pace, toward the monster ship.

He stopped short of it, and again looked up. Now it

towered over them. Barton said, "How many times bigger do you suppose it is than the ships we know?" Not like the great ship on Sisshain, he knew, but somewhere in the middle of sizes.

Before Limila could answer, bright light struck. Barton turned, shielding his eyes from the spotlights. An amplified voice shouted, "Stop where you are!" And Limila slumped to the ground.

So Barton, with his own Shield flipped on as a matter of instinct, and knowing that nobody from the second fleet had portable Shields, pulled out his personal sleep-gun and sprayed its radiations until, from out there behind those spotlights, he heard no sound at all. Then he picked Limila up and carried her to the big ship's ramp and climbed to its airlock. No one stopped him; no one even met him. He went inside and set Limila down, then turned to look back outside, because Arleta Fox was still there. But she was up already and to the ramp, making a shaky job of climbing it. Nothing else moved, that Barton could see.

He started toward Fox, but she waved him back. "I'm all right. Just caught the edge of it, I guess." So he picked Limila up again and waited until the small woman was inside. Then he thumbed the airlock-closing button, and watched the thing shut. "What are you going to do?" Arleta said.

Barton tried to shrug; the burden of Limila didn't let his shoulders move all that much. "For now, there's only one real answer. This ship seems to have a status outside the second fleet's authority. And sure as hell, there's more space in it than anybody could search in a hurry."

So, not breathing too hard under Limila's weight because he was somewhat back in shape, and downstairs was easier than climbing, Barton descended. Arleta played rear guard. Barton had the sleep-gun in one hand, but nobody showed, so he didn't need to use it. He kept going until they were past everything that looked to be quarters, down where cargo holds should start—and then three more levels. There he tried a big door, and it opened. Cargo, all right. Going in, Barton made sure the door closed behind them, after he hit the switch that kept the lights on. He walked around until he found a place, way back in the hold, with soft stuff they could lie on, and set Limila down.

"This'll do for now," he said. "Wait here." The doctor nodded, and Barton went back to cut the lights. Then, first stopping in a corner to pee on the floor since there wasn't any other place to do it, he retraced his way to where he'd left the others. The scattered dim standby lights had stayed on; he could see well enough not to run into anything.

Limila still slept; beside her, Fox sat upright. She said, "How long do you intend that we stay here?"

Barton sat, too, at Limila's other side. He listened to her breathing; it was slow and regular. "We can't do much until she wakes up," he said. "Three up and walking make a better team than two up and one flat out." It wasn't much of an answer, he knew, so he continued. "For now, Arlie, I think I'll just lie down here and see if I can rest."

So he did. And until he felt the ship shudder and rise under him, Barton hadn't thought he'd gone to sleep at all.

Limila was awake now. The last thing she remembered was the sudden glare of light; Barton had to explain to her where they were, and why. "It seemed like a good idea at the time."

Fox was either awake again, or still; Barton didn't ask which. She started to say something, but just then the ship bucked and rang with vibration, so she waited for the jarring to pass. When it did—and even through the grav-field Barton could feel, subliminally, the increased rush of acceleration—he said, "We're up out of air now. There's no way a ship this size is going to waste the fuel to go back and land, and have to lift again. Not even to extradite a bunch of desperate criminals, such as us."

He grinned. "I'm not awfully hungry yet, but I'm getting damn thirsty. Now that the ship's finished plowing air, and everybody upstairs can relax, let's go up and meet our hosts."

Limila was walking better already, but still the climb was slow. Barton, leading, kept his sleep-gun holstered but had a hand on the switch of his Shield, just in case.

The strange part was that climbing through level after level of this huge spacecraft, they saw and heard no one at all. When they reached the first deck of quarters, Barton peeked into a few compartments. They were all deserted. In two he saw odds and ends of people's belongings, the kind of thing somebody might not bother to take along when leaving. But those cabins, as well as others less littered, had obviously been occupied and then vacated.

"Running with a skeleton crew, maybe?" Barton asked himself out loud. "All moved into officers' digs, farther up?" This thing was so much bigger than Ship One, or even ap Fenn's ships, that he had trouble visualizing what size of crew it would need. Whatever it was, they had to be around here somewhere!

When they found the galley empty, Barton used a few curses he hadn't remembered for a long time. On any ship at any time, there were *always* folks hanging around the galley; it was the natural social center for everybody who was off watch. But in this monster dining area, nobody at all.

He smelled coffee, though—and fairly fresh, not left-over battery acid, simmering into oily bitterness. The over-sized brewing urn at the end of a long counter seemed the obvious source, but when Barton went over and touched it, it was cold. Then he tuned his nose in and spotted the small pot steaming on a unit heater. He looked into it; it was nearly full, so he picked up three cups and poured them full. Turning to Limila and Arleta, he said, "I don't know about you, but maybe a little of this could help me think better."

Nobody else spoke; they moved to a table and sat. Barton set himself to face the main entrance, and scanned to watch the two side doors, too. He was taking his first sip when Limila pointed and said, "There, at that table. Someone has eaten, recently!"

Sure enough, there was a tray, left by some sloppy diner who hadn't picked up after himself. Barton got up and walked to look. Remains of egg and toast, dregs of juice and coffee, smeared tableware. Somebody whose watch-sked made this breakfast time.

But *one* tray? It didn't make sense. Barton rejoined the two women and sat, and sipped again. "Well, it's not bad coffee."

Limila had begun to answer when the man came in, and yelled. "Who the hell are you? What are you doing here?"

The man was short, blond, young, curly haired—and

most important, Barton saw, not armed. Barton got up and walked toward him—not fast, and doing something with his face that he hoped would look like a friendly smile. He reached to shake hands. "My name's Barton; I was Exec on Tarleton's fleet. You've heard of it?" He wasn't being entirely sarcastic; who knew what might be happening nowadays, on Earth? But the young man nodded, and accepted the handshake, so Barton went on. "I got in a little jam with the second fleet, so we hitched a ride on here. I hope you don't feel obliged to tell the second fleet everything you know? I mean, it's not your mommy or daddy, is it? Because that could cause us some problems, here."

Looking puzzled, the man shook his head. "This is an independent mission, and a very important one. Acting-Admiral Hennessy tried to opt us into his own forces, but our captain refused, naturally."

"Your captain," Barton said. "That's somebody I'd like to meet."

The man's eyes widened. "But you can't. Not now. Didn't you know? The whole crew's debarked on Tilara; the captain, too. I'm a volunteer, the only one aboard for the mission. Or rather, I was supposed to be."

Even the first parts, for some sort of bare understanding, took a lot of sorting out. The young man, who was singlehandedly crewing the biggest starship Barton had ever seen get off the ground, gave them guidance on fixing themselves breakfast in this luxurious, semi-automated eatery. Barton introduced his companions, and their host said, "I'm Honus Hayward. They call me Honey." He did a double-take at his own words, and his face reddened. "Don't get any wrong ideas. It's just a nickname."

Barton hadn't been getting any ideas at all. He said, "Sure, I know how it is. No problem." He stood, and got himself more coffee, from a fresh pot Hayward had made. "What I want to know is, what's this important mission you're on?" He saw the stubborn look come onto Hayward's face, and quickly said, "Or if that's Top Sphinx, how about, where the hell are we going?"

Keeping in mind, Barton was, that courses can be changed.

Except on the great ship that brooded, immobile, on Sisshain, Barton had never seen a control area that this

418

ship's didn't dwarf. On the rearview screens he could see that Tilara was nearly twice as far behind as he would have expected in such short time; another few hours, and Hayward couldn't reach Hennessy with signals, even if he wanted to. And to give the kid credit, he seemed to have no such intentions in mind.

The screens that interested Barton were the ones with the map spread across them. He recognized the galactic Arm well enough, and a number of landmarks on it. The dust cloud with the pocket that hid Sisshain's primary didn't show that sun, but the cloud itself was there.

And the Demu volume of space, the same version that Tarleton's maps had shown. Of course Barton had seen better data now, but this was fairly accurate. And then, down-Arm from Demu space, the wide belt, clear across the Arm, where no habitable planets existed. The Great Race had somehow done that, according to the Demu Sholur, Keeper of the Heritage. But how or why, no one knew.

Still the map unfolded, reeling jerkily across the screens. Below the dead belt, no data showed. But toward the far side of what was known, a dim light blinked. "That's our rendezvous point," said Honey Hayward.

"With *what?*" Barton shook his head, and heard Limila gasp. "We don't know anything, down there. Do you? Because if this is some kind of wild-goose chase—and don't get antsy just yet, because if you do, I'll drop you, Hayward—I may have to change the plans."

"*You can't!* I mean you mustn't. It's terribly important—" Then, looking Barton in the face, Hayward slowly nodded. "I guess I'm going to have to tell you all of it."

"Now that," said Barton, "sounds like the best idea I've heard yet."

It began with rivalry between the two major branches of the Space Agency, keeping secrets from each other. While one group worked to improve the Demu drive and help Tarleton get his forty ships together, the other went its own path and didn't give Tarleton the time of morning. "But within days after your fleet lifted, Barton, they sent a ship out."

To where? To scout the dead belt, from the far side. To try to get another angle on the Demu. But, trailing Tarleton's fleet, wasn't it a little late? No, because Group

B made a breakthrough into a new principle, based only partially on the Demu drive, so that sizes and velocities went up a *lot*.

But why? Barton meant, why weren't these two prongs of effort coordinated? But before Hayward could answer, Barton shook his head, because he already knew why: to some people, including most politicians, nothing was more important than revving up their egos and listening to the echoes.

But none of that crap was important now; Barton said so, and added, "The Demu are taken care of, but the horseshit isn't. I don't know what your mission is, yet, but so far you haven't convinced me that it's more important than getting to Tarleton, to give him the handle he'll need to get the second fleet straightened out. And fix things with Earth Base, too. So I think we should get up to your control room and start figuring some course changes."

"But you don't know!" In a pale face, Hayward's cheek-bones stood out red. "The ship that went down-Arm, what they told us—"

"What they *told* you? You mean they got back already?"

The young man shook his head. "No, of course not. What they *sent* us, I mean. You see—"

For a moment, while he didn't understand yet, Barton had his hand on Hayward's arm. Then he did get it, and until he saw the cheekbones go pale, too, didn't realize how hard he gripped and shook that arm. Then he let go. "You mean—you mean, Hayward, that those silly Group B sons-of-bitches had faster-than-light communications? All along—*and didn't tell Tarleton's group?*"

"I—I guess so." From Hayward's expression, he wanted to be someplace else, if at all. "But *I* didn't know. Not any of it. Until our captain played us the tapes, once we'd been diverted to Tilara to refuel for this mission, and then asked for a volunteer."

Barton shook his head; none of this was the kid's fault. Couldn't be. So take it easy; ask, but don't yell. "Tapes, you said." And Hayward nodded. "You think, maybe I heard those, I might make a little more sense out of this mess?"

Hayward bounced back good; he smiled now. "I wouldn't be surprised."

The control area again. Quickly now, Barton noted

the switching positions that indicated how major functions of subsidiary positions were multipled into the chief pilot's board. He didn't see how any one person, haywire multiples or no, could land this crate. But Hayward had lifted it, and navigation in free space was easier still.

He asked the one thing. "This bucket's not to land; right?"

Hayward's blond eyebrows raised. "How did you guess that?" Barton told him, and Hayward nodded. "You're right; we make rendezvous in deep space, then this ship's abandoned." Barton tried to speak, but for once the young man overrode him. "There's no choice; we'll be out of fuel, nearly. Our tanks are only about one-tenth filled. And that's on purpose."

Estimating what full tanks would do, if Hayward were telling the truth, Barton shook his head. "Fuel to get where you showed me, though," he said, "is more than enough to land us on Sisshain. Or even swing a right-angle course change"—equivalent, they both knew, to an extra landing and liftoff—"and head for Earth." Frowning, Barton said, "So far, you haven't convinced me I shouldn't do one of those things."

Riffling through a bank of switches, the kid said, "That's what we're here for." The screen flashed a picture, but it blanked before Barton's mind caught the gestalt. "Just a minute." More switch-fiddling. Then: "Hell with the official reports; they didn't get any action moving at Base, so probably they wouldn't with you, either. I'll run the bootleg tape that got us diverted to this mission. It's mostly voice-only, not much picture, and that part's blurry." One final switch; then they waited. "One of the ship's Comm officers got this out, somehow. Obviously, it's no kind of official report; we don't know who the guy was trying to reach. Maybe Base knows, but they didn't send us the lead-in section. What's here, though, made quite a splash at Base. It does with me, too. Why don't you give it a fair hearing?"

Barton did. The tape began, and he listened.

II.

The Others

I have to start where it begins.

We named the planet Opal because you couldn't call it anything else. Approaching from sunward we got the full lighted disk on our screens, and there it hung, at about two million kilos, shining like the most glorious fire opal you ever saw. Even the brass back at Base, I'm told, when they got those first tapes cleaned up by computer enhancement, had to agree. Whatever official name had been planned for that world is off the books and forgotten.

I understand that in the first days of space travel, the thing a lot of people found most surprising was the direct live video coverage from the spacecraft and then from the moon. I expect they'll feel the same way about faster-than-light interstellar communications, now that the Labs found a way to make phase-velocity do some useful work and earn its keep. Someday, I wouldn't doubt, you can sit on Earth and talk with your field man a hundred light-years distant, and have him point his Phasewave set at a patch of weeds so you can tell him which ones to take in for analysis. Or squat at home and watch aliens do colorful native dances, on "Galactic Traveler," live on the Trivia. Not yet, of course. But soon, maybe, the way progress keeps snowballing.

Our planet Opal had indigenes, but we didn't call them Opalites, even though it turned out later that we couldn't pronounce their own name for themselves. They started out as Opalites in the records, but that's another official designation that went down the drain. The Others are the Others, and that's that.

I was off watch when the initial down-party first saw and then met the Others. Lisa Teragni, my ship wife, coming back from breakfast while I was just getting up, gave me the news. Secondhand, because she hadn't been up in Comm herself. "But from what they say, Ren, I can't tell whether these Opalites are more like people, or more not." Xenobiology isn't her specialty; psychology is. "They have all the right number of arms and legs and eyes and ears, but I gather that nobody would ever mistake one of them for Earth-human."

I snapped my other boot closed. "Let me get a bite to eat. Then I'll take you to Comm and we'll both see. Even if there's no locals on the screens at the moment, there'll be a tape or two, we can run." Understatement; the place would be knee-deep in them.

Actually, we didn't get up to Comm all that soon. Usually Lisa and I had our watch-skeds in sync, but we had two Comm people in sickbay and I'd been filling in odd watches, so we hadn't been together much lately. This seemed a good time to make up for it a little; Lisa was by no means the least favorite of the ship wives I'd had. In fact, we were talking of making it permanent, though we knew that when it comes to advancement, Agency policy makes it tougher on people who insist on paired assignments. But then I never did expect to get rich, anyway. The boots came off again.

Up above, when we got there, Rigan, the Comm Chief, had the watch himself. He's a long, thin drink of anti-freeze, but the chill is just his normal grade of manners. Once you figure that "I suppose it will do" is the highest praise in his book, he's all right to work for. The strongest condemnation he's likely to give is: "I think perhaps you might try it over again." You have to read him between the lines, and the lines are awfully close together. So when I brought Lisa into Comm and he said, "I suppose it's all right," she took it as a hearty welcome. Being a psychologist, she'd figured Rigan out in about twenty minutes. It took me six months.

She said, "Good morning, Chief. Ren thought we might be able to have a look at the Opalites."

"We have pics," he said, "of the Others." That was the first time I heard the term; sometimes I wish it had been the last. "You're certainly free to look them over, Second." In case the lead-in garbled, that's me: Comm-officer Second, Renton Bearpaw. The Bearpaw gets a lot of mileage from the clowns I work with, if I knock over a cup of coffee or anything, but it comes from a man who could kill a buffalo with a spear.

I checked the screens first; no aliens showed. A moving view above a tree-covered coastline—that would be the aux craft itself, that had delivered the down-party while we stayed in synchronous orbit, on its mapping run. Some-body was swinging us a hilltop panoramic; another field man showed close-ups of vegetation plus something that resembled a fat, furry grasshopper. A red face arguing into his pickup, and sweating; wherever the voice was going, it wasn't to us. Maybe he was complaining about the heat. There were no Others in view, though; for them we had to go to the still pics.

The trouble was that we expect man-shaped creatures to look human, and these didn't. Skin texture looks hu-man enough, and color ranges from a pinkish-beige to deep reddish-brown. The differences, though. First picture a human head. Now move the eyes up and out to the extreme front corners, nothing above them but a protec-tive ridge. With independent articulation, those eyes have almost a 270-degree scan without even turning the head. Which the Others can do, nearly front to back like an owl, or that carnivorous amphibian on Blaine's Mistake. The ears are leaf-shaped cups, rounded, very mobile, halfway back on the skull, at eye level.

The back of the skull, the cheekbones, mouth, jaw, and neck all look a lot like ours. The nose would, too, except that it comes out of a convex area rather than having brows above and eye sockets to each side. I hear that the Others have different numbers of teeth, top and bottom, but you can't tell by looking.

The torso as such is proportioned slightly longer, nar-rower, and deeper than we consider normal. The arms aren't set where we expect shoulders; they mount lower, move more freely, and can reach backward as easily as forward. The legs have a lot of pivot, too; they're set wide apart, not at the body's "corners" but a little above. And the Others aren't plantigrade, like us and bears; they toe-walk like dogs or horses.

Let's see; what else? Well, they're mammals; the breasts are set so close together that they look more like one udder with two spigots. And on average height the Others are a little shorter than we are, not enough that it's always noticeable in individual cases.

Their hair is a fine, thick fur that grows only three or four centimeters long, in a strip along the median line of the head and body. About five to six centimeters wide, but coming to a point where it terminates. In both sexes, one end is just above the nose and the strip goes up over the head and down the back. With the female it comes down around and ends just below the navel, which is set about the same as ours. The male's fur continues on up the front of the body, and neck and chin, and stops on the lower lip.

We didn't get all this from the pics, just then, because ordinarily the Others wear a sort of loose, sleeveless tunic. And the pics were off on the fur's color, which varies from a bleached sandy hue to a bright copper-gold red, light or dark in accordance with skin tone. But we did get a fair idea of how the Others appeared. And Lisa's comment still held: it was hard to decide whether they looked more like people, or more not.

When Rigan sniffed and said, "Second? Don't you think it's a little stuffy in here?" I tactfully escorted Lisa out, telling her I'd let her know how our watch-skeds meshed as soon as I knew it myself. Rigan takes a little translation: "stuffy" means too many people. Often there are eight or ten working in Comm, and we were only six, including Lisa. But when the Chief said frog, I jumped. Because he could have stood on status and refused to let her in at all. I've worked under worse than Rigan; few better, in fact.

It wasn't my watch, but I hung around, hoping one of the screens would show the Others. None did, so I left. Lisa wasn't anywhere I looked; finally, I remembered it was her day for the weekly treatment she still needed for a recent injury, since she was the one who found out the hard way that the whatsit on Blaine's Mistake had close to 360-degree traverse at the toothy end. By the time she joined me in quarters she was due on watch; I gave her a kiss for later and went back to fiddling with a breadboard circuit I was working on. I hoped it was the pilot model for an automatic tuner for Phasewave Relay. There's nothing like trying to work yourself out of a job.

On my next watch I did see Others live and direct. Funny—first they'd look near-human, and then completely alien. Not like Blaine's Mistakes. (Did the official tape mention that Blaine's own mistake was trying to push some peaceful-looking villagers around? As our first casualty, he rated a fairly impressive gravestone.) Ignoring details like beaks and claws and iridescent scales, the Blaine's natives *move* like humans. The Others don't; until you see the particular grace and economy in any completed action, they appear to be embarrassingly clumsy.

Later we found that they had the same feelings, of part-rightness and part-wrongness, about us. I guess that makes sense.

Two days later, one of our ailing Comm techs was ticketed healthy, so I had fewer extra watches to work and could catch up on time with Lisa. And with the other sick case nearly recovered, soon Lisa and I could get back into full sync. About time, too.

So then Comm-First Blenkov, my immediate superior, broke his stupid leg. Well, that's the way Rigan put it, and I had to agree. Blenkov had been down on Opal doing Comm for the aux boat. Somebody had to take over, and I got the nod.

I made a pitch to get Lisa assigned downside with me, but it worked no better than I expected. Maybe that's why it didn't work; I've never convinced my meager psi-powers to be on *my* side.

The down-party, including the aux boat, was run by Command-First Szabo, who was second only to Captain Soong on the whole mission. I'd always tried to stay away from Szabo; that one had a reputation for being dangerous, and I didn't want to test it.

Szabo didn't look mean—a tall, rangy, Greek-god type with more good looks than anybody needs, and the same for muscles. Smiling a lot—but going by rumor, nobody trusted that smile much. The words to keep in mind, the way I heard it, were "explosive" and "unpredictable." To back them up, incidents were sometimes cited.

This gets important later or I wouldn't be telling it. The trouble with Szabo, rumor had it, was that here was a highly intelligent, capable person who used to be a functional male and now wasn't. It's on the records that he married when he was twenty, and fathered a child before the divorce a few months later. I heard several versions of what happened in between, but the parts that agree with each other boil down to this: Szabo got some kind of minor cyst or tumor, nothing serious, down near the prostate gland. Operating for it, the doctor made a glitch and cut the peripheral nerves that make sexual response possible. Lisa says it used to happen a lot with one of the kinds of prostate operations. The whole idea makes me cringe a great deal.

At any rate, Szabo wound up with all his equipment intact, but disconnected—absolutely no way it could work, any more than an unplugged computer terminal.

Szabo reacted hard. He was smart; nobody ever pinned the doctor's misfortune on him, and although killings show on his record, they're always in line of duty or self-defense. Usually with a commendation for him—presented, I'd guess, by someone who wouldn't look Szabo in the eye because they both knew better.

He became the toughest, most iron-nerved and capable person I've ever known. And dangerous, because he was touchy about his difference; mention it in his hearing and you have real trouble. The existence of sex was an intolerable insult; never remind him.

That's not too easy, all the time.

When I hauled my kit onto the aux boat, Szabo met me. "Cheers, Command-First," I said. "Anything particular that needs doing on here, with the Comm gear? Blenkov was too full of needles to tell me much." As I hitched my stuff along the narrow corridor, Szabo followed.

"Nothing that I know of; it's all working. Bearpaw—have you heard, yet, what they think of the Others, shipside?" He sounded worried; down-partywise, I didn't take that as a healthy sign.

"Not much, Szabo," I said. "But if there's anyone who's not confused, it's being covered up pretty well." You call him Szabo because ever since he lost sex he hasn't used his first name. To him, maybe, it means his former, complete self. Which hints at a strange kind of pride, driving him. Scary. But on impersonal things you can joke safely because it gives him a chance to be human, and he needs it. I didn't figure these things out by myself. Working around Szabo, a lot of the discussion behind his back is how to keep Szabo happy. It seems to help.

"The down-party's confused, too," he said now. "I'm going down for a firsthand look." He shrugged, and gave that angelic smile I always wished I could really trust. "Not that I'm trying to out-guess the experts, of course."

We entered the tiny control room. "So you'll be in charge of the boat, Bearpaw. On our way down, scan the mission instructions. Anything unclear about the mapping tour, let me know." He left, and I felt guilty about how relieved I felt.

Nothing tricky in the instructions, but I looked and found a couple of points I could ask about, because Szabo liked that. So it was another part of the S.O.P. of working with him, and for all I know, maybe he knew it and was amused.

We downed at a field base. I don't remember which one, by letter-designation. Once we'd worked out the routine, on Blaine's Mistake after we crossed the dead belt that lacks inhabited planets, they all set up pretty much alike.

The difference here was the attitude. Whatever I'd expected to find, I didn't. Mostly, it looked as if the group was dragging its feet on studying the place, because what they'd learned already, they didn't like.

As Szabo's new Exec, I sat alongside him and looked official for the folks Upstairs on the ship while he read off his summary and fed pictures to the pickup. "It's obvious," he began, "that we're meeting a species and culture quite different from ourselves. The Others—" For the first time, I saw Szabo's face color. "I mean the Opalites, of course. They're extremely puzzling to our teams."

Somebody Upstairs told him to cut the crap; actually, the phrase was: "Don't bother with details of nomenclature." So be it; the Others were the Others, and Upstairs had signed the memo.

"Very well." Szabo nodded. Maybe he was on pickup, maybe not. "The Others simply don't fit our pattern. Their language appears to be rudimentary, but they learn ours with startling ease. Conclusion: they're highly telepathic, and may have as great a grasp of the so-called 'psi' powers as we have of physics. And possibly vice-versa—as little physics as we have 'psi' control."

He cleared his throat. "Apparently the Others don't fabricate their shelters or clothing; they grow them." He read a field team's summary; the way it translated through the jargon is that if the Others want a house or a tunic, say, they think at a bush and it grows what they want. I've never heard that version contradicted, anyway.

A faint note of disdain came into Szabo's voice, as he said, "The Others seem to have no violent behavior patterns whatsoever." Maybe it wasn't disdain; maybe it was incredulity.

But skepticism, I couldn't mistake. "It's speculated that the Others can directly affect each other's emotions—and therefore, possibly, our own. I don't believe it, and in fact I intend to go to the nearest village as soon as possible, and test the hypothesis. For the moment, though, I have decided to postpone the test until more important matters have been settled." Something about his logic, there, bother me, but I couldn't decide what it was.

"One thing is certain," Szabo went on. "The Others aren't primarily analytical-minded. They seem to operate largely on intuition, perhaps aided by their hyper-sensory talents, if those in fact exist." Well, I knew Szabo hated the idea that E.S.P. or whatever could be of any real use. Maybe he had a bad case of my own problem, that any time my "psi" stuff shows up at all, it's wearing the other team's uniform. But I know it works right for some people, sometimes, and I don't begrudge them, much. Szabo, though, took it all as a personal insult. Which made me nervous, now.

"The Others' culture," Szabo said next, "is apparently a hand-to-mouth affair; if they plan ahead, our people haven't been able to find signs of it. Food, housing, clothes—all seem to grow as needed, with or without conscious control. The same, I'm told, goes for their art forms. The most recognizable one was described as a cross between painting and sculpture, with sound effects, and what they do is pat a mass of miscellaneous material roughly into shape, and go away and leave it. The next day, the thing is fully formed. No research team can explain the phenomenon."

Looking uncharacteristically pensive, Szabo ended on the cheery note that the Others certainly seemed to be friendly enough. And if they weren't, we could blast them off the face of the planet if we wanted to. Not that we did want to, of course, he hastened to add. Somehow he didn't sound quite like the Szabo we knew and walked askance of.

The parley done, Szabo and I ate with the field crew and then I dossed down in the aux boat. But I couldn't sleep. What bothered me was that Szabo hadn't told the Upstairs brass the most worrisome thing he'd told *me*. And why hadn't he?

What it was, a groundside team member working alone would meet up with one of the Others, and then his or her squawktalker wouldn't answer for maybe an hour, sometimes longer. Then when a call got through, the party didn't seem to realize that contact had been broken, had heard no calls during the break, and didn't know what the caller was now perturbed about. And persons who'd had these lapses tended to look sidelong at other people who had also had them, but not to talk together. It all made me wonder.

Szabo proposed putting somebody under drug-interrogation, and maybe get a few facts, but then he turned right around and talked himself out of it, " . . . until later." Well, if he was blind and would not see, I was wearing pretty dark glasses, myself.

Next day it was time to get on with mapping the coastal contours of the island-continent we were on. For some reason, the drill was to do the coast first and fill the rest in later. Blenkov got about halfway before he crunched his leg; the other half shouldn't take too long, I hoped, if we didn't run into complications. Famous last words.

Of the other five people on the aux boat, my next-in-command was Elys Rounds, a Medic-3. Compared to my striking, big-boned Lisa Teragni with her half-share of Polynesian genes, Elys looked as bland as she was blonde, and as fragile as she was tiny. But since no little sugar-cookie would be carrying Medic-3 rating, I didn't go by looks. Well, she handled her watch duties fine, was a fair grade of navigator, superb at weapons control on the one incident we are *not* allowed to discuss, and of course a thoroughly competent medic. Evaluation Reports don't mention whether people are good in bed, so officially she will have to go unsung on that score. Unofficially, she is very nice.

At the coast we picked up where Blenkov had left off, trying to make up lost time. Ten days saw us nearly caught up and close to halfway done with our leg of the tour. And that evening, watching for a good place to land for the night, I saw a village of the Others. For no particular reason, I set down near it.

We hadn't been avoiding the Others, especially, but we hadn't happened to run into them much. Once in a while the brief visit with a small group if it happened to be where we landed to take plant and animal samples— that sort of thing. They always seemed friendly enough; my earlier uneasiness had simmered down. I was even getting used to the way they picked up our lingo so fast, and seemed to know whatever we might need in the line of help before we finished asking. Sometimes later it would strike me that we really hadn't got what we wanted, though I'd been fully satisfied at the time. I chalked it up to natural confusion of meanings; just because they learned fast didn't mean they got it all *right*.

Anyway, I landed close by the village, and we buttoned up our procedures for the day. I called my daily report in to Szabo, to be relayed Upstairs. Then it felt like time for dinner. I was a little grimy and sweaty, so I went to spruce up some.

I was getting dressed again when it struck me that instead of another routine meal on the boat I could be visiting the Others and maybe learning something. I finished dressing and went to try my idea on the rest of the crew. But they weren't there, in the cramped galley. Elys sat alone. I said, "Where is everybody?"

"They've gone ahead, to the village. Shall we go now, too?"

In an open clearing among the odd, organic huts ringed with flowering bushes, our people were being fed profusely; we joined them. The food was delicious—steamy, delicately flavored meat; tangy fruits; crisp, chewy vegetables. I drank a pale wine with a flavor that owed nothing to sweetness, and took a few whiffs from a carved, ornate pipe. That stuff sent my head around the circuit, like the synthetic hash at my Mind Exploration class when I was fourteen. But it didn't lose me the way you can get lost at fourteen, because I'd already been there.

The people from the boat, though, seemed to be lost; except for Elys, I didn't see any of them. Elys and I sat with a few Others, everything so warm and friendly that

I couldn't imagine what all the worry had been about. Well, in the morning I'd figure that out, and reassure Szabo, and Captain Soong fretting Upstairs.

But right now I hoped nobody would mind if Elys and I took ourselves off to a dark nook someplace. Great idea, so I turned to Elys. But she wasn't there. She was leaving the lighted area, leaving with a male of the Others. I made to stand up and call to her, but my legs and voice vetoed the move. A female of the Others came near me. I wanted to ask what was happening, but she handed me a cup of warm fragrant liquid, and when I caught the fragrance of it I had to drink. It tasted as spicy as it smelled. The alien female watched as I drank the cup halfway; then she touched my hand and I let her take the rest.

Then this woman, this lovely woman of the Others, came to me, and I knew how mistaken I had been to think of her as alien. For I loved her, and lovingly we took each other. No matter the consequences or delusions, I can't regret that taking, for she was, then, the most beauty I had ever known. Part of that feeling is still with me, even though now I have a better idea what it means.

Elys, next morning, felt much the same way. We two could talk about it together, a little, because we were already quite close. But I saw why field personnel, alone with one Other, who turned off their squawktalkers for an hour or two, would never say what had happened. No one wants to be thought insane.

When the rest of the crew had straggled back aboard, we lifted and got back to work. Everybody, I think, wanted to finish the map circuit in short order. So from then on, each day we started early and worked late.

Except for Elys and me between us, nobody talked much. I tried to clear the air, saying, "What the hell, it's no crime; we couldn't have known. And don't forget, it happened to all of us."

One woman looked across and glared at me. "Nothing happened. Not to me. If you say it did, you're a liar." But when she'd returned to the boat, she'd had the same look of glazed reminiscence that everybody else had.

Her name was Krehbol, I remembered—Theresa Krehbol. She looked to be facing the end of her youth with fear and anger, with ill grace. I doubted that at any time of her life she could have been called beautiful or pretty or even handsome, but I had seen her in pleasant moods, and then she was an attractive person. "All right," I said to her now, "if you say so, then nothing happened."

"You'd better remember that." So I gave it up. Krehbol was the only one who actively fought my efforts to get people to open up and rejoin the human race; the rest simply clammed it. I couldn't see any way to help matters, really. Especially after the night we landed not more than five kilos away from an Others' village, and in the morning, Krehbol was gone. With more of her gear than I'd have thought she could carry.

We looked for her; we lifted over to the village and asked the Others there. No luck; if they knew, they weren't saying. I called Szabo but someone else answered. "Hold on; I'll check Upstairs." And a few minutes later the answer came. "Continue with your mission. We don't have time or supplies to waste, hunting down a deserter."

I hope the Others have been kind to her. They can afford that much.

So eventually we finished the shank end of the land mass and approached our base camp. Now, I expected, I could report to Szabo and end the mystery, to some extent. And things might get back somewhere close to normal, if there is such a thing.

Szabo wasn't there. The Others had him.

Upstairs, I gathered, was having diarrhea. Up or downside, nobody knew what to do. I was certainly no exception.

The main thing was, no one knew what had become of Szabo, or why. We didn't find out until later, but it will make more sense if I tell that part now. It was simple enough. Szabo got the cup treatment from a female Other, and when the most beautiful, the ever-lovely, *got* to him —well, his only possible response was to kill her. Being Szabo, as he was, what else could he do? That cup is strong medicine.

The Others couldn't have known; it's mostly on the subconscious level that they touch us and each other, and at that stratum Szabo was a healthy male; when the female Other went warm to him, she would have no idea she was pulling the pin on a live grenade.

At the time, though, official opinion had it that the Others had turned unreasonably hostile, that grabbing Szabo was only the first strike. Our orders were to round up everybody, and all the gear we could manage in a hurry, and cut trail back up to the ship in its sync-orbit. Using both aux boats, and I learned that Lisa, not by her own choice, was assigned to the second one.

Once we were all Upstairs, having salvaged more of our equipment than I'd expected we could, orders were to sit there. Until we got word by Phasewave that Base had made up its mind what we should do. That's when I began to learn not to hold my breath until Base got around to put its responsibility where its authority is. Because Base made the great but natural mistake of leaving all decisions to our illustrious Captain Soong.

I hate to cut down a man who shares even a tinge of my own proto-Mongol gene heritage, but Soong is a book soldier. If the answer isn't in the book, he will sit on the problem until one of them rots away entirely.

He can't have been this way all his life, because his record is good. One of the early astronauts, riding chemical rockets. Oh, not Mercury or Gemini or Apollo; he was on the shuttles, later, and was some kind of hero on a rescue mission once. I've heard jokes that maybe he ran himself a little too heroically short of oxygen, that time, too long to keep his smarts going. My own thought is that prestige and political clout notwithstanding, the man's over the hill when it comes to decisiveness. It can happen. And commanding a ship, with Szabo next in line, would make anybody cautious.

Possibly by accident, Soong did one smart thing; he lifted us out of sync-orbit, apparently outside the Others' hypothetical range of control. Because until we moved, I *couldn't* report what had happened in that clearing. And then I could, and along with all the other field personnel, spilled my guts as to what went on, downside, when the squawktalkers went off. Most of us got interviewed, anyway, and a summary was sent off to Base by Phasewave, I understand.

For what that's worth. Because then the two Others turned up on the ship with us.

Either they could teleport themselves or they'd stowed away in the aux boats and then hidden out for a while. Captain Soong leaned heavily on the latter idea; in my opinion, it didn't support his weight too well.

The male, tall for an Other, ranked about medium on

their color scale; his name was Dahil. The female was dark, of average height, and named Tiriis, or possibly T'ries; I've seen it spelled both ways, but that's only in *our* alphabet. Far as I knew, I'd never seen either of them. They greeted Lisa warmly, though, but she didn't respond; she turned and walked away.

I followed her to our quarters and tried to talk; she wouldn't say what was chewing her. Well, she'd been aloof and withdrawn ever since we got back to the ship, but people have a right to their own moods, so I hadn't pushed it—not that there'd been time to push much of anything. Our ship marriage had never been on an exclusive basis, so she wouldn't be clawed about Elys and me, downside, even if she'd had a chance to hear about that part. So for a time I stewed about Lisa's silence, because sometimes I can't see past my own nose, and it's not even all that long. And then I quit nagging, and we talked other subjects on a fairly friendly level, and I went back upship to see what I could learn.

At the open level outside the galley, from a little distance I watched Dahil and Tiriis. Besides their simple hot-weather garb, all they'd brought with them that I could see was one pouch, each, of whatever passed for personal effects among the Others, and a big transparent "wineskin" filled with dark gold liquid. Seeing it, I smelled spice; that color had been in the cup I drank.

Somebody ought to be warned, I thought, but with Szabo gone, Soong was the only one left to tell. Things were confused enough that I got to him at his business console without the usual red tape. But when I got there, he was giving one of his more fogheaded sets of orders. By the time I'd listened through it, one of his guards asked me for my audience pass, so I'd blown my chance.

I'd heard, though. Soong's ideas of how to cope with the shipboard presence of Tiriis and Dahil went like this: capture them, kill them, hold them hostage for Szabo's return, torture them for information, and call Base for advice. In that order. I had no trouble guessing what he'd decide to do. Call Base.

He didn't get that far, because first he decided to interview the Others in person. The same way the moth decides to have a closer look at the nice flame. After they'd turned his friendlies on for him, Soong initiated very few calls to Base. And answered hardly any of the communications from there, that he bothered to read.

Base, I expect, truly had its bowels in an uproar. Look at it their way. Reported aboard with us were two aliens, intentions unknown, with mental powers of unguessed extent, but obviously well out of the pea-shooter class. And Soong wouldn't even answer questions.

Base couldn't order us home; they didn't *want* us home. Later I saw their order to Soong, to blow up the whole ship, including us, if necessary, to keep it out of alien hands. The captain didn't even acknowledge receipt of that one. The potato was getting hotter, and Base was running out of cool hands to juggle it with.

So was the Comm center: Rigan and Blenkov and I and the rest. We had to say *something* to the repeated queries, which became more heated as no answers appeared. The pressure got to Rigan; he was driven to deliver one of his most devastating criticisms, right to Captain Soong's face. "Sir, this latest communiqué carries a definite note of impatience." Soong brushed him off; maybe the man didn't even get the point. When Rigan returned to Comm, he came perilously close to mutiny. He said to me, "I'm not sure the captain understands the seriousness of the situation." For Rigan, that's mutiny.

Meanwhile, Dahil and Tiriis had the run of the ship. How else, when no one could hold a hostile feeling in their presence unless they allowed it? I wondered what they were doing. So did everybody else, except possibly the captain. I imagine he merely hoped they weren't doing anything, or that if they were, he wouldn't hear about it.

Elys figured it out. We saw each other fairly regularly now. Well, Lisa was coolly keeping herself from me and wouldn't say why, so . . . "It's that magic elixir of theirs," Elys said.

"What about it?"

"Dahil's trying not to be obvious, but once or twice I've seen him talking with one of the women and offering a drink. Five gets you ten, it's out of his plastic sack of Hallucin-Ade."

"I think I see it coming, but spell it out."

"Sure you see it. Then they get lost for a while. And next time the woman shows up—"

"—she's not talking to anybody, much," I finished. "Scheist on a shin splint! So *that's* what's wrong with

436

Lisa." Suddenly I wanted to go find her, tell her it was all right. But it wasn't an appropriate time to rush away from Elys, so I didn't. "Is Tiriis playing up to any of the men?"

"Not that I've noticed," she said, and frowned. "One odd thing. Dahil ignores almost every woman who was on the down-party. Could that mean something?"

"Maybe that whatever Dahil has in mind, once is generally enough. Indoctrination by seduction?" I shook my head. "*We* got nothing like that, and Tiriis leaving the men alone—no."

Then I had the idea. "If once is *generally* enough— Elys, has any woman taken the initiative, approached Dahil?"

"I don't know of any." Maybe I had a funny look on my face, because she pulled back, brows raised. "You mean *me?*"

I nodded. "You've been there; it won't throw you. Now, look—this is important." Her expression said I'd checked my brains in a locker somewhere and was indecently exposed without them, but she was still listening. "Share that cup with Dahil again. And the whole works, if it goes that way." I grabbed her shoulders, no harder than I could help. "Here's the thing, Elys. Somehow, get a sample of that spiced-up bug juice, and bring it back for lab analysis. Okay?"

She sighed, and relaxed. "It's nice to know you're still making sense. All right, I see it. Now if Dahil only plays along . . . " I left her then. We both had things to do.

The way things had been going, I'd lost track of Lisa's watch-sked. But I got lucky; she was in our quarters. "Lisa!" I tried to hug her, but she pulled away—as usual, lately. "No!" I said. "Listen to me for a minute."

Dull-eyed and blank-faced, she looked at me. "Whatever you say." Her voice hadn't always been flat like that.

I said, "I know what it is with you. I *know*." She let her head sag forward, and shook it. The hell with that; I grabbed her chin and raised it until we could match eyeballs. "All right, Lisa. So you shared the cup, with Dahil or with another of them. Well, so did I, with one of their women. I've been there, and so has practically all the whole damn down-party. Does that tell you anything?" I hoped it would.

For the first time in a long while, she smiled. Not

exactly the smile I was used to, but better than none. "Yes," she said. "Quite a lot. I—I'm sorry I've been putting you off. I guess if I'd known, I wouldn't have." Then she cried.

We were close, I felt, to getting ourselves back together. So I kissed her, and so on, and although it was a little soon for me, things went well between us. But afterward she cried again, and wouldn't say why. I kept on asking, the way you do when you can't get something to make sense; she still cried. I would have let her be, but it struck me that maybe she was hiding something that could be important to more than just Lisa and me. So against my own feeling I kept pressuring her until she told me.

She was pregnant, that's all. Which may not sound like much, except that it should have been impossible; her contraceptive implant was a one-year squib with ten months to go. And until just now, she'd had sex exactly once since I'd left the ship with Szabo, and at the time I left, she had definitely not conceived. Downside, she had shared the cup with Dahil.

Lisa, pregnant by an alien? I found it hard to believe, but once the impossible is eliminated, you know what's left. So all I could do, now, was try to soothe Lisa. Once she realized that practically every woman in the down-party, and now quite a few here on the ship, was getting the same treatment, she didn't feel like quite so much of a freak.

But then she sat straight up, from where she'd been snuffling gently against my neck. "Ren! What if they *all*—?"

That's when we both *really* began to worry.

The trouble was, we had no one to report our suspicions to. Captain Soong had holed up, talking to nobody except the messboy who brought him his meals, and between all the rest of us there was enough authority to wipe our own noses, maybe.

Two days later, Lisa and I had a chance to talk things over with Elys. She'd approached Dahil, and all she'd say about that was that she'd lifted a sample of liquid love-bomb, all right. As Medic-3 she'd authorized lab analysis on it, but no results as yet. One personal note, though. She, too, was pregnant, and we could take our choice between an Other or divine intervention.

We needed to know whether impregnation was the whole idea of the Others' schtick, so it was my turn—to approach Tiriis, for cup-sharing and all. She smiled and said it wasn't "necessary," but before I could disengage with apologies, she handed me the cup, anyway. Well, what do you do?

I drank, and my mind changed her from an oddly formed humanoid with a mild visual attractiveness that grew with familiarity, to the essence of utter loveliness, and from there you can guess. Even now, after twice at that cup, I don't see a female Other the way you might. I see beauty you wouldn't believe. But without the cup, I'm content merely to appreciate it.

When Elys got the lab report, the results weren't much. "Part of it's hallucinogenic, of course," she said, "and there are some trace items that don't seem to mean much, though we can't be sure. Also, we found something resembling colchicine, which has sometimes been used to stimulate plant growth."

I nodded. "Yes. The Others do mess with plants, don't they?"

"Not the same way, I'd imagine," said Elys. "As I understand it, colchicine doubles the chromosome count." It wouldn't trigger ovulation, though, at any old point of the cycle. But something did, apparently.

So we weren't sure what we knew, what it meant, or who to tell it to, so as to get some constructive action started. Two more days we met for discussion, and got no place at all. Then Captain Soong came out of his cocoon—not as a butterfly, but to call assembly of all officers, and ratings of the first three grades. It was nice of the captain, I thought, to wake up and remember he had a ship to run.

All he said, to the lot of us seated in the galley, was, "Our visitors have something to show us." Then he sat down, and sure enough, Tiriis went to the viewscreen controls and Dahil got up front to speak. I wondered if she could handle those controls, and if so, how she'd learned the skill.

To the ear, the Others talk oddly, because they leave much detail to pass directly from mind to mind. I'm not sure just how much they put into sound waves and how much not; stand by for a general impression.

"You want know on man Szabo," Dahil began. "Here

439

man Szabo." And on the screen, there he was. He'd been missing for weeks now; this had to be a recording, and I have no idea how much of it was played on a real-time basis. All I can say is how we saw it.

I'd never seen Szabo nude before; I doubt if anyone had, on the ship. He looked exactly like any normal man; his lack, which apparently had made him kill once too often, was inside and hidden. Asleep or drugged, he lay supine on a cot, in a bare room.

One male and one female Other came on camera and stood, one at each side of Szabo's cot, looking down at him in silence.

"They think on man Szabo," Dahil said. "On where he not," Tiriis added. Minutes passed; then the two straightened up and came up past the camera to go out of sight.

Dahil said, "Man Szabo make right, now." For a moment nothing happened, and then, pulsebeat after pulsebeat, Szabo's erection grew. Like halfway up to a buffalo, my old grandaddy would have said; I had to reassure myself that size wasn't really all that important.

"Now man Szabo right," said Dahil. The stunned silence broke, everybody talking and nobody listening. Which was all right; none of it was worth listening to, including me.

Then quiet came again, because Szabo was coming awake and sitting up, then getting off the cot. He was half-standing when he realized what had happened, and he froze in that crouch, face writhing. Obviously the poor guy thought he'd gone crackers and was hallucinating. He reached to check by touch, then brought his hand away; probably he didn't dare find out, for sure.

Soft-voiced, Tiriis said, "Man Szabo not know he right. We show."

They showed, all right. Nude, bearing the familiar cup, a female Other came on screen. Gently drawing Szabo upright, she put the cup to his lips and tilted it until he drank; then she took the rest of it. Szabo's face relaxed. He smiled; not the frightening smile we knew, but a completely open, defenseless smile, a shy one. And very gently, he reached to her.

In the next few minutes there was no doubt that Szabo was fully functional. None. "See?" said Tiriis. "Now he right. Now he know he right." Then, when it ended, I think the screened picture skipped some time, for suddenly the female Other was leaving. Smiling his new smile,

Szabo looked after her for a moment, then lay down and slept so immediately that I suspect he had some help.

Elys said, "Then he'll be all right, from now on?"

"No." Dahil looked puzzled. "Why need? Is done for now; can do again."

"You mean you'll make him right when you want to?" She was near to screaming. "But the rest of the time, you don't think it matters?" She took a deep breath. "It matters to *him*. Don't you see?"

"We see," said Tiriis. "We show." And on the screen we saw the time I mentioned earlier, when Szabo as we knew him took the cup, and went berserk and killed the female Other. It wasn't a true picture, probably some kind of thought-projection put onto tape, because the figures were stylized, like line drawings. But there was no uncertainty as to what was happening.

"So you're punishing him?" Elys challenged the Others. "He couldn't help it; surely you can see that."

I had time to wonder why the Others were letting Elys scold them, instead of simply turning down her emotional wick, before Dahil said, "See now, but without try, not know. So make right and try. Man Szabo do right. Soon now, more try, one. Man Szabo do right more, then make right for stay. Or any when need." Elys, now with several of us backing her stand, tried to explain that the shocks of being made right and then reverting to the same old bind would likely drive Szabo *all* the way out of his tree.

Dahil made the odd twitch of his upper torso that passed for a shrug. "Not us to say. Is said, now be done." That was his final word, and the same for Tiriis. Szabo would have to tough it out, was all. Neither of them said what happened if he flunked the test, and nobody asked. I know *I* didn't.

The story went around the ship. It wasn't supposed to leak, of course, but naturally it did. Soong didn't bother to scold anyone; I expect it took all his time and energy to ignore his own problems.

You wouldn't think that in a situation like ours, weeks could pass with absolutely no action taken. But that's exactly what happened. Soong wasn't going to make a move without orders, and Base didn't have enough info to give any. So we hung in slow orbit, now as far from Opal as we could get and keep that orbit stable, what with other gravitational influences. The stalemate was virtually complete.

Not entirely, though. None of us could fire our own misgivings off to Base independently and hope to get away with it, but the routine departmental reports could be sent. These were supposed to go out over the captain's signature, and he wasn't even reading them, let alone signing anything. But to save himself the bother of getting ink on his fingers, he'd long ago given signature-stamps to all his department heads. Thus, we preserved some shadow of legality; we used Rigan's stamp.

Everything that was sent, I read in the Chrono log, whether it went out on my watch or not. I couldn't see that Xenobiology, for instance, had much new to say, but maybe they'd give Base a little something to bite down on.

In the chain of command, Lisa was an odd side-link— a First rating in Psychology, no one out-ranking her in that line, but still under Medical so her material had to be correlated with theirs. It worked out well; we needed to rub together all the ideas we had. One new datum was that the impregnation program, downside at least, was intended to work in both directions. Because Tiriis was definitely showing signs.

Elys had taken our first guesses to her boss, Medic-Chief Mark Gyril. He's small and thin, deep-voiced and long on brains. Nice, informal kind of person; when Elys said she wanted me and Lisa to sit in on the worry sessions, he said, "Fine; bring in two more chairs." And that was that.

Our first think-session, he summed up the mess. The Others didn't seem hostile, but they didn't have to be, when they could keep *us* from feeling that way. Did they mean us harm? Unproven.

Elys, he guessed, could have had her sample of the magic potion by asking. Because she couldn't have swiped it, against Dahil's wishes. She looked shocked, but then nodded, as Gyril added, "Either he doesn't care what we learn, or thinks we can't analyze the stuff; I'd guess the former." Well, so would I.

"I don't have a full analysis, and I couldn't synthesize the fluid here. Back at Base, perhaps, I could do both; so could the people there, for that matter." My impression was that given the props, anything Base could do, Gyril could do better.

His incomplete analysis sounded pretty good to me. The side-trace items, he thought, stabilized the mixture and counteracted our anti-fertility measures. The mind-bender differed enough from other known hallucinogens to give him the idea that it might be tailored to a specific purpose. How specific? Gyril shrugged. Try cup-sharing between a human, or Other, and a member of some other humanoid race, and then we might know more. But without the cup, humans and Others weren't sexually attracted. Or we weren't, at least; maybe they only drank to make it look mutual. But the crux was, the Others deliberately set up these encounters, while our people got hooked without knowing what was going to happen. Well, usually; Elys blushed and I expect I looked sheepish.

The component that resembled colchicine, the chromosome-doubling agent: "I can't prove this yet, or possibly ever, but it has to be the element that makes this inter-species fertility possible, at all." He smiled. "I have tissue samples from Dahil and Tiriis, you know." I hadn't. "There's no real chance of disease-contagion between us and they know it, but they humored me.

"Well, by several definitive criteria we're as interfertile with the Others as we are with a stalk of wheat. There are some interesting near-fits to the genetic layouts, but the point is that they do *not* fit. Part of the cup's function, I speculate, is to act on our respective germ cells so that they *will* fit. To produce a viable organism—a hybrid, if you please, between us and the Others."

Lisa blinked. "But what would it be like? How would it look?"

"It's a bit early," Gyril said, "but I'd like to get some X-rays. Because the trouble is that your question is not theoretical. It's very real—to you two, and to quite a number of other women."

That wasn't the only real trouble; another was that if he'd summarized our knowledge again two months later, he couldn't have added much. For one thing, we never did get any X-rays.

It's not really X-ray, doesn't even use hard radiation. The old name holds over, because it's easier to say. But we got no pictures, for many reasons or sometimes none. Women didn't keep their appointments, or the techs were busy and rescheduled them. Or the machine was out of order. Or, more often, the job was just plain botched.

After our think-group got together to concentrate on seeing the work done right, and after four hours had a stack of blurs and fogs and all-black negatives to show for it, Gyril summed the matter up. "I think we can assume that the Others don't approve of this line of research." He grinned in a tired way, and we all went to his quarters and had a drink, to simmer down.

The Others were stacking the deck on us, no doubt of it. Some lines of investigation went fine, but always to logical negative results. And some we simply couldn't get off the ground; we'd forget proper sequence and botch the results. After a time we quit bothering with any approach that ran into that kind of static, but made notes on it, anyway—for there, of course, the answers lay.

Once Gyril said, "I may not be able to feel hostile toward the Others, but sometimes I manage a certain annoyance. My thought is that one day I shall conduct this research *without* them peeping down my brainpipe." Good idea; too bad it didn't really apply.

And so it went. What we knew, what we even guessed, we tried to slip into the reports that went to Base. Looking at some of it, Rigan went cautious and wouldn't let his Soong-signature stamp be used. But Gyril had one of those, too; no problem. The Xeno-folks sent a lot of stuff, too; I hope Base could make more sense of it than I could. If they did, you couldn't tell it by the messages they sent to Soong, which I doubt he ever read. Certainly he answered none of it, or I'd have seen something in the Chrono.

The Others didn't interfere with anything we sent out; either they didn't understand about Base, or they didn't care. In the latter case they were probably right.

Maybe if Szabo had been aboard, he could have been primed to pressure Soong or even go over his head. Dangerous proposition, it would've been, to make to Szabo —but I wasn't the only one getting desperate enough to try something dangerous. No point in bracing Command-Second Nargilosa; she was crowding retirement, and had a sort of myopic crush on Soong, anyway. Command-Third Rocco was a political appointee; enough said. And a doper, too.

It gets nervous, sitting for months in high orbit, doing nothing much about a situation that's scary as hell. Nearly every woman aboard, capable of the condition, was into late pregnancy. All, except those who had been downside, by Dahil. Well, there were five who'd made the grade, by human agency and with official permission, before we hit Opal. Maybe the Others were considerate in not adding an abortive chemical to the cup, or perhaps they weren't up to that stunt; I doubt that anyone ever asked them.

But having every woman on the whole ship, who's not past it, running about six months preggy, doesn't do a lot for morale. Theirs, or anyone else's. For starters, only five were volunteers; the rest had been drugged into it. And knew that whatever they would bear, it was something new under the suns. The idea scared hell out of some; Gyril and Elys got worried that they might run out of a stock of stability drugs that should have been good for ten years, under normal conditions.

I had to think back, to recall what normal conditions *were*. For one thing, we used to know what we were supposed to be doing. But by now, even routine ship maintenance was beginning to suffer.

And that's what blew the whole package. The grav-lift hiccuped while a woman was halfway up it. Her broken ankle wasn't serious, but she began to hemorrhage and then miscarried.

It wasn't one of ours.

Only Mark Gyril actually saw the fetus; he said it wasn't viable so he'd destroyed it. He took no pictures for record, which gave us a good idea who was pushing his buttons at the time. With Elys and Lisa and I all questioning him, it got embarrassing; he couldn't look either gravid woman straight in the eye when they asked him what the unborn creature *looked* like.

His strained voice came out a lot higher than his usual mellow, bass growl. "It wasn't . . . what you might expect. I can't describe it. I'm sorry; I can't." And finally we realized he told literal truth; he couldn't describe it because the Others wouldn't *let* him. Which gave me to think, and I didn't like it much.

Especially I didn't like thinking how the women must feel, each carrying Something in her belly—and this good friend, the only one who knew, couldn't or wouldn't say *what*. Elys probably had it worse, because a few days earlier, she and Gyril had affirmed ship-marriage together, and now he was clamming up about the biggest personal worry she had. What a way to run a honeymoon!

Not that Elys was in any better shape for frolic now than Lisa was—but the principle, I thought, still applied.

Muttering something, Elys turned away and began fiddling inputs into the holo-projector. A man's image flickered into being; then it vanished and an Other's appeared. The man again, then the Other, faster and faster. She pushed the sequence-speed to tops, far past normal usage range; the two images began to blur into one.

Gyril shouted "No!" and reached for the control. Too late; something blew and we had a lot of smoke in the place. But for an instant, first, we saw both pictures at once. Heads and torsos superimposed, but arms and legs separate and clear.

In the dim back rooms of my mind, hackles raised. What scared me was, that grotesque mishmash looked *right*.

We left Gyril trying to soothe Elys down out of her screaming tizzy. Considering everything, I thought she was having the only possible reasonable reaction.

Back at quarters, Lisa and I needed some cleaning up; over the past hundred years or so, I understand that the stink of burning insulation hasn't improved much. Ordinarily we'd have hit the wash-off booth together and had fun at it, but with her extra bulk now, that wasn't feasible. So we hugged, and then I took myself off to the communal officers' showers, which are handy for relief breaks during watches if you happen to feel the need then.

Those compartments have G-control; I put mine on low so I could float on strong spray and be pelted all over with mild. Great! I needed to relax, and now I did. When the warning buzzer rang, meaning that someone else wanted in, I put G back to normal and stood up. I could have punched "Wait," but it's more polite not to. And the spray dwindled off, so the door could open and let someone in.

It was Szabo. None other. Not the Szabo I'd known—from the way his face looked, this was Szabo "made right," as Tiriis had shown him on the screen. He grinned, and stuck his hand out, and though I knew he could still break me in half if he wanted to, he didn't scare me now. I took the hand.

"Hi, Ren," he said. He'd never called me anything but

Bearpaw or Comm-Second, and that had suited me just fine. But now . . .

I said, "Hi, Szabo. Good to see you." And before I thought: "But how'd you get up here?"

The question didn't seem to bother him. "I'm not going to ask," he said. "I'm afraid Dahil or Tiriis might *tell* me." So it had to be the teleport thing, and Szabo didn't like psi stuff. But he said, "My first name's Ferenc, Ren; feel free to use it. It got changed to Frank when my folks went American, but I think I'll go back to my ethnic start." Before I could think what to say, he reached for the compartment controls, and said, "Low-G?" I nodded, and then we floated on spray, and had to speak up to hear each other over the splashings.

I didn't know what to say, except to ask if he had anything to tell Base about the Others that might help the ship get off the dime. He didn't, so I was stuck, because I wanted to stay off the subject of his personal transformation in case it was still dynamite.

But he cut through all that. "Look, Ren—you're pussy-footing, and you don't have to. I was what I was, and I am what I am. The Others didn't owe me a thing, either, except a fast blast in the head. In case you didn't know, I killed one of them." Not out of fear, but because this was his story, I said nothing. He said, "If it matters, I'm sorry for the way I had to be with everybody, just to keep going. I envied *eunuchs*—at least their drives are gone, along with their abilities. I was like a bird with its wings cut off."

I damn near cried. For murderous, frightening Szabo. With the water spraying, it wouldn't have showed, and when I got my voice back, I said, "I'm glad for you. Okay?" And he smiled, the new way I could trust, and I flipped up to stand and leave. Low-G is nice.

"Just a minute, Ren." I paused. "I skimmed the Chrono log; I know how the ship stands. You know as well as I do, something has to be done." I never in my life made a more sincere nod. "I haven't talked yet with Captain Soong. I will, shortly. When I do, either he will take action or I will." He shook his head. "Needless to say, I won't *harm* the captain in either case. But he may go into storage for a time. I think the log, in itself, will justify any action I may need to take."

I couldn't argue with a word of it; I nodded, we shook

447

hands again, I toweled and dressed and left. To go tell Lisa.

I found her leaving our quarters to meet with Mark Gyril and Elys. When I said I had news, she said to save it for the whole group, and took off as fast as her condition would allow. Well, as she said, she moved pretty well for a fat lady.

Elys let us in, and we all got sat down, and I sprang my news. It brought quite a lot of startled comment, and Gyril said, "Does this change anything we're trying to do?" Before we could come up with anything that quacked like an answer, Ferenc Szabo was on the intercom screen, announcing an all-ship broadcast. Looking a little mussed up, he stated that since Captain Soong had refused to abide by Regs, such as answering queries from Base, Szabo as Command-First was stuffing Soong away for future reference and assuming the title of Acting Captain. And shortly we were all heading back for Base at the high lope. All complaints, I gathered, would be more than ignored.

Well, it figured. But who was the man speaking for: us, or the Others?

Later we heard how the takeover had gone. Under pressure, Soong had agreed to let Ferenc move the ship and inform Base. But as soon as he was alone, Soong called in his personal bully-boy guards and sicced them onto Ferenc. The personal-guard thing isn't *in* Regs, but doesn't violate them, either.

Even Soong should have known better; there were only six guards. At least he had the sense to send them unarmed; six armed men can't help but get in each other's way in a confined space, and then it doesn't take a Ferenc Szabo to disarm one and use the weapon to cut down the rest while they're still wondering which way is Christmas. Officer-level combat training is quite effective.

Ferenc killed one. Not by choice; he caught a full tackle from behind while he was bending someone, and the impact broke the man. Two more were injured but recovered; the other three had the good sense to run, luckier than either they or Soong deserved.

So, like it or not, soon we'd be on our way back to Base. But not until ship's maintenance was up to snuff;

people began working long shifts. A major problem was that a fair proportion of our best tech-ratings were women, and most of those simply weren't in any condition to move or climb normally; the work went slowly. But eventually we moved out; behind us, Opal dwindled.

Earth with no stops, after all the delay in orbit, meant pretty close to running out of groceries, but not quite. Elys said we were bound to run short of baby food, with so many women expecting sooner than not. Lisa said this proved the acting captain was under the Others' control. I said, why would the Others want their own offspring to starve?

Gyril brought up the point that if the Others were backing Ferenc, how did Soong's six heavies manage to tackle him at all? That was the best question of the semester, because it was our first hint that the Others' powers had limits. Thinking back, none of us could recall any instance of group resistance to the aliens' wishes. It gave to think—and with hope, this time. Sometimes, even parts of the problem give some of the answer.

No one looked forward to the time when the ship's complement would suffer a forty-percent increase, all tiny and fragile and loud and messy. But the classic nine-month mark came and went, and that increase didn't happen; the pregnant, for the most part, stayed pregnant. Well, the five human conceptions delivered on time, with great relief, and actually there were six; one woman had worried needlessly all this time, because apparently she'd slipped her implant schedule and been secured before she went down to Opal. Well, once in a while somebody has to get lucky.

The next months in transit were pretty miserable. Women wretched with fear, and with wombs too bulky and heavy to carry around. Lisa, bless her sturdy bones, could still stand and walk. Elys couldn't, without help; she looked like a small girl clinging to a large rock. Men were sick with worry, trying to take care of the women and afraid it wasn't going to be good enough; they were so hyped up that it didn't take much to set off senseless fights. I expect the women would have fought, too, sometimes, if they could have moved around well enough to do it.

To visit Mark and Elys, Lisa and I had worked out a

way to travel together through the standard-G corridors.
And on stairs, for no woman cared to trust the grav-lift
now. I walked bent over, crouching a little, with Lisa behind me—her hands digging into my lower ribs, her great
belly resting against my lower back. Not the greatest way
to fly, but it got us from Point A to Point B. The ship's
few invalid carts were for people who really needed them,
and some of those had to do without. By contrast, Lisa
and I felt we were lucking out. So far.

To see Elys was heartbreak. Not too long ago, that tiny,
bouncy wench could run your legs off in an uphill sprint.
Now she couldn't stand without a helper. Yes, it hurt to
see her.

Gyril looked like the wrath of God, and who hid My
thunderbolts? Heavy in study, he looked up as though
we were skunks at his picnic. Lisa tried to jolly him.
"How's the research, maestro?"

He did try to grin. "I'm studying the old Caesarian
operation—delivering the infant through an abdominal in-
cision." The grin faded. "You didn't expect, did you, that
any of you could deliver normally?"

That line was a stopper, but Lisa said, "You can do it,
can't you?"

"Correctly, with minimum risk? That's what I want to
ensure."

"Good answer," she said. Then she pouted. "Mark,
come here and hug me; tell me it's going to be all right.
I'd go to you, but these days I can't get there from here."
So Gyril did, and Lisa did, and I knew who was reassur-
ing whom. Gyril's the Medic-Chief, but Lisa's the psychologist.

A week or two later, Gyril delivered the first of the
Children, as they're called now. Dahil and Tiriis were
there and observed, not interfering at all. What they did,
though, was set up their own infant-care ward. As soon
as the baby was out and obviously viable, they left Gyril
to take care of the trimmings, and a little later, Dahil
came back and trundled the infant off to the Others' own
bailiwick for further care.

So for some time, most of us had no idea what the
Children looked like. Only that after nearly fifteen
months' gestation, they were big lummoxes that had to be
cut out by main force if their mothers hoped to live.
Though, come to think of it, we never heard how Tiriis

was delivered. But any way you look at it, that's not much of a recommendation.

One thing that happened. When Dahil and Tiriis left the delivery room, Mark Gyril got the acting captain on the viewscreen and showed him the infant. "This is what we've been waiting for. Your orders, sir?"

And Ferenc Szabo said, "You'll have to kill it, of course."

"Come down here, if you please, and give me that order in person." And Ferenc went there, looked at the first of the Children.

Then he shook his head. "The order is rescinded. Doctor, we are born at the wrong time."

If you think, as I first did, that the incident shows carelessness on the part of the Others, take a second thought at it.

Quite some time passed before most of us learned much about the Children. There were about thirty born and living—three died—when I first saw one.

Describing them isn't exactly difficult; it's more like impossible. If you haven't seen one, you can't really imagine it very well; if you have, you realize it's like trying to describe a cow to a cabbage. As a starting point, remember how the Others look; then try to visualize the double exposure we got when Elys burned out the projector. The first impression . . .

*

. . . move separately, or any adjacent pair track for two-eye focus, to front or rear or . . .

*

. . . between the left legs, and female between the right. As with humans and Others, elimination is centrally located. It appears . . .

*

Gyril refuses to speculate whether this means a tendency to multiple births.

Later insert here. I find some of the tape erased or garbled, and when I record it again, the same thing happens. I think I'm running into the same kind of censorship, from the Others, that stopped us from getting X-rays. Maybe they'll let this explanation through and maybe not.

Either way, I'm splicing from here directly into the next part they haven't tampered with.

. . . sounds like a bunch of little monsters, I realize, but they're not. Once you get used to them, which does take some doing, they're quite an attractive form of life. I don't know how much of this is objective and how much their own doing, because the Children's powers of mental influence, when they use them, are cards and spades over what the Others can do. Consider: newly born, the first one changed Ferenc Szabo's mind, about killing it, as soon as Ferenc was in the baby's presence. After ten or twelve days, we found, they can reach you any where on the ship. We have no way to test the effect over longer distances.

Base does, of course, but for obvious reasons would rather not make the final test. Which is to say, letting us come close enough that the Children's influence could reach Earth. And since it turned out that Base knew the problem, apparently the Others hadn't stopped Ferenc from reporting the situation as he saw it. Well, I never claimed to understand the Others, and I still don't.

So Base finally did something; they sent us a directive. Per orders, Ferenc Szabo assembled the officer complement to hear it together, and piped it through the intercom broadcast circuit to the rest of the ship. The directive made more sense than I expected.

"Attention, Captain Szabo and all present," it began. "You must not—repeat, *must not*—return here with the creatures you call the Children. We realize you are low on supplies. Consequently, a ship, basically similar to your own, will be diverted from its present mission to resupply you in space. Rendezvous coordinates in space-time will be given you as soon as possible. Meanwhile, to simplify rendezvous, maintain your own vectors constant."

I thought, but what about the other crew, when Dahil and Tiriis get at them? The person reading the directive must have been reading my mind, too. "Except for one male volunteer, your supply ship will be uncrewed. The volunteer will join you; the ship will be abandoned once you have transshipped your supplies. To ensure this outcome, that ship, after achieving rendezvous, will be left with no appreciable amount of fuel."

That part impressed me; Base was *serious*. I have some

idea of what these ships cost. Enough pure fright, apparently, could overrule even budget considerations.

The voice continued, and I was surprised to detect in it a real note of human feeling. "To pronounce exile on innocent, loyal Agency personnel is a hard thing. But we have to do it. After you have, as rapidly as possible, re-supplied your ship, reverse course. Proceed, at max acceleration, back across the dead belt that lies beyond the Demu planets, and continue until your fuel supply falls below the point of no return. You understand, I trust."

I got it, all right; what surprised me was that it made sense. Now the voice came slower. "From there, you will be on your own, to search out any habitable planet and settle there. When you do, your ship's drive must be completely disabled, and all technical literature concerning it, destroyed."

The throat-clearing, then, sounded embarrassed. "This order, we know, demands complete sacrifice of your own future plans. But we have no alternative. These aliens cannot be allowed to take over the human race." I wondered if Base had already made the decision when they had only the Others to fear. Then I decided it didn't matter what I wondered. What mattered was whether Base had missed one vital point, here.

Not entirely, they hadn't: "The Others, if not yet the Children, will put mental pressure on you to disobey this directive. We ask you now, all of you listening, to concentrate together on the thought, the purpose, that you *will* remove this threat. Awake or asleep, never let that group purpose leave your mind, and you will win. Despite this alien attempt to force you to betray . . ."

Well, then it got hokey. But up to then—I don't know where they dug him up, but *somebody* at Base had some brains. Picked up the group concentration thing, how the Others hadn't stopped Soong's goons from jumping Ferenc, from Mark Gyril's report. Well, their idea, now, might work, at that.

The wrap-up was: "You are heroes, all of you. You will never be forgotten. Thank you." Funny thing. Given the tone of voice, it sounded convincing.

As a matter of fact, we did start working on group concentration to resist mental pressure. Hung around and even gave each other pep talks. Anyone alone, with no one else's thoughts to help, is vulnerable, and we are beginning to know it. The next . . .

*

' . . . was changed, for rendezvous. Remembering co-ordinates isn't my department, but the least-fuel compu-tation had us already slowed to "rest," whatever that means in the twisting Arm of a spiral galaxy, and moving back down-Arm into the dead belt, before the supply ship could reach us. Ferenc Szabo's been following instruc-tions; I hope it works.

I hope you got all this, too. Hasn't been easy, getting it on tape in chunks, putting it out on Phasewave the same way. When it wasn't having to dodge Rigan—who, to give him credit, hasn't snooped on me lately—it was stooges of Soong's for a while. And a time there, I was some cautious about Ferenc Szabo.

But either it's all gone out or it hasn't, and either you've got it or not. We know a ship's coming, and there's only two or three there could be, finished and launched since we left, but we don't know which, or from where. We'll find out, I guess.

And I don't know how long until rendezvous; Szabo hasn't said.

But now at least you know why we won't be back.

If you're lucky.

III.

Decisions

"Do you believe that, Hayward?" Barton was finished with the tape now. They hadn't tried to hear it in one sitting, he and Limila and Arlie Fox, because Barton kept turning it back to check on earlier things to make sure he had them straight. So they'd had two meal breaks, and to Barton, his day was getting into evening.

The young man spread his hands. "It all fits." He turned to the console once more. "I'll punch up the official-reports tape for you; just skim it, if you like. But then see what you think."

"All right." Barton had plenty of time; he began with the earliest message relayed to Base from the down-party on Opal, and at first he skipped nothing. Then he nodded, and began sampling only the first phrases of each entry and punching ahead to the next start-code. When he came to Base's order for the ship to get itself permanently lost, he listened all the way through. Then he turned the playback off. "I guess I believe it, too."

He paused, thinking. From the start of Bearpaw's odd tale, Barton had been piling up questions. He'd saved them, because maybe the answers would be later in the story, and a lot of them were. All right; Bearpaw's ship, and the one Barton was on now, were magnitudes ahead of those he was used to. But the grav-lift and variable-G showers were certainly derived from the original Demu ship Barton had swiped on Ashura; Tarleton's fleet could have had those, except that it would have taken longer and they were in a hurry. Barton remembered the day those things were decided; for a moment he wondered whether any areas of these big ships had the Demu pee-through floors, then shook his head. The matter simply wasn't important.

And what was? Barton was tired; concentration came hard. But before he slept, he wanted some answers. So he began asking.

What Bearpaw's ship had and what this one had, it turned out, were two different buckets of clams. "We're going to leave this one adrift, remember," said Hayward. "A total loss. So as soon as we accepted the order to divert, the ship was systematically stripped of everything not essential to the mission. And that equipment was unloaded on Tilara."

Barton asked for details. The faster-than-light communication gear was gone; after rendezvous, Bearpaw's ship could do the report to Base. Maybe Hennessy on Tilara would get his hands on the apparatus, make use of it, and maybe not. Barton had had another idea, but now he dropped it. He cleared his throat; it felt dry. "How about weapons?" He didn't know what he might want to do with weapons, but it would be nice to know what he had, just in case.

Hayward shook his head. "They dismounted the big laser; it's gone. Of course we still have the Demu Shield; they couldn't send us out totally defenseless, in case we met Demu raiding ships. And—"

"And since the sleep-gun works from the same power supply and some of the same wave-form generators, we should have that, too."

"I'm not sure," said Hayward. "It's not my line of work."

Barton stood. "Let's find out." They went up a level and Barton tried those controls; the indicators showed no power going out, so he led the way to the generator turret and saw where components had been removed. For a moment he was stumped, and if he hadn't been so tired he might have done a little cussing. Then he grinned. "Hayward? Do you know how to check your spares inventory?"

Barton's faith in human inefficiency was rewarded.

When Hayward showed him where to find the parts stocks, and Barton plugged things in where they belonged, the sleep-gun came operative.

"I still don't understand," said Hayward, "why you *want* that thing working." It was Barton's morning now; in the Command-First's quarters that dwarfed the compartments on Ship One, he and Limila had slept well. Arlie seemed happy enough living in the style of a Command-Second. Hayward, of course, had captain's digs.

Pausing between bites of breakfast, Barton said, "How should I know? What I want is all the options I can get." He shrugged. "Who knows? Maybe we could fake out all those super-psi types and solve the whole mess with one good shot of sleepy-bye." He grinned, then, so that nobody would take the idea seriously. Because, he didn't. But Limila nodded. So she knew he'd decided where they were going.

One serious idea, he did have. Done eating, they went above and Barton had Hayward put the galactic-Arm map on the screen. "Show us our course, huh?" he said, and Hayward produced a thin, curving line that arced from Tilara to a point in the dead belt. Leaning forward, Barton studied it.

Finally he sat back. "Too far. No time and not enough fuel." Before Hayward could speak, Barton said, "I think you know already, but I'll make it official; I'm not going to interfere with your mission. But still—" He slapped a hand against the side of a console. "Those aux boats Bearpaw mentioned. I don't know their range, anything about them. But Tarleton needs some warning. And maybe, if the budget-minded types hadn't been so pinchpenny about stripping this ship . . ."

He saw Hayward gulp, and the man said, "They left me an aux craft. In case, you know. One man to handle the whole ship, and if something should go wrong—well, I'm a volunteer, but not any kind of kamikaze."

"What's its range?"

Hayward told him, and Barton sat back. Again he looked at the screen, and said, "We can do it. Bend course enough to get within safe distance for the aux boat to Sisshain, and this ship still rendezvous as planned."

Hayward's eyes widened. "Then you're taking the boat to Sisshain?"

"No," said Barton. "You are."

"But why?" All three asked him that, and Barton had
no real answer. The real answers had been censored out
of Renton Bearpaw's tape, by the Others. All that Barton
had to go on was a hunch—a hunch, and a memory.
But whatever had happened, and would happen on that
ship he'd never seen, he wanted to be there.

What he said was, "Tarleton needs information, not
me. I'm trouble for him, and dealing with Hennessy, he'll
have enough of that." Hayward tried to talk; impatient,
Barton waved him off. "If they'd left us F.T.L.-comm
capability, there'd be no problem. Well, not so big a
one. We'd call Earth, is all, and get things straight. Now
we can't. So we'll do it the way I said." He stood. "You
can navigate, Hayward. Or you wouldn't be here."

The young man nodded, and Barton said, "Then rig
course to let yourself off for Sisshain, with a safety margin. Meanwhile, I'll tape the stuff for you to take to
Tarleton."

Nobody argued. Barton expected to finish his taping
in maybe fifteen minutes, but it took him nearly two
hours. Because every time he thought he had it right, he
found he'd forgotten something.

The course changes looked right to Barton, and the
computer agreed, so Barton watched while Hayward put
them into effect. Then everybody gathered in Hayward's
plushy quarters. Now that things were decided, even
though Barton had made most of the choices, the situation felt more relaxed to him. He couldn't take the sweet
wine, though, that was all Hayward had in the way of
alcohol, so he ran a computer check on the cargo, and
Arlie Fox went along and helped him find a case of
tolerable bourbon.

After that, the party went better, and when Barton
and Limila left, he knew he'd bagged about as much of
a load as he could use.

He got away with it without a hangover, but that was
the only time Barton came anywhere near getting smashed-
drunk. He guessed he'd needed it, though, the once, to let
some of the tension off.

Now as days passed and the ship plowed space-time,
faster than the ships he'd known but still measuring in-

terval by the slow movement of chronometers, Barton studied this new ship. For he needed to know it, and was determined that he would.

Hayward didn't seem to be so sure. One day he said, "Do you really think you'll be able to take over, so quickly? I mean, what if you miss something, and I'm gone, and there's no one to ask?"

Barton rubbed sweat off his forehead. He'd run into some trouble, with the haywired circuits that grouped all important controls to one central pilot's position, and he didn't welcome the interruption. Looking up, he asked how long it had taken Hayward to pick up his own briefing. Hearing the answer, he nodded. "About the same time as I have, now. So quit worrying."

"But I had training by experts!"

Barton snapped a refractory connector into place and eased back onto his haunches. "You ever land a ship, Hayward?" Headshake. "Well, I have. The first time, with no training by anybody at all—and I damn near put it in the drink, but I didn't. On my second try it was bat-ass sideways, and the drive knocked dead at the last of it; hadn't been for the Shield, we'd've splattered halfway around Sisshain." Realizing how he must be glaring, Barton felt silly. "All I'm saying, Hayward: I've done new stuff before."

"Of course you have. I know that, Barton. But—"

Fed up with the argument, Barton sighed. "Put it like so. I don't see how any one pilot could land this crate. But if it came up that way, sure's hell I'd have a try at it."

Hayward still worried, though; Barton wished he wouldn't do it out loud so much. At lunch once, puzzled frown on Hayward's face: "What happens if you make rendezvous and they don't? I mean, there you are, practically out of fuel and no F.T.L. communications."

Well, no end to the kid's frettings, it seemed. Barton set his plate back—he was near enough done with it as to make no difference—and said, "We miss connecting, the other ship'll be yelling a lot; wouldn't you say? So Base sends out more troops, and I doubt they'll forget us entirely." He couldn't help but shrug, then. "Meanwhile, this is a supply ship. Three people aren't going to run short of anything."

"Three?" said Arleta Fox. "Make that two, Barton." He looked at her. The regrowing curly auburn hair didn't make much bulk yet, around her head, but now there was enough of it that no hint of scalp showed through. Neither did her thinking, Barton realized; maybe it was a little too long since he'd last talked with her.

He knew she was sharing quarters with Honus Hayward—his, since those were the better accommodations—after the first ten days or so aboard this ship. It was something he hadn't asked about, because it was none of his business. Now he said, "Sure, Arlie. You want to leave in the aux boat, for Sisshain, that's your right. Care to tell me why, though?"

As her hand squeezed Honus Hayward's, then released it, she gave the little bulldog smile. "Several reasons, Barton. One's phobic. The idea of creatures that can influence my own mind, directly—well, I might jump ship without a suit."

Thinking back, Barton smiled. "Any connection, Arlie, with why you let me off the hook about hypnotic drugs, back on Earth?"

She nodded. "Positive connection, yes. But even without that, Barton—at this point, I wouldn't leave Honus. What we have—"

Sure. Permanent or not, they had to give it the chance, if they could. And now, no reason why not. Barton's hand signified agreement, but he said, "I don't think you're done, Arleta."

The way she pushed Hayward to one side, and leaned forward, looked a little brusque. "Barton, do you think you're going to clear all the mess up, back on Tilara, and with Tarleton when he gets there, with one *tape?*" She ignored his attempt to answer, and said, "I'm a witness all around. I can fill in to Tarleton, and then testify some more, back on Tilara. Do you see, Barton?"

"Or on Earth, if necessary," said Limila, and Arleta nodded.

Barton did, too. "Yeh, I see it. And I guess it's just as well, I won't be there. The screw-ups with the ap Fenns, and all."

A touch on his arm, and Fox said, "How do you feel about what you plan to do?"

It took a little thinking, but not much. He turned and kissed her forehead, which was easy since her hair hardly grew down to cover it all yet, and said, "All these years, Arlie, since the Demu grabbed me. I must be as loose from Earth as anyone ever has been. More than those poor bastards on the ship we're going out to meet. By a long way. So I guess I'll just go do what I can." He saw Limila looking at him, and took her silence for agreement. After all, she'd been uprooted for a long time, too.

And over the next days, while the ship's course curved to its nearest approach to Sisshain, nobody talked up anything touchy. Hayward and Limila checked out the aux boat's supplies, to make sure everything was sufficient. When the time came for the boat to launch, there was a lot of talk and hugging, but as near as Barton could remember of it, the talk said little that they hadn't all said before. Once the boat dropped away, and Barton saw on the main screen that its vector was optimum to hit Sisshain, he put Honus Hayward and Arleta Fox out of his thinking.

Because now there wasn't room for them.

So he turned the big ship away from the vector that gave the aux boat an easy ride to Sisshain, and upped his accel so that rendezvous would be accomplished.

It was a long haul, and first Barton was moody and then he would come alive and feel animated. He knew the whole thing had to be as hard on Limila as it was on him, but he couldn't help it.

And then, way out in the dead belt, his detectors found signs of a drive wake. "It's a whopper, too," he said. "Not that there's much chance anything else would be out here, besides the ship we're after meeting." Also, the wake appeared suddenly, at full strength, rather than building from faintness, which fit with a ship slowing to "rest" and reversing course.

When their own began to vibrate, Barton knew they'd hit the part where the one ahead passed light-speed, and he steered outside the wake's cone. Saying, "To jar us, this far back, that thing had to start off with a *lot* of power."

For it was two more days before their quarry showed up on visual. It was the one they wanted, all right.

Eager to learn what had been happening on the ship ahead, Barton was all for giving hail immediately. Limila put her hand on his arm. "Barton, should we not first decide how much we wish to appear to know? Some of the knowledge from Bearpaw's tape may be more useful if we are not known to have it."

Politicking wasn't Barton's forté; he hadn't thought of

such aspects. Now he did. "Sure; you're right. Honey, sometimes I *am* the dumbest man in the world. Look, now—only Bearpaw and his little group of cronies, probably, know he got those tape segments out. This Szabo character may know or may not. So, in general, we can't seem to know anything that's not on the official tapes. Which means we'd better give those another quick scan, while we have the chance. But all the personal stuff—" Yeh, he thought; there was more than a little, that they'd have to play close to the vest.

An idea came. "We are of one advantage, though, Limila. If need be, we can be of conference in their presence." Then she smiled, because he had spoken in Tilaran.

The man who answered Barton's call was Renton Bearpaw; Barton recognized his voice in the first few words, but didn't let on. He looked younger than Barton had expected, dark-skinned with black hair, from the Amerind side. Barton had a touch of that heritage himself, or so his grandfather had told him, but it didn't show. This man appeared to be a little taller and slimmer than Barton, but in the same size range. He gave his name and rank, and said, "You're here a little early, which is good. I imagine I don't have to tell you how much we appreciate your volunteering. Joining our exile, all by yourself—well, it takes dedication, and—"

Turning his head, Barton saw that Limila was off camera, at that. He beckoned to her, and when Bearpaw saw her, his eyebrows raised. "Not exactly by myself," Barton said. "There's two of us." The brows still hovered, and suddenly Barton saw what the problem was. "I guess you wouldn't have seen any Tilarans before."

Before Bearpaw could answer, another man joined him —a taller, blond man. The way he moved reminded Barton of a big cat, and his expression gave him an air of confident power. So Barton wasn't surprised when the man said, "Ferenc Szabo speaking; I'm acting captain. And your name and rank, please?"

All this crap about rank, again. Well, use what works. Barton said, "Barton. Vice-admiral of the first fleet. Now on detached service."

Szabo's forehead wrinkled, then cleared. "Oh, *that* Barton. Well, we're honored, I'm sure. But you people didn't carry military rank. Or even quasi-military, such as ours here. I—"

"We had to pick up on that," Barton said, "in order to make sense with the second fleet." No point in divulging that the "we" in his statement was the editorial kind. "You want to hear how the Demu war came out?"

"It's over? That's wonderful news. That is, I assume we won, or you wouldn't be here."

"Basically," said Barton, "we called it off without any real shooting. On our terms, though, so you could say we won, I guess."

He'd made a dent in this Szabo, but the man was resilient. Now the frown came again. "I'm certainly glad to hear it, Barton. But, this vice-admiral business. Do you mean that you intend to assume command of this ship? Certainly you outrank—"

"Hell, no! What kind of sense would it make for an outsider to move into the middle of a touchy situation and try to take over?"

"But then—"

Barton had him going, now. "Look, Captain—Acting Captain, whatever—you're in command and you'll get all the cooperation I can give you. You started talking rank, is all, so I thought I'd clear it, right now, that I'm nobody's flunkey."

Jeez!—less than two minutes, and in a hassle already. But Szabo nodded. "Yes. Yes, of course. Barton, once we match vectors, it's essential that we transship supplies as quickly as possible. That means every able-bodied person who can handle a spacesuit, working long hours. Including me. But once that's done, I want us to take time, you and I, to sit down to a solid briefing. There's a lot you need to know about this ship, that you won't have found in the official tapes."

"I'm sure." And the briefing *would* help, because then he and Limila would have less cover to keep. Tricky keeping track, though, it was going to be. "And thanks, Captain. Now, do you want to talk me in yourself, to match up, or turn it over to the pilot on watch?"

"I'll do it," said Ferenc Szabo. He did a good job, too.

When the ships neared closely, they had to cut their Shields to get any closer. For moments, Barton was tempted to sleep-gun the other ship and run the show his own way, from scratch. But he put that thought aside; Barton was given to doing things his own way, but this would be a little too much like playing God, and that had never been one of his inclinations. So he listened, instead, and learned something new. Which was that two ships at very close range—these new big ships, anyway —could synchronize their Shields into one, holding the two in a fixed configuration. "Theoretically," said Ferenc Szabo, "it can be done with three or more. But as far as I know, that's never been tried." For a moment he looked surprised. "In fact," he said, "I believe this is the first time it's actually been done at all."

Barton was glad Szabo hadn't told him that until they'd done it.

The only times Barton had ever worked outship in a suit had been in drills while the first fleet drove from Earth to Tilara. He remembered well enough to do a fair share of work, but expert wasn't the word for his performance. Well, he didn't see too many others doing much better. All available personnel, he gathered, or as many as there were suits for, were sweating on this job. Even with the power equipment on both ships, it took a lot of muscle. Soon he was all over aches and pains and blisters, and once a crate dropped on his foot but didn't break anything. One man, he heard, had a heart attack, but not fatal. And he saw Ferenc Szabo, during a galley break, wearing a splint on a smashed thumb. He saw Bearpaw, too, but had no chance to talk with the man.

Then, finally, it was over, and Barton and Limila gathered their meager gear, to take to the other ship. She hadn't tried to work in transshipment because she'd never worn a suit: Barton helped her into one and towed her across the gap between ships. And then Szabo, controlling the other Shield over a wideband circuit, cut both Shields for a moment and the derelict dropped away. Barton saw him restore his own ship's Shield, and felt acceleration resume.

Well, he'd bought this situation, Barton had. Now he was stuck with it, for sure.

Whether somebody had been moved to give him and Limila quarters, Barton didn't know. But from his stay on the other ship, he knew they were in officers' country. He felt like sleeping for a week, but one day and night

464

brought him around, a little stiff and sore, otherwise feeling not too bad at all.

As soon as he was alert enough to think to do so, Barton began checking his own reactions to see if anything—Others, or maybe Children—was messing with his mind and feelings. If so, he couldn't spot it. Well, he'd keep checking. . . .

Limila was out prowling the ship, getting acquainted. They'd decided she might as well, while Barton was resting up after all that work, and that it might be interesting if at first she pretended very little grasp of human language. She hadn't detected any sign of fiddling with her own mind, but maybe Tilarans were immune.

So when the door chime sounded, Barton was in his nakeds, standing by the coffee-maker and wondering why it didn't work right. He hesitated, then decided to answer the door. And to take no chances that this outfit might be touchy about nudity, he grabbed his shirt and pants, and got them on and padded barefoot to the door.

Renton Bearpaw stood there. Barton said, "C'mon in," and went back to the coffee gadget. He heard the door shut, and Bearpaw's steps following him. "I'd offer coffee if I could make this thing cough it up. Or maybe you'd rather have a drink. I think we got some."

"Coffee's fine." The man moved to touch a switch Barton had overlooked, and the machine operated just as it had, earlier, for Limila. So Barton poured for both of them, and they sat, and Barton waited. Until Bearpaw said, "We have to talk. There's a lot, on this ship, that you probably don't know about. That you need to know, and it wasn't in the official reports."

Barton took a deep breath. This man's cooperation had been one of the big question marks. Now Barton said, "Some of it, I do know. I've heard your tapes, Bearpaw."

Word-for-word recall wasn't one of Barton's strong points, so it took a few minutes to clarify how much he knew, and how much not. Finally the younger man nodded. "You have most of it, I think. Maybe you'd better ask the questions; it might be faster."

Barton thought back. "You never mentioned how your Lisa came out. Or the little blonde, either." If you want people to be on your side, he figured, you should show

465

a little interest. And as a matter of fact, Bearpaw's story *had* got him concerned.

Looking surprised, the man said, "Yes, you'd know about them, wouldn't you?" His expression relaxed. "Well, Lisa did fine. Elys had a bad time, but she's rallied pretty well. You'll have to meet them soon, and Mark Gyril. Because you and the Tilaran woman need some intensive coaching, in how to keep the Others off your mental backs."

Barton nodded. But his next question was: What kind of stuff had been coming in from Base, lately?

Not much, was the answer; Comm wasn't busy, these days. During the transfer of supplies, the whole place had been held down by a sixty-five-year-old woman and a man with one leg, working alternate twelve-hour shifts and sleeping a lot. What the ship received was routine announcements that went to everybody. "Maybe somebody just forgot to cut us off the distribution list. Lisa says not; she thinks Base wants to keep us feeling part of the team. A way of reinforcing our drive to follow orders and get lost." Bearpaw shrugged. "I don't argue; she's the psychologist."

The statement didn't seem to call for comment. While Barton was trying to think what to ask next, the intercom came on. Announcement: officers and ratings to meet in galley. Bearpaw stood. "That's Ferenc's idea. Get us together and hammer on our group-purpose button a little, every so often. You're included, I'd imagine. If you want to come."

"Sure," said Barton. "Let's go." He put shoes on first.

Sitting beside Renton Bearpaw, watching Szabo get up front to start talking, Barton tried to settle his impressions of the man. Somehow the deepset blue eyes, the high cheekbones, and gaunt jaw gave Barton an odd feeling. Like a picture he'd seen once, of an avenging saint with a flaming sword. But that was silly.

One thing wasn't, though. Barton had never considered himself a combative type, but on the other hand there had been damn few men he'd back down from. Looking at this one, the way he moved and the implicit surety of him, Barton knew that against Ferenc Szabo he would stand no chance at all. And the man was a crowder; given his history, he'd have to be that. Well, Barton had set up a good start. Maybe with luck he could keep it that way.

Now Szabo began talking; belatedly, Barton tuned his ears in. " . . . have to stay on our guard, against the Others' influence, for a considerable time. Nearly a year, we estimate, before our fuel supply is down to the no-return point for re-crossing the dead belt and reaching an inhabited world. Which we must *not* do."

He hesitated, and from the way it looked on him, Barton decided he didn't do it very often. "I'm afraid Base made an error," he said, "in ordering us to return exactly the way we had come. For this puts us passing near Opal again, while we still have fuel enough to undo all our endeavors. I don't look forward to being within range, at that point, of the Others' massed influence."

"Why not change course?" Barton didn't see who asked it.

Smiling in no happy fashion at all, Szabo said, "Yes; obviously, that would be the ideal solution. The only difficulty is that I can't seem to manage to do it."

His further explanation was clear enough. Concentrating on following Base's "get lost" order exactly was hard enough. Making changes on it was impossible, because such a move laid minds open to the Others' manipulation. Szabo had tried, and barely stopped himself from turning the ship back toward Earth. No smile, now.

"If *anyone* here is capable of deviating from the letter of our orders, changing course to avoid Opal, without losing the purpose to carry out the spirit of those orders, I will turn command over to that person."

A few hands went up, wavered, and were withdrawn. Barton's wasn't one of them; he didn't want command, and he had no idea whether he could resist a mental pressure he'd never felt.

The meeting ended with the whole group reciting Base's "get lost" directive. Barton gathered that this had become a ritual, and looking at the faces of those around him, it seemed to help.

Bearpaw, standing with another man and two women, beckoned to Barton and Limila. Barton wasn't surprised to be introduced to Lisa Teragni, Elys Rounds, and Mark Gyril; they all fit the descriptions Bearpaw had given in the tape, except that words didn't do justice to the bold modeling of Teragni's features. And Bearpaw

467

hadn't mentioned the way her coarse black hair frizzed out, as if electrostatically charged. She shook hands like a lumberjack, and said, "We're heading for a conference. Consider yourselves invited."

They went to Gyril's office, and the slim man offered brandy, and said, "Ren, you were filling them in, and you know how far you got with it. Care to continue?"

So, starting from where the tapes had ended, Bearpaw began bringing things up to date. Dahil and Tiriis, the two Others, kept to themselves in the nursery, at the far reach of the quarters space. With them, helping out, were several non-pregnable women who had volunteered for the work. Szabo had arranged a buffer zone of vacant, sealed compartments between the nursery and the crew's living space. "The feeling of insulation may be purely in our heads," said Bearpaw, "but it's more comforting than you might think. Maybe not all that comforting to the volunteers, though."

Impatient, Barton said, "Okay, so that's the quo of it. Any plans, though? And any results?"

Bearpaw shrugged. "Lots of ideas that haven't panned out. I still like one of mine. To fake an order from Base, up in Comm—with confirmation, if necessary—to change course and miss Opal."

"It wouldn't work," said Lisa Teragni. "Ferenc would see through it in two shakes. That man couldn't let himself be fooled, even if he wanted to in the worst way." She turned to Gyril. "Mark, tell them how you're fighting the Others' veto on your research."

Barton liked the man's smile. "They can't stop the empirical approach, because they can't know where it's going next. And they've never managed to bollix *everything* I try to do. I think they spot-check us and stop whatever might be close to working."

Current project was the chemical approach to mental resistance. "You mean," Barton said, "get zonked on the right stuff and you can tell the Others to scoff off? Put them out of commission?"

"Something like that," said Gyril. "Not to harm them, though; none of us wants that. And I prefer to think those are our own feelings, not the result of mental influence." Well, Barton could go with that. Especially since he had some ideas of his own, as to what was happening.

"To approach the matter as randomly as possible,"

468

Gyril said, "I used nearly a hundred different drugs, labeled only with numbers assigned by chance." Anything from aspirin and caffeine through hash to L.S.D., Barton gathered. Somebody picked a pill or whatever, marked the number on Gyril's list, then started thinking anti-Others thoughts. The game was to see how near the person could get to the nursery before the Others changed that thinking.

"I tried Number 32," Bearpaw said. "Turned out to be coca extract. Twenty feet down the corridor, they had me purring like a pussycat. On the same stuff, somebody else stayed hostile all the way to the nursery door. So the Others are playing the random game, too, right back at us."

"Of course," said Gyril. "But if we find something they can't block, no matter what, the game's over."

Maybe. But somehow, Barton wouldn't have bet on it.

The party broke up. Elys Rounds hadn't said much. She looked older than Barton had expected, but he remembered she'd had a tough time carrying her alien fetus. Bearpaw said, later, that she'd aged badly during that time but was slowly coming back from it. "She hates the scar, though—keeps her belly covered at all times. Gyril's studying up on cosmetic surgery, for when the scar tissue stabilizes." And Barton found himself wishing for Raymond Parr, who had done such a superb job on Limila, with worse to start from.

The trouble was, Barton thought, that these people were in a rut. They were trying to make some headway, sure, but after so many months they couldn't seem to find much urgency about it.

Then suddenly there was some. Barton was at Gyril's when the woman came bursting in with a full load of hysterics. After listening, Barton didn't blame her a bit.

She'd delivered a routine consignment of supplies to the nursery, but this time Dahil had pulled her inside and gone into his cup routine. With the usual results, of course.

"I won't go through that again! I'll kill myself!" She wouldn't, Barton knew; several had tried that on the first round, but never succeeded. The Others simply wouldn't allow it.

Gyril seemed to have an idea, though; maybe in his trial-and-error way he'd learned a few things. He got the woman up on the worktable and began mixing a solution, and filled a syringe. "Excuse us a minute, Barton." As Barton, in the interests of modesty, went into the next room, Gyril was repeating, "It's only a minor infection, but we'd better take care of it."

When Gyril called him back, the woman was gone. "What'd you do?"

The Medic-chief smiled. "The rigamarole was to throw the Others off the track, in case they were monitoring. I filled her womb with a harmless colloid jelly that solidifies at body temperature, then breaks down after about three days and drains out again. It has other uses; I didn't invent it on the spur of the moment. But meanwhile the fertilized ovum is stuck; it can't implant itself in the uterine wall in time to survive and multiply. She won't be pregnant."

Quickly now, Gyril used the intercom. Without asking anyone for authority, he pulled all women off nursery-delivery detail. He needed Szabo's okay to post male guards and keep women out of the nursery vicinity entirely, but before he obtained it, two unlucky women got the cup and the rest of it. Gyril had them come in immediately, but apparently the Others weren't about to be fooled twice by the jelly thing, because he couldn't make it work. He kept getting the clumsies and spilling things. Modesty or no modesty, he got Barton in to help, and they both tried. Now Barton saw what the Others' influence was like; he couldn't *feel* anything from outside himself, but he kept making mistakes. And he knew something was suppressing his natural anger at such frustration.

Finally Gyril faced the two frightened women and shook his head. "I'm sorry. I've tried my best, but I can't help you."

The younger one said, "You mean, we're stuck to bear *Children* again?" When Gyril nodded, Barton saw tears jarred loose. The other woman put an arm around the one who had spoken; without further words, they both left.

Gyril said, "It's the same as when we were trying to get the X-rays. And experience, it seems, is no help at all."

The next reaction that hit the ship was something the Others couldn't stop; Barton saw what Bearpaw had

470

meant about group concentration, because with *everyone* savagely determined that no more women would be impregnated to bear Children for the Others, things got a little bloody. Mark Gyril wrote the instructions and Elys Rounds checked them without advance knowledge of their contents, and absolutely nobody said anything out loud to help clue the Others as to intentions, while the men read those instructions off the various screens.

Luckily, contraceptive implants weren't stuck very deeply into the muscle tissues. Most of the men cut them out of the women's thighs without making too much of a mess. Afterward, the Others didn't interfere with various medics' work in cleaning up the damage; there wouldn't have been much point in doing so.

Barton wasn't sure they all had the best answer, but it was one they could depend on. You can't get pregnant if you're *already* pregnant, they'd learned, the first time around.

So for a time, with people hanging around in groups for mutual support and the hell with privacy, getting pregnant was the name of the game. Getting safely, *humanly*, pregnant. And mostly, they did, what with removal of the implants giving an immediate fertility backlash. Including three who, Barton gathered from what Gyril said, had thought themselves past the capability but wanted to be on the safe side, just in case.

The Others' second round, then, gained them only the two victims that Barton and Gyril hadn't been able to help. Plus Tiriis, the female Other—a young man reported, much embarrassed, that when he delivered a consignment to the nursery, what he thought was a cup of coffee turned out not to be. Barton could take it from there.

"When the rush started," Bearpaw told him, "I suppose some of the younger studs thought it was the answer to their prayers. Not for long, though." He frowned. "It can't be much fun making love with a frightened woman who sees you only as a source of seed. And a lesser evil, at that."

Still, near as Barton could tell, the feeling on the ship was one of victory. At least the burden of fear was mostly lifted. Elys Rounds said once that she wouldn't bet against the Others being able to abort the whole lot and start over. But whether they could have or not, nothing of the sort happened.

Barton and Limila had talked it over and decided not to enter the sweepstakes, because she was by no means recovered from her injuries, so it could be dangerous for her to conceive. If she would ever have ability to bear child again; they didn't know.

They counted on two things. First, the normal Tilaran control over ovulation: Could the Others override it, or not? Second, if the Others could intuit Limila's difficulties, would they risk her safety? Lacking any solid answers, the two decided to stand pat. And didn't feel like hanging around in groups that were taking the other option, because they didn't feel at home with them.

So one day Barton returned to quarters and found Limila sitting up in bed, nude, and rubbing her belly. She looked wide-eyed at him, and said, "Barton, it may be we have made a mistake."

"What—?" The story came short enough. Knock on the door, and she opened it to admit no human. Bearpaw's description of the Others, she said, was quite accurate. This one, male, had to be Dahil, and that was what he had called himself. And he had the cup with him, and its odor made her drink. "Before I realized . . ."

"But how did he *get* here, past the guards?" Oh, sure; if they could teleport up from a planet to a ship! Barton shook his head. This is what they got for not going along with the group thing. He didn't ask, "Then what?" But she told him, anyway.

"There is one thing I know," she said then, "and one that I do not. I think Dahil thought inside me and healed me; the long, nagging pain is gone now. The thing I do not know is, whether he and his cup overrode my own control of ovulation, at crisis moment."

Not liking it at all, Barton had to settle for that. Then he thought again, and decided that if she had it right about the healing, everybody was still ahead of the game. He didn't say so, because right now she might not see it that way.

Barton had had several briefing sessions with Ferenc Szabo, and by now he was beginning to feel more at ease with the man. He realized that a lot of his misgivings came from what Bearpaw had taped about the original edition, and now he recognized that Szabo emanated tension because on this ship, it naturally centered on him. Barton still played his cards close, though, sticking to what he'd learned on the ship itself, near as he could keep track. Because his own ideas differed a little, from everybody else's.

He was in Szabo's quarters, the two of them talking while Barton sampled a kind of wine from Blaine's Mistake, that had a faint tinge of pepper to it, when Ferenc Szabo said something about feeling sorry for the two women he'd helped impregnate, recently, during the rush.

And without meaning to, hearing his mouth work without benefit of brain, Barton said, "Must have been a nice change, though."

And saw Szabo, catlike, lean forward. Face taut, not menacing, but certainly feral. "You know. Who told you?"

Barton's nape prickled, but he shrugged, and said, "Coming out here on this mission, wouldn't you expect I'd get a scan on the records?" Always nice, he thought, to avoid an outright lie.

"Oh." Even letting the air out of himself, Szabo looked graceful. His smile looked forced, but Barton gave him points for trying. "With people I know, I'm not self-conscious about it now. But you're largely a stranger, so you gave me a jolt."

"Then let's quit being strangers." Barton had the initiative, he knew. To hold it, he poured himself more wine, and then some for Szabo. Taking a slice of the host role couldn't hurt. And now Barton did the leaning-forward bit, and waited.

Until Szabo said, "What it's like. That's what they all wanted to know, the medics and psycho-techs and such. The truth is that at the time I couldn't tell them; I didn't know." He shook his head. "It's a subtle matter, Barton. Something that isn't felt at all unless there's something to compare with, and sensory memory fades so soon! But change!—when the Others made me right, when they turned me back off, then restored me—change can't be mistaken." Pausing, Szabo seemed bewildered. "Have I answered you?"

Barton nodded. "Yeh. Yeh, I think you have. And, hey—Ferenc, I'm damn glad for you, man."

Then, talking about nothing at all personal, they drank

473

the rest of the Blaine wine before Barton left. He still wasn't sure he'd cleared the air all the way, but for now it was the best he could do.

As the ship neared Opal again—"that beautiful trap," as Bearpaw put it—Barton watched everybody begin to tighten up around the edges. He saw Ferenc Szabo, pushing for group support of the directive from Base, leaning on everybody at officers' meetings with the full force of his personality. Which, Barton admitted to himself, was plenty. The tight policy of need-to-know had long since been junked; meeting proceedings were screened to all the ship except the Other-controlled nursery. Like it or not, all the crew knew the score. Some, Barton gathered, didn't like it too much.

But when there aren't any good answers, he thought, you have to take the best you can get.

Nobody had to guess about the point when the ship came close enough to Opal for the Others there to exert influence; the pressure hit like a great wave. Barton, walking into quarters, staggered and almost fell. When he caught his balance he found that he had turned and was heading for the control area, so that he could change course and take the ship to Opal.

"No!" He grabbed a door handle, closed his eyes, and forced himself to stand still while he fought his mind back to purpose. When he had a stalemate—he couldn't get rid of the pressure entirely, but he could withstand it—he hurried up to Control, anyway. But now, to make sure nobody else did what he'd wanted to do, only minutes before.

Before he got there he could hear the noise, and he ran in to find maybe half a dozen people in a free-for-all wrestling match. Two others were down already, and as Barton tried to guess who was on which side, another fell. Leaning over someone in the chief pilot's seat was Ferenc Szabo; he pulled the man up and out, and hit him once; the man dropped. Szabo leaned over the controls and did something Barton couldn't see.

A woman screamed, "Opal! Opal!," and came at Barton; he gave her a jab of stiffened fingers in the solar plexus and doubled her over. He ducked a man's haymaker swing and chopped the side of his hand against the neck.

Except for Szabo, the rest were thrashing around together on the deck; Barton ignored them and approached the acting captain. "Stop right there, Barton!"

"Sure." Barton stopped. "Just one thing, though." Barton breathed deeply; if he had to tackle this man, he needed all the oxygen he could get. "I hope we're still on course. Are we?"

And Szabo relaxed. "We are now. Jessup had started to turn us, but I set it right again." His sweating face grinned. "In fact, I think I managed to overcontrol a little, being a bit shaky, you understand, so we'll pass wider from Opal now."

For those who had succumbed to the Others' sudden onslaught, there was no talk of punishment; once their directed actions were stopped, they came back to normal, fighting the nagging pressures as well as anyone. Barton was surprised at how quickly the group spirit was restored —and at how much it seemed to help him personally.

The way Bearpaw put it was, "We built unity on the determination that no woman would bear Children again if we could help it. Add fear to unity, on top of the basic sex urge, and it's an act that's hard to beat." The Others were still trying, though. Barton could feel it all the way through, and it hurt.

Next time he saw Bearpaw, the man was heading from Comm to captain's quarters, carrying a flimsy. He said, "Base figured out that they forgot to tie the other shoe; now they're trying to fix it, too late. This is the first non-routine message we've had since the crucial directive. Top Priority, which is why I have to deliver it in person."

The Comm-man sounded a little rattled; Barton got in step with him and asked, "What's it say? Or am I supposed to know?"

"Here; read it." Barton took the paper, skipped past the usual gibberish that tells who's saying what to whom, and read:

TOP PRIORITY. Change course immediately to avoid vicinity of planet called Opal. This urgent; repeat, urgent. Change course, avoid planet Opal. If this is impossible, destruct ship at once. Repeat, destruct ship at once. End, TOP PRIORITY.

He handed the message back, and said only, "Destruct,

huh? How did that silly word get into the jargon? Destroy says the same thing; why not use it?"

"Let's hope we don't have to do either one."

At his quarters, Ferenc Szabo invited them in. As he read the message, Barton saw strain grow in his face, ridging muscles. "Too late. Why are they always too late?" If he wasn't close to breaking point, Barton had never seen anyone who was. He tried to think what to say, that might help, but came up blank.

Bearpaw spoke. "We're making it, Ferenc. *You're* making it. We're almost as near Opal as we're going to be, and nobody's cracking. We're taking all they can throw, and still holding."

The man shook his head. "The Children, they're not in it yet. Can we take *that?*"

"They're not developed enough, Gyril says, to influence us, except for direct self-defense. I think he's right. Because, do you think the Others would be holding anything back *now?*"

"No," said Ferenc, "they wouldn't. And they're not." He nodded toward the door. It opened; two Others entered, and he said, "I was expecting you."

Again, Barton thought, Bearpaw's descriptions had been accurate. Even so, he wasn't prepared for the effect the two aliens made, his inner confusion: were they people, or weren't they?

The door closed. "Man Szabo," they said, together.

"That's man Ferenc, if you don't mind. What do you want?"

The male—Dahil, that would be—said, "Turn ship and land our planet, man Ferenc."

"Like hell I will!"

"Any way, so you do. You do. You do now." The aliens moved forward, flanking him, ignoring the other two men.

"In a pig's hat! This is my ship. Get out of here."

"Yes," said Dahil, "will get out."

"Yes," echoed the female, Tiriis. "Soon will go."

But they didn't, just then. They both looked at Ferenc Szabo, and in about a minute he grabbed his crotch and went pale.

"Yes, man Szabo," said Dahil. "Land our planet or be not right, so ever."

"Land, you be right," Tiriis said, and nodded vigorously. "Land?"

On the man's face, Barton saw it happen. The humanity went out of it; he saw the killer that Bearpaw had feared. Barton shivered; he was seeing a monster reborn. He looked away, but he couldn't stop hearing.

"You *fools!* You utter, ignorant fools! Do you know what you've done?"

Dahil smiled. "Yes, man Szabo. Now we land our planet."

"No," said Szabo. "Not now, or ever. This isn't how I'd have wanted it, but it's a way out." He turned to the other two men; Barton wished he hadn't. "Get out of here; I don't want you dead!"

Neither did Barton, but he figured to have to stay, anyway. He shook his head and backed away, hoping his face looked more friendly than frozen. Bearpaw didn't leave, either.

Szabo turned back to Dahil; the man was panting like at the end of a long, hard run. "You had to pull the pin out of the grenade, didn't you? You had to explode something you don't even understand."

Close to screaming, now, he said, "Don't you *see?* When I was this way before, I killed one of you. Didn't that tell you anything? Then you made me right, and for the first time in fifteen years, I was human again. And you can control humans, can't you?"

Not too many things scared Barton, usually, but Szabo's smile did, then. Almost casually, he took Dahil by one arm and threw him across the room. About halfway up the wall, the Other hit; when he dropped to the floor, he didn't look too well.

Szabo turned to Tiriis. "You made a mistake." Quietly, he said it. "You thought this would make me obey you. Instead, it will let me kill you. And," he added in a thoughtful tone, "the Children, too."

He reached for Tiriis, gently, or so it looked, but she wasn't having any. She tried for the door; he was there ahead of her. Clearly, he could have caught her if he'd wanted to. He said, "To end this, to allow the ship to go home again, I will kill you two, and the Children. Not the women who are bearing more Children, for they can still be aborted. But the Children first."

And the two Others, the only ones who could make

477

him right again, last? Barton wondered if that was a conscious part of the man's thinking.

"And there's no way you can stop me now, is there?" Szabo whispered. "No way at all." Going out, he slammed the door so hard so that the door chime jingled.

Bearpaw gave a nervous laugh. "If that's a victory bell, I'm not sure it's worth it." Barton didn't answer; he was thinking that with the Others' powers, there must have been a number of changes they could have thought into Szabo, that might have sapped his will instead of unleashing the tiger. But Szabo himself had said, downside on Opal, that logic wasn't their strong point. Well, the tiger wouldn't give them another chance; that was for sure.

Tiriis tugged at the two men, urging them to help her with Dahil. Barton couldn't see the point; he didn't especially want to see the aliens dead, but he wasn't calling the shots. For now, though, the injured Other might as well be as comfortable as possible, so feeling like a soft touch, Barton helped move Dahil onto a couch. He wasn't exactly unbroken around the outskirts, the way Szabo had played billiards with him, but given the chance, it looked as if he could heal up all right. Except for the arm, maybe, that Szabo had used for a throwing handle.

Tiriis waved the men off and bent over Dahil, chanting something under her breath; Barton caught a sort of tune, but no words. After a time the alien came awake, which Barton wouldn't have bet on for a day or two, and they put their heads together and chanted low-volume harmony. Then they sat back, Tiriis apparently trying to comfort Dahil in ways that weren't clear to Barton.

The wait stretched out, but Barton didn't feel like leaving. Then the door opened, and Ferenc came in. Not Szabo the monster, but Ferenc the human; the difference was all over his face.

He looked at the two Others and shook his head. "I'm not sure who won this round, or whether I'm glad or sorry. You were in time; you caught me well short of the nursery." He shrugged. "As I say, I don't know who won. Obviously, I'm better off right and you're better off alive. But what this means to my race, I don't know."

His voice hardened. "We won't try this again; I assure you of that. You will go to the nursery, and not leave it again without my permission. I've increased the guard throughout the ship, and given shoot-to-kill instructions.

I think your abilities fall short of ensuring that *no* guard will be able to follow my orders."

He wasn't done yet. "Don't think to tamper with my sexuality again—not for blackmail, or revenge, or plain spite. If you do, I will wipe your kind of life off this ship *and*, to the best of my capabilities, off your home planet. Is that fully clear?"

To Barton it was. This ship's giant laser could wipe out villages like so many anthills, and the sleep-gun's field, on wide spread, could turn escaping stragglers into drooling zombies. Of course, no human, close enough to Opal to use those weapons against the Others, *could* use them. But Szabo could, the Szabo that Barton had seen briefly. So the way to keep Opal safe was to keep Ferenc Szabo "right." Barton figured they'd get the point.

The Others went back to their own area and stayed there, and the ship passed Opal and receded from it until the pressure from the Others on that planet diminished and finally vanished entirely. The battle was over, and until Ren Bearpaw told him, Barton hadn't even thought of the scariest part, the thing that hadn't happened after all.

"If we'd come within their teleporting range," the Comm-man said, "and suddenly the ship had been full of Others, we'd've been cooked for sure."

"Thanks," Barton said. Then seeing puzzlement, he clarified it. "I mean, thanks for not telling me any sooner."

As Opal fell behind, Barton could feel the tensions ebb. After the mass influence from that planet, the efforts of Dahil and Tiriis were easy to resist, even for Barton. As Gyril put it, "We had mental muscles we hadn't known about. Now that we've exercised them, they're in better shape."

Now and then Barton felt a really heavy wave of pressure, very general, not concentrated; for seconds it practically knocked him on his head, but didn't make him want to *do* anything. Mark Gyril said it was the Children, warming up under direction. The ship was still a time short of no-return when the surges became more than petty nuisance. So there was still a race on—the humans and the fuel supply against the Others and the Children.

"But why don't we just *dump* some fuel?" Lisa Teragni

asked. They were in meeting at Gyril's and Elys's quarters, and Ferenc Szabo had joined the informal cabal. Ren Bearpaw shrugged; Barton, sitting alongside Limila, waited to see who had an answer. He wasn't sure how he could have jettisoned fuel from Ship One, in space, but he expected he could have managed it if he'd had to. This ship, though, he knew very little about, really.

When Ferenc started talking, Barton realized he knew even less than he'd thought. To beat light, a space-drive had to do two things. Get traction on space-time, and hold your space and time vectors closely in line to those of the rest of the universe, so as to avoid mass-increase and time-dilation. The Demu ships did those things, and so did Earth's first and second fleets, and this big tub had to do them, also. But this drive wasn't adapted from what Barton had swiped from the Demu; it did its jobs in a considerably different way. Not just the efficiency-improving multiplex of components that he'd seen in the great ship on Sisshain, but an all-out different approach.

The bottom line was that you couldn't mess with the fuel supply, in any way, without cutting power to the whole ship. So refueling was done only in dead orbit, or downside.

"There's standby power," Ferenc said, "for essential items such as keeping the computer's memory alive, and minimum Comm-gear. But that doesn't even cover life-support; in orbit the maintenance crews would work in suits. Of course, in the drive areas they'd need those against radiation, anyway." Which surprised Barton, because with the ships he knew, radiation was only a problem if you went too far up another ship's drive wake, above light-speed. Well, he hadn't planned on doing any drive maintenance, on here.

Another thing that surprised him was that ship's personnel wouldn't know all this stuff already. But he'd seen that with a crew this big, people specialized a lot more. Not like Ship One, where everybody did a little of everything.

Lisa wasn't done, though. "Then why don't we look for the *nearest* planet we could settle on? And leave the ship in orbit with the power off? Why couldn't we have done that, weeks ago?"

"Same reason we couldn't change course to avoid Opal," Bearpaw said. "Base didn't think of it, and we can't monkey with orders, or Dahil and Tiriis take over;

school's out for sure." She nodded, obviously she had to buy it, but Barton saw she was looking for still another answer. That she didn't quit easily . . .

Teragni's pregnancy was well along, but any time Barton had seen Ren Bearpaw getting solicitous about it, she'd laugh and put him off. "Compared to last time, this is like having eaten a little too much for dinner." And of course Barton realized another difference: this child, the two of them had begun on purpose. And the woman didn't have to be *afraid* of it.

When he and Limila' left the meeting and went back to quarters, Barton had occasion to think more on such matters. Because that was when Limila told him she was pregnant.

By Dahil, of course.

He looked at her, realizing that he'd been so taken up with the ship's problems, lately, that he hadn't been paying her more than perfunctory attentions. Her hair had grown long enough to hang nearly to her brows, in front, obscuring the high Tilaran hairline. But not yet long enough to pull back. Her silver-irised eyes stood wide now, and if she hadn't had her lower lip between her teeth, he thought it might have trembled. Probably not, though; she wasn't much given to that sort of thing.

Barton cleared his throat. "How do you feel about it?" Even to him, it sounded dumb, but he couldn't think of anything else to say. "Is there anything I can do?"

"Possibly. I want to see the Children. I want to know what it is, that my body carries."

Well, that was certainly reasonable enough. He stood. "I'll talk to Ferenc. We'll see what can be done."

Barton knew that the Others had let the Children be seen earlier, because Bearpaw had said so on the tapes, the censored parts that didn't tell much more than that fact. But later, Ferenc told him, they'd blocked attempts to observe the nursery—covered the eye-pickups, for instance. "I don't know why," the man said. "Maybe it's time we found out."

Limila accompanied the two men to the nursery. One of the human attendants met them there, and after a certain amount of argument, agreed to fetch Tiriis. At first the Other refused to let them in. Then Limila said, "You and I will bear the same kind of young. You know

481

what it will be; I do not. I think I have the same right, Tiriis." She stepped forward, and Tiriis gave a little ground, but not much. "My name is Limila."

Surprising Barton, Tiriis stepped back and aside. "Come, man Limila, and man Ferenc, and—"

"Man Barton," Barton said, and followed them. "You remember me, I think."

"Remember, yes. To help Dahil, did. To help man Limila, now?"

"Something like that." Tense, alert for mental pressure, Barton felt none. A few doors along the corridor, they entered a small room. The important thing in it was a viewscreen with fairly sophisticated controls. Tiriis turned it on.

Barton saw a number of smallish creatures climbing around in a three-dimensional lattice. Reaching, he zoomed in on one and froze the picture for a moment, then let it run again in real time.

It took him some while to absorb all the details, but in that first moment, Barton knew what he was seeing.

He turned to Limila. "This is of our prior knowledge."

And in the same language, she said, "And I think it will be of good, Barton, that of this time, at least, it remain so."

The head was almost pure Other, except that there were two more eyes, one at each rear corner of the braincase. Yes, Bearpaw had said, in one fragment, that any adjacent pair could work together. The median fur strip came to points above and below the rear pair of eyes, leaving a bare space between.

The rest of it: on a blocky torso, four arms and four legs, each with more digits than Barton was used to. He concentrated on details. Upper arms set about human style, lower—Other?—pair on movable shoulders with fore-and-aft traverse. All four legs shaped like a blend of human and Other; Barton saw that the Children walked flatfooted like humans but ran on the toes of their long feet. The outer pair of legs swung from hip joints that moved ahead and behind those of the inner pair. Same as the arms; yeh. *So this is what they're like.*

"As infants," Ferenc said from behind Barton, "they're clumsy. Remind you of a drunken spider. But they learn coordination fast. You see how they streak through that low-G jungle gym in there. Well, they can do that, long before they tackle prosaic things such as walking." He paused. "If you haven't noticed, they're male between the left pair of legs and female between the right. All elimination, though, is centrally located." Barton zoomed the picture; near as he could tell, it confirmed what Ferenc said. "The adult, it appears, will have four breasts, set approximately where humans and Others have their different placements." He repeated Bearpaw's quote of Gyril, on possible multiple births, but now it had context.

A little longer, Barton watched. There was no question about the Children's intelligence; watching the moves in a sort of flying tag game, he guessed they were using human-style logic and Other-style intuition about equally. Then one of them, startling Barton, disappeared from one side of the room and appeared at the other. And in moments they were all doing it. Just fun? A different stage of the game's rules? Barton didn't know, but one thing was clear. The only reason the Children weren't teleporting all over the ship—*if* they weren't, and just keeping out of sight—was because they didn't want to.

Then Dahil, injured arm strapped to his chest, entered the Children's room and made one slight gesture, and Barton had an alternate hypothesis. Because the game stopped; all the young creatures turned to face Dahil. The Other's mouth moved, but Barton could get no sound with the picture. Well, he couldn't know the language, anyway. But the point was, the Children gave Dahil instant obedience. So maybe the Children kept to the nursery because Dahil and Tiriis told them to. Barton had a quick thought that turning the Children over to the Others at birth might not have been the best move he'd ever heard of. But then he remembered that nobody had had much choice, about that.

Not that it mattered, because Barton knew, now, that sooner or later he was going to have to cross every Earthani on this ship.

He hoped he was up to it.

He turned to Limila. "Seen enough?" She nodded; so did Ferenc, and then Tiriis led them back to the nursery entrance. There Barton paused, and looked at the female Other, seeing things about her that nobody else on the ship was likely to see. Except Limila, of course. He said,

"Tiriis, I thank you, for what you've shown us just now."
Then they left her, and went up the several levels to
officers' country. Ferenc accepted Barton's invitation to
come in for a drink or so. And once everybody was sitting down with a full glass, Barton had some questions to
ask. For starters: "Ferenc, what's our timing?"

"Until our nominal no-return day? About a week. It's
been some time since we could have reached Earth, or
Tilara. But if the charts are accurate, we could still make
it to one of the Demu planets. And refuel, and go again
from there."

Barton had been ready to laugh. The idea of the Others trying their cup routine on the exoskeletal Demu
struck him funny. Come to think of it, that business
would hardly work with the Larka-Te, or the Filjar,
either. But with the Tilari it sure as hell did. So he didn't
laugh. Instead, he asked, "For now, what's most important?"

"Not to relax vigilance," Szabo said. The door chime
interrupted his next remark; Barton went to admit Ren
Bearpaw, got him sat down with a drink of his own, and
waved for Ferenc to go on. The man said, "I was pointing out, Ren, that we should be braced for a last-minute
mental push by the Others. We're so close to securing the
situation that it would be easy to let down and be caught
off guard."

"Not when you keep telling us," Barton said. "And it's
good, your doing that. Change of subject, though." He
looked at both men, and at Limila. "What do you think
of the Children? How do you feel about them?"

"Scared," said Bearpaw. "Oh, not of anything they'll
do, directly. I think they're no more given to violence than
the Others are, and maybe less." For a moment, Barton
took exception; then it struck him that the fighting in
Control had been *human* reaction to the Others' influence. He shrugged, and listened. "What I'm afraid of,
I guess, is what the Children are going to *be*."

Ferenc Szabo scowled. "I know," he said. "It's a hard
thing to say, but the thing I wish most is that I could be
one of them. Since I can't, obviously, I wish they didn't
exist."

Before Barton could say anything, the man continued.
"It would be meaningless, as well as cruel, of course,
to eliminate the young creatures on this ship. Even if

484

such a terrible act were possible. For their counterparts exist on Opal, as well."

Barton chilled, a little. *This man's coming close.*

Bearpaw stood. "I'm due on watch. These days it's about as busy as a chess match between two corpses, but that's what I get paid for." Suddenly he looked surprised. "Except that there isn't any pay now, is there? We just keep doing the job because it's there."

Barton had to smile; since he first left Earth with Tarleton's fleet, he hadn't thought much about pay. He said, "There's a lot of it going around, Ren. Might's well get your loyal butt on duty."

So Bearpaw left, and the other man not long afterward. Then Barton said, "Limila. You haven't said. Seeing the Children, how do *you* feel?"

Maybe without knowing she did it, Limila clasped her hands across her swelling belly. "I am not certain. I think —Barton, I am torn between two things. Fear is one; the other may be honor."

For a long time then, until Limila calmed, Barton held her.

When the sirens woke Barton, he didn't know a hoot in hell, what was going on. He didn't find out in a hurry, either. He grabbed clothes and shoes, told Limila it might be a good idea if she stayed put, for now, and went out in the corridor, moving fast to go see what was happening topside. When he stuck his head up past the next-level deck, somebody came close to blowing it off with a standard explosive bullet.

Well, the hell with *that*. Faster than he thought he could, Barton snaked back down to quarters and rousted his luggage for what he wanted right now. The sleep-gun's indicator showed a fair grade of charge; his portable Shield-harness, its charge lamp, gave an intermittent blink. Maybe it would hold up for a while, and maybe not. Hardly an optimum situation, but you go with what you have, so Barton went.

This time, climbing, Barton wasn't Mr. Dumbjohn; he kept his head down and his gun up. His infantry stretch, in Nam, was a long time ago, but the techniques came back fast. Only the first person to shoot bullets at him got off more than two. Nobody hit him, but that, of course, needed him a lot of luck. Though it did strike him that he'd never seen so many lousy shots in one fracas.

Going up, he met Ren Bearpaw coming down. Then they got cornered on a landing; no way to go, at all. Barton was trying to figure whether he could jump and catch the next-level railing, or maybe the next one down, if it didn't tear his arm off, when somebody on a bullhorn offered truce.

So while there was still enough confusion that he might get away with it, Barton dropped his sleep-gun and Shield-harness down the stairwell. If they didn't break, maybe he could find them later.

Then he surrendered. He and Renton Bearpaw, both.

And once it turned out they were disarmed, nobody wanted them for anything. Seemed stupid, but Barton wasn't going to argue.

And after all the shooting there were only five casualties, none fatal.

To find out what had happened, though, took Barton a while. The answers, then, were simple enough. In the best defense, there's always a hole. This one was, the Others had got on a young medic who was running a fever and not concentrating too well, and influenced him to drug the man guarding Captain Soong's detention quarters. Since the mental command was totally outside the resistance pattern everyone was focusing on, it caught the groggy man unaware.

Freed, the captain got on the intercom and rounded up his personal guards. Working for him, they'd had privileges; under Ferenc Szabo, they didn't. The goons came running. Armed, they took Comm and Control, and had Ferenc Szabo bottled up in Soong's former quarters; their orders were to blow his head off if he showed it. "Poor old Nargilosa, in Control—she's working with a gun at her head, too," said Bearpaw. "Not necessary, that; she's always saying how Ferenc overstepped the bounds by stashing dear Captain Soong away." And probably, he added, the only reason she hadn't freed him herself was that she shared his profound horror of taking any initiative.

But when Soong was up against it personally, he could act, all right. He had a message sent to Base, in the clear, and read it aloud over intercom broadcast. Besides the official gibberish fore and aft, he said, "I have taken command. The mutinous Szabo is confined to quarters. Since I was wrongfully deprived of command when your latest order was received, and was unable to give you the correct information, the order is invalid. I cannot be bound by it. Accordingly, I am reversing course and returning to Base as soon as possible. Soong, Commanding."

Looking at Barton, Bearpaw shook his head. "I wonder who wrote that for him; he never said anything that well in his life."

"Doesn't matter," Barton said. "He's only the mouthpiece for Dahil and Tiriis, anyway. And maybe the Children, too, by now." He made a lopsided smile. "He hasn't checked the fuel situation, though, if he still thinks he can get back to Base."

But that didn't matter, either, Barton realized. Somebody would tell Soong the facts of life, and if the ship couldn't reach a Demu planet, it could still make Opal. Which wouldn't give the Others the whole galactic Arm, right away, but human women would bear more Children. "For what good it might do," he said, "could we sneak a message through to Base somehow?"

"Not a chance." Bearpaw shook his head. "Once Rigan had sent that message, Soong disabled the F.T.L. transmitter. Wouldn't have expected him to know enough, but he did. Pulled out a couple of key components, and the spares are gone, too."

Damn it, there had to be something they could do! Barton said, "You been in touch with Ferenc yet?"

"Don't dare," said Bearpaw. "Anything on the intercom can be monitored, from Comm." Then, after a moment, he grinned. "I'm due on watch in a few minutes. Stay here. If it's safe to talk, I'll call here and let you know."

When he had left, Limila said, "What strange game do you play, Barton? When the time comes, to which side will you jump?"

Well, he hadn't expected to fool her, and come to that, he didn't want to. "I know. What must happen, will. But right now I'm on Elys Rounds' side—hers, and other women who aren't physically up to taking another of those long pregnancies. You saw the holo of her, taken two years ago; you can see how she's changed. And I don't imagine she's the only one."

Nodding, Limila said, "Yes. But Lisa Teragni, for in-

stance, does not seem to have been harmed. And I—"
She patted her belly. "So far, I feel no ill effects."

"Sure, and that's great." Time for a hug, Barton figured, and Limila responded. "If the Others would settle for volunteers, give full information instead of that sneaky cup business—"

The intercom interrupted him. "Bearpaw, calling from Comm. The coast's clear, and I've checked for taps; negative. I guess Soong figured that with our Phasewave out of business, Comm isn't important enough to waste his muscle on."

Well, either the Comm-man knew his business or he didn't. Now he brought Ferenc Szabo on the circuit. Barton gathered that Bearpaw had filled the besieged man in on any developments he hadn't known already. Now Ferenc said, "Hi, Barton. All right; things are about the way I had them figured, but it's better to know than to guess. I'm safe enough, for now; they can't get to me in here. Not without a lot more men than I think Soong can muster. But I may have a little trouble getting out." He'd made one try at it, he said, but no luck. They had him boxed, all right.

"We have to get you free," said Bearpaw, "and start thinking how to retake the ship. Any minute now, Soong could reverse course and lock it, under code. I can't imagine why he hasn't, already."

Ferenc laughed. "Because I locked the damn course myself, and changed codes when I did it. Soong couldn't break that in ten months, let alone ten days, and that's all he's got." Barton waited; the man would tell it without needing a question. "We're locked into match and orbit a planet I spotted on my last watch. Would have told you today, but all this mess came up. It's definitely a no-return stop, even for Opal. So stop worrying."

Stop worrying. Beautiful, Barton thought. Well, Ferenc was all right—plenty of food, and all. And Soong, Barton gathered, had his original quarters armored against anything his guard-boys could find to use now. Maybe he'd been more paranoid, all along, than anybody realized.

Fine. But Barton wished that *he* could stop worrying.

After a little more talk, Bearpaw signed off fast; Barton guessed he had company of the wrong persuasion. Ferenc was sure he had enough data to guarantee that his no-return planet was livable; Barton wished he could believe

488

that. He said so. "From this far out, how can you be sure?"

"I sent a high-G drone on an expendable fly-by. Launched it as soon as I made the sighting. What its pickups show—"

Under his breath, Barton used strong language. How many more gadgets had Group B kept to itself, that nobody told him about? And when would one of them trip him up?

Three quick buzzes came over the line; Barton guessed they were Bearpaw's warning that the circuit was being monitored, so he signed off fast. At the end he heard a few words in a woman's voice. Did Ferenc have a roommate now? He asked Limila.

"Had you not heard? The tall, fair woman, named Racelle." Yeh, Barton knew who she was; hadn't met her directly, though. The thing he remembered noticing was the way she moved, like a lazy tiger. He had a hunch the laziness was deceptive; in that case, the two would make a good team.

And Bearpaw had mentioned that she was the only woman who had managed to avoid carrying one of the Children to term. "I don't know how she did it, and the miscarriage nearly killed her. But that one, Barton, is something special." Which, from one who obviously admired his own ship-wife as much as Bearpaw did, was real praise.

Now Limila said, "I do not know if they have ship-married, as is the custom here, or not." She smiled. "On Ship One, things were not so formal, were they?"

"No." Barton thought about it. "I think what it is, maybe, is that with so many more people, like they have here, they need some formalities. To keep things from getting too scrambled." And with a few established customs to curb him, Barton thought, maybe Terike ap Fenn wouldn't have got so badly out of hand.

But that was fuel down the pipe. Now Barton stood. "Going to take a little walk," he said. "See if I can find my sleep-gun."

He wore a loose jacket over his jumpsuit, to hide the thing if he found it, and a belt inside to hang it on. With no trouble he found the landing where he and Bearpaw had been cornered, and began working his way down. He had no idea where gun or Shield might have landed; he'd tossed them without looking, and other noise had covered any sound of impact below. Descending, level after level, he felt less and less hope; either the items had been picked up or had fallen far enough to smash them.

On the gun, though, he lucked out. There it lay, in the corner of a landing far down the ship, with only a couple of chips out of the butt. He saw the marks where it had struck and dented the railing, then skittered. He couldn't test it to be sure, but the test-indicator lights said it would work. So he clipped it to the belt, closed his jumpsuit, and kept looking.

His Shield harness had taken the full drop; when he picked it up, things rattled inside that never had before. If only he'd thought to turn the thing *on* before he threw it! Too late now, though. But in case somebody aboard might be able to fix the device, he tucked it inside, also. And began the long climb.

Something new had been added; twice, he was stopped by armed guards who hadn't been there a half-hour ago. When he told them where his quarters were, and that he was going there, they let him pass. For a moment he thought the second one was going to try to search him; as Barton braced himself for action, he wished to hell he'd stashed the gun a little more accessibly instead of quite so well hidden from view. But the man waved him off, and Barton saved his sigh of relief until he was out of earshot.

Finally he reached quarters. As he entered, he heard Ren Bearpaw's voice on the intercom. Calm, the man wasn't.

" . . . make any difference; I'm not saying anything a listener wouldn't already know. Anyone who doesn't realize the Others are behind Soong just hasn't been paying attention. So Lisa and I wanted to go confer with—with someone who's studied them more than most. And *that* conference we didn't want tapped, so it had to be in person. You see?"

"Yes," said Limila, at the same time looking over her shoulder toward Barton. "Ren? Barton's here now."

"Oh, good. Should I start over?"

Barton gave Limila a quick kiss, then said, "You wanted to go talk with somebody about the Others; I heard that much. Anything before that, I need to know?"

"I guess not. Well, we started off to see, uh, our colleague; we didn't get there. It was all of a sudden Goonsville—guards at all the bottlenecks. If you didn't have a pass from Soong, the guard called in to somebody, and unless you're headed for your duty station and on schedule, you go no place but home to quarters."

"I noticed," said Barton. "They sure mounted this operation in a hurry."

"Yes, they did. And it's sure going to play hell with *normal* operations, if there are any such things by now." A pause. "Well, we came back home. And one of the dumbskulls wasn't even going to let us do that, until—"

Lisa's voice. "He was really stubborn about it. Until I told him, quite sweetly, that unless he let us go home immediately, I was going to commit an unsanitary nuisance on the floor right in front of him." She laughed. "Thank heavens, there are limits to what even massive stupidity can put up with."

Barton didn't laugh, but he came close to it. Then there was some more talk, but by now Barton knew the gist of it. Bearpaw needed to let off some steam, was all, so Barton didn't mind listening.

When the call was done, Limila poured them a little wine and they sat together, not saying much. Her hug jammed the hidden equipment against his ribs, so he opened the jumpsuit and got the items off his person, telling her what worked and what didn't. When he went to close the jumpsuit, her hand was in the way, so he changed his thinking. Lovemaking had been less frequent as her pregnancy advanced, but if Limila was in the mood, so was Barton.

To Barton's mind, the next few days were what you might call odd, if you couldn't spell ridiculous. He and Ren Bearpaw were probably as silly as the rest, he supposed; they kept thinking up flawed plans to spring Ferenc Szabo out of siege, and he kept telling them not to bother, just yet. Judging by cryptic remarks over the intercom, Mark Gyril was going all out on his chemical warfare. Loading people up with drugs, to see how far they could get against the wishes of the Others, didn't work now; Soong's guards turned them back before the Others had a chance to. So Gyril, if Barton had this right, tried doping the air in the corridor where Soong's gunmen guarded Ferenc's quarters. But maybe Gyril didn't know the air-supply system too well; that's what Barton de-

duced when he heard about the sudden hay fever out-
break in an entirely different part of the ship.

Barton also deduced that if Soong ever figured out
what was happening, he'd have a few people shot. It was
quite a circus, Barton thought, but did it have to be *all*
clowns? Because it wasn't funny at all. Not when he
thought about the stakes, it wasn't.

Barton hadn't quite believed Bearpaw's tape on the
subject of Base back on Earth, the idiocy of its earlier
directives. Now, on the basis of flimsies that Ren smuggled down from Comm, Barton had to believe. Soong had
killed only the transmit side of the Phasewave gear; messages still came in. In reaction to Soong's proclamation,
Base first demanded that Soong crawl back into pokey
and leave Ferenc Szabo in charge. Next, that he acknowledge and comply with the original "get lost" order. And
finally came a confused-sounding plea that boiled down
to: "Just *say* something!"

So nothing happened, and Barton stewed. He didn't
have to stew all in one place, though, because he and
Limila had enough semi-official status, which Soong
hadn't got around to revoke, that they could visit various
working areas of the ship without challenge. And, of
course, the galley. That's where Barton first saw Soong, in
person.

He and Limila were sharing a snack with Mark Gyril
and Elys Rounds when Gyril's elbow dug into his ribs.
"There's Soong now." Barton looked. Flanked by two
armed guards, a fat man walked with tired step, and
took a seat at an empty table. One guard went to bring
him a tray; at distance, Barton couldn't see what was on
it. He was looking at the man, anyway. Looking, and
remembering. A long time ago, before the Demu had
taken Barton and changed his life. And, as it had turned
out, their own, as well. . . .

Picture on the front page, Arnold Soong, lean and serious. The dedicated astronaut. The shuttle had malfunctioned but Soong brought it down with minimum damage
and no casualties. That incident made him a minor hero;
the one that made him a major one had occurred while
Barton was in the Demu cage on Ashura, and he'd never
learned all the details. Merely that Soong had endured
more fatigue and deprivation than most people could survive, and by the doing had saved some lives. Including a

V.I.P., but Barton didn't count that in for points; what he did count was the guts the job had needed.

Looking now, all he saw was a paunch, and a slack face that showed no determination. *What changed this man?* Well, he knew some of what could happen; he'd seen it in Nam; there were people who could transcend themselves once—twice, maybe—and then they collapsed into less than they'd been to start with. Too bad, but when the mainspring breaks, there's nothing left to wind up again.

Gradually the galley had gone quiet; by tuning his ears in the right direction, Barton could pick up most of what was said at Captain Soong's table. It came clear that the captain thought he had everything under control; he resented the idea that he was supposed to take any action. The older woman—Command-Second Nargilosa, and Barton had seen her before—tried in a gentle way to persuade him, but Soong wasn't having any of it. What he had in mind was griping at his strong-arm boys for not breaking Ferenc Szabo out of the quarters into which Soong had assembled so much comfort and luxury. At the same time he made it clear that they were not to damage so much as a thread of his precious carpets.

Barton shook his head. Some people didn't seem to think, at all. Himself, he had an idea. He didn't figure his companions would like it, so he didn't ask them. Instead he got up, empty coffee cup in his hand, and started over for a refill. Two tables away he set the cup down and changed course. When he came to Captain Soong's table, he expected a guard to stop him, and that's what happened.

"What do you want?"

Walking over, Barton had prepared his lines. "I'd like to pay my respects to the captain, since we haven't met. And present the greetings of the first fleet, from Admiral Tarleton."

He'd figured to make a splash, and it worked. Soong said, "It's been so busy, you know—so hectic. But I've heard rumors. You are . . . ?"

"Barton." He reached out a hand for shaking, and the guard moved back until the reach made it. "Vice-Admiral Barton. In case nobody told you, we won the Demu war without a fight." And while he had the initiative, Barton sat down without an invitation. The guard gave him a hard look. Barton looked back, trying to look innocent but not feeling very confident about that. The guard turned away, and came back with wine and coffee for Barton. Well, you never know until you try. . . .

Soong coughed; Nargilosa patted his back until he gulped a time or two and could speak again. "But I don't understand. What are you doing *here?*"

Good question—and Barton had no answer prepared, so he faked it. "Ambassador plenipotentiary." He hoped to hell he'd said it halfway right, and that he and Soong had the same idea of its meaning. But the main thing was, for now, that it sounded good.

It meant nothing, Barton knew, but the afternoon in Soong's displaced quarters gave him a real kick. He frowned at the text Nargilosa had written, and sipped at Soong's good wine. " . . . to be respected by both parties in perpetuity. Yes, good; I like that. Now, then," he continued. "Section two, clause three. In the event that . . . " He shot the whole afternoon that way, Barton did. And the only way he could have enjoyed it more would have been if he believed it. Because the thing they were discussing so gravely was the draft of a treaty between the human race and the Others on Opal. Which meant that Soong still thought he could get the ship back there.

The funny part, Barton thought, was that Soong was really a likable oldphart. He shouldn't have been in command of anything, was all. It wasn't his mind that had gone flyblown; it was his perceptivity and initiative. Within the limits of his understanding of a situation, his logic worked fairly well. The trouble was that those limits didn't stretch very far, so he came out looking more stupid than he should have.

What Barton was after, in a vague sort of way, was to probe the extent of the Others' influence over Captain Soong. Hints weren't getting him anywhere, so when they came to the end of the treaty draft, he asked straight out. "When we get to this planet we're aimed for, what do we do then?"

Soong's heavy shoulders moved a little. "Go into orbit, I suppose. To save fuel, and avoid adding any more distance between ourselves and Opal, while I convince my mutinous Command-First that we have to get back to that planet."

"Why do we?" Soong looked blank. "Have to go there, I mean."

"Why, it's necessary! How else can we negotiate the treaty?" So the Others were learning. Now they didn't merely use straight mental pressure; they'd given Soong a *reason* he could accept. And of course he was a soft touch for them because he'd never been any part of Szabo's mental-resistance group effort. Along with his rank, that vulnerability made him an ideal tool.

Idly, Barton asked, "Who's putting us in orbit, when the time comes?"

Soong blinked. "Why, I will, I suppose, since Szabo's not available." Ferenc had programmed the course to end in orbit, but the fine corrections couldn't be set up in advance; all his program could do was get the ship to approximately the right place, then leave some time for maneuvering before automatic timing cut the drive. So the final jiggling had to be done accurately.

And Soong's reflexes, Barton had noticed, were woefully slow; he dropped things, for instance, and grabbed too late. Well, Barton was done here, anyway; it was time to go do something.

He thanked the captain for his hospitality and made a point of being equally gracious to Geta Nargilosa. She was older than Soong, but still slim and erect. And now Barton remembered who she was, from the old days: one of the first of the women astronauts, but for years she'd been kept out of space, and when she did get upstairs it was in subordinate roles. Maybe, he thought, that was why she seemed to have no force to her, now. Too many years spent trying to please, to get the assignments that were her just due, by not offending anybody. It could happen; too bad it sometimes did.

Finally he got back to quarters, and called Ren Bearpaw. "Why don't a bunch of us eat together, for dinner?" he said. The galley was one place they could meet, without interference from the corridor guards. "Eighteen hundred hours; right." Before they met, though, he told Limila what was on his mind.

Barton and Limila, Ren and Lisa, Mark and Elys—there were more in the cabal by now, but six were as many as could meet in public without drawing attention. They took a central table, because the guards got nosy about groups that retired to the far corners. They had two conversations going: Barton giving his pitch to Bearpaw

495

and Gyril, and Limila to the two women, all looking quite natural for low-voiced talk.

At the end of it, Bearpaw nodded. "You're right; we have to break Ferenc loose *now*. If Soong blew the synchronous orbit, we could spiral into the planet or drift away with no place else to go."

"It's going to be tougher than it would have been at first," said Gyril, "before we had the checkpoint guards."

"Yeh, and Ferenc admits he goofed, there," Barton said. "But that's all down the spout; forget it. Now, is the gear ready, Bearpaw? And your stuff, Mark?"

They talked, and Barton decided he was as satisfied with the planning as he was going to be. He really thought Lisa Teragni should be in on the action if she wanted to, but all three women wanted in, and Elys purely wasn't up to it. Limila would have been, if not for the pregnancy, but she was slowed down, now. So with Bearpaw strong that Lisa shouldn't risk herself, Barton couldn't single her out from the three, as the one who was suitable.

Finally, after drinking too much coffee as an excuse to linger at table, the group adjourned. Bearpaw and Gyril were to alert the rest of the conspirators. And everything was set to move at noon of the next ship's-day, right at watch-change.

With a standard projectile weapon stuck in his belt, in case his sleep-gun ran out of charge, Barton walked a little ahead of Bearpaw. He didn't know where everybody else had got their armaments, but his had survived two searches of quarters, by Soong's guard-people. He hadn't been in the Army for nothing.

He was a little high on the antidote pill for the aerosol sleep-gas Gyril had come up with, and he hoped he could remember the beep-code their hand-talkies had been changed to use. Vaguely he recalled that the sets worked by induction, along the power and signal conduits that spider-webbed the ship. So they might hit blind spots, but mostly they could communicate between themselves and the opposition wouldn't catch on.

He wished to hell he had his Shield, because nobody seemed to know whether the other side was using sleep-guns.

Barton dropped his first goon before the man could get a shot off. The second was female, and either she was faster or the sleep-gun was losing charge, because she spanged one slug off the bulkhead beside him, a lot closer than Barton liked, before she fell.

Things seemed to move awfully fast; maybe it was Gyril's pill. They passed two checkpoints where the guards lay sprawled flat, and Barton smelled the sleep-gas there. Then someone shot at him, and he shot back and nothing happened, and from behind him, Bearpaw's gun gave a crashing report that made Barton's ears ring. The man ahead, slumping back against the bulkhead, clutched his right shoulder and let his gun drop. Barton pulled out his slug-gun.

That was at one end of the corridor where Ferenc Szabo was trapped. Bearpaw worked his code-beeper. At the far end of the corridor, two goons. As Barton upended one of them with a deck ricochet to the lower legs, a door came open. Looking around it, using it for a shield, Ferenc Szabo put the other foe down with a sleep-gun. To Barton, it seemed that the man certainly took his time about it.

From behind, now, some people came running, but they were friendly troops who went past, to secure the other end of the corridor before any more of Soong's partisans showed up.

Who got there first, though, were Dahil and Tiriis. AWOL from the nursery.

Barton could have used a quick council of war, but there didn't seem to be time for it. Ferenc waved thanks to him and Bearpaw as they walked to greet him, then turned, frowning a little, to watch the two Others approach. Aside, he said, "Let's wait and see what they have to say, shall we?" Barton nodded.

Nearing the men, Tiriis raised an arm. "No more fight," she said. "No kill. No need for fight."

"I'll decide that, I think," Ferenc said, "but go ahead, anyway. What's your point?" Either the business in the vicinity of Opal had built Barton's resistance to the Others' mental hanky-panky, or they weren't trying, now. He couldn't feel a hint of push.

"We tried Soong," said Tiriis. "Was mistake."

"Yes, he was." That was Bearpaw. "At all times."

Ferenc shushed him. "Go on. What is it you want now?"

"No want," Tiriis said. "No need. Just no fight more."

Ferenc shook his head. "It takes two to stop a fight. What does Soong say? Or his storm-troopers? Do you speak for them, too?"

For the first time, Dahil spoke. His bad arm still didn't look too useful, but if he was holding a grudge, it didn't show. "Soong mistake; Soong nothing. Say nothing. You want, we stop Soong people. No need fight."

Well, it go along and it go along, Barton thought, but the way it wound up was, no fight. It hadn't all been fun and games, by any means. Three humans were dead, two of Soong's and one of Ferenc's; Comm-Chief Rigan, that one was. More had been wounded, and were hurting.

But now maybe all that stuff was over and done with.

The aftermath seemed like anticlimax—but, Barton reflected, that's the way it went sometimes, with wars. Soong went back into seclusion in his surrogate-quarters, not even guarded now, and Ferenc actually had his luxury items transferred there, as much as was feasible. Barton suspected that Ferenc would have let Soong have captain's digs back, except that the screen circuits there, no longer disconnected at Comm, were awfully handy for command purposes. The F.T.L. transmitter was working again, too, but Ferenc wasn't ready to use it yet.

The Others, near as Barton could tell, were sincerely horrified at the carnage they'd wrought. The deaths were final, but Dahil and Tiriis sat by the wounded and "thought on them," and recoveries proceeded faster than Barton would have believed. He found it impossible to keep feeling hostile toward enemies who wouldn't *act* like enemies. Well, if he had it figured right, the enmity part was all a big circumstantial mistake, anyway.

If he didn't, of course, then it was a whole new ball game.

Things had run a little close, there, but Ferenc Szabo at the primary pilot's console warped the ship's path into synchronous orbit around the planet ahead. The indicators looked right to Barton, but Ferenc watched for a time and made a couple more twiddling adjustments, before he took a deep breath and cut the drive. The ship's hum dropped to a new level, barely audible.

Barton, sitting beside him and keeping his hands off any controls, had been watching the world that now, somehow, was below them rather than "out there." He'd watched Ferenc, too, and while Barton figured he could have achieved orbit here if he'd had to do it, he was just as glad it hadn't been his turn this time.

The planet looked good. Barton took Ferenc's word that the axial tilt was small, meaning mild seasons, and that there was a good wide belt of temperate climate in each hemisphere. Cloud cover was considerably less than Earth's, more than Tilara's or Sisshain's. Land-to-water ratio was greater than Earth's, but the land was broken up into smaller, isolated masses. From this high, Barton couldn't tell about mountains or such.

Somebody, entering, broke Barton's train of thought. The man was bringing coffee that Ferenc had asked for. It was one of Soong's ex-goons; disarmed, those people were back at the nothing-jobs they'd held before Soong recruited them as bully-boys. Well, thought Barton, on a ship this size, somebody has to do that stuff, and nobody with any brains will sign on for it, so there we are. He thanked the fellow for the coffee when he was handed a cup.

Ferenc hadn't said anything for a while; Barton turned his head to see the commander watching him, and said, "Something?"

"Yes. I've punched up a draft of the message I intend to send Base. Here's a readout. See what you think."

Barton took the flimsy, and read it, out loud:

"Ferenc Szabo commanding. We are past the no-return limit, and preparing to settle on a planet that appears attractive and promises comfort." Barton skipped the coordinates. "At present there is no mental coercion from the Others or from the Children. In a short while, such coercion will be immaterial, for I shall have evacuated this ship and totally cut power on it, as ordered. As you know, there are no facilities to restore it, this side of the dead belt." *That we know about, you mean.* But Barton didn't say it; after the brief pause, he read on.

"I suggest, strongly, that any human forces entering this immediate volume of space in future, do so with utmost caution. Ferenc Szabo, commanding."

"The last words Base will ever receive from us," said Ferenc.

Barton found them fitting enough; he nodded. Then another thought came. "You're leaving them hanging, aren't you? The last they knew, Soong was in the saddle and spurring hell-for-leather for the home corral."

Ferenc grinned. "You're right." So when he read the message into the F.T.L. Phasewave transmitter, he adlibbed a P.S. to the effect that while the latest transfer of command had entailed a certain amount of conflict, Captain Soong was unharmed and would remain so. For a moment, Barton thought the man was going to say something more. But after a brief hesitation, Ferenc shut down the Phasewave, both send and receive sides, and shook his head. "There has to be an end."

Now, even without the side-effects of any weird pills, Barton thought things moved pretty fast. After he met Limila in the galley for lunch, and brought her up to date on the things he'd forgotten to tell her during their first meeting after all the shootout, he went back up to Control. He didn't know why; he had no official status. But that was where things were happening, so that's where he went. And found Ferenc talking at a viewscreen that had Dahil on the other end of it, in the nursery.

The gist was that Dahil and Tiriis and their human helpers were to get themselves, and the Children, and all supplies of the Children's needs that were in the nursery area, to the aux boats' docking facility within the next six hours. Barton thought that was a little quick for the job, but he'd misguessed Ferenc Szabo before, too.

Dahil wasn't buying it, though. "No do. We stay here."

Ferenc didn't argue. "Suit yourself. I'm evacuating the rest of the ship—taking the crew and all supplies and removable equipment outside your area, down to the planet we're orbiting. If you get lonesome up here, or hungry, you can give me a call."

Barton had to like the way Ferenc did it; it was much the same thing he'd have done himself, probably. The screen went blank, and Barton said, "You want everything downside fast; is that it?"

Ferenc nodded. "Yes. The sooner we're down on Endatheline, irrevocably, the sooner I can relax. Whatever happens, after that."

Barton must have let his puzzlement show, for Ferenc said, "Endatheline? What else? This world *is* the end of the line, for us."

500

"Yeh. I guess you're right." Or, Barton thought, maybe not . . .

After a little more noodling, Dahil did what he'd been told in the first place. Not quite in time to meet Ferenc's original deadline, but at least the nursery was evacuated. Barton decided the deadline had been more of a psychological necessity than any other kind, because it was going to take the two aux boats a lot of trips to get everything downside.

The Others and the Children were the crucial part, of course. At first Ferenc insisted that no one but himself could ferry any of them down. "I'm the one man on this ship they won't play games with, I think."

"Bullshit," said Barton, and saw the other man stiffen, then relax. "I mean," Barton said, speaking quietly now, "once they're in an aux boat going downside, they won't screw around with their pilot."

Slowly, Ferenc smiled. "You're right, of course. Possibly I've been getting a bit paranoid. I don't suppose you'd know about that."

"Sure not." Ferenc blinked, and Barton couldn't leave it at that. "Sometime we'll get us drunk, Ferenc, and I'll tell you."

There was no question about Ferenc Szabo handling one aux boat; the other was up for grabs, though. Ren Bearpaw had toured half a continent with one, but all in atmosphere, never coming down and plowing into air from the outside. Whereas, Barton had never tried to run one of the things in his life but sure's hell he'd landed bigger craft. Soong and Nargilosa weren't even in consideration, though both had the training, and Command-Third Rocco—well, Ferenc said, "I don't know what kind of dope he's on, but I wouldn't trust him to carry me on a piggy-back ride."

What governed, finally, was that somebody had to stay on ship and occupy the saddle, and Bearpaw had official status and Barton didn't. So, after a quick instruction session with Ferenc Szabo, Barton got the nod to play Charon with the second aux boat.

First trip, Ferenc took Dahil down, along with about half the Children and their human helpers; supplies filled the rest of the landing vehicle. Following instructions, Barton waited with his own load until Ferenc had landed, and passed up the okay for Barton to follow. Riding with Barton were Tiriis and the rest of the Children—larger now, and being very quiet. Some of the nursery supplies were going to have to wait for a later drop; the boat was about as full as Barton figured it could handle.

Coming down, Barton tried to get the feel of his controls. He wasn't worried, really; he was riding good equipment and had pretty fair confidence in it and in himself. When he hit air, he found he was right; the boat handled fine, and he homed in and landed alongside Ferenc's.

The other boat was open, and people standing outside looking healthy enough, so Barton unbuttoned his, too, and got out. He felt a slight decompression, a whoosh of outrushing air, when he cracked the first seal; nothing big, though. When he got outside, himself, Barton smelled scents he hadn't known before. He was reminded of the difference between the fragrances of Tilara and those of Earth, but here the strangeness went a bit further.

Breeze and temperature were mild. As a child in school, Barton had first learned temperature in Fahrenheit; he still had to pause a moment to translate. All right; in the low twenties Celsius, it felt like. Either scale, it was pleasant enough.

Underfoot, the soft blue-green stuff that looked not much like grass or moss, either one, smelled a little bit like mustard. The aroma was light, though, and after a few minutes he didn't notice it any more.

Off a way he saw gnarly trees with long, pointed leaves, and bushes clustered in a shallow ravine that probably hid a stream. Looking up at the pale sky, Barton took a deep breath. If they were stuck here, he thought, they could have picked a worse place!

As Barton had figured, downloading took a lot of trips. When dusk came and they stopped work for the night, he estimated they were maybe a tenth of the way done with the job. Of course, they'd been less than a full day at it. Planet's days at this longitude were several hours out of synch with the ship's days he'd been observing; he'd been up a long time, and went to bed as soon as he'd eaten.

The funny part, next day, was that all of them nearly forgot about Soong. When Ferenc remembered, and they went to get the captain and begin loading his stuff, the man simply wouldn't believe that someone couldn't just kiss it and make it well. He wanted Humpty-Dumpty put back together, and never mind that everybody was fresh out of king's horses. Finally, Nargilosa put her arm around the shoulders of the tired, fat old man, and led him off to the aux boat where his comfort goodies were being loaded. At least, Barton thought, Soong would have an easy life downside, as long as he lasted.

The next things they took down were several loads of miscellaneous metal and plastic, for building shelters. Nobody downside had minded sleeping outdoors the first night, but to the "west" a cloud front was approaching, bringing rain. The odd-looking trees were big enough to provide wood for framing, but none of the tools on ship were well adapted for cutting wood. Barton wished he'd brought a hand-laser, though, of course, he wouldn't have dared use it in the fighting—too easy to slice through essential circuitry in the bulkheads. But when he mentioned the idea, Ferenc set a couple of technicians to work, and by evening they had cannibalized together a unit that one now could carry. It looked pretty haywire to Barton, but it worked, and speeded up construction quite a lot.

The next day he and Limila moved downside, bringing along all the stuff from their quarters whether it seemed useful or not. As Barton said, "You never know."

They worked long hours now. Before dawn each morning the aux boats first lifted, and made their last landings of the day in twilight. Barton lost count of the days; on the eighth or maybe the tenth, the ship was gutted of everything it was feasible to remove. A lot faster job than transshipping cargo had been—proportionately, anyway—because the aux boats had little fold-out loading cranes, and the operation could use more machinery and less muscle than in the earlier chore.

On his own boat, or so he thought of it now, Barton downloaded a few items he didn't bother to tell Ferenc Szabo about. The thing was, he wasn't sure, yet, about Ferenc's plans for the ship. Since he might not agree with them, he wanted to keep his options open. And for the same reason, when Ferenc gathered a party to go up one last time, inspect the ship and shut it down for keeps, Barton unobtrusively joined the group. Making a full passenger load on the aux boat, along with Ferenc, Ren and Lisa, Mark Gyril, and a youngish, heavyset woman whose name Barton couldn't remember.

They rode upstairs without talk; Ferenc docked the aux boat, and the party gave the ship a final inspection, taking longer about it than Barton thought was strictly necessary. Well, maybe Ferenc hated what he had to do now, and was delaying. No harm done.

They wound up in the power control center, and Barton saw a great pile of tech manuals, and microfiches of circuit drawings. Ferenc said, "Let's get those into the Destruct box," and sure enough, that was the way the bin was labeled. Barton didn't say anything; as requested, he helped. Then Ferenc unlocked the main power switch, and Barton moved forward.

"You haven't said, Ferenc. Just what you plan to do now."

"All of it," the man said. "I was going to push only two buttons here, one to cut all ship's power so it couldn't be restored without going through the refuel cycle, and the other to operate the bin and destroy all written information that could possibly help restore it."

Barton nodded. "That sounds pretty thorough. Let's do it." At the back of his mind, something pushed for a moment, then ceased.

"Not enough," said Ferenc. "The information's also in the minds of ship's personnel. And the Children will get that knowledge from us, Barton; you have to realize that. It won't be like our fighting off mental influence; when they get around to it and are capable, I think they'll read us like so many books."

"So?"

"So instead I'm going to turn the drive power back on, and mistune the exciters to blow the whole ship, a little after we leave it. Half an hour leeway, maybe, for safety. In that way—"

Barton shook his head. "No need, Ferenc. All the books in the world won't synthesize fuel without a lot of high-grade equipment. Or get it upstairs, if we disable the aux boats. *Or* . . . "—he waggled a finger—" . . . *or*, let anybody stay alive on this ship even if they could get here. What we do is, we let the air out."

It was working, but Ferenc still hesitated. Barton said, "This is too much ship to blow up when we don't really have to." Hoping he wasn't going to need it, Barton kept one hand on his concealed gun. And then the man nodded agreement.

"All right, you've convinced me. I'll stick with the original plan." His fingers reached for the two buttons.

And just as Barton was beginning to let himself relax, a wave of mental pressure hit the ship.

Barton staggered, and caught himself; for a moment his vision blurred. This had to be the Children as well as the Others, acting under adult direction. He saw Mark Gyril fail to catch balance, and fall. Ferenc steadied himself with one hand against the bulkhead, made a tight grin, and pushed first one button and then the other. Barton felt one last burst of pressure, like the final outraged howl of a child's temper tantrum, and then it was all over. Through the ringing in his ears he heard the sound of the air system's impellers beginning to wind down. Funny; he hadn't consciously heard their steady hum in a long time.

And as the group, after waiting while Ferenc checked through the power switch settings as if he hadn't already done so twice, walked slowly back to the aux boat, Barton felt the deck-gravs losing pull. That wasn't the way it would have worked on Ship One, so he asked, "How come it didn't cut off all at once?"

"This system works differently," Ferenc said. "The field derives from a rotating magnetic torus. While the superconductor fields hold, the rotation will take some time to slow down, even without external power feed."

"I see." Barton didn't, except in a sort of way, but he wanted to keep Ferenc's thinking busy. Then they entered the aux boat area and Ferenc gimmicked the entrance door so it couldn't close, and by-passed the safety interlock so that the launching gates could still be opened.

They got into the aux boat. "Strap in," said Ferenc, "because we're going to have a jet-assisted launching, when the air blows. I hope we don't hit the gates too hard, while they're opening."

They didn't; the aux boat shuddered but made it through. Still, Barton thought, it was one helluva bang, there.

Once clear, Ferenc turned the aux boat to face the ship for a moment, and looked at it. "That was a fine ship," he said. "It's too bad we have to leave it dead, forever."

Barton, in his mind, agreed with the sentiment. But not with the prediction. What Ferenc Szabo didn't know about was the crate of spacesuits that Barton had smuggled downside. And Barton certainly wasn't going to tell him, right now.

IV.

Answers

All things considered, Barton thought the transition from ship to colony status went pretty smoothly. Nobody had told him that one of the original planned options had been to plant an outpost base with a skeleton crew to maintain it at first, so he was surprised when people began cultivating ground and breaking out seeds from the crated supplies. The stuff seemed to grow well.

Getting started was a lot of work, sure; nobody was working the kind of hours Barton and other folks had worked during the downloading, but it wasn't exactly like a union job, either. Still, now he and Limila had more time together, and that was good for both of them.

The two Earthani women who were carrying Children came near their times, and Limila conferred with them now and then. When Gyril did the Caesarians, Tiriis came to take the Children as she'd done before, but this time both mothers insisted on joining the nursery. Barton had no idea whether it was their own motivation or something new in the Others' repertoire.

He asked Limila what she thought, and she said, "It is different now, Barton. Or so I think. We shall have to be a community, here. We, and the Others, and the Children. The isolation must cease."

And it was happening that way, Barton noticed, when he stopped to think about it. Since the last-ditch try at stopping Ferenc from disabling the ship, Barton knew of no instance of mental pressure from Others or Children. Certainly everyone mingled now, in daily routines, without any tension or suspicion to speak of. Maybe there was no pushing, he decided, because there wasn't anything left to push *for*.

Dahil had promised, when Ferenc was making up his mind whether the Others and Children would live among humans or apart from them, that he wouldn't play any more games with his trick cup. Privately, Barton wondered if maybe Dahil hadn't simply run out of joy juice. But since he'd kept the promise, it didn't matter either way.

The Children, growing fast now, fascinated Barton. Considering their powers—extent unknown, as yet—he figured it was lucky that these youngsters seemed to show no trace of the "me-*me*-ME" stage that makes normal human kids a little hard to take, sometimes. They kept to themselves a lot, or worked with Dahil or Tiriis on a plot of ground the Others were cultivating by themselves—whose seeds?—Barton had no idea. And when they came around humans, mostly they seemed to be observing. The couple of times when one or another spoke to Barton, the few words were in good English.

All in all, Barton decided they were pretty nice kids. The only thing that worried him was what they were going to be when they grew up. Assuming that he and Limila were right about that.

On the human side, of course, it was really Kiddie Corner. When practically every woman from the ship began delivering human babies on schedule, from the Great Pregnancy Race as Barton thought of it, things had been truly hectic for a time. He doubted that anyone was planning on having any more kids for a while, because it was all the community could do to handle the current crop.

Bearpaw and Teragni had a boy; they named him Ferenc. Gyril and Elys produced a girl, and Barton was pleased to see that this time the pregnancy left her looking better rather than worse. And a little later Ferenc Szabo's mate, Racelle, gave birth to a male child. Bearpaw said, in an aside to Barton, "In the old days, if anybody'd ever told me I'd see *Szabo* as a doting father—!"

But the thing that puzzled both men was why Ferenc and Racelle named the child Dahil.

Then Limila was the only woman left carrying child. Barton had lost track of the timing; he didn't know when she was due, for sure. Mark Gyril told Barton not to worry, just yet. So Barton didn't. Except that one night he got home from a stint of scouting for ores in the foothills to the north, and came into his and Limila's hut, and stormed out again and found Mark Gyril and grabbed him by the front of his jacket. "Where the hell were *you?*"

"Where—I don't know what you mean!"

"Then come and see, goddamn you!"

But when Barton dragged Gyril into the hut by the scruff of the neck and threw him halfway across, Limila said, "Barton—there is no need to be rude to Mark. I did not call for him. Why did you not, when you came and saw me, give me time to explain?"

Barton looked. Well, Limila wasn't really dying, after all, he guessed, even though it still looked like one hell of a lot of blood splashed around. And her Child was suckling peacefully enough. Barton shook his head and helped Gyril up. "Sorry, Mark. Limila—you mind telling me what's been going on?"

"No, I do not mind. If you will prepare some herb tea for all of us, then sit to listen." Feeling as confused as he had for some time, Barton followed instructions. Then, sitting, he waited while Limila sipped tea before she said, "It was because I am not Earthani, Barton. Earthani women, to be delivered of Children, must all be opened by Mark's knife. I did not wish my body cut; I did not feel it needful to do so." Limila shrugged. "But had I said as much, there would have been argument. So I thought to speed development slightly, and do this thing in my own way." Wide and silver-irised, her eyes sought his gaze. "Do you understand?"

For moments, Barton couldn't talk at all. *This woman!* Then he said, "You're all right?" and she nodded. But: "You mind if Mark checks you over, though, just in case?" Headshake. "Then I think I'll go unload my ore samples. Be back in a little."

He did the routine work without thinking about it, his mind chewing on what Limila had said. Deliberately speeded-up growth of the fetus? From the beginning, Barton had realized there was a lot he didn't know about his Tilaran love. Now he wondered if he'd ever catch up to all of it. But at least she was past the birth.

Gyril, when Barton returned, didn't seem offended at the way Barton had horsed him around, earlier. "I can't blame you. Seeing the mess, I suppose it would have scared me silly, too. Anyway, she's in absolutely fine shape, and I certainly wish I knew how she did it, so that I could use the knowledge to help other women in the same situation." Gyril sighted down a forefinger, at Limila. "If Earthwomen could manage as easily with their own kind of babies as you did with this hybrid birth, they'd have a much tidier time of it." He shook his head. "I can't do any more good here. And if nobody minds, I'd like to get home and put some notes on paper before I forget the details."

"Sure." Barton was glad the Medic-chief would still shake hands with him. When Gyril had left, Barton sat down beside Limila. He stroked the head of the Child who lay against Limila's breast. One rear-corner eye opened, blinked once, then slowly closed. In the iris, Barton had seen silver specks.

Not sure what to say, Barton began with, "You letting this one go to the Others' nursery, or do we keep it ourselves, or what?" Another thought came. "You got any ideas what we should name it?"

"Each question in turn," Limila said. "I keep this Child, but we spend some time each day with Tiriis and the other Children, also. For there are needs, I think, that you and I cannot fulfill." She shook forward-falling hair away from her eyes.

"But here we have no 'it,' Barton; my offspring is fully of both sexes, as you know. Use which gender label you prefer, or either, at whim. But not the neuter, please."

"Sure; I see it. The language doesn't work right, but I'll try. How about the naming part, though?"

The way Limila smiled, then, puzzled Barton. "The name," she said, "is not ours to give. It is Conjuldephane, and it was during birth that Conjuldephane told me. Gently, in my mind."

To that, Barton didn't have much to say. So he hugged them.

In a way, Barton thought, the next year (a little shorter than Earth's, but not much) went by like back home on the farm, and howdy, neighbor. All that; no real turmoil in the settlement.

When Conjy, the Child that Limila had borne to Dahil's siring, was weaned from Limila's still-petite breasts, Limila wanted to begin another baby. "All of you and me, Barton. To replace the one we lost on Tilara."

Barton could sympathize, but too much else kept bothering him. So he asked her if she'd mind holding off for a while yet, and she agreed. "But not of indefinite extent, Barton." And *he* agreed. But to keep his various worries separate in time, would take luck.

Being no farmer, having the exact opposite of a "green thumb," Barton stayed out of agriculture and did other work. For one thing, he took his aux boat to have a look at adjacent land masses. On the third one he scouted, he saw evidence of intelligent life.

Such as villages. And when he got back, the villagers were there ahead of him.

They looked mostly like the Others, but not quite. Distribution of fur was different, and so were general bodily proportions. But it was a cinch that the Endatheliners were related to the Others in much the same way that Tilari related to Earthani. And the natives here picked up language as well as the Others had done.

Barton went to Ferenc Szabo and said what he thought. Almost.

The way it worked was that the first-born of the Children had hung around Barton quite a bit, and Barton liked the kid and felt that maybe here was the way Barton might find out how to play this hand he'd never asked to be dealt.

He addressed the Child by name. "Chiyonou," Barton said, "I think we got a problem, here. Any good ideas, how we cope?"

Barton couldn't interpret the movements of multiple eyes and extra shoulders. But Chiyonou made a whistling tweetle-sound, and then said, "You *know*, Barton. Time that all were told."

So that evening a full gathering was called. Tiriis told part of the story, confirming Barton's hunch that the Others carried a certain ability for racial memory, and Chiyonou did the rest.

As Barton listened, he couldn't be sure who said which

parts. None of it surprised him totally, though; he'd figured some pieces out a long time ago. So Barton sat, and he listened. And wondered if things had any chance of working out the way they must have been planned to work, so long ago that he found difficulty in trying to imagine the time gap.

A very long time ago, there was the Great Race. From wherever it came, it grew to inhabit nearly a third of this galaxy. It could have expanded farther, but other races were there, and the Great Race respected other people's rights. Instead, it sent its excess to seed other galaxies.

The Great Race fought no wars. It didn't have to; its powers were that mighty. Some of its achievements are literally beyond our power to comprehend, let alone duplicate. Combining logic, intuition, and mental forces, the Great Race not only controlled most physical aspects of its universe, but also strongly influenced the structure of probability, and time-flow itself to some extent.

If there were no gods, the Great Race made a fair substitute.

That's why the next part was so hard to understand or believe. To such beings, what could possibly be a serious menace? But some threat came, so dreadful that even the Great Race could only seek to hide. To hide so thoroughly, so completely, that it could never be found. And being the Great Race, it found a way.

How do you find what does not exist? It was that simple.

The Great Race vanished. Where it had been, lesser races appeared. Up-Arm, humans and Tilarans and the like. Down-Arm, the Others and those like them. All sprinkled among star systems holding existent species that are superficially similar but not at all related—Blaine's Mistakes, the Larka-Te, the Filjari.

And between the two groups of seeded species, the dead belt.

It was a master stroke. The knowledge and skills are lost, but what they did can be roughly understood. By microsurgery they divided their germinal cells into viable complementary halves, such that similars, when mated, produced simplified organisms. And complementary species were separated by the dead belt.

A simple splitting wasn't enough; some parts were vital

512

and must be duplicated in both halves. So that each, essentially, had to be more than half.

Deliberately, the results were made varied; the Great Race may have used misdirection to confuse whatever terrible search they worked so desperately to evade. So besides Earthani there were Tilari and the like; besides the Others there were their analogues here, and no doubt more variations elsewhere.

But with the aid of a catalyst, such as Dahil's cup, any humanoid became interfertile with any Otheroid. And always the resultant Children would be the same, the sum of the parts rejoined.

Long ago, there was the Great Race. And now it was come again.

Barton had thought he'd accepted the idea long since, but now the full impact hit him. Makes a man feel lost, he thought, to realize in his gut that his species has no destiny of its own, and never had. That humans had never been anything at all in their own right, but only the carriers and conservators of half the heredity of a race he couldn't even begin to understand. He found it hard, at gut level, to believe something that made him feel so utterly god-damn insignificant.

He had to believe it, though. When the gathering broke up, a group of them talked it out—Barton and Limila, Ferenc and Racelle, Ren and Lisa, Mark and Elys. What it boiled down to was that once you looked at it, there was simply too much evidence.

On Earth the advent of Cro-Magnon man had never been satisfactorily explained. And too many myths pointed to a time when a few of the Great Race shared Earth with man and with some Other-type beings; after they were gone, they survived in legend.

The Greek fauns and satyrs, for instance, have Other-like aspects. The Great Race became the centaur, such whimsies as many-armed Kali, and the two-backed beast riven into man and woman eternally striving to reunite.

Oh, there was no doubt, if you looked at it right. They were there. Stories got mixed up a little, over the millennia, but not too badly to recognize, once you saw the real thing.

How long ago? Not even the Others had a guess, on that. The dead belt was a safety factor, to make sure the danger would be past before a comparatively half-smart

513

species could develop star travel enough to meet one of its complements.

Another fail-safe device, it had to be, was concentrating the intuitive and mental-force powers, and the touch of race memory, into the Others and those like them. So that they, at least, would have the instinctive drive for recombination, would have ready the cup and what it must contain, and would know how to use it. No, the Great Race hadn't missed a trick, that Barton could see.

"So now we know," said Ferenc Szabo. "We and the Others and the rest—all through our long separate histories we've been nothing more than self-perpetuating strains of sperm and ova, waiting no one knows how long, to combine and re-create the Great Race." Barton saw the man's arm tighten around Racelle; her long, tawny eyes, slanted a bit, widened and then relaxed.

"What bothers me," said Lisa Teragni, "is what were they hiding from? And how do we know the danger's really gone?" When nobody answered right away, she said, "Oh, I'm just as shaken up as everybody else, at finding out we're nothing but sperm banks. I refuse to think about that, just now. But this other—"

Mark Gyril cleared his throat. "It's not my field," he said, "so I may not explain it too well. But I have a guess at what it was, that the Great Race couldn't withstand."

When the man paused, Barton said, "Give it a try; all right?"

"Radiation," said Gyril. "There's some evidence of a wave of stellar explosions, time not too well pinned down, that occurred in the galaxy-proper and would have flooded this Arm with more quanta than would have been healthy to most organisms."

"But *we're* still here," said Elys Rounds.

"The more complex the organism," Gyril said, "the more vulnerable it is to radiation damage. Genetically, I mean, as well as with individuals. The Great Race, you know, carries roughly double our chromosome count. At least, the Children do—and of course that's what the colchicine-surrogate is for, in Dahil's cup. To allow full addition of our chromosomes with those of the Others."

Barton frowned, not angry, only thinking. "You mean, the Great Race split itself into simpler organisms that could weather the radiation?" He nodded. "Yeh, I guess I got it the first time. Seems like the hard way, is all."

Limila touched his arm. "Perhaps. But we cannot

understand their motivations." And Barton had to agree with that conclusion.

Everybody was tired; the discussion had ground down to repetition. "Let's let it rest until morning," Barton said. "I have some ideas, but they can wait that long."

In the morning, though, they were up against the matter of the suicides. Nearly twenty percent of the human adults, during that night.

"Damn it!" Barton said. "We should have thought. Some people just weren't going to be able to take it."

"What could we have done?" said Renton Bearpaw. "Hold a pep talk? We were too busy, getting our own selves sorted out."

"Yeh." Barton shook his head. "Couldn't do everything all at once. Well, let's round up some muscle and get to work."

The work was burying the dead, and the mindlessness of digging gave Barton time to think. Part of his thought had no bearing on the immediate problem. If the Great Race was so almighty, how come it couldn't handle the radiation problem? Assuming Gyril had the right of it, there. Then Barton shrugged. Maybe they overreached themselves; maybe one of their own projects got out of hand. No way, for sure, that he'd ever find out, one way or the other.

Right now, though, he had to start putting some feelers out, and the first place to start was with Chiyonou.

He found the Child off to one side of the settlement, engaged in some sort of game with other Children. They were—Barton blinked, and then knew what he'd seen, briefly, before the Children noticed his presence. They were teleporting, vanishing and appearing, but now they stopped doing that. With no word or gesture on Barton's part, Chiyonou came to greet him.

Barton steadied his thinking, and held it, and said, "You see what has to be done? Can you do it?"

The Child nodded. "We knew it yesterday; we have begun. The ones coming and going, as you saw—they help begin our work, at some distance from here. What we need to know, we read from many minds." The kid couldn't frown, exactly; the equipment wasn't there for it. But Barton thought Chiyonou looked puzzled, as the next words came. "I see only so far, Barton, along the line of action. Do you see farther? The difficulty, I think, is that we are so very young."

"Don't knock it," said Barton. "It's all too curable." He set an image in the front of his thoughts, and said, "Read me now; it's quicker than talk." And after a silent pause: "What you think?"

"For your people," Chiyonou said, "perhaps it is the best solution."

Barton had been squatting beside the Child. Now, feeling a little like a cat petting its master, he ruffled the fur on Chiyonou's head, and then stood. "All right," he said. "But let's keep this just between us for a while. I still have to sell it to Ferenc Szabo."

Ferenc, after the evening meal, was in philosophic mode. Maybe, thought Barton, the wine helped. As Ferenc said, "Even from the human standpoint, I think it's worth it. The way the Children are, I mean, even as relative infants. They deserve the universe a lot more than we ever did. They'll enrich it."

He shook his head. "I have to feel sorry for the human race, though. Not for any tangible harm the Children will do it; they don't hurt people. But the shock—the shock I'm only now getting over. A lot won't be able to take it. Like today's dead."

"Close to twenty percent, was it?" Barton said. Ferenc nodded. "With the Demu, it's more like ninety, when they find out. Of course, maybe having been pets is worse than being gametes."

He'd said it to jolt Ferenc loose from introspection, and the ploy worked. Now Barton leaned forward. "Who says the human race has to know? The rest of it, I mean?"

Bearpaw hadn't said much; now he spoke. "This isolation won't last; you can't believe it will. Either human ships will come close enough to be drawn here by mental influence, or the Children will find a way to take over the ship and make it work." He looked harassed. "Can you deny those possibilities, Barton?"

Barton grinned. "Sure not. The only thing is, why wait for them to happen?" And before anybody could take the wrong reading from what he'd said, Barton added, "Why don't we give them the ship *now*?"

For a while there, the party got a little noisy. Then Ferenc got the floor, and said, "You're talking as if such a thing were possible. But there is no fuel. No air in the ship, so no way anyone could work in it if we *had* fuel. You saw to that yourself, Barton." For a moment, Ferenc looked almost reproachful.

That's when Barton told them about the Children's fuel-refining project across the hills, and about the spacesuits he'd smuggled downside. "It won't take all that long," he said.

"But I don't understand," said Bearpaw. "Turning the Children loose, sooner than necessary—what good will that do?"

Barton savored his punchline. "Who said we're turning them loose in *this* galaxy?"

It was a good thing, Barton thought, that the fuel wasn't ready any sooner. Because until little Conjy was old enough to leave her and be with the Child's own kind, Limila wasn't about to let her offspring go. And of course there was no question of one of the Children, isolated, staying with humans of any sort. But the timing worked out, well enough.

Most people, now, tended to avoid the Children, but Barton didn't. He knew they outclassed him, and that as adults they'd be totally outside his comprehension, like as not, but he didn't let it bother him. Some people were bigger or stronger or faster or smarter—that was the way things *were*—but Barton was Barton and he was satisfied being himself. Ferenc, he noticed, was another who spent time with the Children, and Racelle often joined him in that pastime. Limila, of course, took Conjy for playtimes and teachings, and seemed to feel no unease.

She hadn't said any more about starting a normal humanoid pregnancy, so Barton didn't push it, either. Actually, he didn't feel he needed any new complications just yet. For one thing, he was thinking over a conversation they'd had recently, and wondering how he felt about it. She'd been trimming his hair for him, and said, "The parts at each side, that were gray, now are not. Barton, I think the Tilaran treatments are having effect on you."

Well, hell, Barton thought. If she had it right, if all the misery he'd suffered on Tilara would really make him live young for a long time, well and good. He didn't really believe it, though.

Quite a lot of the colony, including Bearpaw and Lisa and Gyril and Elys, opted to stay on Endatheline; for sure, sooner or later there'd be more people coming from Earth to join them there.

Barton had a few jitters about passing so near the glorious spectacle of Opal, but Dahil and Tiriis kept their promises. No matter what the Others below might have felt, they made no mental moves against the ship, and Dahil and Tiriis did their teleport trick at the ship's closest approach to Opal. First, though, the number of Children aboard the ship was approximately doubled; Barton took the Others' word that all the Children from Opal had transferred up. He hoped so, because that was the way his plan was supposed to work. But from Opal on, passing Blaine's Mistake and crossing the dead belt, the ship held only Earthani and Limila and Children.

There was no point, Barton and Ferenc agreed, in calling Earth Base; people there might not agree with what the two men intended, and they were going to do it, anyway. It worried Barton that the F.T.L. transmitter got no response from Sisshain, but when they came within range for light-speed talk, things cleared up a little. "Tarleton got the obelisk in shape," Barton said to Ferenc, "before he left. Now all we have to do is get hold of it."

Sholur, Keeper of the Heritage for the Demu, was another matter. "It is," Barton said to that gold-robed worthy, "that even those Demu who have become—even yourself—may not have become sufficiently to withstand what will be seen when we arrive. It is, perhaps, that all should leave the place of becoming."

But Sholur stayed, and withstood. Even when the great ship, Mecca for the Demu race since its beginnings, lifted to take the Children away beyond return. Pulled the lower third of its two-kilometer length out of the mountain, and lifted and was gone. "It is," said Sholur, "that they are well removed from us."

Maybe, Barton thought. But for himself, he wasn't entirely sure.

From her own ship, Thirty-one, Estelle Cummings was running the Earthani embassy. She and her husband Max, the surgeon, filled Barton in on the news. Tarleton was back on Tilara, and a recent ship had brought word that after some hot F.T.L. talks with Earth Base, he was in charge of both the first and second fleets. Arleta Fox and

Honus Hayward had gone to Tilara with Tarleton. Too bad, Barton thought; he'd have liked to see them again. Well, last reports had them still together, anyway; that was nice.

Barton's own status, Cummings said, was still a gray area. So when he and Limila went back to Ferenc's ship, Barton got help to put an F.T.L. call through to Tilara. But Tarleton wasn't available; he was off-planet and not due back for a few days. Barton shrugged and thanked his helper. "I'll try again, then."

The next contact he tried to make, Barton had better luck, and about an hour later he welcomed two guests aboard the ship. Eeshta had grown; the young Demu wasn't quite full-sized yet, but coming close. And while Barton was fairly certain that the exoskeletal Demu weren't given to hugging among themselves, Eeshta must have picked the habit up from Barton, because now she came to him and did so. "Barton. It is good to see you."

"And to see you, Eeshta. You're well?" The young one signed assent, and now Barton looked past her, to the adult Demu. "Hishtoo?" No hugging here, nor did Barton think Hishtoo would have picked up the custom of shaking hands. "It is that I greet you, Hishtoo. That I wish you good health." And thinking, things *do* change—because, unmistakably, Hishtoo lifted his stumpy tongue in the Demu smile.

"It is, Barton," said Hishtoo, "that I would have died before changing as I have changed. That in part I can never forgive what you forced on me. But that I am more now, than before that change." The chitinous, serrated mouth flexed; a sound came that Barton had not heard before. Then Hishtoo said, "It is, Barton, that although you have not correct appearance, you are Demu. Not animal." And while Barton was trying to find an answer, Hishtoo turned abruptly and left the compartment.

Barton looked at Eeshta. "What in the—will he be all right?"

"He will, Barton. I did not know if he could say to you what he has said, but he did. Now he needs, for a time, to be alone."

Barton relaxed. "Okay, I guess. Hey, you want some coffee? And I'll tell you what's been happening lately." So they sat, and he did. Eeshta was disappointed, though, that she hadn't had the chance to see the Great Race personally.

Picnic on the mountainside, below the vast pit the great ship had left. Barton and Limila and Ferenc and Racelle. "Which do you think we were," Ferenc said, "and which were the Others? In terms of sperm and ova, I mean."

The question took Barton a moment to figure; then he knew. The humans had been like sperm, traveling blindly in search of their own extinction as a species—an extinction they didn't foresee and bitterly resisted. The Others waited like ova, knowing, and drew humans into a unity the Others intuited and welcomed. Now, though, with a little caution the gamete species would survive on their own.

He must be a little drunk, Barton thought, to be speculating on this kind of stuff. He said, "What does it matter, actually, which was which?"

But he could see how it might matter to Ferenc Szabo.

The fourth day, Barton got through to Tarleton to Phasewave. The picture was better than he expected, but Tarleton looked pooped. First he talked about fleet doings, and to Barton it sounded as if he had things pretty well in hand. Then he said, "Have you heard what Helaise did?" Barton shook his head. "Locked herself in her room and kept zapping herself with a sleep-gun until she couldn't remember how to use it." Barton wondered if he looked as shocked as he felt. The other man said, "Mentally she's about fourteen, I think, and a rather cheerful youngster. Ap Fenn's taking care of her, and he's quite patient about waiting for her to develop grown-up attitudes. I don't think it's going to take too long."

A lot of things Barton wanted to ask, then, but he couldn't think how. Finally he said, "Where do *I* stand, Tarleton? I mean, last I knew on Tilara, I was in tough. I asked Cummings but she didn't know."

Tarleton frowned. "Well, there's a little problem. We have your tape, explaining what happened, and the testimony of Doctor Arleta Fox. But Hennessy, when he was in charge here, set up a Board of Inquiry, and that Board still wants to do some inquiring."

Barton grinned. "They may have quite a wait. Unless

they want to convene on the other side of the dead belt, that is."

He saw Tarleton lean forward. "You mean you're not coming back here?"

"Not hardly. I'd like to hoist drinks with you, but Ferenc's heading down-Arm again, and—"

Tarleton cut in. "What happened there, anyway? I've heard rumors, and now I'm told the great ship's lifted off from Sisshain and gone God only knows where. I think somebody owes me some answers."

Barton considered, decided Tarelton was right, and told it—the bare bones, anyway. At the end, the big man nodded. "You and Szabo did right; that bombshell must *not* get out in public. Matter of fact, I don't expect to sleep too well myself, tonight. Oh, there'll be leaks, but without any solid proof . . ." He shrugged, then frowned. "But if down-Arm's a trap for humans, what can you do there?"

"Plenty." Barton explained some of it. First-off, take auxiliary fuel pods and a prize crew out to the drifting derelict supply ship, so as to return it to Tilara for re-fitting. "Group B wants to look good in the budget.

"And two more of these big ships, full of colonists, we're escorting to Endatheline. Plus a contact team for Blaine's Mistake, to negotiate colonization rights on the uninhabited continent."

"The down-Arm mapping project's dead, though, isn't it? I mean, we can't risk having this whole thing happen again."

"We won't." Barton grinned. "The job needs a crew trained in group resistance to mental force. Just happens, that's exactly what Ferenc has, aboard here."

"And you feel you have to go along?"

"Right, boss. Vice-Admiral Barton, on detached service."

"Yes. Well, Alene and I would like to see you and Limila, and I did have the funny idea you were working for *me*—but I guess I can't argue." A pause. "Barton, it's been good."

"That it has. And, Tarleton—we'll be back sometime." He cut the circuit.

Lying with Barton, Limila again opened the ongoing discussion: should she ovulate now, on Sisshain, as she

521

had done before? Barton wasn't sure. "This place wasn't so lucky for us, the last time."

"But now it may be. Barton, why do we not try?"

The thing was, they got so involved that they didn't notice when the ship lifted. So whether conception took place on Sisshain or in space, they'd never know.